The Diam

Pamela Haines was b
educated at a convent in the Midlands and then read English at Cambridge. As a child she wrote prolifically but she did not take up writing as an adult until her late thirties, by which time she was married with five children. In 1971 she won the *Spectator* New Writing Prize with a short story, and in 1973 completed her first novel, *Tea at Gunter's*. Acclaimed by the critics, it was joint winner of the first Yorkshire Arts Association Award for Young Writers. It was followed by *A Kind of War* in 1976, *Men on White Horses* in 1978, *The Kissing Gate* in 1981, *The Diamond Waterfall* in 1984, *The Golden Lion* in 1986 and *Daughter of the Northern Fields* in 1987.

By the same author

The Kissing Gate
The Golden Lion
Daughter of the Northern Fields
A Kind of War
Tea at Gunter's

PAMELA HAINES

The Diamond Waterfall

This edition published 1995 by
Diamond Books
77–85 Fulham Palace Road
Hammersmith, London W6 8JB

Published by Fontana 1985
First published in Great Britain by
HarperCollins*Publishers* 1984

ISBN 0 261 66719 X

Set in Baskerville Printed in Great Britain

In loving memory of my father

HARRY BURROWS
1898–1978

CONTENTS

Prologue	1887	9
Part One	1897–1918	25
Part Two	1922–1945	297

PROLOGUE
JUNE 1887

She screamed. Then again, but much louder. As loud as she could. Just standing there, scream after scream. Then, her throat rasped, she battered instead her fists against the bedroom door: pulling at the doorknob, rattling it, straining at the lock.

But no one, none of her family, came to protest. She must be alone in the house. It was stifling in the room – hot, stifling air. Helpless with anger, she walked over to the window. Then back to the door. It seemed to her suddenly that the room had grown smaller, the door thicker. A bedroom that she had known for at least ten of her seventeen years. Now it was her prison. The door – a dungeon door.

'Let me out!' She banged again, shouting. 'I want to come out! I *shall* be an actress, I *shall*. You shan't stop me. I'll go on the stage – I will, I *will*.' She drew breath. Then: 'You'll have to let me out for the Jubilee. I shall petition Queen Victoria. *She* wouldn't want her loyal subject imprisoned. And anyway, it's against the law, there's something called Habeas Corpus, you can't keep someone shut up . . . *Air*, I want air!'

The window was open, just a crack. Only – it was barred. Right to the very top. Bars that had been put there for their protection when the room had been a nursery for the four girls: Daisy, Ethel, Lily, Amy, the little daughters of Alfred Greenwood, founder of a chain of grocery shops serving the clothing trade of Leeds, in the West Riding of Yorkshire.

Big daughters now, though. Except for Amy, dead from scarlet fever. Daisy already married – but a runaway marriage, a family scandal. Her name must never be mentioned. Lily in disgrace too: locked in her bedroom. Until she comes to her senses, that is. Only eighteen-year-old Ethel in favour.

She would be, Lily thought now, *she* would . . .

'I want to go on the stage,' she had said, six long months ago now. 'I want –'

But she had said it without much hope. People like Dad

didn't struggle to make money and to live in a smart district of Leeds, in order to have a daughter living a dangerous, flashy, immoral life. For that was how he saw it:

'Never. Never, Lily. That I should ever *see* the day . . .' And Ma, who always agreed with him (who didn't dare do otherwise), stout, soft Ma, who should have been a refuge, a lap to sit upon, a bosom to weep on, but who herself looked always in need of comfort – crumpled, creased, forever on the verge of tears:

'You've upset your father now, Lily – with your foolish ideas. All we want for you is . . .'

But Lily knew well enough what was wanted for her. And I *shan't* be that sort of person, she thought. Ever. That suffocating life of bombazine, of predictability, where a visit to Scarborough was a great event. Where she too might marry someone like Dad, and then have four little daughters, and perhaps five years later, at last, a son. (Even if one as dear as her *dear*, dear brother, Harry.) And then to grow stout . . .

No. It would not do. It would not do at all. When I might be out there on the stage, applauded by thousands – however humbly I have to begin. When I might go, *shall* go to Paris. When life, through my own making, could always be exciting, exciting, exciting.

Later, there had been the scene she didn't want now to remember:

'You think because I've spent money on you, lass – because your Dad's spent money on you, you can do what you like now – *eh Lily*? As if there'd not been trouble enough with Daisy, without we've *this* now. What'd folk say, eh? Alfred Greenwood's lass, *gone to join the lakers* . . . It's no life for a lady.'

And now, over and over, all through this Jubilee Week:

'You'll promise then? Give us your word, your mother and I, that it's all done with. No more of this lock and key . . .'

'I'll promise *nothing* –'

'You will –'

'I'll not –'

'What's that, eh? Say "Dad", "Father".'

'I'll *not* – Dad. *Father* . . .'

The indignity of the chamber-pot, the one with the blue violets on it. She was going to need it any moment now. The chamber-pot – for everything. It was as if she were ill. Ma hoped she *was*: only being poorly could make Lily behave like this, she told her. Ethel had said something quite else, but Ma had turned on her, and said she was lucky to be healthy, and it was no fault of Lily's these ideas had overcome her.

When she came in to see her, Ma's eyes would fill with tears – and then Lily would very nearly give in. Ma had suffered enough over Daisy, she didn't deserve all this unhappiness. If I had it *in* me, Lily thought, to promise . . .

Downstairs, the piano had started up (the new cottage upright, a Schiedmayer and Soehne's, seven-octave, in walnut, that Dad had paid a whole *thirty-five pounds* for at Ramsden's). Ethel, who couldn't tell a flat from a sharp, playing as if her fingers were croquet mallets. *Berceuse*. No baby would be rocked to sleep with *that* . . .

A knock on the door:

'Lily – Lily. You there?' Harry's voice. Full of love for his big sister.

'Of *course*, daftie. How could –'

'Lily, we're back. I saw them – Hussars, Mounted Police. Practising, they were. There's to be a *twenty-one* gun salute –'

'Yes – and?'

'Ma's coming up in a little, Ethel too. Lily, I've on my new sailor suit. It's got a lanyard *and* a whistle. And you know what, Lily? It's meant for a lad of twelve –'

'And you only nine . . . Listen a moment, Harry – listen now. I want –'

'Lily, there's *Ethel* coming . . .' She heard him being pushed from his place at the keyhole.

Ethel's voice was breathy: 'Ma's on her way. She'll have something to say to you. Or rather, Dad will. We heard you screaming when we came down the road. Folk'll think you're touched . . .'

But Lily had only one thing to say to her sister:

'I'm going to be an actress, Ethel –'

'You're acting *now*, Lily. What you're doing now in that bedroom, that's *acting* . . . You ought to do what Dad says. You know what happened to Daisy . . .'

Lily said angrily, her mouth too near the keyhole, tasting the brassy flavour:

'Marrying isn't wrong – what if he doesn't ever speak to her again? And anyway, Daisy married the man she loved. *That's* not a sin in the eyes of God.'

'But Father had said No. He forbade it –'

'He's not God the Father, is he? Is he?'

'Lily, *please* . . . Anyway, marrying a *Jew*, fancy marrying a *Jew*, they're awful those Jews here in Leeds. Common Polish people, Dad says. Taking the bread out of honest folk's mouths. You know it . . .'

But Lily didn't know it. Not at all. She had been completely on Daisy's side, from the very beginning. She was on the side altogether of the newly arrived Jewish community. Even more so now: now that she knew just a little, a very little, of what it was to be persecuted . . .

Daisy's drama had begun the day she went to help Mrs Mandelbaum with her party. The Mandelbaums, who were not strict Orthodox Jews, had lived in Leeds for twenty or thirty years, and through wealth, charm and kindness had become part of a wider social circle than was usual. Ada Thompson who knew Herbert Varley who was married to a Jewish girl, asked Daisy, one dank and drizzling November afternoon two years ago, to come with her to the Mandelbaums'.

'It's a party for refugees, I've promised to help hand round cakes – I've done it twice before. You'll come, Daisy, won't you?' And Daisy, the gentle, the endlessly kind, who never refused anyone anything (and yet was to show herself later so strong, so tenacious of purpose, so immovable in her loyalties), gave up whatever else she had planned – and went to meet her fate.

The year was 1885. The first really large wave of Jewish immigrants had been in 1881 with the pogroms of Alexander III in Russia. They had been coming over steadily ever since, in spite of warnings about the difficulties of living in a foreign land – warnings given them by the English Jewish establishment.

Many were from the Polish part of Russia. They would travel to Hamburg, then by boat to Hull: many of them intending to go on to Liverpool and from there to America. Frequently they hadn't the money. What they did have was the word 'Leeds': often the only English word they knew, passed on to them by relatives who had been early immigrants. By the time of Mrs Mandelbaum's party, they were arriving at the rate of about fifty a month . . .

Daisy knew little about them (Lily and Ethel even less), except that they were numerous and had formed by now a ghetto in the Leylands district of Leeds. Dad was rude about them (but who wasn't he rude about?) and there were notices in shop windows – jobs advertised with the message, 'No Jews need apply' . . .

About twenty boys and girls were at the party, ranging in age from ten to nineteen. Some had been coming for a year or more and spoke quite a little English. Ada and Daisy's task was to hand round food, and to talk to those who could manage some conversation. Ada, because she had been before (the parties were held every month), showed off a little.

'This way, Daisy. Over here is a girl who dances like a – wait till she does her piece . . . That boy there, Stefan something or other, he plays the fiddle . . .'

Three minutes later Daisy met Joszef. She told Lily afterwards that from the first moment she saw him, she knew. 'I just stood there, with the dish of fruit salad – staring. Till he smiled and took it straightway from me. And then he *dared* to start eating . . .'

It was his beauty, she said. In spite of the ill-fitting clothes. His dark shadowed face with its high cheekbones, the eyes, almost black, which she thought laughed at her, the hands with their long fingers: 'I felt so pale and fluffy, Lily – beside him . . .'

When the food was all served and before the entertainments began, she had gone over to speak to him. She discovered that he was nineteen (a year younger than her), that he came from the Kovno province of Poland and had escaped with his widowed mother and two elder brothers and young sister. He was apprenticed to a jeweller and hoped to become a watchmaker.

All this she learned from him, with the help of two girl immigrants, who laughed and blushed either side of him. He himself was only a little shy – and obviously very proud of the English words he'd acquired in the few months since his arrival.

Daisy had determined there and then that she would – somehow – see more of him. And in spite of being quiet, compliant Daisy (so very, very unlike Lily), that was what she did.

It hadn't been too difficult at first. For three or four years now, Mrs Mandelbaum had been giving free English classes in her home. She limited the numbers to those who wished to write and read as well as speak. So far natural selection had kept the group small enough to be manageable; usually it was filled from among those who came to her monthly entertainments. Rachel, Herbert Varley's wife, had been helping since the very beginning.

Daisy heard about the lessons that afternoon. When the tea-party was almost over, and the singing and fiddle-playing done, she went over to Joszef and very prettily told him that he must come to Mrs Mandelbaum's: 'to make your English better and better'. Already he'd learned an unbelievable amount, she said. Here was a chance for him. Later she spoke directly to Rachel. She would like to teach. 'Even though I'm not Jewish, I want to *help* these people . . .'

She told Lily everything, but no one else, except Aunt Millie who was Ma's older sister and the two girls' greatest ally. (If she were alive now, Lily thought, I would not be in this sorry mess . . .) At home, Daisy said that she was helping with Sunday school teaching. Neither Ma nor Dad were really interested. Aunt Millie went with her as chaperone, and kept her secret. Not that it was much of a one then: discovery would have meant at the most punishment and a diatribe against immigrants generally, with the chief worry, what contagion she might have picked up. A litany of nits, ringworm, fleas and unmentionables . . .

But as the weeks and months passed, everything changed. Daisy was irrevocably, desperately, in love. And it was not, she told Lily, just her. From the blackboard where she or Rachel pointed: 'take took taken', their eyes met continually. When she corrected something with his pencil, their fingers touched . . .

He stayed behind once and talked with her after class.

Then – every time. Aunt Millie looked unhappy. Daisy invited herself to his home, and *he* looked unhappy. Aunt Millie even unhappier. But she went, taking Aunt Millie with her. His mother spoke only Yiddish, his two brothers were suspicious of the visitors, the young sister hid and would not come out at all. An uncle from Hull, a cabinet maker, visited while they were there. A great bald-headed man with a scar on his temple from a Cossack sword: three years in England, he spoke good English. The whole Ziolkiwski family it appeared would like to have gone on to America. It seemed unlikely now.

That was April, six months after their first meeting. In May, Daisy proposed. 'I know it's very forward – but otherwise, how? He can hardly ask Dad for my hand, can he?' Indeed, that very week, Dad had been holding forth again. 'Yorkshire for Yorkshire folk,' he said three times in one evening after reading that immigration figures were up.

Somehow, with Aunt Millie's help, it had come all right – if being turned out, forbidden to see your sisters or brother, cut off without a penny, your name never to be mentioned at the family dinner-table, could be called that . . . But she *had* her prince – triumphing first over his diffidence, her non-Jewishness (she had taken on his religion), the problems of his family who did not know what to make of her. She had poverty too, and ostracism . . .

For Dad, Joszef was no prince. He was – but Lily wanted to forget . . . For the noise of that scene had filled the house. Daisy, seeking above all not to betray Aunt Millie, had stood her ground, trembling, white-faced. Sent up to bed in disgrace, she had left the house within the half-hour, taking refuge first with Aunt Millie. Then secure in the knowledge that she was of age by six weeks, she had become Mrs Ziolkiwski – and written to tell Dad so.

The disgrace, the shame, had been terrible. Ethel had taken her parents' side. But little Harry had wept for his beloved sister's absence and Lily had taken him secretly to visit her. Soon they would be moving to live in Hull with the uncle. This Christmas she expected a baby.

Although Daisy's name could not be mentioned, Dad was ruder than ever now about the immigrants. 'Yorkshire for Yorkshire folk, let America have them . . . They took the paddys when I was a lad. In the Famine. Aye, let the *Yankees* have them . . .'

Her bedtime drink. Tonight, June 20th, the sixth night of her imprisonment. It was drugged. She was sure of it. The bottom of the cup was gritty. It might be of course possibly just a different, poorer type of cocoa, something Dad was trying out in the shops. But it made her feel odd, strange. 'I do feel strange,' she said out loud. Perhaps her tantrum had worn her out? She had all day to sleep if she wished, but: I sleep less than ever, she thought.

I am a prisoner. But no one can imprison my spirit. She tried to remember some poetry, any poetry about prisons. But her mind kept going back to singing, dancing, *acting* . . .

I am the Countess, no, the *Princess* Ludmila Hohenkopetal, imprisoned by my cruel stepfather because I wish to marry the impecunious Lieutenant Longlegs who is really a king's son in disguise. He hears me singing, and so learns where I am imprisoned . . . He comes to my rescue. Rescue. Cue. Cue for a song . . . It was difficult to invent a song for a princess. Maybe, in her nightgown, the gas mantle turned down, the curtains drawn back, moonlight across the floor (and if they don't like the noise, let them come and complain), she could sing . . .

'Ladies and gentlemen, the famous *Jack-in-the-Box* song as performed by Miss Fanny Leslie –'

Her feet dragged. I am drugged, she thought . . . so feet drag . . . Drugged, drug. Dragged. Best to lie down now . . .

She dreamed – about the Golden Jubilee. She was in Leeds, in Duncan Street. The tram was coming towards her from Boar Lane. The people on top crowded, standing, hanging over the edge. The horses wore golden plumes, tossing gilt. Excitement filled the air. She thought: I'm glad I'm awake and not dreaming. A man, dressed poorly and without gold dust, stood near her. 'What's happening?' she asked. When he didn't answer, she looked closer and saw that he was one of Joszef's brothers. 'We just arrived,' he said, 'we are not stopping. We go to America, you know . . .' As the tram drew nearer the crowd could be heard cheering. 'Who is it,' she asked urgently, 'who are they, what is it?'

'They are cheering you,' he said.

And then suddenly, coldly, she was alone on an enormous stage. No audience – just a dark emptiness. She saw that she was dressed entirely in jewels . . . Rubies like pigeon's eggs; sapphires, emeralds, rope upon rope of pearls. They are *paste*, of course, she thought. And indeed they weighed next to nothing, lying lightly along her arms, over her wrists, round her waist . . .

It was then the diamonds came. More diamonds than she had ever seen in her life. They fell on the boards at her feet and she rushed to pick them up. But the necklace, or corsage – she did not know which – was heavy. With disbelief and joy, she saw that this one was not paste, but *real*. She turned it over and over in her hands. Held it up – seeing the diamonds catch the light as they moved, changing colour again and again. Streaming, falling . . .

She woke with a start. Sitting up, searching for a light. *They put something in my cocoa.* These are opium dreams. They are making me into an addict, so that I may never leave home . . . She tried to calm herself, but her heart raced. Going over to the window, she could make out odd moon shadows on the garden.

'Miss Lily Greene,' she said out loud, 'not Miss Greenwood – Miss Lily *Greene*.' Then, the curtains round her face like a veil:

'For insertion in *The Stage*,' she announced, 'the week of June 21st, 1887: "Miss Lily Greene. Disengaged. Available for singing, dancing, acting roles. Address: 1, Wycliffe Avenue, Far Headingly, Leeds, West Riding, Yorkshire . . ." '

She had been intended for a respectable life. Respectable. Ma used that word. Dad used it. Even Ethel used it. Everything was respectable, or not. The stage was not. And especially so, it appeared, if you had done well from nothing, like Dad.

From nothing: in 1850 he'd been just one of the hands at Wm Paul's Tannery in Kirkstall Road. Now he never spoke of it – except once when they were passing, and the smell of it had been blown down on the wind. Hard labour at the tannery, but also: going to Sunday school, learning to read, add, subtract, divide, multiply. Above all, to *multiply*. Starting from a job as shop assistant, gained through his new skills; then, greatly daring, his own small shop in the Marsh Road area. Then another in Kirkstall. At first selling just food, then some clothing, and utensils . . . Next, real multiple shops, some even selling furniture. Greenwood's. By the time Lily knew anything about it there were ten branches. The Greenwood tree. She was Lily Greenwood . . .

Except on the stage. There she would be Lily Greene. That idea had come from no less a person than the famous Sylvia Grey – who could sing, dance *and* play the piano, divinely.

Lily had been to dancing class – but so had Daisy and Ethel, just as all three at Dad's especial wish had spent many hours learning the piano. It was the dances she'd invented *herself* which she wished to go out alone and show the House. (How she loved that word for the theatre . . .) Singing: her voice was very small. She feared often that it might not fill the House, but it was true and strong and she'd been told it was pleasing. Her looks too: she had hair that could be called golden. It curled naturally too . . .

She did not see herself as Miranda or Juliet or even Portia. It wasn't straight acting that had captured her imagination, but rather the stage itself. (*The Boards* – another word she loved . . .) Vaudeville, burlesque, attracted her. Her heroines, the stars of the Gaiety Theatre in the Strand. Last summer in Leeds she had seen the burlesque *Little Jack Sheppard*, when the Gaiety's new manager, George Edwardes, sent it on tour. She had loved Nellie Farren as Jack – but it was Sylvia Grey she admired the most . . .

From the theatrical magazines on which she spent every spare penny, she learned all that she could about her. Sylvia had been asked to arrange Sir Henry Irving's dances for *The Dancing Girl*. So pleased had Irving been that, in congratulation, he had shaken her foot . . .

And I have met her, Lily thought . . .

Six months ago now, the last show at the Grand before the Christmas pantomime. A Benefit for someone: Fred Leslie, I think. Moore and Burgess were there and G. H. Chirgwin the

White-eyed Kaffir, Ballyhooley Lonnen, Hayden Coffin singing *Love of my life* . . . And – Sylvia Grey.

Oh, but it was a wonderful evening. The special seats were had, for we were there by invitation – Dad was, *is* Someone in the city of Leeds. I renewed my vow that evening. The vow I made four years ago that *someday* I would go on the Boards. Then, my head full of dancing rhythms, lights, applause, I thought: Not someday – Now . . .

As we were leaving the theatre, we had to wait for Dad to shake hands in the foyer with some dignitaries. It was then I slipped away. Quick. I had to be quick. Asking the way to the dressing-rooms. Imagining that four male admirers at least would be waiting outside Miss Grey's room, be already inside . . .

Her voice: a light 'Come in –' She was made up still for the stage. The room struck me as chill. She had thrown a shawl about her shoulders. And she had a cold: she sneezed almost immediately after I came in.

Quick, quick. Again, quick. My breathless self-introduction. Her surprise. (Although she did not seem so *very* surprised.) She was blowing her nose. Then she rubbed her wrists and her forehead with a cologne stick.

I said: 'I want, you see, to go on the stage, and . . .' Then out it all came: what I could do, would do – *if* given the chance . . . And Miss Grey, smiling at me now, a smile of such radiance. Her reddened nose, showing now through the greasepaint, only enhancing her beauty.

'You have learned Deportment?' She was smiling still. 'I see that you have.'

'Yes. At school . . .'

She was young. Not so much older than myself. But greater. Already successful. She did not ask me foolish questions such as – 'How do you propose to go about it?' but instead said with easy grace, reaching into a capacious velvet bag, handing me a card:

'If you come, *when* you come to London to try your luck – please visit me. When I am not on tour, the Lyceum finds me. If I can help . . .'

Her voice was so pretty: 'Greenwood, did you say?' She put her head on one side: 'Yes, that is nice. Nice. But . . . don't you think . . . How about Lily *Greene*?'

But of course. I should have known. Greenwood is all right – but for me, it is a shopkeeper's name . . .

'Lily Greene,' she said again, 'Yes, I like that . . . Miss Greene, goodbye, and good luck . . .'

In the foyer, indignation. Our carraige was waiting outside. Almost everyone else gone. 'What's the meaning of this, eh, Lily? Eh?'

'Yes, Dad. No, Dad. I wandered off, then I couldn't find my way back . . .' I whispered something to my mother and then Ma whispered to Dad. Needing suddenly . . . natural functions . . . But Dad said only: 'You should have taken your sister with you –' (As if I would take Ethel anywhere I didn't have to – and certainly not the lavatory.)

I was so happy, though. And proud too, when the next day I had caught *her* cold . . .

She had never meant to run away. She had thought that, difficult as her father was, he would see the reasonableness of her ambitions and send her to London with some sort of blessing. If not immediately, at least when she was a little older. So just as Daisy had done a year or so earlier, she had made her announcement . . .

With similar results. But sadly there was no longer an Aunt Millie to run to. She had died soon after Daisy's marriage. I shall run away, Lily had thought then, it's as simple as that. I shall run away to London.

Money was the main problem. She had a small legacy from Aunt Millie, but it was hidden away, waiting for when she married. ('You'll have a tidy sum to bring with you, Lily . . .' Dad had said.) That was the trouble with money, in Yorkshire: you never had it *now*. Hers sat in the Yorkshire Bank or the Leeds Permanent, meant for marriage, when it would not really seem hers.

And so on until the Last Day, when it was always: 'How much did he leave, what was he *worth*?' Dad, reading the Wills in the *Yorkshire Post*. Old Higging ('best Angel and Bride Cakes in the West Riding') worth only half of what had been expected – a failure at the time of his possible greatest triumph.

'No one'll say that of *me*, eh, Lily, eh, Ethel? If things go the way they should . . . Another three shops by eighteen-ninety . . . I'll have the Co-operative off the map, eh?'

She had seen an advertisement in the newspaper: '£5 – £100 lent to respectable people only on their IOU's and promissory notes without bonds – W. Trees Esq., Park Villas, Heeley.'

'Respectable people.' She liked that . . . She went, taking Harry with her: she took Harry everywhere so that she might go out alone. She gave her name, a false one. Said what it was about. The parlourmaid went off.

And then, the enormous figure with rust-coloured moustaches walking towards her in the hall. 'Well, little girl, eh? My little lassie. *Well* –'

She fled.

In the end she had sold bit by bit anything she could lay her hands on. Any trinket, small unwanted gift. Anything larger she pawned, intending to leave behind the tickets.

All those elaborately laid plans. The timing: when best to go, *where* to go. She had the grand sum of ten pounds, and her wicker canvas-covered dress basket packed. The advertisement in *The Stage* had read: 'Well-furnished Rooms to Let from 3s.6d. per week . . .' She had worked out how long the money would last. In so many weeks she must find work.

The best laid plans . . . Harry in her confidence but no one else, not even Daisy. (Daisy would be upset for her. She would write to her from London.) Late at night was the best time to leave. The last train was half past midnight. It was important to be at once on it so that she couldn't be followed. But Ma was in bed always by ten, Ethel even earlier. And Dad was away, gone for two nights to Halifax.

Or so she thought . . .

'*And what might you be doing?*'

He said it twice, three times. Each time growing more angry. Standing at the bottom of the stairs, turning up the gas, revealing her in a pool of light. It would not do. Her stammered explanation. Then her defiant declaration. His stunned horror. 'What's this? *What's this?*' She had not seen him so angry since Daisy's marriage.

Bundling her up the stairs. A door on the landing opening and Ethel peeping out, nightcap pulled over her forehead, mouth open. Dad shouting at her, too. He was rough. She had hold still of her wicker basket. Dad pushing her into her bedroom: basket, cloak and everything, snatching the key from the inside, and then – but this she could not believe – locking it from the outside. The key turned – and removed.

Five days ago now. They thought that they could wear her down. That in the end she would give up her foolish notions. *They really believed that . . .*

'Lily, Lil – it's Harry. Listen –'

'Harry, are you alone?'

'Yes, hush – I've got to be quick. You know about the key, Lily? – I've found where Ma keeps it –'

'Harry, dearest Harry – go on. Yes. Yes?'

'She locks it in her desk and the desk key is on her belt. But, Lily, there's a second desk key somewhere. I heard her say . . .'

'Harry, you've got to help me. I won't do anything terrible, it's not *her* fault – but I *must* find a way –'

'Ethel's after your blood, Lily. She thinks you *might* do something, she says she's always coming up with Ma. Every time.'

'Oh Lor'. Harry, listen, I'm desperately, terrible unhappy. And I know I'm wicked but –'

'I'll set you free, never fear, Ensign Greenwood to the rescue. God save the Queen. And trust me . . .'

Already the second Sunday. Perhaps the worst day of all – Sunday. With the smell of roast beef from nine-thirty in the morning and a horrible hush everywhere: no piano, not even Ethel, no Harry with his tin trumpet. Just Dad's voice outside on the landing. 'She'll be coming to her senses soon enough, will the lass. Don't fash yourself . . .' And through the window, only the sight of people going to church . . .

To church. She could not believe her good fortune when it happened. When suddenly the door opened and Harry stood there.

He was in his sailor suit, dressed for church. And breathless too, as if he'd been running.

'You got in here,' she cried. 'You got the key!'

'Quick, quick. You've got to be quick, Lily –'

'Harry, how did you do it?'

'No time to say really – but we were just about off, and I was holding the books for Dad when he said, "I'd best get those papers for old Holroyd." I followed him, Lily, and then – I couldn't believe it – I saw where he'd a desk key hidden, so then I put the books down sudden, and bent double. I was poorly, I said – and now I'm meant to be lying down in my room. Only, Lily, you've got to be *quick* –'

It was too much, now that it had happened. She was all fingers and thumbs – and worry. About Harry.

'I don't want you in trouble –'

'Don't reckon to me. Honest. And Lily, Sunday trains, you're sure? You know?'

'Yes, yes, I do. By heart. Harry, push this in the hamper for me. Harry, Harry, Harry . . .'

'What'll you do, will you change your name? They'll be after you, won't they? Won't they, Lily?'

'How long have I got?'

Without Harry, it would have been impossible. Hurry, Harry, *hurry* . . . In case someone should come back from church early.

Then, down the stairs, out of the door, look right at the front gate, left . . .'

A kiss, a hug. 'I'll write to you, Harry, I'll find a way . . .'

Free, free, free, at last. Hurry, hurry.

'Harry, I love you best of all. Best in all the world . . .'

Hurry . . .'

PART ONE
1897–1918

1

Roses, roses, roses. Waiting for her this evening, as always. Yellow, white, and deep dark red. Roses. From Edmund.

In another part of the dressing-room, a great basket of fruit tied with ribbon – hothouse peaches, grapes, nectarines. 'Miss Lily Greene, star of *The Duke and the Shopgirl*, Carlton Theatre . . .' She looked inside casually, flicking the card over, finger skimming the heavy raised copperplate. The Hon. Herbert or Algy or Whatever – the very same who had said (how original!) that her skin was like a peach . . .

Evie, her dresser, said, 'Over there they are, ducky – the roses from You Know Who . . .'

But Lily had seen them already.

'He's out of Town,' she said, 'my Viscount – till Thursday.'

'Some other gentleman giving you supper?'

'Yes. It's the one you don't care for. Mr Firth.'

'Romano's, is it, ducky?'

'No, the Savoy. But it's a party. We shan't be alone.'

I am just filling in the days, she thought – until Edmund returns. Anything, anyone else, it is nothing.

1897. And another Jubilee. Diamond now. *My* year, as well as Queen Victoria's, thought Lily.

How everything dazzled, this summer of the Jubilee. Day after day of sunshine, and excitement. The air shimmered with it. And then the great day itself – June Two Two, as they called it – it was as if the excitement could no longer be contained.

It had been a while coming. Sound of hammers and saws, smell of yellow pine. Carpenters putting up stands along the procession route. Scrubbing up of statues. Food imported for a million and a half people. Celebrations. Illuminations. Coloured glass and gas jets. 1837–97 in fairy lamps. VR in cut glass, and brown paper.

A Procession to St Paul's. The hero, General Roberts, on his white Arab pony (six medals hanging from its breast):

'God bless you, Bobs,' called the crowd. And inside the Cathedral, someone from the States paying two thousand dollars for a seat. The fabulous Indian princes, their coats sewn with real diamonds . . .

For Lily, starring in the most popular show of the Jubilee Season, the excitement felt almost unreal . . . That in ten years she should have risen from a frightened, defiant seventeen-year-old to this. Her name on every smart person's lips . . . And – but wasn't this the most important? the betrothed (well, almost) of the Viscount Tristram. Of *Edmund.*

It was that, wasn't it, the real excitement? Fairy-tales *can* happen in real life, she told herself.

He was altogether too handsome, she had thought at first. Mistrusting such good looks. Then – why not? she had thought. Since for him at least, it was love at first sight. And for her at the most, third sight.

It had all seemed part of the wonder: that it should have happened just this Jubilee summer. As if everything had conspired, as if it had been ordained.

Heroine of *The Duke and the Shopgirl*. Suddenly to be offered, fruit of ten years' hard work, this plum . . . It had even caused Dad to get in touch with her (although apparently for the past three or four years, he had been collecting cuttings . . .) Now he was actually proud of her. Even spoke as if her success were *his* doing. While she – she was in quite a bargaining position. She did not want to see him, and did so as little as possible. As for her mother: Ma, she felt, had let her down. Taken the wrong side. Ethel . . . well, Ethel was simply jealous. But what it *had* meant was being able to see something of Harry again . . .

Meantime the wonderful enchanted season that had begun with the opening of the show in April went on. She had never looked so well, and knew it. Her new way of doing her hair: waved and brushed back high from her forehead – so much better than last year's fringe. Those photographs: a silk thread held either side of her nose, just tilting it up slightly . . . A year, too, when it was the fashion to show off the figure. And hers was good . . .

Oh, those lovely dresses, silk, batiste, ninon, lace, all

stitched by hand, all paid for by Max Hochoy whose show *The Duke and the Shopgirl* was. Ascot Sunday, and an attentive Edmund – straw boater, white flannels. Herself, lying back on the punt cushions. Taking care not to be burned by the sun (had she not promised Max?). Her parasol of orange and grey chiffon, with its Dresden china handle. At Bolter's Lock, a crowd singing, as soon as they saw us, songs from *my* show . . .

And always Edmund. So much in love. (No sooner leaving me in the evening, than he must write to me.) Suppers, suppers, suppers – Gatti's, the Savoy, private rooms at Kettner's, Romano's with its butter-coloured front, and our favourite table, just behind the glass at the entrance.

Then, every evening – oh, the danger of it – home by hansom. Not any old hansom cab – Edmund's own private one, with its glittering harness and liveried driver (he *is* a Viscount, after all . . .). Dark green plush velvet of the upholstery into which I sink – and struggle. But not too hard. Oh, but there is nothing quite like a hansom cab – as it shakes from side to side, throwing us against each other, deliciously . . .

Edmund, Viscount Tristram. He had held the title for a year now, since just after his twenty-second birthday. His father's death, of a heart attack, had been very sudden. Edmund spoke of him movingly, as a devoted parent, completely wrapped up in his Suffolk estate and the care of his tenants. 'I intend to be like him,' Edmund told her. That meant marrying, settling down, bringing up a family, thought Lily. How fortunate that she, at twenty-seven, was just ready for that. And fortunate too that he should be so much in love . . .

Her mouth full of pins, Evie said, 'You're all right with your Viscount, Ducky. But – I wouldn't be too much with Monsewer Firth –'

'Why's that, Evie?' said casually. 'He's not the marrying kind, for a start.'

'He's here often enough, Ducky.'

'Only when there's no one else. When Viscount Tristram's away . . .'

But then when Evie said nothing further, perversely she

felt a flutter of curiosity. She said, 'He seems interested enough in women, if that's what you mean. Why haunt stage doors here, if *men* are the interest?'

'It's . . . Well, ducky . . . it's to do with things that aren't spoken of . . .'

Lily, laughing, said, 'Oh, go on. Tell me, do –'

'He's – the kind as . . . He buys little ones. What they call unripe fruit . . . Little girls what haven't been touched. He's to pay for them, mind you – they don't come cheap –'

She felt faintly sick. 'I wish you hadn't told me,' she said, in a light voice to mask the shock. She felt unclean.

'Time to dress, ducky. I seen to them stockings . . .'

A little close to the knuckle, she thought sometimes, this tale of shopgirl turned Duchess . . . (*real* life was the highly moral tale of a Yorkshire chainstore-owner's daughter, likely, before 1897 was out, to become a Viscountess . . .). Indeed, recently a journalist from *The Lady* had hinted at some connection between the heroine and Lily.

> INTERVIEWER: Miss Greene, is it true that you know perhaps, a little, about the life of a shopgirl? That your part is not *all* acting –'
> ME (*coldly*): I have never served in a flower shop if that is your suggestion – My father owns a chain . . . His daughter would hardly expect to stand behind the counter . . .
> INTERVIEWER: (*hastily collecting notes together*): There is, has been, a break with your family – now happily mended, I understand. Perhaps you could tell our readers a little about your early life? You ran away to go on the stage –
> ME: Yes. My father forbade . . . Since I have done well, he is quite proud . . .
> INTERVIEWER: Your family? You said a brother, two sisters?
> ME: Yes, one sister lives at home. She is unmarried. My brother works for my father.
> INTERVIEWER: And the other sister?
> ME: Married. With children . . .

And I hastily changed the subject. I had expected the cock to crow, that day. It was as if I had denied Daisy and Joszef. Even Harry a little.

There was a photograph of Daisy on the table in her theatre dressing-room. Daisy from the Wycliffe Avenue days. She would have been ashamed to have up the present-day Daisy. (Yes, I send her what money I can, and whatever I send, feel always that I should send more . . .) She did not like to admit that she was embarrassed by her sister. Moving upwards, how could she not be dragged down by the truth about Daisy? (For that, she thought, *I hate myself.*) Yet she continued to keep on her table the photograph which told so little. Only that Daisy had once been far prettier than her . . .

What she wanted was to send the whole family to America. With enough to set themselves up. (I have heard too many tales of immigrants' early days – their second state worse than their first.) If, when, Edmund and she were married, it would be easy: I shall have only to ask. He will help. For he has a kind heart . . . But first, she thought, I have to tell him. And that I do not look forward to . . . I have become a snob.

The truth was that Daisy had absolutely, but absolutely, lost her looks. Her figure with its dragged down look, her colourless, drawn skin – once pink and white. And Joszef, the last time seen: receding hairline, dark velvety eyes bloodshot and anxious. She could not have believed ten years could so alter two people.

Yet in everything that really mattered, their concern was always for each other – and of course the children. Two sons, two daughters, born in less than six years, brought up in simple surroundings with no help. Poor Daisy, disapproved of from both sides (for Joszef's family had still not come round, though she had adopted their religion).

The eldest was little Joe, then Anna, Sam, Ruth. Any money Lily gave went straight into their mouths and on to their backs. Or into the small money-box that each child had. Harry told her:

'Daisy says that *their time*, it's over . . . But the little ones are to have, one day, the best . . . And Lily, as soon as I'm rich – they *shall* –'

Dear Harry. So carefully dressed when he came to applaud me and, with money given by Dad, to take me out to Simpson's. Already becoming, just a little, the person Dad wanted him to be.

All those years ago, Harry had suffered on her account. She only learned the details now:

'. . . I didn't know a lad could be so black and blue . . . He hadn't the truth out of me for going on three days. "I'll have it, I *will* –" he kept saying . . . He was that certain I knew something . . . But he never made to go after you at all. Every day it was: "If she's expecting I'll rescue her off the streets . . ." Ma was worried, though . . .'

And how Dad had punished him . . .

'The thrashings, Lily – they weren't much. It was the disgrace – Ethel and Ma not so much as allowed to speak to me . . .'

He spoke of it a lot that evening: not to bring home to her all he'd done but rather because it'd been perhaps the biggest single event in his (now rather dull) life. And of course, because he loved her. Over and over he told her, 'I'd do it again tomorrow . . .'

'Overture and beginners . . .'

This hot June evening, Lily could sense already another excited expensive Jubilee audience.

'They've been turning them away again, Miss Greene – in their droves . . . Miss Greene – the Duke of Sedley has the second box on the prompt side . . .' (She thought: I mustn't forget to sing a few notes in that direction . . .)

'Overture and beginners . . .'

The Carlton Theatre was a little larger than George Edwardes's Gaiety. Playing the fringes of the metropolis, Lily had used to hope that one day, looking up on the prompt side, she would see one of George Edwardes's scouts. Better, that one of his scouts would see her . . .

The curtain rose on *The Duke and the Shopgirl*. The chorus sang plaintively of their long hours in the shop, and short nights in the attics above. Woken at five, wash, comb, and downstairs to receive the day's stock.

Enter Mr Malcutt, manager. No real life shop could support so many assistants for so small a stock, but how the audience loved this bevy of beauties who bowed, and side-stepped, in stately fashion (the great stunning picture hats for Jubilee Year would not appear until Act Two – not reach their apogee until Act Three).

Roll-call '*Where is Miss Dainty?*' The girls look at each other, finger on lips. '*Three more minutes* – and Miss Dainty is dismissed . . .' Consternation. And then, just in time to save her skin, the bow of her shop dress defiantly askew, here is the tomboyish, the naughty Cynthia Dainty, alias Lily Greene.

An ovation. But Lily is used to it – a quick glance now up to the box where an evening-coated Duke sits, double-barrelled opera glass trained on her. (It was from *that* box, three months ago, that Edmund first saw me . . .)

Miss Dainty is safe, for today. Mr Malcutt leaves. And the Duke of Moberley, Hero, enters.

'I come to buy flowers and fruit for the most beautiful woman in London . . . the actress Bathsheba Rebecca.'

And then since we have a real life Duke in the house, what about an apparent *ad lib*? Turning, throwing his voice – (Miss Dainty: 'Why do you stare so?') and the line with extra meaning: 'A duke may look at an actress, may he not?'

He has a song in praise of Bathsheba and when he has left, Lily sings it too – in praise of him . . .

Thirty minutes to go . . . soon all the complications (rival for the Duke's affections, villainous uncle-solicitor, Duke in disguise as a shop assistant) will be resolved. A Happy Ending beckons . . .

As Lily stands centre stage, a basket of fruit in her hand, the Duke sings:

'What a skin, what a bloom,
It's the very finest peach
If only I could reach
("if only he could reach" sings the chorus)
Up to her room . . .
What a bloom, what a skin
Would it be such a *sin*?'

Any moment now, applause. Encores. Calls for Miss Greene. Lily Greene née Lily Greenwood. *I am a success.*

The Duke back again behind his opera glass. In the interval, she had been presented to him. It would do for excitement, since Edmund could not be there . . . Then next, supper at the Savoy with Lionel Firth. Since Edmund . . .

'My dear Miss Greene, may I introduce a new, but *very* fervent admirer . . .'

Although she had dined with Lionel alone twice, she was happier with him in the company of others. His dark good looks had about them something raffish, sinister almost, which at once attracted and frightened her. Cynical and astringent too, which she found satisfying after too much flattery. (No need to take him seriously, though – even less so after Evie's disgusting revelations . . .)

'A new admirer,' said a deep voice, 'and already your devoted slave.' An older, stockier than Lionel, but equally dark-haired man.

Lionel explained:

'. . . My brother has left the family seat for two weeks of the fleshpots.'

Of course. The brother, the older Firth – so often thrown casually into Lionel's conversation. ('. . . As my dear brother said only last week, evenings spent with actresses . . .')

Sir Robert Firth. *Sir* Robert. I think, she remembered, as he walked a little behind her, it was a title received for some public work or other . . . A widower too. Always a pitiful sight. Rich, too. Money enough for Lionel to idle away his days, to be all the Season in London, to be up in Yorkshire when it pleased him . . .

A firm, almost too firm handshake. A deliberate, slightly monotonous voice. But in many ways – another Lionel. Although not, she suspected, an amusing one . . .

Gilt, plush, chandeliers, cigar smoke. It was cigar smoke she noticed first always – every time a slight, pleasurable stinging of the eyes. As she came into the restaurant, the Hungarian band was playing Leslie Stuart's *Soldiers of the Queen*, revived for the Jubilee. At once they broke off, and in her honour played *What a skin, what a bloom* . . . Heads turned.

They were a party of six. She and Lionel, a Mrs Kingswood (a widow – hoping perhaps for Sir Robert?), Captain McArthur – a friend of Lionel's whom she knew a little – and a Miss Bateman, young and pretty.

Captain McArthur was a musical comedy aficionado, and not pleased when Mrs Kingswood spoke critically of the form. For him, Lily's show was quite simply the best . . .

Lionel said, 'Anything to do with rags to riches is sure of a welcome if brightly done – as happens of course at the Carlton . . . Although,' he added, 'I'm surprised we have not had yet *The Duke and the Typewriter*.'

'Ah yes,' Sir Robert said, 'typewriters. Those ladies who use the new machines . . .'

Captain McArthur said, 'Typewriters haven't the romance of Shopgirls. There's something too worthy about them – an odour of the New Woman. But it would do for a comic sketch –'

'It has been done, I rather think,' Lily said, spooning her crayfish bisque. Lionel agreed. Mrs Kingswood shuddered at the mention of New Woman.

The band played *Dear little Jappy Jap Jappy*, and *The Amorous Goldfish* from last year's hit, *The Geisha*. Conversation turned to Yankee heiresses. Always a fruitful subject, Captain McArthur said. He would not refuse one, if offered. Lionel who had been catching up on news from Yorkshire, said, 'My brother tells me Hawksworth at the Hall has netted an enormous fish. A Philadelphia – or is it Chicago? heiress. And very oofy, very oofy indeed. That family won't want . . .'

'How was it done?'

'A visit here. Earlier this year. He did not even need to cross the pond. They marry at Christmas, I believe.'

Mrs Kingswood turned to Sir Robert. 'How is young Miss Alice? Any improvement?'

'A little. Her governess finds her difficult still.'

'Your daughter?' Lily said to him. 'Lionel told me you have one . . .'

'Yes. Alice. She is twelve. She took her mother's death very hard.'

Further down the table, the subject was the Jubilee again. Captain McArthur said: 'I was here a few evenings ago, when the band played the anthem. God save Her if the whole restaurant didn't stand up, cheering and waving napkins. Food grew cold on the plates . . . Really one may have too much of a good thing.'

'Oh,' cried Miss Bateman, the first time she'd spoken. 'How too too TwoTwo, don't you think?'

'. . . and such jams with the traffic,' Lionel was saying, 'I saw a fellow walk along the tops of the cabs in Berkeley Street. Quite a circus turn . . . And then the day of the Procession itself . . .'

'Ah those Indian princes,' said Mrs Kingswood. 'Their coats . . . the *diamonds* . . .'

Lionel turned to Lily. 'Diamonds indeed. Diamonds galore. My brother here is the owner of a remarkable piece of jewellery. A family possession since the 'sixties . . .' He bent nearer. 'You've heard of a rain of diamonds? Well, this is a *waterfall* of them. A style favoured by Empress Eugénie and very fashionable at the time. The diamonds are articulated, you see, and move with the wearer . . . It's a necklace so lavish it is almost a corsage. We call it simply *The Diamond Waterfall* . . . It is very spectacular . . .'

Lily made no comment. He went on:

'Naturally these past few years it hasn't been worn. My late sister-in-law, of course . . . It is a piece too that wears the woman, not the other way about.' He spoke in a confidential tone, his voice low.

Miss Bateman, who had nevertheless been listening, said, 'I should *adore* to see –'

Sir Robert, he had heard too, leaning forward said gallantly, 'You shall, my dear, you shall.' He turned to Lily:

'And you, Miss Greene – would it interest you?'

She had hardly been listening. 'Oh, I scarcely think so,' she said carelessly, 'I am not much set on jewellery, you know . . .' (Although I have, have I not, a sapphire bracelet from Edmund? I broke all the rules for that. Never to accept . . .)

'Oh come now,' Lionel said. 'That doesn't sound like our Miss Greene –' He persisted, saying to all the table, 'It is a beautiful sight. On or off. No mere rain of diamonds. A waterfall –'

'Yes, indeed, yes.' She caught his brother's eye. Sir Robert stared at her. To show she had meant nothing by her remarks, she smiled.

At that moment the Hungarian band launched into a selection from *Dorothy*. First a light, prancing number. Then a quieter, more romantic one. Sir Robert – she saw that he watched her still – said:

'You know it – what show is this from?'

'Yes, yes, I know it.' She thought again: He is a widower

and that is pitiful. '*Dorothy*. Frank Cellier. Always popular. It wasn't new, even ten years ago –'

Pity. I don't care for pity. Once, it was nearly my undoing . . . She felt that she could not bear it: this rush of memory, emotion.

Sir Robert was insisting, though: 'This song – what is it called?'

'*Queen of my Heart*,' she said promptly. 'It is called *Queen of my Heart* . . .'

2

I had to be hard in those days, she thought. Yet hearing the song now, she was reminded only of pity. And the irony of that pity. I concerned myself with the wrong person, she thought. A foolish heart (mine) betrayed me, blinding me to what I should have seen.

Two memories the song brings back. One shameful. The other of a sadness I can hardly bear now to remember . . .

Escaped! That first terrifying, wonderful day. Ten years ago now yet seeming so much more. Afraid and happy. I was both. Afraid they would come after me, that Harry would be punished on my account; that worse might befall Daisy and I not there to help . . .

Sitting there in the London bound train (I had thought it would never come into the station, that the whistle would *never* blow), I saw myself in a play, a melodrama perhaps – I felt I had Runaway Daughter written all over me . . .

It was a mixed carriage in a corridor train and the man sitting opposite me, heavily bearded, wrapped, though it was a warm June day, in a food-stained Ulster, watching me, watching me. Outside Peterborough we ran into engine trouble and lost nearly two hours. I was beside myself with wild imaginings. How should I *not* be discovered?

When eventually we arrived at Kings Cross it was raining. Summer rain. I had made no arrangements for that first night. But at once, for very fear that the bearded man who had reached out as I struggled with my hamper ('No, no, I do very well, thank you') might follow me and find out everything, I hailed a porter and then a cab, assuming a confidence I did not feel. (I knew nothing of London. Might not my pocket be picked, my person assaulted?) Deep in my hamper was the little notebook with its precious list of theatrical lodgings. I said miserably, throwing myself on the cab-driver's mercy:

'If you know where I might lodge, where a young woman alone –'

'Does your mother know you're out?' He scratched his head. Laughing at me. Catch-phrase or not, it was too near the truth. In those few seconds I saw myself returned to Leeds like a misrouted parcel . . .

Then, 'Berridge's', he said, or something that sounded like that. 'Gray's Inn Road, just off. There in a jiffy, miss . . .'

Oh blessed relief. It was a good hotel – but more expensive than I had intended: next day I must arrange everything. All night, exhausted, I made plans. I could not sleep for sheer fatigue. Train wheels, bustle. Noise in the kitchens late, and early.

I did not feel completely safe – for I had signed the register with my new name. Proudly: Lily Greene. But then I had thought: It is too like. Anyone searching for a Greenwood, of a certain age and description . . . I wanted to be out, quickly. I told an uninterested reception clerk that I had to catch the boat train (let them look for me in Calais, I thought. In *Paris*!), then took a growler and made for the first address I had. Theatrical lodgings, in Westminster.

When I was almost there (and how would my money do, if I must be always taking cabs?) I thought: Perhaps they will ask me what play I am in, where I am engaged, and I have no fiction ready. I turned the cab back, deciding to breakfast somewhere and wait until I could speak to Miss Grey . . . (But would she find me work at once?) Fatigue, indecision. I changed the order, and then changed it back again. I had lost the cabby's good will ('Make up yer mind – can't she?') If I was traced, he would certainly remember me . . . By the time I reached the address, I could not decide whether I should ask him to wait. I could decide nothing.

It was not quite half past nine. I stood on the step with my hamper. The door-knocker was stiff and my nervous hand rapped too loudly. A great battleaxe of a woman opened the door a little. 'Yes?'

'I want – you keep lodgings, theatrical lodgings?'

I thought she was going to hit me: her hand which was already formed in a fist, went up – but she used it only to swipe at a cat scuttling from under a bush towards the door.

'Not a room, no. You might get, perhaps, *half* a room–'

'I'll pay in advance –'

'You *have* to pay in advance.'

It had begun to rain, the same sad summer drizzle which had greeted me at Kings Cross. The cat had done well to run for shelter . . . 'Seven and sixpence with attendance, five shillings without. Attendance means you buy the food – and I cook it.' She lifted her fist again but only to push an insect away. 'Well – yes or no? Yes or no?'

'Yes. I mean –'

'Come in then, if you're coming – and don't bring mud with you.' I looked for a scraper but couldn't see one. She led me into a parlour. I remember it as horrible, with a smell of cold cabbage seeming to come from the upholstery. The curtains were still drawn. She did not bother to pull them back. 'Your boots are muddy,' she said, then before I could answer, 'You may use this room for hearing cues if you wish – and going over parts. But no *visitors* . . .'

I agreed to everything. To paying at once, to sharing a room, to buying food for this evening, to waiting in this unpleasant parlour till she would agree to show me the room.

'Of course they're all out. They had rehearsals at ten. How is it you're alone, then? I never –' She was used I supposed to lodgings arranged by an advance man, coming ahead of a company and making the arrangements for them. (Surely she would guess the truth about me? Runaway Daughter blazoned my forehead, shining in the darkened parlour . . .)

I had come, I said, to see a certain well-known actress, who would be arranging work for me.

'Well, draw the curtains back – if you're to wait in here. And your boots away from the tiger, if you please.' Daylight revealed a mangy skin lying in front of the unlaid fire.

Half an hour later she took me upstairs. The room was small and dark. In the double bed was a large hump. 'Miss Malcolm!' She shook and prodded the hump. I stood in the doorway uncertainly, arm aching from bringing up my hamper. 'You should be out. Wake up *at once*!'

'Never,' said a muffled voice. 'Nevermore. Nevermore.' The sheet covered her face.

'If you're taken sick – this is no infirmary, Miss Malcolm –'

There was no answer. I thought she would grow really angry but instead she just pushed past me at the door. 'Please yourself, Miss Malcolm, do. And you, Miss Greene, can wait till her ladyship decides she'll speak. It's her you've to sleep along of –'

As the landlady's footsteps died away, Miss Malcolm (how could I ever, *did* I ever, think of her as 'Miss Malcolm?') stirred. She lifted a ravaged face from beneath the bedclothes. Her dark, waving hair had not been tied back; instead it stood out from her face, wildly.

'Dear Lord, I have lost it, you know. Gone, gone, *gone*. I am undone –'

It was a deep voice of great beauty even when as now, she was over-emphasizing. Dear Vicky – larger than life (too large for little life . . .) She had sat up and was pulling her fingers through the tangled forest. 'Oh dear God – I must take your name in vain. Gone, all lost . . .'

I said, and felt foolish, 'Is something wrong?'

'But absolutely a *disaster*, I couldn't sleep for thinking about it. Now I sleep too heavily. I *lost* it –'

'Lost what?'

'It wasn't very large,' she said desperately, 'it wasn't as if it were *important* – but I have lost it.' Just as I was about to ask further, she went on: 'My part – the *little* part that I had – it is *gone* . . .'

'You are unemployed – does it mean that?'

She said dramatically, '*Indeed* I have the frost . . .' She had climbed out of bed, pulled on a wrap. Suddenly, looking at me for the first time, 'Tell me,' she said, 'oh, tell me – what are *you* in?'

'Nothing,' I said, 'I am *in* nothing.' Enough, but I had had to spoil it then with a little arrogant turn of phrase. 'Miss Grey, Sylvia Grey –' (how I squirm to remember!) 'An introduction. I expect soon to be engaged, you see.'

'No, but you are *very* fortunate –' She looked, it seemed to me, suitably impressed. 'When do you take this up?'

I explained that I would go to the Lyceum today. She nodded, all the time moving about the room which was in an incredible confusion. Clothes and underclothes on every chair, 'I shall move all these for you,' she said. 'And in any case I shall not be here long. I *cannot* be here long . . .'

Presently she went downstairs for hot water. She washed behind the flimsy Japanese screen, telling me all the while about everybody in the house, in the company. 'And the first time we performed it was a screamer, Miss Greene – what doom . . . and the second time I had not learned my part, not at all, and they said, "If you are going to corpse continually . . ." ' She told me of Mrs Bullivant, whose voice was true still but whose weight was such that – *really* . . . 'And little Mr Zulueta who thinks himself God's gift. But not for this child! You will know the kind of person . . .' There was Barry Gerard. 'He is the romantic ju, juvenile, and very aware of it. *His* star is rising –'

She tidied the room a little, attended to her hair, while I sat in the basket chair watching her. She had not asked me of my previous experiences. Over-confident, I would surely be found out soon . . .

Then, her mouth full of hairpins, she asked, 'Why should we not go together, now, to the Lyceum?'

The rain had let up and we walked at first, then as the first drops turned into a steady drizzle, we took a cab. I clutched to me the note I had written to Sylvia Grey.

Oh, but I should have guessed . . . Fool that I was, I had not even looked in the newspapers, let alone the stage journals . . .

'Miss Grey?' said the man in the deserted foyer of the Lyceum. His brow furrowed. 'She's on tour, miss –'

On tour. On tour. Where? (Cambridge, Canterbury? – please God not *Australia*.)

I took the note and all my foolish hopes. Miss Malcolm was waiting in the cab.

'Well? You have left your letter?'

'She's not there. She is in *Scotland*.' And then it all came tumbling out. I said, 'I have run away from home. Run away in the *wrong direction* –'

I had not meant to tell anyone – or at least not so soon. But at once she was warmly sympathetic, giving directions to the cabby, then, clutching my arm: 'Oh my dear,' she said, 'we are both in *such* trouble.'

My mind raced but I could not speak. After a few moments: 'We stop now,' she said. Then, paying the cab, pushing my money away: 'There's a teashop here. We must talk, at once. We are rowing the same boat, I think –'

Inside, she asked: 'What are you going – or rather what are *we* going – to do now?' Adding: 'You might as well tell me *everything*.' As I did so, she said, nodding, 'Yes. That's right. You did right. Especially everywhere to *add to your age*. It is wiser. And I had thought you twenty . . .'

'But your trouble,' I said, 'you have told me nothing of your trouble –'

'Sacked. I lost my part yesterday *and* my place in the company. I answered back, you see. No more. And in defence of someone else – a stage hand merely. But it goes deeper than that. I tell you in confidence, of course.' She leaned forward and said in a dramatic whisper: 'Mr Zulueta wanted what I was not prepared – what I *should* not be prepared to give – and I repulsed him. And I was too strong in that, you see. So now he is my enemy, I have touched his pride, and he has been waiting only the moment to humiliate me . . .'

She told me some of her story then. A lot more, later. Her father was a man of the kirk in Scotland, in Linlithgow:

'*He* could have been, should have been an actor. Instead he frightens people with Hell every Sabbath. Including my mother. And then she is not certain whether it's him she's more frightened of, or Hell.'

'But you are on the stage – what do they think of that?'

'At first, angry. No, sad first. More in sorrow than in anger. And yet – any talent I have – it is from him. The same gifts are needed, after all.' Pause. 'I left home at twenty-one. With *some* sort of permission. His words were: "I can no longer forbid you. Satan has won." But of course it has been all right. Until now –'

She seemed more interested, though, in my tale than hers: 'To have been locked up. *Imprisoned*,' she said in wonder. 'You see, I knew nothing like that.'

But of course our talk kept coming back to our plight. Our joint plight. We discussed money.

'Have you some savings?' I asked her.

'For a week or two. And then I shall be in diffs.' She leaned forward, stirring her tea.

'I know,' she said with sudden resolution, 'we must find something *out* of London. Immediately –'

Together we went back to the lodgings, she packing her belongings, both of us braving the landlady. Her fellow actors she wished to say goodbye to, and this was arranged.

We took the night train to Scotland. Sylvia Grey, we had discovered, was billed this week in Edinburgh. We sat up all night. As we passed through Yorkshire I was terrified – and a little homesick.

In Edinburgh I discovered all too soon that Sylvia Grey was not their either. She had been taken ill at the weekend and had had to stay behind in Liverpool. Vicky, however (for in that long night's talking we had moved to Christian names), was not daunted. I thought perhaps we should go to Linlithgow. But she said proudly, 'I would never visit them without work. To seem even to be in trouble . . .'

But it looked now like trouble. That afternoon, between summer showers, we walked disconsolately through the streets. We visited all the theatres. And then . . .

A grubby building in the Old Town. Outside, a filthy and torn bill: 'Jubilee Song and Dance . . .' We were trying to decipher the remainder, when a man came out. He said: 'Will ye buy your tickets now? We *shall* play tonight. Dinna fear.'

A devil got into me: 'We don't watch shows,' I said haughtily. '*We* perform –'

'Yes,' confirmed Vicky, 'we are players,' and she made as if to sweep on majestically.

'And can you sing?'

'Of course.'

'And dance?'

'Yes, yes.' (Now was not the time to say that I had danced only on the boards of my Leeds bedroom . . .) Vicky said, 'This is Miss Lily Greene. I am Miss Victoria Malcolm.' She paused. 'And now – we must leave.'

I would not have risked turning away. A moment's silence, then: 'What has happened,' said the man, 'it's this, see . . .' That very morning, it appeared, they had lost a couple of turns – one of which had been two sisters: a singing and dancing act. One turn missing, yes, but two – no.

'Tell your manager,' Vicky said grandly, 'that two first-class artistes are by chance free . . . Up here on holiday.'

It was she who did all the talking. By evening we were in business. That afternoon she and I devised in the small front room of our lodgings (pliant landlady, audience of children) a double act: the Carruthers Sisters. Vicky sang *O Bird of Love*, and although not quite sure of the words, I did Fanny Leslie's *Jack-in-the-Box Song*. Sharing between us our repertoire, we turned up two comedy songs, *But I couldn't* and *Just in the old sweet way*. Vicky could play the banjo. 'Shall I black up?' she asked.

We were a success, in a small way. At least we did not get the goose. On the Sunday, after five performances and with another week to go, we went through to Linlithgow to see Vicky's family. Her father was as fierce as she had described – but only on matters of religion, when his face and his whole bearing would change. At other times he watched Vicky with pride, nodding gravely as she recounted truths – and untruths. For myself, I pretended that I had left home with full approval, inventing for myself a Harrogate doctor father, fleshing out an imaginary family . . . Vicky's mama watched all the while with sad eyes: Vicky's but without the fire. Two of the three brothers only were at home, and one of her sisters, who hung on our every word. She said to Vicky often, 'When you are famous . . .'

I never took up Sylvia Grey's offer. Although she was due a week later in Glasgow, I did not go there. The last night in Edinburgh we were approached by a man, a dubious-looking character who turned out soon to be of an unimaginably boring respectability. He had a small touring company which had just suffered a couple of deaths in a carriage accident, and he was looking for two versatile and experienced (yes!) players. I told a few more lies.

Three months later the company folded up. But we spent the winter of 1888 with another, and the next year had some experience in pantomime. Staying always together. A summer season on the East Coast, another in Wales . . .

We worked hard, but we had fun. Vicky was the friend I needed. Before, I had had Daisy: when I had lost her, I had lost both sister *and* friend.

So it was that although in those days I was often homesick, missing Harry, missing Daisy, it was never unbearable. I worried, though, for Daisy and Joszef – how could I do otherwise? But even for the sake of seeing them again, I never longed to be back . . . I wrote to them, saying only: 'I am *well and happy.*' I sent money and a small gift for Harry: 'If you can speak to him, that is – he will have been in enough hot water already on my account . . .' I said that I would try and secure a *poste restante* in London. They were to tell him that I loved him . . .

I became seasoned, gained experience, all the while preparing myself for the lucky chance that would surely come. In the meantime it was not a bad life – this small enclosed world, more hard work than glamour, with its private language, its unsociable hours. A life of travelling Sundays (proudly I noticed less and less wicker on my hamper, so covered was it with railway stickers), shunted into sidings to move on later with the consignment of coal, or worse, kippers. Crewe station at times the beating heart of the universe. Inhospitable lodgings, homely ones. The sudden rivalries and petty jealousies. The sheer *drama*, so often greater off stage than on . . .

We travelled up and down and across Britain. I never doubted that I was on a road that led somewhere. We acted, sang, danced – hoping always for temperate weather, dreading the sudden heat waves which lost us audiences as surely as rain and snow kept them at home – burlesques with preposterous titles (*Very Little Hamlet, The Vicar of Wideawakefield*), comedies, farces. The principals would change depending on what the current manager could afford. Sometimes he would be able to hire a premium artist, one who paid *him* for the privilege of playing. But these turned usually to more distinguished companies, those with a classical repertoire. Everything we did was of the very lightest weight – however heavy the humour.

Vicky and I, although occasionally playing roles that had something to do with the (slight) story, were more often in a group (Country Maidens, Serving Wenches, even Coifed Nuns . . .). We stood out from the rest, who would be played by girls or women – supers as they were called – hastily chosen early on the Monday of our arrival in the town. Vicky or I, as a singing nun perhaps, would skip forward to chant: 'Oh, but I am mother prioress/And they would *wall* me up!/Sir, have mercy, sir, have mercy . . .' And as the chorus of supers took it up, 'Sir, have *mercy* . . .' we would skip back again – until our next big moment.

I did not mind that often the work was well below what I felt certain I could do. Did not the road lead uphill all the way to Olympus? I was in no hurry. With greater beauty, I would perhaps have been sooner there. Vicky was beautiful – but had no ambition. It surprised me. I had thought her, on our first meeting, prima donna material. (Looking at her, I was often reminded of the famous Lina Cavalieri as I had seen her in photographs. It was Vicky's bearing, I think, and the maturity, the ripeness, of her beauty.) Yet when a chance came to her – a few extra lines, a small but important part – she would forget to learn the lines, forget to come in on cue – and for a while would not be asked again. Late for rehearsals regularly, she was as regularly fined. She seemed hardly to mind at all.

But all that time we were friends. We would not have dreamed of changing companies unless we both moved. We giggled together backstage, boiled up tea in railway compartments on Sundays, grilled ourselves sausages late at night on reversible gas-rings. We flirted from time to time with good-looking or not-so-good-looking men in the company. Sometimes we were escorted out by some admirer in the current town. We went whenever we could in foursomes . . . Very innocent. Very happy. Too happy?

We were in Hartlepool in the March of 1890 when Mr Frobisher, our then actor-manager, told us all as we assembled for a Monday morning rehearsal that he had secured the services of a great singer. A tenor. He mentioned no name, saying only that now we should be able to extend our repertoire . . . Offstage, rumour proliferated. It was, *must* be . . . It was Hayden Coffin, Frank Leslie . . . When we at last learned his name, we had not heard of him at all. Frank Donovan? Frank Donovan? Everyone shook their heads.

It appeared that once, and once only, Mr Donovan had had a success. He had understudied Hayden Coffin for three months and had on two consecutive nights gone on for him. But since then, nothing. He had not risen. There was no history of greatness. But Mr Frobisher, who had been having trouble with his male leads, assured us he was just what was needed. Instead of untried young men, we were at last to have a pro, and moreover, one with an excellent voice.

We learned soon that the money for Frank had come from the wife of our new romantic juvenile, Laurence Wheldon, a blonde and willowy man whose good looks far exceeded his acting powers but whose wife's money was underwriting the company, to say nothing of her husband's ambitions. Laurence Wheldon. I did not care for him. I did not like the calculating way in which his cold eyes appraised each girl in the company.

Frank joined us together with his wife two weeks later at Sheffield. (We were often alarmingly near Leeds. Too near for comfort.) He would be playing only male leads: *Mrs* Donovan made that clear. She did not play opposite him, but was second soubrette usually. Her voice was not very strong. She herself did not expect to lead: she had all the success and power she needed, offstage.

I did not like her. Nor did Vicky. Perhaps because Mrs Donovan snipped at her:

'Miss Malcolm, I'm surprised that such a powerful voice, such a powerful *manner*, that we should not hear it out of the chorus . . .' Or: 'Frank, Frank, do look! There is Miss Malcolm blown in late again. In *total* disarray . . . Frank, it is *too* much –' And she would fall about laughing.

Me, she scarcely noticed. 'The little one,' she called me, although I was at least as tall as she was. When she was not drawing Frank's attention to Vicky's faults, she was correcting him for his, her high-pitched voice shrill with reprimand. 'Just remember,' she would say very loudly, wagging her finger at him, 'we don't want your trouble again. *Remember*?' And she would turn for confirmation to Reginald Forrest, who played the comic characters or heavy villains and whose deep voice could often be heard singing, falsetto, some of the women's songs. He was our light relief. Constance Donovan thought him extremely amusing.

Once, Frank must have been very good-looking, with his head of curly hair, grey now, and his tall athletic build, grown heavy but still impressive. His voice. Ah yes, his voice. A light but strong, caressing tenor and even if past its prime, still an instrument of beauty. Certainly, it seemed to me, he deserved better than our little company . . .

We toured Scotland in a bitterly cold spring. There was even talk, Frank's idea, of going to Ireland (European tours, filling me with excitement at the very thought, were not for the likes of us). The outskirts of Edinburgh, Peebles, Alloa. We played Linlithgow, Vicky and I staying with her family. It was about this time she began seeing more and more of Laurence Wheldon . . .

At first it was just to help hear his part: 'Darling, he looks so utterly beautiful just reciting – and getting wrong – those quite ridiculous lines. He really cannot act at all. But –' and here she sighed, 'Lily darling, I could look and *look* at him the whole day . . .'

'Well, if that's all you do,' I said easily.

'Ah, if he touched me,' she said. '*Then*, then I think – I think that I might burst into flames.' She waved her arms histrionically to mimic raging fire . . .

A week later I fell ill. A neglected cold turned to a bad fever and I was forced to stay behind in Newcastle, in hospital. While I was away, Vicky wrote to me regularly. She said little about herself, instead giving me colourful, often verbatim accounts of everyone else. In her last letter she announced: 'SCANDAL!!! Can you believe – *Mrs Donovan has run off with Reginald*! It is truly the greatest excitement . . . And by the way, Laurence advises you to hurry back, as you may have *the chance of a part*. He has heard something . . .'

Truly, I thought, our lives were more exciting than any of the crackpot dramas we acted on the stage . . . I hurried south immediately. I joined them in Gloucester where they were playing a particularly foolish burlesque based on *As You Like It*. The show following was to be Frank Cellier's *Dorothy* – a true musical play, or comedy. Because I had been understudying Constance Donovan I was now to play Lydia, the second lead. Vicky was happy, so happy for me. 'It is your *chance*. You will never look back . . .' She spoke from her place in the chorus without envy. It was what she would have wished for me: her sister, her friend.

And at that time did she not love *everyone*? Loving Laurence, she loved all the world. 'Oh, I love, I love,' she told me over and over, 'I put nothing in my letters to you. Only – darling Lily, I love and love and *love* –'

'But Vicky – he is *married*.' (I was ever the shocked little Yorkshire Puritan.)

Her eyes opened in wonder: 'But he loves me!' She

frowned, knitting her dark thick brows. 'Passion, Lily. It is a *great* love!'

'And his wife?'

'Oh – but she don't care for him *at all*. She cannot even bother these days to tour with him.'

'Perhaps she has children she must look after?'

'They have no children.'

'Oh well – if they have none . . . Then . . .' I weakened.

'She is – has no interest, Lily. Does not care if he is a success. He has told me that . . .'

She was completely taken up. And I was excited by my new importance. Proud and pleased to be playing opposite Frank Donovan who had once stood in for Hayden Coffin. Occasionally perhaps I should notice that he was not the jovial, easy-going character I remembered from my humble place in the chorus. The elopement must have hit him hard.

Dorothy was set in Kent in 1740. The costumes were picturesque and the songs attractive. The plot was foolish. Dorothy and Lydia, the heroines, are at a Harvest Home in disguise, calling themselves Dorcas and Abigail. They meet there Geoff (Laurence) and Harry (Frank). Geoff is on his way to marry the rich Dorothy, to pay off his debts . . . From then on: a tangle of marriage-avoiding stratagems, faked robberies, fresh disguises – all happily ending with the weddings of Dorothy and Geoff, Lydia and Harry . . .

Then one afternoon, three days before the show opened, we were rehearsing a scene where Dorothy alias Dorcas and Lydia alias Abigail are recognized by Geoff and Harry and . . . When suddenly Frank without any comment turned and walked off stage. Laurence said at once, to the theatre at large, 'The bottle, the bottle. My God.' Then to Polly, who was playing Dorothy: 'Dearie, run after him. Do.' She looked prettily blank. I said, 'I will. Let me –'

I found him near a pile of stacked ropes. As predicted, he was holding a bottle, but I saw that it was almost if not quite full. I pulled at his arm. 'Are you sick? Shall I say you're sick, Frank?'

'Yes – sick,' he said. 'Sick. My *soul*. Sick . . .'

I heard the piano strike up: Polly was to go over again a difficult duet with Laurence.

'You don't need any of that,' I said. (Yorkshire temperance. Greenwood again.) 'It won't help your soul, you know. *Or* your body.' When he didn't respond, taking his arm, I said, 'Come back. On stage. They need you. They love you. And the audience next week. You will see . . .' (And dear God, I thought, if this show doesn't go on, I shall lose my chance . . .) '*Please*, Frank, Mr Donovan –'

'Yes,' he said, looking vague. 'Yes. I could . . .'

Back again, he behaved as if nothing had happened. Mechanically correct. Singing to me, faultlessly, the best-loved song of the show, *Queen of my Heart*. Once Laurence said acidly, 'You are meant, you know, to be *amorous* of little Lily – You cannot leave all the passion to Polly and me . . .' Polly simpered embarrassedly. (Vicky had told me she would not be averse to some of the loving attentions *she* was receiving.)

That evening, Frank asked me to walk in the town with him. 'To keep me from temptation,' he said. 'The devil and all that . . .' We walked solemnly around Gloucester in and out of the Cathedral precincts while he told me about his childhood. He did not mention Constance at all. The next evening the same, and the evening after.

But – the performance itself. How he played . . . Even Laurence was agreeably surprised. *I* knew, though, that it was my doing – that Frank sang not for Lydia, but for Lily Greene. I knew myself to be, for those few hours, Queen of his heart. I felt pity then, immense pity. I could see, as he sang, the years drop away – so that I *knew* him: the young and hopeful singer, all the best to come, a bottle no more than something to be cracked among friends. '*Queen of my Heart*,' he sang. I scarcely noticed Laurence and Vicky (passing of messages, quick touching of hands in the wings . . .)

Afterwards, as we all drank together (only a bottle of stout for him), he said: 'I did it for you.'

'Did what?' I asked, all innocence.

'Played. Went on. I'd else not have done so. I had a mind not to.'

After that, I thought my support could perhaps be less, that I had done the *work*. But it was only beginning . . . And I, I was not without feeling. A bond had been forged. Pity (mine), need (his)?

'Help me,' he said, the second evening. 'Walk. A short walk. A drink. No, *no* drink –'

'No drink,' I echoed. Well wrapped up, we walked a little way out of the town. He sang to me, mainly old Irish airs. 'It is not serious, my drinking,' he said. 'I can live without it. Surely I can. *If you help me . . .*'

Vicky told me: 'Laurence says it was the bottle that first got Frank into diffs. He goes on binges. That's the "trouble" Mrs D used to wag her finger about. To think we didn't . . . Are we not deliciously innocent?'

The next time out with me he broke down and cried for Constance. 'Her little . . . she has such little *feet*,' he wept. 'Such *pretty* feet.' He was rather ridiculous. I wanted to take him in my arms, but did not. Instead (and I was to regret this) I said pertly: '*I* have pretty feet too . . .'

'*Be wise in time, O Phyllis mine*,' Polly and I sang each evening. And each evening after the performance, Frank and I walked, and talked. He did not cry again. On the Friday morning we heard that by popular demand we were to stay on another week. 'A Sunday without even *smelling* a train,' exclaimed Vicky, 'what shall we do with such riches?'

Riches indeed. For the November weather which had been cold and damp changed suddenly to mild and sunny, the sky unbroken blue. St Martin's summer . . . Eyes sparkling, Vicky told me: 'Laurence and I are to spend the *whole* day together.' Then, 'And you, dearest, what shall you do?'

But we had arranged already: luncheon in an inn, followed by a walk in the country, and then back to Frank's lodgings for tea. The perfect weather held all day. Then as the light began to go: tea-time. Closed curtains, the kettle singing, warm room. Muffins on the hob. Their pleasant yeasty smell. The scent of the tea as I poured it . . .

I should have thought. It is unbelievable that I did not. Frank, as we approached the house, had said: 'Now you'll not mind, I'm sure – but my landlady . . . I told her it's my wife come down for the day . . .'

The key firmly turned in the lock ('She's for ever wanting in – to dust her little bits of this and that . . .'), we sat over our muffins, our toast, our cakes. We spoke this time of my ambitions. Leading roles, visiting Paris, travelling, being seen in London, Rome, New York . . . Above all, showing Leeds and Dad, especially Dad, that I had *made good*.

I did not make good that afternoon. Frank listened to me

sympathetically. Head on one side, nodding encouragement. When I had done, he took hold of my hand: 'You'll do it – aren't I sure of that? Even though I'm just an old has-been who's lost his only love. And surely will soon lose his voice . . .'

'No, no,' I assured him. 'No, of course you aren't, of course you won't –'

'You really think that now?' Unsure. A little pathetic. Both his hands now enclosing my one. 'Of course, I had my chances – The Almighty knows I had my chances . . .'

And he began to tell me yet again (I liked to hear, though – I *loved* theatre tales) of his early days, his few triumphs. Of how he had met, courted, wed Constance. He brought himself – and me, for I was brimming over with pity for him, always damnable pity – to the edge of tears. All the time, he stroked my hand. Played with my fingers. 'Take care of me, won't you, won't you now? See that wicked, wicked bottle doesn't get me . . .'

Then he sang to me. He should never have sung to me. For I knew, just as he did, that he was doomed now to smaller and smaller parts in smaller and smaller companies. That without Constance (even *with* Constance), eventually the bottle would win and he would lose – everything. But for now, he had still a beautiful voice. And touch. For I liked – I was amazed, never yet having had time for or interest in such delights – I liked to be touched by him. The further his hands explored, the more I liked it. And that I should be giving such pleasure too. My boots off now. My stockings rolled down and off. My bare feet (but this was ridiculous) caressed, kissed, praised and praised. And then his hands wandering upwards . . .

A sharp knock on the door. Another. Frank's angry reply: '*Please*! My wife and I are rehearsing. Did you not hear me *sing* just now?' The footsteps going away. Then Frank bursting at once into song, laughing and winking at me. A moment later and his hands were exploring further, further. 'My princess, my little princess. Take care of me. My little princess . . .' My head was pulled on to his chest.

Taking fright suddenly, I mumbled, 'I'm not your princess –'

'No, no, of course not. You are *queen*. Queen of my heart,

aren't you?' Stupid words from a stupid song. But they were my undoing.

He too was undone. Unbuttoned. I was amazed at what I saw. Terrified. The more so when he thrust this fearful object at me, shamefacedly, hurriedly. Pushing me back where I sat, opening my legs, thrusting it between them –

'*No*!'

'Queen of my heart – just wait now till I – only a moment – still, lie still . . .'

'But you're *hurting* –'

'Quick, quick now. No, don't –' For I had begun to struggle. 'No, little love!

It was at just that moment the bells began. For evening service perhaps. But a great carillon pealing, pealing. The room seemed to shake with them. Their crashing echoed my trembling, my fear, my disgust.

'Have pity,' he was pleading, 'have pity, and let me –'

'*You* have pity, Frank Donovan! You're hurting –'

'Queen of my heart, a little moment – there, there,' he was panting, 'and I shall be done, shall be –'

I pushed him away from me. Out of me. So that he fell awkwardly, knocking over an unfinished cup of tea. A dark stain spread over the grey patterned carpet. Outside, the bells called good people to pray. In Leeds . . . but what had I to do with Leeds now?

He looked ridiculous. I looked ridiculous. We were both ridiculous. And to add to it, he was crying.

'For *pity's* sake – no more tears! Please.' And then at once, I realized what I'd said. But did it matter? Uncomfortable, sore, frightened, I had *spent* all my pity.

It was an embarrassing week. I could not avoid him, since we had to play together. When he sang to me – and he did not sound now as if he meant it very much – I tried to think of something else . . .

Then half way through the following week, when we had moved on to Lichfield, Constance came back.

It was Vicky who first heard the news. She rushed to tell me, fearing that I might be upset. She knew I was no longer close friends with Frank, but of the rest I had told her very little: her own love-affair would be soiled, I felt, by my tale – so disgusting, so absurd.

'Does it worry you, dearest?' She sounded a little low-spirited. Fighting a heavy cold. Winter had set in truly now. St Martin's summer behind us . . .

If Constance expected her role as Lydia back, she did not get it. Mr Frobisher said, 'Miss Greene must finish the week out. She is billed here.'

'Ah let her, let her,' Constance said. 'No matter.' She was very pleased with herself. She had not come running back to Frank. She made that quite clear: it was a triumphal return, although what the triumph was, was not vouchsafed. About her escapade: 'We were not suited,' was all she said. Reginald had found work with a company about to leave for Australia. She approved of the 'heavy merchant' who had replaced him with us. She wagged her finger at Frank, even for the first week behaving flirtatiously with him – while he tried to hide an obvious mixture of embarrassment and pleasure.

I did not care. Why should I? Only a week later I was noticed by a scout and engaged for a pantomime in Manchester, to play the Princess in *Jack and the Beanstalk*. I was certain that from now I would never look back. What was more I had secured a place for Vicky in the chorus. It would be good, I thought, to get her away from Laurence for a while . . .

Coming off the stage one afternoon, Vicky swayed and fell. Laurence, standing behind me, said irritably: 'What's happened now?'

'It's your little favourite – fainted,' Constance said. (Although away, she had not missed any gossip.)

'It's nothing,' Vicky told me, as I rushed to her side. 'I haven't been sleeping, you see. That is all –'

But two evenings later, as I stood in the wings about to go on, she came off stage and, separating from the others, clutching my arm, she whispered, 'Lily, Lily, dearest – the worst, it is all the *worst* –' Her eyes, against the wet white, the rouge, were large, frightened. 'I shall *die*, it's so terrible –'

'Tell me quickly,' I said. 'It cannot be so very, very bad . . .'

But it was. And after she had told me, I had to pirouette,

sing, laugh: a fairy in a burlesque *Midsummer Night's Dream* . . .

'I am certain,' she said that night, as we were preparing for bed. 'Quite, quite certain.'

I wished only that she had spoken to me before. She was wringing her hands, pulling at her lovely mane of hair. I said: 'But what shall you *do*?' (It could have been me, I thought. So nearly – it could have been me too.) 'What does *he* say?'

'Ah him. Him. He said only, when I told him (since I must. I had to, had I not?) he said only, "That's really too bad, dearie. You *are* in trouble, aren't you?" It took my breath away, Lily. I had thought – even though nothing had been said, and of course he has his moods when he is difficult and cruel . . .'

'Did you not press him? You must press him, Vicky. He must acknowledge –'

'But I am ruined whatever –'

'He must pay you. Then you may have the child – and return.' I hardly knew what I was saying. My mind whirled with ideas and anger. I asked how long she had? She thought until about July. 'Well then,' I told her, 'you will be back on the boards for the autumn, when the season begins. And none the worse.'

'You know I am finished, do you not?'

'He must be made to pay . . . and if he will not, you must speak to Mr Frobisher. He is after all manager, and cannot wish for a scandal . . .'

But she saw little hope in that notion. And she was right. I saw by her face next day that she had not succeeded. She had learned only that she must leave the company soon, Mr Frobisher not being at all disposed to cross swords with Laurence. As we might have guessed, the importance of Laurence's wife's money overrode any other consideration.

I said: 'You could tell his wife . . .'

'*She* has done no wrong –'

'Vicky, Vicky. If you cannot help yourself . . . Tell them all, all of them, that you will noise it abroad. Create a scandal.'

'And be believed?' she said bitterly. 'Who will believe me? Something like that happened once before. A girl in my first company. It cannot be proved, you know. He will deny it. It is I, after all, who am to have the child . . .'

And then: 'Oh but I love him,' she said. 'The sad truth is – I love him still.'

Stupid Frank, drinking too much in those last weeks before the Christmas season. Being scolded by Constance – and enjoying it. I found I had always to be looking at her feet. I was fascinated to think of how they might be, bare. Frank abased before them, worshipping them. Then I would feel faintly sick.

But not as sick as Vicky, who every morning now staggered up to retch helplessly into the slop bucket. I counted the days until we should leave for Manchester. She thought that she could manage at least the pantomime season before her condition would show. And then she would go home.

When we had been in Manchester only a week, a week of arduous rehearsals and long hours, Vicky could keep little food down and, frantic with worry for her, I urged her to go home *now*. I knew she was homesick. I had heard her cry for them in the night. Without making too much difficulty, she agreed.

Laurence had given her some money which fortunately she hadn't been too proud to accept. A replacement was found for her and she arranged to travel two days before Christmas.

'You'll tell them at home?' I asked anxiously. 'And you will write to me at once. We shall meet . . .'

'Oh but yes,' she said, that chill December evening. A damp cold trying to sleet. Manchester was still a strange place to me. Like and yet unlike Leeds. I saw Jews going about and thought of Daisy and Joszef this fourth Christmas of their marriage.

'I'll take a cab to the station,' Vicky said. Then: 'No, you dear thing, you may not come too . . .' But just as she was stepping into the cab, she clutched me: 'I have loved you so much, darling Lily.'

I hugged her back. 'And I too, dearest. Take care, take care – and you will tell them – at once?'

They loved her too. She would be all right.

The pantomime was a success. It sparkled like a Christmas tree. I was happy on stage, happy with the glitter and the applause. And on Christmas Day itself, although I was lonely, I thought of Vicky in Linlithgow surrounded by her family – and was happy for her. But on the Sunday, perhaps because it was a strange town and I had not yet made friends, I felt all day a sense of doom. I walked in the deserted public gardens with the woman who acted the Queen in the show.

The next day was icy cold. In the evening I was in the dressing-room after the show when a note was brought to me. 'Please come. Soon. Please.' It was signed – no, not signed, she had not written it; it was crudely block printed, and misspelt. The name: Vicky.

A boy waited outside. I went with him immediately. I could hear him sniff as he went before me. Occasionally he wiped his nose on his sleeve. I wondered if we should have taken a cab. When I had asked, 'What is it, where is she?' he had stared, uncomprehending. As we hurried now beneath the gas lamps, in and out of the dark patches where the light did not reach, I wanted to cry, 'But I thought her safe in Scotland!'

I did not know Manchester. In the time we had been there I had learnt scarcely more than the theatre and the streets about our lodgings. We had come now to a poor area. Mean streets. I had thought where we were lodging, so far from the wealthy industrialists' villas and mansions, to be humble enough, but these . . .

At last he stopped in an alleyway, turned suddenly. 'Light,' he said, speaking for the first time, 't'light's low.' The gaslight flickered in the alley – and then I could not bear that he should be out of my sight. Afraid, I touched his arm. He pushed at a door in the courtyard. The hallway was dimly lit. I stumbled tiredly up the stairs in the damp chill. A bang on the door. Almost at once a head came round: a woman's.

'Is that her – t'friend? She'd best –' She opened the door a little. 'Well, come in,' she said to me. 'Come in. This way.' Then, as if to herself: 'This is a fine kettle of fish, a fine to-do – I don't know.' And turning back to me: 'You'll do something, eh? Arrange something?'

Inside the small low-ceilinged room a light showed a bed

in the corner. There was a curious smell. In a saucer something burned. I hurried over . . .

'There's to pay, too, you know. I'd to get t'doctor. I said to her, "Do ye know no one here?" She asked then for *you*, miss. And my boy, t'lad, he went . . .'

Kindness, fear and, a little on the make. I saw them all war in her face.

Vicky. Vicky. I would not have known her. All that wild hair spread thin, strawlike, limp on the crushed pillows. Her eyes stared. Enormous, dark. They burned.

'It's Lily,' I said. 'I'm here, darling. I came at once –'

I wanted to ask questions. But I knew I must be careful, careful. The woman brought me a chair as I bent over her, both my hands enclosing the weak one which lay on the bedcovers.

'My God,' she cried out suddenly, 'my God, God help me!' Then head from side to side, muttering, moaning.

'Vicky, what happened? Tell me, dearest –'

'T'doctor,' said the woman, 'he'll be back the morrow. He'll maybe – t'hospital. Happen it's too late, thought.' She stood behind me at Vicky's bedside. She added righteously, 'And she'll not tell us who did it. They'll never tell, will they? I'd not have taken her in . . .'

Who did it? Why, Laurence, of course. I would have condemned him, betrayed him at once. Innocent as I was, ignorant rather, I did not realize it was something else she spoke of. I said to her, 'Would you leave us, please?' Then when we were alone: 'Darling, *tell me* –' I could not bear it that she suffered so.

Her lips were dry, cracked. 'The pain,' she said. 'I shan't be all right. It cannot be all right. The pain – you see, it is . . . everything. All wrong, all has gone wrong . . .'

There were sounds in the street outside. Drinkers returning home. Rough sounds, from another world. The light by the bedside flickered. I noticed the bedclothes . . .

'But, darling, you were going home. What *happened*?'

'Lily, I *couldn't*.' Her eyes were enormous. But sunken. '*I could not do that to them*. You understand? Tell me you understand –'

'Yes, yes. Of course, darling. But the pain –'

'I thought, you see . . . Mrs Swarbrick, in the show, she's

from here. She knew someone who knew a woman. I was going to be here just a week. Less. Tell no one. No one. It was all arranged. I had the money. I got rooms. They think I am married, you know. You won't say? *You won't say?*'

At first I could not understand – but then when she had, whispering, explained properly, I was filled with a desolate, despairing horror. Why, why, why?

'But Vicky – oh, darling, *why*? I would have helped . . . Something, anything – but not . . . No, never *this* –'

Pain. The pain had gathered again. The doctor had left some opium. She said then, between cramps, 'I don't understand. Why. This pain. It's so much. *She* said – they told me it would be all over soon and that when it was, I would be – all right. But it, *it* has left me, you know. And yet still – Oh Lily, everything is worse, *worse*. Lily, dearest, *what will become of me?*'

I could think only that we must get, at once, the very best of help. 'The best, Vicky, you shall have the best man. At once. I shall see to it.' I was Dad's daughter. Lily Greenwood now, never Lily Greene. But as the pain came again, she twisted my hand.

'No – I cannot.'

'Hospital, Vicky. They will care for you. I'm going to send now –'

'I *cannot* – Lily, don't leave me, darling!' She clung to me, as I bent over the bed. The place was terrible. It was all terrible. I did not know the full story – would never know it. (Some woman botching it up? Filthy money for filthy instruments. Or just – an accident?)

'I'm afraid. I'm so afraid, Lily. The pain. I am afraid of the pain. Because I did wrong, it was because I did wrong –'

'No. You are not to say that.' Laurence, I thought. Laurence shall pay . . .

The bleeding began very suddenly. In only a few moments the sheets, the bedding, all drenched. I shouted for the landlady.

The boy was sent for the doctor. We tried, with growing despair, everything. A jug of icy water brought up from the yard was splashed on to her, from as great a height as we could manage. Brandy was sent for and forced between her colourless lips. Opium. More opium.

But in that next hour, before even the doctor had arrived (what, I think now, could he have done so late?), she bled to death.

My dear, dear friend. The smell of that room. The sad confusion. The dawn breaking behind closed shutters.

'Sweet wine, for the ladies,' Lionel said. The waiter poured Barsac into their glasses. 'Sweets to the sweet, of course. I only say what is expected of me –'

'James eleven,' said Sir Robert. ' "Doth a fountain send forth at the same place, Sweet water and bitter?" '

'The Bible, at the Savoy? Really, he is impossible . . .' Lionel, looking around him, shrugging his shoulders helplessly.

'Yes,' said Sir Robert affably to Lionel, but looking at Lily. She felt again his gaze on her. 'We are not *all* savages up in Yorkshire . . . I remember that I was put (and you too, I think, Lionel) to learning the Collect for the day . . . I say it again to show there is no ill will – "Doth a fountain send forth at the same place, Sweet water and bitter?" '

It is meant for me, Lily thought: hardly able to drag herself from the journey she had just made (bitter enough surely?) into the past. It is meant for me.

3

I am sharp, Alice thought, coming down the stairs in the afternoon. The great wide wooden staircase into the empty hall with its patterned marble floor.

So empty. No servants about. Papa was in London. He had been there for almost two weeks now, visiting Uncle Lionel. I prefer it like that, she thought. It's better than when Uncle Lionel comes here. *I don't like him.* He's sharp too, but in a different way. I like much better Papa's fine soldier brother, Uncle Thomas, who's away serving in India now.

An afternoon that was all hers. Her governess, half an hour ago: 'Alice Firth, surely you can amuse yourself? A lovely home like The Towers . . . the garden, the orchard, the fountain, the copse. And in this beautiful September weather . . .' Perhaps to Miss Fairgrieves, who was rather elderly, just to be young might seem amusing?

Down the great wide wooden staircase and into the hall: I am sharp, she thought. She saw herself, all of her, as sharp. Pointed. Spiky elbows, heels, toes, fingers. Sharp as a fox, always watching and waiting. I have something to watch and wait for, she thought. I must always be on my guard. Anything at all, and probably bad at that, might happen at any time . . . Sharp, watching . . .

But only for myself, she thought. Sadly. It's not as if I have a sister or brother to worry about. I am an alone child.

She had said just that to Miss Fairgrieves on her first day as governess. 'I am an alone child.' And Miss Fairgrieves had said: 'You mean, Alice, an *only* child. It is called an only child, my dear . . .'

But she had persisted: 'I am an alone child. It is not the same thing,' she had said, 'they are not the same thing.'

She often persisted. They didn't like that. Just as they did not like her being sharp. They call me that, she thought, when they are talking about me, for they talk about me a great deal even when I am there. Almost as if I were *not* there . . . ('And how is the child doing – she is quite over the loss?

That little upset after. She eats well? No more of that refusing to eat, eh?')

It was then, of course, I became sharp. I felt sharp all over, like a needle. I did not want to eat. I did not want to put anything in my mouth because if I didn't, if I *ate nothing*, then I would soon go to join Mama. (They said at the time, 'If she doesn't take something, she will join her mother soon . . .') It was for Papa's sake only that I ate again. So that he might not be sad twice.

Gazing at her in the hall was the stuffed body of Grandpa's black clumber spaniel, Pickwick. He looked very fierce always, even though his eyes were glass. She thought: What shall I do with the afternoon? Perhaps she could go and find Fräulein Schultz, the German governess? They were, in a way, friends . . .

Fräulein had been two years already at The Towers. Very fat, stouter even than when she'd first arrived, with a great soft moon face and little spectacles which looked lost. She'd just come back from a visit home to Germany and was still sad. She wept easily and often anyway: frequently dissolving in front of Alice, who would then coax or bully her into all sorts of concessions. German Conversation would become English . . . Although the subject of course was, as always, Fräulein's brother Augustin.

It must be better to be an alone child than to have a brother like Augustin. Younger than Fräulein, he had just finished his first year at university, but was already in trouble. He spent money that he hadn't got and twice he'd been in a duel. One of his opponents had almost died, and he himself had a huge disfiguring scar . . .

'This alone – we don't worry, although before he made the fight he is so beautiful. But he does *nothing* for his studies. *Und* the money, Alice – I should not say to you this – it *walks away* from him . . .'

She thought now, she might be better to go and sit with Nan-Nan who had been Mama's nurse but who in spite of that was not so very old. Only moody. She complained of too little to do now that she lived in the village as companion to an elderly lady.

'All I ask for, Miss Alice, is another baby in the cradle . . .'

Alice knew she was talking of Papa's marrying again. Now

that it was three years since Mama had died, people did. At first it'd been: 'if he marries again.' Then, more lately: '*when* he marries again.' But there were some things one did not think about because they were unimaginable. And Papa, so sad at her going, *could* not mean ever to replace her. Mama could not be replaced.

Mama's going. Before and after. Like the Red Sea of the Bible, divided exactly in two. Before, although everything wasn't always perfect, at least it was not cold and unkind. After, even if people tried to be nice, it was cold everywhere, and dark.

Most of all now she missed that sacred half-hour in the morning after breakfast, in Mama's sitting-room. Before other people claimed her. Before my lessons began at nine o'clock, when Mama was just up, not even her hair done . . .

She talked to me then. She needed me (I think). I wasn't just a child, an alone child; she used to say, 'Alice, you are my friend. Darling, sometimes, *you are my best friend.*' And then she would take my hand and lay her cheek against it. She would let me brush her hair some days. It had a lovely smell, something like roses but not so sweet. I used to bury my face in it, and laugh. I used to laugh a lot then.

But perhaps the early evening was better still? Because often I would be alone with her up there: not like other children, having to come down to the drawing-room at five o'clock, brought by nurse, on their best behaviour. I would sit with her often for a whole hour, she with her feet up on the sofa, resting. From as long as I can remember, she had to rest a lot.

I had to tell her about my day. 'Yes,' she would say, '*everything. Of course* I want to hear it all.' Then if something wasn't right – her indignation: 'No, no! They *shan't* say that, Alice/do that/rob you of that . . .' She even took sides against Nan-Nan who had been her own nurse. ('Alice, we shall speak to her nicely, and it will be all right.' And it *was* . . .)

I was allowed to be her friend. Because she wasn't always happy, I know that. But I would never have asked her. She would say to me: 'We shan't bother today with how I feel. We mustn't ever bother with that. This is *your* time, Alice.'

Sometimes she complained, very slightly: her head ached, she was a little tired . . . Sometimes Mrs Anstruther, Aunt

Violet, came to see her. Her friend. (My friend. Since Mama went, she's been mine too, although Papa doesn't like her very much . . .)

She thought now, standing quite still: I might go and see Aunt Violet. She wasn't a relation but she had been told to call her Aunt Violet. She was a Roman Catholic, which Papa didn't like. He said Romanists were bad on the whole – though not as bad as Jews. She heard him say once to Mama: 'Violet is a bad influence on you.' But she, Alice, had never been forbidden to go and see her. She could talk to her about Mama. Now, when things got too bad, she would say to herself, 'I can go to Aunt Violet.'

The evenings Mama went out, or people came. Dinner-parties. Mama would say of those evenings, 'Something I have to do, for your Papa. People can't choose, Alice, what they must do.' She'd come in to see me when she was dressed – always with so many jewels. Sometimes even, the Diamond Waterfall. Then, after she'd kissed me goodnight, she would take my hand in hers and, half closing it, fill it with kisses. 'Shut your hand up quick, and they will last *all night*.' (And they did, they did . . .)

Rubies, sapphires, emeralds – she wore jewellery always. Even in the daytime. Papa liked her to. Sometimes, alone, with me, she would take it off. 'It breaks my back, my neck –' And she would give a little laugh, unclasping a heavy bracelet: 'It breaks my wrist too.' But often I wanted her to keep them on because, wearing them, she was beautiful. Without them she wasn't. She was just lovely, plain Mama, with the little face that crinkled up when she laughed, showing small white teeth.

Such jewels. They were beautiful all by themselves, without people. It was enough just to look at them. The stones too: kept in a special room in heavy glass cases inside strong cupboards. When Alice had been smaller she'd been surprised to find that every other home didn't have a room devoted only to precious stones . . .

But the most beautiful, among so many, many things of beauty, was the Diamond Waterfall. Not just a rain of diamonds (and they were hardly common, Mama had explained), but a whole *waterfall* of them . . . They gleamed not only about Mama's neck but tumbled almost as far as her waist – and could seem all different colours. They were fastened together, too, in such a way that they moved with the person – who was Mama. Lovely, lovely.

Grandfather had been rich enough to buy the many diamonds it took to make it up. Just as he had been rich enough to build The Towers . . . Grandmother, Alice was told, had been very, very proud of the Waterfall when it was new. Although Aunt Violet wasn't often rude about other people (she explained to Alice that Catholics were not allowed to be uncharitable), it was she who'd remarked: 'Just a little bit vulgar. She wore it, you know, *before* luncheon.'

It was Mama, though, who wore it in the painting half way up the great staircase – so that all who passed by could see it and admire. Grandmother's portrait had been there before but was tucked away now in an alcove in the dining-room. Only those in certain seats saw it. Mama looked frightened and unhappy in the portrait. Alice thought perhaps she'd known already she was ill. Dying, ill.

She didn't look at the portrait often. It was not necessary. She had her own picture, in her own shrine: one like Aunt Violet's for the Virgin Mary. *Hers* had a photograph of Mama, taken by Papa. In his youth Papa had been an eager photographer. He had had his own darkroom, and had always been taking pictures. The new wing being built, the sunken garden being sunk – everything. And soon, when I'm old enough – he has said that I may have his camera, and take pictures for myself.

In the shrine also: a small bunch of flowers, some heather, a pair of gloves that had been Mama's (and still, but only a little now, smelled of her), and her little gold notebook and gold pencil. Mama had stopped using the notebook when she'd become too ill for them to have any more happy times together. She'd said then that Alice must have it.

By that time she was in bed all day, too weak even to joke. Some days she had a fever and spoke very fast. Her face would be pale except for two red spots high on her cheekbones. Towards the end, she had been moved to the big green bedroom in the West Tower, where she lay propped on high pillows, often delirious, each day weaker and weaker.

Aunt Violet never spoke of that time. 'Let's talk about happier days,' she would say to Alice, 'I was *so* careful with your mother always. We only spoke of happy things . . .'

Going out through a side door, she stood a while in the courtyard. A gardener came by with a barrow, but didn't turn his head. In the distance she saw Fräulein, carrying a flower basket. She thought of joining her. They might pick flowers together. I might do this, I might do that . . . Already it was after five. In a very little, it would be the time when once she had used to sit with Mama . . .

Mama's sitting-room. It was no use to go in there. It was furnished still, but it was cold, cold. Like Mama. It was covered with dust sheets. It waited – for what?

4

'Tell me, Miss Greene, what would amuse you? What would you like to do tomorrow? My brother, you see, has persuaded me to stay in Town, a further ten days at the least.'

Lily looked at him. Ah yes. Sir Robert, Sir Robert Firth. And beside him the smiling, sardonic face of Lionel. But she had not been listening.

'Some idea for the weekend perhaps?'

What? What idea? She scarcely heard in her humiliation. She could only think: everybody knows. They will all have read *The Times*, the *Morning Post*. They will know. I am humiliated.

Yet all was glitter in this room, as it had been glitter two months ago when she had been so happy. The Savoy again, but this time a private room for their, quite large, party. Twelve people. Everywhere masses of hateful chrysanthemums. Everywhere extravagances of decor, ordered no doubt by Lionel whose party it was. There is money in that family, she thought.

He was giving the party for his brother, visiting London again now, at the end of the summer. Lionel, in his bright red cummerbund. Ah yes, he knows, she thought; and I don't trust him not to suddenly humiliate me further – to send some remark flying the length of the table. The image of the newspaper burned behind her eyes, pricking them. This very morning, the Court and Personal column of *The Times*:

> An engagement is announced between The Viscount Tristram, son of the late Viscount Matthew Tristram and Mary, Viscountess Tristram, and Miss Augusta Mayhew, only daughter of Sir . . .

She had not been able to read on. Just thinking about it now made her tilt her chin higher. She tried to change the anxiety in her eyes to a proud gleam. I *do not care*.

'Miss Greene – I know I sound like a deuced newspaper reporter . . .' There was the Honble Freddie Moore, leaning forward eagerly, his turn to speak to her (it could not be about that; it must not be), 'is it true that George Edwardes is after you, and means you to star in his next . . . The thing is that I should so like to be the first to know, officially . . .'

I do not care.

She had read the announcement alone in her bedroom over breakfast. At first, she hadn't believed it. She peered more closely. The name could be mistaken, but – no, it was *not* a mistake. And *who was she*? Miss Augusta Mayhew. Some little girl . . .

She had sat there, anger and humiliation struggling inside her, so that she was locked. Even her heart: she felt as if it had barely room to beat. I expect a letter, she thought. He will write, surely. Or he has written and I have not received it. Perhaps he will even write and say that he knows nothing of it – that it is the Mayhews, Augusta's family, who have announced a marriage. She had heard of such mistakes. Only recently – a prank played on some young man by his friends. An enemy, too, could do it. Soon perhaps there would be another announcement. And in it the wonderful words: 'will not now take place . . .'

Then the fresh waves of humiliation. '. . . *will not now take place*.' But it is Lily Greenwood, shopkeeper's daughter, it is *my* wedding which will not take place. The pain was such that in her anger she could not remember how much, or even if, she had loved Edmund. The image of his face flashed past and together with it all the days of early summer, Jubilee summer. Of happiness. Of being wanted. She had been secure in her hopes. He had promised, had he not? But then – not exactly . . .

But perhaps exactly enough? Still in her wrap, she had hurried over to the drawer where the letters were kept. They were tied with white ribbons, as if, she thought contemptuously, I were a silly young girl.

They hurt. How they hurt. But trying to calm herself, she thought: I'll read them through now a second time, but as though written to someone else. Her head was suddenly hard. Dad's daughter.

The letters, they showed a progress through that summer, marking the enchanted moments, the highlights, where pride and vanity could not now be separated from notions of love. She tried to tell herself now: It is only my pride. But then she thought: I have a right to that pride. I have earned it . . .

Each letter, and how many there seemed now, for she had kept each note, even the hastiest ('half past two a.m., Dearest, I have been away from you only fifteen minutes and already I am dreaming of my dearest Lily and our next happy meeting!'). Had kept all of them just for the proud thrill of his in truth rather badly formed hand. Read now, one by one, they formed a chapelet, a commentary on that summer.

Hurry on, and pass *this* one. Ironic now, referring to the evening out with Lionel when she had met Sir Robert for the first time.

> Dearest, I know that when I am away my darling goes out with others. I think perhaps I must try never to go away unless with you – And yet I know when you are out at supper with *others*, that you are all the time thinking of me, as I am of you (and last evening in the hansom! Your lips are not cherries but strawberries, and that is why I crushed them. I wish, dearest, that I was a poet and not just a silly twenty-three-year-old man about town . . .

And so on and so on – until August, and his departure abroad. He had had no choice about that. He had told her, again in a letter:

'. . . I know, dearest, that *you* could take a holiday this summer – You mentioned it would be possible. And I would have liked to invite you . . .' But she had not thought much about it because of the hint – reading between the lines – that soon they would be together always. She would become Viscountess Tristram. There would be the headlines, 'Carlton Star Weds Peer'. And the customary nonsense: '. . . one of the loveliest flowers adorning our English stage has been plucked by the aristocracy . . .'

'I *wanted* to invite you,' he told her again later (his hand over hers beneath the tablecloth). 'The trouble is – Mother.'

Lily had thought: I should have guessed. Earlier she'd said to herself: 'There will be trouble there. But she had thought herself equal to it. After all, his mother would be the Dowager only. I would have always, in the end, the last word.

'. . . Mother. She hasn't been strong, or well, since Father's death. The shock. And upsets over the Will, and claimants. She would like to go to Austria or Germany, you see.' His dear face, the vivacity dimmed but shining with affection, with anxiety to please. (Might not that be, even now, the trouble?) 'She wants me with her, although a great friend, Lady Bartlett, goes with her sons, and I believe too an aunt of mine. It will be good for her in the mountains . . .'

Lily remembered that she had hoped even then that it was not too late to change . . . She had said to him, saucily enough:

'Has she ordered you, Edmund? Is it a *command*?'

'Not a command – just a plea, darling. She asked in such a way . . . She said, and she's right, dammit, that Father would have wished – that she *expected* . . . So, how not?' He had looked pathetic, torn both ways, distressed and (how to think of that now?) so terribly, terribly in love with her.

That same night he had written a letter which she first saw on opening her eyes, which she had read over her coffee, wearing, she remembered now, her new negligee with its neck of coral swansdown.

> Perhaps I wasn't able to say earlier this evening, when your dear sweet face was looking at me. I could not say how *very*, very much I am going to miss my dearest – except that I know she will understand. Soon we shall be together again. And next time – who knows, forever? You *do* understand, my darling? It is not just the duty I owe my mother – but even more, my Father. A man, that King, Country and Empire could all have been proud of. I could not let him down, could I?

Their last supper together, at Gatti's. The promises of undying love, of daily thoughts. The drive back to her house in the hansom cab, his importuning, her fear that she might yield . . .

And then the long weeks: the rest of July, half of August. Letters had come. Shorter it was true, but no less protesting. Gifts. How she was to know, how could she ever have known? In the middle of August, his note:

> I have been ill – the result of a fall. My wrist was sprained and they think it quite serious [he wrote with his left hand.

It looked like an old man's wavering]. I do not know who I can get to write for me. How could I dictate to some amanuensis all the love I feel for my darling Lily, the loveliest flower . . . This has taken nearly two hours to write. I cannot, dearest, do this very often. Shall you take the silence for my love? Do you still receive flowers three times a week? I have wired that you should receive grapes now, and a fruit basket each weekend . . .

Had it been the truth – that damaged wrist? She had never questioned it. But now . . . The silence had seemed long after the habit of receiving notes, letters. He wrote once more with his left hand. The wrist, he said, was not improving. 'Next week, I will try to write again. I have some news . . .'

He had not written. Indeed he had had news. News which surely she might have expected to hear from *him*?

'An engagement is announced between . . .' The truth had not been too difficult to discover. Even in the little time she had had since yesterday (and she had sent out at once for gossip papers. A picture of Augusta in *The Queen*: 'a blushing rosebud, soon to be a blushing bride. The wedding, planned for November . . .') she had learned that she was the god-daughter of Lady Bartlett (that mother of sons . . .) and had joined them at the end of July. For the rest – Lily thought, I can imagine it all. Certainly Augusta would be different, younger, well connected, suitable (oh, how suitable). And – proximity. There was nothing to beat proximity . . .

The story was an old one. But it would not do. I am a woman scorned, she thought now, in the private room in the Savoy, lifting her wineglass, sipping without tasting. He has behaved very badly. And *why*, in God's name, *why should he get away with it*?

She turned to her neighbour, Colonel Crossley-Payne, and very lightly touched his arm. She smiled sweetly.

'Dear Colonel, please, the name of your solicitors? A person you could – recommend? You see I have a problem of a –' and she smiled again – 'a rather delicate nature . . .'

She was up early next morning. Nothing came for her by the first post. She took a cab and was in the City just after ten.

The solicitors were in the shadow of St Paul's. She was able to see Colonel Crossley-Payne's man at once. He was amiable, grizzle-haired and portly, with a wide smile. His frock coat strained whenever he leaned forward at his desk.

'. . . My dear Miss Greene, cases of this nature . . .' he rubbed his hands. 'Er . . . Some experience . . . A good barrister . . . I have in mind a QC who cannot be too highly recommended – if he is free and will take the brief. Essential, of course, that counsel be first class . . . these cases can be – Not to say tricky . . .'

She was in it now, and could not back out. She could see events, already out of her hands, moving faster and faster . . .

'You have the letters with you, Miss Greene?' A strange man, hands unknown to her, reading Edmund's schoolboyish phrases. There was something wrong. She felt suddenly weak – last night she had scarcely slept – wanted to snatch them back, saying, 'But these are *private* . . .' After all, if Edmund was happy what did any of it matter?

Within seconds the mood had passed. She felt her anger grow colder, not hot, strengthening her resolve. *He shall not get away with it.* She could see the solicitor, his eyebrows lifting occasionally:

'Ah yes,' he said at intervals. 'Ah yes, certainly this would appear to be, if not a proposal, a promise. The words are not there, perhaps, but the sense – it would be difficult to take the sense as otherwise . . .' He looked up from the desk, caught her at a moment when, against her will, tears had filled her eyes.

'You say that you have heard nothing from him – as regards the future marriage, that is? Not that, I think, anything he might say now would affect the case . . .'

When she arrived at the theatre, a letter had just come by the evening post. The familiar handwriting. She thought: I shall read it later. I shall not let it spoil my performance. But it might have been better to read it, for all during the show, creeping into her mind at every lull (whenever, standing still, she had to gaze up adoringly at the hero, her Duke), an idea . . . Perhaps. Perhaps he has changed his mind. Perhaps after all I shall end this evening, this year – in happiness?

But she might have guessed. It was as she had expected

deep down. A letter which, attempting to excuse and explain – succeeded in neither.

> . . . this may arrive *after* you have perhaps heard from others. Although my wrist is not quite right, I could not of course have let anyone else write this particular letter . . . I know I should not allow one of my *dearest friends* to discover so late on of my romantic attachment . . . You must have wondered sometimes whom and when I would marry? You, Lily, who gave me such a happy summer with your delightful companionship! In days to come as a staid married man and paterfamilias I shall remember my darling Lily with affection . . . I should like you to meet Augusta, but think that your two worlds are so different – And that is why I think there was surely never anything *serious* between us two . . . But what *fun* we had, did we not, Lily?

She could hardly bear to wade through it all. Her contempt for him was total. Before her eyes, prince turned into frog . . .

> And so goodbye, *dear* friend of my youth – for now I am no longer the boy you knew, but a *man* . . .

'Oh rot!' she said out loud. 'Rot. Rot. Rot.' Her hand made as if to tear the wad of paper, then halted. This too must be shown . . .

That evening she turned down a prior supper engagement, pleading a headache. She went straight home to bed. In the small hours she woke, her heart beating. She could not remember her dream, only that it had been about Edmund and that he loved her. She felt as she lay there that it was she who had done wrong. Tears crept down her cheeks, and she wept silently. It could not be *all* pride . . . She lay for a long while, the tears falling. In the dark, Lionel's face passed before her. Dark, saturnine. Man about town. Idle memory. What was he saying?

'. . . and of *all* the jewels – the Diamond Waterfall – it must be seen to be believed . . .'

She was to have worn a diamond tiara. Edmund had said once (oh, his foolish streak of poor poetry), 'Your tears – they are jewels. Diamonds.' And now, she thought (because I have in spite of all, a heart): I weep for him, because of him, a whole *waterfall* of diamonds . . .

Events moved swiftly. Later that month she learned that Edmund would like to settle out of court. In a letter, he admitted that an intention to marry might reasonably have been supposed from 'certain phrases'. But he had quite simply changed his mind – and was willing to pay for the privilege (usually a woman's, he commented).

'It is possible that by going to Court we shall get a larger sum.' The solicitor's even voice. 'It is also possible – so unpredictable is the Law, even with a special jury as we would have – that we might get less. Or even, nothing. And the, er, publicity. While it *might* be good for your career . . . One cannot be sure. You will be exposed to comments of the public, the judge, his counsel. And you realize that all, any of these letters may be read out?'

'No,' she said. 'I shall not take him to Court. And – the sum mentioned – that is completely acceptable.'

That evening after the show she sat in her dressing-room and wrote to Daisy. She was sending her very soon, she said, the sum of seven thousand pounds. 'My darlings, you are at last going to America! And buying a lovely house of your own and sending the children to *good* schools. Joszef shall have a business of his own. I shall explain later . . . I am so happy for you both, for us *all* . . .'

That night, strangely, she did not weep.

It seemed to her a happy coincidence that Robert (she thought of him now as Robert) should write inviting her to Yorkshire for the weekend. He suggested two dates: the second involved travelling on the day of Edmund's wedding. A Friday. It must have been meant, she thought. She had due to her a free ten days and decided to take them then. She would go on to see Daisy.

On the Thursday night, which was to be her farewell to her public for ten days, she allowed an admirer, Frederick Calthrop to take her to supper. He was an elderly bachelor ('I shall never marry, my dear,') and also very rich. They went to Romano's. The menu had been arranged earlier together with the wines. He had taken a great deal of trouble. He offered that evening to buy her a little dog. In passing she had mentioned once that she missed the fox terrier, Rex, they had had many years ago as children.

'You have only to say, Miss Greene, and the very best, a King Charles, don't you think? will be yours. I should ask only a smile in return . . .'

But of course. And how *kind* . . . She would let him know in a fortnight. 'I go north tomorrow . . .'

They were a party of six travelling up from Kings Cross. As the train left, looking at her watch, she tried not to think that Edmund was by now already surely married. She had seen mention of it on a newspaper placard earlier that morning. Tomorrow or Monday there would be photographs.

Her companions were a married couple, a young man of about thirty, and an elderly, forthright, General's widow, a Mrs Beeley. It soon became apparent to Lily that the wife and the young man were in the midst of an affaire, which by secret signs and language they seemed able to carry on during the journey. Perhaps purposely, the husband appeared unaware. No doubt tonight, thought Lily, there will be tiptoeing along the corridors. She tried to imagine such a life for herself, but could not.

At Darlington, so that they would not have to wait for a connection, they had hired a special train to Richmond, where they were met. There was some light left as they motored the few miles to The Towers. Looking out, she was reminded that East, West or North Riding, she was Yorkshire. Her emotions were mixed: anticipation, a little (pleasurable) fear, a tingling feeling of going into the unknown. Something, anything, might happen. After all, had not Lionel said, lightly enough it was true, 'My brother is not, you know, immune to your charms . . .'

I could do, she thought now, with being wanted. Perhaps with being wanted a lot. She thought even of a proposal which she could have the pleasure of turning down. She wondered idly if what she had heard about Lionel's proclivities or tastes in sexual matters were his brother's also? (Ten pounds – the price of a little virgin, she had learned.) She wished Evie had not spoken, since she found it difficult now to look at Lionel without wondering whether that day, or the day before, some poor child had been sold to him. But then, she thought, perhaps it is none of it true? And in the meantime, he *is* amusing company.

She had thought that the village of Flaxthorpe would be larger. But it was little more than a hamlet: a fine but small Norman church, an inn, a few houses and cottages and in the distance, farm buildings. The Hall, pleasant, Georgian, walled: it was here the Hawksworth family lived. The young heir who was to marry the rich American . . .

The Firth home, The Towers, could be seen from the village. Even in the fading light it impressed her, if only because it was worse even than she had imagined – or Lionel had said. Who could have dared to blot the landscape so? That wonderful stretch of unbroken moorland, the softer hills below, some woodland – and then this monstrosity . . . Confused as to its intentions. Partly baronial, partly (but only a very small part) classical. The rest – what?

Robert came to greet them. He seemed different, perhaps because he was in his own home, his castle (and it *was* almost a castle). More forceful, assured.

'Will it keep fine for the shoot? November – We are often better favoured in the last weeks of the season . . .'

Everything had been laid on for their comfort. She was impressed to see they had electric light. But the house itself seemed vast, echoing. Upstairs the bedrooms ranged either side of the wide straight corridors. It was her first experience of staying in a country house. She distracted herself now with little worries about 'doing it wrong'. She had no maid. But one appeared, a local girl with butter-coloured hair. Her clothes were unpacked and the low-cut coral chiffon evening dress laid out, with its underskirt of black silk, its yards of ribbon and lace.

But first they had had a late tea in the smaller of the drawing-rooms. Just before she had gone up to rest and change for dinner, Robert's daughter, Alice, had come down to see the company. Lily had almost forgotten her existence.

A thin, nervous child, with drab mid-brown hair and pointed features, she was ill at ease. Her face had a close, guarded look – one that Lily had seen already on Robert. She supposed her to be about twelve or thirteen. The only person with whom she spoke at all easily was Mrs Beeley, the General's widow, who somehow struck the right note –

chaffing her about learning French, to which Alice responded with spirit. To Lily, something almost despairing came from the child. She felt a softening: seeing how Alice placed her feet reminded her of Daisy and how, when in trouble with Dad, she had used to stand just that way.

Poor child, she thought. I may have had a foolish mother but at least she was there. To be motherless? To have no one to run to . . . But Alice did not look as if she ran to anyone.

Downstairs before dinner, Robert paid Lily very little attention, spreading his duties as a host equally among them all. She began to wonder if what Lionel had said was true? Her charms . . . It was during the meal that everything changed. As well as the house party there were some local guests. Mr Hawksworth, Charlie Hawksworth as they called him, was not there. He had gone 'over the herring pond to see his betrothed', she learned.

It was Robert who took her in to dinner. They ate by candlelight ('Electricity, my dear, is so cruel,' Lionel told Mrs Beeley), and from where she sat throughout the meal she could feel his gaze, steady, as if he took the image of her inwards. In speaking to others, he seemed to be listening for, watching, her reactions. Now he spoke to his neighbour. Shooting – the eternal topic. Broken phrases floated towards her:

'. . . after deer . . . stalking with old Egerton . . . the sort of chap that uses scattershot in a twelve-bore . . .'

Mrs Hunnard, the young married, watched by her lover, Mr Johnstone (as she, Lily, was being watched by Robert):

'Oh well,' said very prettily, 'I can put up with mosquitoes since they only take a little nibble. But *midges* –' and she gave a shudder – 'this August in Scotland. Quite ruined. Tell me, Sir Robert, that you haven't them here . . .'

They made a little fuss of Lily. She was asked what it was like, *really* like, to be on the stage. 'I imagine,' said one rather earnest, heavy-jawed man, 'it to be like any other job of work. Plenty of toil and tears . . .' A rush of disagreement to this: 'Oh, but the excitement – and you cannot call it *work*' (this from Mrs Hunnard).

After dinner Lily was coaxed into singing several numbers from the show. Then a duet with Mr Johnstone who had a pleasant light tenor. She felt that really he sang for Mrs Hunnard.

Lying in bed later, she thought: Edmund is married now. It is all over, quite, quite finished. Of the rest, of what would happen tonight, she did not want to think. But her body, free now of all the lacing, the trammellings, could feel, as if in memory . . . In the darkness, Edmund's face came into view. He was over her. His hands touched her face. Remembered touch. The hands, wandering hands, so often reprimanded, restrained, searched her body now. She shuddered in memory.

Angry with herself, she sat up in bed, turned on the light (wonderful electric light), and reaching for one of the three modern novels laid out for her, forced her self to read.

It is over, over, over. *I do not care*.

The next day there was a shooting party. Lionel surprised her by his skill. She had not imagined him a sportsman. Little Mrs Hunnard stayed behind at The Towers, resting, while Mr Johnstone said that he did not shoot and would prefer a country walk. Lily was not deceived.

She and Mrs Beeley walked with the guns. Lily had not realized how large Robert's estate was. His grouse moors stretched further than she could see. Their colour gone now with the setting in of winter.

There was a luncheon-party at a neighbour's house. Lionel said to Robert, 'Miss Greene, you know, is more than a little interested in the Waterfall.' He said it where only Lily and Robert could hear. She was about to say, 'But – I never . . .' and then, could not be bothered. Robert said only, '*All* women are interested in the Waterfall . . .' and smiled to himself. The remark made her angry, and for a moment, she would have protested. But then she thought: Why show I care?

That evening, he approached her after dinner. 'Mrs Hunnard,' he said, 'also on her first visit here, has expressed a wish to see – the stones. Not the Waterfall, of course. But my – collection . . .'

So in the company of Mrs Hunnard and Mr Johnstone (who appeared, an awkward fourth, at the last moment) she followed Robert for a viewing. He had been first to collect the keys.

Jewels, jewels. A whole roomful of precious stones. She would not have been surprised if The Towers had had dungeons to store them in. But these were kept in a tall airy room, admittedly with a double door, in locked heavy glass cases. Sapphires, emeralds, pearls, rubies, peridots, tourmaline, topaz . . . Row upon row of them. All indexed, described, places of origin, dates, histories, interesting facts . . . To Lily it was an Aladdin's Cave.

'Spend as long as you wish – I would like visits to be at people's whim. But of course I cannot leave such a place open to – anyone.'

Mrs Hunnard was soon bored.

'And what does little Mrs Hunnard think?'

'Oh, they are too utterly – they are quite –'

'You prefer – jewellery?'

'Yes,' she said, and dimpled.

Lily was not asked. Only, on the way back, as the other two were talking, he said to her: 'I too prefer jewellery. I have a considerable amount. My father, after indulging himself in The Towers, invested what was left in stones. And some jewellery. Notably of course, the Waterfall. I have merely developed the interest – and extended it. I like them to be on the premises, however. A bank vault would be meaningless . . .' He spoke without looking at her, but as if confiding. 'Lady Firth. A great deal of my collection, of the jewellery that is, was bought for Lady Firth.'

The words rushed to her lips: 'I am sorry,' she said. 'That you should have lost your wife. A man needs . . .' Then: 'Your daughter,' she went on quickly, 'she is perhaps lonely?'

'Perhaps,' he said. 'She does not confide.' He changed the subject abruptly, awkwardly, saying, 'Ah, but here come the – friends, caught up with us . . .'

He was equally abrupt, as if embarrassed, when on Sunday afternoon, finding her a moment alone: 'The invitation,' he said, 'was till Tuesday only. But – could you be persuaded to stay a little longer? Say, Thursday – or even, dare I ask, until the weekend?'

She told him that she did not play again for over a week.

So, yes, it was possible. Some rearranging . . . 'My sister,' she said. 'I had planned to visit my sister and her family –'

'But that is no problem, that may be arranged. Where? Leeds? You can be taken there and back . . . I shall see to that. You *will* stay, I take it? I should be honoured . . .'

An invitation perhaps. But she felt it more of a command. She was at once attracted and annoyed. In some ways it was like Wycliffe Avenue, Headingly, all over again. And I did not like that . . .

Daisy came alone. They had arranged to meet at the Metropole Hotel. It is not, Lily thought, that I am ashamed, but – then she thought again of the photograph in her dressing-room and blushed. I have become, and *am still*, a snob . . .

Daisy's face above the frayed collar of her old black coat had shed ten years. She glowed with happiness. In repose, she showed still the strain she had been under, but it was otherwise a new Daisy. She who'd never been one to chatter, prattling away now like a child:

'. . . Joszef couldn't come, wouldn't come, Lily, because he says he will cry if he sees you, tears of happiness and gratitude, and also that we are sisters and must be alone with each other . . . I can't say, there are no words. I tried to write, but you must have thought it not much of a letter, for what you had done. To have saved *so much* from your stage success . . .'

She told Daisy nothing. At least, even with my sister, let me keep my pride. I am ashamed still of that money. Good only for what it can *do*. (But what happiness is was giving!)

'We sail on January the first. We begin eighteen-ninety-eight in the most wonderful, wonderful manner – Joszef's second cousin, he's in Boston and we shall go there first. Ah Lily . . .'

She spoke quietly, but flushed and non-stop, of their plans, of Joszef, of little Joe, nearly ten, of Anna, nine, of Sara, of Ruth who at five sang enchantingly. 'And *that* she gets from your dear self.' She said with quiet passion, 'Ah Lily, Lily, it is after all wonderful to be married and have children. You, dear, really must marry soon. Soon, Lily.'

The visit to Leeds was on the Tuesday. When she arrived back, a little late and with only about forty minutes before she should go down to dinner, she found a small packet on her dressing-table. The sight filled her with childlike excitement.

Lying on silk in the round leather box was a bracelet. Emeralds and rubies. Gold. Beneath the dressing-table light the stones shimmered. Vibrant peacock colours. She lifted it, laid it against her wrist. She saw that her hand shook.

Her response to its beauty alarmed her. I am used to gifts, she thought, used to returning them politely, if not on every occasion at least on most. (That King Charles spaniel next week? A decision to be made there . . .) Always excepting Edmund, of course. She looked at the bracelet again longingly. But it's beautiful! She desired it – there was no other word. I yearn to possess it. *And it could be mine* . . .

Her day out had exhausted her. I cannot decide anything she thought. Accept, or refuse. She put it quickly back in its box, and into her locked case. When the little maid came in to do her hair, she had chosen as her only ornament a simple mother-of-pearl choker.

Lady Firth, she said to herself suddenly. And then thought: I might still have a title.

I did not really love Edmund. That was not love. And do I, anyway, need it? What, really, has it done for Daisy – if I had not been able to help materially? And for Vicky – what else there but false notions of romance? Ending in tragedy. Frank. Frank, she did not wish to remember. She thought: When not unhappy in love, I am instead a little ridiculous . . . I am, I think, not made for love.

Then she thought with simple and hard resolve: *It is time to get married.*

Downstairs, she did not know where to look. But he solved this for her. After the first glance and greeting ('All was well with your visit to Leeds?') he ignored her. However, once again it was he who took her in to dinner. As they walked together through the hall, she was about to speak to him (such a gift, *something* must be said . . .), but before she could do so, he said, his voice hard, displeased:

'You are very – as to ornament – simple tonight, are you

not?' When, discomforted, she didn't answer at once, he went on: 'You received nothing – interesting?'

'I – yes,' she began. She felt certain that Mr Johnstone and Mrs Beeley walking behind could hear. 'Sir Robert, I –'

He cut in angrily: '*Then why are you not wearing it?*'

She thought him more hurt than angry. Nor did she see how she could explain here, now. She said coolly as they came up to the stuffed spaniel, 'What do you call him, that very fierce dog?'

An unbearable meal. Robert stiffly angry – surely the others must notice. Lionel, mercifully, was dining out. Then an interminable wait till the gentlemen joined the ladies. She was filled with dread. There was talk of playing cards, or perhaps Lily would sing for them? Mr Johnstone was detailed to search for a duet from *The Geisha*. Mrs Hunnard gave delighted little cries. 'If only *I* had a pretty voice – I'm *quite* without tune, am I not?' Her husband seemed deep in conversation with Mrs Beeley. Lily felt out of patience.

She left the room for a moment. As she came back towards the drawing-room, Robert was waiting in the hall. He took her arm, pressing it beneath the elbow, on the nerve.

'I must speak to you, Miss Greene –'

She did not refuse. They walked, he directing her, to the small drawing-room where they had had tea the first afternoon. There, he asked her to marry him.

She said, 'The message of the bracelet. It was not clear . . .'

'I think it was –'

She was surprised to see that he was trembling. She said, saucy with nerves, 'Do we speak of love?'

'I am a widower. My child needs a mother – as you pointed out. And I – need a wife.'

'And you think that I –'

'I feel quite certain or I should not have asked.'

'Then – I shall.' She had surprised herself.

It was he now who seemed suddenly embarrassed, ill at ease. There was a pause. Awkwardly, he added:

'Of course – I want a son. I think I should make that clear.'

She said lightly: 'Oh that, that will be no trouble.' She turned to him. 'Accepting – if I am to consent, I should like to make a condition or two –'

'Indeed.' He looked mildly curious, not displeased.

'The honeymoon. I would want to go to France. To Paris, *especially* to Paris.'

'Of course. Of course.' He took her hands and crushed them between his. It was not unpleasant. She thought even that she might grow to want more of his touch. 'The honeymoon. And what if I have a condition or two? Nothing so important of course, but –'

'Yes,' she said, laughing now. Suddenly happy. *I am to be married. I have made the decision.* 'Why, yes. Fair is fair, is it not? Do you tell me now?'

5

I cannot bear it. The most terrible, awful thing that could have happened. Everything is spoilt. I don't believe it, I don't want to believe it. It shan't happen.

And then – that I should hear it first from Nan-Nan. I think she truly didn't realize I knew nothing of it at all.

'Well,' she said, come up to The Towers for the afternoon (who had she been talking to?). 'Well,' she said, seeing me mixing rose madder and burnt sienna in my paint-box, 'what's all this I hear about a new mother?'

'What, what?' I said, 'What?' Papa wasn't even there for me to ask.

And then her funny pinched look. She pressed her lips together:

'Oh well, if you don't know, Miss Alice, then it'll be only a rumour – hearsay.'

I ran from her then and rushed into Mama's sitting-room. Then I rushed out again, and went to my shrine, her shrine, *our* shrine. And I knelt for a few moments, head buried in my hands. I was so stupid I didn't even wonder who it was – it was just the idea. That was enough to set me weeping.

And then, only a few minutes later, the knock at the door. Uncle Lionel wanting to see me. Downstairs, he made me sit on his knee. How I hate to sit on his knee. He held my hand too, and pulled at the fingers one by one. His knees were not comfortable. They are not safe. And also, I'm too big for that. I am twelve.

'Your Papa has asked me to tell you . . .'

Yes, that is how it began. Not even Papa himself to tell me. Oh, and then, and then that it should be *her*.

'Oh,' I cried, 'not that one!'

'But Alice dear, yes – that one. She –'

I didn't like her when I saw her. I remember now that I saw neat features, a nose a little hooked, and a very good figure. She had a firm speaking voice, which I suppose some might think pretty. And a tinkling laugh which is horrid. And expensive, fashionable clothes. And, worst of all – she is an actress. Yes, she is an actress. And quite, quite hateful.

Aunt Violet is away. I'd have wanted to run there at once. I spoke again to Nan-Nan, and she said she was sorry I should have found out like that. Then she cried a little, and I cried a little. And she said there would never be anyone like Mama. But that I must try and look at it like this: that Mama had been her very special baby – and so had I. So *that* could never be the same again.

They are not to be married until Easter. Miss Greene has contracted to stay in her show (I shall not go to see it!) until March. She does not plan to continue working. There are to be two features on her in the illustrated papers, Uncle Lionel says. She is determined to be a good mother to me as well as Papa's wife. I don't like that word 'determined'. Often when someone is not pleased with me, they say 'you are very determined today.'

They are often not very pleased with me now. Yet I don't think I used to be very naughty. I don't think I often wanted to be. It was easy to be good *then*. But now when Miss Fairgrieves must write about me, what Papa calls a 'moral report', whenever he is away from home for more than a day, then it is always full of: 'Alice has been as usual rather headstrong, argumentative, even secretive . . .' But why should I not be secretive? I *have* a secret. It is that I loved Mama the best . . .

6

It had grown dark. The sea glimmered in the March evening. Lights were strung across the promenade; around the Casino.

'*Marquez vos jeux, s'il vous plaît, messieurs, marquez vos jeux . . .*' The croupier had a high-pitched voice, insistent.

Lily looked at the faces above the dazzling white shirt fronts. Alert, tense, some wary, some knowing. Here in the *salle privée* were those willing to play for high stakes. Those who could afford to lose – or perhaps could not . . .

'*Tout est marqué, messieurs?*'

I have played for very high stakes, and I have lost.

'*Faîtes vos jeux, s'il vous plaît, faîtes vos jeux . . .*'

Tonight, the fourth of their honeymoon, Lionel was playing, but Robert not. Later, probably, Lionel would want to play *trente et quarante*. Robert would watch quietly, indulgently. He never suggested she should gamble – it was Lionel only who attempted to persuade her: ('Not gamble? Shan't you essay *any* alteration in your finances? It is only light-hearted, after all . . .') It did not seem to her always so light-hearted. Just as the size of the winnings amazed her, so did the size of the losses terrify her. Two thousand, three thousand, more, in an evening. She saw it all in terms of Edmund's settlement: a brief holiday on the Riviera, and such a sum could vanish as if it had never been. (Or, less likely, magically become £20,000, £60,000 . . .)

'*Les jeux son faits, les jeux sont faits?*'

Clatter. Turn of the wheel. Fortune's wheel. Everything, but everything, she thought, is a gamble. (Some though are more foolish than others. And I?)

Lionel had lost heavily yesterday evening at Monte Carlo. Robert had only laughed. Tonight, Lionel had said, he would do better. His theory was '*suivez la couleur*'. Red, for him. He explained that for that patience and courage were needed. Lily could think only of him paying for little girls. She imagined it done with his winnings. Ten pounds a guaranteed virgin. Had that not been the price?

'*Le trente . . . le rouge . . . quatre fois rouge . . .*'

Earlier that evening she had been recognized as Lily Greene by some people staying at Cannes, to whom Lionel was slightly known. Invitations had been extended. Although Robert might not know the *beau monde* here, Lionel did. Enough of them to make their days and evenings full of distraction. Jewellery sparkled, all about the *salle*. Her own – so newly hers – shone from her head, her neck, fingers, arms. She knew that it had not gone unremarked . . .

'*Rien ne va plus, monsieur. Monsieur, rien ne va plus.*'

Oh how the company glittered. Lionel, winnings amassed, was having a good evening. He would attend the other tables. It was no use her wishing to leave. He said now, looking across the room:

'What an *omnium gatherum* . . . That couple there – no, to the right, he with the magnificent broidered jacket – they are Hungarians. Quite an *embarras* of Slavs this year. And Rumanians. There are *Rumanians* rumoured, I hear. The Balkans are fearfully represented just now. The Casino quite ablaze with them . . .'

She lifted a hand to her hair. Touched the hard edge of diamonds. Jewels, jewels, jewels.

'I shall not take on any Hungarians. The year before last – no, 'ninety-five, there was quite an imbroglio with a Count Andriyadi. You would not credit . . .'

Lionel, Lionel. On and on. She wondered that she had ever found him amusing. Ten days on the Riviera. She could think only that she would rather be in Paris. Perhaps, in Paris, everything would be better. She had been promised Paris.

'But first, my dear, Nice. It will suit Lionel better. Then we can be three weeks in Paris. Your heart's fill of Paris . . .'

But why Lionel anyway? My honeymoon. *Why Lionel*?

They had arranged March for the wedding. Her contract for the play ran out then. She had decided anyway to leave the stage. Had not Robert said, 'Of course, I want a son . . .'?

It was not naturally as smart a match as the failed one of the summer, but the reactions were all the same gratifying. She frankly enjoyed the extra publicity, the little notices in the press. The congratulations. The surprise of her family.

There was an unexpected sense of achievement, as of a decision sensibly made. She was doing a *wise* thing.

The conditions. Ah yes, the conditions. She was to honeymoon in Paris. He asked only that Lionel might accompany them on the trip. 'We are not only brothers but friends. And he is, of course, excellent company . . .'

He had barely noticed her raised eyebrows. Had taken her surprised silence for consent. And the matter had not been mentioned again. Until perhaps too late. Lionel's trunks labelled Nice. Paris . . .

One of the more pleasant surprises, on a protracted visit to The Towers in January, had been to meet the new bride at the Hall. Sadie Hawksworth. Petite, vivacious, full of common sense and bubbling over with ideas for this and that: for life in England, Yorkshire, Flaxthorpe. She said within hours of their meeting, 'I can't *wait* for you to come and live here too. My, what fun we shall have . . .'

The Greenwoods were to say the least taken aback at the match. She did not know what they would have said if it had been Edmund, but it was the title now which amazed them. (Although Dad, she knew, saw himself as in line for one some day. Services to the City of Leeds . . .)

Difficulties had arisen almost at once. Robert informed her (he did not ask) that the wedding would be in Flaxthorpe. It would be expected of him, he said, which to her seemed reasonable. But to Dad, it was an insult. She feared he might have an attack, apopleptic, so high his colour, so great his anger. 'Not *good* enough, eh? Is that it – only tradespeople, are we? And what are *they* – have we heard *that* yet?' Ma, standing by, looking anxiously from one to the other, face puckered, tears hovering.

But if I'd not run away, and made good . . . Irritably she had said to him, Lily Greenwood again now:

'If I'd not escaped when you made a prisoner of me . . . Do you want me telling everyone how my own dad behaved? If I hadn't run away and made good, you'd never have been the father of *Lady* Firth. You may say that soon – "My daughter, Lady Firth . . ." '

Next it was Ethel to make difficulties, because she hadn't been asked to be a bridesmaid.

'Of course I'd have said no. But that I wasn't *asked* – you always were uppity. *Honour thy father and mother and thou shalt have length of days* – you never read the Bible, do you? Your pride won't go unpunished. If it'd been *me* wed . . .'

But it was not Ethel to be wed. Grown now into a heavy, sour-faced thirty-year-old, who bullied Ma, when not doing good deeds (how often her victims must have had to remind themselves: the deed, not the doer . . .).

Harry complained good-naturedly of life with her. Counting the days and months until he would be twenty-one and could join Daisy and Joszef, happily settled in New York now. He dare not tell Dad his plans, he said. 'I'd not put it past him to lock me up . . .'

In the end it was not Ethel who boycotted the wedding, but Alice. Not that Lily had had great hopes, so early on, of winning over Robert's daughter. Indeed the first meeting after the announcement had been a sullen affair, with the child, pinched face, eyes cold with anger, scarcely able to speak to her. Her only remark, when impulsively (and foolishly?) Lily had opened her arms to embrace her:

'I have noticed – actresses are always acting . . .' And she had backed away in such a fashion that Lily could only let her arms drop.

Lily had told her, she hoped tactfully, that she was asking six girls from the show to be her attendants. 'I thought that – best. My own sister, she is not asked either.' I must not do anything, she thought, anything which draws attention to my taking her mother's place. I could not expect her to be bridesmaid.

But she had not bargained for a complete refusal to attend. It had been more than awkward. Robert would not discuss it. 'She is often difficult. I take no account of it. Lionel frequently finds her impossible – especially if thwarted.' Nor did he ever speak of his first wife, her mother. Lily, left to her imaginings, pictured a termagant, for no good reason. Lionel had mentioned her only once: 'Florence, *Flora* rather – we had to be careful not to ask of her more than she could give –' and had left Lily to puzzle out the meaning.

In the end it had been simply: 'a high fever unfortunately kept Sir Robert's daughter from attending the wedding ceremony, which was blessed with unwontedly blue skies, as if Someone above were more than glad to know that The

Towers is to have a mistress again. All Flaxthorpe rejoiced. The new Lady Firth is of course Lily Greene, the actress . . .'

More than one local reporter suffered from a runaway pen. But the sun *had* shone, and the small church, massed with early daffodils, narcissi, hothouse lilies, was full to overflowing with guests in spite of the heavily whittled down list. Lionel had been much in evidence. Harry had looked handsome, very. She had caught his eye as she came down the aisle. And in that second had made her glance say: 'Thank you, Harry, for opening the door . . .'

Luggage, so much luggage. Although she and Robert arrived at their London hotel quite late, and admittedly she was somewhat tired from the journey, the strain of the ceremony, she was all the same a little surprised when they booked in and were shown to a suite which Robert explained was hers – alone.

'I have two rooms on the floor below –'

'And Lionel?'

'He is also on the next floor. You were – not expecting him to join you?'

She wondered if that were a joke. If humour, it was heavy. She said: 'I'm afraid that really –' she shrugged her shoulders – 'really – I don't understand.'

He laughed then, and put his arms about her. 'It's a simple matter of consideration. I am not tired, you are. You need a sound night's sleep to prepare you for the taxing journey tomorrow. A stranger in the bed – is not restful.' He paused. 'Later – in France, things will be quite different.'

And so they had better be, she thought, a little indignantly. She felt a frisson of gratitude at his thoughtfulness; then, reminded absurdly of Ethel (who had not so much wanted to be a bridesmaid, as to be *asked*): It is not that I look forward to it, she thought, if Frank was anything to go by, but at least I would expect to be, tonight, a little irresistible . . .

A night on the train. That *did* exhaust her. She slept badly – again in a compartment to herself, with an adjoining door which Robert had locked on his side. (She had tried it.) She locked her own door against Lionel.

He and Robert had in any case disappeared to drink and play cards (the express had a gaming saloon) soon after dinner. She had pleaded, more than truthfully, a headache, and had settled to read. She had brought with her Tennyson's *Idylls*, and the latest Mrs Humphry Ward. But her head hurt too much for either. Most of the night, the sound of the train wheels kept her awake.

Nice. She would have liked Nice – if she had not been in such a hurry to be in Paris. They had a suite, very sumptuous, in the Hotel Excelsior. Beneath their balcony the sea shimmered blue. Almost the end of the winter season now, but a freshness about everything. The cypresses, the olives, green to grey to green in the ever-changing light. And roses, climbing, rambling, hanging over walls, draping archways, luxuriantly in bloom.

That first night when she was ready for bed, the maid dismissed, she sat at the dressing-table, moments, adjusting the lace jabot of her wrap. When Robert came up, before going through to the dressing-room he rang for brandy. And champagne for her.

'You should not have,' she said. 'Truly, I want nothing. We drank very well with dinner . . .'

After he had taken two large brandies, very fast (too fast for what looked a very fine *marque*), he led her over to the sofa and sitting beside her, put his arm round her. His eyes looked softer than she had ever seen them, but he wasn't looking at her. He chatted of this and that, idly. Then getting up: 'Wait,' he said, 'please wait there.' His voice urgent, constrained. Then he said: 'That must come off.'

'What?'

He fingered the silk nightgown showing a little at the fold of the wrap. 'That. The garment. I want it off. It's not cold in here, I think?'

What a way of speaking, she thought, as he began to walk away. While he was in the dressing-room, she took it off, placing her silk wrap round her shoulders. Waiting for him, she thought of getting into the big bed. He appeared suddenly in the doorway: he was in a dark blue dressing-gown, frogged. He carried a large box – red leather, with black corners. Worn. She recognized it from their luggage. He had kept it with him always in the compartment.

He knelt by the fireplace. She sat on the sofa still, pulling the folds of the silk wrap over her bare belly, her thighs. It is the waiting and his strange behaviour, she thought, which makes me shiver. He opened the box then, and inside she saw – oh, but he could not have brought with him so much jewellery. And this was but the first tray . . .

'Hold out your arm, please.' She did so obediently.

Old-fashioned bracelets. Broad gold; gold network, fastened with ribbon of gold; blue enamel medallions, each with a small bouquet of brilliants; a broad gold chain, each link separated with a ruby; aquamarines with twisted gold. Sapphires . . .

One, then another, another – he placed them reverently first upon one arm, then the other. Bewildered, she tried to smile:

'Some of these – they are very lovely . . .'

Already the wine from the meal had worn off, leaving her tired, and hollow. A feeling of haunting anxiety.

Now he was placing the last, low down on her wrist. 'These – they belonged to our mother. This one, so simple, is what they called a 'sentimental bracelet'. There is some of her hair, you see, fastened in with gold . . .' He was breathing deeply.

Her wrap had fallen right off. She saw her own skin – velvety, glowing. Already, she wore on her arms all the jewellery she could ever have dreamed of. But not like this . . . She thought: I should at least have been a little drunk. It would have been better to have had something, anything. The champagne I spurned so imperiously . . .

She said, since he did not move: 'And now?'

'What is the haste?' It was the tone of voice, cold, edged, which had reproached her that evening at The Towers, when she had not worn the bracelet.

She saw then he had lifted the next tray from the box. More gold, more stones glittered, shone, reflected light. Wanting him to use again his pleasant, bluff manner of speaking, she said: 'Ah, I'm sorry. Do what you will . . .'

She shut her eyes, breathed slowly, hoping that the shivering would stop. She felt him pass over her head a chain, heavy, cold. Now, she couldn't open her eyes. Shut, they somehow protected her. To move would be impossible (and yet I have only to stand up, pull off the bracelets, announce an end to all this . . .).

Breathing heavily again, he said:

'Good, good. Your eyes are shut.' His voice thickened. 'My – flower. Such a gleam against flesh. No flesh is anything unless it's adorned. It changes, changes quite – when the stones touch the flesh. One needs the other – I need, I need . . .' She felt the clasp of another necklace. Then something about her waist. His hands were behind her. 'The body adorned. It will not do. I –'

Rings were being slipped on her fingers now. Some were loose, some went on only with difficulty. She thought, if I keep my eyes shut, perhaps, perhaps this charade will soon be over. His hands were warm, but the stones were not. The cold feel of the stones – and their weight. I might as well not be here. I am a dummy to be decorated. A tree to be hung with rings and necklets.

She felt the weight of something fastened on her head, circling her brow. Then her ankles.

She said, opening her eyes, ' "Rings on her fingers, bells on her toes . . ." '

'Ah yes,' he said. 'Ride a cock horse, ride a cock horse.'

She thought the remark unfortunate . . . He told her, ordered her, to stand up. The cheval glass opposite: in the subdued light, she saw herself – surely not a woman, but a freak? Weighed down with rubies, sapphires, emeralds, pearls, diamonds. Ringed, belted, fettered . . . It seemed to her she must have on every piece of jewellery the family owned. Everything bar the Diamond Waterfall. There seemed little of her flesh left. Her shoulders partly, her thighs and legs above the ankle, the lower part of her belly. The blonde triangle of hair . . .

He gazed at her without speaking for what must have been at least a minute. Contemplating. She hoped then that perhaps it was all to end here – that the act would be something separate. For another night, or day.

'Well – have you seen enough?' she asked jauntily. 'I am a fine sight. Not even a queen –'

It was then he took her. Removing first only the belt. It would not have been terrible – only like Frank – if it had not been for the pain of stones, metal, pressed into soft skin. (If I had even dreamed . . .) She tried to remember she had thought Robert pleasing once.

And ludicrous – it was all ludicrous. That was the word for it. She had been once already, with Frank, ridiculous. And here it was the same again. But more serious. She could not now shrug her shoulders. Escape.

He hardly spoke. Not even the momentary flattery she might have expected, to make it tolerable for them both. His only words, just before he took her, 'My God, but they are lovely . . .' Speaking surely of the jewels. I, she thought, *I* am not here . . . There was just the clumsy pushing, prodding. Touching, stroking not her but the jewels – touching them with an awful tenderness. *They* must not be hurt. Then, stabbing at her.

A convulsive movement – and he turned away. He said without looking at her:

'Take them off. The jewels. Dress again, please. Dress.' He was embarrassed, awkward.

When he had gone through to the bedroom, tired, shaking, cold, she stripped herself of all the finery – fighting with clasps, pushing and twisting rings. She laid everything in an untidy heap in the leather box. Humiliated, disgusted, she joined him. She said in an unsteady voice:

'I have left – them, next door.'

He said from the bed, where he lay already on his side, 'No matter. No matter. Shall attend to them. The morning . . .' His voice was thick with sleep.

She curled up on the other side of the bed. She bit her lip, wanting to cry, but too proud. As a girl she had lain always on her back, proud, determined. Now she curled up in a ball, hunched, defeated.

What have I done?

There were marks on her skin where the jewels had pressed – weals almost. Some of them still visible in the morning.

Robert the next day seemed urbane, sure of himself, even, she thought, pleased with himself. He treated her with the greatest courtesy, concerned that she should not be tired, or bored; that the holiday should be nothing less than perfect.

'You look forward to Paris?'

Paris in April. In the public gardens small children built forts with the gravel. Girls with skipping-ropes. Punch and Judy. In the Champs-Elysées there were roundabouts and goat-drawn carts. The particular quality of the light in the early mornings, lilacs after rain, the scents of spring. Those first few days, it seemed to her very terrible to be in Paris, and not in love . . .

Paris. Her dream fulfilled. But, what have I done? was all she could think. *What have I done?* It was as if she had made her decision, her momentous decision to marry, sleepwalking. I must have been asleep. Yet I seemed at the time to be thinking rationally, to be making common-sense plans. Even now, she thought, if ordeals like that first night in Nice did not happen again, it might yet be possible. Indeed, in the eleven days since, there had not been another. If only the memory, and the humiliation, were not still so alive . . . She feared that the air of Paris would be poisoned with it just as the air of the Riveria had been . . .

And yet, the days were not too bad. Certainly nothing was spared to make her happy – if money, and attention, and general spoiling could do that. Their hotel: the Grand, near the Opéra, with its nine hundred rooms. Their own suite. Every luxury. Lionel a knowledgeable companion. Usually it was he who organized their days and evenings. They went to the races so that he could study form, so that Lily might be seen in the outfits chosen with such care in London in February. They dined out late. Were brought back one early morning by a drunken cabman – his red plush waistcoat unbuttoned, white shiny hat toppling on to the pavement, when at last he delivered them. Robert refused to pay the three francs asked and, supported by Lionel, left a ranting cabman outside . . .

She saw them for the first time about half way through the second week. Teodor and Sophie. Afterwards she was never sure what she had noticed first: Teodor's enormous size, loud voice, even louder laugh, or Sophie's nearly equal bulk, plump, cushionlike. Their arrival could hardly have gone unremarked, preceded as they were by a number of attendants with trunks, hatboxes and assorted luggage, a little yapping pomeranian on a lead . . .

That evening at dinner in the hotel they were a few tables away, just out of earshot but plainly visible. They had a group of friends with them. Voices were loud. There was much gesticulating, Teodor banging the table, his thigh, his friends' thighs, throwing wide his arms. And everything, but everything, made Sophie laugh.

Lionel looked at them with faintly veiled distaste. 'An hotel such as this, and filling up already with Slavs. Depend on it,' and he sighed, 'they are from the Balkans. It is to be Nice all over again . . .'

Robert commented, 'Not Russian, I think –'

'Oh, but look,' Lionel said, 'now they are greeted by *more* friends.' And indeed, four people had just arrived to join them at the table. Waiters were bringing chairs, making space.

'I shall ask,' Robert said. He summoned a waiter. Gliding over, the waiter bent his head as he was questioned. Lily could not catch the reply.

'A Count Baltaretsu-Gadea and his lady,' said Robert. 'From Rumania.'

'Oh, fearful. Not Slavs at all but *Latins*,' said Lionel. 'Remains of the ancient Romans. They are for some reason most dreadfully at home in Paris –'

Lily said, 'They look pleasant enough –'

'They are boyars, the crème de la crème, the best that the country can do. They have only just, very lately, sprung from the soil. They are savages –'

'I know nothing about Rumania,' Lily said equably.

'They've only recently wrested their lands, or some of them, from the clutches of the Holy Roman Empire. The usual bloody battles. Their crown was peddled around Europe and now they have a German Royal family – including a quite absurd Queen who writes sentimental novels. And only yesterday, it was a land of wild forests and even wilder gypsies . . . Frankly, dear Lily, I saw too many of them last year . . .'

Later that evening there were other people to look at, other amusements. She, Robert and Lionel were out till late, drinking chocolate and brandy in a café.

The night was peaceful. Robert sat up in bed reading before turning over to sleep. 'Good night, my dear . . .' If only every night could be like this, from now on and for ever.

Next morning about eleven, in the hotel foyer, a little white dog, a pomeranian, ran into her skirts. Under them. She had been standing alone, hatted, pulling on her gloves, ready to go out. They were to drive in the Bois de Boulogne. The dog – it was the pomeranian from yesterday – was pulling at her hem. Nipped her ankle. As she jerked her skirts, throwing him forward, he rolled over on his back. Then up again, yapping excitedly. She bent forward to push him away. He snatched at the glove she held . . .

Then, suddenly, there was the Rumanian countess. Laughing and scolding, rattling words in low-voiced French. Looking over her shoulder, perhaps for her husband? She couldn't rescue the glove. A messenger boy had joined them, was trying to help. The dog gripped and shook, as he would a rat. Sophie threw her hands up in despair. Then leaning forward, an arm on Lily's sleeve: another flood of French.

Lily, feeling rather helpless, said, '*Je suis Anglaise . . .*'

'My dear, oh but yes – pardon, pardon – what shall we say? The Count – Teodor, where *are* you? He speak English better . . .'

Two of the hotel functionaries had come on the scene. Also at last, Teodor. The glove, chewed, wet, unwearable, had been rescued. More French from Sophie. Then she told Lily it must be replaced. She said:

'We send buy today. I am so desolate – oh, but please, it is all arranged and say no more.' She slapped the dog, '*méchant petit, diable*.' Then she patted Lily's arm again and clasped her hand warmly. 'Oh, *what* can I say?'

The Count beamed. Seen close up, he was even larger than remembered. Pinker in the face behind the thicket of white beard.

When the incident had been over several minutes, Robert appeared, flustered because Lionel was not yet ready. He took out his watch. 'Without him, perhaps?'

'Lionel is not necessary on *every* occasion,' she said.

'But he so looks forward to the Bois. To be seen –'

'I have had trouble with a glove,' she said. 'I have only one. I must go up again.'

'If you could hurry,' he said, 'Lionel comes now.'

That afternoon three pairs of gloves, in lilac, dove grey and white kid, were delivered to their room. It was from the card inside that she had learned their first names: Teodor and

Sophie. Later, at dinner, a message was sent over inviting them to join their party at the table.

'For cognac. After, we are all going to a fine place,' Teodor explained when they had sat down. Sophie said, 'There we drink only champagne . . .'

'What the deuce,' Robert had said when first asked. But Lily, suddenly desperate to go, had argued: 'They wish to make amends for this morning – they must be allowed . . .'

'Come, come. *Three* pairs of gloves. They already exaggerate –'

But Lionel had taken her side. Insisting: 'Why not? This is Paris – not Flaxthorpe.'

The conversation was partly in French, isolating Robert and, some of the time, Lily. She found that though she could not speak up herself, she understood snatches. An effort was made to speak English most of the time. But what English . . . The other friends were all Parisian except for a young couple, Rumanians living in Paris, distant relations of Teodor.

They discovered Lily was on the stage – had just left it. That she was a 'name' in London. Sophie clapped her hands to show delight, to applaud. 'And that we shouldn't know! Just now this evening the manager here he has told us. And that you are only two weeks espoused . . .'

Robert was pleased. It was as if, Lily thought, someone had praised, wondered at, a costly purchase. (A bargain perhaps?)

'You have seen Réjane here? Gabrielle Réjane. you know her? *La Belle Héllène, FrouFrou* . . . You meet her?'

Lily had not. She knew only of her fame. Later when Sophie remarked to no one in particular, 'Imagine, it is already five years since we was sitting here in Paris –' Lily said:

'And I – It is my very first visit . . .'

'*Comme vous avez de la chance, tout voir pour la première fois* –' someone said.

'Like Eiffel Tour,' said Teodor, and roared with laughter.

Sophie looked hurt. 'But no – it is great monument. Truly.' She turned to Lily, then back to the company: 'And you know it is a Rumanian who has a *médaille d'or* because he climb it? Yes, alone *by himself* he do it. Such courage.' She said very seriously, 'He was engraver of wood, very precise, he can write on one postcard three hundred thousand words . . .'

'My dear,' said Lionel, stifling a yawn, 'who would *want* to write three hundred thousand words on a postcard? As to *reading* them . . .'

They went out to drink champagne as promised. Lily was enjoying herself, although she thought: I am easily pleased. Anything was better than being in the hotel bedroom. Robert too did not seem to be unhappy. When Sophie praised a necklet of rubies that she was wearing, it appeared to give him great pleasure. Then Sophie had added: 'It is *she* makes it beautiful, no?' begging Teodor to agree at once.

They did not mention children, and Lily did not ask. They spoke easily, happily, of their life at home. They had a house in the capital, Bucharest, and another in Sinaia in the Carpathian mountains where they spent their summers. Teodor spoke of shooting ('quite the favourite of his,' Sophie explained). There were scurries to translate. Dumb shows, laughter. Bears, it appeared, were hunted. Lynx, chamois, wild boar. Robert was led to speak of, to compare, his shoot in Yorkshire.

Also in Sinaia each summer were the Royal Family. Their castle, built by the present king twenty years ago was a mixture of styles, German gothic predominating. Peleş castle, pronounced 'Pelesh' – Lionel remarked that The Towers (which he described rather cruelly, Lily thought) was like 'Pelesh', a mish-mash. He, all of them, delighted in the sounds the words made . . .

Sophie spoke now of the Royals: '. . . Carol, our King, he works you know always standing up. It is the army has made that. And she, the Queen, she write – oh, so romantic. And now there is young English Crown Princess, this Marie of Edimbourg as you will know. For her it is not being easy. She was used to live warmer, not so stiff life. For us, we go to Court or not, as we please. We are true Rumanian . . . But because my mother – twenty years ago, she is part of Court . . . And then I, young married . . .'

Lily listening, wondered: Where am I? Realizing she was pleasantly drunk. Robert, seen through a champagne haze, looked distinguished, kindly. So delightfully muzzy was she that it seemed to her the night in Nice had never happened . . .

But that very evening, back in their suite at the Grand, holding her arm roughly, he ordered her to undress. The drink wearing off had left her tired, happily so, ready for sleep. Taken aback, fearful – this second time she was more afraid – she hesitated. Then made as if to leave the room.

He pleaded with her then. 'Oh, if you would. Dear, I don't ask very much. I must see you, so that I can . . . Lily, *adorned*.' His face, close to hers was taut, anxious; his eyes hard. It is he – another person, she told herself, I must think of him as *another person*.

Again, she was festooned with the contents of the treasure chest – the terrible red leather box. But this time he took longer to arrange everything – sometimes changing for better effect. Twice he asked – no, ordered – her to kneel. She was shivering now, could not stop, even though a fire burned in the hearth. She tried to control an urge to pull at the ropes of jewels, coils of bracelets, the heavy tiara pressing into her scalp. (Somewhere, back at The Towers, the Diamond Waterfall lay in waiting. *That* too, must be worn. Whether in or out of the bedroom had ceased to matter . . .)

She saw herself once again in the cheval glass. She thought wildly of dashing to the windows, out on to the balcony. There in the moonlight tearing them all off, throwing them to the street below. Down, down. Crowds appearing to amass them. Lily Greene the actress – she has gone quite mad . . .

'Wait there,' he said. His handiwork was finished. 'Do not, I implore you, move – or alter *anything*.'

She did not. She did not dare. It was so hateful. *Hateful*.

The door opened and Lionel came in. Robert was just behind.

'What –' she cried. 'What?' She reached angrily for her wrap.

'No, my dear, *no*.' He pulled it from her. 'Let him see. Let my little brother see.'

'Now,' he said, turning to Lionel. 'Look. You wanted – see what I have . . .'

She could not bear to look at Lionel's face. At either of them. She was more naked than if she were wearing nothing. I would prefer he saw me naked. I am a slave girl. Fettered.

She trembled with fear. Were they to be three in that huge bed? If Lionel is to touch me too . . . If, *if*. But Lionel yawned.

In the silence later, in the darkness, she thought she would never forget that.

'Oh dear,' and he yawned again. 'Very nice,' he said. 'Such a white skin. Just like a lily. So *apt*. Yes, yes, I *do* approve.'

It seemed an hour, was perhaps only five minutes – and he left, saying only, 'I must to the arms of Morpheus. It's late. Good night – frère Robert. And the fair Lily. *Amusez-vous bien* . . .'

It was worse, far worse this time, because she was expecting the pain, the discomfort, the sharp jabbing of the stones. And of him. After, she did not get into bed, but took her volume of Tennyson through into the sitting-room. Sat before the dying fire. The room seemed strangely without air.

She browsed among the *Idylls*, trying to still her heart, her shaking, used body – looking to be soothed by the rhythm, the romance . . . She read:

> Advance and take your prize
> The diamond; but he answer'd, 'Diamond me
> No diamonds! For God's love, a little air.'

She closed the book and wept.

She thought afterwards, and was to think for a long time, that it was Sophie and Teodor who saved her. From that first evening together began a series of shared outings: days that were so nearly enchanted – evenings too, when she could forget what might await her return. When she could just be Lily Greene, on holiday in *Paris*.

The Opéra, invitations to their suite, a cinematograph show at the Grand Café (the thrill: a train arriving at a station, steam directly at them . . .), drives by the Seine in the spring sunshine.

It had almost ceased to matter that she was in Paris, and not in love. For she was almost in love. With the city, and this couple, Sophie and Teodor. If she could have told anyone of what had happened, what might happen again any night, it would be Sophie . . . Often when Sophie admired her jewellery, as she did almost every evening, she wanted to tell her – and could not. I would not. But if I were to tell anyone . . . She fancied that somehow the blend of sophistication and cosiness that was Sophie would be able, if not to help (how could she?), to understand a little. *And how I need that . . .*

She supposed they had no children, since none were mentioned. Instead all their talk was of their nephews: the sons of Teodor's brother. Valentin, Ion, Nicu – their names were often invoked.

'. . . When Valentin hear of this naughty dog – *pom* you call it? and how he is comporting self in Paris, he shall be *not* pleased. They don't like, I think . . . By the way, all have English governess some years. The Count's sister, she is anglophile. It is from them that I learn what I have. Valentin most especially, he has such English. It runs and runs. He is in your university of Oxford, but only one years – last, no, year before. Play, how he *plays*! Nothing is *au sérieux*. Ion too much – he is *very* so, he have philosophic thought. And politic one. Too many . . . that can be danger, *chez nous*. As you, perhaps?'

One afternoon in the last week of their stay she went to a reception in the Rue de Varenne given by yet more of their friends. Robert had a headache and stayed behind: he wanted to be well enough for the Opéra that evening.

Lily, feeling unusually calm and peaceful that day, enjoyed the gathering. One elderly man, eager to speak English, talked to her about her new friends.

'It is so sad they lose a daughter. Yes, they lose one. They have never I should say make the recovery. She was dying of inflamed brain, I think. She was dear little thing, not pretty, *jolie laide*, it is big loss they have . . .'

So that was *their* secret sorrow. She thought yet again: I make a great fuss of nothing, and have not suffered at all.

Today Sophie was the centre of a circle of admirers. She threw up her hands in mock horror as the little pomeranian ran yapping among the guests. Teodor, with good-humoured exasperation, picked him up and handed him to a footman. Lily, half listening to the woman talking to her, watched Lionel. He was deep in conversation with the daughter of the house, a little girl of about twelve. He had stopped her as she was walking solemnly round the small onyx coffee tables, among the guests. She giggled and pouted as he chatted to her. His arms encircled her waist. She giggled again. 'My little butterfly,' Lily heard him say.

It was Bizet's *Carmen* they went to hear at the Opéra. Half way through the second act, she began to feel ill. Leaving the box, she went to the cloakroom where she was violently and unexpectedly sick. She thought at first it was something she had eaten. And indeed for the rest of the evening she felt a little better. But she awoke next morning to acute nausea. Her sickness came and went throughout the day. She said nothing to anyone. Lying down, having pleaded a headache, she only felt worse. That evening at dinner, seeing the dish of swordfish cutlets in a rich wine and herb sauce, she knew that she would be ill.

Ten minutes later as she sat in the Ladies' cloakroom, smelling-salts to her nose, Sophie joined her. Bent over her, concerned. She said in English, while the attendant, impassive, continued with her crocheting:

'No, it is not Robert send me. No. I see with *me*, what is not right.' She took Lily's arm. 'I have order you some bitters drink. We are going upstairs. We speak there.'

Lily, without protesting, let herself be led. Up in Sophie and Teodor's suite, she said faintly, 'I don't know – I've drunk none of the water. It can't be that. And I have no fever. The *wine*, perhaps? The white, acid . . . ' She thought suddenly of the swordfish and nausea returned. Her throat filled.

Sophie said, 'Oh my dear.' She raised her eyebrows humorously. 'What do you think – perhaps *you* are not thinking as you should – you see – it's permitted to be frank?'

Yes, yes. She was beyond caring. 'I speak of certain matters,' Sophie said. 'You are just married, yes? one month? So you forgive me because I am your friend when I tell you it is perhaps – baby. No?'

At first she could not answer, for the shock. For the nausea too. How could I have been so simple, naïve? Her ignorance embarrassed her. But of course, *of course* . . . What she had been used to see every month, postponed she had thought by the excitement, the travel. Often in the days when she had been touring, had not the same thing happened – and nothing thought of it?

Yet had it been anyone else – I would have guessed. But as she sipped the bitters, as they dried her mouth, she could think only: these last days, this oasis of friendship, it is all over. Everything is over . . . My life.

I played for high stakes – and I have lost.

'I can't,' she said, 'oh, but I can't.' She wanted to tell Sophie – all. She saw the leather coffer, with its massed jewellery . . . It seemed part of her nausea.

'No, but I am certain, yes, I am right,' said Sophie. 'Yes. And you shall be happy, so *happy* that it is so. Soon, happy . . .'

Never. Never.

7

It would quite ruin Christmas. No doubt about it. And so much fuss being made too. The grave faces: Dr Sowerby calling twice a day. And *two* strange nurses, one for day and one for night. The night one had spoken to Alice in the corridor. 'So you're the lucky young girl who has a baby brother! We must take great care if he's to stay with us. Mother needs care too . . .'

'Don't you dare call her "Mother",' she'd muttered under her breath, hurrying away.

The worst was: *no one had thought to tell her*. Not a word until September. She had guessed nothing. She was annoyed with herself since she knew after all that babies were carried inside, and once she'd heard the news she saw clearly the difference in Belle Maman's appearance. (And that was another thing – fancy being told to call her by a name which meant in French not only 'stepmother' and 'mother-in-law', but 'beautiful Mama' too . . . How dare they?) Angry too that she had not been trusted with knowledge which concerned her so much. Knowledge which would change her whole life.

Not only am I expected to love Belle Maman, she thought, but now I must love IT as well. The son and heir. And sickly. She was terrified when the rogue thought came to her: I hope he dies . . .

Belle Maman had looked tired and wan in the weeks before the birth. But when Alice was taken in to see her on the second day, she was sitting up in a swansdown wrap, surrounded by flowers. The baby, lost in drapes and frills of white lace and organdie. (Her cot, it had been *her* cot once.) She could think only: It should be *my* mother sitting up there, with *my* brother beside her. Then someone said, 'Shouldn't you like a closer look at your little brother?' and she realized – oh, make it not true – that he *was* her brother . . .

Aunt Violet tried to help. When Alice told her a little of how she felt (some of it she could tell *no one*), and how she was angry with God as well as Belle Maman, Aunt Violet said God would understand: 'He is All Wise, Alice. Al*mighty*. And your mother, dear, in Heaven, will understand.'

'But *I* don't understand . . .' Alice wailed.

Nan-Nan let her down badly. Greeting Alice with: 'What a wonderful start to eighteen-ninety-eight – back in my nursery again!' Only Fräulein, dear Fräulein, with her moon face, her hair in that absent-minded crooked bun, only she could be relied on. Although probably she was thinking about her brother Augustin who was in some fresh trouble at the University. But when Alice said, 'Fräuelin, repeat after me: 'We don't need a baby here . . .' she had smiled and nodded that great head, floppy on its neck even with her stiff collar.

'. . . *Ja, Ja*, we are so happy, how we are *now*. The life before . . .'

Christmas Day. At church the Vicar, Mr Nicolson, preached only a very short sermon. His voice trembled as he stood in the pulpit. She looked at him with awful fascination because she had heard his wife was dying. Mrs Nicolson hadn't been seen out for four months now. A friend brought her little boy to church.

Presents. Papa's to her: a camera. Waiting for her beneath the tree, with all the other equipment she might need, packed in a box. A new camera. Not his old one as she had been promised. He told her the gift was Belle Maman's idea. She knew that she should be grateful, pleased, surprised, but instead she felt only angry and somehow disappointed. First she was tongue-tied, then very ungraciously she said, 'Thank you.' I shall never use it, she told herself.

But later in the day, after the Christmas meal, alone in her room for an hour's rest, she unpacked it with all its effects. Papa had said that she might use the rooms in the small tower. She would set up there her very own darkroom. It will be my *own*, the photography, she thought. She began to think of whom, what, where she would photograph first. For a moment she felt almost happy . . .

Early in the New Year Belle Maman seemed much better, and the baby, they said, was safe now. He was to be called Henry. He held for Alice altogether a great fascination, but she steadfastly refused offers to go and see him in the nursery, and ignored him the few occasions he was on show. She wasn't sure really how long she could keep it up – since after all, he was most probably here to stay . . .

The second week in January, Mrs Nicolson died. Alice overheard Nan-Nan and Mrs Platt, the housekeeper, talking. 'Quite horrible, a growth like that – and lingering so, it was a merciful release. They say she was no more than a skeleton. And then at the end . . . the little lad was there, they let him, I'd not have allowed . . .' Alice remembered again the tall figure in the pulpit, with the trembling voice. She shut her eyes and tried not to think . . .

Later that same month the Hawksworth baby was christened in the Norman church. He was to be called John. Belle Maman was one of the godmothers (she and the American Mrs Hawksworth had become great friends) and Alice was invited also to the ceremony and the family party afterwards. After the ornateness of The Towers, the simple lines of the Hall always seemed to her a little ordinary, but nice. Mrs Hawksworth was very kind. She asked Alice about *her* baby:

'Those two are going to have *such* a good time – isn't it just so lucky, their being born almost together?' She asked too about Alice's photography. 'I hear you've gotten so good at it, your parents want *you* to photograph the christening . . .'

Well, that was true. For very soon after, Papa asked. Again, it was Belle Maman's idea. It is only flattery, Alice told herself. Toadying up to me, like that . . . She is an actress, and not sincere. It would be quite on the cards too if, on the day, they were to produce an official photographer as well, saying they never meant it.

'All right,' she told Papa. 'I will take them.'

He asked her then where her smile had gone. She told him, hearing her voice sharp, cold, 'It flew out of the window when Mama died.'

On the day of the christening, they played fair. There was no official photographer, and before tea they were all assembled on the front steps, and she was allowed her moment. She made the most of it. She bossed them all. Aunt Hetty come down from Cumberland, fearsome old Aunt Minnie . . . She wished Uncle Thomas could have been there. Uncle Lionel she ignored and hoped he would ignore her. Belle Maman looked white and drawn beneath her pink velvet and chiffon hat, in her arms the baby in christening robes and shawl.

She wasn't very skilled with the camera yet. And nervous. Too much to think of at once . . .

'One more,' she insisted, 'I have to have one more!' She put her hand up. 'Papa, tell Belle Maman that if she looks at the baby like that, I shall get only her *hat* in the picture . . .'

But then it was over, and the tea-party began. She went from person to person, taking care to avoid Uncle Lionel. He seemed, though, to be absorbed in conversation with Belle Maman. She grew a little bored, restless.

She was sitting in a corner of the drawing-room, nearest the door, when she saw a Miss Hutton coming towards her. She had by the hand the Vicar's son.

'Alice, dear, just the *very* person. See who I have here . . . Gilbert,' she said, 'say good-afternoon to Alice . . .'

He stood there, in black jacket, black knickerbockers. His brown, nearly auburn hair clung to his scalp as if with misery, sad eyes stared out of a freckled face, his hands were clenched tight.

'Well –' Alice began. (*Well*, she thought, we cannot surely be meant to *play* together? He is only ten, and I am thirteen . . .)

Miss Hutton smelled of mothballs and good works. She was the daughter of an old and scholarly man (whom Alice thought to be about ninety-five) and lived on the outskirts of Flaxthorpe. She handled Gilbert with a firm, no-nonsense grasp. Letting go of him now, she turned to Mrs Kent, wife of the Master of Foxhounds:

'What a joyous occasion this is, is it not? And the Hawksworths too, all in the same year.' She lowered her voice, half glancing at Gilbert, 'I am doing all I can, here, of course. Poor dear Mr Nicolson . . .'

The boy continued to stand in front of Alice, where he had been placed. She could not think of anything even remotely polite to say. She had been intending to go in five minutes' time, when she had drunk her cup of weak tea. Up to the darkroom to begin *at once* the pictures she had taken this afternoon.

She saw that he was looking at her. 'Did you eat some of

the christening cake?' she asked. 'Have you been given some?'

He shook his head. 'No, thank you.' His voice was so low she could scarcely catch the words. 'I had enough, thank you.' His tone was very polite.

She said, 'I'm not hungry either. I don't eat very much. I don't believe in it. If you eat,' she said, 'you can't fly.'

He looked up suddenly; interest flashed across his face. She could not think why she had said it. Although it was of course the truth . . .

He frowned. 'I don't partic –' and he stumbled over the word, 'particular*lely* want to be a bird . . .'

She said then matter-of-factly, 'Let's leave all this food and – people. Come with me.'

Where to go? She could not take him to Nan-Nan who would soon be, if she weren't already, fussing, supervising the nurserymaids, the care of the baby . . . Fräulein was not in her room but down at the party.

'Come with me.' She went out into the hall, not looking to see if he followed her.

'He's called Henry,' she said idly as they walked along, 'after my grandfather, and also I think after my father's elder brother, who died in a railway accident. But we are to call him Hal.' ('See if I care,' she said to herself, 'see if I care . . .')

'Did you notice me taking photographs?' she asked. 'You were not there, I think. We could go up to my especial photograph room. You may see then how I set about developing . . .'

They went up the stairs to the darkroom. She rattled the keys importantly. He may come in this once, she said to herself. It is a special occasion. Then as she opened the door, she regretted her offer.

'Well, here it is.' But he only stood there politely. *Too* politely.

'Come over here,' she said. 'These are tin dishes for washing the plates – I've coated them with bath enamel myself.' He gazed wonderingly, she hoped admiringly.

'All the real work has to be done in the dark, of course,' she said importantly.

Once or twice he asked her a question but it was with great

effort, in a small closed-up voice, as if his throat were sewn too tight. At one stage, he said suddenly, very politely:

'Thank you. It's all – very interesting.'

'Do you want to go?' She thought that perhaps he had had enough by now. And she – she would rather be alone.

'No. I mean, yes. No, I –' his voice faltered. Then broke. He caught his breath. She saw that he was shaking. Almost in tears.

She could think of nothing to say. Nothing to do, either. After a few seconds:

'Is it about –' she hesitated. The word was sacred to her too. 'Is it about – your mother?'

He nodded. The tears spilled over. And then he was weeping in earnest. She did not know what to do. She was at once elated and frightened. *She* must deal with this.

He stood quite still, shoulders shaking, tears coursing along the freckles. There was no sound except for his sobbing. He should not, *must* not cry alone for a mother.

'I heard – that she died . . .'

Still he wept. She laid down the printing frame that she held. She stretched out her arms, and drew him towards her. (Almost, she thought afterwards, as if it were done *for* her.) Her arms enclosed him just as she would wish to be clasped and comforted.

They were the same height, almost exactly. As she pulled his head against hers, she felt his tears dampen her cheeks. His body was bony against her.

She wasn't sure when *she* began to cry, but it seemed staunchless. A great well of tears. They rocked, sobbed, rocked in each other's arms.

It was he who stopped the first, suddenly drawing himself up, searching in the pockets of his jacket for a handkerchief. While he blew his nose, she said, surprised by the steadiness of her voice:

'If there's nothing else you want to see, we must go back, I think. They will wonder where we are.'

He didn't speak on the walk back. As they neared the hall and drawing-room, she said lightly, 'If you are interested – in photography – then I could invite you again. To see how it is done . . .'

'Yes,' he said, his voice still flat. 'Yes – please, Miss Firth.'

'Oh, but I am *Alice*. And you're Gilbert –'

'Gib,' he said, and smiled suddenly. 'I'm Gib.'

Before her supper that evening she had to go upstairs and see Belle Maman, to say goodnight. Belle Maman had gone to bed early and sat up, not in swansdown this time, but lemon chiffon ruffles and a cascade of lace. The room was a bowery of hothouse flowers. Nowadays she didn't have the baby with her ever. He slept in the night nursery that had once been Alice's.

'I wanted to thank you – for everything, Alice. You did very well. It was altogether a lovely day, was it not?'

She felt light-headed, as if she walked on air. Almost light-hearted. She would like to smile, perhaps even at Belle Maman. To say: 'I think I have made a friend today.'

She turned. Better not to look at Belle Maman's face. She stared at a watercolour of a moorland scene which hung between the two windows.

'I hope my photographs come out all right,' she said.

8

Languor. As winter turned to spring, then slowly into early summer – that was what she felt. Languor. A word she had once associated with ease, happiness: 'A delicious languor . . .' Lillie Langtry (a name there, to be reckoned with). Lily Firth. Lily. Lily Languor. So weak, so languid, that every action, every word, was too much. Tired before she spoke, tired afterwards. And always hopeless.

Where, oh where was the Lily of yesterday? I should not, she thought, really should not feel like this. In a world full of want, I have more than I need. Above all, I have a fine baby boy. Safely delivered. Whom I love.

And yet, all was not right. In the long months after her return from Paris, she had felt certain that after the birth (if all went well – and it must, it would) she would be herself again. Lily. No longer the much cosseted bearer of Robert's son (he had never thought it would not be a boy), a being set apart: real life suspended until it should all be over.

In those days of waiting, she had been spared any dread of Robert's approaching her. From the moment he knew of the baby: 'We must do nothing,' he said, 'nothing to endanger my son . . .' His tone as matter of fact as if he spoke of arrangements for a day's shooting. Now, she wondered if this very languor, passing almost for bad health, did not protect her?

She should be thankful for it. Perfect excuse on the mercifully rare occasions when he hinted, showed any interest. She held her hand to her head, visibly drooped before him. That was enough. It would not do for always, but it would do for now.

'It takes time,' she told him, 'to recover from a difficult birth.' Dr Sowerby had said exactly that. She had made sure he had a word with Robert. An exact time was not mentioned: 'Strain on the nervous system . . . delicate tissues . . . the internal organs . . .'

Certainly her relationship with Alice was no help – to

either of them. God knows, she thought, I have tried. The fund of goodwill, of love even, which she had brought with her just a year ago, must be almost exhausted. With Alice, she could not get it right. Affection was spurned, interest misunderstood as interference.

And for Alice herself, how often things went wrong. The christening, for example. Those photographs. All that fuss over photographs. And then at the end, that they should be complete failures. It appeared she had put the glass instead of the film side of the plates next to the lens. The upset had been terrible. Lily had wanted to be kind and had arranged another grouping – herself dressed up again and as many of those originally present as possible. But Alice's mood: little better than a sulk, and behaving as if it were everyone's fault but her own . . .

Social life continued. She could escape some of it, but not all. Bejewelled, she sat through dinner-parties, often drowsy before the soup course was through, longing only to escape into sleep. Once, she had been sparkling . . . Paris.

Teodor and Sophie. How she missed that time – those few weeks, which now she would have to live on for the rest of her life. Or so it seemed. Sophie had promised to come to England, even to stay in Yorkshire, but she knew they would not.

They had not forgotten her, though. She did not expect letters but on hearing from her the news of Hal's birth, they had at once despatched an enormous bearskin: a gift for the child. She treasured it, feeling that Paris, and all that it meant, was perhaps not *quite* over . . .

Gifts. It wasn't as if Robert were not generous. If generosity were to be measured by gifts. For seeing her like this, so low-spirited:

'Shall I not buy you something? Tell me what you covet. Name anything –' a slight pursing of the lips – 'anything within reason, and it shall be sent for. Surely *something* will cheer?' He sounded almost impatient. But anything she might want (and what *do* I want?) would not be 'within reason' . . .

'Of *course* you don't want more jewellery, you poor, poor thing,' Sadie Hawksworth told her with feeling. Lily had confided in her – not all of it, but the general idea. Where she did not want to be exact, she hinted: secreting at the back of her mind the disgust, the shame . . .

She wondered what she would have done without Sadie's friendship. Sadie wasn't Vicky, whom she would always mourn. She was different, but good. Now several mornings a week when perhaps she should have been concerning herself with the house (she delegated more and more to the housekeeper, who after all had run everything before she, Lily, had come), she would go and sit with Sadie, who was expecting another child at Christmas. Sadie was not languorous, but complained of a restlessness:

'I mean to organize and overthrow the whole of this part of Yorkshire. I figured that if I can just get involved in whatever's going on, in some sort of work that *helps* people . . .'

Sadie's Jack. Lily could not boast of Hal when once Jack was seen. He was the perfect child. A full head of hair – the fine baby growth had not dropped out – several teeth. He sat up and gurgled. Hal, dark like Robert and Lionel, had only scanty hair yet. A large, lolling, anxious head. Lily was anxious too. She could not bear to watch him bathed for fear he might be dropped.

Now Sadie was expecting again. She did not seem to mind (but then, Lily thought, she is not bedecked in jewels before the act. Perhaps it is all ordinary, whatever that may be). Sometimes, sitting in Sadie's room, temporarily energetic, talkative – cups of tea, coffee, perhaps a madeira – she would fall to thinking, looking at Sadie – and imagining. How was it? How would it be? and to thinking pleasantly of her not unpleasant husband, Charlie. So much younger than Robert. At the most twenty-eight, nine. Fair-haired with a luxuriant drooping moustache. Easy charm.

The only cheer, solace, was all the good news of Daisy. She and her family had been in the States over a year now, and had moved from Boston to New York. They lived on East Broadway where they had been able to afford property. Joszef had put capital into the real estate business of a distant cousin. The cousin was astute, far more than Joszef, Daisy said. And now with the extra money, making it possible to take out smaller mortgages on apartments for letting on the East Side, they were already doing well . . . They were sometimes homesick – she for Yorkshire, he for Russia, but all in all they were *happy* – and hopeful . . . The children were in school and already Sam and Ruth had been promoted twice, and Joe once. She herself found time now to help with poorer immigrants. She had thought of a little simple nursing.

> And to think, darling Lily, my darling sister, if it hadn't been for you, I'd as likely be selling herrings on Orchard Street . . .

Towards the end of May, Robert sent her to the seaside: Filey on the east coast. Alice too, because she looked peaky. (What kind of a rest is it meant to be for me with a querulous adolescent? Lily thought.)

He said too: 'I shall see if we may not go back to Nice in the autumn, or Austria or Switzerland. Mountains, you need mountains.' But when the time came she did not expect he would want to leave his shooting . . .

They stayed in a Georgian house in the Crescent at Filey. Days of uncertain weather, riding out, walking over the sands, in the beechwoods. Fräulein was a heavy presence. In the absence of Miss Fairgrieves Alice was meant to have lessons with her every morning. For the last week they had the company of Violet Anstruther, which Lily found trying, although it perked Alice up. There was much fussing about religion. A day was spent visiting a convent in Filey.

Lily said tartly, 'I am surprised Sir Robert is not worried you may influence the child –'

Violet Anstruther replied, lips pursed tight: 'There is no fear of that. I was her dear mother's friend . . . a special relationship . . . She trusts me . . .' But Lily, who avoided her socially when at home, found it difficult to cope with her here. A scene or two. Words, Alice bursting into tears. ('Look what you have done!' exclaimed Violet Anstruther.) Really, it was impossible.

She worried too, as soon as The Towers was behind them, about Hal. She wrote almost every day to ask for news. The weather, so cold for May. What good would it do her, this holiday, if she were all the time *anxious*?

One night she dreamed that Sophie and she were alone in a fairy-tale, turreted castle. Sophie wore the Diamond Waterfall. She said to Lily, 'It suits me much better, yes? You were wrong to want such things . . . Come to my country and I show you . . .' Suddenly she was among mountains carpeted with dark green forest, pines, larches. Water tumbled headlong down narrow channels into the valley. The light was dazzling. She thought at the time: This is a vision. She did not want to wake up. I will not wake up, she was saying, as the morning sunlight flooded into the room from the opened curtains . . .

She liked to think later that the dream was in some sort prophetic. For on her return to Flaxthorpe, in balmy early summer weather, it was to find a letter from Sophie, postmarked Geneva. Part French and part halting English, it said that they planned to visit London and then Scotland, and though it would be almost the grouse shooting season there, they would come for August 12th to Yorkshire, taking up Robert's invitation. Teodor was very keen. 'Instead of Scotland he decide he shoot *you*,' Sophie wrote.

Lily said to Robert light-heartedly, 'I have heard from our Rumanian friends. Teodor wants to shoot you, it appears.'

He was at the tantalus, pouring himself a whisky. 'They're coming here? Why not – if it cheers you . . .'

She held the letter with trembling hands. She was filled with longing to see them again. New breath, life, hope. It *must* come to pass.

'Why not?' Robert said again. 'If it'll make you even in the smallest degree more cheerful.' He lifted his glass. 'Lionel must come up, of course . . .'

They arrived, from another world, on a rainy evening in early August. But it was as if they had brought the sun with them. She wanted to run straight into their arms.

While longing and longing for their arrival, she had feared they would seem larger than life in the sedate village. They brought noise, surprise, colour. Indeed it was the colour which amazed . . .

Sophie wore an outfit in tartan. Three tartans, since the skirt, jacket and blouse were all different. She had had them made up to order while in Edinburgh. Lily supposed the tartans to be fictitious: no self-respecting Scot would have accepted the commission if real clans were to be insulted.

Sophie asked at once for it to be admired. Reminding Lily with delight: 'Our Crown Princess is daughter of Duke of Edimbourg – so I wear this for her, who is so little, so charming . . .'

'We are spared Teodor in the kilt, I see,' remarked Robert.

Lionel, who had been up now a week at Flaxthorpe: 'Naturally. They cannot be made *wide* enough . . .'

But to Lily, ridiculous or no, they seemed utterly lovable. And how they bubbled over with enthusiasm. The first evening, within half an hour of arrival, Sophie:

'I must see this baby –' It was half past nine at night, the nurseries sacrosanct. 'But yes, please, I *must*.' And of course she had.

They loved everything. The heather, purple now, they went into ecstasies over. It was like but *not* like Scotland. When the villagers stared, they smiled and waved as if on a royal tour. They needed to rest, they said, but showed no signs of doing so. So many places they had been to, so many people . . .

'And happy everywhere. Laugh, we are all day laughing, you see, look at his face – a laugh, a smile –'

'At or with us?' Lionel asked.

'Oh, we laugh at with them all one together,' Sophie said. 'It is happiness. And also we see *Ox*ford. *Ox*ford because our nephew is one year there. We meet friends of him, of Valentin, and also it rains and rains . . .'

Alice was allowed down to dinner one evening. As feared, she did not behave too well, staring at the visitors beneath a furrowed brow. Teodor chucked her under the chin suddenly, affectionately, and as suddenly Sophie threw an arm about her.

'What a lovely maman you have! *And* a new baby . . .' The remark was not a success. Alice rolled her eyes upward rudely.

On Sunday they insisted on attending the Protestant service in Flaxthorpe church. Lily had suggested they go in the carriage with Violet Anstruther, since Roman Catholics resembled Orthodox more, she thought. Sophie shook her head at this.

'No, no, you see, we are in Rome and must be as Romans . . .'

Alice, overhearing, shook her head pityingly.

The village, when the staring had worn off, regarded the visitors warily. People even from other Ridings were foreigners. Many of the villagers had never been out of the dale. That someone had come from abroad – be it Calais, Cairo, Boulogne or Bucharest: they scarcely distinguished.

In the Fox and Grapes, Lily didn't doubt that The Towers' staff discussed the servants Sophie and Teodor had brought with them. Goodwill, sign language, a few misunderstandings. Common sense and friendliness triumphed over problems. Her own maid asked her:

'What is it they talk, m'lady?'

'Rumanian, Taylor.'

'Higgins says their mistress talks *French* –'

'Educated people in Rumania speak French, Taylor. Rumanian is spoken by the peasants, and servants.'

'Thank you, m'lady,' said Taylor. And Lily felt at once, as so often now, that she had done it wrong. Who *is* this 'm'lady, m'lady'? Plain Lily Greenwood. I am ashamed of what I have become . . .

They went to dinner at the Hall. Sadie, her figure thickening a little now, was a sparkling, proud hostess. For Lily the evening was spoilt a little because she was persuaded, no, ordered, to wear the Waterfall. (And I look well in it. I wish I did not. *Very* well . . .)

It was a successful evening until Robert and Charlie initiated a boring discussion about trouble with the Boers in South Africa, and the possibility of more armed conflict there. It filled Lily with fear. Anything of any sort which might rock the world, her world, and her thoughts flew to the cradle. Might it only be rocked by Nan-Nan's loving hands, she prayed.

Sophie was being drawn out about their visit to Scotland:

'This bagpipes, they are sounding that remind us of our *doina*. Sad, very sad. We cry.'

'Pibrochs, laments,' Lily said.

'Yes, yes, pibrochs. Pibrochs and *doina*. The same . . .'

At the end of one day's shooting, Teodor said to Robert: 'My dear fellow, you shoot us – soon, yes?'

Robert, who had never taken the invitation seriously, brushed it away. Sophie said to Lily, later the same day:

'The little one, the baby make you happy, no? He is strong now. Very strong. I *know* strong look . . .'

'Yes, he's all right.'

'But you – not good, not all right?'

'No.' What a relief to say it.

'You dance. Theatre again? You know.'

'No. I don't. I shan't.' She had thought of this. She had not the energy. And how to fight? It would not be allowed . . .

'He, Robert, shall say no?'

'Yes.'

'And to come little visit with us?' Sophie put her head on one side. 'He says no? *You* say no?'

'I don't know. I –' Truly she didn't know. She had not taken seriously, because Robert patently hadn't, the original invitation. Nothing could have come of it. It had not been a *serious* proposition.

But *what if now* . . .

Events moved with lightning rapidity. It seemed nothing less than a miracle. No, Robert insisted, he could not, would not, pay a visit to such distant parts. But had he not offered, Lily reminded him, anything (within reason) to revive her spirits? Within reason . . . What else was this?

Even Dr Sowerby was brought into it. Sophie's enthusiasm, Teodor's delighted encouragement pushed matters along. There was Lionel's lifted eyebrow. Sadie's unselfish envy, out and out. 'Why, I'm *so green*! The very notion. The very notion . . .'

It was done. It was to be. Lily Firth, Lily Greene the actress, née Lily Greenwood of Leeds, was to holiday not in the South of France or Austria or Switzerland, but in deepest, darkest, furthest Rumania . . .

Alice showed no interest. 'Let me show you, dear, in the atlas . . .'

'I don't want to see, thank you. You may go where you please.'

It was not yet decided how long she should go for. But it

would be at least two months. The baby. Hal. He would be all right. She thought that she must be a little mad to leave him so easily, so willingly. She could not hope for news every day . . . But, so far away, might not her anxiety lighten, take on some perspective?

'And when you bring back your traveller's tales,' Nan-Nan said, 'he'll be a big bonny boy, won't you, my love? Your mam back again with roses in her cheeks . . . Baby have a *bonny* mam . . .'

It is for the sake of my child that I am going . . .

9

'We don't see Bucharest yet,' Sophie told her, 'we go straight for Sinaia, in the mountains. These mountains make you well again.'

She was surprised not to suffer more from heat, from fatigue, as the so-called express dragged its way across Europe. Sophie and Teodor, thoughtful for her comfort always: wines, brandy, cushions, fans, ear plugs, boxes of sweetmeats, mosquito nets. Sophie, gazing from the window, fanned herself and said she had become too old for travelling. 'I don't understand, really, what for we are so *mad* to do this . . .'

Their route was through Vienna, then Budapest, and on into Transylvania. They had been two nights in London first so that all the formalities could be arranged. From the moment of leaving, at Charing Cross, Lily's excitement had been complete. She forgot the sick foreboding which after visiting baby Hal for the last time had kept her awake, heart thumping at three in the morning.

Some excitement in reaching Budapest – and then on and on through flat countryside. They stopped at a small station where some peasants danced and sang to the mouth organ. Then climbing up: through the Tomos pass to Predeal and the frontier. Half Predeal station was in Hungary and half in Rumania. A guard, wearing black kid gloves, snatched Lily's passport from her and added to the Grand Imperial Austro-Hungarian stamp something further. She could not read it.

On and on into Rumania. They stopped, hot and dusty, at Asuga and drank some of its famous beer. The Bucegi mountains rose up, snow-capped. The fir trees grew high up them. The lower slopes were covered with flowers. It was strange, it was exciting; she was light-headed with fatigue. The air through the open carriage window was like champagne.

'Oh, but now we are here,' cried Sophie, as the train drew

into a small station. 'This is what we are calling our *Pearl*. Pearl of Carpathian mountains. Sinaia . . .'

Dearest Sadie,

. . . I am still in a state of excitement – and I want this letter to arrive soon, so that you can share everything with me! Dear, dear Sadie . . . But first of all, the *air* – and the countryside – if you can imagine mountains like Switzerland but with the trees growing much higher up: great wild, wild frightening forests of fir and pine. And yes, just as in the fairy tales, in the cold winter months the wolves do come down. This winter past, three children and an old man lost in a village near here . . .

And now – the house in Sinaia! (They have of course their big house in Bucharest which I shall see later. One must not visit a country without seeing its capital.) The district here has not been accessible for very long. Less than fifty years ago there were only shepherds and hermits, and the track through only passable by horses. It is the Royal Family who have made it fashionable lately. Indeed, as we drove up from the station we had to pass Peleş Castle, where they have their summer court. Well, well. My! If I was ever rude about The Towers – They say *La princesse soleil*, as they call our English Marie, doesn't like it outside *or* inside! Inside is apparently disgustingly Old German in decor . . .

The house here is a wooden chalet, long and low and roomy, with the hall, where I'm writing this, serving as a drawing-room – bearskin rugs everywhere, walnut beams, and today a roaring fire as it's been raining since dawn. I sleep in the guesthouse part and have a room complete with a great wooden bed, and a sitting-room and washroom of my own. Wood everywhere – and no wonder, for all around are larch and beech (when they turn fox red I shall think myself in heaven – if I am still in Sinaia, that is!) The pine forests are higher. From my window I look out on to trees, and a stream with a small waterfall coming from the mountains. Down with the Diamond Waterfall and *up* (although it flows down!) with the divine little Prahova waterfall . . .

The life here is very simple . . . I have breakfast by myself at nine, after which Sophie joins me and we discuss the day's plans – for there are so many people staying or about to! It seems to be a Rumanian habit that the most casual of invitations is taken up. Among others are two boys, Mihail and Radu, their sister Alexandrine, together with their mother – they will be here for at least three more weeks and came I understand quite on impulse because she had had words with the mother-in-law with whom they usually stay in the summer. She is called Madame Xenescu (apparently there are a lot of *escu* here and it is enough for any foreigner wishing to settle to add it to his name and hey presto, he belongs!). She is rather haughty in manner and told me frankly that she prefers things German to English. (She must beware as I believe an Englishman comes to dinner this evening . . .) She said, 'I find more purpose and order in their (the German) way of doing things, and we Rumanians do not have order and purpose ourselves, so that it is most attractive.' Personally I think *we* do, but she insists that we are only amateurs – which is not serious enough and will bring us to grief! I learned later that her eldest daughter at just seventeen was this summer married to a German who is part of the Court entourage. So much for impartiality! Madame Xenescu has been beautiful, with hair that is still red but faded. Her skin is dry and her figure beginning to go. About forty and obviously past her best (listen to me, who will be thirty next year! But thirty is not forty, *n'est ce pas*?). I think she has settled in to be disagreeable if not to everyone then at least to me. Her husband is with the army and often absent.

As family and on a lighter note, there is Cousin Alecco who chatters away all the time – and no one listens! He looks about ninety and is I believe seventy-five – a little dried, hard apple, *very* friendly. There's also Tante Elise, in her late sixties and apt to tell Sophie off and even Teo. She is very industrious, always tatting. 'Hands which are making something cannot make mischief,' she says. I translated for her our 'the devil finds work for idle hands'. '*C'est exactement ça*,' she said. I have this picture of her tatting even in the bath! (Sadie, dear Sadie, I can just see your face now . . .)

I pick this up again at just after midnight. I heard it strike from the monastery, but I shan't be going to sleep for a while. I have already had so much rest today! Three hours every afternoon – followed always by refreshments: little cakes and coffee and some conserve of rose petals and sugar in a little glass with a very long spoon, together with a glass of water. First you eat the confection, and then drink. I eat very well, Sadie, already. There is a great deal to tempt me. Oh, the wild raspberries from the woods above us – and the cream we eat them with, so rich and yellow. (Every herd has always two or three buffalo, you see!)

We have overnight guests – two naval men stationed at Constanza. Their train came in this evening, bringing also, just as I had been promised – an Englishman! Not especially for me, of course – he is at the Embassy in Bucharest and has been their friend since last winter. His name is Ogilvy, and he is about fifty-five and a widower. He was seated next to me at dinner and told me lots of Rumanian history and background – all about their Roman origins, and their years of being under Turkish domination – and the great fight for independence this century. In fact the table was quite weighed down with the seriousness of his discourse, and one guest remarked, 'When are we to be allowed to hear the English milady's voice?'

He was telling me, Sadie, they *still* do not have the whole country rightfully theirs. Transylvania, just a little way from here, although really Rumanian belongs to the Hungarians, who are of course much disliked. The magyarization of everything. The Rumanians want so much to be united (who can blame them? After all, you are the *United* States of America and would not like still to belong partly to *us*!). The area they have now is about the size of England, but all the population together only so many as in London . . .

He explained it so well that I scarcely noticed that I was eating which was a pity . . . We had some fresh caviar which was delicious but grey and quite unlike Russian, and an unusal sour cream fish soup, and oh, much else. By this time some were complaining, 'You are monopolizing our guest' . . .

Tomorrow I shall be received by the Royal Family – paying a call only, but it will be interesting and will give me topics for dinner-parties for quite a while! ('As the King of Rumania was saying to me . . .') Am I not vulgar? The truth is, I have had a *lovely* evening. Perhaps I do rather like men in their fifties – especially when they are so distinguished and silver-haired and make such a fuss of me. By the way, he was in England for the Jubilee, and actually saw *The Duke and the Shopgirl*, and enjoyed it! '*The* Lily Greene?' he said when Sophie first mentioned my acting days . . .

Now it is really time for bed. I can just hear fiddles playing faintly – from the town perhaps. The clear air after the rain carries the sound.

What will tomorrow bring? Of course – a King and a Queen! and dear Mr Ogilvy who has promised to be there also. Shall I have just a little teeny quite harmless flirtation? Write back and advise me. By which time the danger will be quite past . . .! Goodnight, dearest friend. . . .

She was outside the chalet in the sunshine, playing with the borzoi dogs, when the visitors arrived. She was surprised: she would not have thought the chalet could hold any more people. At once the dogs turned their attention from her, and the silk scarf she'd been teasing them with . . .

A slight fair-haired youth leaped out of the carriage. And at the same time the younger Xenescu boy, Mihail, came running through the front door. Both put their arms about each other. Mihail cried, 'You're not alone?' An older, very dark youth got out too. A servant was already unloading luggage. 'You'll stay, you'll stay?'

Sophie appeared in the doorway. She gave an excited cry, clapping her hands like a child. 'Ion! And Take! Oh, but I'm so happy –' The borzois barked wildly.

A third person was climbing out, slowly. Lily thought: Ah no, he is not possible. He was tall, unusually so for a Rumanian, and enveloped in a large silk cloak. He had gathered it about him as he stepped down. She imagined that he must have waited in the carriage so as to make the greatest possible effect. For he was very beautiful.

He was in Sophie's arms. 'Oh happy visit, happy visit!' she insisted. Then suddenly they were all of them before Lily. Introductions must be made at once. Sophie was all excitement: here, for them, was a famous English actress, met in Paris. And for Lily – here was Ion who was Teodor's nephew. And the dark youth, this was dear Take. Take was the student friend of Valentin. He of the silk cloak . . .

Valentin had a high colour and dark heavy brows meeting

almost in the middle. He took Lily's hand very firmly and kissed it a little too long. Sophie was saying, 'Valentin, *Tino*, is Ion's brother, and is so also Teodor's nephew . . .'

Mihail had dragged Ion away. Take, left standing beside Valentin, had a wide, eager face, the expression intent.

'Oh, how we love to make surprise visits,' Valentin said. 'Dear Sophie, I was to have been on a yacht to sail from Constanza for Athens, then the idea was suddenly *ennuyeux* and I thought of here. Take consented to come too. We shall stay for ages and ages!'

Oh dear, thought Lily. Oh dear. Sophie was explaining now that although Lily managed so well in French, Valentin must practise with her his beautiful English . . . Lily smiled politely, prettily, while in front of the chalet the borzois ran in excited circles, whimpering, nuzzling the visitors.

'Take', she discovered, was the diminutive for Demetre. He belonged to one of the oldest families in Rumania, but Ion, sitting next to her at luncheon, explained to her in his rapid French: 'He's not what his family expects, not at all, they think him almost anarchist. *Take anarchisticu.* But it is only that he's very, very much for the cause of unity. There's a group of them, in Paris . . .'

'But he's your *brother's* friend?'

'Oh yes. I've not been in Paris yet. I go in January perhaps. But my brother – you should be talking to him, Lady Firth, he has excellent English. I've only a few words. "How are you, I am very well, at what time is the train in the station?" I used to know more – when I was small there was an English governess, *very* smart to have, but she left because of ill health when I was still only seven. Valentin was older so he learned more. And then he has had his time in England . . .'

'Yes, yes,' she said. As he talked she glanced down the table to where Valentin sat, next to Madame Xenescu. He appeared to hang on her every word. She wasn't looking at him but straight ahead, smiling, pouting a little – occasionally shrugging her beautiful shoulders.

'So you must talk to my brother all about London,' Ion was saying.

'Yes,' Lily said. She saw then that Valentin was looking at

her. At once he turned away, back to Madame Xenescu. 'Of course.'

Mr Ogilvy returned that evening from a short stay at Sighishoara to spend a day or two with them on his way back to Bucharest. Seated next to him at dinner (something she would have welcomed a week ago), Lily wondered how she could have even contemplated a flirtation. She felt restless, angry with herself. The charming, complimentary, *civilized* Mr Ogilvy, with his silver hair, his long, distinguished face. Why bother?

Why bother either that Valentin had as yet hardly spoken to her? He had been out between the afternoon siesta and dinner admittedly, but whenever there had been a chance he had not taken it – and *she* was not going to seek him out. Yet now, during this meal, she knew that he looked at her often.

Madame Xenescu noticed. While they were eating a pudding of lemon and white wine and eggs, Lily glanced up and saw that she stared at her: with dislike.

Then afterwards as they drank Turkish coffee in the long sitting-room, Sophie cried suddenly, 'Tino – you haven't spoken *at all* to Lady Firth . . .' She touched his arm, 'Come at once with your lovely English . . .' He had been deep in conversation with Madame Xenescu, seated so that his knee touched hers. Now he looked up, annoyed. Letting his fingers trail lightly over Madame Xenescu's skirt:

'Of course I come in a moment. I've just been telling the story of the Munteanu summer ball and *that* scandal – I had almost done . . .'

Lily was angry. He was making an event of speaking to her. She began: 'Do not bother –'

But he stood before her:

'How ungallant of me, how uncourteous, to wait till now – please, dear Lady Firth, may I sit beside you?' Then to Mr Ogilvy: 'Now I'm going to be talking, in spiffing English, so that you'll both be amazed.' He ran on, telling Lily that he'd already had a long conversation with Mr Ogilvy earlier. 'He's told me of your show in London, and my aunt had spoken to me already that you're famous . . .'

Soon, perhaps because Valentin spoke about nothing in

particular but was doing all the talking, Mr Ogilvy gently excused himself. Valentin said:

'Alone – at last. Except of course for everyone other in this room. I hope now you are going to sing for us. I can tickle the ivories for you . . . I'm so amazed, you see, that someone so beautiful and famous is staying here at Tante Sophie's. You must have noticed how flabbered I was? And that I've fallen totally heels over head in love –' he waved his arms about, then dramatically held a hand to his heart: 'We were to stay one week, now we shall stay *three* – because of you.' His voice was laughing, mocking. 'Say now you feel the same about *me* –'

Joining in the (foolish) game: 'Oh, but *certainly*,' she said.

At once he lay down full length on the rug at her feet. 'Look, everyone,' he called out in French, 'I am prostrate in adoration of the beautiful English actress, Lily Greene –'

'Don't be stupid,' she said sharply, 'please get up at once.' Madame Xenescu looked over at her. Her eyebrows were raised angrily but her expression was pitying.

Valentin, sitting up again, said wonderingly, 'Don't you *like* high jinks and horseplay and bearfights?' He sounded like a disappointed child. 'I thought, because you were English –'

'Tell me about Oxford,' she said.

He did. But what he had to say seemed dull and predictable – perhaps he was sulking, that he hadn't been allowed to posture. After a while he changed the subject and spoke about the theatre: drawing her out finally on her stage career. She must, absolutely *must*, sing for them . . . 'Hum the tune,' he said, 'any tune which you're famous for. And at once I'll be able to thump it –'

She felt curiously irritated. 'They are not *thumping* tunes . . .'

But at last persuaded, she agreed to sing. She did not think she did it very well. As she was crossing to the piano, she saw Madame Xenescu leave the room, speaking first to Sophie, then in an aside to Valentin.

'Ah, the poor treasure,' Sophie cried when she had gone, 'she is a martyr to *such* a headache. Tomorrow we keep her from the sun . . .'

Later, dressing for bed, she worried about Hal. Stories of infants dying suddenly, without obvious cause, in their cradles . . . To calm herself she sat down with pen and paper and for a few moments talked to Sadie:

'. . . and one of the new arrivals is a nephew, a beautiful young man much too pleased with himself. He'll quite spoil the holiday (and my flirtation with Mr O.?!). His name is Valentin but they call him Tino which I don't like, and he was one year at Christ Church, Oxford. He seems to think one year makes him an authority. And, so rude about actresses! ("We stormed the Gaiety when we're visiting London – I was very rich so could afford whom I pleased. I took out . . .") Ugh!'

'I'm awfully sorry, Lady Firth, awfully sorry. *Honestly*. I know that I behaved badly. It's my way. I showed off and played the fool and you don't like me at all. Yes?'

'No,' she said, a little coldly. Then because her answer must be ambiguous, added: 'It's quite all right –'

'But I am a nasty person, my behaviour – you don't think all Rumanians are like this? Please say –'

He shan't get round me in that fashion . . . 'I was not particularly pleasant either,' she said. 'Let us leave it at that . . .'

But all that day he seemed to be at her side, returning again and again:

'Do you like our wine, that we have at luncheon? It's from Tante Sophie's family – their vineyard in the Dobrudja.' Then:

'How is your little baby? You have a *son* yes?'

She was disarmed a little. He said, 'Tell me about him, please. What he's called?'

'Henry. But he is known as Hal.'

'I cannot believe you are a mother. So young . . .' That evening he said, 'I want us to be friends, please? Tante Sophie has already remarked – she says, you know, that she thinks we look awfully well together. A spiffing couple. Since I am dark and you are so fair –'

'I am sure Sophie did not say "spiffing".'

It was not so easy to deflate him. 'But I've translated – I do it pretty jolly well, don't I?'

She was seated next to him at dinner. Madame Xenescu was not there – she had spent the day in her room, while her children amused themselves with Ion and the others.

Valentin said: 'Now I want to ask some questions about London because I'm only there a few times – taking out these actresses . . .'

Even though annoyed, she found herself talking, telling him. For one so lively, he was a good listener. She had seen the night before how he had listened to Madame Xenescu.

Towards the end of the evening he told her: 'I've arranged everything that we do tomorrow. There is to be an expedition – we all go on ponies up the mountain. We shall eat up there . . .'

And what of Madame Xenescu? Really, Lily did not know what to think. Perhaps, she decided in the scented darkness, the wind sighing in the larches outside, *perhaps I should not think*? Just before she had settled for bed, Sophie had come in, saying mysteriously, 'You have been making great conquest, you know. Please allow that he pays attention – He is such a dear boy and you will find certainly you are amusing together . . .'

Dear Sophie.

The ponies were small and shaggy with long flowing manes and tails. Usually the saddles were only rough wooden ones but hers was sheepskin and comfortably padded. They climbed slowly up through the forests, where it was cool in the glades. The peaks of the Bucegi mountains, inaccessible, snow-capped, filled her with longing. The fir trees grew right to the tip of the Piatră Arsa. The air was champagne again.

'The flowers, you see how many grow here – we have them all spring and summer – roses of the mountain, violets, gentians, carnations. You will find even edelweiss . . .'

They saw a bear. They had been sitting resting and Valentin was adjusting the cloth of her saddle for her:

'Bruno's very daring, to come so far down – he's after the wild raspberries. Because they're so very, very delicious.' He said easily, 'I think perhaps your mouth tastes as they do.'

When they arrived back, the Xenescu children heard that they were to leave in the morning. Their mother was still not about. Valentin appeared unworried, but Sophie told Lily:

'Ana Xenescu – there's a little upset. She has jealousy.'

'Whatever for?'

'Oh, for you. Because he look at you. But Tino is not her *amant*. That is being over with one year. She think it begin again but it don't . . .'

Tired after their expedition, most of them went to bed early. The next morning only Take and Tante Elise were about. Take sat at a table in the garden surrounded by papers. Some fellow zealots were coming from Paris soon for a meeting . . .

Sophie joined them outside. 'Oh, these politics,' she said. Tante Elise looked up from her tatting:

'I'm not sure that all this should happen in our house – it is dangerous. I ask myself what the Castle would say? He would not be *persona grata* –'

A little later, noticing few people about, Lily heard that Valentin and Teodor and some others had gone off shooting. Sophie said, 'They go very early, before the sun rises, and will sleep in some huts. They pass some days with it . . .'

For Lily it was as if the sky had suddenly darkened. She was horrified at the strength of her feelings – was certain that everyone present must have noticed something . . . But the Xenescu departure soon after with its noise and bustle – the children reluctant, Madame wan and proud-looking – served to distract . . . All the same, it was a long day. She wrote to Sadie. To Robert. To Alice. She did not sleep during siesta time, but walked to and fro in her room. *What is happening to me*? Sweet reason: but she could not stay still long enough to apply it . . .

In the middle of dinner, he reappeared.

'My apologies, my apologies, I am late –' He opened his arms as if to embrace everyone.

'But, Tino – where are the others? Where is my Teodor?'

He said, surprised: 'In the mountains of course, dear Sophie.' He explained, 'It is only I who've returned. It was suddenly *ennuyeux* – to be away . . .'

All the while he hadn't looked directly at Lily at all. Her heart thudding, the colour rushing to her face – oh, but surely she could not hide her delight. A place made for him at the table – near to Sophie but opposite to her. The food tasting now quite different, bright colours of saffron rice, tomatoes, flavour and texture of quails. Wine: amber and jewel red. A bunch of small white grapes. She was possessed by a feverish excitement so that as the candles glowed on all the colours, she hardly knew where to look – it was as if everything had been touched – with what? The very air hummed. (Oh dear God, what is happening to me?)

'Please, may I come inside your bed tonight?'

'Certainly not,' she said airily. 'Whatever will you think of next?'

'But I'm especially back from the mountains, just so that –'

'I don't care if you travelled from Manchuria. The answer is No.'

'Please – I'm so sad otherwise, too sad. *Please* – Lily. I shall be very careful, I am always very careful –'

'You're very free with Christian names, aren't you? And perhaps – just a little absurd?'

'No, no, it's you who are foolish. But I don't pay attention. I come inside anyway.'

Her bedroom door had a lock. The window had shutters, which she fastened tight. It was only when she was already in bed that she realized she had not after all locked the door.

I never meant, she thought afterwards, I could never have meant to lock it. She lay very still then, as if waiting. Her body didn't move but her heart thudded still, and all her skin felt as if fevered.

Just after midnight she heard the door handle turn.

He didn't say anything at first but just placed the light he was carrying beside the bed, and then knelt down near her pillow.

'*Whatever*? You know what I said –'

'And you remember what I said? Yes, yes, you *do* – oh, but you are a silly lovely lily and now is not at all the time for *talking* . . .'

Certainly it was not the time for talking. The great wooden bed so wide and generous – the flutters of thought, she was soon rid of those – she was all body, feeling. All that glowing of skin, thudding of heart, had been for this. The same body which all those years ago – the fumbling of Frank, clumsy eagerness of Edmund, dreadful bejewelled pain and humiliation in Nice, in Paris . . .

For a while afterwards he tried to still her trembling.

'Just lie very quiet please in my arms – you're not frightened of me that I make you so happy? And that I don't talk, only to say what beautiful breasts you have and other things that I only know how they're called in French . . . You do like me a little? It's not that you're angry I'm so naughty? No, I don't go to sleep – *you* may, but I stay now to talk to you, and touching, always touching, until it is time we begin again . . .'

She wasn't sure which were best, the days or the nights. Those enchanted days which she and Val (for she called him that, preferring it), spent now always together. By common consent a couple. Days which rushed by. And yet stretched out, each one a great length of shining cord. Days joined to nights . . .

Somehow in all the excitement she had not expected to *like* him. She distrusted charm, good looks even more (what of Edmund?), self-satisfaction most of all. A rich and probably spoilt young man. That was what she had seen – yet been unable to resist. Her happiness she put down to the pleasures of the bed, the mountains, the scented pinewoods, the long late summer days . . . So how to explain her terror, her sudden glimpses of the silken cord snapping? The woods growing dark, bears hunted in the mountains, hungry wolves making their way down to the villages. Cold winter. Endings . . .

But of course it was the nights which were the best. Then after pleasure and more pleasure, there would be the quiet talking.

'Sophie told me that perhaps you're not very happy, so I watched always. Now you can tell me about this Robert, and Lionel and – everything . . .' It was easy, good even, to tell the story which was like a shameful secret. She told every sad detail, no veiled hints and half-explanations as when she'd confided in Sadie. Val took it matter of factly – 'Ah but there are people like that,' and then exploded with anger on her behalf. He went round the room, kicking at furniture, thumping the end of the bed. 'It shan't be, it shan't be . . .'

'Oh, but it is,' she told him sadly. Feeling the sudden cold wind of hopelessness. For what could Val, would Val do?

What else could all this happiness mean except – endings?

And the necklace, the Diamond Waterfall – how to explain that she had sold her soul for that? 'Ah no,' he said, lying still, hands cupped over her breasts, 'you sell your *body* – and that is not important, not important at all.' He stopped for a moment: 'Oh, what frightful tosh, that I talk like that. *I* mind that you did, I mind, I mind – and *that* is important . . .'

'You think yourself, your darling self, very important –'

'But I've always been so – to my mother, my sisters, my brothers, to Ana –'

'Ah yes, Ana.'

She had thought there would be upset about Ana Xenescu, his former mistress. But almost from the beginning he'd spoken of her, although not often, always quite naturally. It was she, Lily, with her sudden spasms of jealousy, of nagging curiosity, who asked, and asked . . .

'. . . But you see, when I am sixteen, seventeen, I had to learn of course – to be so pleasing. And then she, who has a husband so always away from home and very *complaisant*, she chose me and I am very proud. She is altogether very beautiful then and it's only just now that she becomes so fat – it is easy for Rumanians to become fat. She and I, we have many, many funny days together. So of course, I become very good for other women. Then after some time what happens is that when it should all end, she doesn't want. And because she is older and of a jealous temper, she minds that I look at others and is angry. But all was over for me nearly two years ago, when I'm twenty. Then, she sees me here – perhaps she *hopes* that I come – and I'm weak and give her little attentions, but because I don't come to her room any more, and you are here and are so beautiful – there's a *crise de nerfs*, and what can I do?'

'I found her difficult, a little,' Lily said. 'I think too that before this, she didn't like me. Now I'm sorry for her –'

'Lily, I also was giving – you understand what I mean? It's not right that because she had been the teacher, she shall be *accaparante* . . .'

Lily thought: I must not monopolize him either. I must never become like that. And yet she could see it so clearly, how it might so easily be that way. When, oh when, did the light easy conversation, the badinage, when did it suddenly hint at boredom? ('I like women very much,' he had said . . .)

She said lightly: 'It's my turn to tease you now. Your English is so good – but we say, you know, "come to or *into* bed". Not "inside" as you said. "Inside" is for when you come into me.'

'But that is what I was meaning . . . Whatever else did you think I spoke of?'

Time passing. Autumn crocus everywhere already. Pale blue. 'It is only here in Transylvania that it is this colour.' Excursions, walks in the pinewoods, an evening of dancing with the peasants, above Sinaia, on the grassy plateau outside the monastery . . . Music, the wild, sad sound of the pan pipes . . . trying to take the sound inside herself so that one day she would be able to call their music up: to remind me . . . For surely she would wish to be. Reminded – or haunted?

September melted into October. October. And now its days ran away too . . .

> I shall certainly be home for Christmas, Alice. I have told your Papa so. Really I would not have believed when I first left that I should agree to stay so long – two months already! But I know my son is in safe hands (and two of those hands are yours!) and Papa is very pleased that I am now so well again – my spirits completely recovered. I wish that you too, Alice, might have a visit such as this! Many of the guests mentioned in my letters have left us. Take is in Paris, and Ion grew bored and returned home. There are just a few relations left now. In three days' time we leave for the capital, Bucharest . . .

They were so silly together. It was as if she had missed somewhere in her life the time for being silly. (Vicky, even dear Vicky, we weren't *really* so . . .) All manner of stupid games. They joked about anything. The story of Red Riding Hood . . .

'What a big – I don't know the French – you have!'

'*All* the better to – how do you say? – prick you with – Oh, oh, ah *yes*. Now kiss me. And Lily –'

'Yes?'

'What a little *trou* you have . . .'

'All the better to – oh, Val . . . Never leave me, never leave me . . .'

She asked him: 'But what about Bucharest? You have a home there. We cannot –'

'I shall arrange myself. Us. I shall go home – every morning.'

And that was how it was.

A different life. A town life, to which she'd become quite unaccustomed. The weather not yet settled into winter: days of blue skies and high clear air. She was to amuse herself, meet people, and indeed she did take part in the comings and goings – drives out, calling on others returned to Bucharest from the country or abroad.

'What a pity that you don't ride . . .' But all the same there was driving down the Chaussée with its avenue of linden trees. Like Rotten Row, the Park, the Bois, this was the place to be seen. *Le tout Bucharest*. Clothes were from Paris and to be shown off. Smart victorias sped by, drawn by jet-black Russian horses with long flowing tails. Lily saw, and was seen. The drive back down the Chaussée was more leisurely – one could be seen, and see more closely. Some 'painted ladies' were pointed out to Lily. They seemed to her the smartest of all.

Sophie and Teodor lived, as did Val, in the fashionable quarter. Lily loved to roam instead in the older parts of the town. Houses roofed with shingle and moss, roads and squares paved with round cobbles. Often neglected, already forgotten.

The town ended so abruptly. On the fringe there were gipsy camps. Toothless old women coming up to the carriage with cards, offering to tell her fortune (but I would rather not know, *dare* not know). A horde of children, naked or with only a few tattered rags, scrambling up the carriage, calling out for alms – '*Cinci parale, cinci parale*' . . .

Val contrived to spend some part of each day with her. Each evening he either dined with them if they were at home, or called late, often very late. By morning (oh, those cold early dawn partings) he was back in his home. He woke always in his own bed. She was happy, happy, and tried not to count the days and their ticking away.

But, what was this – for she had not counted the days *at all* . . . She had noticed nothing, and it was not until one Sunday when together with Teo and Sophie she visited the metropolitan church. Its dim frescoed background, yellow-tinted walls. Against the nasal chanting, she prayed for Hal, and Alice. She thought then, suddenly, idly: How long I've been without a Visitor . . . The last time was – when?

She had never been regular, less so since the birth. Could it be, could it be? Among the tapers, silver lamps swayed, the air incense-laden. And now? she thought. But it was already the middle half of November. She was to stay another four weeks . . . In that first sudden flash of thought, she knew with certainty what had happened. *What was not meant to have happened* . . .

During the next few days, she said nothing; pushed the thought to the back of her mind – it could wait for confirmation. It gave her a slight air of nervousness though, a subtle change of manner which Val noticed. And was concerned.

They visited the Bucharest Museum. He said to her:

'I know that you aren't happy about jewellery and precious stones, but here you must see our *Cloşcă cu Pui*, our Hen and Chicks – they are treasures that some quarrymen in Transylvania found maybe sixty years ago. They didn't know the worth of them – they were tricked later. But look – three gold brooches, they are work of the Goths, so thick with emeralds, and sapphires, and turquoise, and pearls.'

But she could not admire their beauty. Sick, doubly sick with the thought, feel, weight, texture of gold, of precious stones. For she knew already what was to become of her . . .

'You worry because we must part – leave each other?'

'No, no, it's nothing. A little tiredness.'

Because she didn't as yet feel sick (and I was so sick, so early, last time), she wondered still if perhaps . . . But, those swollen breasts, the vague darting pains, what was she to make of those? Swollen breasts which cried out more, more and more, to be sucked, to be kissed, caressed.

She had begun to think: If I tell him what will he do? At worst she imagined some resigned, cynical reaction: a suggestion perhaps that he knew a woman somewhere who . . . and that *he* would pay. It would be all right, he'd say. It had been so with Ana. These things happened every day . . .

I at least am a married woman . . . But Vicky? For two days her mind was sickeningly full of images. Memories kept in hiding . . .

Then came the nausea – not so bad as before, but unmistakable. She made love more and more frantically in the faint hope of losing it naturally. While part of her didn't want to lose it at all.

And then she told him: after he'd asked again and again, 'What's wrong? *Qu'as tu? qu'as tu?*' At once his face, it was like a little boy's. Panic. Emotions racing over it. Panic.

'Darling. But I have been so very, very careful . . . Always. What do I . . . You are really sure?'

'Some signs – yes. Almost certain, now.'

He changed suddenly then, saying, his arms about her, 'I am proud. I can say only I am so proud. Of you, of me, of *us* . . .'

He cried. She cried. They clung to each other. Words of love:

'No, no,' he protested, 'it's not "I love you" like I say when I'm wanting your *trou* – really, please, this is quite different, this is *I love you* . . .'

'I must go home, as soon as possible. So that it may appear natural . . .'

'Your husband – Robert?' But no more was said. She didn't want to remember, neither of them must mention it, what must be done to make it 'all right'. She had thought of it already when he showed her the *Cloşcă cu Pui*.

Her departure. She had been going in three weeks' time – but this was not the same. This was undue haste, agony of mind, rush of practical arrangements, the decision to tell Sophie and Teodor only that someone was not well at home. The sudden wild notions (*his* usually) that she should stay after all, she would somehow become his wife – for he could not get over the delighted discovery of his love, his *real* love. She listened, sick at heart, with loving patience to elaborate fantasies of honourable divorce, of the three of them (and somehow Hal too) living happily ever after, here in Rumania. But then, realizing the absurdity he would grow angry, sometimes with her, sometimes with life. Once again they would both cry. It seemed, those last five or six days of her stay, a fount of tears, as if one supplied the other. And love, they made love now with such care. 'We must not hurt our baby, our own dear little baby . . .'

The last hours were the worst. She did not think she would ever want to remember them again. She who could see no future, he who had put aside now all the wild ideas: who was just simply, desperately, unhappy.

Arrangements to write – it would be through a friend in Paris: the letters in new outer envelopes, some story to be concocted. She too would write to Mme Billaud in Paris. The false cheerfulness, protestations to Teodor and Sophie that it had been the most *wonderful* visit (and had it not?). That she was so very much the better for it . . . Yes, yes, of course she would return.

(*How ever, how ever are we to see each other again?*)

A difficult future. A hopeless one. Images of jewels, of precious stones – crowding into her dreams . . . As she woke in the morning of her last day she hallucinated, seeing in all its hateful beauty the shimmering, priceless, many coloured Diamond Waterfall.

Their last night. His head between her breasts. 'Lily, lily of the valley. So much more pretty than *muguet des bois*. My Lily. *My* valley . . . Lily, Lily . . .'

10

She thought she would never forget the misery of that journey back. The weather had turned very cold and although she was supplied with hot bottles, she felt chilled through and could not seem to get warm. She'd hoped at first there would be someone to travel with at least as far as Paris, but in the rush that had not been possible. She was lent a German maid, but as she didn't speak German . . .

There were delays, late starts: her luggage was opened, presumably with false keys, between Budapest and Vienna. Three summer dresses were stolen, she lost also two hatboxes and their contents. Still there, though, was the shirt of Val's which she had begged from him (he had lifted it over his head at once, surprised: 'But it's not clean – I've worn it already three hours . . .'). I shall keep it, she thought foolishly, and never wash it. Hide it at the back of a clothes tray – no, tie it up in brown paper – a secret parcel.

And the ring he had given her? A Lover's Opal and plaited gold. Traditional joining of hands and pledging of troth. Misfortune to come to the faithless one . . . That too must be hidden away.

The train was dirty, gritty, and after leaving the Rumanian side of Predeal there was no food. Hungry, heartsick, she sat in the cold carriage and felt as if she had been torn apart. It had not been necessary to fall in love. It was to have been *fun*. It had not been necessary to make a child . . .

And now this terrible hurrying back. She could see only black ahead. She was to produce a seven months' child, but before that . . . As she drew nearer to England, the dread of *everything* clutched at her. Why not just tell Robert the truth? But this child must live in his home, call him father. If he were to give it only hate . . .

'You don't look much better. You don't have the appearance of one *rested* . . .'

She spoke sharply in reply.

'After a journey such as I've just suffered? Whatever did you expect?'

What indeed? Not, oh *not*, this secret. Bad news, which must be forever kept hidden.

But here at home again, all was not bad news. Even Alice came to greet her and was not too churlish. Best of all was Hal. Four months had altered him completely. She *hoped* he recognized her but had to admit he didn't. It was as a friendly stranger, nothing else, that he greeted her. A great wide smile. Teeth now, to be counted. He stood up in the iron cot and shook the bars. She marvelled at the rounded knees beneath the full skirts.

Letters too, awaited her. All good happy news from America. But from her brother Harry, a disturbing note.

She had taken little account of what had been going on in the world outside. Before she left there had been rumours of war. Letters from home mentioned: 'the conflict in South Africa'. But no one in Sinaia or Bucharest had spoken of this argument between Dutch settlers and the British, a continent away. On the journey back, some people in a French railway carriage spoke critically of the British (so arrogant, and their *mauvais comportement* in this unjust war . . .). Lily had kept quiet.

Unreal, irrelevant, it had seemed, this Boer war. But now, with Harry's letter, how different. He who was so soon to have left for America and a new life. Telling her now:

> You'll expect to hear that I'm off to New York and Daisy – Well, the States will have to wait, because I've enlisted! For Queen and Country. So it's the West Yorks Regt, and following the Flag. We sail in early December . . .

Death at sea. She thought of everything. Already the letter was old. She could do nothing now but wait.

So long had she been away, that she thought it would be only natural Robert would want to go through the dreaded ritual. She had resigned herself beforehand, wondering only how much of the jewellery she would have to wear . . .

Perhaps she could plead exhaustion from the journey? True enough, God knew. But that was only to postpone the horror. Worse would be if he didn't approach her at all . . .

'You were long enough away,' he said, 'perhaps you missed us after all, that you have come hurrying back before the date given.' He stood there in his dark red dressing-gown. 'I hope at least you have some zest for life again.' He paused: 'Did you miss me, a little?'

'Yes, of course –'

He talked idly for a few moments, then in brisk tones: 'Undress, please – the nightgown off.'

Why, why, so spirited usually, do I obey? Head hanging, waiting to be draped with gold. But tonight it was to be just the Waterfall – that should have been so beautiful. The fire in the bedroom was quiet, glowing red. She thought that she could smell fear. Her own.

Before she had not liked him to see her body, had hated as much as anything this standing naked before him – to be hung with trophies. The diamonds were cool against her flesh. Cruel against her skin. Facets caught the light. She felt suddenly a wave of sick misery, a longing quite desperate for Val, *for it to be as it had been* . . . All evening she had kept it at bay, telling herself: I shall feel again when it's all over. Only then would it be safe to feel . . .

He had taken off the gown. Underneath he was naked. She saw with horror that as he gazed at her, he grew – what was once unattractive now appeared obscene.

'Lily, my dear –' The deep voice. He was walking towards her.

I cannot, she thought, cannot, cannot. *Shall* not . . .

She said, in a dull but loud voice, 'Don't. Please do *not*. I'm with child.'

'What?'

Then a moment later: '*What?*'

She still didn't answer. But began to tremble. Looked behind her for a chair, sofa. Weak-kneed, she sat down. What have I done?

'You must be mad – You mean to tell me – Dear God, is that the truth? Say now –'

'Yes, it's the truth.' What good to lie now? There was a bitter taste in her mouth. The taste of fear.

He dragged his dressing-gown on angrily. 'My God, it surpasses all – an actress, yes, dear God a cheap *actress* –' As he came near her, she flinched. 'Give it me, the Waterfall, give it me. I want it *off* you.' He pulled impatiently at the clasps, cursed as they would not open fast enough. 'I want it off you. Off!'

He let it fall over the head of the chair. 'And now, if you dare – tell me *who*, eh? Dare to tell me –'

'No one –'

'Autogenesis, my God.' He was walking to and fro.

'No one – especially. A casual encounter, an accident –'

'*Who*?'

'A Rumanian.'

'Naturally, why not? His *name* – if you dare –'

She hesitated, her mouth dry with invention. 'Alexandru Crisan.'

'A friend of – our friends? *Eh*?'

'It was . . . he's a happily married man. Middle-aged. I said – an accident. These things . . . I can only – would have asked forgiveness. These things happen –'

'So ill, so *weak*, that you have to leave home. But well enough to *whore*. Aren't you?' Leaning forward, he struck the side of her head so that she fell against the chairback.

'Don't! Robert – how . . .'

'Don't, don't – You don't care for what you deserve.'

She said, sobbing now, 'These things happen –'

'They do not – to me. In the world you came from, perhaps. Or the fast set maybe. The usual disgusting ways of Society. Lionel may live that life if he pleases. These things, they don't happen to me, in *my* home –'

She cowered in the chair as he came near again. But he stood over her only, head thrust at her.

'You meant to pass it off as *mine*, eh? That's the filthy truth – is it not?'

She avoided his eyes, the angry colour of his face.

'You've heard me before – on the ways of Society. Chipping at the very foundations of the family. And the older families, they are the worst. Not the *parvenus*, so-called . . . You know what I think about that sort of conduct? Eh? Yes, say Yes.'

'Yes.'

He leaned nearer.

'I have my son at least. You've given me an heir. But if this bastard's a boy, don't think he stands second in line.

Offspring of some gypsy, and a shopkeeper's daughter – for that's what you are – Do you think I want the Waterfall coming into such hands? Do You?'

He hit out suddenly with the back of his hand, this time her face. A whiplash. A second later he hit her again, about the shoulders. Right, left. And again. The blows rained down. A fist in her face . . .

She was too shocked to fight back. Afraid too. Between blows he shouted, railing against her, against Val. This Rumanian gypsy . . .

'You are never to go back there. Nothing to do with any of them, understand?'

In her terror, as he belaboured her, his voice not so much loud as threatening – and righteous, she thought: Dad. (In the hall. Leeds. My wicker basket beside me. Discovered. Wicked. In the wrong. Hopeless. Imprisoned.) I have married my father . . .

'Was he a Jew? Tell me that –'

'I don't answer you. You've knocked me about, like a drunken husband on Saturday night . . . Now leave me . . . Go on, get out – if you haven't killed the child – Get out –'

He threw her nightgown at her. For a moment it covered her face. She wrapped it over her belly, her knees. Her head she kept down so that she didn't have to see him. She heard the door close behind him.

The next morning, after an almost sleepless night, she saw in the mirror that she was marked: her face worst of all, livid bruises on cheek and temple. Her throat and upper shoulders too were stained.

She spent all that day and several days after in bed. She wrapped silk scarves around her neck, pleading a sore throat after the journey. A fever too – so that she had become dizzy and fallen heavily in the bedroom, hitting her face against the fireguard . . . It was a story for the domestic staff, for Alice, and a few others. She was surprised at how easily it succeeded. Robert, whom she sent for after breakfast, made no comment. 'That is the story I am giving out,' she told him. 'The matter will not be referred to again.' They treated each other with icy politeness.

She would have told Sadie. But there was not really the

occasion. For Sadie the next day, after a horrified concern at Lily's appearance and a (surprising again) credence in her tale, poured out her own anxieties:

'. . . Charlie, two days ago, darling Lily. He wants to fight for your Empire. As if it wouldn't be just dandy without any contribution from *him* . . . And not telling me till too late – isn't that just like a man? Someone or other's Horse they call the Regiment and oh – it's *crazy*! Only eight weeks to the new baby. Why, I'm so mad at him I just haven't been able to stop crying. It's crazy. The eldest son . . . I mean, Lily darling . . .'

What else but crazy? But now there was Sadie to comfort. Her own troubles could be put aside for the moment . . .

She heard that Harry had landed safely and was at Pietermaritzburg. The first of Val's letters arrived through Paris. She sent one off herself. Charlie left straight after Christmas. Sadie's world seemed all saddlery, revolvers, Zeiss glasses . . . A little after his departure she had her baby – a girl whom she called Amy, after her grandmother. Lily told Sadie she too was expecting. In September, she said.

Her greatest consolation now was Hal. She spent so much time in the nursery that Nan-Nan, rather than being pleased, showed signs of resentment. But I only want to be *with* him, Lily thought . . .

For the new baby, she felt a mixture of longing and fear. Strong it must be, since it had survived the journey back, the beating, her emotional upset. But unlike those far-off days when it had been the precious secret of her and Val, now it was – a burden. All the love and longing she had felt, and still did feel, somewhere underneath – buried now in fear.

Winter still, always winter. Every afternoon, when meant to be resting, she would gaze out of her window and see that nothing changed. Sometimes she would try to bring back the summer, the autumn she had just known. Pan gypsy pipes, violins, chamois leaping from rock to rock, the spread of blue autumn crocus in the meadows of Sinaia . . . She could not.

Late in February she watched one darkening afternoon the steady fall of snow, blowing, drifting across the garden, watched the last leaves on the spectral beeches and thought only: How time stretches out. It will always be a winter afternoon . . .

The next day the baby quickened. She was not able to still her excitement. The good news. When she saw Dr Sowerby, he remarked that she seemed perhaps more advanced than he had thought ('calculations with irregular menses, um, very difficult'). Her absence abroad was tactfully not mentioned. For a while, feeling physically better also, she was almost contented: hugging her treasure to herself, hands sensing every movement. Val, who would be so proud . . . She wrote to Paris. With Robert there continued the veneer of polite concern they'd agreed to show each other in public. In private, they scarcely spoke to each other.

It was a warm summer. She sat outside, increasingly large now, eight months that should have been only six. She was in the summer-house or on truly fine days, on a garden bed. She was lying there the afternoon she was brought the news about Harry. That he had been killed on June 6th at a place called Diamond Hill.

11

On the whole, Alice thought, she preferred this new baby. Although Papa plainly did not. He wasn't even proud of her, in the way that he was of Hal – who would be two any day now and with his solemn round face and dark almost curly hair above his little white dress, wasn't *too* bad . . . He didn't seem sharp at least and that was a mercy.

True, Nan-Nan fussed over him, but then so far, she wasn't enchanted with the new one.

'We've had girls before, haven't we? Nothing like *my* girl – who's *my* girl, eh, Miss Alice?' (But Mama had been her girl, too . . .)

The baby had been christened in October, and this time Alice's photographs had been successful. Very. The baby had been named Theodora which meant Gift of God. She was red-faced and loud-voiced and cried throughout the ceremony. She was also very large: *nine and a half pounds*. Theodora was after the Rumanian Count who had stayed at The Towers the summer before last, but who could not be a godfather because of his religion.

Papa had not said that he disliked Theodora. It was just that she, Alice, was sharp. At the ceremony he had not been at all jovial. Once or twice she saw him drum his fingers on the table when a guest praised the child. Later when she interrupted, and should not have, he was short with her:

'Seen but not heard, please. Go and look to your brother. You're a big girl now and should be a help with him . . .'

Big girl . . . Of course, yes. That meant growing up and becoming more responsible. But there didn't seem any more of her than a year or even two years ago. Perhaps it was being sharp that kept her so small . . . And what of it? Except that Nan-Nan kept dropping hints.

'When it happens, you will tell Nan-Nan, won't you?'

'When what?'

'When you get your poorly time –' She looked knowing.

'*Ill?*'

'Well, not quite ill,' Nan-Nan said. 'Poorly for a few days. Your mother went to bed often then . . .'

When her throat swelled up at the beginning of November she asked, 'Is this it, am I – poorly? That way?'

'No, no,' Nan-Nan said hurriedly, 'that's not it.' She added fiercely: 'You're to tell Nan-Nan at *once* . . .'

But on the whole, really she was much happier now. She did not have too much to do with Belle Maman who gave so much attention to Hal these days, and now had Theodora to fuss over.

While she – had Gib. She would tell herself often: I have a *friend*. The only sadness, that he would go away to school next September. What if he became someone different then? Someone not interested in photography?

For that was their greatest bond (aside from what had first brought them together. And they didn't, now, need to speak of that again . . .). She was his teacher, although he was already almost her equal. Indeed at the beginning she'd felt humble, after the disaster of Hal's christening photographs. She had read aloud from her photography manual: '*Do not be discouraged by your failures* . . .' Gib wrote it in illuminated lettering for her and fastened it to the back of the darkroom door. Later he had watched, and then helped her develop the second, horribly artificial set of pictures.

All through the summer of 1899 they had been on outing after outing with her camera. In September for his birthday he was given one. They compared their pictures. The moors, grouse butts, Flaxthorpe church. A waterfall swollen with autumn rains. The spray was like a million diamonds, Gib said. She had not liked that. *A diamond waterfall*, she had thought, remembering her mother . . .

She spent some time at the Vicarage, but not so much as Gib spent at The Towers. He was looked after now by his aunt. She was not like the aunts Alice had read about who came to take care of orphaned nephews and nieces. No ramrod fierceness: Miss Nicolson, his Aunt Ettie, was small, fluffy and delightfully vague. She managed somehow the duties of the Vicarage but had little time or energy left to be strict with her nephew. She referred to him always, in her slow dreamy voice, as '*little* Gib'. Even though he towered above her already, and indeed topped Alice now by at least three inches.

'Perhaps little Gib should have a darkroom too,' she had said, and about the time of his birthday, one was rigged up at the Vicarage. But it was too small and not truly dark and could not be used in winter as it was unheated. He was soon back at The Towers.

Gib had a book of war photographs – a large red volume, *With the Flag to Pretoria*. They had looked at it together out on the lawn this summer. She thought now of Belle Maman's brother, killed nearly six months ago. Harry. She had never met him because she had not been at the wedding. But she felt she recognized him among the sad faces in the hospital photographs: death from enteric fever. Even though she knew he had died in action. Other more lively pictures reminded her of Mr Hawksworth, *Captain* Hawksworth now; and too, a distant cousin of Gib's who was Galloper to a general. 'A galloper,' Gib would say with relish. They imagined for him a life of ceaseless movement, his steed thundering over the sandy veldt . . .

She and Gib, a team, were they not? They had begun to think – Gib's idea, this – that they might set themselves up, not as portraitists (unless perhaps to start with, in order to build capital, since surely Papa would not finance a commercial undertaking of this nature?), but as some kind of roving photographers, working on commission. Arabia, India, or nearer home – wild Rumania that Belle Maman had written of so excitedly. Travel, travel, travel. The idea was enormous. It glowed.

'But first,' Gib had explained, 'I must get myself an education. I have to go to school, to Marlborough – And then to Cambridge. Because that is what my father did. Although, I suppose –' pause – 'I could always *run away* when the time comes . . .'

The daring, the courageous, the intrepid Gib! Three years younger than her, yet it was he who had the ideas . . . She was filled with excitement: *The Great Adventure*. And it might be, could be, as little as five years away. She would be only twenty, he seventeen – but what of that? As for the Proprieties which people spoke of (whatever they might be), she was sure they'd manage those as well . . .

But meanwhile, here and now, there was Christmas to enjoy. Days free of dear silly Fräulein, of Miss Fairgrieves; time to spend with Gib who would be free too. The only cloud in the sky: Uncle Lionel.

He was to spend Christmas with them. (If only it could have been her dear Uncle Tom . . .). He made it worse this year by arriving a week early. At once he made a great fuss of her.

'Well, mistress Alice, where are you roaming, come and tell your true love . . .' His hateful kiss and embrace lingered longer than usual. She pushed him away a little. She knew she would have to show him the photographs, the work of the last few months.

'Let us see what our little budding Lumière has been up to?' but said in an offhand manner, because already he had begun regaling Papa and Belle Maman with the latest, absolutely the latest, scandal from London, from Town.

'Wait,' Belle Maman had said, 'wait, Lionel, please. Until it is more *convenable. La petite* . . .'

'Let me see the darkroom,' he said. 'Please, Alice.'

'You know it,' she told him. 'It was Papa's.'

'Let me see it now that it's yours.' He pleaded, persuaded. But she didn't want him to, because in there was private.

'I want to see how you have made it different. The impress of your personality.'

'No.' But in the end, he just simply walked in. Without knocking too. Because Gib had only just left, she hadn't locked the outer door.

'Hallo. Hallo.'

'The light,' she screamed, 'shut the door!' She had meant to say, '*Get out.*' Now instead she had invited him in.

'The Nicolson lad was on the stair. He told me you were here.'

'But, you see, I'm at work. You may not disturb me . . .'

'Alice?'

'Yes?' She was taken unawares.

'Alice, you know how quite too, too sweet you look in that light, that *red* light –'

'I don't know what you mean. And anyway this will spoil if I don't take care.' She had almost finished, would have done so before Gib left except that she had thought of one last thing. 'Why are you here?'

'To see your little house –'

'In a moment I shall turn up the light, the ordinary light, so you may see how it all is nowadays – and then you can go.'

'So eager to be rid of me – your own uncle?'

'I don't like people in when I –'

'What about young Master Nicolson, eh?'

'That's different . . .' His hand stretched out. He stroked her ear. 'Don't,' she said, 'that's ticklish.'

'Allie, Allie, Allie – such a little child, aren't you?'

'Fifteen,' she said coldly. She moved the white ebonite dish with developer in it.

'Hardly the young lady, is it? is it now? and you look, bless you, darling little niece, you look only thirteen. A *child*. That's why you could almost, couldn't you, sit on my knee still?'

She said angrily, 'I don't like to sit on your knee. I never did. And I don't wish to be treated as a child –'

'Then why do you behave like one? Refusing to be friendly with me . . . what about filial love, filial embraces and all that? If you can't show affection to those near and dear . . . Charity, Alice, begins at home.'

'Not in the darkroom, though –'

But he was breathing into her ear. 'Alice. Alice. Alice.' His hot breath smelled of brandy, of ginger too.

She said: 'Anyway, I shall be going out of here in a moment.'

'Without showing me anything?'

'What did you want to see, then?' She thought of flinging open all the cupboards and being done with it. 'I'll –'

'Show me something else, please.' He spoke rapidly, edgily. 'Show me – will you show me, here, just by the ruby lamp, darling. Allie, you are quite my favourite. I have been so jealous of Robert, that he has all of his own such a little darling –'

I don't hear it right, she thought. Standing absolutely still in the half darkness. And then, feeling his touch.

'I want to see. Look, I want to see, let me see, darling, I won't hurt you. I just want to see . . .' He spoke so fast, couldn't be halted. His tone kinder than she had ever heard.

'I can feel, those little buds, where you just begin to be a woman. So small, so small. And the other, Alice, let me touch – I won't look, darling, if you just tell me, is it small and perfect down there, do you have hair – hair there, just beginning? No, no, I won't hurt – can I feel, I shall only feel –'

It is not real. His fingers *are not there*. The pain too. The pain is not real . . .

'Yes, but yes, Alice. No, don't mind, darling – let me. Let me feel, you darling, darling half-*child*. Darling –'

Suddenly, she was another person, escaping from his grasp, that hateful arm clutching her shoulders, holding her tight, those fingers, feeling. She stood alone, shaking. Then she hit him very hard across the face. The very hardness of the face she hit, surprised her. As did her satisfaction. She was amazed at her sense of power. She hit him again. He stepped back. Three plates, a bowl, some bottles. A crashing sound.

There was a terrible smell of chemicals. Sulphur. Ammonia. 'Stinks,' he said, 'stinks.' His voice trembled. 'My God, stinks . . .' He said agitatedly, 'Let's forget, quickly, shall we? Forget your uncle was ever silly. For that's all it was. A moment's silliness, eh?'

She did not reply. She had turned up the light. 'Some of these chemicals,' she said after a moment, 'if they get together, they could poison us. We might die. Gilbert, although he's only small, *he* knows better –'

'So we shan't say anything, shall we?' His voice was pleading, his appearance dishevelled. She had never seen her perfectly groomed uncle in such disarray. 'Shall we?'

'Please move out of the way. I have to clear these up *at once* . . .' She was very composed.

The remainder of that evening, she continued to feel composed. Icy cold, and quite unreal. I don't have to think about it, she told herself. Once in bed, she did not sleep for a long while and when she did, was woken soon by stomach cramps. By morning they were gone. She wanted, though, to tell someone about yesterday. She was feeling sick. Her body heavy, her head aching. Uncle Lionel, thank God, had gone out shooting. She was asked to the luncheon, but refused: 'I have to go and see Mrs Anstruther.' She would take her a Christmas present. And because she had been Mama's friend she would know, somehow, what to do . . .

Aunt Violet was in her small sitting-room tying up parcels. She was delighted to see Alice: 'Such a long time, my dear. Always busy now with photographs!' She turned her frail prettiness towards Alice. '*I've* been busy too. Arranging the Mass centre for Father Proudfoot – and then the convent at Thirsk – a little carol service. These are presents for the orphans –'

She looked so gentle, so kind. Mama's friend. How many times had she not wept in those arms? Had they not *both* wept when Mama was betrayed by Belle Maman?

'Alice dear, what a lovely gift? May I – shall I *guess*?'

'Please, dearest Aunt Violet, something dreadful has happened –'

'Yes, dear.' Her eyes opened wide. But she was not quite, not quite concentrating.

'My uncle. He – you see, when he was alone with me, he –' But she did not know what words to use. If only, without explanation, Aunt Violet would take her in her arms (beautifully smelling, faint flower scents . . .).

'Aunt Violet, what he did was to ask if he . . .' She stumbled over the words. '. . . And then he asked if he might touch me, there. And he hurt me, so I hit him.' She wasn't crying, but her voice, she could hardly control the tremble in it. Any moment now, and she would break down.

'. . . So you see, I hit him, you see, because it was so dreadful. Aunt Violet, I'm so *unhappy* –'

'This lovely little carved bird is from New Zealand,' Aunt Violet said, holding up a toy in smooth pale wood. She looked over towards the window. 'I think we shall have snow. Should you like a white Christmas, Alice?'

'*Didn't you hear?* He, he –' But she could not remember now what words she had used.

'The nuns have arranged such a lovely crib, with quite the most beautiful *bambino*. I would have liked you to see it, Alice.' She reached for her scissors. 'Would you hold this string now, please, my dear? I don't see, you know, how I am to get it all done. And Christmas only a week away . . .'

Her cotton drawers were stained. She thought she had cut herself. Then when she was in the downstairs cloakroom – outside, sounds of people returning from the day's shooting – she was appalled to see blood in the water. Mine, she thought, it is from *me*. White and shaking, she made her way upstairs. Locked the door of her room. She didn't want to look but forced herself to. There was a wound, *must* be a wound.

It was something *he* had done. When he touched, when I wasn't sure what he did . . . She saw now a thin sluggish trickle of blood. She stood on the towel, her legs apart, the china washbasin beneath her. Then with the jug of cold water she poured and poured, over *that* place. To wash it away. To wash everything, all of it, all to do with it, away.

The wound healed. By Christmas Eve it was all gone. She tried to forget about it, and what had surely caused it. Uncle Lionel she avoided as much as possible.

On Christmas morning, walking by Belle Maman's room, she caught sight of herself in the long cheval glass. Casually, she paused. This is me, Alice. But then suddenly, to her horror, she saw that she was not clearly Alice at all. She was a blurred mass – a *mess*, rather . . . She peered at her body. Thin? No, *fat*. She didn't understand how Uncle Lionel could have thought her so childlike. I am fat. All these months while I've been happy with my camera, with Gib, with the new baby – I have been eating, eating. I was hungry and ate meals and hardly noticed that I ate and ate. Now I am fat, puffy even. It was that very puffiness which Uncle had wanted to grasp in his hands, whatever he had said. Whatever he had said, that was what he *meant* . . .

It was better then not to eat. Or so little that it hardly mattered. Just like after Mama's death. If you were clever, no one noticed. (I could even *be sick* if by chance I have taken too much.) And at Christmas dinner it was not too difficult since there were so many people: visiting aunts and great-aunts, elderly cousins, chubby Hal brought in to be made a fuss of . . .

But she did not go quite unremarked. Hawk-eyed Aunt Minnie, at eighty-five missing nothing:

'Alice has no appetite. On *Christmas* Day – The young,' she said in a loud voice, 'eat sweetmeats all day from the first unwrapping of the stocking. They are incorrigible. But a child of that age – she should know better.' And when Alice mumbled something: 'Speak up, child!'

Five minutes later Alice was very rude to Uncle Lionel, refusing to answer a polite question. It was bad enough when she was pert but this, it could not be allowed. Belle Maman spoke sharply.

'No, no,' Uncle Lionel said. 'If Alice wishes to play the little madam – let us salute her. Peace and goodwill to men, and all that. Eh, Alice?'

'Oh, go and boil yourself, *why don't you go and boil yourself*?' She heard the words. They did not come from her. 'Don't speak to me,' she said. 'Don't speak to me.'

'Alice! *Alice!*' A shocked Papa and Belle Maman. She must go up to her room. At once. Gaps. Snorts of disapproval. 'She is impossible,' someone said.

Uncle pleaded for her. 'I don't mind. I like spirit. No, I *insist* she stays.'

It was horrid that he should take her part.

Aunt Minnie said: 'It is all the sweetmeats. Injurious sugar, you may depend on it.'

12

The Towers,
8th December, 1901

My Valentin, my darling,

Last night I dreamed about that little waterfall in the Prahova valley – and was sick with longing. (You know really of what waterfall I dreamed . . .) And then this evening for a dinner-party I was obliged to wear the hated *other* waterfall. It's become useless to make scenes about it, so I tell myself little follies such as the one that every diamond is a tear of sorrow that we are parted – for ever (I try not to think that. And while I can still write . . .). My twentieth letter only, how is that for discipline? (You have cheated, who put *five* in the one envelope! It was lucky no one but I saw the post that day!) Four weeks ago I managed a visit to Oxford. And somehow sneaked a sight of Christ Church (wet and cold, alas) but at least I could walk about and think: *He* looked on these stones, he went up *that* staircase . . .

I have too much time for memories. Idle and pampered. My friend Sadie expects her third child already. Her husband is safely back from the War in Africa, although very weak on his return. Enteric fever . . .

What stories I make up about what Madame Billaud tells me of Paris – I am *really* the actress again! Such practice too for the stories I shall soon be telling three-year-old Hal – who is not slow to invent stories himself! (That day so long ago when you asked so sweetly all about him. And I thought you tried only to ingratiate yourself . . .)

Now, *our child*, dearest! Yes, yes, she *is* like you. Staring at her, I convince myself that it is true – and it *is*! I enclose this little drawing I've made, which is no feat of draughtsmanship, and a small lock of her hair (she has so much!). Next time I shall send a picture that Alice will take (that dreadful photography is sometimes a boon).

My darling, about Other Women – there is no need to say anything and it is best that I don't think of it and *you* don't speak of it again. The kind of life you lead, the sort of person you are – it would not be natural. And since *we have no future*, it would be madness, such fidelity on your part. For me it's easy, and will I think remain so – but that is different! It was a mistake that we should try to discuss it in letters, which lend themselves so easily to misunderstandings . . . Those letters which are so precious to me because they have in them the very sound of your voice (Yes, we *did* in the end look 'spiffing' together – but it was not to be . . .) And the writing paper which smells of your cigarettes . . . The letters are safe, of course – you should see the stoutness of the lock on my leather case. I read them in the middle of the night . . .

Theodora, gift of God. I am still surprised that the name should have been allowed – except that he was not angry with Teodor and Sophie, only with me . . . The something terrible that happened on my return, it is all long behind now. But he is determined not to like her. I pray God others don't notice, above all that *she* will not . . .

Meantime you and I may love her. No, my darling, I can't think what you can send her. Even the simplest of gifts, it would be too difficult. Perhaps through Sophie, just this once?

Nearly a whole year of the new century gone. That you and I should have to say: 'We have not seen each other this century' . . .

Now I must say goodnight, dear heart. Tomorrow I write more. I shall not be able to stop myself, I shall write of what *it was like*, – do the memories tormet you as they do me, yes, I know that they do – it is only with my eyes closed I can taste you, and sometimes I wake in the night and cry because I thought I felt your touch, your *secret* touch. If it is never to be again, never, I don't think that I . . .

Alice, seen standing directly under the great light in the music room, dressed in her new frock of red faille. It seemed to Lily that under the stiff material there was scarcely a body at all. She told herself that Alice had had always that pinched look, had all the time she'd known her been thin. And yet . . . February now, and in three months the child would be seventeen. She was scarcely developed at all . . . It was difficult to think of her as more than about thirteen. (Is that why I push out of my mind always that boy from the Vicarage – already so tall? No one has as yet made any remarks, but if we suggest there should always be a third person in the darkroom, will that not put ideas into their heads?)

The painful thinness, that was a different matter, and must be dealt with *now*. Dr Sowerby must examine Alice thoroughly. But first she must speak to her . . .

Embarrassedly she asked: 'It's – is everything all right with you each month?'

Alice looked puzzled.

'But, dear – at sixteen. Nan-Nan spoke to you, of course. I –' She floundered, ashamed of her neglect.

'No,' Alice said when Lily had explained. 'Nothing like that happens.' She had flushed painfully. She said with head averted, 'Yes, once, a few years ago. I didn't think –'

Her mother's disease, tuberculosis. Surely, Lily thought, that is our greatest fear. And should be, must be Robert's too. And yet, no cough, no fever. Perhaps after all it was only the 'green sickness' she remembered from her girlhood. Chlorosis. With iron the remedy.

And indeed that was what Dr Sowerby thought. He suggested a visit to Harrogate, to take the chalybeate waters with their high iron content. Also she *must* put on weight. Must have cod liver oil, cream . . .

But Alice rebelled at the cod liver oil. 'I shall be sick.' Then later: 'I've *been* sick . . .' There was no means really of making someone of her age take it. Yet something must be done. What would be her future otherwise? Talk of her 'coming out' in perhaps a year's time, doing a London season – was no more than talk. An idea of Robert's glanced at in conversation with Lionel, mentioned only once to Alice, who would have none of it. Lily doubted it would happen. With an excellent dowry, although no longer the heiress, Alice would have to take her chance among the local eligibles. For that, both her looks and her health would have to improve . . .

In late February she was sent to Harrogate for three weeks. It was suggested Mrs Anstruther went with her, but Alice refused. Then, surprising Lily: '*You* could come instead, I suppose,' she said ungraciously. But in the end a cousin on her mother's side was sent. Forty, kindly, she was delighted:

a rest from her elderly mother to whom she was bound hand and foot.

But if it was a success for Cousin Dorothy, Alice came back as thin as ever, and with as an extra a streaming cold and cough. Dr Sowerby said he could not rule out the possibility of tuberculosis. By now Robert had become very concerned. Another change of air was recommended. It was no good to speak of Filey and the seaside since the bracing air of Harrogate had not helped. Four to six weeks in a warm climate, Dr Sowerby suggested. The Riviera perhaps?

Lily thought afterwards: It was meant to be. The idea came to her almost at once. They would go to the Riviera, she and Alice (had not Alice actually asked for her company in Harrogate?). It would appear quite natural. And then . . . Ah, but I am wicked, selfish, she thought, and will be punished. But not before I've had, *we* have had, the most beautiful reward . . .

Her hand trembling with haste, she wrote, 'We are to be at the Hotel Colony, Beaulieu – concoct what alibi you can – are you at all known on the Riviera? Arrange whatever you like – get yourself introduced. After that, something, anything, will be possible . . .' She sealed the inner envelope with their joint seal. On the outer envelope the name of Madame Billaud.

Now she had only to wait.

The mimosa was out. In the early morning the sun came through the slats of the jalousie. A spell of cold weather, but the sky was blue, the sea jewelled. They sat on the terrasse of a café where a coke brazier glowed. Clean and light. Another world and already, Lily thought, it was doing Alice a little good. She had enjoyed the day in Paris and then in the train *de grande luxe* going to the Riviera had slept, she said, all night.

Lily had not slept. Nor could she the following nights. She felt certain Alice must notice something – but it seemed not. She said to Lily,

'I hope we don't stay so long that I miss all Gib's holiday . . .' She had brought a folding camera with her. Lily wondered – shall we be photographed together, he and I? (When will he come? Oh my God, when will he come?)

She tried, now that Alice was a little more receptive, to give her some of the affection she had always wanted to show her.

Perhaps now, she would be allowed? She began to long that Alice might confide in her, that they might miraculously – for it would have to be a miracle – become friends . . .

As they walked or drove along the promenade, among the shaggy palm trunks, or sat quietly over their meals, she spoke of her own childhood: growing up in Leeds, Dad, Daisy. Ethel. The death of Harry. Alice, although she said nothing, *seemed* to be interested. Lily felt only shame that all the time, while wanting to give love to Alice, her heart, her watching nerves, her whole being really, were somewhere else . . .

He walked across the foyer of the Hotel Colony, to where they were taking afternoon tea. It was the sixth day.

She thought that she might die. A violin trio were playing, badly, the waltz from *La Belle Hélène*. Alice had been laughing with her at the frequent excruciating wrong notes.

'Lady Firth? Forgive me that you don't know me, madame. I've heard that you're staying here from a mutual friend. May I present myself . . . Valentin . . .'

She didn't know what to do with herself, how to behave. She wanted suddenly to laugh, with relief, with wild happiness. He is here. *He is here*.

'Please forgive me, Monsieur Oleancu. I laugh – we've been laughing at the trio. Look – no, the small one with the long moustaches, it's very wicked and ill-mannered but my stepdaughter and I . . .'

Introductions to Alice, explanations: he was Rumanian and had been asked by Madame Billaud of Paris to look out for them. And then had seen their name on the Beaulieu Visitors' list. That he should happen to have arrived today at the *same* hotel . . .

He sat with them. More tea was ordered. Yes, he would love some gâteau and had an enormous appetite. This coincidence was delightful and he hoped, really hoped, that since he was here for several weeks they would perhaps allow him to take them about? Did they know Mentone?

He was the same, yet not – heavier perhaps. She tried not to stare, to meet his eyes. How to keep up her acting? Oh, the theatricality of it all . . .

'Your English is so good,' she said. 'Really quite remarkable –'

'I was one year at Oxford. Christ Church.' He turned on

Alice his beautiful smile. 'Miss Firth, do you know Oxford at all?'

She could not wait for the night. She thought that Alice, who was plainly enjoying Valentin's company, would never leave. She could not send her up before ten. And it would be best, would it not, if they all three said their goodnights downstairs . . .

But it was worth it, the wait. She cried, before he came to her room at midnight (Alice safely asleep two floors up). Cried when they made love . . .

'Oh, but my darling Lily, it's not sad, not sad, it's so *happy*. Valentin has been so clever and we have three weeks, four weeks . . .'

'But I *am* happy, that's why I cry – because I'm so happy and have been so *un*happy – and because it will all end, it has to end all over again –'

'Hush now, hush now . . .'

'Ah no, but it does –'

'Stop this at once, I stop you like this – and this – and *this* – you see I've not forgotten what you love best of all . . . And now this, and this, yes? . . . Then we lie quiet for just a little while, and you tell me how clever I've been, how very, very clever – that I arrange our meeting so *perfectly* . . .'

And so the happy days began . . . She promised him, herself too, that she would use them one by one. 'Each one preciouser,' he said . . . It worried her sometimes that she deceived Alice. Even more that Alice might take seriously the compliments, the attentions shown her by Valentin . . . He spoke of this to Lily. 'I want so much it is all natural, and that I don't show for you anything at all. Only perhaps, I do it wrong?'

But although Alice showed pleasure in his company, she often appeared removed from it all. She said once when asked playfully for her thoughts, 'I am arranging a series of photographs I shall take. When I am home again –' Her appetite, alas, was no better. She toyed with *médaillons de bœuf*, cutting a little off the edges and making it last the course through, ordered profiteroles and left them after just a bite of choux pastry . . .

'She's a sad little girl,' Valentin told Lily. 'Even for me, she won't eat –'

Never alone together in the daytime, it was at night, after love-making, that they would talk and talk.

'. . . One delicious piece of gossip – Ana – Ana Xenescu, she has had another child, and at almost forty-two! The talk is wild as to who is father – (no, it's not me, not at all, and no, not even in teasing must you try that), since it is absolutely *known* it cannot be the Colonel . . .'

Gossip. Their love, news from Sinaia, Bucharest, their love again and, of course, their daughter . . .

'You're wicked that you don't bring her here now, to see me –'

'What – and with her nurse, and all other manner of unlikelihoods? We'd be discovered in a trice . . .'

'My face. Expression of pride that she's so spiffing – *that* would give me away . . . And also you know, Lily, we are so fortunate that no one of ours, Rumanians, that they don't visit here. If I have that fence to jump . . .'

'You may think yourself a great actor, but shouldn't you congratulate me too? I think I *shall* go back on the stage after all –'

'But you've other greater gifts, yes? Lily of the Valley. Let me admire, ah come now, let me talk to the smallest *trou* in France, in *all* the world – hold my head – no, better still, love me as I talk to it . . . To think *our* child has come from there . . .'

Then one evening, her despair again, washing over her. I should be braver. I have been brave before. But this time it is worse, worse . . .

'Listen, Val, I'm sick, I tremble, I shall never go back to England, never, I shall send for the baby and for Hal and we can . . . we could . . . it might be . . . people have done these wicked things and prospered, have they not? Tell me they have. Tell me we *could* . . .'

Alice thought: I am almost happy. The feeling had grown slowly through the sun-filled spring days. She felt at home in Beaulieu, perhaps because it was smaller than nearby Nice. She loved to sit on her balcony and gaze at the snow peaks, a romantic distant world – then to look down on to the hotel gardens: mimosa, orange trees, stone seats set among the flowering bushes. Often when the light seemed to her right, she went down and took photographs.

If only Gib – it was his absence made it not quite perfect. But about that Belle Maman had been strangely thoughtful, even suggesting that it might have been nicer for Alice had he been invited too . . . All in all she was a far more pleasant companion than Alice would have expected. And since this Valentin had arrived (already, at Belle Maman's direction, she was calling him 'Valentin'), it would have been difficult to be bored or unhappy. Their days were so full now – mornings out driving, always the three of them, excursions or walks by the sea. Then in the afternoon, for Alice the prescribed rest which Belle Maman took also. Tea together, perhaps another outing. Then some evenings to the Casino here or at Nice.

She thought sometimes that she had never seen anyone so beautiful as Valentin. Not handsome, but beautiful. She would say the word over to herself often as she rested in the afternoon. *Beautiful.* She would have liked just to gaze at him if that had been possible and not rude. Also, he was fun – making her laugh, including her in every remark, even on two occasions telling her lightly that *she* was beautiful (which I am not, but it is oh so wonderful to be thought so . . .), and soon would be *elegante* too. There must be a dress-buying expedition, he said . . .

Belle Maman liked him also – that was evident. Hadn't she said to Alice at least twice: '*Wasn't* it the most wonderful chance that someone so delightful should turn up? If you had had only me to amuse you . . .'

Yes, it was almost happiness. Or – perhaps it was what people called contentment? For she slept well and took exercise and enjoyed herself and *even* (yes, even this!) had an appetite for the delicious meals. She surprised herself by the way she'd been able, for almost a week now, to eat the whole of what was set before her.

Yet it was not *just* contentment – or why that little frisson of excitement every morning when Belle Maman cried: 'Why, here comes our knight, Alice!' And Valentin, kissing their hands, saying, 'Another lovely day – how are we to spend it – the three of us?'

'Another lovely day,' Belle Maman said, that Friday morning. 'I wonder how we are to spend it without Valentin? We've grown so accustomed . . . I've written him already a little note about the theatre tonight.'

It was their third week. A few days earlier some friends of Valentin's staying at Cagnes had been in touch with him. Yesterday afternoon he had left to see them. They expected him back next day.

How then to pass the morning?

'It is not the same without him – our *friend*,' Alice said. And Belle Maman, understanding perfectly (perhaps she had the same feeling of dullness?) said that they might take an expedition to buy Alice a *hat*? There were some lovely new models in the windows of Mireille's . . . And then some hot chocolate perhaps at their favourite café?

Yes, yes. That would do well enough . . . They were standing in the foyer about to call a cab when Belle Maman looking in her reticule found that she had left her notebook upstairs.

'I don't care to be without it. It's always then one is certain to need it – a nuisance . . .'

'I can hurry and fetch it.' She offered willingly. More and more she found herself having kind, good thoughts . . .

Upstairs in Belle Maman's sitting-room she found it exactly where she had been told: little ivory pad with its worked gold pencil. She glanced around. A blue silk peignoir in Japanese style, patterned with iris, flung on the sofa. With her free hand, she stroked the silk. The whole room and probably the bedroom next door had taken on a look of Belle Maman. She thought that it might be interesting to photograph it?

She rearranged the peignoir, so that it looked more careless. The desk was not quite tidy – a letter in Papa's handwriting lay open on the blotter. She read the first few sentences but found in them only the news that she too had received. Looking then at the blotter, its white paper scored with blue, here and there a blob, she wondered idly what Belle Maman had written?

I shouldn't, she thought, hurriedly holding it up to the glass. And then – oh and then, as word after word yielded its mirror image, she said out loud: 'Ah, *no* . . .'

What was all this? This talk of *love*, and *Valentin*? Her hand holding up the blotter trembled. It could not be – Belle Maman could not have *fallen in love*. So soon – it wasn't possible, and also wrong, and horrible, horrible, because she was married to *Papa*.

'. . . even this one night apart . . . the terrible longing . . . your body, the velvet touch . . . but it's *you* who are velvet . . . how am I to live after . . .'

She pushed it back on the desk. Her lips felt stiff, almost numb. Soon, very soon, the room would be cleaned, the blotting paper replaced, the hateful words removed. But not from her mind. They will never, never go, she thought, hurrying now down the corridor, shaking a little, wishing, wishing, wishing that she could turn back the clock five minutes, three minutes even – *to be as I was before. Not to know* . . .

'Why, Alice dear, you're quite out of breath. Was it difficult to find? Not where I said?'

Such a smile. Charming everyone, *seeming* kind and nearly, oh so nearly deceiving me. Going out to the carriage now, wearing a costume of creamy white cloth showing off her beautiful (horrible) figure and small waist. The fashionable tricorne hat. Oh, but she is hateful.

And so was that dreadful morning – that was to have been so pleasant, such fun, so easy.

'But, Alice, that is the very hat you admired on Wednesday, when we saw it with Valentin . . .'

With Valentin, yes. And had he not said (thinking all the while surely of Belle Maman?): 'Alice would look quite absolutely spiffing in that one . . .'

False, false, false. In her anger and distress, she slouched before the milliner's glass, her mouth turned deliberately downward. White straw picture hat with blue chiffon, brim folded one side over a black velvet bandeau. Pinned to it, an inexpensive ornament.

'It's all a terrible mistake. I look a fright –'

'I could easily lend you, *give* you, dear, my little sapphire and gold butterfly. That would be quite charming.'

'*No*.'

She astonished herself by her rudeness. It was like old

times again. When she had mourned her own mother and hated the interloper. Now she hated the person, the *persons* who were deceiving her father. But Belle Maman only said mildly:

'If you're not in a hat-buying mood . . .'

But there was still the rest of the morning to get through. And then at luncheon, oh horrid surprise: the return of Valentin.

'And how have my darlings been amusing themselves? For me it's been so *ennuyeux* as you can't imagine – but duty is done now . . .'

'Alice is a little low-spirited today. Perhaps you've been missed –'

'I am always missed. I am so greatly loved . . .'

Half way through the meal Alice felt that she could bear no more. 'If you'd excuse me? I'm going up to my room. One of my headaches –'

They were both of them at once all tenderness. 'A cachet, I'll fetch you one. We'll order a tisane to be sent up. You *must* be well for the ballet. Rest, as long as you can . . .'

Up in her room she couldn't sleep or even lie still on the bed. After a while she raised the jalousie, letting in the afternoon sun. She sat on the balcony, in the shade, and tried to read. It was only half past three. She looked down below, and saw strolling past the judas trees, Belle Maman and Valentin.

They were deep in conversation, circumspectly walking a little apart. Belle Maman wearing her new lemon écru lace and silk coat. (How fitting that she walked among the judas trees . . .)

Now they had stopped, where a garden seat stood against a wealth of bushes. They sat, and Valentin took Belle Maman's parasol for her and folded it. Watching, Alice thought suddenly: I want to hear them. As they talked, surely they would condemn themselves out of their own mouths? And she, she would surprise them, *embarrass* them. It would be worse, far worse, than telling Papa. (How could I ever, would I ever?)

She strolled into the garden through the side entrance leading to the tennis courts and croquet pitch. Few people were about. Along the other side of the bushes, she crept stealthily. I am searching for a lost tennis ball, she told herself – and to bear the story out, bent occasionally to look in the undergrowth.

Voices. Belle Maman's tinkling laugh. Valentin's deep one . . . She stood still, holding her breath to hear the better. Ahead, she saw where she might walk round, and then as they spoke their words of love, spring out on them and . . .

'. . . your *affaire* . . . what would you have done if Ana Xenescu – if there'd been a child there? I often ask that because you –'

'But my darling there wasn't, so . . . Anyway, she has now this charming little Corina. *Not* mine, of course.'

'Of course.' Belle Maman's laugh again.

'Don't I do enough fathering an English Miss? Even so, it'd have been being all right with Ana – she has after all a husband. Society understands. As in England . . .'

'Not Robert, not Robert. The King, and his Set, that's another matter. *There* it doesn't do to peer too closely into the cradle – certainly not to remark on family resemblances, or lack of them . . .'

'But my Theodora –'

'*She'll* always be all right. I may be fair-haired but Robert is dark enough, and so is Hal, and then – Lionel! He is *very* dark –'

'What you've been saying of him, God forbid anyone should think . . .'

'No, never! And Robert least of all . . . It is now all quite safe. It is only that – when people – when they say "How like . . . such a Firth . . ." I would laugh if I didn't want to *weep* –'

'Darling, you *mustn't*. Nearly three years now that we love –'

' . . . I want to cry out and tell *everyone*, "Look, look, she is the daughter of the most beautiful man in Rumania –" '

'Lily, sweet one, it will be always all right. I shall be loving her from far away. And when she grows up – you don't cry, darling, or I too –'

'How can I help it? How? If I count the days . . .'

'Kiss me. Let me kiss you –'

'Where all the world can see? *And* Alice from her window!'

'Later, later. No, don't cry . . . Indoors now. And back to the play-acting . . .'

'Yes. Back to our play-acting . . .'

She could do nothing. There was nothing on earth she could do. She had heard things now which she could not ever have wanted to know. *I do not want to know any of it.*

What she had learned was so terrible that she would never, never tell anyone. Horrible, disgusting, *too much.*

If I could only go back, she thought, not just to this morning, but to before Uncle Lionel in the darkroom. To before Mama died. When she loved and needed me. *Before . . .*

I am an alone child. They think I am grown up. And part of me is. Old and sick and sad. It is all a tangle past unravelling . . . One thing is certain though, after what I've seen, I never want to marry. Never. *Never.*

13

From *Country Life*, March 1903.
Our photograph this week is of Lady Firth, wife of Sir Robert Firth of The Towers, Flaxthorpe, in the North Riding of Yorkshire. Before her marriage Lady Firth was the well-known actress Lily Greene. She returns to the stage this spring playing the lead in *Princess Violet*, a new musical play by the Irish composer John Plunkett, with book by Ernest Harley . . .

From *The Lady*, March 1903.
'Miss Greene, where do you expect to go from here? Can we hope for a permanent return?'

'That is for the public to decide, I think!'

Miss Greene lights a cigarette in a beautiful holder, studded with small rubies and pearls. I continue: 'Miss Greene, ladies' ages are a delicate matter but our readers will surely wish to know – do you plan to continue playing heroines such as your Shop Girl, and of course this new Princess?'

'Certainly. When apt . . .'

'*Princess Violet*, Miss Greene. Perhaps you could tell our readers a little about it?'

'With pleasure. It's a very simple tale. Princess Violet, heiress to the throne, has so far rejected all suitors. She is thirty. The kingdom is worried. When the play opens she has just consented to marry a rich but rather elderly prince from a neighbouring kindgom. Then she meets in the Castle grounds a young man – he tells her he is being pursued by foreign agents. She agrees to hide him . . . and – to say any more would be to spoil . . . The music is delightful and gives me some enchanting songs . . .'

I ask her now about her family. 'Surely they will miss you? You have children –'

'Yes, Henry – Hal – four and a half. And Theodora, we call her Teddy, is three . . .'

'Miss Greene, recently Miss Fannie Ward in *The Clim-*

bers wore some of her own diamonds, about twenty thousand pounds' worth, I believe. There has been mention not only of your home, but also of the precious stones and jewellery there. Particularly the remarkable waterfall of diamonds. Is there any possibility that as Princess Violet you will –'

'No.' Her tone was crisp when she interrupted me: 'No. None at all.'

There was no eseaping it now: her return to the stage. It was in the end quite a sudden decision, although the idea had been growing in her mind all through the long, lonely summer of 1902. Her children: on the one hand such a joy and yet – seeming to belong to other people. Nan-Nan, Alice. Even one August afternoon when she had been sitting in the garden, little Teddy running with a bloodied knee into the arms of – Gib Nicolson . . .

As for Hal, often she felt that for him, she was not real at all . . . A visitor perhaps – who might or might not stay a while. ('Was that story all about *Mummy*?' he'd asked Cousin Dorothy, reading him a fairy story about a beautiful princess . . .)

Yet Sadie's Jack, how confidently he ran to his mother . . . to show her this, tell her that – and as confidently ran away again. Sadie with her three beautiful children (and all of them Charlie's . . .). She is still my greatest, my only friend, Lily thought. It is Vicky again, without the unhappy ending. But just as I never told Vicky about Frank, I've told her nothing of Val. Now it is too late. I could not, now . . . And then – Teddy . . . The rest of the story . . .

To become an actress again. Not only the summer of heartbreak, parted it now seemed for ever from Valentin (and feeling more than ever wicked, wanton, deceitful, all that she would detest in others . . .), but the despair of the cold dark winter following, decided her. A casual remark at a dinner-party to the effect that had she remained on the stage, it night now be *her* playing opposite Seymour Hicks in *The Earl and the Girl* . . . ('It would quite match *The Duke and etc.*, do you not think?')

Robert had surprised her then by saying, lightly: 'But she

has my permission to return when she wishes. She can only do us all credit . . .'

Later when, the idea grown in her own mind, she had spoken to him of it, also lightly, he had not seemed quite so willing.

'I – of course – a remark on a social occasion . . .'

'People no doubt took you at your word –'

But she let it go. Two weeks later she raised the subject again only to find him suddenly agreeable. 'It will do no harm – and you will tire of it soon enough.' He added brusquely, 'But one breath of scandal . . .'

She knew well enough what he meant. The matter of Teddy's birth, now never referred to – about that he was scrupulous as was his behaviour towards the child – was only lightly buried. It would not take much . . .

To her surprise and Sadie's delighted excitement, she found almost immediately a suitable play. Possibilities for Billie Burke or Gertie Millar, neither of whom were available . . . She felt that it must be *meant*, and wrote at once to Val, certain that he would be able to come and see her. Despairing, though, of any real time together. 'One breath of scandal . . .'

She scarcely knew where to turn for excitement. The music, easy, charming, made little demand on her light voice. The storyline she glanced at only: seeing with pleasure that thirty-three playing thirty would strain no credulity.

She rented a small, pretty flat, began rehearsals, and travelled home on a fast LNER train at each weekend. Her photograph was in three magazines and she was interviewed twice.

It was about three weeks before the opening that she finally admitted: I have made a mistake. But only to herself. Not even to Sadie did she hint that it was all of it about to go terribly wrong . . .

She had expected there to be some difficulties, returning to the stage after six years' absence. But she had expected better than this. *The Duke and the Shopgirl* had brought excitement, comradeship, little or no rivalry, and a great deal of fun. *Princess Violet* was its mirror image.

She thought at first it was her leading man who was the culprit. Also not the impresario's first choice, he was too young, and worse did not convince. Physically clumsy, his voice raw, too loud. Who would believe him a prince in disguise? It seemed no one else saw that he was miscast . . . But she had not enough of the prima donna to say: 'He goes, or else . . .'

And the story – was not that too part of the trouble? It was to her a faint reflection, mockery almost, of the love-story between her and Valentin . . . A woman of nearly thirty about to marry for security, the 'beautiful' younger man from a far away romantic country, their secret and apparently doomed love. A stupidly happy ending only compounded the mockery . . .

Even the music, which she'd thought she liked, she now found thin. Sole consolation was Muriel, the second female lead. Gentle, yet strong, she reminded Lily of Daisy (to whom an excited letter had already gone off: 'Perhaps, who knows, the show will come to Broadway and your sister with it!!').

A disastrous dress rehearsal gave her some hope that on the night all would be well. Yet – how? Everything was against it. It wants only peacock feathers, she thought.

The first night. Robert in the front stalls. And Lionel, the mocking Lionel. Afterwards the fulsome praise for something she knew to be bad, bad, bad. And in the morning, the critics. As she could have predicted, they were rude about the hero. 'Gauche . . . wooden . . . insufficient colour in the voice . . .' Muriel's debut was rightly praised.

As for herself: 'Miss Greene delighted us,' said the *Morning Post*, 'she might never have been away. Indeed perhaps she does not realize that she *has*. And that she is no longer playing Shop Girl turned Duchess, but a Princess deeply and hopelessly in love. She does not sing her love songs as if she meant them . . . Her performance is pretty but wants passion . . .'

Well, she thought as she read it, well: this caricature of my own plight and I cannot even convey it on stage . . .

But the public liked the play – and her. Advance bookings for the London Season were already excellent. She realized then that mistake or no, she would have to continue. She had heard nothing from Valentin. And she was homesick: the weekend journeys were not possible now the show had opened, and she arranged to go once a month only. Alice came up for a week, and was difficult. She said, 'I'd really prefer to be in Flaxthorpe. Gib is on holiday . . .'

Each night she went through the motions of being Princess Violet. In a dress of mauve chiffon embroidered with paillettes, she sang nonsense:

> 'Every diamond a tear I shed for you
> My jewels and my crown I would
> Forget, if only that I could
> Bring together with my love we two . . .'

Really! There must be an honourable way out . . .

Early June, and Robert came to spend three weeks with Lionel. Suppers again at Romano's, the Savoy. Almost like old times (if I wished for them . . .). But she could think only that Valentin might come during these weeks. And what then?

Although Robert stayed at the flat, they had separate bedrooms. She would have pleaded tiredness had he suggested anything. But she was glad to see the red leather jewel case had not accompanied him . . .

One night during the second week, they returned after an exhausting supper together in a *cabinet privé* during which he had repeatedly accused her of flirting with a Mr Coleman, a financier, the evening before: 'He's a Jew, and has his eye on you – I am not blind to these things.'

As soon as they reached the flat, he began again:

'You do *realize* he is a Jew?'

'Yes. For all the importance it has. Yes. And now, isn't that enough? I tire . . .'

He said suddenly, 'Oh, but you are so beautiful. Now. Stand like that. When you are angry –'

'I am not angry. Just tired. And I dislike thoughtless prejudice . . .'

'Yes, angry. And beautiful. No one, you know, no one has ever looked as you do in the Diamond Waterfall.' He paused. 'If I could picture, imagine that you wore it now – I might . . .'

She thought wearily: Why not? Why not have another child and be out of all this? The quinine pessary that was to have protected her for ever after . . . Why not just submit, and see?

It was bad, but at least no worse than she had feared. He said afterwards: 'The Waterfall, my dear, your next visit to Flaxthorpe – would you wear it? In the bedroom . . . My camera,' he spoke offhandedly, 'if I had one still, I would pose you –'

'With nothing on?' she said. 'Whom for – *Country Life*?'

She suffered it three more times. Wearing on one occasion an ornate Egyptian gold necklace, just purchased by Robert as a celebration gift for her success in the show – which it was now thought would run till Christmas. A few weeks later, the morning after a performance attended by King Edward and Queen Alexandra, she was very sick. Fatigue, excitement, too much champagne?

She knew better. She explained to her producer that as soon as he could make satisfactory arrangements she must leave. 'I am expecting a child, I cannot afford to take risks . . .' It was given out that she left for reasons of health: the full truth to come later . . . The convenient folding of another show, releasing an actress who had first been mooted for Princess Violet, made it all simple.

In early July she travelled back to Yorkshire. She felt a sense of relief but also, of failure. She thought with longing of her two children. Of the happiness she had had with Theodora, the late joy (please God not too late) with Hal . . . She could not wait to be a mother again.

A letter from Paris awaited her. 'My darling, my darling, it's so absolutely spiffing as I can't say – Now I am quite, *quite* certain to come the end July! Mimie Billaud writes she has *forgotten* to forward a letter and what is she to do? I have been since Christmas on a world tour, far far East with a dear but so ill uncle. Write *at once* that it's all good for my London visit – I can't believe we are really to be together – O my lily of the valley, we shall . . .'

She grew much larger, much sooner, than with either Teddy or Hal. Nan-Nan assured her it was a boy. Alice she felt embarrassed to tell and hoped that, as before, someone else would do it. (That curious and short-lived rapport in Beaulieu, lost even before the holiday ended – we shall not see that again.) Told to her face, she would surely greet the news with scorn – or coldness. Lily did not think she could bear either.

Of the missed reunion with Valentin, she thought: It was too much the fairy tale; I never really expected it . . . Her first despairing letter written, his heartbroken reply received. She told herself: One day, I shall have to admit it is all The Past. Meanwhile she sent him cuttings of Teddy's uncompromisingly straight hair, photographs, two large-fisted drawings . . .

A week of violent winds and gales towards the end of November. Standing at the drawing-room window, she saw moving among the trees a bent shabby figure. It was late afternoon, the light was going fast.

She rang the bell. 'There's some sort of – tramp outside. If the matter could be seen to?'

Only a few moments later a breathless parlourmaid knocked.

'A gentleman's here, m'lady, that'll not give his name but you'll know him and be glad, he says . . . please, have I to show him in?'

A disreputable-looking figure. And surely the one she had seen outside. He smelled, of dirt, of drink. His thin brown overcoat was torn and stained. Red-veined bulbous nose, watery eyes set in a dry, wrinkled skin . . . She thought with sudden disloyalty: Someone from Joszef's family. Someone who will trade on my love for Daisy . . .

'I rather think –' she began, but she was interrupted:

'Lily!' The voice, although cracked, husky, was well bred – exaggeratedly so . . . Then: 'Queen of my Heart,' he cried, 'Queen of my Heart tonight!'

She saw, thankfully, that the maid had left. She felt a sudden overwhelming nausea. Don't let him touch me . . . The smell as he came nearer was worse.

'You're drunk,' she said, moving back a little. Her condition of obvious pregnancy embarrassed her. He said more quietly:

'Is that the welcome, I get, my *Queen*, eh?'

'Frank, my dear.' She hated her tone of voice. But when she spoke again she sounded, she knew, even brusquer. 'Are you hungry?' (Surely yes? But if so, where was he to be fed? Not in the kitchen, and certainly not in the house. *I could not sit with him* . . . She imagined with horror what tales he would tell, how he would boast, blab . . .)

'Well, yes my dear, I could, I think, eat a good meal.'

'What is it you want?' She spoke sharply. He'd come now into the centre of the room, and was fingering the raised embroidery of an antimacassar. She saw that his hands were not only dirty, but blue. It is not the time for pity, she thought.

'What is it you want?'

'How can you ask? Didn't I come just to see you? Weren't we very close now, once. Ought I to say *how* close?'

She didn't answer. He shall not refer to that time. *When I'm carrying a child, I must never think of what happened to Vicky.*

'The surprise I got now. You've done very well for yourself, Lily. I knew nothing –'

'I've been married over six years, Frank. I value highly my peace – and privacy.'

'Not a thing did I know . . . Didn't Frank try to make a living Down Under? Australian touring companies . . . Constance died, you know. 'Twas then I came back. The Old Country, all that. Only – these days they've nothing for Frank – nothing at all . . . Didn't I learn then of your comeback? Except I'd heard nothing – that you'd been famous *before*. And a Lady too, since. You've done better than Frank –'

She said, 'It's drink, isn't it?'

'Yes,' he said, and began to cry.

She didn't soften. I am not the Lily Greene of 1890. 'What is it you want? Money? It's not, I'm sure, a visit for old times' sake . . .'

'Yes, money.' Then he added: 'Or else –'

'Oh nonsense,' she said, 'you wouldn't. And shan't. Sir Robert wouldn't believe a word of it. Menaces indeed!' She turned away from him. He had taken out a large red handkerchief and was alternately blowing his nose and wiping his eyes. 'If it's money you want, you shall have it. As a gift. Only

– do not ask again, or I shall inform the police.'

She crossed over to her desk. There she wrote out a cheque for three hundred pounds on Coutts. Blotting it, she placed it in an envelope and handed it to him.

'Now – go.'

An hour later the children were brought in by the nursemaid. Teddy wrinkled up her nose.

'Funny spell.'

'*Smell*,' said Hal. 'You ought to talk better. Ye're nobbut a larl small un, and likely a beggar . . .'

Lily remonstrated. 'Darling –'

'*Ach, du lieber Gott* and – no, *und – mein Gott, das ist nicht gut* . . .' He looked up at her for approval. 'I can talk in any person's voice. That was Fräulein . . .'

14

This must be the sweetest dearest baby ever. Alice's darling, Sylvia. With a cloud of fair curls, and in this summer of 1905, already fifteen months old. Mine, Alice thought, if wishing and caring could make it so . . . Sylvia, universally adored. Even at this age it could be seen that her nature was sweet and gentle. Not like Teddy who showed off and seemed alternately to exasperate and delight Belle Maman. Nor Hal, grown unpredictable, disobedient. Indeed if the baby could have managed to be Papa's child only, all would have been perfection. (Best not to think, *even for a moment*, that this baby might not be a Firth.)

For me to think well of or to love Belle Maman is a lost cause. I am twenty, we are *two* grown women, but since Beaulieu three years ago, there has been *no chance* at all. I have hidden away what I learned: for weeks at a time Teddy is just my little stepsister . . . Then the betrayal comes back to me. *I don't want to know if she still behaves like that.*

They had been dark days, those first weeks back in Yorkshire. Her lack of appetite – food had become not only uninteresting but *disgusting* – the hypocritical concern (on Belle Maman's part) about her health, her own feelings of despair, hopelessness and above all, unreality. *I am not real*, she would say to herself. Reality was holding a letter up to the looking-glass, hiding behind the oleander bushes, hearing *those* words . . .

If she left home, perhaps it would be better. But where to go, what to do? She had made difficulties already by her refusal to do a London season (what else could *that* be but a painful attempt to marry her off?). Anyway, to leave would be to lose the one certain, most important thing in her life: her friendship with Gib.

And yet even about that, how difficult everyone made it for her! With their nonsense talk, their hints that perhaps it was not seemly now Gib was such 'a well grown boy' that so much time should be spent in the darkroom . . . She and Gib should not even be so much together each holidays. It was disgusting, what went on in their minds. It was even suggested that Fräulein should go up with them to the darkroom, to sit in the little ante-room as chaperone. 'It is only convention, Alice. Another word for common sense . . .'

She and Gib were *friends*. Between friends such things did not happen. She had not been able even to discuss it with him, so embarrassed had she been.

This, she thought now, is my future. Little trips here and there, abroad, in England, continued studies in German (just because we have Fräulein), visits twice a week to the poor (who really cannot be pleased to see my glum face), horrid social appearances in the hope someone will pay court (which they won't, for I shan't let them), and over the years, less and less time with Gib. Until we are separated and there is none at all . . .

But I smile and manage well enough. I am sharp, she thought, opening the nursery door: going in to where Nan-Nan sewed by the firescreen, and Hal seated on the rocking-horse, Teddy pulling at the reins, waved a mock sabre.

'Give it *me*, Hal –'

'Shan't –'

'*Shall*.'

'It's *my* horse, I was born first –'

'Nan-Nan says it's not yours, not now you've cut its hair.'

'Didn't. Sucks. The Wizard did –'

'The Wizard's not real, he's imadge – imadgeary –'

'It's *you* not real.'

'I am. I am. I'm Theodora Firth, so!'

'You're not as pretty as Sylvia, Alice said –'

'Hal, give it me – *let me on Angelica* –'

'His name's Thunderer –'

'He likes to be called Angelica, he told me so.'

'That's a girl's name –'

'He *is* a girl.'

'*She's* a girl, you mean –'

'Know-all, know-all – I hate you, I hate you . . .'

Then the reassuring voice of Nan-Nan:

'Whatever's all this and my back turned only two minutes? Both of you away from that horse! I don't know whatever

Baby will think – look, the little dear, she's nearly in tears and all your fault! There, my sweet thing, come to Nan-Nan . . . You'll have tea with us, Miss Alice? Master Hal and Miss Teddy will be nice to each other, won't you – and you may eat some of those funny cakes sent from London . . .'

And I shall eat, Alice thought. When I sit with them I shall eat too. Nowadays, I eat. I may still be thinner than many people, but I don't reject food any longer. Because of Gib. *For his sake* . . .

It happened the July after the Riviera visit, when he came home at the end of his third term at school. He seemed to like Marlborough well enough, or at least was not actually unhappy. Letters had come fairly regularly, although he had had to obtain especial permission since she wasn't a parent or close relation . . . (the same silly rules . . . what is it they *think*?). He'd enjoyed, he told her, some acting: dressing up, singing, that sort of thing. It didn't please her too much. She didn't care for that side of him, that liked to play the fool. When he clowned, for her he lost something. As when last Christmas at the Vicarage he'd done a comic turn with an officious girl cousin whom Alice had hated at once.

But that summer she had Gib to herself, and, still smarting from the episode on the Riviera, she found to be with him was peace. Excitement too, for they were to experiment with Alice's new camera, bought with her birthday money.

There was to be a portrait of Alice first. She had stood happily, while, cloth over head and camera, he had busied himself with the focusing. Straightway after she said:

'The shutter, Gib, it oughtn't to stick. I rubbed it with a really soft pencil –'

But as if he hadn't heard her, he burst out:

'I can't bear it –'

'What?' she asked at once. 'Can't bear *what*?'

'You are so thin. So thin. I can't –'

'What do you mean? I'm the same as ever, I'm *Alice*.'

'No, you look like, I can't – it mustn't be –' his voice trembled. He said urgently, 'A shadow, that's what you're like. Hardly there . . . when I looked through the lens, I almost said –' he laughed nervously – 'I almost said, "Come here and see for yourself" –'

'I look perfectly all right,' she said sharply.

'No. No. Look, you mustn't . . . Thin like *that*, it means . . . She, my mama, she was thin when the sickness began. Then always thinner, Father and I could see it – I heard him say to Aunt Ettie, "It's the thinness – that she fades before our eyes . . ." And I – it was so dreadful, I . . . *Alice*, I *cannot bear it that you are so thin* . . .'

Profoundly shocked, she wasn't able to speak for a few moments. When she did, it was to make some technical remark about the Watkin's actinometer. And had he the pendulum?

That evening when the dish came round she took a second helping of potatoes, and a little later, one of summer pudding too. No one noticed. Curiously, she enjoyed the food, relishing it not for any pleasure it gave her, but because by eating it she *gave* pleasure.

Curiously also, after a month of eating, when she looked in the glass she did not seem much bigger, nor more rounded, but rather, softer, calmer. The bleeding too started again. This time she shrugged resignedly.

When he could get away from everybody – which meant really Nan-Nan and of course Teddy – Hal liked best to wander about. Downstairs, library, conservatory, gallery, unlocked bedrooms, in the guest wing, or down below in the kitchens where, if he was lucky and the mood was good, they made a fuss of him. But best of all, when the weather allowed, was to be in the grounds of The Towers. For the whole north part of the garden, stretching from the rose walk to the copse, was his kingdom. While he walked there, it was his.

The Red, the Violet, the Green, the Blue, the Yellow Fairy Book. To be read to by Alice, by Mother (best of all by mother). To read on his own. Then afterwards to tell himself the story, to talk in *all* the voices – witch, beggar, princess, goatboy. If that wasn't the greatest fun . . . In the evening Mother might come in to see him, sparkling with diamonds and rubies and emeralds . . . and be seen to *be* the Princess, the Queen . . .

My kingdom. I am King Henry. King *Hal*. I reign over the kitchen garden, the Lily garden, the Rose garden, all, all. And especially this little wood behind the orchard. They call it a copse: willow and hazel and ash – it was here long before they built The Towers. It is my ancient (I love that word), my very ancient kingdom . . .

Now I walk boldly into it. My voice is full of echoes . . .

Once upon a time the king of the Goldland lost himself in a forest and try as he would he could not find the way out. As he was wandering down one path which had looked at first more hopeful, he saw a man coming towards him. 'What are you doing here, friend?' asked the stranger; 'darkness is falling fast and soon the wild beasts will come from their lairs to seek for food . . .' 'I have lost myself,' answered the king, 'and am trying to get home . . .'

'Daft beggar,' said a voice. 'Who're ye talking to?'

A stranger. A stranger in the kingdom. But not the one who said *friend* . . .

The boy was about Hal's height, but older. He had on very thick breeches of rough material and his jacket was torn. As he stood there he broke a small twig off the hazel bush.

'I say there, don't! Who *are* you, what are you doing in *my* grounds?'

'Nowt. Do I *look* as if I'm doing owt?' He broke off another twig. 'A lad can walk an' all, can't he? Tak a look about him . . .'

'I am Henry Reginald Francis Exelby Firth. I command you to leave my kingdom –'

'Kingdom. Daft. It's nowt but a little smally –'

'I –'

'Sir Henry – right fluffed up wi' yourself, aren't you? Well, I'm *Stephen*. Ibbotson.'

'Leave now – go on!'

'Don't talk on so – I'd not stop *you* if ye'd a mind to visit *us*, Sir Henry . . .'

'Don't tak on *yoursen*, reet fluffed up beggar . . .'

The boy grew suddenly angry. 'Mocking me, are you? Ye've no call to tak off way I talk.'

'I'll speak as I please in *my* home –'

Stephen kicked at a piece of dead wood. 'Any road I'd not want to talk your fashion, *grand* like . . .'

Hal said, in a conciliatory tone: 'That stuff, the furry stuff on the wood where you just kicked – they call it "fairy butter".'

'I ken.' His voice wasn't unfriendly. 'Me dad told us. When we were little uns.'

Hal said, 'I've two sisters, what have you got?'

'A sight more. We've Will, then Meg as died. Our James, and Ted. Then Olive. She's eight year. And I were ten a week since . . .' He added, 'But Ted is badly, he's been two days badly, can't fetch his breath – can't swallow, like . . . Our Dad says we've to call doctor if he's not mended soon . . .'

'What do you do all day?' Hal asked.

'*That's* a daft one . . . You was talking sense a moment past –'

'I have lessons in the schoolroom. And I have to say where I'm going always –'

'I don't doubt. A grand place like The Towers – I reckon they'll want to see as ye *stay* grand.' He paused. 'I'd best be gone. Ye'll not tell on me?'

Hal said solemnly, 'No. I shan't.'

The boy turned to go. He shrugged his shoulders. 'I've taken nowt. It were just a notion I had – to walk about, see for missen, like, how it is. How grand folk . . .'

'We're not grand, we're just the Firths.'

'Get away, not grand? *Sir*, *Lady* . . . Our Will, he says folk'd be best all having t'same – in France they're rid of all rich folk, he says. They had their heads off, king and queen and all. Years back it were. It'll happen here too, he says . . . one day.'

Then as he made towards the fence, he turned a moment. 'I like ye – Sir Henry,' he said, and grinned.

Gib sang:

> 'Teddy, I've a little canoe
> Room for me, my Teddy, and you . . .
> Teddy, you'll have nothing to do
> When I've told my worries to you
> Then, Teddy, we might *canoodle*, we two.'

He swung her. She giggled. '*My* birthday song, sing it again, more, Gib, please!'

He told her: 'I specially changed it for you. It should really be *Maimie* – but that's not half as nice . . .'

'Gib, enough,' said Alice. 'You'll make her queasy. After cream cakes . . . Really . . .' She felt impatience rising, but kept her voice steady. She could not bear the look his face would wear if she showed disapproval. And yet – all this afternoon, Teddy's birthday, he had played the high-spirited fool. That song from a London show he'd seen: *The Schoolgirl*. Enchanting Teddy with it, going on and on and on. Belle Maman approving . . .

'Gib, dear, what a delicious light tenor! Too late for me, alas . . .' Then her terrible laugh. A little high trill that *some* found attractive . . .

'Gib, Gib, what's a canoodle? Sing to me again, *again* . . .'

Everyone out there on the great lawn before the house, eating birthday tea. Jack Hawksworth playing with Hal. Mrs Hawksworth and Belle Maman talking, laughing. Trying to include Alice. I can I suppose be polite, she thought, planning to leave them in a moment and, until Gib was hers again, talk to poor Fräulein.

Voices wafted over.

'. . . Dr Sowerby told Charlie there's a second case. The same family. I guess – well, diphtheria – if they can just keep it down . . . Alice dear, you've not been visiting, sick peopling, about there?'

'No, Mrs Hawksworth. Just my old people . . .'

'Sadie –' Belle Maman speaking now, 'that cricket bat's nearly the size of Jack! And Hal . . . Let the Nicolson boy give a hand . . .'

Fräulein, sitting alone, was pathetically glad to see Alice. Moon face, great smile. She went home next month for six weeks, but meantime, as ever, there was trouble with Augustin . . .

'. . . I have certainly to speak with him in the *stern* manner for he is not staying in this new employment – I hear yesterday they don't like in the morning he is always in the bureau at ten and not half after eight. Alice, the *cares* I am given from this brother . . .'

Gib, always anxious to please, bowling gentle underarm cricket balls for Jack and Hal. And then tomorrow morning, setting off with his uncle and two boy cousins walking in the Swiss Alps. When he came back, there would be only two weeks of his holiday left. He had almost finished with school. A year to go, and it was Cambridge.

She remembered now her one visit to Marlborough, to Speech Day. Flushed, proud, he had introduced her, shown her about. Afterwards he told her, 'It was really frightfully jolly. The other chaps had their mothers – but I had *you* watching out for me . . .'

Voices again.

'. . . Charlie says when Consols are low like that . . . But the market's bad, so all this South American stock my family bought . . . They did right, Charlie says . . .'

15

'Darling, *Hal*, it's Alice here, Alice is with you.'

The road through the forest is long and dark, I don't know the way out, there is a thicket, tangled branches, leaves, *I cannot find my way out*, the prince finds his way through to rescue the princess, she has long golden hair, she hangs it out of the window and he climbs up it like a rope . . . where is the witch, the witch who spoils everything, she is old and wizened, she pretends to be a sewing woman, Princess Violet pricks her finger and falls asleep, I want to sleep, how do you sleep when you are hot hot hot, so hot, now the forest is on fire and . . .

'Hal, darling, Alice is with you, I'm holding your hand . . . Fräulein, fetch Lady Firth. At *once*. His condition gets worse . . .'

. . . I want to *sleep*, how do you sleep when you are hot, where is the ice maiden, Gerda the ice maiden . . . the whole palace was made of ice, ice is like glass, the points pierce the heart . . .

'. . . probably some salt-water injections. As a medical man, Lady Firth, that would be my first suggestion. Continue of course with the tepid sponging. The pulse just now at 144, a little less, but the temperature will continue to be raised for some time. It is for the *heart* we fear, of course. The great strain on the heart. To use the lay term, a murmur . . .'

The wicked witch grew and grew until she was twice the size thrice the size of him and then she leant over him and took him by the throat and he could not breathe, *he couldn't breathe*, she sewed thick cobweb over so that he would never swallow or speak again, the witch lived in a hot country, her fingernails were very long and black, she was all dressed in black, her fingers came round his throat and dug and dug so that he could not swallow, *he could not swallow*.

Once upon a time the king of the Goldland lost himself in a forest and try as he would he could not find the way out. . . . 'What are you doing here, friend?' asked the stranger: 'darkness is falling fast, and soon the wild beasts will come from their lairs . . .'

'Really, Dr Sowerby, I *cannot* understand. He is never allowed out alone. Never. And the only cases, you admit this yourself, at Lane Top farm. It's not possible . . .'

. . . *'I have lost myself,' answered the king, 'and am trying to get home . . .' 'But darkness is falling fast,' said the stranger, 'and soon the wild beasts . . .'*

'Frankly, Lady Firth, I would prefer there to be a little more strength. Although to wait – while there is such difficulty with breathing . . . You understand my dilemma? I should wish to balance the risks, but I feel that you and Sir Robert should be *prepared* for the worst . . .'

'Listen, Hal darling, can you hear Mummy? Even if you can't, I'm here, and shan't leave you all during the operation . . . you are going to be a *very brave* man . . .'

'Diphtheria of the pharynx, yes, well, *if* the tracheotomy is successful . . . I have to say *if* . . . there has of course been little nourishment lately, even with the œsophageal tube . . .'

. . . Mummy, help me, help, *Mummy, help me*!

The Queen of Goldland had a tiny waist, she had long fair hair and her voice was like the water falling, falling, she wore diamonds in her hair like a crown, and diamonds all over her bosom and to her waist like waterfalling . . . falling, falling, forget everything, black and blacker, down, down, down . . .

16

I never realized till now, Lily thought, how much deep, deep down, I still *hoped* . . . Even after the heart-wrenching visit, and parting, in Beaulieu. And after my return to the stage, darling Sylvia's birth, the terrible week two years ago when Hal brushed with death – and survived. After all that, did I not have still at the back of my mind – such a small, and quickly fleeting notion that one day *perhaps* . . . If I were to be widowed . . .

Oh, and then (but the notion must never be pursued) it would be simple, somehow possible to arrange everything. *He* would come from Rumania to live here (since she would have to take care of Hal till he came to man's estate) . . . With God and man's blessing – together. She, running, running, to join him. So clear, so glorious a picture. She ran to him, he wore the cloak in which she had first seen him – no, it was the Val of the Colony Hotel, coming to her across the crowded foyer. She melted into him.

No longer would the nights be furtive. I was never really one for intrigue: the creak on the stair – I only thrilled because it was Valentin, because *he* was coming. (Coming, coming, that most wonderful of words . . .). She would allow herself, wickedly, to dream a little of how it might be . . .

But now I am punished. I am punished, she told herself, that early autumn evening of 1907. Reading the letter, sitting at her dressing-table, hair intertwined with diamonds and already up for the evening.

> My darling [he wrote], my darling, I don't think it's possible that you will hear from other persons what I have to tell you – but I don't wish there is any risk . . . I have decided to marry . . . Now it's written down, what I have been afraid about saying because we have been talking together of this moment so many times . . . I am thirty years now and the head of family. Ion was married last spring – I told you this – and so there has been a lot of care that I too shall be serious, because of the fortune and the

many lands and family name . . . My wedding will be at Christmas time. I don't insult with telling you of her, who you surely hate, but she is quiet and dark and already a little fat . . . she is nineteen years and will do what I tell her. So you see that is how it is. Life must be going on – but oh my darling, *how I wanted* for you to be the mother of my sons – only the day gets very late – I say this not to rub in salt but so you are understanding what I am doing . . .

I don't expect to be faithful, in the body (who is?) – and *you* know well enough what little they mean all those *aventures* that aren't with you . . . *You are the only love of my life* . . . And now I come to write the dreadful thing, that I hate, which is saying because I begin this new life and everything changes for me, the best for us will be – goodbye. That we don't write no longer. You see, it has become *adieu* and not *au revoir* – And it *is A Dieu*, because I will pray to God that he look after both of you. You, my darling, and our little Theodora – God's gift, and she is, is she not? . . . But it will be better, really, that she's growing up without knowing of her father or any things of me at all. It will be better, won't it? *Won't it?* Write to me, my darling, *your A Dieu* . . .

Hope must have been stronger than she thought. Now that it had happened: *I cannot lose him. I will not lose him* . . . But there was no choice. And as she sat with guests at dinner – a shooting party for the weekend – she felt weighed down by memories. Once treasured, even if painful, now best jettisoned . . . I shall not always feel as raw as this, she told herself, but could not imagine how that might be.

The autumn of eight years ago returned to haunt her. The plaintive sound of the pipes, the *doina*, the lament that she had so loved, tinged as it had been already with farewells. The gypsy violins with their frenzied sound, faster, faster . . . She had been so happy . . . Yet why happy? for the music whirling, twirling, always more frantic, had said to her, far more clearly than the plaining *doina*, 'Never, never again.'

Never. Never. Over the next few days she took to wearing as often as possible the ring, the Lover's Opal, remembering how they had joined hands to pledge their troth. (Misfortune to come to the faithless one . . .) The plaiting of the gold was attractive and opals were just now very fashionable. A visitor that weekend, a slightly affected young married, remarked on it. 'Oh pwetty, pwetty,' she exclaimed. Lily told her, 'It is just a little thing I bought in Nice – it took my fancy . . .' That she still had, hidden away, Valentin's shirt, she tried to forget.

He the faithless one, to whom misfortune . . . Yet why should he not marry?

If she only had someone to confide in. Far, far too late now to tell Sadie: the time for that had been many years ago. They who had shared so much – but never this. Who shared most especially their joint pride in their children. Lately, Jack and Hal, so close in age, had become more and more friendly. Soon they were to share a tutor, leaving their governesses to the girls. Later Jack would go to Harrow. Hal, because of his damaged heart, legacy of the diphtheria, would not. They had been advised by a consultant that it would be foolhardy.

But all that lay ahead. For now they were too happy small boys who bird-nested, collected moths, and on rainy days played bagatelle, diabolo, or raced wildly about the corridors of the Hall or The Towers.

Even had she felt able to confide in Sadie, it might have been difficult. Sadie was often away from home now for several days at a time. When she had lost her last child (a boy, which had made her grief all the stronger), she had soon after thrown herself into work for charity. Her concern was child poverty. She'd said to Lily many times over the years that she had a conscience about the money she had brought with her – so much over and above what was needed by the Hawksworths. And the manner in which that money had been earned. 'By using other people, by *ab*using them.' She had added, 'But then, it's a luxury is it not, to worry about having too much money when some don't know when they will get a meal. And while there are children that go hungry . . .'

Now she had become very involved, partly helping, but mainly campaigning. In public she spoke well and movingly, and was much in demand. I too, Lily thought, should be more useful.

She sent for a Braille apparatus that she had seen advertised, and several pounds of special paper, then set aside an hour three mornings a week to work on it. She had to select articles and extracts from books, and write them in Braille for the blind to re-copy and make money. She took care that Alice did not know. Alice would be both curious, and superior . . .

As she worked, she would find herself remembering suddenly something she had meant to tell Valentin: usually to do with Teddy. Of how this summer when King Edward's horse had won at Ascot, the crowd had called 'Good old Teddy!', and an enchanted but puzzled Teddy had asked, 'But how do they know me?' No use to save such anecdotes now . . .

Often she would be alarmed by the strength of her feelings for Teddy – both love *and* hate. Hal, saved from the dead, object of her fierce pride. Sylvia, gentle Sylvia, hot hand clasped in hers. But Teddy . . . Some days, visiting the nursery she would want suddenly to pick her up and shake her till the teeth rattled: those slant eyes, heavy-lidded, that thick black hair, confident pretty little voice . . .

I don't understand what is happening to me, she thought, as slowly the days passed. I would rather feel *nothing*. Remembering Valentin, anger would catch her unawares, taking her over like some giant uncontrollable nausea. Better to feel nothing. Better to feel dead.

A week later: an invitation to a house party in the Midlands. Shooting, excellent hunting, Robert promised a mount. Their hosts were a couple Lily did not much care for. She said to Robert, a little irritably:

'*You* may wish to go – I shall not know what to do there. It is an uncomfortable house. And the company – I see from the guest list that it is mainly cronies of yours. Midlands *nouveau-riche* . . .'

'That is good, coming from you. Your family. Grocers –'

She interrupted him, 'You who are so rude about Jews – if you look, you will see for certain Jewish financiers.'

'I shall not need either to borrow money – or to do business with them. Certainly I shall not invite them under *my* roof –'

'The King is not so fussy.' She spoke only to annoy.

He said tiredly, 'We have had this exchange before – If it's with the idea that I may permit or encourage your idle Jewish, Russo-Polish relations to come and call here –' He warmed suddenly to his subject: 'What good will it do our son if we are to see, walking round here, the Leeds ghetto with Yankee overtones? What will people say?'

'What will people say?' she mimicked. 'Nothing. Nothing that they do not say already –'

'Oh pah!' He turned in disgust back to his newspaper, riffling through it for the financial pages. Later he told her that he would be joining the house party. 'You may do as you please.'

She did – accepting another invitation received the next day, a week in a castle in the West of Scotland. Her hosts were friends of the Hawksworths, who were of course on the guest list. She looked forward to journeying north with them.

She had already settled in the carriage, cushions about her, stone hot bottles filled, reading *The Lady*, when, looking up, she saw Charlie Hawksworth.

'Oh, but – alone?' she asked, puzzled.

'Yes. She cannot come, Mrs Hawksworth doesn't come. The time *was* free of meetings, and excursions – but not apparently, alarums.' He began unfastening his ulster: 'A meeting this evening at which Lady Fordyce was to speak – but the good woman telegraphs from her sick bed – struck down by an ague. Nothing will do but that my Sadie should drop everything and talk in her place. The exciting venue is Derby, I believe – further speeches during the weekend . . .'

She was disappointed. As the train moved out of the station, she thought that not only would there be no Sadie, but also she would be left for many, many hours in Charlie's company. Handsome, pleasant, probably kind-hearted but someone she scarcely knew, except through Sadie. 'Charlie says, *we* think, Charlie feels, Charlie believes . . .' At shooting luncheons, dinners, outings, a charming and polite host, or guest. But not known, not known at all . . .

The journey went well enough, though. She did not think that she bored him, did not care anyway, and in turn found him amusing and, occasionally, interesting. She enjoyed it when he spoke, with just a little malice, of social life in the South African War. Sadie, who never gossiped, had not mentioned this. Capetown, a hotbed of gossip: the Duke of

Westminster and Mrs Tommie Atherton, garden-parties at the Rondesbosch, races at Kenilworth. Scandal about one, intrigues of another. 'All very *vieux jeu* now . . .'

'You like that sort of thing?' she asked.

'Now and then. Now and then . . .' He pulled at the luxuriant moustaches. 'A country boy at heart, though.'

Then as they were eating luncheon, he said, 'I've often wondered – forgive my asking – why a woman who would look so fetching in hunting dress is never, never seen on a horseback?'

'Simple. I feel certain to have said it before – I am terrified of the animals. From the front, from the behind – no, do not laugh, it is true . . . Sadie suggested, perhaps the new astride –'

'Most likely. She is all for the new.'

'But that would not help. Nor a really gentle mount. One must begin as a child. It's true that in Rumania I rode a mountain pony and there were persons there who *might* have persuaded –'

'Some day perhaps *I* shall be able to persuade you?'

'No, not even you –'

'Not *even* me? Then I am a little – special?'

She ignored this flirtatious remark, saying rather seriously, 'I wonder sometimes that you can be so devoted to riding, to hunting, after your sad loss. And your mother, that she goes out with the hounds . . .'

'She will be riding to hounds when she is ninety.'

'And you are not afraid?'

'If your father had been run down by a cab, would you cease to cross the road?'

'That is different –'

'How?'

She could not think how; only knew that it was so. She said: 'I can't approve of hunting anyway. Hares – did you realize that their bones become soft when they are dying? As in the Bible – "My bones melted like water . . ." '

'Chapter and verse? I believe you, of course . . . But a change of subject perhaps? Have you for instance the same theme in your home as with us? Bicycles. Young Jack speaks of little else – and I understand Hal is as enthusiastic. Rudge-Whitworth is the name most often mentioned. Would you agree that we should wait till ten years old – possibly even eleven?'

The Castle was large and draughty although architecturally pleasant. It stood above a loch with woods of pine and fir rising behind. Real winter had not yet arrived and the wind that blew across the water was a mild westerly one.

Charlie was asked to take her in to dinner the first evening: she and he seemed to have settled into a relationship of amicable sparring, foreshadowed in the train. Conversation at the dinner-table was predictable. The poor cubbing season, the lock-out at Paisley Thread mill. Dreadful ever-present fears of revolution, of anarchy . . . 'Let's hope that Messrs Coats will resolve it *soon* . . .'

She ached dully. Loss. Perhaps because she looked less frivolous than some of the other women guests, she became on the second day the confidante of one Teresa Mildmay: just twenty and married for about eighteen months. She desperately wanted to conceive, since the family anxiously awaited an heir, but had had no success so far. Her mother-in-law reproached her continually. She showed a touching envy on learning of Lily's 'honeymoon' baby . . . The third day, during afternoon tea, a packet was brought to her by special messenger. She opened it in view of the other guests. Inside, a small celluloid baby doll, dressed in blue. The sender was her mother-in-law. She ran from the room in tears. Lily would have followed her, except that her husband coming in a moment later, went himself . . . Yet again she felt ashamed of her own, intractable, pain.

The gramophone was quite the thing. Every evening, walnut cabin, immense brass horn, it blared out from the minstrels' gallery, Lionel Monckton's *Gollywogs*, a selection from *The Girls of Gothenburg* . . . The daughter of the house, fourteen, allowed down to dinner, turned the handle between, and often during, records. A young barrister guest asked for a cake-walk. Someone cried, 'Oh, but this is absolutely, it is quite the most . . .'

Charlie said to Lily, 'They play nothing from *The Duke and the Shopgirl* –'

'No records were cut –'

He said, 'I worshipped at your shrine that summer. Jubilee summer.'

'Oh, fooey. You were in Philadelphia.' His mood irritated her a little.

'How clever of you to remember. I visited the show in the autumn.'

'So you told me the first time we met –'

'Am I really so boring?'

Later that evening as she stood by some bookcases, leafing through a travel volume, he came up behind. 'What is that?'

'Our host's grandfather – some quite remarkable travels in Greece, with sketches to prove it. In the days when brigands lay in wait –'

'Lily – may I say Lily? – I think we cannot possibly be overheard – I'd like to know – a visit to your room, later – would you?' The question hung.

'It's for you to see,' she said, 'whether the door is locked.'

She thought that perhaps she had gone mad. Later, upstairs, after her maid had brushed her hair, she lay in bed in the darkness – and waited. She was quite unable to think. A faint excitement hovered. She said out loud, 'There is still time to change my mind.'

The corridor creaked outside. Footsteps, slow, then growing quicker. They went past her door. *This is ridiculous*. Ten minutes, twenty minutes . . . the clock struck one. Then again the creaking in the corridor. Steps, nearer, stopping outside. *Now it is too late.*

Perhaps the best was to sleep afterwards. She did not do so, but lay awake, thinking, remembering. I must not compare, since one *cannot* compare. She was grateful: what she had most dreaded had not come to pass. The encounter had not mocked Val and her memories. Rather, it was something apart. Sufficient unto itself.

She waited to feel guilt (my best friend . . .), but it never came. It is as if I have done nothing, she thought.

Home again, she sealed up in a leather box everything to do with Val. Letters, pressed flowers, his shirt, even the opal ring. Lover's Opal. It was all over.

17

Yesterday, Easter Sunday, there'd been enough sun to make you think it was May or even June. Today, decided Hal, didn't look half as good. By afternoon, when he thought of going out on his own, the sky had grown dull and heavy. The tutor, Mr Pettinger, that bandy-legged purveyor of Latin and Greek, had gone home to his family in Leicestershire. Otherwise some horrid idea would have been thought up for today: a nature outing perhaps with Mr Pettinger (who knows nothing about anything unless it's out of a book, and who has *never been fishing in his whole life*).

But 'Jack has the measles, Jack has the measles,' he chanted now, going through the thicket, out at the back behind the orchard. Probably there wouldn't be any lessons for a while, since he mustn't go near the Hall (soon something would be arranged – Mr Pettinger would come to The Towers, Alas . . .) And all, he thought, because I have to be extra careful, on account of my – my – but he didn't want to say the word, or there might come suddenly that beating in his chest, thump, thump, thump . . .

I nearly died. They told him that, often. Worse, the suggestion that for a nothing, it might happen again – if he didn't take care. The shadow on the bedroom wall when the wax nightlight flickered: the enormous shadow with its changing shape, open shut open, *got you*! Death.

This afternoon he didn't want to be with the girls, or indoors at all. Nan-Nan said he might do as he pleased, so he thought that he would go for a walk. He said to Fräulein who was walking along the corridor, hatted and gloved, 'Fräulein – if anybody looks for me, I'm over the hills and far away –'

'Yes, yes,' she said, 'Good. And nice.'

'*Die Wetter, das Wetter ist gut, ja, nein?*' he said. But she had already passed by.

For a while he followed the stone wall as it went up the hillside. Looking back, he could see The Towers and the fenced thicket behind, all growing more distant. It was cold and wispy clouds had run together, become solid. He was walking briskly and kept warm. Above, lowering almost, were the brown outlines of the fells. He knew where he was more or less, but wasn't sure what happened when you climbed over and into the next valley. Further up, he looked back till he could see where the river ran: Flaxthorpe bridge, the houses grouped on the green, the church tower square and dark; the patterns of the drystone walls as they crossed and re-crossed the hillside.

The ground was dry and springy from yesterday's weather. As he came down into the valley he wasn't so sure where he was. I *might* go back now . . . He wouldn't anyway climb up on the high moor. He followed a grassy lane for a little, passing a cow house. Below was meadow, and he could see farm buildings.

Then a sheepdog, brown and white, rough haired, came through a gap in the stone wall higher up the hillside. Running in his direction. A moment later a boy appeared. He was carrying two rabbits on a string. Seeing Hal, he stopped, stared a few seconds. Then began walking towards him.

'Tess,' he called to the dog, 'Way here, way here, Tess –'

The chill air, the lowering sky. I wish now I'd turned back, Hal thought. Faint rumble of thunder . . .

The boy drew nearer. 'Tess, Tess, way here!'

(*Once upon a time the king of the Goldland lost himself in a forest and try as he would he could not find the way out. As he was wandering down one path . . .*)

I know that face . . .

(*'What are you doing here, friend?' asked the stranger, darkness is falling fast . . .'*)

'Bye hell,' said the boy, 'if it's not his lordship from The Towers . . .' He grinned. He had still that friendly grin which at once altered his face.

Hal shivered. The sky, darkening rapidly, the air growing chiller.

'They call me Stephen,' the boy said. He pointed ahead. 'Ibbotson. Lane Top Farm. You mind we met afore?'

'Yes, yes,' Hal said. 'Yes, I remember.'

'And ye never told on me, eh?' He stood, swinging the rabbits from his arm.

The wind was getting up stronger. Earlier, Hal had noticed the sheep huddled together.

Stephen said: 'Look at sky. We're in for a hap up.' Tess the dog was crouched at his feet, head on ground, eyes only darting warily from side to side. 'Birds – they've hushed singing. And Tess, she knows right enow . . .'

'Tess, way home. Home then!' He shooed her suddenly. 'Me dad, me brother Will, he'll be vexed and all – that I've took her. He's forbid me –'

The lightning came first. Flashing the grass to the west of them an electric green. Tess, who'd been moving reluctantly, shot forward in sudden fear. Claps of thunder followed.

'Bye – hear that! We'd best –' Stephen's voice was drowned.

Down it came, across it came, sleet, great hailstones, battering, stinging, against his ears, his cheeks.

Stephen grabbed the sleeve of Hal's Norfolk jacket. 'Come along of me. Come by our place . . .' Together they ran down the stony grass to the track leading to the farm. Looking too near his feet, Hal stumbled over the cart ruts. Now, Stephen was ahead of him, the rabbits' bodies swinging.

The violence of those hailstones. He was running into them, it seemed. And then it seemed they came at him, icy, from every side . . .

As he went through the gateway, he saw a door slightly open. Stephen's face came round it. 'Bye, but ye're slow.' He pulled him inside roughly. Both of them shook themselves like wet dogs.

Seconds later he found himself in the big farm kitchen which seemed full of people – more than he could count, all staring at him. Or perhaps they weren't? When he looked again he saw that two of them at least were paying him no attention at all.

'Come close to fire, then.'

But he was afraid to move. A man sat one side of the fire, mending something, tying, or was it untying, knots. He wasn't noticing Hal at all . . . In a wooden armchair a little bit away there was an old woman wearing a grubby cotton cap. Her feet, planted firmly, were in what looked like men's boots, without laces. She appeared to be asleep.

'Who's this now?' the man asked. He didn't look up.

A boy and a small girl, about his own age, sat at the kitchen table. The girl who looked like a little brown bird *was* watching him, gravely, with interest. A lanky boy of about eighteen who'd been standing by the fire, crossed the room towards them.

Stephen said: 'We got ourselves wetted and all –'

'Aye, I see that.' He was dark-haired, with a jutting underlip. He looked over at Hal. 'Who's this, then?' But when Stephen told him, he only looked sour. 'What were ye about, the two of you?'

'Just walking, Will. And him here, Mr Firth, I found him. He were walking . . .'

It must have been their mother came in then. Pale, thin, tall: origin of Will's lankiness. Her head drooped on her neck. She spoke in a tired, kind voice.

'. . . Summat hot to sup. Poor bairn. And a bite to eat.' Cloths were brought to rub down his hair, trousers and a heavy shirt found for him. Too big, but warm, dry. He changed in the room downstairs that Stephen shared with Will and the other brother, James. Stephen showed him the little cupboard under the stairs. 'That's where me sister, that's where our Olive sleeps.' Outside, the hail battered still.

'How many are there of you?' Hal asked.

'Will, that you've seen – he's all but head of us . . . Dad minds nowt. Then James, and – and me and Olive . . . Mam, Dad and Granny Willans – her with the boots.'

'I noticed those,' Hal said.

'Deaf as a post, she is. And never sits near the fire. She's afeard she'll crack her boots. Allus worn them she has, "I feel *safe*, like," she says, "I like to move me toes about . . ." '

Back in the kitchen, his Norfolk jacket, his sturdy tweed knickerbockers with their now damp leather knee bands, were hung by the fire. He said: 'I really ought to go –'

'Not in this weather. No.' Mrs Ibbotson sounded firm in spite of the faint voice and the feeble way of moving. She insisted that he sat by the fire.

It was Dad, Mr Ibbotson, who hadn't much to say for

himself. Nor James. Will spoke the most. The little girl, Olive, smiled twice at Hal, her mouth widening slowly.

Will asked, fixing Stephen with a look: 'Where were ye then, our Stephen?'

'Out –'

'Ye didn't mebbe tak Tess along t'walls? Ye weren't after rabbits –'

Stephen shrugged his shoulders. Will said, 'Dad, he were out again.'

'Bye hell – what if I did?'

'We'll not have any of that talk, son,' his mother said. 'There's words we don't use.' She paused. 'And ye boots . . . When we've rugs down and all –'

Hal looked round the kitchen. Cotton handmade rugs covered part of the flagstones. Above him, something like a ladder on the ceiling had lengths of what looked to be dough hanging over its slats. He asked, 'What are those?'

Olive answered first. 'Havercakes.'

'She fashioned them,' her mother said. 'Olive fashioned them.'

'I like to bake.' Olive said it solemnly. 'Even rest days.' She pointed to an iron plate beside the fire. She said proudly, 'It's there I bake them, after I've pulled the dough out, like.'

'Give lad a bite of it –'

'Do ye want some, then? Will ye eat some?'

It tasted very good. It had a thick slice of cold bacon laid across it. It tasted like nothing at The Towers.

After a while, not much notice was taken of him. There was some talk, about lambing mainly. He liked the way Olive watched him all the time. Whenever he caught her eye, she smiled at him.

James said: 'She can't manage her school work –'

'It's a rest day –' she began.

'It's to be done,' Will said. 'If you've brains you'd best learn to use them while chance comes your way.'

'Fuss, fretting,' Mr Ibbotson said. 'Content yissen running farm, or learning to. Day'll come, soon enow, I'll not be able . . .'

'Nowt much amiss with ye *now*,' Will said a little sulkily.

'There will be, lad, there will –'

By way of answer Will fetched over a large red book with

gold lettering on the cover, and buried himself in it.

Hal asked Olive: 'What is it you've to do?'

'Sums,' she said promptly. 'Like this.' She slipped down from the table and brought him over the copybook.

' "If a draper sells braid at sixpence three-farthings for nine yards, what is the cost per foot?" '

'Easy,' he said. 'There's three feet in a yard, so that's three times nine to find your feet, and . . .'

Some time later, and after he'd eaten a meal with them, Mrs Ibbotson said, 'I reckon they'll be worried at Towers. So if ye're warm and dry, lad . . .'

Home. But he didn't want to leave.

Will said, 'It's let up, the weather. It's faired up enough. He can be away.'

They discussed it among themselves. 'Light's going fast . . . He'll have been missed . . . He could go wi t'pony . . . He'd be best in cart . . .'

Mr Ibbotson said: 'James, tak t'cart, then. And Bluebell. Stephen'll go along of ye . . .'

It was further going down by the road, and round and up again. Over the moor. Strange dark shadows . . . A lamp swung from the cart. James didn't speak. To look at he was like his father. Occasionally he murmured something to the grey horse, with its shaggy winter coat. 'Hoa there, easy there, Bluebell . . .'

Stephen talked. About fishing, rabbiting, going to market. About how clever Will was.

Fishing. 'I know t'best places,' he boasted, hand pointing over to where in the darkness the river ran away as a beck. When Hal said nothing, he said, 'I could mebbe show you – if ye've ever a mind.'

'I might,' Hal said. (I shall, I *shall.*) A curtain drawn back, showing a bright warm different world. Dangerous, even. *Different* . . .

Hailstones lay by the road still. The lamp on the cart showed them up. A white landscape now, where this morning there'd been sun. But on the lower road there was little sign of the storm.

'It's allus worse up our way,' James said. 'We was snowed off *eight week* t'year Ted were born.'

'Ted?'

'Ted that died,' Stephen said. 'He'd the same sickness as I took. He were first – then Will and me . . . Diffy sickness they call it, when there's poison right across t'throat . . . I were took bad three days afore Ted went. Our Mam thought we'd all be lost. Eh, James?'

'Aye,' James said, without moving his head. 'That were a bad time and all. Diphtheria,' he enunciated slowly. 'They brought it up from Settstone village.'

Hal said, 'I was sick with it.' He added, not without pride. '*I* all but died too.' He kept quiet about his heart.

'You're a wicked boy. A bad wicked boy . . .'

His mother, his beautiful mother.

'I thought, we thought – *dead*. Some terrible accident. We've been *out of our minds*, Hal . . .'

But how? Why? The King of Goldland safe home who had been lost in the forest. Saved by the stranger . . .

Mother cried over him. Father was *very angry*. Alice fussed and looked pinched from the upset. He protested:

'But Nan-Nan said –'

'No excuses, young fellow-me-lad. No excuses, sir. Eight o'clock of an evening – and last seen at *two* in the afternoon. Outrageous . . .'

His clothes, tied up in a bundle. Nearly dry now. The feeling of disgrace (the same feeling as when his nightshirt, his sheets, were discovered wet – when he was much, much younger. He thought he'd forgotten how that felt . . .) Everything spoilt. Gold that was really dust. Like in the fairy tales. King of Goldland . . .

'The Ibbotsons. Yes. They will be thanked, and the clothes returned.' He heard money mentioned. 'A small token, some appreciation naturally. Although it was only their duty . . .'

Later Nan-Nan, cross too, said:

'We've the worry already that you don't catch measles off Master Jack – then you go putting on farm boy's clothes –' She sniffed, and held up the trousers with their frayed leather belt. *Farm boy's clothes*.

'He – the boy whose clothes those are, he's going to show me, about fishing. Stephen's twelve. He goes anywhere by himself. He takes one of their collie dogs along the walls, after rabbits . . .'

Such tiredness, such happy tiredness.

'And I'll be seeing him again. Soon.'

'That's as maybe,' Nan-Nan said. '*What* a bag of moonshine . . .'

18

Sadie's mouth trembled a little. She said, 'The boys – Mr Pettinger won't have finished yet. For Greek, they have always an extra half-hour.'

Her manner was very odd. As Lily stepped forward to embrace her: 'Lily – no!' She stood back a little. 'I don't care that you should. I've –' Her fingers were clawing at the silver clasp of her belt. 'There's something – I want to say something to you. I was going to – maybe call . . . but seeing you're here . . . I –'

'Whatever is it, darling?' It wasn't the Sadie she knew. Overtired, yes, a little overwrought, and prescribed three months' rest by Dr Sowerby before beginning again on her child poverty work. Six weeks of that had passed already. For Lily it had been like old times again. To sit together, talking about anything, everything (no, *not* everything, not everything . . .)

Long days of summer. Hal and Jack still taught by Mr Pettinger at the Hall. Often Lily would go up to collect Hal, then stay to tea. Play with and admire Amy and Edith. Admire Jack. And who could not? His father's son but with Sadie's vivacity and lively eyes. Mischief, not true naughtiness. Headstrong, impulsive, often obstinate but never sulky.

Sadie had said once: 'Let others be angry with him. I can't. Perhaps he'll go to the bad, with my spoiling.' She had smiled fondly. 'And perhaps not . . .'

Indeed Lily couldn't imagine it. Hal and Jack, inseparable, although lately often making off to that farm where Hal had sheltered. Going fishing with one of the boys. At Christmas, when they got their Rudge Whitworths, they would become cyclists . . . Beside Hal's seriousness, intensity, Jack was the perfect foil. Both had two younger sisters, both expressed scorn for them . . . Each son was quite different. And quite perfect.

Today, she was bursting with news from America. Sadie followed always so closely the fortunes of Daisy and her family. A letter from New York today that said all was well. Daisy's daughter Anna, at nineteen had just married a lawyer's son. It was a really good match. And so happy together . . . Joe, Daisy's eldest, he was doing well too. Daisy was helping with immigrants at Lilian Wald's Henry Street Settlement . . .

'No,' repeated Sadie, 'No, don't, Lily – *don't* sit down!'

'Sadie –' She grew more alarmed. 'Darling, has something happened? I can't –'

Sadie, turning the key in the lock, moved round to face her.

'Stand there. Don't move, please. I'll stand too.' Then she burst out: 'Lily Firth, I'm so *mad* at you – and you call yourself my friend! I just don't know how you *dare* –' She was breathing deeply. Trying to hold back tears.

My God, thought Lily, my God, I know . . .

'You've a husband of your own and anything you want, and yet you . . . *What did you want with Charlie?*' Her voice rose hysterically.

'Sadie – just a moment –' Lily's voice shook. 'It's not like that –'

'It's not like, it's not like – It *is* like that! He's been unfaithful. And with you, you, *you* –'

'Last year, Sadie, all right. Yes, last year. Three, four times – in Scotland –'

'I don't want –' her voice was a screech – 'don't want to hear how many times. Or why, or when – no, Lily, *let me finish*. I just want to tell you that you're no friend of mine! *Friends* don't – they do *not*, Lily Firth –'

Perhaps, to calm her . . . Lily's voice – she heard herself: a little hard, cool:

'How did you find out?'

'That's all you care about, Lily Firth, you whited sepulchre. Being *found out* . . . I'm so mad at you, *mad* . . . I guess you thought it just didn't *matter* . . . It's – Charlie told me himself. Yesterday. He was – we –' She had calmed down just a little. But she clawed desperately still at the silver clasp.

'He couldn't – bear it another moment. We'd . . . there'd been words about – I don't recollect. He told me then. Confessed . . .' She gave a little sob. 'He said he'd wanted for months – wanted to confess. And that he felt mighty bad because there'd never been – he hadn't before. Other women.

I don't care, but there hadn't. . . . He asked me that I shouldn't say anything – But I'm not like that. If I get mad I . . . Lily, I'm just so mad at you, I could kill you!' She burst into tears.

What, what, what have I done? thought Lily. Most of all now, she wanted to throw herself in Sadie's arms. To tell her *everything*. Valentin, Teddy . . . To beg forgiveness for the unforgivable. Instead she felt her features settle: sophisticated, slightly offhand, an almost amused reaction. (I at least am not hysterical . . .)

'If I thought an apology, or even an explanation –'

'Don't bother,' Sadie interrupted. Her voice calmer. 'What good would it do? None at all, I guess – if I'm to live here among your sort of people, I've just to – well, it's the way of Society, isn't it? Moral climate – it's just the climate, I guess. There's nothing you can do really about *climate* . . .'

Lily began, tentatively, 'Sadie, if we –'

'I tell you, though, I tell you, Lily Firth – something other. *It's all over between us*. I don't ever want you as a friend. Ever, ever again.' She was sobbing once more. 'We're going to be mighty polite with each other *in public* – I don't ever want Jack or Hal, or any of them to suffer – because you . . . No one'll ever know but you and me –'

And Charlie, thought Lily.

'No one'll know, no one'll ever know that we're finished. My word, I'll act. You'll see, Lily Firth, who's good at acting!

'And now, just clear out . . .'

19

With the coming of the warm weather, Alice's spirits rose. The treat, which she had carried around with her like treasure ever since Gib had gone back to Cambridge in January, was that she should visit him in June. He was now in his second year at St Catharine's College, where he was a Scholar (dear clever Gib). In the Lent Term of his first year she had visited him for the day from London with Papa and Belle Maman. But it had been a stiff affair: going out to luncheon at the Blue Boar, and not meeting any of his friends. He was in lodgings in Little St Mary's Lane but had not shown them his rooms. She hated the way Belle Maman was charming and at ease with him – how he was suddenly not *her* Gib any more.

This time it would be different. She was to spend several days there, to watch some of the May Races, and best of all, to go to his College Ball. A May Ball. Some of his friends had asked their sisters up. A chaperone, a cousin of Gib's, Mrs Radcliffe, had been arranged.

How to wait? And would it never be summer? The month of May was unusually cold and earlier in the spring she'd been particularly upset by the assassination of Manuel of Portugal and his Crown Prince. The illustrated papers had been full of drawings, even photographs. She couldn't help thinking that one moment they had been alive and confident, and the next, were not. Because of violence. She found it hard to imagine. Violence within – ah, that I understand. Although, too, it could be physical: as that hand which had shot out seven years ago and struck Uncle Lionel. (Nowadays he kept a distance from her which was almost insulting in its obviousness – although she fancied nobody really noticed.)

Now at last it was June, and Gib and the Ball. What she hadn't liked in the days before was the fuss and interest shown by Belle Maman in what she would be wearing. She would have preferred just that money should be given to the dressmaker and the affair arranged between the two of them.

The ball dress was perhaps the most important, and for this, a number of spring patterns were sent for from Paris. Alice was part grateful, part resentful: the suggestions were so much better than she would have dared to think of herself. Two or three day dresses, hats – at least two. 'There are sure to be some smart persons from London, and really there is no need to look as if one has come from the country.' Alice wanted to say: 'Oh, any old thing will do to go on my head.' (She was reminded of that, oh so dreadful hat-buying morning in Beaulieu . . .) But Belle Maman didn't notice, or perhaps had become used to her moods. Clothes and hats were arranged. Once I'm out of Yorkshire, Alice thought, they will be none of them anything to do with her.

Gib's cousin, Mrs Radcliffe, turned out to be older than she had expected. She hadn't known much about her and rather suspected that Gib did not either. He had arranged it all by letter rather hastily. As she lived not far from Peterborough, she joined Alice's train there, and they finished the journey together.

She had heard about Alice. 'You're the little girl with the camera.' (And I am twenty-two! Alice thought . . .) She seemed disappointed that Alice hadn't brought with her photographic equipment. 'You could take such nice pictures of the undergraduates amusing themselves . . .' Her main interest, it appeared, was food. She confided in Alice that it was her misfortune to be almost continuously in good appetite, and yet always to have to pay the price. She was not sure what she would find at Cambridge. 'I think some of these boys eat very rich foods when they send out . . .'

For all that she ate so well, she was only moderately stout, but her colour was high and she was short of breath, needing a long time after she'd got into the train to get her puff back. They were in a Ladies Only carriage, and when after a while she took her hat off, Alice saw she was wearing one of those made-up combs with a fringe of hair attached. Unfortunately her own hair didn't match the brown with chestnut lights, on the comb. Alice wondered suddenly: Shall I ever look like that one day?

'So you're the Miss Firth, the Alice Firth that Nicolson speaks about incessantly?'

Gib said, 'You won't have met Saint. He's not a Marlburian –'

Saint said, 'I'm not even Cat's – forgive me, St Catharine's. My college is John's –'

Gib said, of another undergraduate who had just come in to join them for tea: 'But Vesey here, he's a Marlburian – not that you ever came across him, I think . . .'

Vesey was slight, with thin pale brown hair, and gold-rimmed spectacles. His face was kind. She didn't think Saint's looked particularly kind. His real name was George Andrew Sainthill and he and Gib had met through sharing the same classics coach last year.

'You could say Thucydides brought us together . . . We get along like smoke, Nicolson and I. Though I can't pretend to share his brilliance –'

'Cut that,' Gib said. He told Alice, 'He's always ragging me. It's just that *I* work –'

Saint said, 'My father's coach – the best a man ever had – told him it was "absurd to work in the afternoon, a great mistake in the evening and almost impossible in the morning". My governor managed on about ten minutes a day. Fifteen's very fair.'

Mrs Radcliffe looked distracted. Her mind, Alice realized, was on the tea-table. Chocolate cake, large current buns, sandwiches, marzipan fruits, dough cake, tea, lemonade . . .

'Take a pew, Vesey, take a pew,' Saint said, for all the world as if they were his rooms. He was sitting on the leather sofa, Alice and Mrs Radcliffe either side of the fireplace in basket chairs.

She looked around. Firescreen, with college crest. A Wedgwood biscuit barrel which she remembered from the Vicarage. On the door, his black gown, his cap, with its stiffening board removed, draped over the firescreen. A clutter of books – many marked, others lying open.

A Toussaint engraving of the College gateway. And photographs. Examples of their joint work: views of The Towers, the Hall, Flaxthorpe Bridge, Lane Top Farm. She herself was there: a picture he had taken two years ago when she had begun to eat again, done with her new portrait lens. She had forgotten that picture.

'Be a decent fellow and offer the sandwiches . . .' They ragged each other all the time. She wasn't sure really how she had thought it would be. Saint talked the most. He would be going to his own college ball, he said. 'My sister and a friend of the most breathtaking beauty will arrive in three days' time.'

He teased Gib and Arthur Vesey. Their college, 'Cat's', was small, only some sixty undergraduates. 'That size,' he said, 'it can only be the exclusive, and the excluded.'

Gib said that they took care to exclude the exclusive, and were perfectly happy.

Saint said, 'Did you know that this fellow has just got a Gold Medal? For a Latin ode, in imitation of Horace. Written effortlessly –'

Vesey said to Alice, 'Didn't he tell you, Miss Firth?'

'No,' Alice said.

'Well, that *is* clever,' Mrs Radcliffe said. Her stomach rumbled suddenly in the silence.

Vesey said quietly: 'Nicolson's human, though. Example – we've to sign the book in the Porter's lodge instead of morning chapel. Four minutes to eight Nicolson puts a coat hurriedly over his pyjamas – gets there just as the clock strikes. He can be asleep again before ten past.'

Saint affected to be shocked. 'He must have a good gyp (which is a sort of valet),' he explained to Alice, 'to warn him . . . And surely it happens only when he's been burning midnight oil? Always up and about when I'm a breakfast guest. Yes, life's serious for Nicolson.'

'Life's serious anyway,' Vesey said, smiling.

Gib said, Vesey and I – we row well together. He sits there quietly puffing his pipe . . . We have the same view of life.'

'Which is too serious,' said Saint. 'I'm here like my father before me, to amuse myself. If I get pilled – too bad . . .'

Mrs Radcliffe asked him what were his ambitions for the future?

'I might care to startle the world. But *that* isn't done by putting your head in a book. Certainly I don't intend to become famous for gathering fragments of Praxilla – or polishing Pindar . . .'

Vesey was going into the City, he told Mrs Radcliffe, 'Unless something wonderful happens, and I get a fourth year.'

'And you, Gib dear?' Mrs Radcliffe asked, almost as if she had to earn each slice of cake she was so eagerly accepting, and which Alice feared she would later regret.

'One or other of the more obvious,' Saint said, 'Parson or pedagogue –'

'*Si vis ut loquar, ipse tace,*' interrupted Gib. 'Martial. In other words and translated for guests – Saint, if you want me to speak, be silent yourself –'

'Oh dear,' said Mrs Radcliffe, 'that's a foreign language.'

'I'm not capping that,' Saint said. 'You and Vesey can play quotation matches – I don't have the equipment . . . *Quid afferre consilii potest, qui seipse eget consilio*, Nicolson –'

He turned to Alice. 'And now Miss Firth, be honest – are we at all like you thought we'd be?'

Mrs Radcliffe's stomach rumbled again loudly. And as if she felt in some way responsible for it herself, Alice spoke quickly to muffle the sound.

Gib had found them rooms in a house on the corner of Benet Street, so that they looked out on to King's Parade and also were not far from Cat's. That night she was too excited to sleep. Standing at the window, she saw the Proctor go past with two top-hatted porters, Bulldogs as they were called: searching the streets for undergraduates without the cap and gown obligatory after dusk.

She was happy. As she lay in bed she thought: I am here, and Gib is here. All is well. The same feeling, only better, as when he came home for the vacations (I am at The Towers, he is at the Vicarage. *All is well* . . .)

Gib and Vesey took her to the last day of the May Races, when the college boats tried to bump each other. They watched Saint rowing for John's, but took care to cheer only Cat's – who alas were bumped, but did not bump. They crossed from Stourbridge Common over to the tow path on the horse drawn ferry, the Big Grind. She wore the best of her hats and tried to forget that Belle Maman had chosen it. It was an interesting blue, and very big, with lace, kilted, a small wreath of roses and long blue ribbon. Kingcups grew in the meadows. The river smelled quite different from a Yorkshire river.

Saint had a friend with a motor and they went right out into the country one morning. The next evening to a concert in his college. They walked over to Grantchester, to the Orchard, for tea. These are charmed days, she thought.

Mrs Radcliffe of course was there all the time. She insisted that she was thoroughly enjoying herself. 'Their talk is so *clever* . . .'

The day before the College Ball, which would bring the visit almost to an end, they went to tea in Saint's rooms. Vesey was asked too. Saint's sister, a tall lively girl, had arrived earlier that morning together with her friend, a Miss Fox, whom Saint had described as 'enchanting'. Miss Fox spoke a lot in a breathy, nervous voice. She seemed to take amiss Alice's few polite questions, so that Alice was glad she would not be of the party the next evening.

Saint's rooms, more colourful than Gib's, had theatre bills on the walls, and a rented pianola in one corner. There was much talk of theatre and entertainment. Both Miss Sainthill and Miss Fox were very keen, it appeared. Although Alice didn't mention Belle Maman, Gib did. Miss Fox looked with new interest on Alice: she told them her older brother had pictures of Lily Greene in *The Duke and The Shopgirl*, and that she herself had seen *Princess Violet*.

Gib had been looking among the pianola records. He put one on the roller – a cake-walk, *Ma Tiger Lily*. The sitting-room filled with the prancing sound.

Saint remarked: 'I borrowed those. A Yankee who keeps in the next staircase. They are his . . .'

Saint's sister said that she just *loved* that sort of music. 'It's the *dernier cri*, and quite deevy. Lots more fun than all those stupid lancers and waltzes from gay Vienna.'

'You'll have to be happy with those tomorrow,' Saint said.

Gib put on another – *Happy Darkies*. Alice thought that she hated the sound: it seemed, she didn't know why, to take him a long way from her. Mrs Radcliffe merely looked surprised. Miss Fox tapped her small foot. Vesey asked permission to smoke and, trying to light his pipe, filled the air with tobacco.

The window was thrown open, sending the cake-walk into the court below.

Saint said he would show them the rest of the college: 'We go through to the New Court . . .' Crossing the Bridge of Sighs: 'Cockney Gothic,' he remarked. And then: 'Mr Wordsworth was unhappy the other end, among the kitchens – I wouldn't care to have kept his rooms . . .' He was in the Tudor court – much the best to be. The new buildings, he said, were a great mistake.

They walked in the gardens, and in a place called the Wilderness, heavy with trees and the scent of wild flowers.

Towards the end of the afternoon Alice realized that Miss Fox, confused by the stepmothers and stepsisters, thought she was Gib's elder sister. Oh, thought Alice, if only that were so. Standing there among the trees, her happiness as fragile as the wild flowers about her feet: if only . . .

She who had never wanted to attend any social occasion she could possibly avoid, was now longing for and full of excitement about – a Ball. She hardly slept the night before. Heard every quarter of an hour strike from Great St Mary's Church. She sat up in bed reading Mrs Humphry Ward's *Marriage of William Ashe*. Other Balls were held that evening. Voices, laughter. Once a party came up the street. When the horse trams started up, clopping by on the stones, she realized that the night was over. She did not feel tired.

Her dress, Belle Maman's choice, was mostly cloth of gold and chiffon, sparkling gold tissue on the tunic. Lace too, just enough not to make the dress heavy. She saw that the gold warmed her skin. Looking in the glass, she realized that just as the blue hat had completely altered her, so – the dress. She did not look sharp any more. Rather, soft.

The party for the ball was held in Vesey's rooms, which were larger than Gib's and had, she suspected, been very tidied up for the occasion. They were a party of eight. Vesey's sister was there and two men who had invited twin sisters from their home town of Chichester. After a dinner-party at the Blue Boar, they walked down to the college. Coloured candles, lights, were strung along King's and Cat's. Mrs Radcliffe had had trouble with her dress: too tight in spite of extra corseting. She told Alice: 'When I have the chance, dear, I think I shall just loosen something here and there.'

There was a marquee with orchestra: waltzes, lancers, veleta. They danced to *FrouFrou*, *Kissing is no Sin*, *They all love Jack* . . . Alice didn't think of herself as a good dancer. And she had never, formally, danced with Gib. But like everything this evening, it was easy. Perhaps because he did it so well, perhaps because . . . The Gib of the gently swaying waltz was not a cake-walker.

The evening wore on. It could only become happier. She wasn't tired at all. About three o'clock in the morning they were to visit Saint and his friends at John's. Now four of them were sitting up in Gib's room with Mrs Radcliffe, who appeared a little wilted. Alice noticed her surreptitiously loosening . . .

There was to be a recital of comic songs in the marquee and they were about to make their way down there, to secure a good place. Mrs Radcliffe said, 'Perhaps, my dears, you will excuse me? I don't feel very comic.'

As they went down the staircase, she and Gib last:

'How fearful to be a chaperone,' he said, 'I fear she will yawn till dawn.' He said it exaggeratedly, drawing out the rhyme. Alice laughed. Vesey and his sister were ahead of them as they crossed the court. In the marquee they were playing the waltz *Catch of the Season*.

'I say, I shay,' came a voice, thickly. A young man in evening dress, but with one of the tails torn, his tie hanging loose. He put out a hand to block their way: 'I shay, damnation. You Wesley-Dutton?'

'No,' Gib said. Then politely: 'If you'd perhaps excuse us?'

'No, will *not*. Bloody damnation, will not . . .' He continued to stand in front of them. His eyes had an odd boiled look. Gib said, raising his hand very slightly:

'If you please. There *is* a lady with me –'

'Whash lady? That lady? *Ship's* a lady. Hey and ahoy and – Whoah, oah she *goes* . . . Putrid bilge . . . Whoops –' He leaned forward, swaying, pressing his shoes on Gib's toes.

Gib said, 'Look here, cut it, would you? Make off. I don't know you. *And* you're drunk –'

The man lashed out suddenly, hitting Gib hard across the cheek and temple. Then again quickly, on the nose and mouth. Alice thought for a moment that Gib was going to turn the other cheek. Instead, he pushed the man hard, with his forearm.

By now the others had turned round. The college porter came up.

'Now, sir, now, Mr Nicolson. You all right, sir?' He and another man had hold of the drunk. 'This won't do at all. Very inebriated. He's not one of our gentlemen, Mr Nicolson.'

The drunk had perhaps decided to be quiet. The porter said, 'We'll soon have his name and college, sir. A bad night's work it'll be for him.' A lot more people had gathered round. The blood ran freely from Gib's nose.

Alice said anxiously, 'Gib?'

'I'm all right,' he said. 'Perfectly all right. I'll just go back up –'

She held on to his arm as they went up the staircase almost as if it was she who had been hurt. They came into the sitting-room not particularly quietly, but without speaking. Mrs Radcliffe lay head back in the armchair before the fireplace. Her mouth open, probably snoring, deeply asleep. There was a jug and basin in his bedroom. She said, 'I'll bathe your face for you.'

She thought he was a bit shocked, although he laughed nervously. He said, 'A fine thing to happen to a chap –'

'You were only protecting me –'

'It's quite usual, gatecrashers – but several together, and good-humoured. *He'll* have worse than a bloodied nose, I fear. Shouldn't wonder if he's rusticated – sent down temporarily.'

She wiped his face carefully until all the blood was removed. 'Thank you,' he said. When she had quite finished, she took his face, all clean now and tidy (I am his mother, his sister), between her hands and kissed his cheek. Once, twice. His temple, his cheek. Blood was flowing again from one nostril. Some ran into her mouth.

I am his mother, his sister. I kiss him better . . .

He said awkwardly, 'Really, I'm rather a mess.' They went back into the sitting-room. Mrs Radcliffe had not moved. She was snoring now. Voices then on the stairs. Others of the party coming up. It was time for them all to go to Saint's.

'Well, old chap,' Vesey said, 'well. *Si sapias, sapias?* Be wise, if you are wise . . .'

Gib said, 'I think it was *Vinum incendit iram*. He was *very* drunk.'

'My turn,' said Vesey. '*Si vis pacem, para bellum*. If you wish for peace, prepare for war. Next time you must be ready with *your* fist . . .'

Somehow the rest of the night, the visit to John's, the coming of the first light, was enchanted still. As Gib's face and eye began to turn slowly yellow, brown, black, they joined up with Saint in the Market Square. At about four-thirty it was light enough for their photographs to be taken. The Market Square was deserted – the early farm wagons just arriving. They were pictured by the fountain. Gib wanted to hide . . .

Then, she was in some sort of dream, they took, ten of them, punts up the river, where they ate breakfast.

Several times on the journey home she would suddenly taste the metallic flavour of his blood, remember the smell of his skin. Why? He had not remarked on it. Everything was the same as before. And yet . . .

She was going home ahead of him. He followed next week. She hurried the train on. Hurried time on, to when it would all be *ordinary* again.

She called on the spirit of her mother. She liked to imagine their two mothers, in heaven, talking together. 'Alice will take care of Gib,' her mother told his. 'I know no one better . . .'

She hurried the train as it rattled over the rails. Back to Flaxthorpe – and the long summer. Gib at the Vicarage. She at The Towers.

Hal said, 'Tomorrow – Jack won't be coming for the hay.'

'Summat up with him?' Stephen asked.

'Mrs Hawksworth says he mayn't. It's sneezing. He sneezed all the way home. Then his eyes went all red and puffed up, and his nose . . . he could scarcely breathe. And he's got to be well to go to his school in September . . .'

'Hay seeds, it'll be,' Stephen said.

'But *I'll* be up,' Hal went on, 'unless that beastly Pettinger keeps me. I can't really cut any lessons. Bally things . . .'

What a nuisance they were. All part of the bad luck that made him Master Henry Firth (aged twelve) of The Towers and not Stephen Ibbotson (aged fifteen) of Lane Top Farm. Not that he would for a moment have changed *mothers* – privately he didn't think much of Mrs Ibbotson, who drooped. But what he'd realized gradually was that really he simply wished more than anything else to be a farm boy. And after that, a farmer.

But one didn't speak of such things. What one did, was to spend every free moment, every moment that could be spared from Mr Pettinger, up at the farm. Sometimes that meant hasty, badly done Latin parsing for the next day, but mostly it was easy enough, especially the arithmetic and Euclid. Once or twice it occurred to him that perhaps he was clever, and that was why he could often do in fifteen minutes what might take Jack an hour or more. Most of the work set, anyway, was to do with Jack's requirements for school – Harrow, in two months' time.

Hal's life would change then, because Gib Nicolson ('I think you should perhaps call him *Mr* Nicolson now,' Alice said) was to be his tutor instead of Mr Pettinger. Gib would leave the school where he was presently teaching, Marlborough, and live instead at home, coming each day to The Towers. Life, Hal feared, might become serious. Because even though he was not strong enough to go to school (sports, fights, general rough and tumble – the dangers had all been explained to him) he was expected to go to University – for no reason he could see, except that most chaps did. Gib had, of course. Cambridge in the summer, Alice told Hal, was 'the most wonderful, beautiful place'. (Maybe she thought so . . . But how could it be compared with evenings on the lower moor, creeping over the beckstones while the brown water gurgled below and the sky above faded and darkened, watching and waiting with Stephen for the trout to rise?)

His heart: in a way it had done him a good turn. For it gave him no trouble he could notice, so that he was no longer frightened by it, although sometimes it beat wonkily, and then he would wonder if *that* was the trouble . . . Luckily most of the things he wanted to do were the very ones allowed. All part of the exciting, happy life he led. He and Jack and Stephen. A trio. A triumvirate.

It had been gradual, really, beginning with that Easter Monday adventure, caught in the hailstorm near Stephen's farm. Then the sad silence afterwards, as if a door had been slammed in his face. ('But Stephen *promised*, he *said* we would go fishing.') The disapproval of his elders. And then – Jack becoming interested because fishing was his new craze. Alice being roped in to plead for them. And finally, a visit to the farm: Alice, Jack, Hal, and yes, Fräulein, all setting out in the yellow dog-cart. Mr Ibbotson was spoken to. Stephen was asked to take them fishing. Hal hadn't liked the formal atmosphere but was happy at the result. He was to be allowed to spend time at the farm, provided he did no heavy work. It was even considered good, since days spent indoors marshalling his lead soldiers, Jack as the opposing general, were nothing like as healthy . . .

A happy summer. Fishing, sheepclipping, haymaking, leading in bracken (even swimming in the icy becks until he was found out and, with horror, forbidden. 'The *shock* you might give your heart . . .') Jack there too, nearly always, for he was as bored by Edith and Amy as Hal was with Teddy and Sylvia. Ugh. The worst thing about them, and Jack felt the same, was that they whined. They also giggled which was horrible and, silliest thing of all, fought each other to get attention from the grown-ups. (He and Jack could do with a lot less . . . '*Don't fuss*' ought to be the motto in every mother's Christmas cracker.)

The next winter, 1909, Will Ibbotson died in the cold days of February, of pneumonia. He was just nineteen. Two of the four boys gone now. Stephen didn't speak of it much – he stayed away a while from Hal and Jack, and they from him. The bad weather made visiting difficult. When Hal was back there again, Mrs Ibbotson still had red eyes. Olive kept running up to put her hand in her mother's. Although he would never have asked Olive out with them, he liked her pretty well. She didn't behave like a sister. Often he did her sums for her, as that first time, but later he made sure that she understood the answers. 'A farmer's wife,' Will said, 'she's the reckonings to do often as not. Olive'd best learn . . .' She'd finished with school now, leaving the year she'd turned twelve.

1911. And this hot, hot summer. Haymaking time. He woke every morning to a sky more blue than white, to what they called a 'hayday'. If at all possible he went up to the farm, even if it could not be till afternoon. His whole, his *real* life was up there.

The 'paddies' had come to help with the hay. Tim and Pat O'Rourke, brothers, had been coming for fifteen years, and their father and uncles before that. Large men who got through more bread, milk and cheese before their day's work than Hal could in a week. He rejoiced in them. Adding their accent to his repertoire. But when he spoke back to them with a brogue they didn't even notice. Pat taught him some songs. Tim had a mouth organ. When the haymaking was all over there would be a feast, a 'mell', with plenty of beer and singing and dancing. Hal wouldn't be there, of course. Jack thought him very odd for wanting to. 'Tim and Pat, they're good sorts,' he said. 'Only – not *our* sort.'

Perhaps. Yes. Maybe. Tim and Pat lodged in one of the two big fieldhouses a little way from the farmhouse, sleeping upstairs where later the hay would be stored. They mowed with a skill which gained respect from all. They brought their own scythes with them, with very soft blades so that if they hit a stone they would not break. Tim, Pat, James, Mr Ibbotson, all in a row – it was a fine sight. On days of close heat they wore buttermuslin over their faces to keep off the midges. Hal, Stephen and Olive were straw boys and girls, tossing the hay first over one shoulder and then the other to keep it light.

Now Jack must stay away. He was angry, Hal knew, not so much because he liked haymaking but because it meant he couldn't be with Hal. Lately, perhaps on account of being about to leave home, he had been reading a lot of boys' school stories. Before that it had been adventure. Fairy stories he'd never liked. When he'd caught Hal at nearly eleven reading *The Green Fairy Book*, he had mocked mocked mocked. *His* book at the time had been *From Powder-monkey to Admiral*. When he'd finished it, he declared that he would join the Navy. 'When the War comes . . .' What war? Hal had asked. '*The* War – I dunno. The Pater says, everyone says . . . Germany. They're spoiling for a fight, and it'll be at sea. We shall have to show them probably, sooner or later, that it doesn't do to get too big for your boots.' Only a month after that, he thought the Foreign Legion was the thing. Then it was Canada, and the Mounties . . . Hal marvelled.

'It's beastly luck,' he said to Jack now, 'about the hay fever. After it's all over, we'll try and do something jolly, if the sun keeps up, which it *will* –'

'*Bonus, bene, melius, melior*,' Jack said. 'Meanwhile I'll just have to stay indoors with Cæsar and his bally Gallic Wars. Beastly lingo . . .' Then: 'I say,' he went on, 'when I'm back with you and Stephen, why don't we all become blood brothers? In this story I read . . .'

The hay had been led in. Loaded on the sledge, tied up with rope at the back because they were going downhill. Stephen led Bluebell. The next day while Tim and Pat were sleeping off the feast, and after an hour's cricket practice with Mr Pettinger, Hal and Jack went over to the farm on their bicycles, stopping as always for Hal whenever the incline was steep.

Jack didn't expect to sneeze again. Some folk, Stephen said, sneezed all summer. 'Grass here is that herby . . .'

He and Jack were together again, and soon would be even more so, for lessons finished completely in a week's time. Jack had caught up, more or less. Gib could help at the last minute, if necessary. Mr Pettinger was about to leave for Switzerland with two boys he was to coach for the summer.

'It'll be ripping to see him go,' Jack said. 'He thinks I'm an absolute duffer at everything. But I wouldn't be bad at cricket if I hadn't his beastly mug to look at when he bowls – it would put even W.G. off . . .'

There was a new calf at the farm. While they were admiring it, Jack said again: 'Let's be blood brothers. It'd be awfully jolly –' When he had an idea he would never let go of it.

'Whatever's that, then?' Stephen asked, a little scornfully. Jack explained.

'And then you mix the bits of blood together . . .'

'Sounds daft to me –'

'It's a very old custom. Gypsies do it.'

'There's no call for us – on account of some gypsy folk –'

'But I'm off to school, and we'll all be parted.' He said desperately, 'Haven't you heard of the Three Musketeers? We could –' Then he broke off because Stephen was laughing at him.

Stephen said good-naturedly that he wasn't bothered. If it was what Jack wanted . . .

'We can any of us call on the others if we're in trouble, for the rest of our lives,' Jack said. 'It's a *bond*.'

To Hal it seemed a good idea. He would if possible have chosen a brother over a sister any day. They did it that afternoon, using the fishing knife for the cutting. They cleaned it with earth first. When their blood was all mixed together, Jack said to Stephen, 'Now you're one of us . . .' Stephen still thought it daft, and said so. Hal supposed it was because Stephen was almost a grown man: fifteen and three months. Although Hal had nearly a head over him. ('Don't grow too fast for your heart,' someone had said only the other day.)

They idled, spoke of fishing later, but hadn't brought anything. When they learned the trap was going into Flaxthorpe, they put their bicycles in the back and climbed in. Stephen came with them. When they reached the Hall, Jack took his bicycle and left them. But at The Towers, Hal said to Stephen, 'Come in. Stay a while with us.'

Stephen looked uncertain. James, holding the reins, grew

impatient. 'It's aye or nay, Stephen lad.'

Stephen jumped down. Hal said, 'All right then, I'll show you everything. We're brothers remember?'

'Right. Aye.'

'I could show you my room – my treasures. Everything.'

Stephen had been to The Towers once before (not counting his stolen visit). Last summer, dressed formally with a stiff collar and billycock hat, to a tea-party held for all the villagers and tenants of surrounding farms. They had sat at long tables outside, while their hosts watched the sky anxiously. Recitations, singing, some dancing. The local brass band in which James played cornet.

Today the first thing that went wrong was that as they came up by the summer-house, who should be in it but Teddy and Amy, dressed in ridiculous kimonos. He *ought* to have paid no attention, but of course had to call out:

'Just look at that –'

And Teddy at once: '*You* aren't invited, you know . . .' They giggled. Both of them, quite horribly. Amy said:

'It's a Japanese tea-party, by the way. You can come if you want.' They had stupid little flowered cups and were sitting on the floor.

'I say, that's awfully civil of you,' he said in a mocking voice. Then added, 'I wouldn't want to go to anything so piffling, thank you . . .'

He was ashamed in front of Stephen, who was looking at them with wry amazement. It was not at all like the home life of the Ibbotsons.

But when he'd walked Stephen about a little, he began to loathe that very difference. The natural authority Stephen had in his own home, around the farm, when he took them fishing, rabbiting . . . where was it? Here he looked awkward. Hal had heard it explained that people like Stephen used the back door rather than the front: '. . . because, Hal, they wouldn't feel comfortable. It's important to make people feel at their ease. A gentleman, or a lady for that matter, does so instinctively . . .'

Perhaps Stephen was thinking of just such matters, for he said as they went downstairs into the main hall, after Hal had shown him his bedroom:

'Reckon when Jack's been at that school awhiles, he'll not

care so much for days at t'farm and the like.' He said it easily, though: as a fact, rather than a sadness.

Hal knew it to be true and denied it at once. 'Of course he will. Specially now we're brothers.'

'*That* –' Stephen's voice was scornful.

'Well, it was his idea, after all. And a jolly one too.'

He tried to think, after they'd been to the kitchens and begged some scones and butter, of some treat to offer Stephen who had politely but not very enthusiastically looked at everything – and who said now, amiably enough, amused almost:

'There's room enough here, and food too, I reckon . . . You could bed and board every beggar for miles about and not be tight . . .'

'Daft beggars?'

Stephen looked puzzled.

'Joke,' Hal said. 'You're always saying "daft beggars" . . . So, I'm just jolly well asking –'

'*Them* daft beggars, they're not beggars, they're buggers, you daft beggar . . . It's just, I've not to use that word.'

'I don't know what it means –'

'Aye, well, don't ask me about it.' He grinned suddenly. 'Ye ken when sheep – I reckon it's best not spoken of – but sometimes ye see them, like – they . . .'

Hal wasn't sure if he understood the explanation. A moment later, Stephen, standing at the bottom of the stairs, asked: 'Who's that?' pointing to the large oil painting half way up.

'That's Alice's mother. The Lady Firth who died. She's wearing the Diamond Waterfall –'

'Bye hell!' He went up and looked closer. 'I like that. Aye, it's grand, that. Shines like a real waterfall . . .' He shrugged his shoulders. 'Bye –'

It was at that moment Hal had the idea. Maybe –? He said, 'There's *masses* of other jewellery. Stones, things like that – my father, my grandfather – there's this big collection. Shall we?'

'I'd mebbe heard tell. I don't rightly recall –'

'If you'd like. I'll have to see – because of getting it opened.' He didn't want to ask his parents, and didn't know where they were. He had to find Alice: she was allowed in there and would perhaps take them round. He suddenly wanted, desperately, to show Stephen.

Alice was with Fräulein. It took only five minutes to find her. She had a hat and gloves on:

'Oh, but Hal dear, I can't say. Mr Nicolson and I are just going on an errand for his father.' She thought for a moment. 'Dear Fräulein, *she* could take you round –'

Hal was not too pleased at this idea. There was something damping about Fräulein. Her heavy soggy presence. Although she surely didn't spy for the grown-ups, he would feel that he couldn't be natural with Stephen.

Alice went off with her to fetch the keys, for she didn't know where they were kept (nor did he, for that matter . . .)

Stephen began: 'I'd not have agreed on it, if I'd known there'd be such a –'

'No. No,' Hal said, 'I *want* to show you them.'

He was glad he'd persisted when he saw Stephen's wonderment and admiration and, he thought as well, pleasure. He wished then he knew more about the different stones, that he'd bothered to listen when Alice or Mother had talked, explained.

Emeralds, rubies, topaz, tourmaline, opals, aquamarines, amethysts, sapphires, pearls – on and on and on, as the iron shutters were unclasped from each case. The afternoon sun streaming into the room caught here and there the colours . . .

'Bye –' Stephen said, and then again as if he'd been holding his breath. 'Bye – they're really summat.' His hand went out towards a cluster of fire-opals, lying on their velvet bed.

'*No*!' Fräulein spoke sharply. 'We are not to touch. And – *ach* –' she looked down – 'those hands . . .'

They weren't that dirty, Hal thought angrily, looking at his own which he'd kept in his pockets till then. Sunburnt, working hands, Stephen's were, but even as he thought this, Stephen hid them – cheerfully, but not looking at the governess. Hal wanted to shake her great fat face. She said now:

'This boy, he is so fortunate that he may look. Enough – *Ja*?' Her voice was soft again. Silly Schultz . . .

'Bye, though – they'll be . . . what's the money in that lot, then?'

Fräulein interrupted, mildly this time, 'We are not speaking of this. Please.'

Hal said, grumbling, 'Everything my *friend* does is wrong . . .'

She didn't answer, but wore her foolish face suddenly. He decided to ignore her.

'They're just stones,' he said to Stephen, 'examples really, because my father and grandfather liked to look at them. The real stuff's the jewellery. That's – well, if you saw *that* . . .'

Stephen grinned good-naturedly. 'Aye. I don't doubt –' He looked over at the last case which Fräulein Schultz was about to cover. 'Our Will'd've said summat . . .' He was frowning now. 'So few wi' so much, and so many wi' nowt – he'd not think it right. But –' he hesitated. 'If we'd a different world – that's what Will did his reading about, and all –'

Fräulein was looking impatient. Hal said (spiritedly), 'My father gives away a *lot* of money, so that people shouldn't be hungry. He says it's his duty. Charity, that's what. It makes the world go round, he says.'

'*Charity*,' Stephen said. 'Bugger charity . . .' But he said it cheerfully enough. Fräulein must have been pretending not to hear, or perhaps better still, didn't understand . . .

'Bugger charity,' Hal replied, to join in the mood.

Most of the time Stephen wasn't argumentative, didn't echo half-remembered sayings of Will, and was just Hal's easy-going friend. With Jack as a third life was near to perfection: the friend he'd grown up with, and the friend he'd acquired by himself and now shared – someone in whose world he felt really at home. Stephen knows that, he would tell himself sometimes. Although he'd never say it to me, he knows that when I'm at the farm, I'm part of the life. It's always 'Master Hawksworth' when Jack goes up there – but for me all that stopped long ago. Unless they've a visitor it's Hal always, or 'Mister Hal' if they're mocking. Granny Willan calls me that . . .

The summer wore on. August now, and still it was hot. Towards the end of the month, the Hawksworths were to go to Scarborough for three weeks: he was invited as a companion for Jack. After that it would be nearly time for Jack to go to Harrow. These last weeks he seemed to have rather gone off the idea. He'd stopped reading school stories. Now, perhaps to get as far away as possible, it was all the Indian Mutiny . . .

Because of the dry weather, the fishing was not good. Earlier in the summer the Ibbotsons had been worried that the drought would affect milk for the lambs: soon now they would be weaned. Then there would be tupping, and in September the Sheep Fair. Hal loved it when there was talk, and worries, and plans made which *he* could feel part of. Twice recently, Mr Ibbotson had said, 'Well, what do you think on it then, Hal lad? What's best to do, eh?' Mrs Ibbotson had whole days now when she looked as if she kept her head on her neck only with effort. 'Mother's not herself today,' Mr Ibbotson would say then, and Hal would know they were all thinking about Will.

The week before going to Scarborough, there were two days of rain. Jack and Hal, with their fishing rods, got lifts up to the farm and permission to stay out till dusk, since the trout might not rise till late.

From the beginning, the day went well. Although Hal had to admit Jack was in a rather annoying mood. Not that Stephen minded. 'What's he on about?' was the most he said when Jack, full of *Barclay of the Guides* which he'd just finished reading, began all his remarks with 'By the beard of the Prophet . . .'

They had climbed quite a way up the dale when they stopped to eat their food. They were going to explore wherever Stephen led them, then stop for fishing on the way back down. The weather, with sun again after rain, did not seem too hot for exertion.

'*Malus, pejor*,' said Jack. 'Every crumb of cake is finished. Salaam, O Ibbotson Sahib – let's have a bit of *your* grub.' When Stephen obliged, passing him a chunk of spice bread, he said: 'I thank thee, Dinga Ghosh, and be sure that my father will reward thee when he comes back –'

'Where's he gone?' asked Hal.

'Pig of a Purbiya, do you insult me by asking? In fact, you duffer, he's gone shooting. And I dare say I could have gone too . . .' He added, 'I'll probably get a gun at Christmas.'

And how different it all might be by then, Hal thought. A Jack home from Harrow, happy or unhappy, would be another person. No amount of talk of Three Musketeers and blood brothers could alter that . . .

'Verily, Oh verily this bread is made by Missy Sahib,' Jack said, licking the ends of his fingers. 'And jolly good too –'

'He means our Olive,' said Stephen, giving Hal a wink. 'You're a right chatterwallet and all today, Jack.' He emptied some beer dregs on to a clump of moss. They frothed quietly. Then: 'We'd best be away – if we're to see all I've reckoned on showing you . . .'

The sun beat down as they crossed Wadsworth Bridge. For a while they were on open moorland. In the distance the ling-covered fells were blue-purple. They went down again, back towards the river, narrowed now to a beck. With the sudden rain, the waters had swollen and as they crossed by the beckstones, some greasy with damp, Jack wobbled deliberately from side to side. Rod slung across his back, bag with tackle and remains of lunch. 'By Allah, the Feringhis pursue me – let them be ground between the upper and nether millstone –' He righted himself with agility. 'The *dogs* . . .'

Hal said, 'You do talk the most appalling rot. Chuck it, can't you?' He had begun to feel irritated, especially as he hadn't read the book. He knew too that if *he'd* wanted to imitate that sort of talk, he'd have done it much better. Jack being a Mahommedan sounded exactly like – Jack.

'We take forward path now,' Stephen told them, when all three had reached the other side. They made their way up, and gradually the rocky bank by the water grew steeper and steeper. Here and there a tree grew out of the crag. Between the rocks coarse grass grew and near where they walked, Hal caught the smell of wild garlic. Stephen said, 'We call it Jack-by-the-hedge.' He looked over his shoulder, 'Hear that, Jack lad? A right stink, and it's after you they call it . . .'

They could hear the beck rushing below. But ahead of them the bank curved, and the trees and foliage at first hid what Hal was certain he could hear: a waterfall. Then they came upon it. Stephen stopped.

'Harkersgill Force, that is. Reckon you didn't know it. It'll be well hidden and all . . .'

The water tumbled down the rocky face, white foam to a brown pool some thirty feet below. A fine spray misted the air around. A rowan tree grew in the rock, its berries almost ripe. Hal's boots slid on the shale, where the velvety reddish moss grew. He could see pink flowers and, dangerously out of reach, forget-me-nots.

'Mind your step, then,' Stephen said. 'And you, Jack.'

Jack came up behind them. 'Salaam, hazur, I am here! What is this boiling ravine that yawns beneath us? Move, son of a dog, that I may see –'

He stepped in front of Stephen. Went right past him. His arm went up. 'The battlecry – Din! Din –'

His foot slipped. His arm, wildly, reached out to save himself. Caught and lost the branch of the rowan tree. He gave a sort of strangled cry as he fell.

For a couple of seconds, as if blinded, Hal could see nothing. Then it became clear. Jack, head down in the pool, body sprawling awkwardly across a rock. Stephen, white in the face, his mouth working, pulled Hal back.

'Ruddy hell – Ruddy hell.'

'Stephen, what do we do?' His voice came out in a frightened scream.

'I'll get missen down there. Stay put –' As Stephen made his way to Jack, scrambling down the steep side of the bank, slipping and slithering, Hal tried to follow. Bewildered and frightened, he followed the path to where descent was easier. By the time he reached Stephen, he was sobbing uncontrollably.

Stephen had turned Jack over, and was holding him half propped up. When Hal saw Jack's face, the front of his head, he began to scream. '*It didn't happen, it didn't happen* –'

'Give over,' Stephen said sharply. 'Give over.' Then more kindly: 'That'll not bring him back . . .'

It was not true. It was not true. Somehow, something, someone must make it all right again. But the seconds passed – and now Stephen, undoing the rod, the strap of Jack's bag, was lifting the body tenderly. He was smaller than Jack, and had to struggle. 'Give us a hand, then . . .'

On the difficult, seemingly endless journey back down the beck and through some woodland which Stephen said was the fastest way to a road, Hal took only a small part of the weight. Every now and then he would find himself sobbing again, even shouting, not knowing what he was saying.

Stephen did not speak again. Not long after coming on to the Wadsworth road, they met a pony and trap. The farmer who was on his way back from market, turned about at once.

Lily said: 'I've come, Sadie, because –' She hesitated. 'I thought, first I thought – but if it had been Hal . . . then I thought –'

Sadie opened her arms, and embraced her. Her face, hidden now, terrified Lily. The eyes, too wide open, too staring. Yesterday, when Sadie had heard the news, she had gone into a state of shock. Alone at the Hall, when young Stephen Ibbotson, accompanied by a farmer, had asked to speak with her . . .

'Lily, stay close to me. Darling Lily. If I ever needed a friend. We shouldn't ever let friends go – for anything. I – just – I don't know how I'm to live, I just don't . . . I don't believe any of it, you see. I think maybe he just hurt his head a bit, and it's going to mend . . .'

Lily thought with shame: Hal is alive. *I have a son.* If his heart couldn't take yesterday, the trouble would show by now. His fever is shock only. Dr Sowerby said so. Disasters don't come in tandem . . .

'But it *did* happen, Lily. It did. I guess I just loved him too much or something . . . You think you're having a bad dream, then you don't wake up – oh, Lily, stay close by me. *Close by me . . .*'

21

The Christmas tree for 1912 had been placed in the main hall and Alice, as she came near, saw the heavy figure of Fräulein busying herself with the holly, just brought in. With clumsy cold fingers she was tying tinsel, but Alice could see from her face (that revealing one known for so many years) that all was not well.

She would be going home for Christmas. Nowadays she went always for Christmas as well as several weeks in the summer. She was very much the family retainer now. Teddy and Sylvia were her pupils, and Amy and Edith Hawksworth came for German conversation. Hal, who still imitated her excellently, had little to do with her – his time was spent with Gib. And that means, Alice thought, that Gib is every day at The Towers. Perhaps if she'd tried to think of something almost perfect: Gib, at The Towers, every day.

They all three ate together at midday. She had had more time with him since the autumn of 1911 than in all the years she'd known him. She remembered that she had kissed him (yes, I kissed him) years ago, at Cambridge, that warm June evening. Gib of the bloodied nose. He had never ever in the slightest way alluded to it. She had wanted so much that everything should be ordinary again, and lo! it had been.

After the two years as a junior master at Marlborough (his degree had not in the end been as good as expected), here he was tutor to Hal. Beginning only a month or so after the terrible afternoon of Jack Hawksworth's death.

In the atmosphere of hysteria then she'd been surprised at her own calm. She had thought at first something had happened to Hal: brought back shaking, crying, occasionally calling at the top of his voice. She'd looked to see, expecting him to be injured in some way. And then she'd heard the story . . .

There was Belle Maman rushing over, as soon as Hal had been put to bed – rushing over to the Hall:

'Alice, I must see at once, at once, if there is anything I can do, *anything* . . .' And Alice, who had once so hated Hal, had gone upstairs to sit with him. His fever growing higher all the time, turning and tossing. From his ravings she'd learned more of the story.

At first she had been inclined to blame, as had Belle Maman, the Ibbotson boy, who she felt somehow should have been able to stop it happening. But at the inquest, which Alice attended, mainly to support Hal and Sadie Hawksworth, he had spoken clearly and frankly, and given a good account of himself. The coroner had gone out of his way to commend him. Indeed, it could be seen to have been simply a tragic accident. Jack's high spirits and excitability . . . She remembered that, alas, he had always been one to break away, run off, be just that little bit foolish . . .

And Hal was still friendly with the Ibbotson boy. Very much so. He was with him this very afternoon.

As Alice came nearer to the mound of holly, Fräulein looked up. At the same time she gave a great sigh as if she had been holding her breath.

'*Alice* . . . Such a letter I have had today. And when it is only four days before I shall go home. What sort of Christmas shall it be?' Her face shook. She looked at Alice, then said in a trembling voice: 'I cannot, I can really *not* . . . It is every time the same –'

I know my cue, Alice thought. She said gently, 'It's Augustin, isn't it?'

'Every time the same. Only now, worse und worse. You know how he is used to borrow money from friends and those he is working for? When he is working . . . Now he has visited those who lend money. It is a Jew and he writes me, Augustin writes me –' she paused to try and control herself. 'I tell you this, Alice, only because I have told you many times before, and you know that Augustin is a *good* boy, except as – I don't know, I don't know at all – only that I love him and that I am doing anything for him, *anything* – and that I am very afraid for him. Of course –' and she attempted to speak in a brisk voice – 'it is a Jew. What else? Augustin is borrowing – it is not so big, but it is *too* big, und perhaps he has borrowed to repay that which he has *before* borrowed. Now this Jew says "Herr Schultz, I must have my money." '

'Oh dear,' said Alice. 'Oh dear. Your father?'

'Ach, I already tell you. Last time he has said, "This is the last time . . . Next time is prison." Und so . . .'

The tears were crawling down now. The tinsel knotted round her fingers.

'What shall become of him? Prison . . . When already his health goes – The bowels are not right, I *know* the bowels are not right. He has written me . . . And now what? How is that – Christmas also . . . We shall not be a happy family, Alice.'

She tried to think how she might help. But of what use *was* it to help Augustin? Perhaps if she asked Papa? She dismissed the idea at once.

'I think you'll see,' she told Fräulein, 'that your father will help. When it comes to it . . . I am certain if it were Hal my father would help.'

'You are so sweet. Always so kind. From a little child, kind.' She sniffed: 'I shall start at once to think of other things. Brighter things, yes?'

'Yes,' said Alice.

'I go now, and walk in the garden.'

Alice, leaving her, made her way up to the darkroom. She had a lot to do up there because her Christmas presents were to be mostly photographs. So she was rather annoyed when after only half an hour she found she needed pyro-gallic acid and had run out of it. She thought: I can go and look for Gib and ask him . . . But if he had none? It would have to wait for a journey into Richmond . . .

It would be best, on the off-chance, she thought, to look through the cupboards really thoroughly. She had finished with the first of them when she heard a knock . . . She tutted her way to the outer door (I am becoming an old maid – the way I fuss . . .) It was Hal, and behind him, the Ibbotson boy.

'I can't find anyone,' he complained. 'We want to go in the Stones Room.' He coloured a little: 'Stephen wants it for his Christmas treat. He saw them, that time, ages ago. And he wants to look again.' He added, 'We could go, if you'd tell me where the keys are . . .'

'I certainly won't,' she said. 'You can wait – can't you?'

'Suppose so . . .'

'You'll have to. I'm looking for something. When I've found it, I'll come down. Meanwhile, *you* look for Gib, and ask him if he's got any pyro-gallic acid at the Vicarage.'

And they had gone. She began to hunt again. All sorts of bottles which, far back in the cupboard, should surely have been thrown out – might, she supposed, even be dangerous. Boxes too. Old plates, old prints. (She had looked at a few once – and very boring they had been. Landscapes, taken on foreign travels – and few of them as good as she herself could do.) One box was right behind all the others, in a sloping recess. Small, and even dustier. She took it out on impulse, and was glad to be wearing gloves.

There were half a dozen plates inside. She thought idly that she might look at those . . . Tissue paper, and then underneath, a handful of prints. She brought them out. Picked one up and . . .

They were all of her mother. But her mother naked. Wearing nothing but jewellery. Covered in jewellery! That very jewellery Alice remembered from her childhood . . .

She didn't know where to look. What to think. She was shaking, breathing deeply. Suddenly very, very hot. She couldn't bear to look at them – yet her eyes went back again and again and again.

'Too heavy,' Mama had said. 'It breaks my back – my neck . . .' But here, she was weighed down with precious metal and stones. Bracelets, necklaces, corsages. A tiara in her poor frizzed hair. In one picture, she wore a scarf over her face (yes, it was her. It was her body. As if she had pleaded in her shame, to be covered . . .)

In the last one of all – there must have been a dozen altogether – she was wearing the Diamond Waterfall; and nothing else. Her face above it, the face of long ago, had an expression that Alice did not know, could not remember, had never seen. It wasn't patience. Nor was it anger. More perhaps, a kind of tired defiance. 'If that is what must be, it must be. But I am still *myself* . . . *Me* . . .'

Why did she allow it? Why? Why ever? That he should ever have thought of or done such a thing. For it must have been him. Must have been Papa. She couldn't still her trembling. Now her mouth had begun to shake as well. It is no excuse, she thought with sudden resolution, that it must, absolutely must, belong to more than twenty years ago. That doesn't make it all right.

My own father, she said to herself, my own father is no better than Uncle Lionel. *Worse.*

She would speak to him. Now. As soon as the trembling stopped. If she did not find him and speak to him *now*, then she never would. In a white heat, still trembling, she cleared up, put everything back into the cupboards, and found that she grew a little calmer. She gathered the prints into an envelope. Washed, and began to walk downstairs.

As she neared the main part of the house, she realized she hadn't thought what she would say to her father. I shall say . . . *what*? Perhaps just to show them to him would be enough? But underneath, the dread thought: once I have done that, where do we, where do I go? *What happens?*

And then in the hall, the worst thing. The two boys and Gib . . .

'It's all right,' Hal said, 'We've been round the stones. Gib took us.'

She said, trying to keep her voice ordinary, 'We should have thought of him. It's just I didn't know he was about.' She'd forgotten in fact that he knew where the keys were. She hoped he hadn't allowed the Ibbotson boy to see where they were kept.

Hal said, 'Stephen has to practise carols at the church before he goes home. I might go with him. Though no one thinks much of my voice.'

'It's all right,' Gib said, 'when you're not borrowing someone else's.'

Alice could hardly bear the teasing, the light-heartedness. The same moment she recalled with a sinking feeling that her father was out. She was sure he had gone out.

'All right, then,' said Hal. 'And thank you, Gib . . .'

Alice said, 'I was just looking for Father.' She noticed suddenly that Gib was looking at her. He said as the boys moved away:

'Something's wrong, Alice –'

'Why ever?' she said in a false voice. 'I'm not *Fräulein*, you know . . .'

He said, 'I wouldn't ask, if you were . . . I'd be too afraid to be drowned in the waterworks.'

She smiled weakly. He persisted: 'Alice, I haven't known you for all these years without being able to realize –'

She stood there, silent. Her tongue seemed to grow to fill her mouth.

'Let's go in –' he looked round – 'the morning-room . . .'

She followed him without protest. When they were inside, she clutched the envelope to her. She said, 'It's in here, and I could never let you see it – *them* . . .'

'Sit down,' he said. 'It would be best if you sat down.' There was a coal fire burning high, and then an easy chair beside it. Across in the corner, a scrapwork screen made by Mama when she was a girl. She sat down – her knees would have given away. Her face felt frozen, even beside the heat of the fire. Tears pricked behind her eyes. Almost without her noticing, they began to course down her face.

Gib leaned forward, took the envelope from her. She said only, 'Don't look at them here.'

He said, 'If they're that terrible, I'll look at them behind the screen.'

She stared into the fire. She knew he was still in the room, but felt that behind the screen, from which there was no sound, he had left her . . .

She realized suddenly that he stood near her on the hearth rug. He had the envelope of prints in his hands. In front of her, very deliberately, he tore them once, twice, and then again. Then he put them on the fire.

'Your mother?' he asked gently.

'Yes.'

He said, 'I didn't ask you before – doing that. It's just in every way the best, and only thing to do . . .'

She sat without moving. The tears still ran.

'Alice,' he began. His own voice did not sound too certain. 'We've always been able to help each other, haven't we?'

'Yes.' (How true that was, how true . . .)

'I've thought, really thought, many, many times, that perhaps we should – help each other – *always* . . .'

She didn't answer. Couldn't answer . . .

He said, 'Do you know what I mean – what it is I'm trying to say?'

'No,' she said, at that moment beginning to understand.

'There isn't any way in which I can actually say it –

without its being either an impertinence, or a cause of distress, or both. The truth is I can't consider myself suitable. The kind of future I have to offer is so much less than you deserve. The life you lead here –'

She interrupted: 'I don't care for it at all.'

He said in a rush, his voice louder now: 'That encourages me to go on – Alice, *will you marry me*?'

The walls seemed suddenly to close in on her, the fire to seem unnaturally bright.

Married. But I was never to be married . . .

She burst out: 'And be like those photographs –'

He knelt down, took both her hands, cold hands, and held them tight. Kissed her hair, all round her forehead. 'Alice, darling Alice, that's not being married. *That's* not being married.'

'Gib,' she said. 'Gib –' Her forehead was against his waistcoat, touched the cold metal of his watch-chain. His hands held her head firmly. Safe . . .

'I would,' she said, a moment later. 'I think I would.'

His face was alight. It wore the expression, the relief, the happiness, as when those years ago she had said to him, 'Yes, I will eat.'

'Yes,' she said, 'I will marry you.'

They sat together, talking almost in their old easy way. Plans, arrangements, ideas. Of course it could not be for a while, the marriage. It might even be several years. He would need money: no question of his living on hers. Her father was not mentioned – not yet. But she knew, and he knew, that approval, although possible, was not probable. It might take much time to persuade him . . .

But, she thought, wouldn't that perhaps be best of all? It didn't have to be tomorrow, next week, next year, even the year after . . . It would be their secret. The most precious they had ever had: that they were, one day, to be together for always. Now, she did not have to imagine any more a life without Gib . . .

A day that had begun so badly, ending so joyfully. Christmas 1912. I shall always remember Christmas 1912 . . .

Christmas 1912, Hal thought, I shall *never* forget Christmas 1912. The most terrible, terrible of my life . . .

On Christmas Eve he had been in the afternoon to a carol service, in which Stephen had been singing. Olive and her mother had been among the congregation. He had caught Olive's eye, and had quickly pulled a face at her, a horrible contortion, and seen her mouth work as she tried to suppress laughter. Mrs Ibbotson, who looked tired and ill, had noticed nothing.

It was later in the afternoon, just after tea, that everything began to go wrong. The atmosphere that he so loved of Christmas had been growing around him all day. Today so lovely because it was anticipation of tomorrow which would be lovelier still.

His biggest present was to be a model steam-roller. He had longed and longed for one – and knew he would get it. They thought they kept it secret, but Gib had let slip something. So had Mother.

Cousin Dorothy who had arrived yesterday had brought her best friend with her. They were to stay till the New Year. Great-Aunt Minnie was here also, and of course Uncle Lionel. Mother and Alice were busy entertaining them.

After tea he had gone up to his room and worked on the rat-trap he was making to his own design. Teddy and Sylvia, he knew, were down in the drawing-room. Each had a song or dance which they would be performing for Cousin Dorothy and the others . . .

There was a knock on the door. Before he could answer Teddy burst in.

'I say,' he protested, 'you don't barge in like that –'

'Mummy wants to speak to you. At once. Downstairs.'

He stood with his hands in his pockets. His mother looked very grave:

'Hal,' she began, 'this is very difficult. I think –' she hesitated – 'perhaps we should wait a few moments? Your father will be with us.'

At once he thought: What have I done? *What have I done?* He ran over in his mind, with alarm, all the misdemeanours, deceits, that might have been discovered. The time he'd overstayed at the farm and kept Gib waiting for a lesson. (But Gib would never . . .) The two panes of glass in one of the greenhouses which he'd broken and just plain forgotten to own up to . . . the result of carelessly thrown wizened apples, gathered up as he walked . . .

Mother, while she waited, seemed to need to keep the conversation going. She said brightly:

'Well, darling, do you think Father Christmas is going to send you your heart's desire?'

It seemed to him a babyish way of talking. And too, he was worried. 'I suppose so,' he said ungraciously. 'I hope so.'

But here was his father . . .

'Your hands out of your pockets, sir!' Grim expression, set face. Clearing his throat.

He began to speak.

The words rolled over Hal. '. . . Your cousin had wanted her friend to visit the Stones Room – or rather, as we conversed . . . I have to say that –' The words seemed to be being weighed. 'I have to say that – I can hardly bring myself – in four of the cabinets, a not inconsiderable number of stones . . . missing. Together with several not particularly distinctive pieces of jewellery . . .'

Silence. I cannot think, Hal told himself, I cannot think that it is possibly anything to do with me.

But he knew even as he thought this, what was to come.

'Hal. *Henry*,' began his father. To stress the gravity of it all, perhaps, he called him Henry.

'Henry, I have to ask you, at this stage, on your honour, if you know anything, *anything at all*, that could help us concerning this –' pause – '*very* serious theft?'

Silence again. Seeming to Hal even longer this time. His father's stomach, as he stood before the fire, gurgled. The sound seemed magnified.

'No, sir. Daddy. No. I don't.' *He knew what was to come* . . .

His father cleared his throat again. 'Hal, we have known about this for only a few hours or so. There is as yet no question of the police. Your mother and I, and Alice, have already spoken together. The whereabouts of the keys are by no means common knowledge. I repeat, *not* common knowledge. I have to say that I would have preferred you not to know . . . the more so, in the present circumstances. But Alice tells me, and Gib Nicolson admits that, foolishly I must say, you and – a friend, were present when he fetched the keys a few days ago . . .'

Why not say it at once? Why this long, long story?

'Henry, the person who has helped himself to these is someone in need of money. Is also, I need hardly add, a thief . . .'

His mother spoke in the pause that followed. 'You know we're speaking of the Ibbotson boy?'

'And,' went on his father, 'what was he *doing* in the first place, a boy like that, in the Stones Room?'

Hal said, looking down at the carpet, 'He just –' he couldn't find the words – 'likes beautiful things . . .'

'Perhaps he does a little more than like them?'

When Hal said nothing, he went on: 'Someone who knows where the keys are kept has helped himself. Someone frequently – too frequently – around at The Towers would not be noticed walking about – even without you . . . Am I right?' He altered his stance before the fire slightly.

'The jewellery could possibly be traced, identified by description. The stones, not.'

Hal began to feel sick. He turned towards his mother, and perhaps from nerves spoke directly to her.

'I can tell you, Mummy – he, Stephen, hasn't stolen *anything*.'

His father protested: 'Henry – this was not a break-in. There are no signs of damage. This was a theft by one who knows the house . . . There is of course always a chance, unlikely, that among the staff someone has stumbled upon the keys' whereabouts – their hiding place. The odds are against it.' He paused. 'Some people might say, have said, that I should take such a matter a great deal more seriously, that it should be more of an orthodox strong room, perhaps even a night watchman . . . If indeed the Diamond Waterfall and other lesser but very valuable jewellery were kept there, it would be a different matter. No, the stones are not of sentimental value. They are insured. But the matter can hardly end there. Nor would the insurance company permit it.'

He saw his father look at his mother. She looked away as he went on:

'What I have to say you may find unpleasant, but I am going to suggest, *ask*, that as soon as possible you visit your friend – who, remember, has been given, foolishly in my judgement, entry through the front door, the run of the house . . . You must visit him, and ask him, as *one friend to another*, if – if it is he, the thief. In that case, if he owns up like a man (and the goods are immediately returned), no more will be heard of it . . . Otherwise, it's a matter for the police . . .'

He saw his mother nod, at the same time frowning. Perhaps, could he hope that she realized how impossible, horrible, *degrading* such a task would be?

'I think you will agree that in the circumstances this is a more than generous offer?'

Hal said, in an angry voice:

'But he didn't *do it*. He hasn't done it – sir . . .'

He said it again a moment later, appealing to his mother: 'But – but –' His voice which nowadays he could not trust plunged downwards and then rose again. '*Stephen hasn't done it*!'

His mother looked at him. She said gently:

'Well, *he* can tell you that, can't he?'

He didn't know whether he was supposed to go over to the farm that day. Plainly it wasn't possible. But how could they expect him to live through Christmas? Later that evening his mother hugged him and said impulsively:

'I know – how you're feeling, darling. But –' she half smiled – 'it'll be all right, truly . . .'

What made them think it would be all right? How could it be all right to have to ask Stephen something like that? Why could not *they* do it?

He didn't see Gib and was glad because he would not have liked to discuss it with him at all. Alice said only, 'I know about it and it's very unpleasant. But it will have to be done . . .'

On Christmas morning, straight after church, he was driven over in the motor.

Of course they were surprised to see him. He thought afterwards that he ought to have brought presents. Except, how could he? He wanted only to die, standing there, saying:

'Could I have a word with Stephen – alone, please?'

He didn't know how to say it. Although he must have rehearsed it twenty times. The words were jumbled together – but the sense must have been plain enough. He ended up lamely: 'They made me come and ask you . . . I have to tell them, that I've asked you . . .'

Stephen had gone very white.

'Bye!' he exclaimed. 'Bye . . . Buggers all, aren't ye? If there's dirty work to be done, let 'em come up this way and do it – and not send the likes of ye –'

Hal said in a tight voice, 'What am I to tell them? I mean, *I know* –'

'Stephen interrupted: 'Mebbe. And mebbe not – eh? Any road, the words – they've been said. They're said now.'

'What words?'

He saw himself again as at Jack's death. Why can't I do it right? he cried inside. Why can't I do it right?

'That I'm reckoned a thief . . .'

'I never said that –'

'I'm deaf, then. And a dunderhead and all. Not just a thief . . .'

Hal said despairingly, 'They sent me up. I had no choice.' (But he had. *He had. He could have refused to come* . . .)

'I'll go back and say, what I knew all along –'

Stephen said abruptly, 'Aye, go back. And when you're back – stay back.' His face was pinched with anger. He turned at once and went into the farmhouse.

There was nothing to be gained by trying to go in there, trying to say anything further. I have made a mess of it – an impossible task. He felt a great wave of hatred towards *them*, those who sat on high and gave orders. *I should have refused*, he thought.

As they drove off, he saw Olive's face framed at the window. Olive was always curious . . .

His father said, 'He denies it, then?'

Hal said, 'Of course he does – because he didn't do it.'

His father said gravely, 'I am afraid I can hardly agree. He has – lost his chance. We shall have to proceed. After that, the matter will be out of my hands. And yours.'

Oh but, Hal thought, it is already out of mine. He wanted yesterday again, so that he could do it right. So that he could refuse, so that even if he approached Stephen it would be as someone on *his* side.

The meal was a misery. It tasted of dust. He could not find

the saliva to chew it. The younger children knew nothing of the upset and were loud and over-excitable, especially the twelve-year-old Teddy. Father was even sharper with her than usual and she burst into angry tears. Nan-Nan had to deal with her upstairs. She came down, chastened, for the present-giving.

There was his Mamood steam-roller. Large, gleaming. His heart's desire. Except that he no longer wanted it. How could he ever have wanted it? He thought of refusing it, to make up for what he should have refused yesterday. But where would that get him or Stephen? He said only, rather ungraciously:

'Very nice. Thank you.'

Great-Aunt Minnie said, 'A spoilt lad, Robert. Lily. That's the trouble with the eldest. Impossible to please. A *spoilt* lad . . .'

The police were called in. They arrived the next day. He did not know whether his father had doctored the date of discovery. All the staff and several people in the house were interviewed, Hal among them. He was treated kindly if a little severely. He was asked some questions about Stephen. To all of them, whether relevant or not, he answered:

'He didn't do it.'

Sergeant Appleyard said, '*Who* did it, is our business . . . Just answer the questions, sir, young fellow-me-lad . . .'

(But they had been blood brothers . . . He wanted to say, '*We were blood brothers* . . .')

Afterwards he didn't know what was happening about it all, and was afraid to ask. His father seemed to be deliberately avoiding him. In the end he asked his mother. She seemed as before, embarrassed by it all. She said only:

'I don't think the police are much farther forward.'

He thought he might perhaps of his own accord go up to the farm. But he did nothing. Then, the first market day of the New Year, he went into Settstone. It was an icy day with snow already falling as he walked towards the market square. He had come on his bicycle, which he'd regretted: he had had to walk a great deal of the way even where the ground was not hilly.

There was a good hope of seeing Stephen at the market. He

felt certain the Ibbotsons would be selling wethers there. And he was lucky – if what happened, he thought later, could be called luck . . .

Where the shivering sheep were penned together, there were James, Stephen, and two boys from Moor Bottom Farm. At first Stephen didn't see him. Then as Hal got nearer, and was about to speak (he kept thinking, if I can speak to him alone only a few moments, *I could explain*), he must have noticed. For he looked straight at Hal – then through him. Beyond.

He was near now. He said, 'Stephen –'

Stephen said loudly, to the others, 'Right. Aye. I'll be away, then.' He touched the shoulder of one of the boys, and moved off. James looked awkward. Pushed at one of the sheep with his hand, then turned his head away. He had coloured. Hal turned away too. There was, after all, nothing to be done.

But he could not, would not, give up so easily. Nothing more had been said about the stones. There were no more visits by the police. When he asked Alice, she told him:

'Oh, I think the insurance people are paying . . .'

It had all been, they seemed to imply, a bit of a storm in a teacup. A storm, yes – but in a teacup? It seemed to him that it had been his whole world rocked . . .

In the end, because he could bear it no longer, he decided to go up to the farm. He would somehow force his way in, make them listen, make *Stephen* listen. I *must* be forgiven . . .

Lessons had already started again. He had some Xenophon to prepare for Gib, and sitting over it one afternoon, Liddell and Scott open beside him, he suddenly threw it down. He set out for the farm.

It was another bleak, icy day. The light, scarcely arrived, was beginning to go already as he came up the lane to the farm. Tess barked as he came into the yard.

'Hush,' he cried, 'hush. You know me – you know me –' That she should bark at him seemed in itself a bad omen.

It was Olive who answered the door. He tried to smile. She didn't.

'Well,' he said. 'Can I come in?'

She shook her head, her face grave. 'You'd best not.'

'Is Stephen there? Because –'

She shook her head again, her hand on the door, ready to push it to.

'I want to come in. *Please.*'

She looked unsure. Then, as if cornered: 'I can't stop you, then.'

The kitchen had only Granny Willans in it. She was asleep, her cotton cap fallen forward, the unlaced boots a little too near the hearth. Hal said,

'I'll be very quiet.'

Olive said, 'There's no call. She'd sleep through a stampede. Her ears, they're going fast.' Her voice had for a moment slipped into its old friendly tone.

His boots slithered a little on the sandy floor. He sat down at the scrubbed bare table. Olive picked up a broom, and began sweeping the sand from the floor. It was a Friday: tomorrow he knew they would lay down rags. Her clogs squeaked.

'Olive – where's Stephen? If I could just –'

She burst out: 'He's gone. And it's your fault –'

'What do you mean, *gone*?'

'Like I said, gone.' Her voice caught, and he saw she was crying. 'He's gone for a soldier . . .'

'*What*?'

'What I said . . . He went through to York. It's Militia or summat. He's – they said a drummer, on account of he's not a very big un. And, well, that's it. He's left us and all.'

'But – why a soldier? Olive, *why*?'

'On account of he was angry. Very, very angry –'

'With me?'

'Have I to talk about it, then? Have I to tell you all? I'd rather not –' She said it in a brave little voice. Then, pushing the broom aside, she sat at the table, and buried her face in her hands. Granny Willans snored on.

'I wish you'd tell me. I can't get anybody – nobody'll talk to me at all.'

She said, tears in her voice. 'What happened was, they came. Police came. Fetched him down to t'station. He was there while breakfast-time – all t'time you're allowed there without they put you away. And there were others up here . . . going through everything.' She said with disgust,

'Prying. Nosing. Great hands in . . . What do'ye think that means to us? Mam, she's took to her bed. She's been badly since. Right since Stephen left us. She took it bad, very bad –'

'I never meant,' he said. 'If only –'

'If only,' she said, '*if only* – then he'd not be gone, would he? I'm that sick at heart. The shame.' She shuddered. 'What do you ken, that kind of shame? *Honest* folk . . .'

He did then what he knew to be wrong – and hopeless too.

'But,' he protested, 'if I can't come back . . . can't come here . . . what shall I do? Tess, when she has her puppies in the spring, I was going – And, Olive, I'm used to lead the bracken down, every year. Every year.' He said desperately, 'You *need* me . . .'

'Nay.' She said it kindly, but firmly. 'You're not needed. And that's all about it, Hal Firth . . .'

There seemed nothing to do then but go home. When he got to The Towers again it was already quite dark. He could remember nothing of the walk back.

22

Lily watched as Teddy sang, her voice surprisingly deep:

> 'I'm Gilbert the Filbert, the Knut with a K,
> The pride of Piccadilly, the blase roué . . .

She strutted to and fro, wearing a silk opera hat. (Robert's surely?)

> 'O Hades! the ladies who leave their wooden huts . . .'

Her fourteenth birthday party, held partly in, parly out of doors. On one of the hottest days in that hot July of 1914.

'Come on, Gib.' She stopped suddenly. 'Come on – you do it *much* better . . .'

Amy Hawksworth urged too. 'Come on, Gib –'

Gib had been at the piano. He got up, and said good naturedly, 'All right, Teddy Bear. Give me the hat.'

When she sang, her face at an angle, shadowed, looked suddenly like Valentin. Familiar stab at the heart. Memory. Then: as we were.

Teddy and Gib sang together:

> 'O Hades! the ladies who leave their wooden huts,
> For Gilbert the Filbert, the Col'nel of the Knuts . . .'

French windows, open on to the lawn. Tea, which had been served outside, was now all cleared away. The party was almost over.

> 'O Hades! the ladies . . .'

Lily wondered if Hal would join in. She suspected him of having more talent than either Teddy or Gib, even if it was at this stage only imitative. But he looked more thoroughly bored by the whole occasion. She suspected he would like to be off somewhere, by himself probably. Where? Certainly he no longer went to the farm. Not since the upset. The Ibbotson boy had anyway enlisted – Thief or no, better that way, perhaps . . .

'It's the cutest little thing . . .
Don't you ask me what it means . . .'

Amy at the piano stumbled over the notes.

Hitchy koo, Hitchy koo . . .

Gib and Teddy dancing together. Teddy in white broderie anglaise party frock, well above her ankles, was at least comfortably dressed. Lily, never able to resist fashion, wore this afternoon a new dress, primrose yellow, ninon, cloth of gold, but so tight around the ankles that she could walk only with ridiculous little steps. She could certainly not Hitchy Koo . . .

Gib and Teddy held hands. Teddy said, 'My thanks to Mr Nicolson. Ladies and Gentlemen, that is positively the end of my birthday recital . . .' She bobbed a curtsey. Giggled. Amy giggled too.

Alice, wearing *her* best frock, was not looking happy. She seemed on the whole to dislike frivolity: was sometimes quite irritable with Gib when he and Teddy fooled together – as they so often did.

She wondered sometimes about this whole question of an engagement between Gib and Alice. It seemed to her altogether a strange affair. I could not tolerate it, she thought. Certainly officially, there was no engagement. Robert was not for it at all. When the subject had first been broached, a year or eighteen months ago, he had not been encouraging. And Alice, Lily knew, would never think of defying him . . .

To Lily, he had said, 'Pleasant enough fellow, Nicolson. Does a good job as a tutor. But – as a son-in-law . . . Hardly a brilliant – even a particularly suitable – match. And how is he to support her? A schoolmaster . . . Too proud, I trust, to live off his wife. We shall see. But it's scarcely, I think – to be encouraged.'

Yet they seemed suited enough. And the situation in the meantime was if nothing else slightly awkward. Unconventional. She wondered if she should suggest to Alice that she intercede for her? After all, she is twenty-nine. Not exactly a child. Nor beautiful. It is not as if many Prince Charmings had come begging her hand (perhaps we should have been firmer about a Season?). To many, Gib with his good looks might well pass as Florizel . . . She thought of Daisy who had left her upholstered home in Westcliffe Avenue for one room in the Leylands – and yet that fairy story, a real one, looked now to end happily ever after . . .

'Can't Amy play the piano for us?'

'I *can't*. I haven't any pieces without the book . . .'

'You know *In the Shadows*,' said Teddy. 'Gib and I want to do a funny dance as an encore.'

'Who encored you?' Alice asked, seeming to joke, but her voice tart.

Robert wasn't there. Fortunately, Lily thought, for he seemed to find difficulty in being anything other than cold and critical towards Teddy. (If he knew about his opera hat . . .)

Nor was Sadie there. Sadie, happily, sat with her feet up at the Hall. She would not be going out again till after the baby. She had stopped, some while since, all her good works for children, so as to give herself every chance to have a baby safely. And although she'd miscarried yet again, at Easter last year, *this* baby, due in a few weeks, would surely be the long-awaited second son – who could not possibly replace Jack, but who might help to blunt just a little the sorrow Sadie felt still so keenly.

Sadie said, 'This cousin of Charlie's, at the Curragh camp, they're really worried about war. I know it's maybe different for me, but Unionists, Nationalists – British fighting British, it's like brother fighting brother. Charlie says the situation really looks ugly. Civil war . . .'

She was lying outside on a chaise-longue. The afternoon even hotter than yesterday. She was dressed in white, lace at her wrists and throat. Her small face, concerned, rose from the frothy white. Her hands, though, lay quiet over her belly, as if she kept the child safe.

She said, 'I'm not sure I even understand it, really.'

Lily said, 'The Protestants in Ulster want to go on belonging to England. They don't want Home Rule for the Irish. And are prepared to fight about it.'

Then, 'Why, there's Charlie,' Sadie cried. Lily rather

hoped he would not come across to them. She still avoided him when she could, but it was not often possible. He too, although no longer rude as at one time, still seemed offhand in her company. She often wanted to say to him, 'What was it, after all? If you could just have kept quiet . . . It was kissing and *telling*, made the trouble . . .'

'I was just saying to Lily, Charlie, that you're worried about Algie.'

'The cavalry cousin. Yes, he's about to resign. Can't countenance fighting against Ulster. A sorry tale . . . Perhaps my wife's country will send back some of its dollar millionaires – who one time fled the Famine – to make possibly an industrial nation of the Irish . . .'

He sat at Sadie's feet, long legs stretched out. After a moment he said, yawning:

'There are matters in Europe I suppose one should at least be noticing. Those dreadful Balkans again . . . Austrian Emperor on his high steed, Russkies getting involved. When I think my grandfather fought them at Sebastopol . . .'

He poured himself a glass of the lemonade which stood on the table beside Sadie. Mopped his brow. 'Good stuff. Perhaps something stronger, in a bit? Shall we?'

A fortnight later, on the last day of July, Sadie had her baby. A son. Lily saw him on Bank Holiday Monday when he was two days old. She was one of Sadie's first outside visitors.

Charlie came upstairs to join them. There was champagne. The baby was perfect, although ugly. They had spoken often of how they would celebrate. Their mood now was odd, fragile.

Sadie said, 'I guess it's not really joyful the way it should be. I just wish – the news . . .'

Charlie said, 'What's happened is that we're going to show Germany you don't do that sort of thing . . . Stern lesson required. Walking over Belgium indeed! There's wild enthusiasm reported in London. I wouldn't mind having a go myself . . .'

'Charlie,' murmured Sadie weakly, lying back against the pillows.

Lily said, 'You had your War – and were lucky.'

In spite of Charlie's robust talk, she could feel only fear

and the fragility of the moment. She was ashamed too of how often she had said to herself these last few eventful days: thank God, Hal will be all right. A fifteen-year-old boy . . . And Sadie – a son in the cradle. Valentin's face came before her suddenly. (But he is thirty-six, thirty-seven. And Rumania not any part of this . . .)

'The German governess,' Charlie asked. 'I heard something –'

'She left yesterday, but would have gone home anyway this week for a holiday. It's sad after all these years . . .'

Embarrassing too. Fräulein had always been emotional, but her farewells this time really exceeded everything . . . The result possibly of worry about her dreadful brother. Weeping and clinging to me, wanting Alice of course, who would not be back from Filey until tea-time. The whole household in a general upset . . .

'I want to say something, Lady Firth, please what I have to tell – there are too many tears . . . I cannot. You are kind, kind, while I . . . Please, help . . . I cannot. Lady Firth, please, I write when I am again in Germany . . .' Her moon face at the window of the motor was the last Lily saw of her. Teddy and Sylvia stood at the bottom of the steps; Sylvia, who cried readily, in tears.

'A toast then,' Charlie said, 'Great God, we *do* have something to celebrate. Another fifteen years or so and he'll be crossing the grouse moors with me. We're calling him Christopher, you know. Christopher. Did Sadie tell you? After that same grandfather who fought the Russkies . . .'

Alice snapped miserably at Teddy. Over-excited, she was rushing about talking of all she would do in the War.

'Why not some knitting? It'll be cold in October, if they're still out there. Wool and needles are a lot more use than a song and dance act –'

Teddy didn't knit well, but began at once a body belt in khaki, casting on enough stitches to girth Goliath. Alice knitted also. To still her nerves. The War against Germany was nearly two weeks old. Gib had applied at once for a Territorial commission and expected, because of his experience at Marlborough in the early days of the OTC, not to have long to wait. In the meantime something must be arranged for Hal's tuition. Gib told him:

'We'll get a retired schoolmaster. Someone out at grass. Gentle. Won't work you as hard as I do . . .'

But it wasn't just her anxiety about Gib and his going that caused her to be snappish – it was, rather, the question of marriage. This marriage that they spoke of perhaps five or six times a year, that Gib had been saving towards, which *would* take place – one day.

She had not been in a hurry. She had felt safe, even in the face of Papa's evident discouragement. If it was necessary she would defy him, *when the time came*. But now, with War declared, Gib was behaving quite differently. He said, almost every day now:

'Alice, dear Alice, let's *get married* . . .'

But it was the maddest of times to choose, with the whole of Europe in turmoil, no one knowing what was to happen. He could not mean it . . .

'Alice, darling, there are hasty marriages everywhere. People who a few weeks ago hadn't even thought . . . *We've* been decided over eighteen months – and have known each other for –'

'All the more reason to be sensible. We know and can trust each other.'

'But if we truly want to spend our lives together, we should commit ourselves *now*. Or at least very soon. For, darling Alice, *men are being killed* . . .'

She did not want to hear of that, of what might happen to him, even expressed in so roundabout a way . . . She said in a voice cold with fright:

'Why would it be better to make a widow of me?'

'I never said – Ah, Alice,' he sounded despairing, and she thought suddenly that she might perhaps be wrong. And yet, if he would wait just a little longer . . .

'I could,' she began, 'perhaps if we – when it's all over by Christmas we can talk again –'

'And if it's not – over?'

But it would be, must be. And anyway, she told him, it was always best to let things rest before hurrying a decision.

'I love you,' she said, burying her face in his neck, just above his stiff collar. 'You do know that I love you?'

She did not care to meet his eyes.

'I just want,' he said, his arms tight about her, so that her face was trapped, 'I just want – *us*.'

23

In the days of Stephen and Jack he had never been lonely. Even when alone. Now he was always lonely. They did not seem to think of that. Teddy, who spent much of her time with Amy and now had a Belgian refugee friend, was no companion.

Everything was wrong and changed and sad. Six months of the War had altered everything. Since the end of September The Towers had been a hospital for officers: a small one, and only for lighter cases so that it was half way between hospital and convalescent home. It had no operating theatre but offered treatment such as electrical massage. The conversion took up most of the house, and the family had separate quarters. Teddy and Amy liked to busy themselves helping: reading to the officers, writing letters . . . Mother was officially Lady Director, and had a lot to do with the organizing of everything, although some man, not a doctor, had come from York or London to be in over-all charge. Father was busy – Hal was not sure with what, but he addressed rallies and sat with Mr Hawksworth on committees . . .

Meanwhile he was a schoolboy (even though he had never been to school). Alice had said only the other day, on five days' leave from London where she was learning to be a nurse, 'You're lucky that you are still a *schoolboy* –' and had paid no attention when he answered sulkily that he would really prefer not to be.

Gib's departure in September – although he was still in England – had meant the engagement, as threatened, of a new tutor. The promised 'retired schoolmaster'. His name was Mr Stainthorpe, and he was worse, far worse, than the bandy-legged Mr Pettinger, shared long ago with Jack. Among other faults, he was critical of Gib, which Hal could not tolerate:

'I think my rather young predecessor, although we must not of course speak ill of those who presently risk life and limb . . . but one would have thought more emphasis on Euclid and perhaps less on Horace (and by the way I do not care for Conington's translation to be used . . .'). He would make also glancing, dry, insulting remarks to Hal himself, adding immediately afterwards, 'Of course you must not take what I say *litteratim et verbatim.*'

Since he lived with them, his presence had to be endured at mealtimes too. He was aptly named, for his large drooping faded auburn moustache was stained always with food or drink. And even (spied during Greek parsing), small particles of meat or vegetables lodging there. Ugh. Oh come back, Gib.

Studying had once been fun; now it was meaningless. What had it to do with what was happening in the *real* world?

From the very first days of the War, he had worried about Stephen. How not? Stephen was in the Army, a Regular. But he was always without real news. Once, he spoke to Olive and her mother outside the church, wishing them a good Christmas. He learned through other sources that Stephen was in France.

Then in the third week of January, he heard his name read out in church. Killed in action. None of the Ibbotsons were at the service. He thought of going up to the farm, but then he thought: I do it only for myself, that I may feel better. He would not want to distress Olive further . . .

For the rest of the day, and most of the night, he raged. He was not sure who he was angry with. God? the Hun? His parents who had caused the break? Stephen, gone now *for ever. We were once blood brothers* . . .

His mother said to him, kindly enough, 'That is sad news, Hal, about the Ibbotson boy . . .'

In his pain the next day he said angrily to Mr Stainthorpe, 'Yes. No. Yes, you silly old basket . . .

'*Henry*, you realize the meaning of that word?'

'Sir –'

'Then apologize. *At once*, Henry . . .'

There was no one to whom he could talk. He did not believe there was anyone who cared. In his free time he walked about the places they had trout-fished together, often going perilously near the farm. It is all hopeless, he thought.

But then, waking up one morning, he knew suddenly what

he must do. He wondered he had not thought of it at once. How often had Mr Stainthorpe said unctuously, 'If only it were possible for me to have a go at the Hun . . .'

But I, Hal thought, *I can.*

It was a little more difficult than he had expected at first, and he had to make perhaps unnecessarily elaborate plans. The essential was that he should not be found and brought back at once. (He remembered a tale of Mother locked in her bedroom for over a week . . . Not that modern parents would do such a thing . . .)

From the moment of his decision he was filled with energy. Where had it all been hiding? Everything he did, everywhere he went, he felt purposeful . . . If he were to join up, to enlist, it would at once solve everything. The dreadful half-life that he led, the chafing, the restlessness. This life where everyone, even Teddy and Amy, seemed to be some part of the War effort. And since too he was beginning to be a nuisance, he didn't expect to be missed – or at least not too much. Mother might worry a little at first. But the hospital, which obviously she found all-absorbing, would soon take care of that.

To keep Mr Stainthorpe off the scent, he did two unasked-for theorems, beautifully set out. ('Well, well, young Firth, we're beginning to pull ourselves together just a *little*, eh?')

Money. He had four guineas, three half-sovereigns and five sovereigns – from Christmas, his birthday, and a secret hoard.

The practical aspects of his departure occupied him a great deal. He thought he would like best a Yorkshire regiment. But he didn't want to go and enlist in Richmond or York. Leeds? The idea pleased him. Mother had run away from Leeds. I shall run away *to* Leeds, he thought . . . Name? He could not dare to be Firth, just in case. (They might go to all sorts of lengths. Father's friends. The War Office . . .) Mother again: *she'd* changed to Greene. So why not be Greenwood, the name she'd left behind as the train for Kings Cross steamed out that Sunday?

Henry Greenwood. The new person took shape. Henry Greenwood spoke with an accent – the one Hal knew best, here in the dale. He was a farm labourer staying with his auntie in Leeds. *And there was nothing wrong with his heart.*

In the event, he managed to get away less than seventy-two hours after he had first had the idea.

He left a note: 'For King and Country. My country needs me, more than you do. *Please do not worry about me.* Love from Hal.'

He reached Leeds about midday. On the way there, he had spoken only with his accent – when he had spoken at all. Now, once arrived, there was a proper order of doing things. He was thinking all the time, with a keyed-up excitement, that it must not go wrong. The sooner he signed on, and was *in* . . .

At the station, he thought: They will want an address. It would not do to invent that. He bought a newspaper to give himself some ideas, taking it with him into the nearest eating-rooms. He had had nothing all day and now, ravenous and nervous, he ordered sausage and mash with a mound of onions. But after a few mouthfuls, he thought people were watching him, guessing, and he left the plate half-eaten.

He took a tram from the station and got off in Briggate. He was in the centre of Leeds. Passing a branch of Greenwood's, he coloured, as if already found out . . .

He had visited Leeds only a handful of times, taken to see Grandad Greenwood. He could remember only that the house had been in Roundhay. Aunt Ethel lived at Huby. She had all Grandad's money, and wanted nothing to do with anyone else.

He was pleased to find a large arcade, which looked to have in it everything he wanted. He began with a cheap suitcase. Then as he walked along the marbled floor, he saw a huge pair of spectacles, the trade sign above the optician's, and thought of buying a pair to alter his appearance. But then: They won't take me with bad eyesight, he thought.

At a draper's he bought underwear and then, two doors down, a dark suit for twenty-two shillings (it was his clothes he feared might give him away), and a cap for a shilling. He came out of the shop wearing them: his Norfolk jacket and knickerbockers in the suitcase together with his new underclothes. Second-hand boots he bought for four shillings. He was ready then for the barber's, half way down the arcade on the right. He asked for a lot to be cut off, telling the barber he'd been ill. Seeing the close crop, the gaunt face: yes, he did look older . . .

By now he felt hungry again. He had noticed the Lyons sign when he first entered the arcade. Now, suitcase beside him, he had two teacakes and a pot of tea. As he sat there, cheered by the tea, mischief got into him, so that, wildly, he thought of pretending to be German. He felt a great temptation to tell the woman opposite him, in the voice of Fräulein, all the woes of Augustin . . .

Before he left he bought from Mooney's a quarter of creme toffee. Then through to the street outside. He had entered the Arcade, Hal Firth. He came out now, Henry Greenwood . . .

'Age?'

The recruiting sergeant had a red face, with one eye larger than the other. His voice was not unkind.

'*Age*, sonny?'

'S – sixteen –'

'Right, well . . . come back when you're nineteen, sonny. Tomorrow, eh?'

Dismissed. After all the care he'd taken, the rehearsals, the preparations. And his accent that had never slipped. Sixteen. Sixteen *How could I?*

He went to one of the addresses he had noted. Albert Terrace. He explained that he'd enlisted and would soon be leaving. He took a room for three nights – the least she'd take – and paid in advance. She was a small, distracted woman who kept looking over her shoulder as she spoke. He remembered he'd neither brought, nor bought nightclothes and wash things. He cleaned his teeth with soap and the edge of the rough towel provided.

'Age, sonny?'

He had it pat this time . . .

'Not run away from home, none of that, eh? Address now. Address . . .'

Heart, troublesome heart. It was that he feared the most. Already it had begun its thumping, its missed beats. It could not, *must* not betray him.

There were others there: boys, men, but he could scarcely notice them. A short, pale-skinned youth, stretching (to appear taller?) said something he didn't catch. Outside it was raining. Inside, it smelled damp and nervous.

'Chest out. Say ninety-nine.'

Ears, eyes, limbs, private parts, reflexes, feet, skull, heart. Heart. Heart. It was all over in moments. Stethoscope on bare chest. Tap, tap. Sandy-haired doctor with a Scots accent, talking to a colleague, not talking to him. 'Sound as a bell, this one . . . farm . . . life in the fresh air. As I said . . . city lads . . .'

Address? Next of kin. 'Miss Olive Ibbotson.' I must be mad, he thought afterwards. I *am* mad.

He was sworn in with thirty others. Hand held up. Holy words. God, swearing. He wondered if it was blasphemous that he'd kept his accent. And who was it had sworn: Firth, or Greenwood?

He had till nine the next morning to report at barracks. He told his landlady. 'I shan't need the third night. I've to report tomorrow . . .'

Never, he thought, had he seen teeth so white, so plainly, triumphantly false. Their owner was stocky, with coarse dark hair, a sallow pitted skin, and a wide smile. He was known as Snowy because of his name, White. Not, he told Hal, on account of his teeth . . .

'. . . they don't fit, like. They *look* good, but they don't fit . . .' And they didn't: seeming to slip up and down as he spoke or ate, or even just thought. Hal couldn't take his eyes off them.

'I'd thought, you see, to go back, have 'em tightened. Folk said as they might fall in the works –'

Snowy worked for Glovers at Wortley Low Mills. He'd enlisted with his next-door neighbour, Bert Varley, who at twenty-five was older than him by six years. Bert's pale brown hair, already half receded, gave him an air of great maturity. He was a grocery assistant at (of all places), a branch of Greenwood's.

'They've said they'll keep my job open. *Said* that, Greenwood's did . . .'

Earlier he'd asked Hal suspiciously: 'You're never one of *those* Greenwoods?'

'Never,' Hal said, and Snowy had added,

'Him here, he's a farm lad, nowt to do with grocers . . .'

Bert said then, but pleasantly enough, 'There's another Greenwood at the barracks so I thought maybe –'

'It's a Northern name.' Hal cut him short.

'Any road,' Bert said, 'there's no Greenwood at the head of it now . . . It's someone else from the family. I've been with 'em twelve years all but – eight behind the counter. Kirkgate branch and then Boar Lane.'

It was important he got the job back because he had been courting Winnie Mason for six years – and would be marrying her as soon as he got his first leave.

'They've to give it me back – after Duration.'

They spoke often of the Duration, because they'd signed on for 'three years or the duration'. It was easy to guess which was the sooner . . .

Leaving Yorkshire. They had marched about midday to the station, and he'd feared that in the crowd there might be someone looking for him. Many of the recruits had parents and relations, little brothers and sisters come to wave goodbye. Tears in eyes. Not France yet, though. Going southwards.

As far as Derby only. They were cheered as they marched to barracks. On the way in the train compartment he'd learned three new swear words, and how to play Crown and Anchor.

Margarine on bread – he had never eaten margarine before. From the Quartermaster's stores they were given straw palliasses: his bed was numberedeight. Sorting themselves out . . . time to kill before Roll Call at half past nine. They weren't allowed out that first evening – what might they not get up to? Some might go into the town and never come back . . . Rushing to the canteen, suddenly hungry, spending the last of his one and ninepence daily ration allowance.

It was there he'd first seen those teeth of Snowy's biting into a pork pie . . .

'Farm lad, eh? Know all about pigs – help put t'pigs in pig pie, eh?'

Then Snowy had called over Bert who bought them both a pint, and told Hal all about Winnie. Snowy said with a wink:

'He'll not be wanting any dick here in Derby, won't Bert. Keeping it all for Winnie, he is . . .'

Bed number nine, next to Hal, had a boy whose face looked nicely wicked. He had curly hair, eyes that darted about, and teeth that were the opposite of Snowy's. Too many of them, crooked and crowding his mouth. He was small too. His pals had been stretching him for two weeks, he said. He'd only *just* made it . . .

Gus Wilkinson. Gus was another who hoped to get his job back – but feared he wouldn't. He loved it. Butcher's boy with a tricycle and a basket full of joints and sausages, and a chance to chat at the tradesman's entrance. Gossip, stories continued week by week, cups of tea, girls . . . Whistling through the gaps in his teeth, getting a song on the brain and taking it all around Leeds. Him and his trike.

'Me and my trike. They said to me, "Right, lad – you go, and there's plenty'll want your place – And they'll get it . . ." '

Snowy. Bert. Gus. Henry. Somewhere in the strangeness and rush of those first days – they had all chummed up together. No particular reason, he thought afterwards. It just happened.

'Squad! Squad *shun*! To the right in fours – Form *fours* – Right! By the left, quick march, left right, left right . . .'

'You may have broken your mother's heart, but you bloody well won't break mine . . .'

Drill, getting punished. Grousing, not sleeping, Reveillé, unbelievably early in the icy cold February dawn. Hungry. The one and ninepence didn't go far in the canteen – and why *was* he so hungry? As if everything he was trying not to feel and trying not to think had left him quite empty . . . Meat and turnips, pie and turnips, liver and bacon, another helping, one's not enough. He was determined not to touch the remainder of his gold. Just the silver change – soon gone.

Easy enough to keep up the accent, easy enough to make them believe he had worked on a farm, since he had. Had he not once felt, wished himself, more Ibbotson than Firth?

There *was* another Greenwood, he learned soon enough, who'd been sworn in before him, so that Hal became 6904 Greenwood, to distinguish him. With all the exercise, he toughened up again, as he had been in those farming summers.

He was Henry Greenwood, and he had his pals Snowy and Gus and Bert – one of the four of them always in some sort of trouble. Even Bert, who tried hard enough but ended each day, each march, each drill, with a patient, puzzled slightly hurt expression. (Sarge: 'Don't look so pained, Private Varley – it's me what's suffering . . .')

Bert: Hal could imagine him at the counter taking down patiently the grocery orders of vague old ladies, demanding cook-generals. When he wrote to Winnie, which he did every other day, he would moisten the pencil tip and then when he'd finished, from habit put the pencil behind his ear. (Just like Snowy who kept a half smoked fag behind his ear – and got into trouble for it.)

Puttees. They ought, with practice, to have been possible. Silly cunts. Roll on, Duration, I can't roll me puttees. A bulge top or bottom. A bulge just when they were *almost* done. Left leg perfect, right leg wrong, right leg perfect, left . . .

He had his pals, though.

Snowy said, 'Best day's work I ever – getting meself them teeth. Always had a ache, like, before, top or bottom, allus one or t'other.'

'My cousin,' Gus told them, 'my cousin Arnold, he saw this notice, Xmas time, for the cycling corps it was. It said large letters at bottom "Bad teeth no bar".'

'Well,' said Snowy, 'so what then?'

'They took him right enough. Only heck, he couldn't ride a bike. He'd never – they give you one, see, he thought it'd be easy, like – but no matter how he tried, he couldn't, he'd no notion. They've put him some other place, me Dad says. He's summat with guns now . . .'

Early days yet – so that it was still novel and weird and not *too* bad. He could be, if not comfortably at least mindlessly, 6904 Greenwood. The pain of Stephen was lessening a little, because just by being here he was going to avenge him. One day.

After a few beers the usually peaceful natures of all four of them would devise what they'd do to the Hun when they got the chance. Bert knew some terrible stories, worse than any that had been in the papers. About women's titties being cut off. Anyone who could do *that* . . . And if Von Kluck came over here, it would happen to *their* mothers and sisters and sweethearts. Winnie was in his, in all their minds. They would all be defending Winnie.

Homesickness caught up with him when he least expected it. Early in the third week he'd been bawled at by Sarge (hadn't they all been saying the night before what they'd do to *him* if they got the chance . . .) for not moving quick enough. He had reacted and for a second only given him the Look which he'd used so often in the last few months for Mr Stainthorpe . . .

Next thing he knew he was up for something called Dumb Insolence. 6904 Private Greenwood got six days Confined to Barracks. Jankers. Gus had been there in their first week and was especially sympathetic: it had been the usual, he said, emptying urinal tubs, all that. Hal got mess waiter fatigues. That way he saw for the first time the officers all together. They were eating, drinking well. One with his smooth freckled face reminded Hal of Gib. The meal had the look of one at The Towers. The room smelled the same: food, drink, wine remaining in glasses, Stilton, whatever. A disorder, expensive, which was no concern of theirs, someone else's work. A manner like Mr Hawksworth's. A pyramid of washing-up.

His last evening, a slight, moist-skinned officer was talking to another, heavier, pouch-faced, dark. Suddenly they took notice of Hal. Earlier in the week the one who reminded him of Gib had thrust on him the end of a box of peppermint fondants – marked 'carminative'. Tonight the pouchy-faced one said,

'I say – you, Private, what's your name?'

'Greenwood, 6904 Greenwood, sir.'

'Right, Greenwood.' He turned a second, then, 'Have a cigar, old chap,' he said to Hal. 'Ever tried one?'

Hal said, 'I don't smoke, sir.' He added, 'Thank you.' Damn you, he thought. Suddenly angry.

'Hungry then? You look lean and damned hungry. I say, what about a Bath Oliver and a bit of Stilton? Know *Stilton*?'

'Yes, sir.'

'Didn't work in a grocer's shop by any chance?'

'That's Varley, sir –'

'Didn't ask who – All right. No, don't go, Greenwood. This, look at this, have a bit on toast. Pâté de foie gras de Périgord, with truffles . . . Food for civilized chappies. Treat for you, Greenwood, eh? Well, *answer* . . . Better than cowheel and tripe, eh? Never seen, tasted it before, have you?'

'Yes, sir. No, sir.' He said it wearily. It must have been eight, nine weeks since he last ate it. New Year. He felt humiliated. Humiliation . . .

After Lights Out that night he found himself weeping, as from somewhere deep, deep down.

Gus was the one he told first. Gus told the others. He didn't come from a farm at all. Hadn't been staying with his Auntie Olive, didn't even really talk like he'd been talking. He was someone quite else, from somewhere quite else, which was *home*. Which he suddenly, desperately desired and needed . . .

If he'd thought and feared that after all this time, his pals might (rightly) be angry with him . . . It wasn't like that at all. Maybe it was too late and some link had been forged: those first weeks of change in all their lives, beginnings of shared experience, reaching out into the future. Perhaps that was the reason. But they didn't mind. They were delighted. It was their 'open' secret.

His Nibs . . .

Bert said only, 'What'd you want to fib about Greenwood's?'

'I don't know anyone that's of it,' Hal said. 'There's a cousin, I think, that I've never met –'

'That'll be Mr Walter. Mr Walter he was round at Xmas. Tall man, big man, heavy. Balding.'

Lord Marmaduke, his Nibs . . .

'Heck, they'll make you a officer,' Gus said, 'a officer. One of them.'

Bert told him that he'd been bad not to think of his Mam. Snowy said the same.

'She knows I'm safe –'

'She'll want to hear, though, will your mother . . .'

'I don't want to be an officer,' he said. It was something he could not imagine, or rather could imagine too well. For every Gib there would be ten like the teasing two he had met on Jankers . . .

6904 Private H Greenwood alias his Nibs, alias Lord Marmaduke, to be known henceforth as Marmaduke.

He didn't tell the others too much about his home. Especially not about matters such as the Stones Room and the Diamond Waterfall . . .

The days ran one into the other. So much to learn. Bull. Everything shone. He was good at that. He had a Lee Enfield and did rifle practice, and was good at that too. The high-ups spoke of making Snowy a lance-jack.

The weather became so bad there was little they could do outdoors. Indoors, bayonet practice made him sick. He was no longer so sure of what he would do to the Hun . . . Sarge bawled at them all, but especially Hal, for half-heartedness.

Snowy said about the bayoneting that if you could spear a sausage over the fire, you could manage that . . . But Gus said he hadn't been counting on *eating* a Hun.

In the middle of March a married man in the squad, three beds down, went on leave. His home was in Nottingham. Hal gave him a letter to post from there. In it he said he was sorry, because he was, but that he was well and happy and had made friends. 'I shan't go abroad without telling you, or seeing you. I don't expect anyway that it'll be for quite a while . . .' He wondered still why he hugged his secret. It wasn't likely they could get him out now, however they tried. An oath was an oath in whichever of his accents he'd sworn it . . .

He didn't say anything about coming home, although he'd decided he'd go there the first time he had proper leave. He had had a weekend pass already which he had spent at Gus's home. He'd visited Bert's home and met Winnie, and Snowy's family who lived next door.

Meanwhile at the barracks, he could amuse them. They found him amusing. Their clown.

'Give us your *Fräulein*, Marmaduke. Listen to his Nibs now. Fuck von Kluck . . .'

'Give us the Sarge talking to his missus . . . Now, Sarge's missus talking to Sarge . . . Better than pierrots last summer, Scarborough –'

'Good as a night at the Empire . . .'

'Don't push your luck after Lights Out . . . Mild and bitter twice, once down, once up. Watch out for Sarge . . .'

'04 Greenwood – I didn't hear you . . .'

'04 Greenwood. *Do you hear me?* You'd soon find it if there was hair round it . . .'

24

The letter, which had travelled through Holland and was over three months old, reached Alice in the May of 1916 when she was already in France. It had been stamped by the censor. She wondered what he had made of it . . . That, to her, so familiar round yet spiky hand, more used to German than to modern script. The letter was in English, but the recognizable confused English of Fräulein in one of her emotional states. Alice could see the great face distorted, collapsed with distress . . .

She began to read. And as she did so, shocked, part of her thought: *But of course* . . .

'. . . all the day now I am thinking of Family Firth, please I don't understand how I lived among you with my *wickedness* which was not being punished . . . That sad day when the God of War struck our two countries, I was trying *very hardly* to make my confession. I was not able. Now, it is *God* who punishes . . .

It is I who take the rubies and emeralds and other matters from your home . . . (I did not *wish* this knowledge where and how the keys are being kept.) In my great dispair concerning my beloved Augustin, I listened to the Evil One. Und he speaks, Alice, with such a voice that it made for me a command: *Save Augustin*!

I cannot speak even yet of the journey I have taken home after and of how every man was for me a police, so afraid I was . . . I never speak to Augustin of this – a life full of worries such as he has, it was not for me to make it more full . . .

These jewels I sold them and it made no difficulty. And I was happy, yes, even though so wicked – because there was so much gold for him, and he isn't going to prison . . .

Then I did not sleep any nights until I have a letter and learn that you find the stones are gone, but no man has arrestation for it. This suspicion of the boy from the farm

. . . Such persons are used to these things . . . I hear when I return in the month of January that all is for now forgotten. I believe then in God's hand, because Augustin works now a serious man – it means from bad I have been bringing good . . .

But I *cannot forget*. So when suddenly I have learned that because of our Kaiser I must leave you – it is not for me bearable. I know then I must tell you *all*. I was thinking they shall put me in *English* prison to be punished. Und after, again we are friends once more . . .

Excuse me that I write in this confusion, I am not in good health and have some 'woman trouble' so that I am going to the hospital here . . . But now because I make confession and ask that you please forgive the wicked thing I do in your house, I ask also God that He forgives me – and that He takes away the *worst* punishment.

Augustin is in Russia. Yes! Such a man, 35 years of age – he was already Oktober '14 in the army – Why dear Gott does he do this when they have not asked for the ones of this age? But He will protect him now I have confessed and pay this debt . . .

Some of the writing was illegible, the paper tear-stained. Tears from that great, inexhaustible source. 'Fräulein's fountains', as Hal had called them – or was it Gib? It did not matter, except that it belonged to the far-off days. *We made jokes then*, she thought.

As of course they did now. But differently – in defiance of this War which already had altered their lives beyond any return. Crowded events of the last twenty months – with their twin peaks of distress: disappearance of Hal, Gib's departure for the Dardanelles . . .

She had found those early months of the War while Gib trained in England and Belle Maman turned The Towers into a hospital, trying enough. The arrival in the village of the Belgian refugees: Teddy settling down to learning French, formally and informally, but seeming to be everywhere, too much, wanting always to be 'helpful'.

For Alice, there was to be definite work in the hospital. Belle Maman had assured her of this, had even consulted her in matters of organization. But, Alice thought, how could I work under, or even *with*, Belle Maman?

Her life then: ridiculous bandaging parties, rolling bandages, or unrolling them in order to encase healthy people like mummies. Always the same sense of unreality. Too easy, she found it too easy, and then too much time was spent travelling to and from these parties which ended up often as a social occasion. So, during autumn as the news worsened – even before the fall of Antwerp in October – when it became apparent that not only would life not be normal by Christmas but that it would never be the same again, she took a First Aid Certificate. After that it seemed the best thing, since she had decided (no, they had *both* decided) not to marry yet – that she should become a nurse.

A VAD. 'Victim Always Dies', Hal told her, having read it somewhere. There was a little teasing generally. Gib was neither approving nor disapproving. A little admiring, perhaps . . .

So by November it was Gib in the south of England, she at a hospital in York. From her window she could see soldiers drilling out on the near-frozen grass. In early December they left for France, and as it was a free period, she went with other nurses to see them off at the station. She'd grown over the weeks to think of them as 'her' soldiers. That night as she undressed for bed she found herself sobbing . . .

She knew that she worried about Gib. That every soldier she saw, most especially those she nursed, was a reminder. Khaki, hospital pyjamas, hospital blue – it made no matter. Once Gib left the safety of England how would she dare to breathe by day, sleep by night?

Fortunately he seemed in no hurry to go. He'd said to her once or twice, 'I don't know why some chaps make such a fuss – when we're needed, they'll use us soon enough. Until then, best to learn all one can . . .' He wrote to her that Vesey had a commission with the Sherwood Foresters, while Saint had surprised them all by choosing the sea, and was now in the RNVR.

She wrote daily to Gib, managing to see him once during her three months in York. Then in early February she succeeded in her aim of getting to London. She could not explain why she had wanted that – but thought it was something to do with putting as much distance as possible between her and Belle Maman. York was not nearly far enough.

I should have left home years ago, she thought. Except – to do what? Photography? Certainly of her own accord she would not have decided on nursing – nor would it have been permitted. When we are married we shall not live near The Towers, she thought.

When we are married. Oh, but that was a thought. She came back to it and back to it, probing like a sore tooth. The girls she nursed with in York, and they were all younger than she was, had discovered she was promised in marriage. They assumed that she was waiting for the first convenient opportunity to have the ceremony . . .

But she knew she – *they* – were right not to marry yet, with the world as it was, the War going so badly, so much uncertainty . . . (Had not Gib himself remarked, 'I can't think it's right to bring children into the world – just now . . .' But such matters, she did not want even to think about . . .) Marriage was difficult enough in a peaceful, predictable world. She had only to remember what her own mother had suffered. How badly Belle Maman had behaved . . . And even for those who truly loved each other, were there not pitfalls?

There had been some pulling of strings to get her to London. She took that for granted. What was the use of someone like Papa if he could not arrange these matters? It had been possible to ensure also that Marjorie Penruddock, her friend at York, should transfer too. (Although it had been more Marjorie's wish than Alice's. She found the plump, always smiling, red-headed girl, eight years her junior, a mixed blessing. From the first day she had thought Alice quite wonderful. 'You *never* get things wrong, Miss Firth . . .')

Within a few weeks of her arrival, she heard the news of Hal. Everyone was sympathetic: knew someone who had a son, a brother, a cousin, who had done just that. But in most of the stories the boys had come home to confess what he had done, to be forgiven, to be supported. Hal had not merely joined up, he had run away – without trace.

Belle Maman's distress. The frantic letter to Alice. The

War Office called upon to help. Papa's friends. The searches promised for a 'Firth, HRF'. She could not understand how those same strings, so easily pulled for her, now seemed useless . . . Worry, desperation and finally anger. A letter from him. At last, his return. His first leave at home . . .

She herself had been terrified – as those years ago when he had come back screaming from the scene of Jack's death. What would become of him? Wouldn't he be, if nothing else, desperately homesick? He who had never been away to school. And, those other worse fears of the family – that he might simply have disappeared? Fallen among thieves. An innocent abroad. Robbed, murdered, who knew what?

In York, she had had time to think. Now, in London, working in the military extension of one of the big teaching hospitals, she did not so much postpone thought as find it crowded out by activity.

She was completely unimportant. Nurse Firth, and Miss Firth of The Towers were two different persons. Nurse Firth was one cog in a giant wheel. She discovered that in many ways she preferred that. All those years of being an alone child . . . She slept now in a dormitory with the thinnest of partitions separating her from her fellow nurses. Almost every minute of her day ordered, prearranged – and shared.

She was good at the work, certainly good enough to pass muster. I must be more practical than I realized, she told herself. And sharp: perhaps it was an advantage to be sharp – here it meant alert, quick-thinking, anticipating wants, needs . . .

Before all this, she would never have believed she would like being teased. But when a boy, no older she would have sworn than Hal, said to her, 'My sister's a VAD too, Victim Always Dies – only I prefer Very Artful Darlings . . . Are you artful or just a darling?' 'I'm a darling,' she told him in her crispest voice . . .

She nursed officers, probably, she thought, because she wasn't obviously pretty or even very young. In fact, not likely to flirt . . . During her second week, a convoy of wounded had arrived. In the non-stop nursing that followed, she discovered about herself many new things, hidden strengths. Where she'd expected to be squeamish or shocked – she was neither. She could do anything however intimate for any of them. She saw a naked man for the first time, and realized she'd been afraid of that, for years. Now when it happened, in a setting of bedpans, dressings, pain, dependency – it did not matter . . .

It was the wounds which frightened her the most, although she would never have allowed her fear to show. Bad enough in themselves – flesh and bone were no match for all that flying metal, sheer weight of weaponry – they were made even worse by the fearful infections which were so common a sequel. These were not the clean wounds of the Boer War, from fighting on sandy soil (oh, those easy heroic days of *With the Flag to Pretoria* when in their imaginings Gib's Galloper cousin thundered across the veldt), but rather wounds quickly infected by bacteria from rich ploughland. The sight, the smell (above all the smell), the suffering, became commonplace. She had seen nothing of this in York – she who had never so much as dealt with a sink of dirty dishes now handled flesh that suppurated, green, black, blue. Often her own arms and hands would be covered in the pus that poured out and poured out. This wasn't the life blood, warm and red, the 'wine of youth' of which people spoke and wrote so romantically, so carelessly. In her mind, this disgusting, stinking pus stood for all the War had now become.

It was from one of these wounds that she had the trouble with her left hand, that first winter. Both hands in the extreme cold had become covered with chilblains – she had not had these since her days in the schoolroom. Some of these became cracked so that even putting on or taking off her uniform in the icy dormitory was an ordeal. Then, pus from a gangrenous leg which she was holding during dressing, ran over her hands. One finger became badly infected. The abscess was lanced but there was some permanent damage, so that she had a stiff, almost useless fourth finger. (And it was there that Gib would place, and she would wear, the gold band when they were wed . . .)

'You're already having a much worse War than I am,' he told her, on one of his weekend passes when he would stay with an uncle in Highgate and she would try to arrange her little free time to fit. He seemed mildly depressed, not so much wishing to see action, as beginning to feel he was being passed over. Still part of the Reserve Battalion . . . (Possibly, she thought, because of his teaching abilities – he was an excellent instructor.)

They spoke of the days when it would all be over. Sitting opposite him in a tea-shop, she imagined instead that they sat over the breakfast table in their own home – which would be part of the school where Gib would teach.

The issue of marriage came up again when Gib heard suddenly that he was to go abroad. Not to France or Belgium. There was to be a new front out East. The details she only understood later: that the idea behind it was to break the deadlock apparent in the trenches since the autumn, by turning the Germans' attention elsewhere. The Dardanelles strait to be forced, Constantinople to be taken.

Where he was going there would be no 'few days' leave'. And – *he might not come back*. A notion so obvious, so horrible, she could not voice it . . . But once again, the same arguments applied . . . What had a hurried ceremony, signing of a register, sharing of a name, to do with what bound her and Gib?

'No,' she said, 'I don't think so. *You* don't, do you?'

'If you don't wish it, no. Better not . . .'

She was able to be with him for his last evening. They went to a revival of *Floradora* at the Lyric. '*Tell me, pretty maiden, are there any more at home like you?*' Her hand clutching his was chilled. Her lips kissing him goodbye, dry with anxiety.

She had volunteered for Active Service but did not know how long it would be before her turn came. Soon after Gib left, in May, Uncle Lionel sent a note to the hospital, inviting her to dine with him. She thought mildly of letting bygones be bygones. And in the end went, but taking Marjorie with her. If he was surprised he did not show it. Marjorie thought him absolutely too fascinating – and yet another reason to envy and admire Alice . . .

Anxious days of the Gallipoli campaign. The long casualty lists. The relief that Gib had survived – so far. She wrote to him three or four times a week, however exhausted she was. She dreamed one night that they had run away together to be photographers. He told her he had a roving commission, and that was why they could not be married. They were among battlefields, not trenches, but some vast windy plain – Gib said, '*Here the ignorant armies clash by night.*' She grew suddenly afraid and knew she must not lose sight of him. But as he went about he did not look at her at all. She struggled with the heavy equipment, something like Roger Fenton had taken to the Crimea, perhaps. Unwieldy, weighing her down. When she protested, pleaded, he spoke to her coldly. It was a Gib she had never seen before.

She woke shaking, dry mouthed, terrified. A moment later the alarm bell went. As she lay quiet in the few minutes before getting up she knew for certain that even if she continued as a nurse, they must as soon as possible marry. All through the day the dream haunted her. She felt, with a cold fear, that it was a premonition of his death.

Not long after she heard from him that he was in hospital in Alexandria. He had had a fever and lost a lot of weight. But they must have patched him up because he was back with his regiment in September, having missed the August landings and battles.

That autumn she worked on a surgical ward on day duty. The sound of the gramophone was in counterpoint with the groans and shouts, often desperate, of men in pain. '*Oompah, oompah, put it up your joompah . . .*' Relentless beat. There was temporarily a Sister on the ward who wore a pained, harassed expression as she bustled about, finding fault. Her face relaxed only for the few seconds after she'd reprimanded someone. Suspected frivolity or a flirtatious manner, she was especially hard on. Alice she found difficult to fault. But then in the midst of the anxiety about Gib, when the news from the Dardanelles was very bad, 'Nurse Firth,' she said one day, 'Nurse Firth, please do try to *smile* more often. What do you think it is like for our boys after all they've been through, to see a face such as yours?'

She was on night duty over Christmas and due for leave in the New Year, before almost certainly going abroad. She was in the ward making lampshades of red crinkled tissue, when someone brought her the news that Gib, safely evacuated from Gallipoli, was back in England.

He had been brought out about the 18th, but was a sick man, weakened by dysentery and frostbite. He was for a while in hospital in 1st London General, so whenever she had a free day, she would spend as much of it as possible with him. Afterwards he would have convalescent leave, and then surely in view of what he had been through, would not be sent abroad for a very long time?

She was shocked at his appearance, used as she was to such sights. But they had not been people she knew. This wasted body, dry haired, dry yellow-tinged skin, eyes sunken – was Gib. Yet he had been worse before, he told her, when he had been on the hospital ship.

'I shall soon pick up,' he said, 'so well looked after. All this milk, and rest, and good treatment. I shall soon be well . . .'

Hardly, she thought. It will take a little longer. But she said nothing. She found it difficult to talk to him. It was as if with the lifting of her anxieties, there were some sort of vacuum. All made worse because they were never alone. She didn't think others in the ward eavesdropped – it was the possibility that they might . . . Once, snatching a hurried half-hour with Gib, she coincided with his uncle from Highgate. They politely discussed the present state of the conflict, and the ethics of gas warfare, across the dozing half-sitting Gib.

Marriage. Well, that was a little way off. First he must be out of hospital, of course. They spoke of it a little, tentatively. She said, 'What I wrote to you – what I said when you were out there, I would still like – it . . .'

'Of course,' he said, 'just as soon as I'm well, and out of here. It's – what I wanted anyway. You know that.' His voice had the tired, patient, brought from a distance quality she'd come to recognize among those she nursed from the same campaign.

'All right though, isn't it, that I should continue nursing? I could not just live at home. Waiting –'

'Of course,' he said.

She said that soon she would get leave – and if he were out of hospital, and better, or well enough, then . . .

'Of course.'

But there was to be no marriage for a while. Towards the end of January he seemed, she thought, a little improved. He told her that in three or four weeks he would be allowed home on convalescent leave. The news came too late to do either of them any good: her posting abroad had come through and she was to go to France after ten days' leave. She spent most of it with Gib: he was allowed some outings, an evening with his uncle. In some ways it was almost a happy time: walking slowly over an icy Hampstead Heath, holding his arm (his nurse, his mother). And he:

'You will be careful in France, Alice darling? Some of the hospitals . . . even base ones – there've been accidents . . .'

She would get leave in at the very most, six months. It was most unlikely any Board would pass him fit for overseas before then. In the meantime he would be safe, first at his home and then – somewhere in England. She liked to think of him in Flaxthorpe, visiting The Towers:

'The darkroom,' she said, 'the little sitting-room, all that's shut up, locked up now. I can't believe, can you, that we ever led such a life? That once we were to be – roving photographers . . . Now we see the world – but in what a different way . . .'

She remembered her dream then. Gooseflesh cold . . .

She crossed the Channel, together with Marjorie who was in the same draft, one icy Tuesday night in early February. Delayed endlessly by fog. On the journey she was low-spirited and fearful, as if Gib were in danger rather than herself.

She and Marjorie were in a hospital near the village of Camiers, between Boulogne and the big base hospital at Etaples. The main railway line to Paris ran between them and the sea. The intensely cold weather, which even the salt in the sea air could not seem to prevent, made it difficult to distinguish the landscape. The whole of the way from Boulogne to Etaples seemed to be made up of camps. Their hospital, like many others, was no more than a collection of huts with marquees for wards. The nurses slept in bell tents. Crouching over an oil fire, or round a brazier in a hut, she thought she had never known such cold . . . And always the sound of the guns . . .

The same guns which she had heard fitfully in the South of England, in parts of East Anglia. A visiting professor had told Marjorie's father that the harsh weather now and the fitful summer just past could perhaps have been caused by the guns.

'All that vibration, he told Daddy, it changes the upper air, affects the climate, you see . . .'

The guns soon became part of their lives. So much so that a momentary lull could seem more noticeable than the sound itself. Sometimes there would be even a sort of vibration – an after sound, as of ghost guns . . .

As the weeks wore on, she began to find Marjorie trying. She would like to have made other friends, but she seemed, whenever she had free time, doomed to her company. Marjorie admired and looked up to her. 'You are wonderful,' she would say on every possible occasion. It seemed impossible to do or say anything which altered this opinion. *If she really knew*, Alice thought. Not admiring Marjorie herself, she found it difficult to feel warmed by this goggle-eyed worship. Oh, for a little acid in the mixture . . .

She wrote as often as ever to Gib. Perhaps they might begin to hope soon that something could be arranged. She expected leave at the end of June, perhaps a little later. He wrote that he had bought a motorcycle. A Douglas, complete with flapper bracket. She wrote back that she hoped he wasn't expecting her to be a passenger. Flapper indeed! She asked him yet again if it was *all right* that she should stay on out here, nursing. 'If you could see (but of course you already have) the suffering . . .'

There was little let-up in the number of casualties to be treated even though, for the time being, there were no major offensives. Verdun, terrible as it was, belonged to the French. Rumoured numbers of dead and wounded seemed to her scarcely credible. Surely, such a battle could not be repeated, death on such a scale happen again . . .

Out at sea there were brown-sailed fishing boats. Between the sea and the camp were the stretches of sand dunes, tufts here and there of coarse grass. As spring grew nearer the quality of the light on the water amazed her – a March wind blowing away sea mist to reveal watery greens and blues. Around the tents, the RAMC orderlies planted flowers, and sowed vegetables.

May, and Fräulein's letter. She sent it back to England, to Hal in Devon. It was more his concern, really. His friend suspected. A friend, if she remembered rightly, already eighteen months dead . . .

In June, expecting to get away before the end of the month, she learned that all leave had been cancelled. Gib, stationed in the Midlands, had already arranged to come up to Flaxthorpe. Her letter telling him what had happened, and his with the good news, crossed.

There was to be a big offensive. A Push. The biggest yet. It was to have been Anglo-French, but the French were still tied up in Verdun, and would only be able to man some fifteen miles in the south. The Big Push was to be decisive. Draft upon draft of fresh troops arrived for the battle. The pick of Kitchener's Army. Hal, thank God, not among them.

The German trenches were well defended – the barbed wire in front of them was yards deep. For the last week before the attack the British bombardment never halted – shell upon shell upon shell, aiming to breach the wire, and to terrify the enemy.

She and Marjorie were both sent to Le Havre during that last week. A real hospital this time, not a marquee. Small, it had been made from the waiting-room and the offices on the Quai d'Escale, where in happier days transatlantic liners had berthed.

On July 1st, something, everything, went very wrong. Not only the battle itself, but the arrangements for the wounded. There were advance dressing stations the length of the line, while three empty hospital trains waited for the first wounded. Twenty more trains were on call – and soon needed. They were not sent for until too late. By night time thousands of wounded were still up the line: fortunately it was a warm night, since many were without shelter.

Over thirty-three thousand wounded came by train during the first few days. The base hospitals were overwhelmed. At Le Havre, where Alice waited, the trains ran straight on to the quay. Altogether, small as they were, their hospital took in some thousand wounded.

She thought she would never forget the plight, the sight of those wounded. Hastily applied field dressings, four days old. Wounds, worse even than any she'd yet seen. And as she worked, the smell of iodoform, ether, never out of her nostrils, all the time under the wards the trains rumbled: bringing wounded, returning to Rouen for more . . .

Gradually she learned what had gone wrong. That all the

intense preliminary bombardment had not damaged the German trenches, so deep were they. Nor had the high shrapnel breached the wire. As the line advanced, wave after wave of men had been mown down.

Yet at home the headlines shrieked Success. Telegrams to relatives, not sent for nearly a week, delayed the truth. Only when the boats and trains in England began to unload these same incredible numbers of wounded, did the truth dawn . . .

It was nothing to her now that her leave had been cancelled. All thoughts of disappointment were crowded out. The windows of the ward open out on to the balcony those hot July nights: out across the sea the white hospital boats arriving, departing, crossing each other, lights blazing. And on the quay the rows of stretchers, waiting . . . It was not time to think of marriage, just to be glad that Gib was safe in England – that Hal had not been sent out.

She lived intensely. She who had a lover, soon to be a husband, safe. *Safe.* She concentrated her energies into relieving pain, and when she could not do that, to consoling. Gentle hands, gentle voice . . . No longer sharp . . . Reality, so peculiarly horrible, smell, sight, sound, was *what mattered* as nothing before had done. It would not do to grumble over happiness deferred. Later they will give us leave . . . A small sacrifice, no more. My, our, happiness, she thought, it is only postponed . . .

25

Honiton, Devon
27th May, 1916

Dear Miss Ibbotson,
Dear Olive,

PLEASE DON'T TEAR THIS UP WITHOUT READING ON. The letter enclosed with this is VERY IMPORTANT. I wasn't sure who to write to in the family and I thought you would be the least likely to destroy it without looking. I know my stepsister won't mind you having it. As you see, it's come a long way – It's a terrible letter really and I wasn't sure whether I should chance upsetting you more, raking everything up. Of course you can never have thought for a second Stephen had anything to do with that horrible business. *I want you to believe that I never did either.*

I was very unhappy about it all when it happened and I know I was very silly to do what my family asked. But I don't expect you'll want to hear about it from me. It was just so sad when we were all such friends and then this horrible mix-up had to happen. I am very, very sorry about it. I don't see how this letter from Germany can make up for anything but it's only right you and your family should have it.

You must miss Stephen very much still. I am a soldier now also, as you will see from the address. Though I expect you may have heard locally. I enlisted about fifteen months ago.

Yours,
Henry Firth (Hal).

PS. Sorry about the beginning bit but I'm not sure what to call you. I thought you might not like me to be familiar just because I used to call you by your first name when we were children. When you reply, *if* you do – perhaps you can indicate which you'd prefer?

Honiton, Devon
12th June, 1916

Dear Olive,

It was the most wonderful surprise to get a letter from you. I meant to say that you mustn't feel that you had to reply to mine. Anyway the things you said were wonderful, but *I would have quite understood* if you'd felt angry with me and our family forever and a day.

I'm so sorry your mother is ill all the time now and in bed. I know she wasn't well before. It must be very strange at the farm now with James gone as well – I can understand your upset especially when he did not need to go. And now that he is in France the worry will be worse.

It will be our turn here – one day. I thought we'd have gone sooner but they arrange things how they like. I'm lucky with my pals – at least I thought they were a bit odd at first but now we are all real friends. But I'm sometimes homesick. What happens about the hay – will the brothers be over this year?

I had forgotten about your aunt in Devon. Is there any chance that you would ever come down to see her?

It was lovely to see your handwriting again – do you remember when I used to help you with your homework?

I am hoping for some long leave at the end of the summer. If you really meant it about coming up to the farm, then I certainly shall.

Every good wish, from your friend,

Hal Firth.

When had he last walked the grassy track? As Lane Top Farm came into view, it was like stepping back into a lost world. He had been nervous about it – how he should dress, whether to go with the motor, walk over, or bicycle. In the end he had settled for his khaki, and travelling on foot . . .

First full day of his leave. Arriving last night, he had found home as unwelcoming as it had seemed ever since it became a hospital. Officers wandering about as if they were weekend guests . . . ('You the son of the house?' he had been asked this morning. He almost answered 'No', such a stranger did he feel.) He wished Gib could have been there. He and Alice, he had heard, hoped to be married next month, when she got leave at last . . .

His parents: happy of course to see him. But busy, and uncertain whether they might not have to entertain him. There was an air of such busyness about the whole place. In fact he walked straight into the midst of some bustle. A patient, meant to be almost ready for convalescent leave, hæmorrhaging suddenly, severely. Even while greeting Hal, Mother was distracted by arrangements to be made, messages, a discussion with the doctor . . .

Teddy, just sixteen and full of self-importance. He found her exasperating. He couldn't believe that anyone would miss her if she went off to boarding-school tomorrow. She rushed about ('Ripping to see you but I have to hurry – I'm reading to some of the officers at half past, they're frightfully nervy and get awfully upset if you're even five minutes late.') She had with her always Amy Hawksworth – and now a Belgian girl too. All full of themselves.

Sylvia was as sweet and dear as ever. She had been in her dressing-gown and just about to go to bed when he arrived. But she'd thrown her arms around him and put her little face up to be kissed. He had thought: She is sugar and spice and all things nice – just what a little sister should be . . .

Lane Top Farm. In the yard, an aged Tess barked as he approached. He waited at the door of the farmhouse. When it opened, he just stood and stared.

Olive said, 'Don't you know me, then?'

Of course. Of course it was Olive. Not very tall – she had scarcely grown at all. But different. How?

'You're different –' he began. Then fell silent. It was suddenly too much for him. Back here, standing at the door – when last time it had been shut in his face.

'Of course I'm not,' she said, laughing. Then, 'Come in, if you're coming. You're very welcome . . .'

First he had to pass the door of the room downstairs where Will and James and Stephen had used to sleep. Then the little cupboard room under the stairs which had been Olive's. It was all the same – and yet not. The smell, it could be baking, oil lingering from the lamps, milk, hay, all scents which seemed to have permeated the very walls.

'Come in the kitchen, Hal.'

The kitchen. It was like the first time, the first visit, when he had felt the room to be full of people. Then, there'd been five. Today, only four. Granny Willans sat by the window. It was as if she'd never moved. Her feet were stuck out and he could have sworn it was the same pair of unlaced boots.

'Here's Hal Firth come to see us, Gran. He's a soldier now –'

But she wasn't sure of him and only shook her head, 'Can't hear owt –'

Mr Ibbotson acknowledged him, without enthusiasm. Grudgingly. I'm not forgiven, Hal thought. Whatever Olive has told them, explained, there is still bitterness.

Two men sat at the table which was already laid up for a meal. Olive said, 'These are Tom Thwaites and Arthur Pickering. They're family now. They help with farm, you see . . .'

He didn't see. He had not thought, really. Without James, and with Mr Ibbotson not strong these days, how were they to manage?

It was then she took him upstairs to see her mother. He had dreaded this. Mrs Ibbotson lay back against the pillows, her hair, thin and lank, about her shoulders. Her face was puffy, and she seemed, like Granny Willans, scarcely to recognize him. He preferred that. If she were to have mentioned the past . . .

'Mam's not having one of her good days – are you, Mam dear? Hal's only come to say good-day. Then you can sleep again, after I've brought you your dinner. She likes, needs to sleep a lot,' Olive explained to him.

He wasn't sure why, but he'd pictured it that he would be at the farm alone with Olive. That the first awkward moments over, ghost of Stephen notwithstanding, they would talk and be at ease with each other.

But it was not going to happen. He saw that, before the meal was five minutes old. Olive bustling about, hurrying to and fro, pouring from the same old green teapot . . .

They made polite conversation. The two new men didn't say much. Arthur was only a boy, really: small and sturdy with a freckled face and a wide friendly mouth. Olive explained that he was too young to go to War even if he'd wanted. Hal's escapade hung about them, was not mentioned. Tom, pleasantly fresh-faced with already receding hair and carrying quite a bit of weight, had wanted to fight but hadn't been passed fit.

'It were only a notion,' he said. 'I'm as well off here. Miss Ibbotson – Olive's – cooking. She bakes a good cake, does Olive.'

Hal thought: My first day here, *I* tasted her baking. Oatcakes, havercakes, it had been. . . . He felt a sudden wave of jealousy. Someone else, a stranger, enjoying it, praising it . . .

'I hear you ran off for a soldier,' Arthur said later. He wanted to hear all about it. But Hal, finding it perhaps an old tired tale, couldn't get it started, or bring it to life.

Granny Willans was silent except occasionally when she would talk out loud to herself. Mr Ibbotson scarcely spoke. Less even than Hal remembered. He wondered now, could not help being curious, whether he, or Olive, had told Tom and Arthur about the jewellery – about that Christmas four years ago. There is something wrong with the *feeling* in here, he told himself.

They asked him when he would be going abroad. Talked about the hospital at The Towers. Then among themselves about farm matters. There was a goose fattening through in the scullery. Christmas wouldn't be all bad. Life had to go on. Up on the dresser was a field postcard from James. It had a tick beside 'I am well'. 'We got that Thursday,' Olive said.

When the meal was finished and the clearing done, he thought: 'It's nearly over and I haven't spoken to her at all.

He said, 'I expect you've work to do –' Tom and Arthur had got up almost at once and gone outside. 'Should I help them at all?' he asked. 'There's lots I could do. I –'

'You're not dressed for mucking,' she said, smiling. She looked like a little brown bird. Brown hair, brown dress under brown apron.

It wouldn't be possible to stay in the kitchen – they couldn't speak there. There was no sign of Granny Willans moving. She looked to be asleep. Mr Ibbotson said, 'I'll mebbe take forty winks – and join lads afore light goes . . .'

Olive said, 'Hal and I'll just go for a walk, Dad. If he wants to. If he'd like that . . .'

When they'd walked, without talking, about five minutes or so, taking the track which led in the direction of the high moor, she said,

'I wanted to tell you I'm sorry – that you've not had a great welcome . . . Dad's not – it's not that he's angry still, it's just he's not bothered with folk from outside. And now that Mam's badly . . .'

'That's all right,' he said, 'I was happy just to be with you . . . I mean, with you all,' he added quickly, embarrassed.

A silence fell on them. What little sun there'd been had disappeared. A dull day in late August, and cold with it. Hints of autumn already in the air. They went through a gap in the cross wall – a hawthorn tree grew beside it. Ahead was open moor, the distant purple of the heather appearing almost brown beneath the leaden sky.

She said, 'I haven't to be long out. There's work –'

'Do you do it all – in the house, as well as farm work?'

'I can't mind a time when I didn't, Hal. I was busy enough before Mam was taken bad . . . Since then – I've had the lot –'

'But if you weren't there?'

'They'd just have to get on with it, wouldn't they?'

He remembered now that side of her: who looked so gentle and could so suddenly be definite and firm. He thought then, sadly: Four years ago, if she'd *wanted* to go on being friends, she'd have done that on her own. Defied them. If she'd wanted. But her own flesh and blood – whatever side could she have been expected to take?

He needed to keep on returning, probing, reopening the scar, looking under to see if it was healed. He burst out:

'I liked all you said, in your letter, about the jewellery affair being over and far back in the past, and how we don't need to speak of it again.'

'Well,' she said, a little briskly, 'if I said that then – why are you starting it up another time?'

They were crossing the sheep bridge now, then along the stone trod by the side of the beck – the water full after the recent rain.

He thought at first she was angry. But then she smiled. Seeing that smile, he realized it was the same he'd always known, only now it belonged to a different person.

Perhaps she was having some of the same thoughts, because she said,

'Being a soldier – or just getting older, or – I don't know, anyway you're like I remember, but *different*.'

'Yes?' He wanted to talk about himself, if she did the talking.

'Your funny voices, we've not had any of them . . . Perhaps that way you've changed –'

'I still have those – I do them all the time for my pals. I do them so much I expect I thought – perhaps I wanted a rest. I didn't think any of you'd want that sort of thing . . .'

'It was really good, was our Granny Willans . . .' She was laughing as she remembered. 'And that Mr Maxwell that reads the lesson in church. You had him, really *had* him –'

He said, 'I do the Sergeant Major for my pals – I wouldn't like you to hear some of it. It's a bit – you know. But – '04 Greenwood,' he shouted loudly across the water. And then two of Sarge's parade ground sayings . . .

'The rest, they're some of them much funnier – only the things he says, I – couldn't, in front of you.' He blushed now as he remembered. ('. . . but at least cunts are useful . . .' '. . . if it had hair round it . . .')

'I expect I'd understand,' she said. 'You see, you hear things – on a farm, and about . . .'

He blushed still. He wouldn't *want* her to understand. He said:

'I hope those two that help on the farm, I hope they're careful with their talk.'

'If Dad's around, yes, they take care. Gran they're not bothered. It depends if they've had a drink or two –'

'Do you like them?'

'They're all right. They're good lads.'

'Which do you like best?' He imagined suddenly that she might be close friends, that there was already something between her and Tom.

'Oh, Arthur, I suppose, because he's only a little small lad. No – I'm not sure. Tom, I think really. He's good, Hal. He's kindly and –'

Interrupting, as if he could not wait to say it, seeing in his mind's eye, the farmhouse door already looming before them. Their time together nearly over . . .

'Olive, even if I don't go abroad for a bit – will you write to me? Getting letters in camp, even in England, it's really good. If you've the time . . .'

'I could find it, I reckon. If I've a mind to –'

She smiled though, and he knew she would do it. They talked little after that – she had taken out her watch and seen that they must hurry back. A faint drizzle was beginning. The distant view quite misted over.

Back at the farmhouse she went in ahead of him. As she took off her hat hurriedly, some of her hair pulled from its fastening so that it hung drunkenly down one side. Thick brown, with just a little wave. There had not been so much of it before even when it hung loose.

'The other thing is – I just thought of it. I'm here for a bit and I wondered if there's not perhaps work – if I could help like I used –' He floundered. He didn't want to go back, yet again, to the past.

'It'd be grand,' she said. 'If you wanted to. If it's not a trouble. You could eat with us. Do you still like fat rascals – you remember, the ones I used to make for Mam? You were a greedy one for those . . .'

Olive, Olive, Olive.

26

'I should have stayed at the convent,' the girl said.

Alice, already in bed, watched her as by the light of a candle she tried to hang a large, shapeless flowered dress. Her valise, gaping open, was disorderly and crowded.

'Were you a nun?' she asked, mildly curious.

'Jesus Mary Joseph. I never heard such a thing. *Me* a Sister! The Lord knows better than to . . .' She held up two unmatching shoes: 'Now wait while I look for the others . . . No, no, I meant only – those were the days, weren't they? Everything nice and ordered and the Sisters thinking well of you . . . At the hospitals now – *that* sort of Sister – you never know what you've done wrong –'

Alice said tiredly, a little coldly, 'I suppose, then, you're a Roman Catholic?'

'What else now? You never mind, do you?'

Why should I? she thought.

She had been almost asleep in the tent which was now home, when the new arrival burst in:

'Aren't I the noisy one, Jesus forgive me – did I wake you? O'Driscoll, Molly O'Driscoll – just off the boat. Did they not tell you about me?'

'Nothing,' said Alice. 'They don't . . .' She felt a headache come on suddenly. Throbbing at the back of her head.

'You're Miss Firth, is that right now? What else do they call you? The girl was sleeping here before, what had she wrong? I heard she was bad –'

'Quinsy,' Alice said. 'Miss Penruddock had quinsy – with complications. She's been shipped home.'

'Jesus Mary Joseph . . . if it isn't enough with whizz-bangs all over without we've to worry about germs . . .'

Roman Catholic indeed, Alice thought. Remembering Aunt Violet . . . (When did I last think of her? Terrible Christmas visit all those years ago, after the trouble with Uncle Lionel. Never the same again, after she let me down . . . Forced occasionally to see her, yes, but never of my own accord. Less and less as the years went by. When in the end, she moved to live with her daughter's family, I could hardly bring myself to say goodbye . . .)

Molly held up a pair of silver shoes:

'I never had so much space before – all my finery, my best shoes now, I've got feet so small you'd never believe – just look at the size of me – would you think it?'

She was a big girl, with close-curling unruly hair, unsuccessfully stuffed under her nurse's felt. She talked fast in a breathy voice, her wide mouth smiling constantly . . . Everything about her large and expansive and, Alice feared, quite irrepressible. A chatterbox too – a chatterwallet as Hal had used to say . . .

Seeing a silver dress join the shoes, Alice said: 'Whenever do you think you'll wear all that stuff?'

'Well now – if I should go dancing with a cavalry man – there're cavalry officers here, aren't there? – then . . . Look at these now, I wore them last in Dublin –'

'But we're not allowed out with officers. People have had enough trouble even when it's a brother or father – so how you suppose –'

'There might be a change, mightn't there now? Jesus Mary Joseph, they can't go on being so cold-hearted. Wicked it is when we work as hard as we do . . .

Since Marjorie's departure Alice had had two temporary companions sharing the tent. The last one had smelled so badly (these were very warm days), she had thought seriously of sleeping outside among the lettuces and flower patches dug around the tents. It was late summer now and it seemed a long time since the first of July and the hectic days after. She and Marjorie had stayed in Le Havre until the end of the month, when they had come to Rouen, to a camp hospital erected on the racecourse. In her free time she had fallen in love with Rouen – although it was as ever almost impossible to explore it without Marjorie's company (I am not as good as I think at hurting people . . .). When Marjorie had had to go home, she hadn't been able to suppress a sigh of relief.

That evening of Molly's arrival, desperate to get some sleep, she wondered if this newcomer might not overwhelm her in a different way. But Molly confounded her almost at once by fastening up her valise, half its contents still muddled up inside – throwing off her coat and hat, splashing herself with cold water in the canvas bowl, undressing, and rolling into bed: 'Don't we both need sleep – dear Mother of God I'm tired, I'll say my prayers lying down . . .'

In the morning, she hardly spoke. Just shook her head to and fro, trying to wake. Splashing more cold water. Tugging a comb unsuccessfully through the wayward hair.

That evening Alice noticed that she'd fastened to the canvas a piece of stiff paper with at least eight or nine photographs glued on. All snapshots. She saw in one a nun's coif. She asked, 'Is that a Sister from your convent?'

'Not at all. That's Sister Columba – Eileen that was. My own sister . . . And that's Pat there who's married – three he has already. And there's my Uncle Denis and my Uncle Ted, and that there's Matt – he's only a little one, but – say a prayer for him now, we're all hoping he'll be a priest . . .'

Willing at almost no invitation to talk about her family, she was curious too in a warm-hearted way about Alice. A day or two later when they were comparing nursing experiences, she clapped her hands with delight when she heard Alice hoped to be married in about a month. That she planned to break her contract, and go home.

'And you never said it. That you were promised! Tell me about him – what do you call him, where's his picture?' She could not hear enough: 'Isn't that romance now? Nearly *five* years . . . My problem, they're all lovely boys – I daren't pray to get any special one for there won't be three days pass before I fall for another . . . Oh, but they're *all* lovely . . .'

She marvelled that Alice should continue nursing until so near the marriage, that she did not go now and wait for him at home. She was sad too, to be losing Alice so soon. 'Just the friend I needed – someone quiet that keeps me in order. Jesus Mary Joseph . . .'

After ten days or so Alice felt Molly had always been there. She could not explain to herself what made her so comforting. She seemed on the surface the very sort of person she would usually try to avoid. But after a little, she realized that in a strange way it was of Mama that Molly reminded her . . .

'Darling heart,' she called Alice. 'Darling heart, did you hear what that Sister called me? I shall never like that woman. Won't I have to say in Confession I wished her at the bottom of the sea – anywhere but Somewhere in France . . .'

Confession. What was all this? Confession. Yes, Aunt Violet had spoken of it, but in a hushed tone as if it had been something 'not quite nice'. Now, sitting in a café near Rouen Cathedral, she asked Molly question after question about Confession. Molly, although glad to tell her, was surprised that something so everyday should fascinate . . .

'And when I've been naughty,' she told Alice, 'like kissing a boy – oh, it's hard to say no, isn't it now, Jesus Mary Joseph, when they want a little cuddle – oh, aren't I glad I can confess it all . . .'

She explained: 'Venial sins, the little ones – you tell the Father those. It's not so bad now if you forget a few . . . It's the *mortal* sins you mustn't miss out.'

Mortal sins killed the life of the soul. She was fascinated by this world where a soul might be killed – and then brought back to life. Absolution. The priest, who was in God's place. 'Even if they're old and cross and haven't listened to a word, when they say, "Go in peace and pray for me," it *works* . . . you really are washed clean . . .'

They went into the Cathedral together. Molly said, 'You see that light burning, the lamp there, that means the Blessed Sacrament. Our Lord's *really* there.'

She emptied her purse of centimes, lighting candles for her whole family. Even with some of them sharing, they nearly filled one of the circular brass stands. 'Don't they make a lovely sight – sending prayers up to heaven . . . Ask Our Lady,' she told Alice, 'if you've anything special, but you think Our Lord mightn't want it for you. Ask Her. She won't refuse or rather her Son won't when She asks. It's absolutely true. If only everybody knew . . .'

On their next visit to Rouen, Alice too lit candles – one for Hal that he would be kept in England for ever, another for Vesey already in France, one for Saint on the high seas . . . Lastly for Gib and herself – together. Oh, make us happy soon. May I make *him* happy, always and forever, amen.

'I hope you lit one now for that lovely boy you're to marry . . .'

What if, she thought, what if one day I were to become part of this lovely warm world – where a mother looks after you, a father is *always right*, and even the most terrible things can be forgiven. (Where *dead souls can be brought back to life . . .*)

But then, she thought, a Vicar's son? When Gib is a schoolmaster again, what will they think of a Roman Catholic wife for a housemaster, a headmaster? It would not do . . .

The next day she received a letter from him, written in great haste, telling her his expected embarkation leave had been put forward. 'Everything suddenly at sixes and sevens' – could she hurry back *please*. She was breaking her contract, wasn't she? so there should be no problems. If she would wire what date she could arrive by, he would arrange the ceremony for the next day but one – 'so that you may have your beauty sleep!'

Molly hugged her, full of romantic excitement. 'Isn't it the best thing in the world? You'll be wanting a baby as soon as ever, to keep you company . . . How terrible that he goes – Jesus Mary Joseph keep him safe . . . Darling heart, how I'll miss you. I can't believe it's only a month we were together – what will I do now when that terrible Sister pitches into me?'

She arrived at Victoria station in the pouring rain after a crossing that had taken most of the night. She had first to sign some papers in Central London before going on to Kings Cross. From there she wired home.

I am too tired to get married, she thought, shivering exhaustedly in the railway carriage. The journey north seemed endless. She could think of nothing but how soon she could lay her head on a clean pillow, clean linen sheets covering her. (Had she left enough time – just one day – to rid herself of dirt and lice and all the unmentionables, to be clean and fresh and beautiful for *my wedding day*?)

The motor came to meet her. Gib with it. She saw at once from his face, even before he greeted her, that something was very wrong. But during the first two or three minutes, he only asked tenderly after her journey.

Then, 'Look,' he said suddenly, stammering a little in his distress, 'l-look, Alice – there's a piece of bad news. Your wire this afternoon – it wasn't the *only* wire today. You see . . .'

He told her gently. But oh, it cannot be, she thought, *it is not true. Who can be so cruel?* He didn't have the second wire with him. He said he could not bear for her even to see it. She protested:

'But if they want you tomorrow, if your draft really goes early – why can't you wire back and explain? Explain that you are *getting married* the day after tomorrow –' Then: 'Oh, but you're so weak, so stupid,' she cried, frantic with distress and fatigue.

He said sadly, 'Alice, Alice. *You* should know – part of the Forces. Life in the Army is not like that –'

'Two more, even *one* more day, they could, they could, couldn't they?' She almost wanted to hit him. As if it were *his* doing . . .

'And France,' she said over and over again, 'it's to France you go. I might never – we might never . . .'

Out of all this nightmare that was the worst. And then, she thought later that evening, at last tucked up in bed (how wonderful that was to have been), *it is all my fault*. She wanted to blame the Kaiser, Field Marshal French, the King, Gib's commanding officer, Gib himself. (Not God. It was not God's doing.) It is my fault. I should have married him in 1914, *when he urged me*.

It was so terrible, they were not really able to discuss it at all. Sick empty fatigue and disappointment, and underlying them – fear, and more fear. She who had so longed for sleep, could not sleep at all. In the morning when he was ready to leave (she had thought once, wildly: Why can't we be married by his father, *before breakfast*?) she insisted on going with him as far as Northallerton. She would have even liked to go on to London.

On the way they scarcely spoke. Too tired perhaps. And as if by common consent, did not discuss any plans for another wedding date. He did ask at one point what she planned to do about the broken contract? 'I don't know, I don't know,' she said. Angry with him for even asking.

She had to leave him. The lips that kissed him, the hands that held his, were drier, more despairing, than those which had said goodbye eighteen months ago, before Gallipoli.

Perhaps they were of some use, all those strings that had been so unsuccessfully pulled for Hal? It was difficult usually to go back when a contract had been broken. To return to France, impossible.

Yet within three weeks, she was back with Molly. Three

terrible weeks – fending off Teddy's sympathy which she found irritating (what does *she* know of anything?) and her proprietary remarks about Gib (just because she has spent so much time with the officers). And worrying always. He was in the reserve lines now. But any moment . . . How could she ever be at peace again?

She had forced herself to take some leave, have a little time at home, while her father telegraphed this high-up, and that high-up. He was successful. So soon had it all happened after her departure that her papers had not been made final yet – a point here and there was stretched. It was in some ways, she thought, almost as *if it had never been* . . .

Molly was overjoyed at her return ('if you'd seen who they put in this tent after you'd gone. Mother of God . . .'), but filled with righteous anger at what the powers that be were capable of. 'Jesus Mary Joseph. It's never true. And there I was praying and praying. Our Lord must have something very special in store for you, that He makes the two of you suffer so . . . I'll begin a novena at once. And a decade of the rosary a day – I can manage that on night duty, honest to God, I can. And I'll write home. Matt's prayers – they're really powerful, darling heart . . .'

Six weeks later Alice spoke to the RC chaplain at the hospital about being received into the Church. She had thought about it, in every free moment, for the last four weeks.

Because of the unusual situation, and the excited promises of Molly to be of great help, the usual quite lengthy course of instruction was waived. In early December she was received quietly. Molly was her godmother. On December 8th, the feast of the Immaculate Conception, they were both free for part of the morning and attended High Mass in Rouen Cathedral.

She would have been happier than she had been for many years – if it had not been for the coruscating worry about Gib's safety. And also, the fact that she had not told him of her change of religion – even though Molly had urged her to. She thought she would wait till after Christmas, which seemed sensible. Occasionally she would have the wild idea of breaking her contract again, of seeking him out, of marrying him *in France* . . .

Then came good news – she had to think of it as good. He was wounded. Leg, shoulder. Serious, but curable with time. The news was slow in reaching her; when it did he was already in hospital at the 1st London General. Now was not the time . . .

When, rarely enough, she read a newspaper, she would seize avidly on the name of anyone said to be married to a Roman Catholic, to see if their career had prospered. It will be all right, she thought. She prayed that it might be . . . Anyway it was unimaginable that anything – What could come between her and Gib?

Icy cold winter of early 1917. Remembering what Marjorie's father's professor friend had said, about the guns . . . In their tents, the water froze. Her chilblains were the worst ever. Sister was rude about her damaged finger, saying that Alice held it in an affected way. 'It would be better to *use* it . . .'

In the coldest days of February, Molly had a sudden bright idea on one of their afternoons off in Rouen, passing by the Hotel de la Poste: 'Jesus Mary Joseph, why not?'

Going in, she arranged for them to rent a room with private bathroom for three hours. 'Why don't we forget we're ministering angels, and look after ourselves a little while? Don't we deserve it? I've the money, if you have –'

Sheery luxury, and such a success that they did it every time they had a free afternoon off together. Molly sometimes made jokes about finding a lovely cavalry officer to be naughty with ('I'd only kiss and cuddle of course.'). But Alice, lying in the deep bath, steam all about her, clean towels beside her, knowing she would soon step on to heavy pile carpet, soft, in a warm room – perhaps an hour's sleep on the bed – could not help thinking: a honeymoon, one day, Gib and I. When it's all over.

She didn't write to him as often as she should. Perhaps because, as she had not told him something so important about herself, her letters were no longer really truthful. His had become duller. It hurt his shoulder to hold a pen for long. He was in Flaxthorpe now at The Towers – he had been able to choose it as his follow-up hospital. How odd, to think of him there – *as a patient*. She hoped his room mates were congenial, that Teddy's well-meaning ministrations were not too over-exuberant – he sounded as if he needed peace – she sensed that he was exhausted not only in body but in spirit. *They cannot send him out again* . . . Belle Maman wrote that he looked better. When I get leave, she thought, I shall tell him.

In April she learned that Vesey had been killed during the Battle of Arras. Gib grieved . . .

Molly was away on long leave for a fortnight in May. Alice missed her terribly – though as the carping Sister had been changed for a more sympathetic one, life was a little easier. Gib was soon to go to a camp in the Midlands. She'd hoped to get leave in early June, but had been told it was unlikely before September. News that Hal was now out in Flanders caused fresh worries.

In late July she and Molly saw a wedding party come out of the Cathedral – a wartime wedding, but still with some finery. The groom in French cavalry uniform, spurs glittering. She wanted suddenly for herself a wedding in *that* Cathedral, which had become so dear to her. If she and Gib could be married like that . . .

Soon after, she and Molly and several others were transferred to base hospital at Camiers again. Once more near the sea. When they had been there only a week or two there was a bout of fierce fighting and a heavy convoy of wounded. She was all day in the operating theatre. When the guns rose to a certain crescendo, the instruments in the steel trays would rattle. She thought of them as teeth chattering with fear . . .

A letter from Gib. She saw the beloved handwriting, and thought with a sudden surge of love: When I am next free I shall write a truly long letter. (He knows how it is here.) She would have liked to read it immediately. Quickly first, and then again slowly, when she was off duty.

She had time only to push it into the pocket of her long skirt before going to assist in theatre with a man who appeared to have lost most of his chest, and the greater part of his jaw. (Oh, let that not be Gib, let that not be Hal.)

It wasn't till late afternoon that she was able to open it. Her head spun with fatigue as she sat alone in the tent, on the edge of the bed, tearing at the flimsy envelope. Passed by the Censor.

When she read it, she thought for a moment her heart had

stopped. She could not believe what she read. Her hand trembled, holding the sheets of paper. 'No, no,' she said out loud. 'No . . .'

'I got some news, in this letter –'

'Darling heart,' Molly cried, 'who's gone West? Your brother – no, don't – is it *Gib*? You're white as a sheet, darling. Mother of God. Let me look now for some of the Comforts, just wait now – a little drop of brandy . . . Sit down, will you now, *sit* –'

'Nobody's dead, Molly. Not even wounded. It's –'

'Thank God for that. Jesus be praised –'

'Gib's marrying someone else. That's what's in the letter.'

'*Never*! Darling heart, it's never the truth . . . Is it *him* says it? These days, there's always women want to upset –'

'He wrote it himself.'

'Oh, but that's – Sacred Heart of Jesus, what can I say? Who could do that to you? It's wicked . . . Wicked when you're out here serving in France, and he's . . .'

(Oh, but this was the indignation Mama showed, when someone thwarted me, reprimanded me . . .)

'Maybe just now, he's not himself – and he's been *trapped* . . . Here's the brandy, drink up now, drink up, will you? It'll be a *bad* woman sure as Mary's in Heaven – you said his nerves weren't right. He'll never go through with it – What we'll do when you've drunk that, is sit and write him a letter that'll *show* –'

'Molly,' she said, 'but Molly, he marries tomorrow. *Today* . . . I don't know . . . But it's too late –'

'We'll send a telegram then – why ever not?'

'Saying what?'

She saw Molly hesitate.

She said, 'Whatever could we put? He's a grown man, he may do what he pleases –' She broke down then, head forward at the table, great dry sobs: 'It's not true,' she said, 'tell me it isn't . . .'

Molly's arms went round her neck. Her voice warm, consoling: 'We could ask Our Lady would she make him change his mind – No, that might – Oh, but aren't men wicked, there's no getting away from it at all. You might feel better if you prayed, though I know well enough *I* couldn't –'

The brandy had made her lips numb. First burning, then numb. 'I'll try – I can't think, just now. Shock.'

'Is she anyone you know at all? I shouldn't have said those things, about wicked and that – aren't I always speaking without thinking? The one he's marrying, do you know her?'

'Teddy. It's my stepsister. Teddy.'

There wasn't any way of managing the letter. She had read it once – and now could not bear to look at it. The phrases he had used burned in her mind. She tried again and again to blot out the thought: *it is worse than if he had died.*

> . . . the most difficult letter I have ever had to write. It would be so much better if I could speak to you . . . I have made a number of, very unsuccessful, attempts to explain everything, and have torn them up. Neither explanation nor excuse are possible, and anything at all I can say is completely inadequate. I ask you to believe that your friendship has meant more to me than . . . I have to ask you formally, to release me from our engagement . . . No way of making the cold words on paper, warm. And yet I feel . . . Alice, it was very wrong of me not to write much, much sooner – when first I had doubts . . . We are so well suited as *friends* . . . But perhaps marriage . . .

How could it all have happened? People did not get married who had not *thought* about it. Yes – three or four months thrown together at The Towers . . . But had no one noticed? And that Belle Maman should not have tried to stop it . . . And worse, worst of all, that Gib said *nothing*. Gib, whom I trusted . . .

The next afternoon, sitting with Molly in the square at Camiers, outside a small café, she wrote a letter. Her hand shook.

'You look very white still, darling heart, should you be having coffee now? It scalds the nerves –'

'I'm writing to my sister –'

'That's a kind thought – I tell you now I'd never be so generous. Jesus Mary Joseph. Strangle her I would, you *should* be angry with her . . .'

Between mouthfuls of *pain au chocolat*, she went on – indignation, concern, consolation. Alice scarcely listened.

She felt in spite of the sun a chill that went deep inside. Inside her head too. But she wrote with great fluency. She had composed the letter during the night. It was all so simple. And she must do it while she *wanted* to. Tomorrow might be too late.

This secret she'd carried for fifteen years . . . The Riviera, Beaulieu, going up to Belle Maman's room – finding *that note*. Valentin, who she'd thought admired her, just a little . . . Valentin walking in the garden with Belle Maman. The *secret* . . .

She had never wanted to know it, had hated even to think about it. If it shocked me, she thought, what might it not do to *her*? She meant at first just to tell Teddy the facts – as she knew them. A simple statement. 'I thought you might like to know . . .' And let the *truth itself* be the upset. But as she began to write, it was not like that at all . . .

She could not stop. She was possessed. Underlining words, block printing them. Insults . . . The curious satisfaction of it all – as once when she had hit Uncle Lionel. It's the right thing, she thought, I must, I must, I must . . .

Molly got up. 'I've to see in that shop have they any soap – I'll be back in no time . . . Jesus Mary Joseph, you look inspired. You'll feel better afterwards, surely . . .'

The sense of satisfaction did not last long. The pain, when it returned, was worse . . . She could not pray, could scarcely remember the consolation she'd felt two weeks, one week, a few days ago. She was horrified, too, by what she had done. Those vicious words, stabs of the pen, who had she helped, what good had it done her or Teddy? She felt now, added to her pain, great waves of shame . . .

It was a mistake to have posted it at once, that same afternoon. If she had waited even one day – until the mood passed. That cold fluent anger . . . She had committed a sin – a very grave one. That much she knew. It clawed her like some animal, something black tearing at her soul, making even more unbearable the raw pain of losing Gib.

All the while everyday life went on. The too long hours, the heat, the smell, the suffering. Gramophones playing in the ward. Trains rattling by. And always, the guns . . .

I shall tell Molly, she thought. It would not be the same as telling the priest, was not the sacrament of confession, but it would help.

She said, 'I've done a *terrible* thing –'

'What's that, darling heart?'

'I – I wrote that letter, but –' How to say? She blurted it out somehow. Just a little of what she had put in black and white. The feeling of venom. *Let Teddy suffer*. she had thought as she wrote it. And could not now call it back.

'Sacred Heart of Jesus, what got into you?' Molly said. She shook her head. 'Poor darling heart, you *were* upset.' Then, 'Write her again,' she said, 'tell her it's none of it true. That it was all a fib . . .'

Alice wailed, 'But it isn't. It's *true* . . .' She hadn't expected to be misunderstood. And anyway, how could a lie sent after help either of them?

'Yes,' Molly said later, 'I *suppose* it's a mortal sin. It can't really be a venial one. Though surely now Our Lady will understand . . .

I killed my soul. My soul is dead . . .

The chaplain was busy. He had the seriously wounded, the dying, to help and console. Matters more serious than the peccadilloes of the nursing staff. Confessions were short and to the point.

'Bless me, Father, for I have sinned . . .'

She murmured, 'I'm recently a convert – I'm not very sure . . .'

'Yes, yes, my child, just make as good a confession as you can. Almight God understands . . . These difficult times . . .'

'I was rude to the Super twice, and Sister once, I've been impatient, I wasted some of the rations, I missed my morning prayers, I . . .' She couldn't, absolutely couldn't, come out with the truth. The list was almost through now. But a mortal sin, because of its gravity, should come first . . .

Surely, if I *tell* God I'm sorry, and I repent? (For I do, I do.) She remembered then a phrase from the small prayer book, the examination of conscience. If I were to call it something else . . .

'And also, I – had *impure* thoughts, Father . . .'

It was over. Done.

'. . . thank God for a good confession. And now, an act of contrition. *Oh my God, I am heartily sorry* . . .'

27

Rags, bones, skeletons, scraps of uniform, debris. No-man's-land of nearly three years ago . . . You could tell by the uniform, Hal said to the others: a white collar instead of a khaki on what had once been an officer. Seeing a rusted bayonet – rust or dried blood – he trembled again at his recurrent nightmare. The bayonet stuck between the ribs which *he could not draw out again*. Twisting, turning, struggling to finish the deed – always a different face looked into his, different eyes, imploring, hating, glazing with pain. Once he had looked into Stephen's face and had woken up twitching, sobbing.

Summer of 1917. They had been out for nearly five months now. He had spent a few days at home first where he'd seen the wounded Gib. 'Haven't they made you an officer yet?' Gib had asked, surprised. Hal had said no, and that he thought they judged him eleven pence three-farthings – 'I keep my head down jolly low . . . I want to stay with my friends.'

And so far, he had. They'd been together a long time – over two years. What he liked was that they never changed. He'd taken on their concerns – they'd taken on his. Bert, married to Winnie, was already the father of a baby boy. Now as a result of Bert's embarkation leave, she was waiting for another.

Oh, that cold send-off . . . Marching down the steep path from the cliffs to Folkestone quay. The steamer, painted grey, waiting. Papers checked, life-jackets on. No going back now. Icy cold winter weather, a sleet-filled sky, a wind getting up. Bert, who'd had a bad experience on a fishing expedition at Whitby the summer before the War, was certain he would be very sick. But in the event, it was Snowy came off the worst: retching before they were two miles out, throwing up over the side, losing his teeth . . .

Base camp was terrible. So was the long tedious cold railway journey later, the train at almost walking pace through the snowy countryside, all of them packed forty to a truck. The jokes about horses and cattle lasted only the first five minutes. Then: 'Form Fours . . .' Hungry, cold, starting the long march.

Fifty minutes at a stretch. As they marched, they sang about the Mademoiselle from Armentières who hadn't been fucked for forty years: '. . . up the stairs and into bed, *parlez-voo*, Up the stairs and into bed . . . *Inky pinky parlez-voo* . . .' Singing to take the mind off discomfort of the body.

New issue boots, and feet that had been icy burning now with blisters and chafing. The weight of the pack: they'd worked out that it was all of sixty pounds. Manure from the officer's horses in front stained the snowy road.

They had spent the first few months after leaving the base in a quiet sector. Bert became servant to a Lieutenant Taylor who came from the same part of Leeds. He was good to Bert, always making him keep the change when he sent him out for cigarettes or food. They fancied Bert enjoyed his work: it was like looking after a customer again. 'Will that be all, sir?' they'd hear him say. 'Because good stocks of café au lait came in yesterday. I'd not leave it too late, sir – if you was wanting a tin . . .'

It was in the last cold days of February he heard from Olive that James had been killed. 'I think I somehow expected it,' she wrote, 'Dad's taken it very hard which is not to be wondered at. Since Mam went he's . . .'

It had been difficult to write back. Mrs Ibbotson's death, just after Christmas, hadn't surprised him. They'd been still in mourning when he visited the farm on his last leave. Olive had said only, 'It was her time.' He remembered now that he'd been jealous of Tom on that visit. Not Arthur. Arthur was too young – she couldn't be interested . . . She said often – he supposed it was natural enough: 'Tom reckons we ought to do this, that, sell this . . .' Natural enough since Tom was there to help – and he was not. But oh, he didn't like it . . . Once, long ago, he'd sent kind regards to Tom in his letters. Now he could not . . .

Letters from Olive came regularly. Never less than two a week. And he the same, although he always thought when he sat down, tired and in the winters months often cold, that he would have nothing to say. But he always did. He could write things he could not say. Pencil covering the paper rapidly, so that Gus who had trouble with anything more than his own name would look on in wonderment, occasionally giving a low whistle . . .

Gus stayed with field postcards, crossing out as instructed the lines which didn't apply. He left untouched always the line at the bottom 'I haven't heard from you for a long time . . .' His family were even worse correspondents.

Hal had felt sad about James. 'I wish, Olive,' he had written, 'I wish there was something better, more helpful I could say . . . I try to remember, and think of what you said about being careful, and I understand how you feel, because now you have no brothers left, friends must be even more important . . .' And he would try not to think about Tom . . .

It was beginning to look really like action now. They had been hearing rumours, latrine rumours, about a big show for some days now. Tales of tunnels dug and mines laid. When at last it was about to happen, the evening before he thought of writing a farewell letter to Olive – in case . . . And then he thought: why? (And yet she was down as his next-of-kin. That had never been altered. Miss Olive Ibbotson . . .) But his hand trembled too much – and then in the end there wasn't time.

All that checking, last-minute preparations. The march off when it was still dark. They were in the first wave for the offensive, so had the furthest to go.

To make it worse, a shell, a whizz-bang, got their rum ration on its way up. It fitted in with the joke they had about the jars of Special Ration Diluted. It should have been called Seldom Reaches Destination . . .

They were silly all the time with their jokes.

'I worry,' Gus said, the evening before they marched. 'I don't want my dick shot away –'

Snowy said, 'You might get a DSO. If you don't take care. Might have to go up to the Palace for it. Have to wear a ribbon, says Dick Shot Off . . .'

Hal was frightened. Not about that, but about all of it. Frightened before. And again after. Not during. It was all too fast. Such a flurry of running, and crouching, and up again, and forward. Doing, for once, what he was told. When he could hear, that was, above the barrage – when he could see the raised arm of Captain Palmer: leading them this way, that . . .

They got separated, inevitably. And as usual afterwards no one told them if the day's fighting was a success or not. *They* had advanced, possibly. But others?

It wasn't till that evening, when they were together again, that he learned Bert had gone. Snowy had been near him when it happened. And no, there wasn't any chance he was one of the wounded . . . He . . . 'Bit of a mess,' was all Snowy would say.

He said it several times, as they lay out on the grass, sipping tea and rum from the second lot of rum jars, safely arrived. 'Bit of amess, old Bert . . . bit of a *mess* . . .'

It was quite a while later he told them, 'It were a Jack Johnson. Twenty, thirty yard away . . .'

A five nine shell. Jack Johnsons, great heavy brutes. 'Bit of a mess,' Snowy said, licking dry lips. His hand holding the dixie shook.

They supposed Lieutenant Taylor, Captain Palmer too, would write to Winnie, but knew they had to also. Hal wrote Gus's letter for him after he'd asked Hal three times how to spell 'Dear'.

Hal wrote, 'Snowy saw him go. It was very quick.' (That must be the truth. The mess which Snowy had at last described *had* to have been quick . . .) 'I know the Lieutenant's explaining that it's sometimes difficult to find the bodies . . . We can only sorrow for you in your great loss. Bert was always talking about baby George and we knew how eagerly he was waiting for . . .' His pen dried up again. The ink wasn't flowing properly . . .

Hot dry summer of 1917. There was a drought so they had to be very careful with water. They seemed always thirsty. The farmers near where they were billeted padlocked the wells – which you could understand, Hal thought. But Swanker Russell in their platoon just shot the bolts away.

Hot dry summer of 1917. The time came and went for leading in the hay at Lane Top. He thought about Tom and Arthur helping Olive. Once he and Olive – and Jack – had been hay boys. Hot dry summer of 1911 . . .

'Roll on, Duration,' Snowy said resignedly. Sitting in the sun outside the trench – they were in reserve now. Cracking lice with his thumbnail. Hated creatures, little white shellfish. Bloodsucking, irritating. Bad enough in cold weather, impossible in high summer. Scratching, scratching, sometimes till the blood ran, frantic with the filthiness of it all. Officers or men, the lice didn't distinguish. (Although Snowy had a theory they preferred Sergeant Majors . . .)

'Chatty for the Duration, I reckon,' Gus said, 'can't ever picture not being lousy. Nice clean soft shirt – me uncle's a tailor, used to give me bespoke ones what'd gone wrong – soft poplin, lovely long thread – really nobby. Scrubbing up in front of the fire, popping it over my head, looking good – and going out with Maggie –'

'Or Connie or Mary or Bridget,' Snowy said. 'You and your backstep carry-ons . . .'

'Best way to meet 'em,' Gus said. 'Nice in their uniform, answer the door, kettle on – never a day I didn't sit in someone's kitchen. All good lasses, they were. Safety in numbers, they say, like – don't they?'

Barechested, sunning themselves. They shared an old stump of candle which Hal lit with a lucifer and, long coarse shirt over head, ran along the inside seams where the little buggers lay in hiding – got you!

Their turn came up to have a bath at the delousing station – previously a brewery. They went in together. Their under-clothes were taken off them to be fumigated. The mail had come up just before they left, bringing Hal a letter. He'd barely had time to skim the first page.

'It's from Olive, is that,' Gus said. 'Blue ink and all. Your folk use *black* . . . Sweet on her, aren't you? Look at him, Snowy . . .'

They were certain he was in love with Olive. He thought it best not to argue. He couldn't just say, 'She's my greatest friend . . .' even though it was the truth. Now, at the baths, he could think only of sitting in the sun, all *clean*, drinking tea and reading that letter . . .

The vats once used for brewing were full of water. Hot, soapy – and dirty. You had to wash off in the first and second, then rinse off in the third – where the water was cold, and clean (or less dirty).

The underclothes he got back after weren't his. It was the same for everyone. But his were the worst: meant for a dwarf, he thought. His vest when he managed to get it on ended above his ribs. The long johns he couldn't get on at all. Snowy and Gus were delighted.

Hal said, 'Give me yours, Snowy – Your vest, it's hanging right down . . .'

'What's hanging down, eh? Gus, look there – look at Marmaduke's johns . . . won't your dick fit in, Marmaduke? Who've *you* been dreaming about, eh? His Dibs dick's too big –'

'Give over now,' Hal said, laughing.

Gus said, before making Snowy do a swop, 'They'll fit him right enow when he gets his DSO . . .'

Oh, why joke about nightmares? They were fooling around. You couldn't have too many laughs. And you had to take them when you could.

'Bet our khaki's not been smoked out. We'll be lousy again by tea-time – Let's play silly buggers, shall we?'

He was always hungry – the others told him he was growing still. The more worried and frightened, the more empty hungry he felt. It was best not to think what some of the food was or, in the line, where it might have been. Flavours of petrol and chloride, dead bodies, fæces. Food fallen, rescued, reflavoured. And some of the tins – what was in them? They sang: '*Oh, a little bit of everything got in a tin one day, And they packed it up and sealed it in a most mysterious way . . .*'

Eating was better behind the lines. And they could supplement it in cafés. They had their favourite estaminet where they would sit for hours. Gus would call for more and more vin blank, though Snowy said it was too acid. 'If I dropped me dentures in that lot they'd be gone in a half-hour.' He drank it all the same with lots of syrup added. Hal drank the pale weak beer. They ate eggs and chips when they were rich, or so hungry they didn't care. Hal had an allowance now from home. They had made him accept it. He shared it with Gus and Snowy, and with Bert when he was alive.

Sometimes Madame's old father would come out and play the piano. They would sing anything they felt like. One evening there was a niece or cousin staying there, helping in the café. Swanker Russell persuaded her to sing – she'd sung the night before, he said. She was about Hal's age and wore a black dress which showed her ankles. Her hair was tied back with a large black satin bow. She looked a bit like Teddy. Hal thought: Teddy's not bad, I suppose . . .

She sang:

> '*Après la guerre finie,*
> *Soldat anglais parti,*
> *Mademoiselle in the family way,*
> *Après la guerre finie . . .*'

The tune had a swaying rhythm and was at once haunting and tender. Heavy French tobacco, Woodbines, Ruby Queens thickened the air, obscuring the Virgin Mary and the Sacred Heart above the bar counter. Smell of sweat, hardly a square inch of unoccupied space. Beside them the pile of saucers which were their unpaid-for drinks. He couldn't believe he had ever been Mr Stainthorpe's pupil.

The girl who looked like Teddy was still singing. Now they all joined in:

> '*Mademoiselle in the family way,*
> *Après la guerre finie . . .*'

Some of the tommies had got French girls into trouble. The thing to do, they said, was to get a transfer elsewhere as quick as you could. And never, never give your real name . . . He couldn't imagine behaving like that. If I loved somebody, I'd *want* them to have my child. If I loved . . . If he didn't, he couldn't imagine in spite of what the others said and told him – couldn't imagine doing it . . . Lectures at the base on the clap, on places to go where it was *probably* all right, on prophylactics (to give them their grand name). But if you kept out of all that, it was easy to go to the grave never having . . . when he had that thought, he often blushed. But the blushing was a sort of sadness . . .

Leave came suddenly, unexpectedly. Near the end of August. They were just waiting to go up into reserve trenches again, when the Orderly Corporal called: 'Greenwood – you're for leave . . .' He was sent then to find Gus and Snowy and three others. But although they got a lift to the nearest station as soon as they'd collected their passes, they missed the leave train for that day. They slept in some goods wagon till nightfall. When eventually they arrived at Boulogne they felt they'd been travelling a week – at this rate it would be time to turn round as soon as they arrived. Even then, he decided to go up through Leeds so that with Snowy and Gus, he could visit Winnie.

Home again – and the biggest surprise: Teddy married. Married to *Gib*. It shook him.

'What about Alice?' he asked. 'I thought –'

But there seemed almost a conspiracy of silence. Mother remarked only on how romantic it all was. Father, Nan-Nan – all said they were pleased . . . 'It's wartime,' he heard. 'What does one expect but hasty marriages?' Only Sylvia seemed a little bewildered still.

It had happened only two days ago. The letter about it must have been still on its way. Now they were on a short honeymoon, in Sussex.

A whole week. After the first polite day hanging around The Towers, he spent all his time at the farm. The second day he came the nearest to fighting with Olive since the unhappy days of the Stephen affair. And of course it was over Tom.

He said outright, as they walked together through the gap in the cross wall (he didn't know why, because he had determined before coming up, on the way over, that it was the one thing he would *not* say):

'I suppose you'd rather be talking with Tom – staying in with him, than coming out now, with me.'

'If that isn't the stupidest –' she began. Her voice quite angry. Then she broke into laughter.

'Hal Firth – when I *think* . . . Me writing all those letters – three a week sometimes . . . Couldn't I be chattering to Tom then? Most nights I'm sat at the table – "That'll be your sweetheart again?" Tom says . . . I reckon, Hal, even if he wanted –' she hesitated. Then, taking hold of his hands:

'No, I'll be honest. He *has* courted me, Hal. I mean, he has asked. He asked –'

'I knew it,' Hal shouted, almost triumphantly. Distressed and yet at the same time vindicated. 'I knew all the while, it's really him. Suitable. He's suitable.' He added despairingly, 'It's just because you're a kind person, because of your kind nature that you go on like this – friendship and letters and . . . If I get killed. When I'm killed –'

It was her turn to cry out. 'What's all this nonesense? Have you gone *daft*?'

'No. No,' he said feebly. 'I just want – you.'

'Well, have me then,' she said. 'In any way you want. Like this, for a beginning.' She had hold of his hands still. Now she leaned forward and, on tiptoe, kissed him on the lips.

He didn't speak. He couldn't. *I* should have done that, he kept thinking. I've wanted to, for how long? She was back smiling at him now. He took her then in his arms, holding her tightly, tighter, squashing the breath out of her. He did the kissing now. Again and again. As his lips twisted on hers, his heart pounding, he remembered, from far away, that out there he'd had a dream once. About Olive.

'I dreamed,' he said. 'When I was in the trenches. Only I'd forgotten. You tasted just like that in the dream. I've wanted for so long –'

'I don't know why you didn't,' she said robustly. 'It's so much better than lots of words. Isn't it?'

Later she said, 'I think you should grow a moustache. Would you, then? You'd really suit it, Hal . . .'

Little brown bird. So much happiness. So short a time.

28

Fourth Christmas now, in a War that was to have been over before the first one. Sometimes, Lily thought, I can hardly remember that world – the one which changed so abruptly, for ever, between our toasting Christopher's birth, rejoicing – and the newspaper placards, mad enthusiasm, the 'We'll teach them . . .' Whatever might have been taught, what had been learned was – terrifying.

To think that once I worried about *love* . . . How did I find the time? Dr Sowerby, himself more than ready for retirement, telling me to do less, hinting that at my time of life . . . A forty-seven-year-old woman. But I have noticed nothing, except natural enough fatigue. And worry. (A son, son-in-law, and stepdaughter, all in France.)

Hal might have been safe in England, she thought, if that wound in September had been a little more severe. Had not healed so quickly and easily. He had only been a week or two back from leave when it happened. The left shoulder, high up, but clean and uncomplicated. He had written cheerfully enough from a French hospital: 'Not a Blighty one as I'd rather hoped. My friend Snowy's had even less luck – his was so light he's back with the platoon already . . .' He seemed to like his stay there. The hospital not too overworked – and the nurses making a fuss of him because they liked his imitations . . . He entertained the whole ward. Sister had come along to see what all the noise was about. There had even been a Chaplin film (one soldier burst his stitches laughing) projected on the ceiling of the ward.

If, when, he does come home, she thought sadly, he won't be around. He will be over 'helping' at Lane Top Farm. He likes to sit there and remember happier times, reminisce with the daughter – funny little mouse of a girl . . .

And of course I have no time to entertain him. I have so little time. Whenever did I *love*?

Love. And Teddy. Was there, I wonder, some vacuum that sent me, incurably romantic, conniving with that most hurried and exciting (yes, exciting . . .) of wartime marriages. A girl, only just seventeen – tied for life to a schoolmaster. To a person I had thought *Alice* was to marry . . . (What was it about those two? It never seemed to me anything but habit – mistaking a childhood friendship for something else. Robert never approved.)

Why then his easy acquiescence in Teddy's marriage? Because she is not his, *he does not care*. The Vicar's son is good enough since if he survives the War he will remove her from the scene. No, it is my own behaviour and feelings that need examining . . .

When she came to tell me, when I saw her face lit by love, I thought – it does not matter, seventeen or seventy, she *loves* (at seventeen I too was in love – with the Theatre . . .). And after all that he, Gib, had been through, and the long years in which I'd grown fond of him, always kind, reliable, polite, almost another son – it was he who had brought this change to her face, texture of skin, hair, voice. She is *altered by love*, I thought.

Also, did I not think at the same time, she is Val's daughter? Mine too, of course. But how uneasy the blend. How restless she looks already. Sometimes, those slanted eyes beneath the bushy brows – and she has no obvious beauty, only vivacity – how I used to be (and still am) so suddenly, irrationally exasperated by her. Once I used to dream of telling her the whole story. But why? It would, alas, be only for my own comfort.

She looked so happy – I was happy for her. She has a good man, I thought, whom she loves and who will take care of her. The haven of marriage so early will save her from complications, torments of her own nature. That hungry look which *I* have noticed if others haven't. Which shows itself in over-excited rushing about, 'ministering' to the officers. (And yet Gib who so obviously needed peace, found it in her . . .) Whatever happens later, I thought, she will have had this. I thought, too, of myself: If *I'd* followed, been able to follow, my heart? Was some of it vicarious, did I live through her?

When I saw her face – when she came back from the honeymoon . . . I knew. So tremblingly happy at first. Then just as suddenly within hours of arrival, white, tearful, shocked almost. Why? I think she realized suddenly, truly realized, that he must *go* again. Leave her.

But what of Alice– and her suffering? When Teddy first told me, I said, 'But *Alice* . . . Teddy dear?'

'Oh,' she said then, 'that has been over some time. After it went wrong, you know, last year. When he was called back. Now she scarcely writes. He doesn't think them at all suited . . . Yes, of *course* he writes to tell her . . .'

Poor Alice. Poor, poor Alice. I wrote to her too, not at once, not as soon as I should have done. I said, 'I don't wish to interfere, I don't know what happened, but Teddy tells me it was all over?' She never answered. But then she is busy, and cut off from us now. And then, she and I, together. It never was, never will be right . . .

Robert's only comment: 'I was not at all happy it should be Alice.' Then a little later: 'Perhaps someone could keep me informed of this game of musical chairs?'

Two bad attacks of bronchitis with the coming of the cold weather. Worry about his heart – it was apparent that Robert was not well. Threats that if he did not slow down he would be a permanent invalid. Dr Sowerby was quite definite. She took a second opinion also from the army doctor working at The Towers. He could not answer for the consequences, he said, were Robert to continue at this rate . . .

Officialdom informed them a replacemet would arrive in the next few weeks. Lily, remembering the impossibility of tracing Hal (but also, to be honest, the speed with which Alice had been able to return to France), had not expected such prompt action.

Accommodation, she thought. The Towers, once so enormous, could not now in the main body of the house provide what was needed. One more *problem*, she'd thought, only to find that conveniently Berthe and her mother, who had been three years in the cottage just beyond the stables, wanted to take up an offer of work in Harrogate.

The cottage, small but pleasant, as warm as anywhere in these days of scarce fuel. She had not decided if he would eat with them or have meals sent to the cottage. Perhaps there would be a wife? They had not said . . .

February 1918. She was sitting in the small panelled room

she used now as her private office when one of the maids, after three attempts, announced a visitor. Lily, used to interesting versions of Belgian names, took little notice.

'A Mr Heartfelt Levissey, m'lady –'

She decided at once, quicker than ever before in her life, that she did not like him. (And now what is to happen?)

He was her age about, of medium height, with brown hair receding, deep-set, almost sunken eyes.

'I must apologize, Lady Firth, that I cause this difficulty with my name ...' Such bowing, clicking of heels. The accent ...

She said in a cool voice, 'It's for *us* to apologize. We have several Belgian families in the village –' her smile was cool also. 'There have been some interesting versions of *those* names ...'

He smiled. 'The correct name is Ahlefeldt-Levetzau. Erik. You will know the purpose I am sent here ... If you should wish to show me now?'

'Oh please,' she said, '*please*, Mr Ahlefeldt, although the work is urgent, I hardly think –'

'But I should wish to work immediately, I am told everything is much with arrears –'

'An exaggeration. Sir Robert, in spite of his health, has been perfectly in control ...' That I should be driven to defending Robert, she thought. She did not bother to look at this face she already disliked.

'I am sorry. I have been misinformed –'

'Certainly you have ...'

The phrase – 'to rub someone up the wrong way'. That is what is happening to me ... She felt exactly as if the skin of her body ... pinpoints of irritation ... I am tired, she thought, trying to keep the edge off her voice ...

She had already forgotten his name. She could not wait for documents to inform her, so humiliatingly – it must humiliate him – she had to ask him.

When he told her, she said, not knowing what possessed her, 'I am sure you see the difficulty. If I hadn't known better I would have thought it a – German one ...' This is unpardonable, my conduct is unpardonable. Fatigue and irritation are no excuse.

She was not sure if he was angry or insulted – or both.

'*Ahlefeldt Levetzau*. If the documents concerning me have not reached you – *Ahlefeldt Levetzau*. It is a Danish name. I am from Denmark, Lady Firth –'

It is laughable, she thought. They would hardly send a German, even one living in England. But though he may be nothing to do with the enemy, I have *made* an enemy.

She saw nothing to do now but to explain as briefly as possible what her own work entailed, and to arrange what he should discuss with Robert on Robert's return. All the while she felt this – what else could she call it? – prickling of the skin. Gooseflesh almost. Positive. It is *positive* dislike . . .

Perhaps it was this irritation, or crossness with herself, or whatever, which caused her to say when the bell was answered:

'Would you arrange, please, for *Herr* Ahlefeldt's luggage to be taken to the cottage?'

A few weeks later Gib was reported missing. A frightened, shocked Teddy walked from room to room – working harder than ever: taking down dictated letters, reading aloud. Sitting in a corner, head bowed, Amy Hawksworth's arm about her shoulders (Amy herself in love with one of the ex-patients, Sadie said). A Teddy who would not talk. She will not let me near her, Lily thought.

'It isn't certain,' she tried to say. 'Missing . . . only means . . . He could turn up in some hospital . . .'

Teddy's face – for she didn't answer – was enough reproach. Would I accept such platitudes? False comfort. Where really was the hope?

She had to tell Hal. But just to think of him, to write his name, was to open the floodgates of worry. Any day the telegraph boy could be at the door . . .

And again Alice. It was for her to tell Alice. An Alice who it appeared had embraced Roman Catholicism, and said that she was 'very consoled'. This latest news could only be yet another test of her Faith.

Lily knew something of the fighting in Rumania. That they had finally entered the War in August of 1916 on the Allied side. That Russia had sent troops to help them keep back the Bulgarians. And that Bucharest had been occupied fifteen months ago. Now the Russian Revolution had altered everything for the worse. She searched out what she could of news. Above all – she worried.

That week of bad news, when they waited to hear about Gib, a letter came from Valentin. Addressed simply to her (the days of secrecy past . . .). She had just opened the envelope, had seen the bundle of close-written pages, when she was bothered by the wretched Mr Ahlefeldt.

She scarcely heard his query. 'I cannot answer now.' (She must read the letter *at once*.) 'Speak to Sir Robert about it, please.' She was barely civil.

She saw that he smiled. 'I would like everything to go smoothly, easily. But it is already two weeks I am here and certain things are not clear –'

She could scarcely conceal her impatience.

'*Later*, I thought I said later, Mr Ahlefeldt . . .'

His eyebrows raised. Quizzically. Sympathetically? But his voice was drily angry.

'I beg your pardon, Lady Firth . . .'

She was alone. The letter. The letter . . .

. . . It is a different Valentin who writes to you – and who should have written much, much sooner.

I have been part of this War. This may surprise you, my darling, because with my age it was not so obvious, but these matters can be arranged. I have not been all the time fighting. I have been just now with the cavalry in the north of Moldavia. Now, Lily, it isn't the Germans which have defeated me, but a more ancient enemy. The typhus germ – which has brought havoc here. I was ill up in Dumbraveni where it was very bad. Although I have recovered, the damage is quite severe, they say. So you will excuse this uncertain handwriting. No more war for me, even though in my spirit I feel with those who deplore the Armistice we were forced to make, and could wish *guerre à l'outrance*. (Although *more* loss of life? I wonder . . .) And also, these days I ask myself, Lily, how could we, I, once have been so light-hearted, so *silly*? We were only children when we were so happy (and then so *un*happy . . .). It is more than eighteen years since we loved – it's one, two, three hundred . . .

First now, what is the news, news that is not War? I say it all to you very simply. (I think my English isn't so good as it was, I don't practise now – though I have met English people these last months.) About my wife, Elizabeta – so young, so specially chosen for children . . . It has been *pénible* for us both – After six years (and I know as do you that it's not with me it's wrong!) there was no child. Then they find something with her and try some operations – but still, no. Now perhaps three or four years ago, they have operated to take away everything. Our chances all gone. I am not interested, she not either, that we should adopt. It is not the same . . . That is my sad story.

It isn't bad with everyone. Ana Xenescu – her little last child, Corina, is enchanting. She is fifteen now, and Ana is already eager she should be married. But when *I* see her, Lily, so dark, so *vif*, she reminds me only of *our* gift. Lily, I *know* although I haven't now seen photographs or talked to you any more of this, that Theodora is a spiffing girl . . .

Older, wiser – I am wiser and I have thought about our daughter. This is very important, Lily – I've decided (and you are free to tell Robert what you wish of this), that because of what I have told you of my own private life, because of this I would wish to leave to Theodora the wealth exactly that I would give a child of ours – *If you and I had married.*

Now, this wealth. I can't tell you exactly anything of this, because such terrible things are happening here also to do with money. And now we must fear Russia as well as Germany. But I was never such a silly little boy as we pretended – Lily, you will find in here on another paper the name and address of a lawyer in Paris, also of a bank – together with other matters. I have made such arrangements that if it is *possible at all*, when anything happens to me then our daughter (our gift from God) will be, I am nearly certain, an independent woman. I know that it can sound foolish because you are not a family without riches! But I know what Robert was saying to you many years ago . . .

You must tell our daughter what you like. It is for you to decide. But I *don't* want gratitude, obligation, embarrassment. I do it, give it, also for *my* happiness. There is plenty for Elizabeta, so there we have no problem. I take in my confidence only Sophie (Teodor died in early 1913. During the Balkan troubles. You know this? His heart . . .)

When I had the fever, I dreamed again and again that you nursed me, you loved me, we were a *long time married* . . .

There were more pages. But she couldn't. She was already too upset. Later . . .

The hundred and one tasks of the day scarcely begun. An unpleasantness already with Mr Ahlefeldt . . . She stood looking out of the window, thinking of Valentin, weeping as she had not wept for years. Not for what had happened. But for what had not . . .

Two weeks later they had a visit from her nephew, David Ziolkiwiski. Daisy's second son. She had heard from Daisy that he had enlisted. It appeared that he would not sail directly to Brest but would be in England a little before going to France. She put off telling Robert. Any mention of Daisy and her family could well set off yet another diatribe against Jews. (When she had challenged him once, saying, 'But what is behind all this?' he'd looked mildly surprised. 'It's a fact,' he'd replied, 'not an *opinion* . . . Only misplaced family loyalty binds you to the faults of that race.')

She wired to David that he should spend a few days with them. Over the years she'd seen photographs of him and the others but remembered him best at the age of six, seven – when they still lived in Yorkshire. (When I was *ashamed*. Before Edmund and the settlement . . .)

When he first arrived she had a chance to be alone with him. He was a fine-looking boy. Large, dark. Except for Joszef's lovely eyes, she could see little resemblance. Harry's hands. A look of Ma when he spoke – how Ma might have been if she'd been confident. Families are funny, she thought. He told her, as Daisy had already done, that his sister Ruth's husband Lew was already in France, working with the ambulances. Ruth had three children, two girls, Esther and Lily, and a boy, Jay. Was expecting a fourth any day now. 'Mother's a grandmother three times already . . .' But Lily told him, 'I shall beat that . . .'

It was unfortunate he should come just when they were having one of their now rare dinner-parties. Another time and Robert might well have eaten upstairs, or been in bed early. She dreaded the encounter.

There was a gathering almost like old times. Sadie, specially asked and for once free. Charlie, who couldn't be *not* asked . . . Erik Ahlefeldt-Levetzau (no choice here . . .). The MO at The Towers. A Mr and Mrs Palmer. A Mrs Fraser . . . All present to greet Lieutenant David Ziolkiwiski.

Food. Short, of course. Although Erik Ahlefeldt had told her that in his native country (I wish he would go back there), the shortage of fats was so serious that health, especially of children, was in jeopardy. She wondered occasionally if he had a wife and family – and if so, where they were? His behaviour, always so correct, left no occasion for personal questions. She was not proud of her curiosity. He spoke freely of Denmark, in which it appeared he had not lived for at least fifteen years.

The problems of food. Game, in season, was the great standby. Problems too of the overworked kitchens, strained to the limits now with feeding patients. This evening they produced charred venison, soup so salted it was painful to the tongue, mangled vegetables. Only the wine was good.

Erik Ahlefeldt came late. She knew the reason must be some crisis in the hospital (how often had it not happened to her?). But she was unreasonably irritated . . . Robert made some light remark which falsely led her to suppose he was in a good mood – he did, after all, seem to approve of the new director . . .

David he had so far ignored. She hoped for this to continue. But no . . . He asked suddenly,

'Don't the Yankees, that regiment of yours – don't they keep all the Ikey Moes in one bunch? Not mix you . . .'

'Sir?'

'Ikeys. Semites, Israelites, what have you . . . You're a Jew, more or less, aren't you? Nothing to be ashamed of . . . Fortunately I don't have the problem. Mix you all together, do they?'

David had gone very white. Lily, faint with shame and anger. Charlie cut in:

'Talking of *regiments* – my cousin, Archer-Seymour, the one in the Princess Royal's –'

Lily was surprised to see Erik Ahlefeldt put down his napkin and rise from the table: 'If you will excuse me. A task I have suddenly remembered. I would like to make my excuses. Lady Firth –'

'But certainly . . .' It made though, a slight chill. Conversation ceased as he moved to the door.

'Well,' Charlie began again heartily, 'Cousin Archie is now fearfully –'

Erik's voice, polite but firm, cut in from the doorway:

'Excuse me. It is not the truth that I have work. I leave your table because I am not willing to listen that another shall be insulted for his race or his nation. Here or anywhere. That is all.'

The door closed behind him. There was an uneasy silence. Sadie turned to David:

'Although I don't know New York like my own city, I want to ask you – the pastry shops round Union Square . . .'

Lily, waylaying Robert afterwards, reproached him:

'How *could* you? How *dare* you?' Beside herself with anger at the upset. And to cap it all that it should have been that annoying Dane to defend David . . .

'I have always said exactly what I like, when I like –'

'Oh?' she said. 'Really? I had not noticed –'

'It *is* my roof, after all. Your Israelite nephew only visits by my kindness . . .'

Impossible. He is quite impossible. 'This,' she said, 'we've had it so many times, this argument. Always about Jews . . . Jews are people, are they not?'

'So are niggers, I suppose, in your book . . . Wisely, until the North American folly, they were kept in their place – as slaves.'

'You are impossible . . .'

'Go now,' he said, 'go and sit with your nephew. Talk to him as much as you like. And,' he added, turning to leave her, 'by the way, I didn't care for the behaviour of my replacement. Damned impudence under my roof. His terrible *correct* English – they say his wife was English. No concern of mine, that. If he keeps himself to himself out in the cottage, does the work properly.'

Lily said, 'There's no complaining on that score.' Even with her prejudice she had to grant him that.

'Tell you what,' Robert said. She saw he was angry still: 'Fellow's a Hun, you know. I'm sure they've sent us a Hun . . .'

It appeared Robert was not the only person to think that. Three days later Lily was in her office before breakfast, writing quickly to Hal. She told him about his cousin: 'They are very keen you should come to New York when it's all over.'

When it's all over . . . One of the maids, a new one from the next village, stood at the door. She looked frightened, rushing her words in a low voice so that Lily had to ask her to repeat them.

'It's summat not right – at t'cottage, where t'German gentleman –'

'Danish. From *Denmark*, Annie.'

'Danish gentleman, m'lady. Summat's up. Hodgson was in t'gardens and he said –'

'Perhaps, whatever it is, Hodgson would care to speak to me?'

Stopping only to put on a heavy coat, she went out. As she passed the stables to reach the cottage, the elderly groom, Wilkinson, said good-morning, and looked quickly away.

'Has something happened, Wilkinson?'

'You'd best see for yissen, m'lady. I don't know owt about it . . . It's nowt to do wi' me.'

She turned the corner then. And saw . . .

Not a window of the cottage remained unbroken. The place looked almost derelict. The contents of several dust-bins, emptied in a pile under the downstairs windows. Red paint on the door and: GET AWAY HOME HUN, YOR BLOOD FOR OUR BLOOD, HANG KISER BUT YOU GO FURST . . .

She hurried to the back. The door, which opened like a stable door, had the upper part swinging open. The bottom had been kicked in. Inside she saw books scattered, torn from their spines, pages lying about. A violin, broken and trodden on . . . She picked up a book, let it drop. She was shaking. Terrible, she thought, this is terrible.

'Good morning and please excuse me, Lady Firth.' He stood just behind her. Dressed, but not yet shaved.

'What is all this?' she said. '*What has happened*?'

'I also must ask what has happened.' His voice was as polite as ever. Only a slight tremor in it betrayed shock. 'The truth is, I remain still a little afraid –'

'It's a vicious attack,' she said. She looked about her. The violin bow, snapped in three, lay at her feet. 'Last night?'

'I am not certain of the hour. Let us say after midnight – it is, I think they are perhaps six, seven, people that live in the village . . . Perhaps some drinking first, and then, they encourage each other. It was – ugly. And, yes, *of course* I have been afraid for myself –'

'What can I say? My husband – Sir Robert and I – we would both –' She kept repeating, 'What can I say?'

'It is enough you are concerned. It is not your fault.' He smiled gently. 'Also it is nothing beside – such things as are happening where is the fighting. Your son, son-in-law . . . We must have proportions about these matters. Besides of that, here is only a game. Naughty wilful children . . .'

She met his eyes. They were blue. She had not noticed, not caring to look at him before.

'The windows,' she said, 'all that. A glazier will be sent for at once. Cleaning up. I shall arrange . . .'

Damaged books, wrecked violin – what should, could she say? She went on: '. . . I shall arrange a room for you at once. You must rest. The shock. Everything will be seen to . . .'

'Yes,' he said. 'That would be most kind.'

She put out her hand. 'If you would accept – I wish to apologize on behalf of – if you can forgive . . .'

Afterwards, afterwards. In years to come, going over and over again the moment when their hands touched (but we must have *shaken hands* before . . .), she found he, they, had lost forever those next few seconds.

She would ask, 'Did I throw myself in your arms? Which of us – did you . . .' And he would say, 'But of course it is *you* who seduce me, how can you think I shall be so wicked?' Then *she* would say, 'What a likely story. Telling it to me too, who would believe *anything* you say . . .'

Her face cupped in warm hands. Then his head, pressed against the heavy wool of her coat. Locked in an embrace. How long, how long, oh let it be for ever . . . We don't compare, don't say this isn't Edmund, Valentin, Charlie . . .

The bedroom upstairs. Berthe and her mother had shared it. She remembered walking first up the narrow staircase. The stripped bed. So neat. She was crying and trembling. Touching, clinging. It *was* me, she thought afterwards.

And yet who had wept (shock and fright at the night's happenings)? Who was it said over and over, that never, never, never . . .

'Never,' he said. 'From the first – when you disliked me so much. From the first moment – When I saw you – a lonely person. You are so lonely. I also, of course. But *you* –'

Lonely. A son, two daughters, a distinguished husband, a full household, a responsible post. Scarcely a free moment. Yes, it is possible to be very lonely . . .'

Stifled cries – his hand, her hand, over her mouth. Icy winter sunlight through half drawn curtains, shattered windowpanes. Floor scattered with glass fragments. And never so happy . . . Since, since – but today I say goodbye, and thank you to Valentin . . .

'You are partly to blame,' she told a visibly shaken Robert. 'It is – was – your attitudes. People are not deaf – they notice. Rumour and misunderstanding. These are ugly matters . . .'

He had taken to humming tunelessly when he did not wish to answer. He did so now.

At midday she went to the village, and into the Fox and Grapes. All talking stopped as she came in.

'Some of you in here,' she said, 'some will certainly know what I mean, when I say about last night – *are you not ashamed*?'

Several of those drinking looked away. The landlord, a man she knew and respected, murmured something. One of the farmers said, 'I told them as they shouldn't.'

Later she told Erik:

'There was that sort of trouble in Leeds, you know, last year. Against Jews. And of course, Conchies have been subjected also. But you . . .'

Gradually, eagerly, because they talked now: she learned

more about him. He had a married daughter, living in Esjbø. A son at Copenhagen University. ('My university also. Unlike our neighbour Sweden, it's by France we are influenced, so I am most francophile . . .') His wife who had died in 1909 had been half Danish, brought up in England because of her mother's second marriage to an Englishman. Erik had worked in her family business for some twelve or fifteen years. Beginning at the bottom. In the early days of the war, he had worked as a censor in London. Later, through friends and connections, he had become involved with hospital administration.

As the days passed – grim with their lack of news about Gib, and constant, draining worry for Hal – she asked how it could be that she had so much emotion left. We are so much in love . . .

She wondered sometimes if anyone guessed. If Robert knew. *How little I care*, she thought. The man who had beaten her before Teddy's birth, who had draped her with jewellery, before whom she'd stood, dressed only in the Waterfall . . .

Such matters did not concern him these days. He had aged remarkably. And the Diamond Waterfall – all that talk of donating it for the War Effort . . . (Perhaps that would earn him a further title – who knew?) The man who if he could not love Teddy gave instead double love to Sylvia . . .

Why worry? This solace, this wonder, among all the cares, anxieties, despairs. She thought too afterwards: I never believed it was just for the moment. I always knew it would be for nearly forever . . .

Nearly forever. For who speaks of forever, now? Not because of broken faith, but because of death. Death . . .

29

Hal started up falsetto (he hadn't much of a singing voice, but they always liked his falsetto):

'Oh they've called them up from Flaxthorpe and they've called them up from Penn, and they'll call up all the women when they've fucked up all the men . . .' It was a parody of the verse from *Keep the Home Fires Burning*. You could use anyone's home town. He said:

'They're the lines Ivor Novello didn't write – he thought of them too late.'

'Jolly good song, jolly well sung, give the poor bugger some beer . . .'

'. . . *Keep the home fires burning, till the boys come home* . . .' And when might that be? Hal felt they'd been over here for ever . . . A long time anyway since the leave he'd had last August, and the time in hospital after for his wound. A cushy time, that, all too short – and not truly appreciated because all he had wanted was to get back, if only for a week or two, to see Olive . . .

Now it was April, and the fourth spring of the War. It was all going badly again. Hurrying backwards, as far as he could make out. Rumour and counter-rumour – the worst one, that soon the Germans might be over the Channel. ('See a Kraut before May's out . . .') On April 11th, Field Marshal Haig's Order of the Day. It was read out to them: '. . . there is no other course open to us but to fight it out . . . with our backs to the wall and believing in the justice of our cause . . . the safety of our homes and the freedom of mankind alike depend on the conduct of each one of us at this critical moment . . .'

Tired. He was so tired. As if he were falling, falling . . . What price his murmuring heart, as they had once called it? He supposed it had been either a mistake in the first place, or else something he'd grown out of. No time here for hearts to murmur, or thump – except with fear. And he was used to fear. Snowy managed the best. Gus had grown jumpy – his colour a yellowy white, his eyes dull. Lighting fags one after the other, when he could get them, or pulling at the skin on his cheek with a nervous angry gesture. He told Hal, 'I don't rightly know – I can't take it, like. Not much more I can't – I'd never thought, you see . . .'

A fine spring evening. Stopping on the march, they lay by the roadside to sleep. Twice in the night motor lorries, mule-drawn limbers, rattled by. Gus said afterwards: 'I never – I couldn't shoot me finger off. Nothing like that . . . But I'd thought – a foot stuck out accidental, like – when the wheels come by. That'd do it . . .'

Hal told him, 'You'll be needing both feet, Gus, to run from all those girls you made promises to . . .'

He hadn't felt at all like joking. Then a few days later, after an action when a number of wounded were lying out on stretchers, a limber rushed by – its drivers killed, the blood-stained horses bolting: wheels rolling over the first of the stretchers. Gus, with Hal at the time, white and sick. Sick all that day.

A letter came from Olive in the evening. Letters came often from Olive. No one teased Hal about her now . . .

> . . . One bit of news is that I'm off to Devon to Aunt Nellie. Dad'll be staying with Uncle Walter, that lives Skipton way. They were always good pals. Granny Willans will go too. Altogether it seems for the best. Tom reckons to wed at Easter – he'll look after the place well enough. It's a right shake-up and no mistake . . . I'm homesick before I've even left. Only that's no way to look at things – thinking of all you boys that really have something to be homesick about . . . Tom'll be fetching up his own collie dog here. Tess is past it . . .

News from a foreign country. Far, far-away places. Yet to think, eight months ago . . . It had been terrible, his jealousy, his fears about Tom last summer . . .

When she'd let him kiss her, he'd thought the worrying would go. Only he couldn't forget her admission: 'Tom *has* courted me . . .' Suppose?

His father hadn't seemed very fit – heavy cough, tired, irascible, critical. Impatient with Hal, still in the ranks.

'Can't see what you've got against it – becoming an officer

. . . They'd bring you home, allow you time here. You might even get to India – somewhere quiet . . . Who knows?' Shaking his head sadly: 'A ranker, Henry. Really. For a Firth to be Tommy Atkins still . . .'

'I could put in for a lance-jack. They've –'

'Are you deliberately misunderstanding me?'

'Probably. Sir.' Then because that hardly seemed fair, he added: 'I'm best where I am. One star one stunt, they say. You've seen the Casualty lists in *The Times*. You can't want –'

No, of course his father didn't wish to lose him. But as he had long ago discovered, attitudes, emotions were not so simple as that. And it was no better with his mother. He couldn't think in the past when they had ever had a *conversation*. Now, the springs dried up within seconds. (For him, ghost of Stephen hovering always. For her too?)

Yet his father had the confidence to speak of University. Cambridge, planned for him years ago, in the days of Gib.

'A little coaching for six months or so to rest you, get you up to standard. Perhaps Nicolson himself . . . Then I really can't see why not . . .'

What fairy-tale world did he inhabit, this father of his? To speak like that when all round him at The Towers was visible proof of what happened in war . . .

A fairy-tale world . . . But then, Hal thought, these few summer days I too have chosen to inhabit one . . . Perhaps it was going back to when everything had seemed safe. Those well-loved Fairy Books, with their different coloured covers, arriving every Christmas. Red, Green, Orange, Crimson . . .

In the evenings, when he couldn't be with Olive, he sat in the window-seat of his room. Removed. In another world. The best was that he seemed to have forgotten the stories: he would read on, breath held, to see what happened next. Yet I must have known once . . . And how could there be surprises, real surprises? The prince always married the princess, the monster was slain, the villains died a horrible death.

He came upon the tale of the King of Goldland. He did not want to remember it. And could do so only with pain. Stephen trespassing in the copse. Stephen sickening for diphtheria. Stephen walking along the walls with Tess, rabbiting. The stranger – Stephen, white with anger, cutting him at Settstone market. Stephen enlisting . . .

All long ago. And long ago forgiven. Certainly by Olive. If anyone could heal it would be Olive. Olive, whom he had kissed on Tuesday and again today . . .

His leave was so short. It wasn't possible to tell her what he hadn't been able to write in his letters. He was shy of many of his innermost thoughts. But if they were not said, if he went back to France without – if she *never knew* I loved her . . .

He opened the Yellow Fairy Book. *The Lovely Ilonka* – An Hungarian tale. He turned the page and read:

There was once a King's son who told his father that he wished to marry . . . 'No, no!' said the King, 'you must not be in such a hurry. Wait till you have done some great deed. My father did not let me marry till I had won the golden sword you see me wear . . .'

He had closed the book, his hands shaking. For what seemed half the night he'd paced his room. Why not? he asked himself. *Why not?* Then the sturdy reliable mature face of Tom would come before his eyes, and he'd think – perhaps it is already too late. Wasn't Tom the sensible choice? There on the spot, wanting to take over the farm. A *good* man.

He remembered then suddenly, the Diamond Waterfall. Hated jewellery, hated stones. But the Waterfall – that was different. It was beautiful, and one day would be his.

Tom. A sensible choice. But I – *I* could make her a princess . . .

'No, no!' said the King, 'you must not be in such a hurry . . .'

He could barely wait for it to be morning. They had arranged an expedition to Aysgarth Falls. She'd managed her work somehow so that she'd be free. They went on bicycles – hers was second-hand and very heavy and they had to stop frequently to rest. She had brought the food – he did not like asking for anything at his hospital-home.

The weather was disappointing, more autumn than summer. They watched anxiously the banked clouds which waited behind the fells. As they cycled through open moorland, the purple stretched around them, dark-shadowed. Sheep clustered, restless, or called to each other.

They reached the Falls before lunch. She wanted to stand and look before they ate, going from one waterfall to the other in wonder:

'I'd quite forgot. When we were bairns, they brought me.

And I'd always meant . . . It's daft when you don't live far. There's even places in Devon I know better . . .'

As she stood there in her light brown jacket and skirt, her hair all wispy from the wind on the moor, he lifted up in his mind the cascade of diamonds that was the Waterfall – fastened it about her neck. He thought how the dazzling of the diamonds would make her skin vibrate almost, set alight the brown flecks in her hazel eyes . . .

She turned to him. 'A penny for them, Hal. They look so deep . . . Not summer outing thoughts –'

He said awkwardly, 'Don't they call that a brown study?'

'What?'

'The sort of daydream I was having.' They were by the largest of the falls. He leaned a little over the bridge, gazing at the water – yellow white, frothing, foaming outwards, upwards. Boiling, churning waters.

Jack falling to his death.

'I was thinking,' he said, 'that time – with Stephen and Jack. *That* waterfall . . .'

'Yes,' she said. 'I thought too . . . You forget, and don't forget – these things.'

'Except,' he said, 'we can't be always not going to waterfalls . . . and Aysgarth Falls, they're quite quite different. It was my idea anyway. I wanted us to come.'

'And I wanted to come . . .'

Looking down, he could see a plain slab of dark washed stone. A bird hopped on to it. A wren, he thought. It stayed there, unconcerned, while a fingerbreadth away the spray rose and fell.

'Olive,' he said, 'would you marry me?'

If she was surprised, she only showed it a little. But first she smiled. She said:

'Oh, Hal love – whatever for?'

He was indignant. Frightened too.

'Because –' He hesitated. '*That*'s not an answer,' he said.

'No,' she said, 'it's a question –'

'Clever,' he said, exasperated. 'All right. I'll ask you one. Why not?'

She turned away from the bridge. Hands on his shoulders, she rubbed her face on his. 'Silly, you're always so silly. I know what you want. Well, you can have it, darling Hal.. We'll find a way, a place –'

For a moment he thought he would cry. He said in a too loud voice, 'But I want to marry you . . .'

'Hal, have you *thought*? You're Mr Henry Firth of The Towers. It's just daft –'

'It's what I want. I've known for ages. All the time in France –'

'You never. What you want, Hal Firth, is *me*. And I've said yes to that. Didn't I, love?'

Oh, but he never could. That wasn't how princesses were made. And that she should even *think* that was all he wanted . . .

He said stiffly, angrily, 'I can get that sort of thing in France – or in London on the way up. I mean, skirt – if that was what I wanted . . .'

She seemed distressed. 'Now *you're* being daft. Twisting my words –'

'I love you. I love you so much, Olive. That's why *I want to marry you* –'

She said then: 'It'd need a lot of thinking on. I'm not sure about wanting to marry anyone . . .'

'Tom –' he began.

'Tom – he's grand, Hal. If I was *looking* for a husband, now –'

'Olive, *marry me* –'

She laughed suddenly, throwing her arms right about him. She whispered, her breath hot in his ear, 'If you say that just once more . . .'

'What'll you do?' He was laughing now too.

'Something that'll really shock you. Wait till after we've had our lunch. When we're somewhere – when we're not overlooked, like . . .'

Olive's breasts, nipples that awoke to his touch. Olive's thighs, his hand in that forest of hair, so warm, damp-scented.

'I don't mind,' she said. 'If you want. I shouldn't mind if you . . . I'd be proud . . .'

'I couldn't,' he said. Then over and over: 'I couldn't unless . . . You'd have to be my wife.'

She smiled. 'You mean it's not seemly?'

'I mean like I said, that I *want you to be my wife* . . .'

'I thought we weren't going . . . Hal, love, dear Hal, I'm only saying there's no need to *marry* me. We could love each other a lot – now, or tomorrow – and it would just be our secret . . .'

He said, 'And if there were a baby –'

She smiled to herself. 'I'd worry about that when it happened. Love-children get along all right – if they're loved.'

'If you really loved me you'd *want* to marry me . . .'

She stopped his mouth with kisses. Then as suddenly, arranging her clothing:

'Get away,' she said. 'You know I love you. Isn't that enough now?' She stood up: 'What of that moustache? I don't see even the *beginnings* of it yet –'

'I thought – when I get back.' How terrible. He did not want ever to think about 'back'. Out there. France. The Front . . . Terrible words. 'I'll grow it then – for when I see you next . . .'

'If you loved me like you said, you'd grow one *at the double* –'

'You sound like Sarge,' he said happily.

Back home, he copied out on a sheet of paper the passage from Lovely Ilonka's tale.

There was once a King's son who told his father that he wished to marry. 'No, no!' said the King, 'you must not be in such a hurry. Wait till you have done some great deed. My father did not let me marry till I had won the golden sword you see me wear . . .

He added underneath: 'I haven't got a Military Medal or anything like that. But don't you think seven months' fighting – and more to come – is worthy of a golden sword? So . . . *PLEASE OLIVE MARRY ME* . . . With love from Hal.'

When his leave was up, and he'd seen her for the last time, he posted it from the station on his way down South.

Eight months now since that August outing to the Falls. And now he had this letter. Tom was to wed *someone else*. But it was the next paragraph which really lifted his heart:

'. . . I've thought a lot of what you asked in the summer – I'm still not sure it'd be *right*. But it's so difficult these days. And I want above everything else for you to be happy. If it's *really* what you want, I could agree maybe. When you get leave next . . .'

He wrote her a long letter. He traded green (uncensored) envelopes with Swanker Russell for the contents of one of his food parcels so that he could write exactly what he wanted (although he fancied they read the letters anyhow). Pages and pages of ideas, plans, and instructions. He kept telling himself that for all his family cared . . . It was no business of theirs – Olive was twenty-one and he, well, *almost*. If he was old enough to die for his country, then surely . . .

He explained that when he got leave he was going to wire her, in code. She was to come straight up to London – where he'd be waiting, having taken care of the special licence. Then as soon as that was through, and if he had enough leave, they'd go down to Devon. (Wouldn't it be difficult to pretend they weren't married? And what about a bedroom?)

Although he terribly didn't want to, he felt he should add: 'If you change your mind, and don't want to do it, then that will be quite all right. It must be what *you* want. Love from Hal.'

They were moved to the area near Poperinghe. Nothing seemed any different. Gus's nerves were no better. Worse, in fact. Hal wanted for him, more than for anyone else, that he should get the right kind of wound, soon.

Cold nights even though summer was on the way. Sleeping in the front line: no wonder he dreamed, never sure if he was awake or asleep. Hard wood of the plank pressing into flesh – so tired that even the discomfort couldn't keep him awake. Taking turn about to sleep in the middle position. And everywhere the rats, bloated with corpses but still voracious – scrabbling for bully beef scraps under the duckboards.

He used to go into Poperinghe, Pop, to the club, Toc H. The garden, if you stopped your ears up, an oasis of peace in the spring days. Because the club made no distinction between officers and men, he could feel there most absolutely himself. Henry Firth of The Towers and '04 Greenwood at one and the same time. Often he would climb to the upstairs room which was the chapel, and think of Olive and of Stephen who had been his friend. Of Jack, and Bert. Gib . . .

Letters, more and more letters to Olive. She was settled in

Kingsbridge, in Devon. Tom was married. Father and Granny Willans had moved out. It was sad, but . . .

He dreamed one night he was with Olive at Lane Top. She sat by the kitchen range. The fire roared. He could feel its heat in the dream. When he looked again he saw that she was quite naked. Except for the Diamond Waterfall. He didn't know what to say. 'I'm wearing it just to please you,' she told him. 'Do you like it?' But he didn't. He could see that it was beautiful, but 'Not here,' he said, 'it's not seemly.' They were words she might have used: 'It's not seemly, Olive.' He was afraid too someone would come in and discover them. He tried to explain to her that they must run away, arrange it all better . . .

Snowy's elbow woke him . . .

The next day he heard that in twenty-four hours he would have leave, for ten days.

Then a golden dress was put on her and pearls were twined in her hair and she took her seat in the Emperor's carriage which was drawn by six of the whitest horses in the world, and they carried her without stopping to draw breath to the gates of the palace. And in three days the wedding was held . . .

He was in London and had arranged everything. But it wasn't any of it very real. Wasn't even how it might have been.

Three days before he'd left, Gus had gone. Hal, working as a runner, had simply come round a turn in the trench, signposted Mornington Crescent, and bumped into a couple of stretcher-bearers, and Gus.

' 'Tis his belly,' said one of them in an Irish accent.

Hal said, 'Gus, you got your Blighty one . . .' The bearer behind his head pulled an 'all up, all over' face. Gus, eyes glazed with pain, mumbled something.

'What's that?' Hal asked, bending near.

'They'll give it me, won't they, then? Me job back . . .'

God forgive me, Hal thought. ' 'Course they will,' he said. 'My love to Leeds, Gus.'

Strangely the face that haunted him afterwards wasn't the dying Gus pumped full of morphine, but the white-faced Gus who'd said, 'A foot stuck out accidental, like – when the wheels come by . . . I don't rightly know. I'd never thought, you see . . .'

Two more days, and Hal had left. Collecting his papers, getting his clearance, crossing on the boat on a fine July evening, and thinking: They don't know at home. If it should be the last time. . . .

He booked in at a small private hotel in Bayswater, with a view of the park. He told the manageress: 'I'm getting married in two days. My fiancée's coming up from Devon.'

He was at Paddington to meet her. Although troops were milling around everywhere it was very different from Victoria. She was wearing a hyacinth blue dress and coat and looked lovely, he thought. He wanted to tell everybody that she was going to marry him. She carried a large hamper. She said, 'I brought eggs, butter, cream – because of the shortage. I thought they might like them at the hotel.'

First thing (he could have bitten his tongue off): 'Are you sure?' he asked. 'About – us?'

'No, I'm not. But I can't get out of it now, can I?' Then she added quickly, 'You fond thing, of *course* I am . . .'

He said, 'If they'd made me an officer like they wanted, I'd have had to get permission for all this. That would have put the cat among the pigeons.'

He told her straightaway about Gus. 'Snowy's on leave,' he said. 'It'll hit him hard when he gets back.'

It was very hot. When they'd put all their things in the room at the hotel and handed over the eggs and the butter, they went for a ride on the top of a bus. He said, 'I hope we don't have an air raid or anything.' Then he asked her, 'What did you tell Auntie Nellie?'

'Never you mind. But it's all right, Hal.'

He looked down from the top of the bus. Sometimes for a minute at a time, when he looked over the rails, it wasn't real. An engine backfired and he jumped so violently that he fell against the seat in front.

The man sitting there turned: 'Whoa up – what's got into you?' After, he kept muttering on and off irritably. Either he thought Hal was talking too loud or else he didn't like his imitations, because he turned again suddenly and said:

'You Tommies – you're all the same. Don't have to pay on the omnibuses, and behave as if you own them . . .'

Olive was furious. 'That's enough, gaffer,' she said. She waved her handbag at him: 'It's thanks to boys like him you're free to get on a bus at all.'

'That'll do,' Hal told her proudly. Later, when there were seats free, they moved to the back.

Still that unreality. It came on again when they went for a walk in the evening before bed. It was quiet in the Park. They filled in all the gaps in their news. He told her more of the hospital in France. She asked him: 'What's it like being wounded, Hal?'

'It depends. That one I had, it was nothing – like being kicked in the shoulder, that time Bluebell lashed out when we were leading the hay in . . .'

'I remember.'

'I've been lucky,' he said. 'I might even be lucky right through . . .'

She squeezed his hand.

He said, 'Olive, afterwards, I don't know what my family – I won't be the same person, however you look at it. I'll go to Cambridge if I want. And not if I don't. It's as simple as that. What's different now is I can make the choices myself. They won't be able to dictate to me. Not just because I'll be twenty-one – it wasn't the running away either as you might think –'

A group of soldiers arm in arm, stumbling from drink, playfully barred their way. Then, turning aside on to the grass, began to sing in slurred voices. As the sound died away, Hal went on:

'It's just, after all I've done, and seen – you don't feel somehow anyone can *tell* you anything . . . Death. Other people's, and your own that could come any second. I saw death around the farm, and – Jack, of course. But it's when you . . . I mean, Olive, we're so reverent about death, aren't we? And you *can't* be out there . . . Bodies – bits of them cluttering up the mud, bits of bodies all stuck in with the sandbags, rats that steal biscuit off you and you're sick knowing what they've been eating just before. And . . . all the *ways* of dying. Those that don't go at once, that take a long time . . . Jack, Stephen . . . Jack in a sort of way died with dignity. Over there – you're as likely as not to go without . . .'

He hadn't wanted to talk like that. But it seemed that once

he'd started . . . They walked back quietly to the hotel, not saying very much on the way.

. . . and they carried her, without stopping to draw breath, to the gates of the palace. And in three days the wedding was held . . .

Mr and Mrs Henry Reginald Francis Exelby Firth. They lay in each other's arms. 'Of course I never,' she said.

'Well, I haven't either,' he said.

She said, as she undressed, 'You don't mind if I'm not very modest. It'd be hard to be –'

He didn't expect anything to be very difficult. It was only, after all, like the time out on Settstone moor last summer, or the day at the Falls . . . But better. It was all those memories *and* the sudden ticking of the big tin clock in the hotel room. Horses clopping by. Motor lorries. A group of people walking past singing.

Because it was hot they had just the sheet over them.

'Don't stop,' she said. 'Don't stop and ask me anything. I think you just – do it.'

'No, no!' said the King, 'you must not be in such a hurry . . .

He shut his eyes.

'My father did not let me marry till I had won the golden sword you see me wear . . .'

'You know in the story, about the golden sword. *This* is the golden sword. I hope you liked it . . .'

'I do,' she said. 'I do.'

'Because I shall be bringing it out often . . .'

She wanted to take him down to Devon at once so they could have as many days there as possible. He'd worried about their being put in separate rooms . . . But she said, 'You know – I told Auntie Nellie. And my Uncle Ben.'

'You did, did you?'

'Yes,' she said, 'and Auntie says I'm a daft thing.' Then she smiled. 'No. Fact is, they're pleased . . .'

He found when he got down there, that was the truth. They were pleased. And they'd moved out, given them the best bedroom, with the view out on to the small orchard and the valley beyond. Her Uncle Ben didn't say much. Sometimes he'd look at Hal and give a kind smile. Her Auntie

Nellie, who talked a lot, looked as if she could be sharp. But it was all bark . . .

They walked out each day. The air was so mild that he felt sleepy much of the time. They went to Salcombe for the day. The sky was a Mediterranean blue and when he saw the palm trees he wondered if he was in England at all. And too, the white houses and glistening sea, what had they to do with Flanders?

Inevitably they talked again of how it would be when, if – he came back . . .

She said, 'It'll not be so easy, like. I mean, I think to myself sometimes – what'll he want with me, then?'

'Oh,' he said indignantly, 'what I want from you now. And *lots* of it . . .'

'Get away,' she said. Then: 'You have to be serious . . . Mr Henry Firth, all that – if you go to Cambridge University –'

'What of it? There'll be married undergraduates, won't there?' He paused: 'We'd be best to talk about –' he could hardly bring himself to say it – 'how it'll be – how you'll manage if I'm – I mean, if I don't . . .'

'Well, that,' she said, looking straight ahead. 'Death. I reckon I'll manage, just like I said.'

He said, 'You would tell my family, wouldn't you? So they could look after you. And like we said too – about, if a baby.'

She said, 'Your family, Hal Firth, *they'd* be pleased. Someone like me – coming saying I'd wed their son . . .'

'They're not as bad as they seem,' he said. 'They have kind hearts.'

'I don't doubt,' she said, sighing. 'But they're just – different, aren't they?' Then she kissed him, nibbling him behind the ears. Arms about his waists. 'You'll see,' she said, 'I'll manage. And not be beholden to anyone.'

The last evening Auntie Nellie took him aside. She said, 'We'll take care of her. Your lass. You'll have no call to worry – not while she's with us.'

When the time came to go, there was as always his dread of how it would be over there. But worse, far worse, was the being torn from her. That last night they clung to each other, sleepless. At the station he couldn't keep his hands off her. He thought: Thank God there's no other family here. I don't have to share, be watched, share the goodbye . . .

As the train left, started to move, her lips were still on his. Afterwards she ran a little way down the platform. He couldn't bear the tears, gathered like diamonds in her eyes.

There was something unreal about those first days back. Disembarking, arriving on French soil. The long journey up to reserve to join his pals. Snowy, made a lance-jack finally, was now in another platoon. He'd have to find ways of seeing him . . . There was Swanker Russell still, who'd been a pal of theirs more or less – but the two of them together without Snowy and Gus and Bert had little to say to each other.

He had felt so strong those last days with Olive. Now in no time, all his fears returned. Which of them the worst? Bayonet. Sliced by shrapnel. Skin, eyes, innards burned with gas. Suffocating, dying on the wire, dying in no-man's-land. Drowning, drowning in a shell hole, drowning in mud . . . There was no end to it. And when he woke from the nightmares, there was no Olive . . .

He wrote to her daily. He went into Pop one afternoon and sat for nearly an hour in the Toc H chapel. Then over in the little undertaker's shop opposite he bought her a lacy post-card. It pictured a woman looking out of a window, holding a baby in her arms. He hoped she wouldn't think it odd.

A few days later they moved out of reserve. For a while the nightmares stopped.

The telephone lines were down. He had this message to take. He never minded being a runner. It was a fine day, had been all week. The sun was high by the time he set out.

He made his way along the trenches first. Then left them, and through on to the open road – ducking once for a stray shell. It was very hot now. He came, horribly, upon a group of three or four bodies. Flies buzzed noisily about them, clustered blackly.

In the middle distance he could see a village – unshelled, unspoilt. The church spire in the sunlight. Closer, a field of wheat, and on his right a small wood. Such beauty, so near, so far . . .

It was cool in the wood. As the sunlight came through, it made a pattern. Something, a squirrel perhaps, was scuffling in the trees. He glanced up. And it was then it happened.

At first he could see nothing. Because of the darkness and the pain he stumbled about. Pushing his hands before him, tripping . . . He seemed now to be lying on his back. His hand, fumbling, touched mossy roots . . .

Once upon a time the king of Goldland lost himself in a forest and try as he would he could not find the way out. As he was wandering down one path which had looked at first more hopeful, he saw a man coming towards him. 'What are you doing here, friend?' asked the stranger; 'darkness is falling fast and soon the wild beasts will come from their lairs to seek for food . . .'

'I have lost myself,' answered the king, 'and am trying to get home . . .'

He put his hand towards his face. Touched. It met – nothing. There was nothing where he put his hand. Nothing. Chin, cheek. Nothing. Something soft and obscene. Pain. Darkness. *Pain.*

It was so dark. Growing darker. Olive. *Olive* . . .

My kingdom. I am King Henry, King *Hal*. I reign over the kitchen garden, Lily garden, Rose garden . . . And especially this little wood behind the orchard. Willow and hazel and ash – it was here long before The Towers – it is my very ancient kingdom . . . Now I walk boldly into it. My voice is full of echoes . . .

The Queen of Goldland had a tiny waist, she had long fair hair and her voice was like the water falling, falling, she wore diamonds in her hair like a crown and diamonds all over her bosom and to her waist like water falling . . . Falling, falling . . . black and blacker . . . down, down, down . . .

Mummy, help me, help, *Mummy, help me*!

30

She was back now where she had been over two years ago, during the first days of the Somme. At the hospital on the quayside, at Le Havre. She was there in mid-July when she heard the news of Gib: alive, and a prisoner in Germany. It was not the surprise it might have been. Somehow, she thought, I never believed him killed. (For me, he is already dead . . .)

She had been able to forgive him – perhaps. But Teddy, no. Herself she could not forgive at all. As the war news improved (next winter *must* see it over – 1919 *will* be the year of victory) she would wonder sometimes: What will become of me?

Molly was gone. Married. Home for leave at Christmas, she had simply not returned. He was a surgeon in Dublin whom she'd known for years. She wrote Alice an ecstatic letter about the joys of being a married woman. She expected a baby this coming November: 'How's that for promptness? Darling heart, I wish you could be as happy. I have started a novena to the Sacred Heart for your intentions – that soon a lovely boy . . .'

Alice missed her. How not? Found it difficult to make a new close friend. She got on well enough with Frances Cummins and Evelyn Parkes – they all three spent their free time together and Evelyn confided in her. She confided in neither of them.

She knew the family worried about her. There'd been a number of air raids recently on the base hospitals. Perhaps in the end that's how I shall go . . .

The second of August. Hot all day, sunshine. Windows open in the ward looking out to sea. Two years ago the hospital ships had criss-crossed, the trains bringing in their interminable convoys. This evening, the light just going, she stood with Frances and Evelyn on the balcony. A boat would be leaving soon – patients they'd been nursing. Now after stripping the empty beds for the night nurses, they waved, trying to pick out faces they knew. Blanket-wrapped figures on stretchers, lying out on the deck in the warm evening, raised their arms in farewell.

These were happy goodbyes, men travelling towards happiness. But as the boat moved away in the darkness, she felt a return of that familiar gnawing sadness. In her billet in the town she slept heavily. Dreamed – of Mama whom she had not seen for over twenty years. Wearing the Diamond Waterfall, Mama appeared in the hospital ward. Walked about, telling Alice: 'I have been looking for you.' It seemed natural she should be dressed for a dinner. Weighed down by jewellery, by the Diamond Waterfall. Ornaments in her hair. Alice said: 'The boys here, show the boys – it will cheer them to see all that finery.' Mama smiled, looked happy: 'Is it true they're pleased? Do they like the Waterfall?' 'I always wanted to do good, to help people,' she told Alice.

When she woke she longed, *longed*, to see Mama again. Walking along the quayside to the hospital, she thought of her all the time.

An unruffled sea stretched bluey green. In the hospital entrance, Frances, her round pink-cheeked face taut with emotion, told her, 'They sank the boat. Jerry torpedoed it in the night. More than a hundred gone, Alice –'

The weight of sorrow, unbearable, lay on them. Passing the beds, now with new patients, remembering yesterday's happy faces. No end to death and destruction, Alice thought . . .

She thought it again when, only three days later, she learned of Hal's death. The news came in a letter from England. It had happened the week before, Belle Maman said. They awaited details still. Alice would realize, she said, that Father was too upset to write . . .

She wrote back: to Father, to Belle Maman, to Sylvia. To Teddy . . . (Hal had been her half-brother after all . . .) Familiar death – what was there new to say? Hadn't it been dreaded, half expected, from the moment he ran off?

How had he died? Quick or slow, painful or unconscious? I don't want to know, she thought. It is better, having seen what I've seen, not to know . . .

The raw pain of those August days . . .

Later that month there was a Sunday evening concert in

the hospital. A piano in one of the wards. They often had these concerts but she could not always get to them. Today she had promised one very young boy in the end bed, a boy with a femur wound that was healing (for him) all too quickly, that she would be there. And Nurse Parkes, he said. Yes, yes, *and* Nurse Cummins too . . .

Comic turns. A recitation. A strong voice leading a sing-song. Thumping rhythms:

'You called me baby doll a year ago,
You told me I was very nice to know . . .'

Oh why was she reminded of Teddy and Gib, who had fooled together? (And who now would fool again . . .)

'. . . You left behind a broken doll . . .'

All singing together, some sitting up, heads nodding with the music.

A local woman, occasionally seen about the hospital, stood by the doorway not far from Alice. She had with her a nun: a black-veiled, wimpled figure, laughing and talking now to one of the patients. Waving her hands about. English with a strong accent . . .

The piano struck up again. Everyone sang:

'*Let the great big world keep turning, Never mind if I have you* . . .'

Alice, watching the nun, thought of Molly laughing that first evening. 'Why, were you a nun?' Alice had asked. 'The very idea!' Molly had exclaimed. And indeed – how could . . . Molly a *nun*. It was laughable . . .

'. . . *I only know that I love you so, And there's no one else will do* . . .'

Gib, in Germany. In Pomerania. Safe. Nothing to do with me. He is *Teddy's* now.

The nun seemed to be enjoying the singing – she caught the eye of someone and smiled. What sort of a life *is* it? Alice wondered. Possibly not unlike this nursing life. Less worldly distractions. Spiritually, perhaps greater satisfactions.

You have simply set me yearning, And there is no one else will do . . . The voices rising, seemed to fill her head.

Oh, *why not*, she thought suddenly. Not Molly. No, never Molly. *But why not me?*

Tears pricked behind her eyes. Hal gone now. Soldiers

singing. Death behind them, until – next month perhaps. The weight of sadness. And more sadness.

No wonder her tears . . .

Let the great big world keep turning, Never mind if I have you . . .

That is what I shall do. That is what I shall be. It was so simple: everything that had happened, all that terrible . . . it was because God wanted her. This was what it was to be called by God. A nun. *Why did I never think?*

Let the great big world keep turning, now I've found . . .

A nun. That was how it would be. She thought, the tears streaming down her face:

I need never be an alone child again . . .

PART TWO

1922–1945

I

'Praise, my soul, the King of heaven,' sang the choir. *'To his feet thy tribute bring. Ransom'd, heal'd, restor'd, forgiven, Who like me his praise should sing?'*

Sylvia, in the body of the church, sang loudly too. It was the only time she was bold, or raised her voice. She couldn't explain why Sunday morning service was something she loved so much. Just being in church: smell of beeswax, summer flowers. I love it. I loved it when I was eight. Now at eighteen I love it even more . . .

Standing beside her singing, but not so loudly, was Mother, looking beautiful, and gracious, and distinguished. Mother has a Lover, she said to herself. She had never mentioned it to Mother, nor Mother to her. Erik Ahlefeldt-Levetzau, who had come during the War – and stayed on. There was something rather grand, she thought, about having a lover. (Oh, beautiful word . . .) Perhaps I should be shocked, but it was Teddy who told me and who made it sound all right (as she makes *everything* all right . . .). Mother needs someone. Daddy and she are not fond of each other, I've known that a long time. And now he is too ill to pay her attention. (If he makes a fuss of anyone, it's of me. He and I have always been friends . . .:

'Fatherlike, he tends and spares us, Well our feeble frame he knows, In his hands he gently bears us, Rescues us from all our foes . . .'

In the row in front, hat bobbing, was Mrs Fisher. Dora Fisher – whom Mother could not stand. A pushy woman who had come to live in Flaxthorpe the first spring after the War (that sad, sad spring) . . . Today her son Bertram was with her. He had been educated abroad and was only just home. Sylvia dreaded she might have to meet him.

If only she might turn her head . . . But looking around in church had never been approved of. Even as a child, craning timorously, she had felt Hal's glare on her. Although not good elsewhere, he had been good in church. Teddy too: Miss Butter-wouldn't-melt-in-her-mouth, as Nan-Nan used to say. But Sylvia aged six knew that Teddy aged ten wore that expression when she was planning something really naughty. I was good, Sylvia thought, and *did not want to be*. I would have loved to be daring . . .

'*Angels, help us to adore him; Ye behold him face to face . . . Praise him! Praise him!*'

If she were to turn just a little, she would see the new doctor. Dr Selwood. He came twice a week to visit her father. Sometimes he and she acknowledged each other on the stairs. Otherwise she knew little about him except that he had been in the War, as a doctor. He was excessively tall, that had been her first thought – and careworn . . .

All the Hawksworths were here today. They could be seen without moving her head at all. Mr Hawksworth had a lovely moustache and always looked dashing, Mrs Hawksworth was just – Mrs Hawksworth. Friend of my childhood, always kind . . . (Jack . . . I wonder sometimes, if he'd lived, whether he wouldn't just have gone in the War?) Beautiful little Christopher, looking more like an angel each day. They say he's *very* naughty.

'*Praise him! Praise him! Praise with us the God of Grace . . .*'

The last lines, and a sudden raucous burst, out of tune, a few rows behind. Captain Gilmartin. Reggie. ('Forget all that Captain lark. The name's Reggie . . .') He'd been staying since Easter, four months now, with his aunt Mrs Fraser just outside Settstone. Sylvia had been invited his second week and from the moment he had seen her . . . I *wish* he wouldn't single me out, she thought. He was exhausting with his loud manner – and even more loud admiration of her . . .

But she had to be sorry for him. He had lost his left arm just at the end of the War. He never grumbled about it.

All part of the sadness of the War: she thought sometimes she would never shake it off. And if she could not – what hope for those who had *really* suffered?

Like Teddy and Alice . . . For them it was much, much worse. Alice, dear Alice, who loved me so and was such a wonderful big sister. Alice-and-Gib – that's how I remember her always. Then suddenly it was Teddy-and-Gib. (Now that Teddy has talked about it, a little, I know they were in Love. But oh, the shock when I first learned . . .) Alice, becoming a Roman Catholic *without telling us*. Then, hurrying back at the end of the War, the first Christmas. Scarcely time to see us. Rushing away at once to *be a nun* . . .

And Teddy – who no longer lives with us . . . Who is quite well off now having been left a lot of money. Enough anyway to make her independent. She lives in a hotel in Paris, but I expect will soon buy an apartment. She's donated large sums to an orphanage which was going to close down, and now her letters are full of the time she spends with the children . . . Her money came from a Rumanian who would have been her godfather, Mother said. So rich he could leave that sort of money to a friend's child . . .

But money cannot make up for losing a husband. Becoming a widow at eighteen. She shuddered now, remembering that terrible winter of the Peace. At nearly fifteen she had suddenly grown up. Gib coming home. Teddy's husband. Thin, sickly prisoner of war. But alive. Safe. And then . . . Oh, I don't want to remember.

And because of all that, she thought, because three persons lost their inheritance, I am to be rich. One day. I hope sometimes it will be never. Most of all I don't want to own that – it seems wrong even to think of it in church – that great cascade of diamonds. The Waterfall . . . Mother hates it. She told me once it had brought her only sadness.

But I'm reminded of it often. Daddy speaks of it. 'It will be yours, Missy,' he says. He often calls me 'Missy'. Then he says things like, 'It's meant for your kind of beauty . . .' What beauty? When he said that the first time, I went and looked in a mirror. It may be . . . my hair. Or my skin . . . But it is none of my doing – And it only makes people like Reggie Gilmartin pester me. It is a burden already . . .

And yet I am a happy person, she thought, pulling her coat collar up to her neck. Her neck was too long, longer than other people's, and so a nuisance. She could not think why it was considered a sign of beauty . . .

I am a happy person, she thought, kneeling in prayer. Oh dear God, keep Peace in the world and let there never be a War again . . .

'Little drinks? Drinkettes? You've time?'

Mrs Fisher, bearing down on them outside the church.

Her mouth seemed over full of teeth and if you got too near, she spat. (In cold weather, Sylvia thought, it would freeze on your chin in little icicles.)

'Lily, my dear. And little Sylvia –' (*I am not little, I am a full head taller than her*) 'you shall come too. I've already asked the dear doctor – so *distinguished*, don't you think? An MC and I don't know what else besides. So *sad* about his wife . . .'

Reggie hovered nearby. She knew he wanted to speak to her. Just then Mrs Fisher swept them off . . . 'Now, at once. The motor will bring you back . . .' Getting with Mother into the high chauffeur-driven car, sitting squashed beside Dora Fisher who smelled of mothballs and Parma violet.

A solid comfortable Georgian house sitting four square. Inside it had been quite ruined. Or so Lily always said. Mrs Fisher looked about her:

'Have we everybody, my dears? Sylvia, my little one, I'd *meant* to ask that boy who admires you so extravagantly – Lucy Fraser's nephew, *poor* Reggie . . . Oh dear, all these War cripples . . . Of course I'm quite distracted at the moment, *full* of ideas for Bertie's little dance. Dancette. Only two weeks now. Dear Lady Firth is coming, are you not?'

Mother smiled in a way Sylvia knew well. It would be a token appearance, if any, on the night.

'Bertram is *so* looking forward to it. It's only the *young* nowadays who know how to enjoy themselves. Bertie dear, come and talk to Miss Firth . . .'

A heavy, acne-pocked young man who'd been standing sulkily by a giant arrangement of dried flowers and feathers, came and sat beside her:

'I say, do you like to dance?'

'Listen to him,' his mother said fondly.

Fortunately, Sylvia thought, nobody seemed to . . . Mother by now was talking quietly with Dr Selwood and the wife of the retired clergyman. Three or four others were grouped near the window.

She managed as best she could, but the conversation died a natural death. She felt shy and ill at ease. She didn't like the sherry which tasted too sweet. She wished she'd had the courage to ask for lemonade, or cider.

'Bertie, you're monopolizing the pretty girls again. Come over at once and talk to Colonel Backhouse . . .'

Bertie left her reluctantly. A voice said:

'I think we have met only at the bottom of the stairs. Or was it the top?'

'Half way,' she said. 'Half way. You were in rather a hurry –'

'Only too likely, I'm afraid. Although it shouldn't be. It's just, what time I have I like to give to the patients. In between, I hurry. But I wouldn't wish to appear a hurrying person.'

'Just hurried,' she said. He smiled. He was sitting now on a leather stool at her foot. He was so tall that he had to lean forward, chin on knees. 'Hurried is different,' she said. 'It's a temporary thing – I think. A *state*. You won't spend your whole life like that.' She paused. 'Or will you?'

He put his head on one side, smiling again. He seemed to be deciding something. 'Yes,' he said, 'I rather fear that I will.'

For a few seconds, they were both silent. Then: 'You –' she began, and 'Do you –' he said.

'Sorry, I'm so sorry . . .'

'My *dears*!' whooped Dora Fisher. 'There goes *another* man monopolizing little Sylvia. Sylvia dear, come and tell all the ladies what you're going to wear for Bertie's party. I expect you to be quite the mirror of fashion – with a mother once a *stage star* . . .'

It was a dress of silk georgette in two shades of orange, made up by their dressmaker. Mother had sent to London for patterns. 'That one,' she'd said of their choice, 'girlish but not fussy. It is never right to look fussy . . .' Then she'd added thoughtfully:

'A little party like Dora Fisher's. It's probably all right – even though you haven't Come Out . . .'

But Sylvia did not want to Come Out. To be a debutante and presented at Court (presentations that had only just begun again last summer after the interruption of War). To be on show. But she didn't dare to rebel, to say (although she wanted to – so much!): 'I think I'll stay at home and not bother – thank you.'

'Grierson will go with you to the Fishers' and wait with the servants, then accompany you back not later than one o'clock. Although you may leave earlier, of course – if you find you are not enjoying yourself . . .'

But she did enjoy herself. At least until the strange after-supper event . . . The dance music (she who spent quiet mornings with Chopin) had a rhythm she could not ignore. Her feet began to tap even before she had stepped out on to the floor.

Bertie was at the gramophone, winding the handle frantically. Then, hair plastered to his temples, he jerked her round the room. Conversation wasn't necessary. Of that she was glad.

Reggie was there. He embarrassed her at once by turning away from his partner and staring fixedly at her . . .

Bertie panted: 'I say, you certainly can twinkle. You're awfully good.' Then looking about him hurriedly: 'The noise box. I must –'

Sitting on one of the chairs lined up against the wall was the younger Hawksworth girl, Edie, looked lonely. She was a sallow, pudgy-featured girl. Sylvia had never been a particular friend – the age difference, although small now, had seemed in childhood impossible. The older sister, Amy, Teddy's friend, was married now. Edie, at twenty, looked already thirty.

Sylvia sat on the chair next to hers. 'I *do* like your shoes, Edie.' Fine silver kid, single strapped, revealing a slim ankle. Edie smiled slowly. Her lumpish face smoothing a little.

'I know scarcely anyone –' Sylvia began, when suddenly she saw Reggie standing in front of them. He ignored Edie.

'Miss Firth, if I could have the pleasure –' He scarcely waited for her to agree. He was very flushed. She hoped it wasn't from drink, remembering some remark overhead. His right hand clasping her waist was uncomfortably tight – perhaps because he had no left hand to hold hers. She could sense the slight imbalance. He was breathing heavily. When he didn't speak, she said awkwardly:

'Isn't that English weather, Captain Gilmartin? Rain like this when dancing on the lawn was planned –'

He said abruptly, rudely almost, 'The name's *Reggie* . . .'

'Of course – Reggie.' He looked for the moment like an angry schoolboy. The expression on Hal's face when . . . Memory slipped, and was lost. Something in the schoolroom? Our darling Gib, his tutor. Jack was drowned. Hal . . .

Death intruded suddenly into the dance.

'Will you mind awfully if *I* call you – Sylvia?' His clasp tightened.

But the music had stopped. It was over. A Mr Scarfe whom she had met vaguely last week asked for a dance. Pale of hair and eye, he was pleasant enough, his ungloved hand cool. He smiled and told her she was quite lovely.

'You're staying with the Hawksworths, Mr Scarfe? Well –' she surprised herself by the sharpness of her voice – 'you must ask Edie for a dance.'

He said, still smiling, 'I shall do my duty . . .' Then just as he left her: 'My dear girl,' he said, 'people come to parties to enjoy themselves. God knows our generation have earned it . . .' But she saw that he moved across to Edie . . .

During supper, when she sat with Bertie, Reggie came and sat the other side. He paid little attention to his own partner but kept staring at Sylvia. She was embarrassed, but Bertie who had a good appetite was busy and seemed not to notice.

Immediately after:

'You promised *me* the supper dance –' Reggie said. When she denied it (where had he got that idea?) she felt her arm suddenly grasped. 'Dance with me now. *Please*.'

She felt angry and thought: I don't *have* to. She thought of Mother's maid Grierson waiting, and how she might go home if she wished.

Waltzing was difficult. He seemed to sway to one side. But his manner was affable again.

'Your hair – Sylvia. Awfully good you don't bob. I'm old-fashioned, you see. Pin-ups, Kirchner girls, when I was out in France – girls with lots of hair. My mother had lovely hair . . . Lovely . . . Haven't drunk all evening, haven't had a drop, you know . . . Don't go in for it much, don't need it . . .'

He seemed to be talking to himself . . . At the end of the record she made an excuse and went upstairs to the room set aside by Mrs Fisher. Her face was very pale and she pinched her cheeks, high up, then bit her lips so that the blood rushed to them. Her hair felt heavy and she thought: Perhaps I might get it bobbed. To bob or not to bob that is the question . . . But then she remembered: Daddy likes it, he praises it often. And he may not have so very long to live.

Looking over the banisters, she saw Reggie in the hall. At first she hesitated, thought of going back – but then he turned, and saw her.

At the foot of the stairs, he said, 'Miss Firth – Sylvia. Need to speak to you. Urgently.'

'Of course.' She waited.

'Not here.' He looked behind him to a half-open door. 'Think that's empty –' Perhaps he noticed her reluctance because he went on, 'Shan't *shut* the bally door if that's what's worrying you. Trust Reggie, can't you?'

They went into the room. Small, with a sofa and two armchairs. He showed her to the sofa and then sat opposite on one of the chairs.

'Would it bore you pallid to marry me?'

She was completely taken aback. Her voice a little shaky, she said, 'It's very kind of you – you're very kind, Captain Gilmartin . . . Reggie – But I –'

'*Would* bore you pallid – that's it, isn't it?'

'No, no. No, of course not. It's just – surely you see you've taken me by surprise?' Then, gently: 'Thank you very much, but No.'

'Offer declined, eh? Not wanted on voyage – ?'

She said, 'No, no. Really, I didn't mean . . . It's – I barely know you –'

'Hasn't stopped chaps from proposing before. If a chap doesn't when he has the chance, another chap comes along. Asks first. I wanted – If you can't say yes now, would you make a fellow happy by *thinking* about it, eh, Sylvia?'

She wondered again if he had been drinking. She thought she smelled it. She felt suddenly more than ever sorry for him. The useless sleeve hanging . . .

'Had it in mind to come up and see your Pater. The family heiress – he'd want to know a chap was all right. Then thought – better find out where I stand . . . if it's to be Aurev or Adieu . . .'

He added rather pathetically, 'There's a title in the family. Second cousin. Through my mother, you know . . .'

She thought: He hasn't said 'I love you', or any of the things they say in books. It can't be meant to be like this.

'If you're wondering about my settling down . . . got a pension, of course. Off at the shoulder, you know, the arm . . .

Can't have a hook. But mean to work . . . Back in 'thirteen I'd a year, year and a half in a shipping office. Family connection, that sort of thing. But jobs now – 'twenty-two, not exactly waiting for a chap . . . I've got business talent. Certain of that. Just need to get started, you know. Have someone, and something, behind me . . .'

Oh, but it was amazing. And alarming. She thought she would never get away. When she did at last, she found that she'd promised him she'd think about it . . .

She went home soon after that. Mother wasn't up, and her light out, otherwise she might have told her about Reggie. She went to sleep at once, but only to dream. It was frightening. She dreamed about Teddy. Teddy and the new doctor. They sat in a teashop and talked about her. She knew something was very wrong, and that she must help. She could not shift this sadness which sat on her almost physically. 'You are in danger,' she called out to them as they sat over the teacups. 'Terrible, terrible danger . . .'

2

'I hate you,' Teddy said. 'It's the most delicious sensation –'

She looked at him. George Andrew Sainthill. Gib's friend, Saint.

They were eating outside, in a restaurant in the Bois de Boulogne. Quenelles just served, piping hot. She burned a finger now, touching the edge of the plate.

'What were your ancestors up to, Saint? *Someone* must have been pious, holy . . .'

'Own that you like me, just as I am.'

She wrinkled her nose, mocking distaste. It came over her in a wave that she was bored. Worse still, perhaps was herself boring? And no amount of badinage between her and Saint, no amount of eating at amusing little places could fill up that quite terrifying emptiness – the cavern yawning beneath . . .

Or was it simply length of days? Life stretching before her . . . interminably. Over before it had begun. ('Poor little girlie, poor lass,' they said. 'She'll wed again . . .' But why? Why bother? Unless it is to have a child . . .)

Teddy does just as she likes, goes where she likes, is quite, quite free. Teddy Nicolson. Mrs Gilbert Nicolson. It is that wonderful, much to be envied Mrs which separates me from those of my age, and older. That is what marriage, and widowhood, have done for me. I am at liberty to dine in a Paris restaurant, on this September evening of 1922, alone with a Man. It is not even necessary to explain what it is I am doing in Paris. I can travel. I have money. Although I take care to give no details of its origin. (If I hadn't confronted Mother with the *facts*, what convoluted version of the truth might she not have given me? Something probably like the vagueness which seemed to have satisfied not only Sylvia but everyone else too. But at least I know now my Father has never liked me . . .

'I hate you, Saint.' She broke her bread roll. 'You shouldn't tease me so. I do have feelings –'

'And I tread on them. And you don't mind – or why else

would you hang around Paris with me? Answer that, now.' Triumphantly, looking at her over his wineglass.

When Gib had spoken of this friend, this far back in time Cambridge friend (and was not 1909 and all that so far away as to be another world?) it had always been with amusement, affection.

'We never kept up as we should have done,' he'd said. 'A few visits to his home when we were first down, then . . . I'm not sure. Letters, yes . . . Then I ran into him after Gallipoli . . . as if it had been yesterday . . . He was always charming – the secret perhaps those few drops of Irish blood . . .'

She had bothered to look out the group photographs from Cambridge days, and seen him smiling there. He could not have changed at all for she had had no trouble in recognizing him when he had called, on leave from the Navy, not long after they had had news of Gib's capture.

It was he who had written to her after Gib's death, in those first blank days of shock and anticlimax. 'I have heard the dreadful news. *What* can I say? I would like to see you . . .' It had been apparent to her at once that he needed, very much, to talk to someone who had known his friend. That they should share a common pain.

And friendship, of an easy sort. Renewed in Paris, earlier this year – when they had become lovers. It was only gradually that this tone had crept into their relations, a tone that was now the everyday mood . . .

Outside on the grass, among the strung lights, two children chased each other down among the tables, unsupervised. The younger ran too fast for his short legs and fell headlong. At once set up a howling. She thought of moving but saw that an elderly woman had already pushed aside her chair . . .

'I had a letter from Sylvia. A *very* long one.' She reached for her handbag, fiddled with the clasp, brought out some crumpled pages.

'The Baby Sister –'

'The Baby Sister. And would you believe it, she's had the most amazing and unexpected proposal –'

'Decent, indecent?'

'Saint . . . Proposal of *marriage*. Captain Reginald Gilmartin, late of the Artillery – one-armed . . .'

'I see. She refused him? A waiter was filling his glass.

'Of course. She can do much better. And he is only the first – she isn't out yet. Mother plans quite a sensation for her. She has looks. Capital L.'

'She has Looks, and you have –'

'Style. No, but she – Sylvia is beautiful. Perhaps she will be the one in the family to get it right –'

'Get what right?' He looked amused, but puzzled.

She said a little sadly, 'Just – get it right . . .'

'If you mean our present way of life, our liaison . . .'

She fingered the tablecloth. 'Partly, yes. Possibly –'

'At least you are independent. Even if I wished it, my means would not stretch to a *femme entretenue* . . .'

'Ah, forget it,' she said impatiently, always wanting to be done with as soon as it arose, any discussion about their life together.

'Actually, the letter's quite amusing. A dreadfully funny account of the Fisher dance. Mrs F too frightful – And son Bertram . . . Gentle Sylvia – sometimes pen in hand she can be quite wicked. Though not of course like you, Saint, when you take it up – and wield it like a sword.'

'Referring to my journalism?'

'Yes. It's better than your painting.'

'For those few kind words –'

'I'm glad you enjoyed them.' Opening her bag again, bringing out the lighter, the cigarette case.

'Is there one for me?'

'They're Virgins –'

'No matter,' he said, 'they're fags not women. Seeing you light up even in the middle of an excellent meal – I *need* one.'

'You're all the same, you ex-Service –'

'I smoked right through. Wardroom, night watch. Can't imagine life without.'

She said, 'If that's the only effect the War had – then count yourself lucky –'

'I do. I do. Though you wrong me. The horrors were not *all* on land. And as a corollary, at sea too there was something . . . a *camaraderie* . . . I tried to convey it in my *Compensatio Belli*, Notes for a Dialogue . . .'

She said dully, 'It's out of fashion, all that now. There's a new Edith Wharton novel, set here in wartime. Even that, I wonder . . .' She shrugged her shoulders. 'All these people with something to say and no one to listen . . . But our ears ache. We don't want to hear . . .'

'The time will come –'

'Perhaps.' She felt suddenly very, very tired. They finished the meal in semi-silence. Waiting while Saint called a cab, she thought she could smell autumn, overlaying the summer evening. Autumn and the death of the year. Death.

Saint's studio. It was very large, very airy – made into rooms it would have housed a small family.

She begun at once to undress.

'Are we?'

She nodded, 'Yes. I supposed that was why you brought the cab here. I'd have gone happily to the hotel –'

'Get into the bed then, sweetheart. Warm it up for me.'

A few moments. He put on a bathrobe, went and stood out on the balcony, smoked a last cigarette. She lay between the sheets, the blankets thrown back. She too smoked as she waited.

He climbed in beside her, enclosed her in his arms, pulled her head down on to his chest. His arms tightened, then one hand wandering, explored, stroking her buttocks, pinching, pummelling. He whispered in her ear, then a quick movement, he pulled her legs apart.

Now it begins, she thought. All over again. Now it begins . . .

*

I am in love, in love, in love. I am sixteen and it is the autumn of 1916. And this wonderful, wonderful thing has happened to me. It doesn't matter if nothing comes of it, it is enough that I *am* and he *is*. Suddenly, I cannot understand why everyone does not feel the same: if all one must do is grow old enough to fall in love. The only other thing I cannot understand – that I have not loved him always, always.

Except that I must have. Surely I felt for him something special, and *did not know it*. For he was always there. Always coming to The Towers, to be shut up there with Alice, talking photographs, taking photographs. Then taller, older, always towering above me – now he's Hal's tutor. He has no mother, I have to remember that. Once I heard *my* mother say,

'Really that friendship has brought out the best in Alice – she is positively motherly towards him . . .' But that was before they were engaged. Before I, or anyone knew about it (and all the complications and difficulties that were to beset it – until, in the end, it was not meant to be. I know, and must tell myself over and over again, *it was not meant to be*).

He liked me. Oh, how fond he was of me. Fat Teddy. My Fat Teddy Bear. He loved my dancing, my singing. 'Come here, Alice – watch Teddy, she has a new dance . . .' I treated him with such ease, such familiarity, pulling at him, dragging him by the lapels, not just to hear me sing, but to sing with me. I liked to make up the words, but he could not or would not. Except nonsense rhymes . . .

Gib, squib, fib, drib, crib. Rib, tib *zib* . . . His face so mock-solemn. Games, tickling, great bear hugs. I am small, swung high in the air, 'Little podge – you're a podge, aren't you? When I'm hungry shall I cut a slice off?'

Alice watched always, never took part. It wasn't the kind of thing Alice did. 'My little Cora Goffin,' Gib would call me, after the child actress who danced and sang (and unlike my uncompromisingly straight hair, had lovely corkscrew ringlets). Gib and I, that last year before the War, we sang together whatever was the latest in novelty numbers, revue songs . . .

War. At the beginning I was still a child. All that summer he had been Gilbert the Filbert. *The Passing Show of 1914*. Basil Hallam. (Dead now too. Killed.) The ladies who left their wooden huts, for Gilbert the Filbert, the Col'nel of the Knuts . . . Singing, dancing, right up to the day war was declared.

We must have danced on the day itself. I remember Alice coming in. Saying, 'Gib, Gib, this isn't a time for fooling around . . .' And Gib replying, 'Half past fooling time, Alice dear – time to fool again . . .' She was annoyed. I didn't laugh. I never laughed at that sort of thing. Nor did I take sides.

Gib enlisting at once. Something between him and Alice. The Towers becoming a hospital, Alice a nurse, Hal running away. But as well as worries and anxieties, excitements. The Belgian refugees in the village: bringing with them a feeling of the Continent, which Fräulein had never done. (How I'd hated the German tongue, and how glad I was now that I could be done with it.) Berthe, and her mother who became our sewing woman. French lessons. (Mother explaining, 'They speak a little differently, certain words and expressions – we can sort that out later.' We have not – although I no longer say *nonante* for *quatre-vingt-dix*, my accent is for ever Belgian . . .) Embroidery, for which I lacked all talent. Even my knitting for the troops was a disgrace . . .

Gib in the Dardanelles, Gib back, the worry of his illness. Gib in Flaxthorpe, convalescing at the Vicarage.

Such a sick man. I didn't realize how sick, although I was used, from The Towers, to every kind of wound and illness. I was very busy with the patients in those days. Nothing official, it was just taken for granted that I was always there, each day, to read out loud, to write letters for the handicapped. And at other times – I was so much part of the entertainments. I loved the singing, the dancing. I made friends, friends. I was every officer's little sister. I was a Flapper – and a child. Amy Hawksworth joined me most days. Berthe who was very shy, almost never. Sylvia in the schoolroom, a leggy twelve-year-old . . .

Finally, he became well enough to go back to Camp in England. Before that, he bought a motorcycle, complete with flapper bracket, and would ride off by himself around the countryside. He said he was starved of that kind of beauty. He took me out a few times, and Sylvia once (she cried with fear, and had to be brought ignominiously home. Amy was bolder). In a still cold May I shivered and clung tight to the stiff fabric of his British warm. I thought how thin as he was, and that he must feel the cold more. He was my brother, my big brother . . .

So what happened? How, *why* did I fall in love? For that was what happened, even though I didn't recognize it. And so precious to me was it, that for the space of seven whole months I hugged it to myself. How could, how *should* anything come of it? Wasn't he Gib, Alice's betrothed?

We were friends, nothing more, when Alice's cancelled leave for the Somme Battle threw aside his cherished plans and hopes – *and those of Alice*. (I must not forget that.) He came to Flaxthorpe and spent the leave due to him that was to have been a honeymoon. He'd asked me already where I thought it best for them to go: 'I so want it to be somewhere that is *all* peace – after the sights and sounds of France – that she experiences now.' (As if *he* had known nothing of horrors . . .) Wiltshire, he thought, where he had relations. He would write about renting a cottage there. She was due for at least a fortnight's freedom.

When the news came of her cancelled leave, he went instead for long walks by himself on the moors. I felt frustrated by my inability to help, and very, very sorry for him. He explained that if she'd only decided to leave nursing on marriage, she could probably have come home at once, but that she was convinced she should continue as a VAD – he showed me a passage from a letter in which she told him: 'I know what would be the *easy* way, but I could not imagine myself content to be just a wife back in England, doing various good works. You see, I think I should have to live at The Towers, and that would be impossible, in the circumstances.' So she would not apply to break her contract. She'd asked instead to be considered as soon as possible for long leave – to get married. (How was officialdom to know that she had already waited for over five years? To them she was just another wartime marriage . . .)

As Gib said to me bitterly: 'It's not as if there were anything *sudden* about it . . .' It was then he told me how he'd urged her to marry him when War was first declared. 'If only . . . Don't you see, all would be well now, wouldn't it?' (And I saw. I saw.)

That dreadful month of July, with the casualty lists growing to unbelievable lengths . . . We had a small chapel in The Towers then, made for the officers. Before, it had been a room for (unimportant) visitors to wait. A simple altar, some chairs and red kneelers. A few religious books and a Bible on a stand. It smelled I remember of fruit, and furniture polish. About that time I took to going in there each day, if only for a few moments. Often it would be empty. Sometimes an officer sitting there, head bowed, still.

I'd never prayed much, because I couldn't stand the weekly visit to church. But now I prayed quietly and with great concentration. I prayed that Hal would be kept safe and never sent to France. I prayed that Gib would stay a long time in England. Above all I prayed that the War would end SOON, so that he and Alice might live happily ever after.

Then Gib's embarkation leave was put forward. Their wedding hastily arranged. He was in Flaxthorpe, waiting for her. Excited, quiet and talkative by turns, he came to the entertainments twice. We sang together from the show *Bric à Brac*. Teddie Gerard's telephone song. *Are you there, little Teddy Bear? . . . Naughty, naughty, one Gerard . . .* I felt I was part of a fairy tale. I tried to forget that he was going out soon. Saw only the romance, the excitement of the happy ending.

And then, the telegram. He showed it me: DRAFT PROCEEDS TO FRANCE TOMORROW 25th INST REPORT HERE BY 7 PM ON THAT DATE ACKNOWLEDGE PROMPTLY . . .

Alice's arrival, exhausted, late in the afternoon of the 24th. The wedding, that was to have been on the Saturday . . . Such persistent bad luck. It might have been almost funny if it had not been so sad . . . *Who could think it funny, who had seen his face?*

And it was his face I saw that day when I went into the little chapel, not to pray, but just to try and understand it all. (Not to escape Alice – for she had already shut herself in her room. She had gone straight up there on her return from the station.)

The sight of Alice, who *was* to have been so happy, now impossible to speak to. She cut me short when I sympathized. I would like to have thrown my arms about her, consoled her.

Her anger, her despair. She mocked me. Said of my work, with the officers, 'I suppose you fancy yourself indispensable. Almost a *nurse*. All that fussing around . . .'

Then soon she was persuading Father to intervene, to write to Devonshire House in his special capacity. Influence, that is what is meant by *influence*. And she *was* sent back to France. Within the month. I think she had the idea that she would be able somehow to meet up with Gib . . .

Hal on leave, but as solitary as ever – all his time spent up at Lane Top Farm. It was about then Father had the idea of donating the Diamond Waterfall to the War Effort. Nothing else was spoken of for days . . .

Leaves died on the trees, bracken turned red, then gold. The weather grew colder. I'd always loved autumn (unlike now). Berthe's English improved a little, my French a lot.

She taught me not only what I should know, but also how the little boys, and the big boys, spoke under her window, or in the village square.

Gib wrote to me that autumn and winter of 1916. Often he would say: 'I have just finished a letter to Alice, and thought that I would like to talk to you too . . .' Then perhaps: 'Teddy Bear, what wouldn't a chap give to be out of this and on a Picnic with a real Teddy Bear? I don't think you realize what a Chum you were in those dark days . . .'

Life was worry, a sort of resignation – and prayer. I prayed still. But now I prayed that Gib would be wounded. Not too much, just enough to be sent home. A Blighty one. I never used any other wording. Dear God (Ask and Ye shall receive . . . it all seemed so easy), please give Gib a Blighty one.

And my prayers were answered. Within three months. (What had Alice been praying? I never imagined anyone else might be interceding with the Almighty. Not even Gib himself.)

The note that came was addressed to *me*. I don't know what he'd managed to scribble to Alice. But at The Towers who else should he concern himself with if not me? I was his Chum. A scruffy piece of paper, a blunt pencil. 'Wounded shoulder and leg but *all right*. Returning to England . . .'

It arrived by the evening post. I took it into the small chapel. It was lateish on a December afternoon. Already dark. I held the paper clutched in my hand. Symbol of his safety. Perhaps only for a while – or perhaps till the end (which *could not* be long away . . .).

I remembered how once, joking, he had said, 'Teddy is my Best Friend!' I began to cry now: relief, happiness, I don't know. I kept saying to myself, whispering aloud, 'I'll be the greatest friend anyone ever had. Now you are safe . . .'

I wasn't looking at the note. I was holding it only. And that was when it happened. I *felt* him, his presence. He was beside me, *with* me. I felt my heart filling up. I thought it would burst. I wanted to sing and shout, run out of the chapel calling, 'There's no one, *no one* like Gib Nicolson in the whole world. And he's *safe* . . .'

Never once in all that time did I think of Alice. Just sat, hugging to myself these feelings: so new, so beautiful, so *right*.

It was two days before I recognized I was in love. Too late

then to go back, to *not* love him. The grown-up cannot be a child again. And I didn't want to. It felt, still, too wonderful. I was his best friend: all through his life it would be the same. He would be able to count on me for anything, anything . . . (And still I never thought of Alice. I swear to God – whom I think of so little now – that somehow I never, in those early days, thought of her at all.)

Christmas came. The third of the War, and the saddest yet. But above all that sadness was my true happiness while I waited for the good news from Gib that would surely come. I must have seemed different, at least a little, though none of my family, or Amy or Berthe noticed anything.

I was seeing less of Amy anyway. She had become sweet on a baby-faced lieutenant, very badly wounded, who before the War had been a cricketer – a left arm over the wicket bowler. He longed to be back with the game. She would beg to run errands for her Basil.

Then one of the officers said to me, while I was preparing a letter:

'There's something changed about you, girlie. Any of the chaps been whispering sweet nothings?' He had a daughter of thirteen at home called Peggy, and often said that I looked like her. I blushed now, and he went on vigorously: 'If one of them fools around – plays with your heart, girlie, he'll have me to reckon with.'

I'd written to Gib at once, but knew that my letter might have to travel around. I felt certain he would read through my handwriting, my words even, that I *loved* him.

When he wrote back it was to tell me the precious news that he was being sent to The Towers *as a patient* . . . I could not wait for him to come. I felt certain that as soon as he saw me . . .

So what went wrong then, at that first meeting? (Forerunner, warning, of times ahead?)

He must have been tired by the journey: his face when I first saw it was tight, his manner tense. True, he didn't look yellowish and grey as last year. Now he had honourable signs: a sling and then a stick for his leg. The very acme of the Wounded Hero.

Those were the words he used to me: 'Aren't you going to kiss the Wounded Hero?'

I flung my arms about him. He smelled of hospitals – but so did everyone here – didn't feel to the touch as I'd remembered, *imagined* . . . We made awkward conversation. A bleak January afternoon. Alice wasn't mentioned at all. I remembered that afterwards.

In the bed next to him in a room of four was a lieutenant in the Engineers, obsessed with racing cars. He drank in the evenings. I knew he wasn't meant to. So did the nurses. But friends and relatives smuggled it in. Often even without alcohol he would imagine himself on the racing track.

'Broom, vroom, vroom – corner her – *there's* a girl, round we go . . . Into the straight – vroom, watch out, bally fools, blasted blithering idiots – here, here, vroom . . .'

Gib had to spend a lot of time in bed. He wanted to read. He said in that pinched, lost way which wrung my heart (I couldn't seem to talk to him, he was awkward with me still):

'I need – just – it's *peace* I need. And Catullus and Horace . . .' I couldn't help him with that. But then nor could Alice . . .

One day when I'd offered to read Rafael Sabatini to them, as I did often, in the hope that it would stop Dougie Durnford from either drinking or driving his motor-car, Gib said politely that he would rather I didn't. 'Just leave me to my own devices. There's a good girl . . .'

Dougie called out then – he'd been drinking: 'You've a regular Pal there, Nicolson. One of the best.' I saw Gib wince. I wondered then if when allocating the rooms they couldn't have done better, and determined to speak to Mother. There was one room with four who were *all* serious-minded. But Lady Director though she might be, she had no pull, and said as much.

The next evening Dougie started up when I was in there watering the plants – which I should have done that morning.

'Vroom, *vroom* – hope enough gas, gas not flowing properly yesterday. Watch, you chaps, here she comes, *watch that bend* – eyes shut – Bloody hell, bloody hell –'

One of the officers said, 'Steady, old chap. Language. Ladies, and all that . . .'

But Gib snapped at him. 'Stop that *row*! Stop your din, can't you, Durnford?'

'Sorry, very sorry indeed. Couldn't be sorrier.' Dougie looked round the room. I was embarrassed and turned away. But he went on and on: 'Really sorry, old chap – have to practise you know, got to keep on form, *tiptop form* . . .'

'Cut it out, can't you?'

'Said I'm sorry, haven't I? Awfully sorry –'

The fourth officer, an artillery captain who seldom spoke unless spoken to, said now:

'Anyone mind if I play the old gramophone? A couple of new records – double-sided. Only came yesterday . . .'

Gib was shaking but said nothing more. Dougie spluttered, blustered a little and then was silent. The gramophone was hurriedly wound. Fay Compton's clear seductive voice sang: *Take off a little bit, and nothing more* . . . Protesting as the song ended, *But I* can't *take off* any more . . .'

I slipped from the room.

Later that evening Father came in with me to see them. He went round once or twice a week, often with me but sometimes with Sylvia also. I suppose as he was owner of The Towers it was a good idea . . . But Mother when she made her rounds did them as if on impulse and as though they were fun. With him it was always stiff. I knew everyone was glad when it was over.

Tonight he passed round the room. I stood beside him.

'Durnford, isn't it?' (Their names were written in large letters at the end of each bed.) 'Well, Durnford, doing all right, eh? Foot getting on?'

But it was his *wrist* (and his nerves, his emotions) damaged. His wrist that worried him. Would he be able to handle a wheel with the skill needed . . .

'Yes – well – not bad, sir.'

To the artillery captain: 'Food all right? Lady Firth organizing decent meals?'

'Fine, sir. Grand. Jolly well chosen menus . . .' The voice died away.

'Lots of gramophone records, I see. Plenty of music hath charms, eh?'

'Yes, sir. Thanks awfully, sir . . .'

And then to Gib, 'Well, Gib, any news of my daughter? The little upset in the autumn, she took it pretty hard, of course, but there's always a next time. They're worked *much* too hard – In my opinion, she'd done her bit and shouldn't have gone out again –'

Gib frowned. 'No letter, sir. Nothing for over a fortnight . . .'

Soon the nurse would come in and settle them. And I would think then of Gib, lying still in the semi-darkness, listening to the breathing of the others and watching the nightlight flicker.

In bed at night I would picture how I'd make him better again – his old self once more. In my mind I would stroke him – always thin in his uniform. Arms and poor wounded shoulder, then, daring, down the leg. And all over his dear face hundreds and hundreds of kisses, healing kisses. Round his lips, never settling on them. Like birds' wings, they brushed, and flew on. In my mind he became calm. He smiled. I made him well – ready to marry Alice. 'I love you,' I breathed into the darkness, alone in my room. '*I love you, Gib*.'

No sign of spring. Even well wrapped up, the patients could not sit outside. But there was crutch practice and on St David's Day, a crutch race. Gib's shoulder was much better. He had begun to have electrical massage which would last for the next six weeks.

One morning he said to me – I had been collecting up letters for the morning post, 'Come out, Teddy Bear.'

I didn't like being called that. I pulled a face, but he went on: 'I want to get *out* of the grounds. I'm not meant to go unaccompanied because of the wretched foot. You'll come?'

As we set out he didn't talk much, but I didn't mind. I was alone with him. I thought: My hands, my kisses, are healing him.

Just near the stone bridge leaving the village, he blurted out suddenly,

'Look, Teddy Bear – I know I'm being rotten. Behaving badly. I shouldn't, you know. But I – Poor Durnford. He's got a right, he's mortally afraid. That liquid fire stuff Jerry used – he escaped, but his pals . . . Often when he's drunk, when he's being a racing car, he bursts suddenly into flames – Then it's all over, and he gibbers and cries . . .'

I was silent, appalled. He went on:

'I can't seem to get a grip on myself. You'd think it was

only a matter of will-power. I mean, damn it – Teddy, *damn* it, if someone – I was brought up, you know, I hadn't cried since the time my – mother died and Alice . . . Now if I'm not careful, I blub – at anything. Sentimental gramophone records. Poetry. And angry, that's the worst. Useless prickly anger – all the time . . .'

I said, 'You've written to Alice about all this?'

'No. I can't talk of it to anyone.'

'You just told *me* . . .'

'That's different, isn't it?'

'Why?' I had the bit between my teeth.

'Oh Teddy Bear. It's *different*.' He didn't appear to want to explain. I was exasperated suddenly.

'Don't Teddy Bear me,' I said petulantly, 'I don't *like* it –' Although I knew I shouldn't, I went on: 'It's babyish, makes me *feel* babyish.'

'I'm sorry, Teddy.'

'I'm almost seventeen. Old enough – to be married. In a year to join up. I could be a Junior VAD *now*. And you call me after a toy –'

He said, dangerously edgy: 'I said I'm sorry, didn't I? Leave it, blast it, *leave it*!'

His voice trembled. And my lips, mouth trembled.

He said, angrily still, 'And now I've made you cry! It was to be such a good, fine outing . . .

I couldn't speak, because although I felt he was being unjust, I knew he could not help it. And if I spoke, mightn't I say the fatal words? *I love you, I love you* . . .

He was walking a little ahead of me – I'd been keeping back purposely because of his foot. I noticed he was limping heavily. I thought we should turn back. I worried also about his shoulder, wondering if it hurt from the weight of his coat. Still looking ahead he said, again in a burst:

'I can't – don't want to marry Alice.' I knew it was to me he spoke, because he stopped then and turned round. He stared at me as if to gauge my reaction.

I said, like the Pal, the Chum I was: 'Well, that's all right. There isn't any law about that sort of thing.' I felt sick. I should have said (as later, so much later, I should have also spoken differently): 'What's gone wrong, what's the matter? Would it help at all to talk about it?'

There was a clump of birch trees. He leaned back heavily against the silvery bark, keeping his right shoulder clear. 'Dear God, but I'm tired . . .'

'We ought anyway to be going back –' I stood foursquare opposite him. There was an awkward silence. Then he said:

'I meant that, just now. About Alice. And I'm horribly ashamed. I don't know anything – Except that suddenly these last few weeks, I just thought – *I can't do it.* It suddenly isn't at all what I want to do. I don't want anybody else, it's . . . Oh Teddy, if I *knew* what I meant, I'd say it.'

I saw that he was near to tears. I thought then: All I have to do is throw my arms about him, *now*, and all will be well. I said: 'Tell me. Anything. It doesn't matter if it makes no sense.'

He spoke, through tears:

'It was a different person, who was to marry Alice. I don't know where that person's gone – and don't care. That's what's so damnable. I *don't care at all.* And yet – the nightmares I've had. I feel – God knows . . . Oh dear God . . .'

He leaned back, still against the tree, not looking at me, while the tears streamed down his face. The air was growing cold and I shivered with fear and emotion. I thought: I cannot bear this, and even as I thought I stepped forward and flung my arms about him. I spoke into the folds of his coat. I was after all only living my dream – I *would* make him well . . . I murmured, 'Don't weep, don't weep. Everything will be all right . . .'

'Ah, I mean it,' he said. 'I can't marry her.' His body felt as stiff and unyielding as the tree. His tears more painful to me than any I might shed. Arms still about him, my head lifted, I covered his face with kisses. Small feathery kisses – just as I had dreamed. My lips, damp from his tears, saltily wet his forehead. I whispered in his ear: 'All right. Really. It will be *all right . . .*'

Gradually he relaxed. I remained with my arms about him until, after a few moments that seemed hours, he pulled his head gently away. He buried it in my shoulder. Rested there without speaking. When we separated he said only, his voice a little rough as if the tears still lingered: 'Thank you.' Then: 'I might have known where I'd find a real friend.'

I said, heartily enough: 'That's what Chums are for, isn't

it?' Then I told him that we ought really to be getting back, at once, or we might be late for luncheon.

'I wish they wouldn't serve parsnips so often,' he said, trying to laugh, sounding false. 'Even in schooldays I never could . . . They taste like stubbed out cigarettes.'

'It's the Lady Director again. She's in charge of the menus, remember?'

'Teddy, forgive me. God, I've –'

I said hurriedly, 'Tease only. Mother's hopeless about it. She has too much else to do. And the food situation anyway. The difficulties . . . There's been a very good crop of parsnips this winter and so . . .'

'Of course.'

The next day as I was crossing the main hall, he came out of the library. He walked straight over to me. 'Teddy, it's empty in there for once. And – I wanted to speak to you.' He looked very firm, very much in control. He was in full uniform, Sam Browne gleaming. 'I've been looking for you.'

'Well, I was out on errands. Sick civilians. We can't be paying attention to sick *soldiers* all the time . . .'

I was tired, trembling with it.

'How well you put us in our places, Theodora. Truly you must have been a gift from the gods –'

'I was, I *am*,' I said over my shoulder, going before him into the library. Inside was a long narrow table spread with the latest magazines and reviews. Nervously, I picked up the *Spectator*. He came to the other side of the table and taking it from me, placed it exactly where it was before. Then, as we stood and faced each other:

'Kiss me,' he said.

I wanted to move, but could not.

He said again, 'Kiss me.'

I said then, saucily, finding a voice, tossing my head, 'It's for you surely to kiss *me*!' I paused and added, 'Gentlemen kiss ladies – even when it's a joke. Even when . . .' My voice died away. I saw the expression on his face.

'Kiss me, I said – *please*, Teddy. Like yesterday, like – any way – but *kiss* me . . .'

So I leaned forward across the narrow table – he took both my hands in his. I brushed his cheeks with my lips. His skin unlike yesterday was warm and dry. But then at once, as soon as I had done, he searched for my lips with his. He kissed me for a long while. And I, I kissed him. Then it was over. He stood back, my hands still clasped in his.

My heart was drumming furiously. I said, 'Really you shouldn't. You shouldn't.'

He said, 'I love you, I think.'

But I could only keep saying, 'You shouldn't, Gib, you shouldn't.'

'Shouldn't love you?' He was frowning now.

'No, silly billy. Shouldn't do – that . . .' So foolish was I that I couldn't even say 'kiss'. 'Shouldn't . . . because of Alice.'

'Please. Not now, not just at this moment. I – You see, I mean to write to her. I've been thinking about it – for weeks.'

'But not about –' My voice shook. 'Not what you just said to me.'

'No.' He was very emphatic. 'No. I've been, you see –' He shrugged his shoulders. 'I wasn't able to explain yesterday. Why should I do better today?'

I said, 'I don't think I understand anything. And I think too we ought to be getting back.'

'Teddy – When you cried yesterday, I wanted terribly to kiss you. Because I'd made you cry and never meant to. But I couldn't. I *could not*. And then *you* –'

Of course, I had thrown my arms about him, comforted him, had not thought . . . Now I did not know what to do with this answer, to prayers I scarcely realized I'd prayed . . .

I said almost rudely, 'Come on. I know its parsnips today because I've seen them go in the vat. You'll miss them if you're not on time.'

'Teddy –'

'Gib, *come on* –'

And so I left him, pushing him almost into the common room where the officers, those who were allowed up, sat for the half-hour before luncheon. A kind of remnant of gracious living: those fit enough to drink sherry or madeira, did so.

I rushed away when I'd left him, up to my room. I wept, stabbing at my eyes with a handkerchief. I had, I supposed, my heart's desire. But I felt only bewildered. Frightened, too . . .

For the next week or so we were awkward with each other. And took care, at least I did, never to be alone together. He had to go twice a week now for massage. He said that it did a great deal of good and that soon he would be right.

'Then I can go before the Board. And perhaps get back out again . . .' He said it with little conviction. Although I knew he meant it when he said, 'I'd like to get back to my men. What's left of them . . .' He had bad news that week, in a letter from his company commander. In the same batch of letters I saw one from Alice.

Two days after that I had to go away to spend some time with Cousin Dorothy. I was glad in a way to be separated from him because I was on fire. I couldn't think of another word for it. As I lay in bed my lips would burn where he'd touched them, and then slowly, slowly, all my body would grow warmer and warmer – till I felt a great glow of longing I *couldn't* understand.

I was away altogether three weeks. When I came back in April, it was just after the Battle of Arras. Gib told me as soon as I saw him that his Cambridge friend Arthur Vesey had been killed . . . His sadness apart, he seemed much calmer. Even occasionally the Gib I remembered.

The entertainments were especially lively that month. I'd brought back with me the sheet music to Teddie Gerard's *Kirchner Girl* song and Nelson Keys' *Walkin' the Dog*, and gramophone records of both. He and I did a turn together. Gib *Walkin' the Dog* was cheerful. Dancing, he scarcely limped.

Meanwhile Amy told me that she and the cricket-loving Basil had been seeing something of each other, mostly in secret. He'd stolen a kiss, a cuddle too while they were visiting the stables, and had been asked to dine twice at the Hall, where he'd been taken, she thought, quite seriously. 'Only, he's almost well again and will have to *go* – and then, what shall I do?'

There had been no letter from Alice lately. We supposed it to be the rush of work. Eventually, a hurried note saying she might get leave in early June. 'It depends . . .' She didn't seem to realize he expected to go abroad again. I wondered if she meant to play Box and Cox until the War ended?

The first week I was back, neither Gib nor I mentioned

what had happened between us. I thought that was how he wanted it.

He was riding the Norton regularly now. I loved the bike, loved to sit on the side, on the flapper bracket, holding on to him, the wind pulling at my hair, undoing the grown-up array of pins and combs. He asked me one afternoon to come over to Settstone with him. Just for the ride. And it was there, on that occasion that he first spoke of marriage.

He said, 'Teddy, you know that time in the library?'

'Yes.' I both desperately wanted and at the same time dreaded to speak of it again. I had made it now into a safe memory. Had learned all over again simply to *love* him.

'That time – I want to say, whatever you might have thought – I *meant* what I said. What I did too – Meant it more than I can possibly express. I – you see, I've felt very wrong about all of it. Alice. You see, Alice . . . I know that I did wrong. But, how can I say this if I don't rush ahead, tell you *now* . . . The truth is, you and I, Teddy – we should be married one day – don't you think?'

'Is this a proposal?' I said it rather acidly. I thought too of saying, 'You're not free to make one.' But instead, gently, as calmly as I could, I asked:

'Have you said anything to Alice yet – about not wanting to marry . . .' I couldn't help thinking of the unbelievable *muddle* of it all.

'No, no. But I mean to – very soon. Very soon.' He paused. 'You do love me a little, you could love me a little? I love you so much –'

He seemed suddenly not twelve years older but younger, far, far younger than me. It must have been at that moment, not before, not after, but exactly then that I felt the façade crack – flimsy, makeshift façade I'd built to cover all the feelings I *must* not allow. I let everything go, let myself love him – in that way. I said it then, in a great rush: 'I love you, Gib. I *love* you –' just as I had once imagined myself doing. I hadn't imagined though that I would burst into noisy tears. Gulping and hiccuping . . .

His turn to comfort me now. Our arms about each other, and my sudden, great, great happiness. In spite of all that happened in the world outside. Far-away France, Belgium. Hal. Alice . . .

'And you'll agree to marry me – one day? When all this is over. After the guns stop . . . You will, truly? Teddy, darling, little treasure . . .'

I said, laughing, 'What's all this about Chums . . .'

'Oh, Chums,' he said. 'Chums,' and laughed and kissed me. 'A man's best Chum is his wife. And you know that, I'm sure you know that.'

Freckles on his face, and the colour back after those grey pinched days. Spring, and Gib safe in Yorkshire, and in love with me, me, me.

I think now I would have been happy to leave it at that. Happy, warm, content . . . I would have waited for him. Would have felt no hurry. And besides there was the matter of Alice. He must as soon as possible ask Alice to release him. The rest he could tell her later. (No hurry, surely, since he and I were in no haste . . .) I tried not to think, as I'm sure he did too, of what it would mean to her.

Two or three weeks later (weeks of such happiness that surely somebody other than Amy in whom I'd confided, a little, noticed?) he was passed as fit by the Board and went to Staffordshire on a course.

In July, the day after my birthday, he came on weekend leave. He hurried over at once, bringing me a present of an Owen Nares record. He had lost colour again and seemed tense. Within minutes he said, his manner urgent:

'Teddy, we've got to arrange something *at once* –' He had tight hold of my hands. 'Darling Teddy, I want us to get married as soon as ever possible. As *soon* as it can be arranged –'

Taken aback, I said:

'I can't. You can't suddenly say like that –' Everything, the whole idea, the *muddle* even, rushed before my eyes . . .

'They told me today – it's almost certain I'm going back. Out again, It's a matter of a few weeks at most. I've been thinking all day, it'd be damnable if anything happened, and Teddy and I . . . That way lies madness . . . Darling, it was the foolish waiting before that finished Alice and me –'

I wished he hadn't spoken of her, said her name. I hesitated then, but in a moment he was urging me again. He wouldn't listen, did not seem to hear any of the practical matters I brought up. My parents, Alice, Alice, and again Alice. The difference in our ages. Trying to arrange everything at short notice . . .

He cut in, 'People are marrying at – well, almost no notice at all. Special licence. A few days . . .'

I felt light-headed with the shock, the joy of it. Had thought myself already blessed enough, but now – we might already soon be *married*! A drowning person, but drowning in happiness I saw not my past but my future flash before me. And loved it.

In the event there were few difficulties. Except the terrible matter of Alice. I let him write the letter himself, did not even want to see it. I don't know what I thought he had written. Nor what I imagined would happen when she got it . . .

Father, because he had always thought Alice could do better, made few comments. And gave his permission readily. It was for me. It didn't matter . . . (After all, what did or does he care about me? Knowing I am not his . . .)

Mother. She surprised me by seeing it as a Great Romance. Everyone seemed infected with fairy-tale notions, born of wartime haste. It was almost an elopement we were to have. A sanctioned, blessed elopement. Unbelievably, everything was ready in time. The eighteenth of August. We would have eight days together before he went back to Stafford to wait for embarkation.

I knew so little. I marvel now how little I knew, and was content to know. Mother said, two days before:

'We were very ignorant in our day, you know. But I, being on the stage – I picked up a lot of information. More than I needed, Teddy. Whereas you – do you think, darling, you know all you should, for next week?'

Since she had never told me anything, except an embarrassed outline just before my periods, I wasn't sure where I was thought to have learned it. Amy and I never talked about things like that. As for Alice – unimaginable.

She told me hurriedly, surprising me by the trembling of her voice, what it was all about. 'That is what happens,' she said. 'What happens to you . . . But – how you will feel, I can't say.' She paused and said, still without looking at me: 'It is possible to be very, very happy . . .'

And those were the words that remained with me. Alone with Gib in the oak-beamed room of the hotel at Lincoln, the night of our wedding, I thought of them.

We were on our way south – he knew Lincoln because he'd been stationed there earlier in the War. Knew the inn, was recognized by the landlady, given the best room . . .

In his arms nestled up close, I felt no dread at all, but rather that same burning glow in my skin that I'd felt months before. He was talking to me too, telling me yet again of all the great, great love he had for me. That's oddly enough what I remember most clearly, perhaps want to remember most clearly – those words, whispered hotly into my neck, my shoulders, my breasts – and then, and then: oh, if all that came after, if he – if we – could only have continued, on and on – I know now that I wouldn't have been afraid, how could I have been, with him? The entering, well, it was only as I'd been told, and easier, much easier – but then as his kisses redoubled, and now I kissed him, kissed him – no feathery kisses these, but frantic sucking, nibbling – I didn't know what I wanted except to be closer, closer. I couldn't be still. I didn't know what to do with my body, could use only my lips, my hands, kissing and kissing . . .

And then – he broke away, and with shocking suddenness turned on his side, away from me. For a few seconds he lay there, his face buried in the pillow. Then, half turning, he reached out, touched my arm.

'I'm sorry –'

'What's the matter then?' I cried. 'We were – It was all right, wasn't it? Weren't we happy, weren't you happy with me –?'

He half sat up, leaning towards me now, crooked on one elbow. He was stroking me gently, gently, through the fine batiste of the nightgown.

'I'd thought, darling, I should have said to you, I know – that it seems to me quite wrong I should give you a baby . . . We never talked about it, I know –'

Indeed we'd never discussed it. To me it had seemed so obvious as not to be worth discussing. I would have a baby after he'd gone away, which would be his, and part of the pride of being married to him, his wife, *Mrs Gilbert Nicolson*. It had seemed so simple . . .

And now: 'You do see,' he said. 'You do see? You're so young and I thought – if anything should happen to me, and you were left with a tiny child –'

'But that's what I want –'

'I oughtn't even to have gone so far . . . It's difficult to talk of these things. One doesn't – can't, but if I hadn't – left you then, there'd have been the risk of a child. Even as it is . . .'

I said obstinately, still shaken, 'It's for me to decide too – if *I* want a child, isn't it, *isn't it*?'

'You're not much more than a child yourself.' He said it sadly.

'Old enough to be married, though? Aren't I?'

It was an argument that was to continue through so much of our precious honeymoon week together. It made us very unhappy at night. The days weren't so bad because we had our love, we had each other, we were *married*, were we not? And the jokes, the ease from knowing each other so long, helped . . .

We spent the next day and night in Cambridge. He wanted to show me everything to do with his life there. It was a sad, wartime Cambridge, out of term, the colleges part hospitals, part garrisons. I fancied too the ghost of Alice and wondered that he should want to come here. But he seemed resolutely to have put her out of his mind.

We travelled on down to Brighton. He had spent a happy childhood holiday there once. Now, when not walking along the stony beach, sending the water-polished pebbles spinning, we sat up on the gorse-covered Downs. Wild thyme scented the air and an August sun burned down on us. High above, larks hung. And in the distance, the rumble of guns in France. Looking out to sea, I tried not to think of Hal – in ever-present danger. Tried not to think of Alice, reading her letter of rejection. We were so nearly happy.

One afternoon as we sat there I watched a hovering butterfly, nearly as blue as the hot sky. Larksong and gunfire . . . I said to Gib:

'How can you go back to – that? After this –'

'I don't have a choice –'

I said urgently, 'You *did*. You didn't need to get yourself a Board so soon. I don't even think you *are* fit, whatever they say . . .'

He said a little curtly, 'I think, Teddy, you could allow them to know their own business.' It was his schoolmaster's voice. I had forgotten almost that he had been a schoolmaster. In that other world, which we, I, had left.

But it was that night that – what happened, what did I do? I think I fought and clutched, clawed at him as he tried to leave my body. 'Gib, Gib the Fib. You shan't, you shan't . . .' I felt such excitement, such certitude: 'You shan't leave me, don't, my darling, you must not leave me.' And by and by, very close together, he shuddered inside me. Then turned his head away and wept.

'Why do you cry, you're always crying? My darling, don't cry.' I lay very still, I was busy comforting him. As I did so, I waited for the blush, the burning ache to die down. I said vigorously, 'I *want* a baby . . . You *know* I want a baby.' I didn't know which excitement was the greater, my need to feel, more and more, as I felt that night, or – to make a baby. And I knew that the shuddering, it was the shuddering would make our child.

Then by tacit consent – for we never talked about it again – it was the same the next night. And the next. And always that frightening, wonderful excitement that I was sure *this* time would break . . .

On the last afternoon we had tea at the Metropole. It was full of officers on leave. We stood and looked at the lovebirds in the aviaries there. Gib said, half laughing, half sardonic, taking my hand. 'That's us, isn't it?'

The next morning early we took the train to London. And in the afternoon travelled on up to Yorkshire.

When we arrived, the Letter was waiting for me . . .

*

Sunday in Paris. Bells. Saint said irritably, sleepily, 'Muffle them, can't you, Teddy – Good people come to church and all that . . .'

'Oh God,' she said, 'I meant to go back to the hotel.'

'You can't believe the hotel think you –'

'I don't . . .' Her hair felt heavy. She could hardly raise her head. She said, 'I think I'll go back to Yorkshire. Or Rumania, or somewhere.'

'Yorkshire,' he said, sitting up in bed, looking at her. 'All right, Yorkshire. But in heaven's name, why Rumania?'

'That's my secret,' she said.

3

It had been one of Robert's more energetic days. In the morning he had been taken out for a drive, had admired the leaves reddening, the bracken on the turn, mourning his shooting days. Now he sat in the big armchair, well wrapped up, his feet stretched out to the fire.

To Sylvia, sitting with him, he appeared to be dozing. She'd just picked up a book, when he spoke.

'Too much fresh air, Missy. Must have nodded off. It's good of you to sit with an old man . . .'

She was about to say – it was the truth – that she *liked* to sit with him, when: 'The new medico, Selwood, he should have been today. What's the time?'

'Nearly seven –'

'He won't come now. Medicos, all the same really. Unless you're an interesting case . . .' He reached for his handkerchief, blew his nose loudly. 'Where's your mother?'

'Dining out, I think.' She herself was meant to be going over to supper and whist at Mrs Fraser's, with Reggie. 'Would you like me to eat up here with you? I've this vague invitation but could go on later . . . Captain Gilmartin's sister – she's anxious to meet me, apparently –'

'Nonsense, it's Gilmartin wants to see you. Still after you, eh? . . . Have to be careful who you marry, you know. Very careful these days. Especially an heiress . . .'

'He's not *that* sort of person . . . And anyway, I'm not thinking of marrying for *ages*.' She said it half-laughing, but feeling fright again at the thought of the Season. *Coming Out* . . .

He must have been thinking of it too. 'All that'll be taken care of – when you get about and meet people.' He patted the chair near him. 'Come and sit down . . .'

He began to cough, getting his breath with difficulty. Watching him now, she felt great pity. The good times over. No more shooting, walking, travel abroad. All the things he cared for best. She looked at the frail, almost bald head with its few strands of iron grey hair. And Mother doesn't love him, she thought. I think I've known that a long time. *Mother has a Lover.* (Oh, daring, frightening thought . . .)

'You've grown very beautiful, Missy,' he said suddenly, 'it won't hurt to tell you.' He was gazing at her steadily. 'Do something for your old father, would you? Just put the Waterfall on for a little while – wear it for me, so that I can look at you . . .'

Of course – if it gave him pleasure . . . The truth was it frightened her. It belonged to, and should only be worn by, Mother. (Three portraits with the Waterfall. Mother's in pride of place . . .)

The arrangements, the elaborate precautions, began. Such an unlocking of boxes which contained keys, which contained keys . . . The secret wall safe. More keys . . . and then lastly, the magic numbers . . .

She said merrily, 'Aren't you afraid I'll learn more than I should, and then tell my Lover, and make off with it?' She liked to tease him.

He replied simply, 'Since it will – soon enough – be yours, it's not so important.'

She didn't like it when he spoke of his death, which had *nearly* happened so many times in the last few years.

Here it was, the Waterfall itself, lying on its satin and ivory velvet couch. Dazzling before it touched flesh, waiting to dazzle . . .

'Well? Am I to see you?'

She was wearing a jersey suit in mauve, with a long sleeved jacket. 'I'll throw this over the chair –'

She knelt at his feet so that he could fasten the heavy silver clasps. He said, 'The main light, turn it off. I want to see the Waterfall glow . . .'

When she stood in front of the fire, beneath the plain looking-glass, she saw suddenly as if it were someone else that it was she who glowed. A trick of firelight, of precious stones against white skin – then (well, it is only me, Sylvia . . .) she looked at her father and smiled.

'Yes. Yes.' He smiled back. 'One more favour though, Missy. Unfasten your hair.'

'Daddy –'

'For me. An old sick man. You wouldn't want to remember that you . . .'

Of course not. If something should happen to him – and she had refused such a small, unimportant whim. Head bent forward, she pulled hastily at the edifice, the combs, the pins. She said, 'It means you don't see the Waterfall properly . . .'

'No. Lift some of it back. Yes, like that.' She stood patiently before the fire while, head on one side, he looked at her. He said after a long pause, 'Yes. Its *true* home . . .'

A knock at the door. He gave an angry start.

But it was the housekeeper. The doctor was with her, she said, just arrived.

'In, bring him in,' Robert said impatiently, picking up his stick, letting it fall again with a bang.

'Oh, but . . .' began Sylvia, hand to her mouth.

Dr Selwood walked in. Embarrassed, she remained where she stood, unable to move. He too seemed embarrassed (or was it surprised?).

'Just checking on family heirlooms, Selwood . . .' And as she grabbed her pins and combs, dropping them again as she picked up her jacket: 'Run along, Missy. Switch up the light as you go . . .'

She could not look at him. Even less at Dr Selwood as, humiliated, she hurried out. He held the door open for her. She could not answer his good-evening.

Bejewelled, smarting, she sat in her room, her head throbbing, waiting until she thought he would have gone. She fumbled, pulled at the clasps of the Waterfall, then threw it down on the bed. Slowly, with angry deliberation, she twisted, lifted, pinned her wealth of fair hair . . .

'Sorry, Angie, old thing . . .'

'You are sickening, Reggie. What ever will Miss Firth think? What *do* you think, Miss Firth, of my absolutely *awful* bro?'

Reggie interrupted, 'She won't marry me, that's what she thinks . . .'

'You're not taking proper care of Miss Firth. Her arm, you sickener . . . Yes, I know that doesn't leave an arm for me, but life's like that. Or *War* I suppose I should say . . .'

If Sylvia hadn't known, she might have taken Angie for

Reggie's twin, so alike were they. In fact, she thought irreverently, she had only to add a moustache . . . Angela, who had been in the WRAF during the War, was as tall and as heavy as her brother but whereas Reggie had on the surface anyway an engaging humility, Angie bounced with self-satisfaction.

'Let's pip off somewhere . . .' She clutched Sylvia's free arm. 'I see we're going to be tremendous friends – don't listen to any rot *he* says, honestly he's the *awfullest* blighter . . . Come on. Let's *ooze* . . .'

Angela was to stay for a month. Sylvia found herself increasingly drawn into threesome outings or evenings of whist which she was too polite to refuse. Sometimes Bertram would be asked and they would roll back the rug and dance. Twice she was asked over to the Fishers'. Mother didn't seem to mind. Then, mercifully, both Reggie and Angela went for a fortnight to the West Country. When they came back, Angie's visit would be almost over.

On the Wednesday of the first week, Mother asked her to go into Richmond with a list of errands. 'The motor will come back for you about five.'

It was a blustery day. But smelling still of summer. The town seemed quite crowded but she surprised herself by the speed with which she worked through the list. Finished early, she browsed a little in the bookshop, saw a copy of Robert Bridges' anthology *The Spirit of Man* which she'd always meant to read, and bought it.

She was just about to leave when the shop door opened and Dr Selwood walked in.

'Oh,' she said with a little gasp. Colour flooded her face. She burned with shame (diamonds, hair down, rushing rudely from the room, *feeling naked* . . .). Then, taking a grip of herself, 'Good afternoon,' she said, at the exact moment that he did.

They both laughed. 'What did you buy?' he asked, and when she showed him, 'Oh,' he said, 'I have that, the edition before, with the green cover. It went to Mudros and beyond – as important as my medical kit . . .'

'I've never read it, and I thought – my sister used to have a copy . . .' She paused and swallowed. The shop owner was half way up a ladder, his arm stretched dangerously. She said feebly, 'I don't expect you have much time for reading. I mean, a doctor . . .'

He agreed that yes, he *was* usually busy. But he was having that rarest of delights, a free afternoon.

'Wednesday *should* be. Seldom is. But today I called on a family who were to have occupied me for at least two hours, and found them fled. So you see an idle fellow . . .'

Afterwards she could not remember whose idea it was, the tea. But not far away there was a teashop, up some narrow stairs, in a little street off the market place.

They sat waiting for toasted teacakes. She prayed, may he not apologize for surprising me in the room that time . . .

'Oh, but this is good. To be quite without purpose for half an hour. I looked around as we came in, and not a patient in sight –'

She felt as if they sat alone on a island. An island in space and time. She could not explain to herself the joy she had felt when he walked through the doorway.

'Thought is furrowing your brow, Miss Firth. *I'm* the one to be furrowed. You're too young . . .'

'Eighteen. Eighteen and a *half*. I hate it so terribly when people speak like that.'

'I'm sorry.' He said it so simply, giving it so little importance, that she was at once ashamed. She made a great fuss of pouring from the heavy brown teapot.

'When you have dipped into that anthology, and I am visiting one day, perhaps . . . Your opinion . . . When a book's been such a good friend, then one wants –'

'Oh, but of course.' She wanted at once to read it. And hadn't he spoken of Mudros and the Dardanelles? Here was a topic of conversation. Gib. Teddy. Gallipoli . . .

'I think your brother-in-law was a little earlier,' he said. 'I went late summer 'fifteen . . . And out there I had more to do with death by disease than with anything Johnny Turk did . . .'

Later they spoke of his children. 'You have three?' she asked, and he told her again:

'I could have offered them this free hour, but they are away. A late seaside holiday.' (Oh, but then, she thought, you would not be here, we would not be here. She could not explain her happiness . . .) 'The sea air, it's of course especially good for my wife . . .'

'I heard she was an invalid. I'm sorry. I hope she'll soon be better –'

He said crisply, 'No. It's disseminated sclerosis. It began in 'sixteen with the birth of our third. It's progressive. She has a wheelchair, and will never leave it.'

What could she say? Silence among the teacups. She stirred her tea, thought it was unsugared.

He said slowly, 'We don't know a great deal about this illness – but to live in a better climate perhaps, it might help a little. Say, one of the Colonies – somewhere we could afford more staff. Some luxuries for her . . .'

'I'm sorry,' she said. 'What else can I say for such a tragedy? One tends to think everything nowadays is the result of the War. Though perhaps you feel the strain of it all caused –'

'Ah, I think it just strikes. The hand of God, and all that.' He said bitterly, 'I wonder sometimes why the more senseless, wanton the pain, the more we hear of God. Why cannot such things – be simply the work of the Devil?'

She said nothing. Then as she looked up, he smiled at her. She thought that she had never seen a face so altered, so lit from within by a smile.

She said hurriedly, 'Will you ask for more water? We've exhausted this and I for one can drink more tea.' Then when he'd done so: 'What do Eva and Peggy and – Brian is it? – what do they think of life in Yorkshire? School, are they at school?'

But then, too soon, too soon, it was all over. The bill paid ('No, I insist. Please.'), her coat held open for her, the stairs negotiated, and back in the market square: Goodbye. ('You are certain I can't drive you back? I have my rather battered motor here?)

Waiting – flat, drained, autumnal – to be collected and driven home . . .

Reggie and Angie were back. They dragged her together with a visiting ex-Army friend of Reggie's to a small dance given by friends of their aunt. Mother raised her eyebrows, but smiled tolerantly. There was a day as a threesome in York.

'Please call me Angie, absolutely everyone does – you call my brother Reggie, after all . . . Aren't we a topping threesome . . . you don't mind we both smoke? *You* should try the weed too . . . What's all this about some absolutely ripping family *diamonds*? Any sort of interesting *curse* to go with them? The blighter says . . .'

From Paris, Teddy wrote a long letter. She was making plans to visit New York in the spring, to stay with Aunt Daisy's family . . . but first she would be home for Christmas. In the meantime she was sending Sylvia three pairs of very special silk stockings from Lefebure in the Faubourg St Honoré . . .

Two days after his sister left, Reggie proposed again. 'A chap has to keep trying, even if it means *being* trying . . . Can't help thinking you say to yourself, "That little pipsqueak, how dare he?" but you don't, do you? Because I shall make good, you know . . . Just got to get a few ideas off the ground. Shan't be staying up with Aunt for ever. But while I'm here – faint heart and all that . . . think about it a bit, would you?'

Now it was October. After a few days of autumn sunshine, bad weather set in. She worried it might affect her father, worried how he would manage the winter. Dr Selwood (she had discovered his name – Geoffrey) still visited twice a week. She had to stop herself haunting her father's room the day he was expected. (Why? Why am I like this?) Once they'd smiled and waved as she passed him by in the family motor.

A Thursday, his visiting day, and by noon, great banked black clouds, a cold spitting wind. The trees outside the morning-room where she sewed, bent their branches. Her mother was in Scotland (with her Lover, thought Sylvia. . .)

She was in the drawing-room, practising Beethoven, when Geoffrey Selwood was shown in.

'I don't disturb you?' He looked worried. 'I'd like a few words – about Sir Robert –'

Her knees were weak. Sit him down. Ring for a drink. ('You *will* have something? My turn to play hostess . . .') Sitting formally, she on the sofa, he in an upright chair, a glass of sherry before each of them. He looked a little dishevelled, reminding her of the howling wind which, moaning round the corners of the house, had formed part of her piano practice . . .

'I should have said, would have told Lady Firth, Sir Robert's condition is substantially worse. I said nothing to him. Would think it better not. But there *is* – when do you expect Lady Firth back?'

'A week tomorrow . . . Is it, what is the danger?'

'Please. I don't mean to alarm, but would rather err through prudence. No, I don't think we should call your mother back. In the first instance it would only alarm *him*. But I must warn you that this winter is critical . . .'

'Yes, yes.' She felt sick with dread. Sick too at the stiffness of this meeting which seemed to be between two different people. Who had been those two in the teashop? If small talk could bring it back . . . But exchanges about the Irish troubles, the weather, her mother's Scottish visit – they ate away the time.

He had got up to go. He was hurried, of course – had perhaps other visits. She wanted to say, 'That book, I have not been able to read it, am afraid to open it even. I found one quotation, but since then . . . I want to know now, *why?* what is in it to frighten me?' But the question (to which I know the answer, she thought), the question itself was explosive . . .

Then as if to accompany the thought came the outrageous claps of thunder they'd waited for all day. A darkening. Rattling of window-panes. Then: cloudburst. As he stood there, she said in a small voice:

'The heavens have opened.'

He smiled. Held his hand out in farewell. 'Try not to worry about Sir Robert. Pessimism is sometimes only caution –'

'You can't go out in this. Have you seen it?'

'And worse. I shall be all right –'

'Please, I insist. It's scarcely safe to drive. In an hour or so – we are just about to eat, you are particularly invited, a thank-you for the tea, we had meant to invite you formally, it is the least we can offer . . .' (I must be mad.)

She saw that he hesitated – then with a smile, yielded easily. 'Why not? When you're so kind . . . But if I may telephone home? They expect me, and of course if I should be called out . . . I must say always where I am.'

From courtesy, after he had telephoned she took him upstairs to her father. But his manservant Coulson said he was already settled for the night.

They sat at opposite ends of the long table. And spoke of – what? She could not remember afterwards. Outside the storm seemed not to have eased at all. Before she rang for coffee, he asked to telephone again: 'to make sure the line is not down or anything dread like that . . .'

'The piano,' he said when he came back. 'Do you play much? It struck me, who know a little, that you do it very well . . .'

'Thank you. I don't practise as much as one should. I'm not very serious –'

'You should be.'

'I do it mainly on account of my father. He likes me to play to him. Since he became ill, he's liked it. Earlier, as a child, I used to prefer the light stuff my mother played. Songs she'd sung. I cut my teeth on those. Then suddenly discovered – the real thing.'

He put his cup down. 'Before I go – you shall play me the Beethoven I interrupted.' He said it in a crisp, businesslike voice. A last duty to one's hostess . . . She got up a little hesitantly, reluctantly. He rose too and as they stood together, the light from the lamp behind fell in such a way that he looked suddenly old. She saw in a quick glimpse how he would be in twenty, even thirty years' time . . .

'I can't manage the *presto*. *Presto alla tedesca*. I'll go straight into the slow movement –'

She sat at the Blüthner and played, not well, the *andante*. He sat in a chair where she could not see him. As she played she felt misery through her fingertips. When she'd finished, the feeling came over her as when she had come down the stairs from the teashop. She sat for a moment, her hands over the keys.

She turned, very suddenly. Caught in that second his expression. As their eyes met:

'Dear God,' he said very quietly. He was looking away from her now.

'*What's happened?*'

He said slowly, 'You wouldn't ask, I think, if you didn't know . . .'

They were both silent. When she thought she could no longer bear it, he said suddenly:

'If you will look at me. Directly at me. Yes, like that. Because I shall only speak once –'

She had come to sit on the chair opposite his. He reached over and took her hands in his (if someone should come in!). The long fingers were dry but warm. He said urgently:

'Listen to me, because I dare to only now . . . I know I do you wrong to speak –'

'Please. please.' She was almost weeping.

'I do us *both* wrong. I know that – Sylvia. The first time I've used your name. It's as beautiful as you. And as you were, that time when I came in and you –'

'The Diamond Waterfall, oh, the Diamond Waterfall. He wanted me to put it on –'

'It haunted me, your hair down, so beautiful with your hair down, I wanted to forget and could not. However busy, I could not.'

'You must,' she said bravely, 'we must. It's both of us . . .' She held back the words: Love me, stay with me, tell me that you cannot live without me, *as I cannot live without you*.

He stood up, taking his hands from hers gently. Outside, the wind had almost died down. Where the rain had been heavy, water ran from drains blocked by the leaves. Standing in the doorway, watching his motor drive away, she shivered.

That first night she lay awake. And the next. Sleeping a little towards dawn. She did not think very much – just lay still, feeling her heart aching.

Geoffrey came three times a week now to see her father. Always at more or less the same time so that it wasn't too difficult to avoid him. She supposed he did this to help her. To help them both. She dreaded they might meet. (And yet I want it so, I want it so . . .)

In the end it was not in the house at all, but in the road that they met. He, coming out of a cottage on the edge of Settstone moor. She, trudging back from a long walk, her father's labrador with her. She took her aching heart often for walks.

He came towards her at once. She said, 'I thought you were going to ignore me – get in your motor as if you hadn't seen me.' She made her voice bright, social.

He smiled. Tired crinkled eyes. She wondered if *he* slept. 'I was in to see old Mrs Aske – she won't have her daughter living with her and the little servant girl can't manage . . .' His voice trailed away. The dog sniffed in circles around him, then leaped up, nudging him.

'Down, Raglan, down.' She pulled at the dog's collar. 'He's being a nuisance.'

'It's just, he recognizes me . . .'

She could not look up, and busied herself with the dog's lead. 'Come on, old fellow.' As she bent a lump, hard and impossible, came into her throat. She said, her voice tight, 'We must let you get on with your rounds . . . I – expect the day's hardly long enough –'

'Sylvia, Sylvia, I can't –'

'It isn't working,' she burst out miserably, 'it isn't working, is it? Is it? Tell me it's not all right for you. I tried and I tried – nearly three weeks, and no sight of you. And yet I know you're so near, so often. I am not very strong, you know –'

'Nor I. Nor I,' he said sadly. 'Sylvia, darling. Darling.'

'If only to talk,' she said, 'just to be together. Not to lose *everything* we glimpsed . . .'

'I've tried,' he said, 'God alone knows how hard I've tried. Because it is you whom I must spare – But darling – Yes – We were too brave, too soon –'

'Yes.' She clutched at the words.

'I must see you. *Talk* to you. But *where*?' He crouched down, caressing Raglan. 'It should be easy, but is so difficult –'

She said in a rush just as the idea came to her, 'The little sitting-room, next to the darkroom in the tower. It used to belong to my sister – the one who's a nun now.' Her words tumbled out: 'It's quite shut off, no one goes there. If you wouldn't be afraid – and you needn't – it would be right. And your car, it could be left – I know where you could leave it and it wouldn't look amiss. There is no danger. If you know when you could be there –' Her voice trembled with happiness. Hope.

No danger. No danger. She was to think many times afterwards: How could I, we, be so foolish? So obsessed, so alive to the danger of discovery, we did not see the danger was something quite else. Only two such truly innocent people – for I was that, she thought afterwards, and he too, for all his greater years – mistaking good intentions for achievements . . .

The rooms could not have been used since Alice's day. The darkroom was as she had left it when she went off to nurse in 1914. The anteroom, a little chill and damp, covered in dustsheets, her and Gib's photographs pinned on boards round the walls. In many ways a sad room – abandoned, forgotten. She didn't feel the need to tell anyone she was using it, but to make an alibi – or perhaps just to feel near him when he wasn't there – she would go in it at least two other afternoons.

At first, it was enough just to be together. The happiness of those first few afternoons. Stolen. Short. He would have to work late to pay for it . . .

If by remotest chance anyone should come, he was to hide in the darkroom (oh, beginnings of deceit . . .). In the anteroom they would hear for certain footsteps on the stairs, which took long enough to climb. It was for this that they did not lock the door. It gave a feeling of being more open, less ashamed . . .

How happiness, though, when almost from the beginning, he spoke of leaving Settstone? 'I'd thought of it before. Now I realize I *must*. I'm not very strong about this, or not strong enough. But it would be better for . . . everyone . . .'

She understood what he said, but it didn't belong to now. *Now* was together on the worn red sofa, holding hands. (Surely it didn't hurt to hold hands?)

He told her about his Somerset childhood. The Great Blizzard of 1891. Early memories of his father. One brother, three older sisters. University, hospital. War (Gallipoli, India, France . . .) His children. His wife. Yes, Patricia. Above all, Patricia.

'My first practice in nineteen-nine – she was my principal's daughter. We married in nineteen-twelve. It wasn't ever a great success. But – a promise is a promise. And she's good. That's what's so terrible, that such a thing should happen to her when she is so *good*. But long before her illness – us together . . . It was she who most wanted the marriage, you see. So determined. So persuasive. Vivacious too, in those days. I've felt guilt ever since . . . She, I don't think she noticed anything. Or ever has . . . I was so busy – not enough money, small children, the War. Then in nineteen-sixteen, the beginning of the disease . . . My obligations, of loving care, responsibility . . .'

Her guilt. It wasn't fear of discovery. Not that. And it began too before the real wrongdoing, before everything went too far – so far there was no going back. Perhaps it was their fourth meeting: November already half spent, grey December in sight.

He spoke, very definitely now, of going to work abroad. 'Patricia thinks she would like it. The children, I haven't said anything yet . . .'

It will happen, she thought. This is the way it will end.

She was often in the room now when he came to see her father. Their attitude to each other, friendly, slightly formal. Her father was if anything growing worse. The worry of that gnawed. He said:

'Selwood can't do much – no medico could. A good chap, visits regularly. Don't think really, though, I want to see this winter. Struggle, you know. The *struggle*.' Yes, the battle for breath. Emphysema. He was always in his bedroom now. No more motor excursions or visits downstairs . . .

Sometimes Mother would be in the room too. In her company Sylvia felt sad, a little lost. She would have liked to tell her everything – but knew she could say nothing. Yet Mother had a Lover. She had Erik. Although he rarely came to The Towers, it was certain she spent much time with him. They went away together . . .

My whole life is altered, she thought. Perhaps this was what people meant by a 'whirlwind romance'. She felt as if she'd been blown by just that whirlwind. Snatched up, and set down in a strange country whose rules she didn't know. Love, she'd thought, would be – what?

Above all, not this alarming tenderness, this corroding worry. Worry for him now, December 1922. Next year, the year after. Saddest of all, in the years to come when she would not be there to help, to protect. For she wanted to look after him: he who looked after others all day, and often all night. Whose wife was yet another charge upon his loving care . . .

When it all began to go wrong, when the guilt began, the *real* guilt – she told herself (they told each other) that they were hurting no one. Lately she had moved to lying gently in his arms. Nothing more. Fear of discovery had left them, if it had ever existed. And since they didn't fear discovery . . .

She said, 'We hurt no one. Tell me that's true. That we can just *be together*.' Then she said, 'It's so little, I take so little from her.' (She could not bear to pronounce her name, just as she couldn't bear the thought of meeting her, of knowing that she might be hurting, had the power to hurt, a *real* person.) 'She has – everything else.'

Of course she hadn't. Patricia hadn't health, hadn't legs that would carry her . . . Life was a wheelchair with the future growing always darker . . .

No wonder, she thought, we feel shame and guilt . . .

The little anteroom never lost its odd dusty smell, its memories of long-forgotten chemicals. But she thought of it as paradise. The day of his visit she would take hothouse flowers for her own room, then steal up to the tower with half of them. She took fruit too, although they never ate, or drank. While waiting for him, she would feel as if she had drunk champagne, heady.

Other people existed too. A world outside that sitting-room. Letters written, received. An outing perhaps with Edie Hawksworth. Reggie . . .

Reggie had developed a passion for exercise and fresh air. 'I'm jolly unfit . . . *You'll* come out with a chap, though, won't you?' Traipsing over the moors, dulled heather, sparse bent, driving wind, walking from Flaxthorpe to Beck Holm. Ending up at the Malt and Shovel. 'They know me in here . . .' Buying her sweet sherry ('Reggie, I don't . . . A ginger beer if I *must*.'). Sleeve dangling, the War hero. Dear Reggie . . . He talked large to anyone who would listen. And took of course this opportunity, *any* opportunity, to ask her again . . .

She said to Geoffrey once, 'You're not jealous of him?'

He smiled. 'How could I be?'

'He can't seem to take No for an answer . . . But he's leaving his aunt soon, so there'll be even less to be jealous about . . .' (But oh, *I* am jealous of Patricia. That is perhaps the wickedest of all . . .)

There were other wickednesses, though. Because in the end it had not been sufficient, just to be together. The kisses at first so shy and gentle, then as they lay in each other's arms, longer and longer. Their mouths grew hungry. It didn't matter that they whispered, over and over, 'We shouldn't, I shouldn't, I shouldn't.' Her hushed, hushing whisper, 'We hurt no one, we hurt no one . . .' (How often now she repeated that phrase to herself, as she lay sleepless in the night . . .)

When in the end they became one person, it was no accident. But perhaps because they had been so near so often, had felt able even to discuss it, his preparations did not seem to her strange or ridiculous. And in every way he took care of her – she would think again and again: Never however long I live shall I forget this sitting-room, and the feel, the smell, the taste of him.

Sometimes her wrongdoing would come over her suddenly, she would close her eyes and feel removed, beyond it all. *We hurt no one* . . . Then she would be open-eyed again, hungry not to miss a moment's sight of her beloved.

So much love, so much happiness – she had not known about that kind of happiness. She could not believe it was not so for every woman, every time. Shy of talking about it, having no name for it, she called it just 'being happy' . . .

His departure: certain now although no date was fixed. In early November he had told her he'd applied for a post in Rhodesia. If he was not successful with this, there were others . . .

'You understand? Darling, you understand?'

She understood, of course, for had they not both decided that it was the best, the only true solution? He told her, 'I search in vain, I'm afraid, for the generosity to wish you some wonderful romantic meeting soon. Even if not till the summer.' (Oh, but I shan't do a Season *cannot* . . .) 'Someone who will make you forget . . .'

'There's no need for that generosity –'

'But you're so young. If I had not – if this hadn't happened . . .'

'Oh,' she said tiredly, 'just don't say to me, "I could not love thee, dear, so much, loved I not honour more" . . .'

A moment later, she was in his arms.

The first week in December he went to London for an interview. Soon after his return he told her that he'd been offered the post. Medical Officer, near Bulawayo. He must leave before February 1st.

Their love. It was one thing to know it had an end, quite another when the end could be seen, darkly gleaming. He said:

'It'll be easier for me – no, no, darling not because I love you *less* – but because I shall have all the distractions. New country. New post . . .'

She would have only the familiar to occupy her. The summer to dread. Some solitude. And memories . . .

Her father's condition: unimproved. Breathing growing more difficult. The week before Christmas he became suddenly worse. On the Friday towards eight in the evening, Geoffrey came for the second time.

Mother said, 'It's pitiful to see – to hear . . . Is there *nothing* you can do?' The room was full already of steam. He was given another injection. She told Geoffrey, 'My daughter's been wonderful . . .'

Teddy had been sent for. She would have come anyway at Christmas. Alice in her convent was kept informed by telephone.

Geoffrey stayed on. He told them, 'It won't be long now.'

The fight for breath – which was life. She had never truly realized that before. He was barely conscious. The overheated, darkened room – a pool of soft light about the bed. Just after nine o'clock, he died. Mother laid a hand gently on his, lying on the coverlet. She turned a concerned face to Geoffrey:

'That *terrible* struggle – you're certain he wasn't conscious?'

'Certain . . .'

Sylvia was amazed at the violence of her own grief. After her mother had touched him, she leaned over and kissed his forehead. Then she felt, she didn't know what, some terror rising in her so that she was unable to look at him. She remembered that he had loved her. How often, lately, had she sat in here: she had read to him, held his hand – she had been his companion, his favourite (one daughter lost to God, another with whom he had never got on. A dead son . . .) She had even, for him, worn the Diamond Waterfall . . .

The need to weep tore at her chest. She left the bedside, ran blindly to the door, choking and sobbing. She heard her mother call out after her. A remark from Geoffrey, low-voiced, came to her from far away.

In her room she sat for some few minutes on the edge of the bed. She could not stop the sobbing: dry-eyed, painful.

She did not at first answer the knock. Her mother's voice: 'Sylvia . . .' Getting up slowly, she went to the door. Her mother stood outside, Geoffrey with her.

'I brought Dr Selwood to see you, darling.' She turned to him. 'My daughter was very close to my husband. If she needs some sedative, drug – whatever you think. I always fear strong reactions.' She added simply, 'I leave her in your care . . .'

The door closed. At once Sylvia fell into his arms. Cradled, she felt slowly the convulsions lessen. Her head against his chest – how often they had stood like this, up in the small tower room, putting off the moment of parting.

'My darling, all right, all right . . .' He spoke to her very softly.

She said in a shaky voice, attempting to smile, 'You're meant to be giving me medicine –'

He said, 'That I should be sent – that I should be asked to care for you . . . But you will be all right, you know.' He was stroking her hair. 'It's *good* that you cry –'

'See,' she said bravely. 'I am so much better already.' She added, trying to make her voice bright, 'You never saw my room before – it seems odd, that.'

He said gently, 'It's a lovely room . . .'

But the shivering had begun again. She clung to him.

'Perhaps I should give you something, wouldn't that be better – no? Sylvia, Sylvia . . .'

It seemed so natural, inevitable, as remembered touch led to remembered touch . . . She cried out, 'Yes, give me something. Yes, yes . . .' Of what use that he said over and over, 'I mustn't, I mustn't –'

They lay entwined on her bed, sprawled across it. She wept now for a double loss: her father gone, and Geoffrey to go so soon. In each other's arms, hungering for solace. Need. Desperation . . .

The most loved part of him deep inside – *we hurt no one* – she covered him with kisses, as he kissed her. Little sobs. 'Ssh, ssh, my darling . . .' Oh, but there is no end to this, no other world in which I wish to be, the darkness, the dark curtains parting. *There must be light* . . .

She cried out then, only a few moments before, shuddering, he clasped her tighter, tighter. They lay still. She felt calm – but strangely desolate.

Soon, too soon, as she sat, head lowered, again on the edge of the bed, 'I – have to go. Darling . . .'

She nodded dully, took his hand and clasped it tight. Heard him say, 'I'm leaving a draught – to help you sleep . . .'

She wanted to call after him, 'Only with you can I sleep . . .' She knew that she mourned not only her father's death, but her lover's departure. *Nevermore*. This is what it means . . .

Teddy arrived early in the morning. Sylvia, who had longed for her to come, could say nothing to her. At midday Geoffrey came. Teddy spoke to him, discussing Father's illness. Sylvia sat there stiffly, feeling the same wooden dread she had woken with. She heard him ask after her, then say (she could not bear it, how they must be in public), 'I ought perhaps to see you a moment alone, Miss Firth . . .'

They went into the morning-room. Stood there with the door open. They spoke in low tones.

'I'm terribly, terribly ashamed. That I should have let – that it should have happened like that . . .'

She said, 'Oh, but I too . . .' Then slowly, because it was so difficult, 'Perhaps – if we should begin to leave each other *now* . . . I couldn't bear to part by slow degrees. And – to run the risks of discovery so near –'

He said hurriedly, 'You know, darling, that we were – that it was without protection . . . I feel so . . . What I may have done –'

'Oh,' she said dully, 'Oh.' Then, eager to console him: 'It will be not to worry, I'm certain –'

'But you'll tell me *at once* if something has gone wrong?'

A doctor who in the course of his work no doubt spoke

quite plainly – could not seem to spell out this . . . She herself did not want to think of it at all. Had it not been in the end her fault? *She* had begun the desperate needing – and now was leaving him in his last weeks here, full of a new worry . . .

Christmas, to be lived through. The funeral. Reading the Will. Except for the life interest set aside for Mother, Sylvia inherited – everything. The Diamond Waterfall. The Towers. Investments. Land. When she was twenty-five they would all be hers.

She wanted only to weep. Teddy told her, 'It's perfectly natural . . . It's just we can't expect Mother . . . When after all it has been so long now. Erik . . .' She asked, was Sylvia angry with Lily about Erik?

'No, no. Not at all.' It had not occurred to her. Since love could come so unbidden, nothing surprised her. 'They weren't suited,' she said. 'I realized that in a way, even when I was a child . . .'

Teddy tried to persuade her to come back to Paris with her. 'Just for a little, until I leave for New York. It's cold in Paris now, but no worse than Yorkshire. I have this lovely apartment . . .'

No, *no*. How could she while, separated though they were, she and Geoffrey still breathed the same air? 'I'd rather stay here, truly.'

It was torture when people discussed, as inevitably they must, the imminent departure of Dr Selwood. Mother, he had told at the funeral. The doctor who was to buy his practice had visited already . . .

Her period was late: she should have had it about the tenth of January. But it was often so. Twice last year she had missed a month altogether. She felt normal. Her body told her nothing other than that her heart grieved. But for several days together she was filled with a deep suspicion – the thought at once so terrible, so powerful, she could not bring herself to look at it calmly, but buried it at once.

She dreamed she told him. Only that it *might* be. His face – such joy . . . No more welcome news she could have given him . . . Cold daylight spoke otherwise. Bringing with it temptation. She knew she should not, must not tell him. If she did, she could *surely stop him going*. Fantasy ran riot.

'Of course,' he would say, 'of course we must get married. I'll get a divorce. She'll give me one. You and I will go to Rhodesia. *It will be all right . . .*'

But she allowed herself only once this wicked folly. Yes, wicked. I will deal with this worry alone. For it was only a worry . . . How doubly wicked then to distress him with a 'maybe' or a 'could be' . . .

The dark days until his departure moved slowly, sadly. They contrived a social meeting. He looked tired with the changeover, the mammoth arrangements to transport a whole family abroad. When he asked if everything was all right, she told him he need not worry about her. 'I shall begin a new life in February. And I'm very strong, you've seen how strong I am . . .' She did not tell him that she had refused a holiday in Paris, with Teddy.

In the last week before he left she developed a kidney infection – she supposed it to be that, since the symptoms were the same as once before. She decided to tell no one, at least until she could be sure it would be the new doctor sent for . . . Apart from the pain, she felt sick – an empty cold nausea. She spent two days in bed, pleading a stomach upset.

She knew that he would come to say goodbye. When he arrived she was sitting downstairs, writing letters. She bit her lips to give them colour. Stood up to greet him . . .

He was carrying a puppy in his arms. Asleep, one paw hanging over coat sleeve, pink stomach just visible beneath the Airedale fluff. For a few moments they were alone. His face, white and strained, betrayed fatigue and pain. His first words when the maid had left:

'You're all right? They said, darling –'

'But *yes*. Just some upset – something silly with, whatever do you doctors call it, *waterworks* . . . I'll get it seen to by your successor . . .'

Silence. They were awkward together. She might have known that was how it would be. She put a finger out and stroked the puppy's sleeping head. He said:

'It's for you, you know –'

'Oh, but darling. I, I . . .' Tears, always near the surface, threatened to spill. *I cry for our parting . . .*

'I thought of it last month, when I saw the litter. But couldn't decide. Most of this man's Airedales are trained as

Ladies' Guards. I somehow thought of him taking care of you –' He paused. 'When I cannot . . .'

She said, 'Mother will be here in a moment. Clarice will have called her . . .' She felt sick with pain, cold, misery. That in their last few minutes together she should be tongue-tied . . .

The visit was almost over. He said, quickly, for at any moment they would no longer be alone:

'I shan't write – as we agreed. But for the last time, thank you – for the sort of happiness I didn't and never could deserve . . .'

The ache, an ache to touch, hung, unbearable. She could feel it still as, cold and sick and small, she told Mother in a bright voice:

'Oh, but look at this gorgeous little puppy – Dr Selwood had agreed to buy it for his children before his new post was settled and now he wonders if we can give it a home? Of course I said yes! Isn't it absolutely dear? How I shall love it,' she stumbled over her words, 'come here into my arms, then . . . see I've woken it – isn't it sweet? Oh, but I shall give it *so much love* . . .'

4

An ocean liner. Teddy Nicolson, aged twenty-two, on her first long sea voyage.

She had come alone of course (although she *had* tried to persuade Sylvia). It was all part of her determination to travel, to be often away from home. Even from Paris . . . This visit to New York, though, would give her mother pleasure. Time spent with Aunt Daisy, a stay with her cousin Ruth, meeting that side of the family. Feeling perhaps part of it.

Meanwhile money bought comfort. A first class cabin, and every advantage that went with that. And dance, dance, dance. Her feet tapped relentlessly. She thought it was almost as if she'd chosen the boat for its dance band, the quality of its dance floor . . . She did not consider herself in mourning for Robert. She did not, to be truthful, mourn him very much. He had never liked her and had shown it (at least now she knew the reason why . . .).

It was easy enough to pass the time on board ship. Gossip, drinks, deck quoits, shuffleboard – and dancing. By the second evening at least two men had suggested a visit to her cabin . . . She did not expect to take up these suggestions. Saint might well not be faithful in her absence, but for some undefined reason, she felt that she should . . .

There was a vast heated swimming bath, marble benches round its sides, a fountain playing at the head of the twin staircases above it. She and Daphne Hillier, another young widow, were there every morning. Daphne's five-year-old daughter Iris was enchanting, with fat dimpled knees which she showed to Teddy daily. 'These – cat's 'jamas,' she said solemnly each time, then exploded with laughter.

Oh, the envy. If that child were *mine*. Berthe, married to her cousin Georges within three months of her return to Belgium, had two little girls already . . . And Daphne had admitted to her, 'Frankly, my dear, I'd accept the first reasonable, and solvent of course, suitor – but everyone I meet, they only want, you know – the other thing.'

(But that is all I am good for. The other thing . . .)

From the second day she sat for meals at Daphne's table. In the evenings they swapped dancing partners. Max Gunning in the diamond business (and fascinated by the Waterfall: 'all those stones, on one person!'), fancy free and keen to remain so. Wingate Stephenson from Philadelphia. Dennis Hobson-Turner in banking ('I do this crossing twice a year and am *always* fortunate – but never so much as now. *Two* beauties . . .').

She was having a good time. She and Daphne were having *a good time* . . .

Gossiping with Daphne just after bouillon time on the last but one morning, wrapped up in steamer rugs on the promenade deck:

'You really don't want to visit Rumania? My dear, it seems crazy. Aren't you *curious*?'

'No,' Teddy said, 'I'm not.' She quickly changed the subject.

It was true. She was not curious at all. The facts themselves, she would confide occasionally, but always to comparative strangers and always in offhand tones as if it were a bit of a joke. Saint she had not told. It was better not to give him weapons for his humour.

She could not bear to examine it, the story of her birth. It was unalterable past, muddled and messy. Wasn't the present bad enough without delving backwards? And yet as so many times before after talking about it, she was hit that evening by a mood of utter blackness. She who never looked at the past, took from her jewel case the frail bundle of cheap paper, pencil already fading, that was Gib's last diary . . . She sat in the cabin armchair with it on her lap – as if it held in it some consolation, some explanation of everything that had been wrong then, and was worse now. And knew that it did not . . .

*

She had been happy that evening, September of 1917, the seventeen-year-old bride arrived back from her honeymoon. Happy because like everyone in those days she had learned to snatch the present. Happy perhaps because of what had just been. And sure. Sure that she was with child.

Pleasantly tired, looking idly through the pile of mail – congratulations, good wishes, offers of photographs, advertisements . . . Then seeing The Letter. Secreting it at once (I must have known, she thought afterwards). Reading it by herself late that night, locked in the bathroom.

> . . . . I *can't think why* I ever loved you or called you SISTER, to think I used to *help* you with your sewing when you were little, and that I went on loving you *after* I knew WHAT I KNOW. You see, you are just like your mother and that is nothing to be proud of, what sort of person steal away a man . . . she is a cheap and deceitful – what I have to call a WHORE, do you know what that means? No, you are too innocent or *think* you are, but really you are *very, very* WICKED and you will be punished. Not him but YOU, because it was *you* did the wicked thing. I think that you are really a *witch* and wove a magic spell, because you are RUMANIAN – there, that gave you a surprise, didn't it? And now I am going to tell you ALL ABOUT IT . . .'

On and on . . . Written in scratchy black, two large blobs where she must have shaken the pen . . . It had smelled too of hospital, even though Alice had said, 'I am sitting in a café filled with HATE and ANGER . . .'

She had wanted to believe it had been written *at once*, without time to think – by an overwrought, exhausted, war-torn woman . . . But that what Alice had revealed to her might perhaps not be true – she had never thought that. Long before she spoke with her mother about it, she had *known* it to be true . . .

She had destroyed the letter at once. The one person who must not know, must not be distressed by it, now or ever, was Gib. Deeply shocked, trembling, she passed off her upset as grief and worry about his departure. She herself felt unclean, wicked – and uncertain who she really was. As if a tree under which she sheltered had been felled . . .

Gib's departure. How soon that happened. Now I shall never know peace of mind again . . . A day like autumn. Up behind the house the wind tore at the trees in the copse. Stray rose petals blew into the lily-pond. A few hours after he left, even as she grieved, came proof that there would be, this time at least, no child.

Berthe and her mother had moved over to Harrogate, to lodge and work with a family there. Amy was more in love than ever with her Basil, who by now had made an almost complete recovery. He was to be boarded any moment and after that, he too might be sent back to France . . . 'We have a secret understanding, Teddy . . . You won't tell a soul?'

Six long months passed. It was the winter of 1918. By now Basil was back out again. She heard regularly from Gib. No mention of leave. Then in March he was reported missing. She thought 'missing' a cruel word, in spite of or rather *because* of its small grain of hope. How many people in the end heard good news? When exactly did one give up hope?

Easter, spring, Maytime, blossom – the War news worse and worse. She began to think of herself as a widow ('it's best, really it's best . . .'). Her mother was especially kind. So much so that often she would almost ask her about the Rumanian story. Even Robert seemed sympathetic. She supposed someone had told Alice – since she had not. (She tried now never to think of The Letter . . .) She was helped, supported by all the officers now at The Towers. Everyone knew, everyone cared. Amy, when she received a letter from Basil, would be afraid Teddy might be upset, would hesitate before mentioning it . . .

In June, Settstone had its Midsummer Fair, held every five years, although there had been talk of postponing it because of the War. Amy and Teddy, taking an afternoon off, made the round of the sideshows: Teddy, for Amy's sake, trying to put enthusiasm into weight-guessing, shove-penny . . .

There was a small tent behind the coconut shies with a notice: Gypsy Eliza Lee, Fortune-teller to KINGS, EMPERORS AND MOGULS.

Amy said, 'Oh, let's – shall we?'

Why not? Inside the tent Gypsy Eliza, a dark spotted scarf down over her forehead, sat at a small table. She had a lot of hair on her face, particularly the chin.

'That'll be five shilling.' Her accent was very Yorkshire. When they had handed over a half-a-crown coin each, she told them to sit down. The tent was hot and smelled of stale beer and rubber. They waited in hushed nervousness.

'You'll have questions then, about loved ones? It's nowt else these days. I'll do best I can . . .'

As, hands still, she concentrated on the crystal ball in front of her, it seemed to Teddy, waiting her turn, that here, last resort of all, must be *the key*. I believe, she told herself – as if she were in church.

'Basil, you said? I'm looking hard – we're – he's over there, is he, somewhere in France? I see – no, it's not clear. It's gone misty, love, quite misty, I'm having difficulty, dear. Wait . . . he's smiling now, he's in white, yes, dear, that's him, he's – I think he's throwing a bomb would it be? No, a *ball* . . .'

'Yes, yes,' Amy said eagerly, 'Cricket, he only thinks about cricket. He –'

But Gypsy Eliza interrupted her, staring at Teddy: 'What's his name, young lady? . . . Well, I see Gib – He's fair, dear, and tall, yes? but thin – was he always too thin? Wait a while, he's lying down, yes, he's . . . what's this, there's sand – where's he fighting, dear? I'm a little confused – but he's moving, don't fear, he's alive right enough. But it's hot, dear, and you'll pardon me, it doesn't smell nice, there's something, some bad smell . . .'

Suddenly Teddy had had enough. She ran out. Hungrily breathing in fresh air outside. Amy followed her. 'We shouldn't have . . .' she was almost crying. 'People are right, you shouldn't – I was frightened even though it's nonsense . . . Except,' she hesitated, 'she *seemed* to think Basil's all right . . . And Gib – she didn't know Gib was meant to be missing . . .'

But Teddy didn't want to talk about it. She said hurriedly, pulling out her watch, 'We're meant to be in the Red Cross tent at four o'clock.'

The evening post brought Amy a letter from Basil. Someone was getting a team together to practise a little bowling when they came out of the lines for a rest next week. Two days later she heard of his death at a casualty clearing station, of head wounds.

For Teddy the wait was longer. When the news came through that Gib, wounded and then captured, was a prisoner of war in Pomerania, relief and joy made her almost ill. He is *alive*. She mourned with Amy, but each night, kneeling by her bedside, prayed that Gib would soon be healed and the War over . . . No longer a widow, she became once again the wife who waited.

Hal, and tragedy again. Mourning . . . Then November and the longed-for Armistice. Hope that Gib might soon be returned to her.

When he arrived, she could not believe what she saw. A tiring journey hadn't helped – he had been continuously sick between Rotterdam and Hull – but this emaciated, dull-skinned man could not be her Gib. She felt it was a stranger she embraced in front of the family, lined up to kiss him too. (Alice, sad Alice already departed. Hurrying to fulfil her vocation, her call from God.)

At first she believed his physical state, the weakness due to malnutrition, would soon be cured by good food, bracing Yorkshire air, and love. But the malaise went much deeper. Alone with him, night after night beside his chilled, almost inert body, she knew that. Rubbing his limbs, talking to him all the while, kissing him, as if the very heat of her breath could warm him deep down . . .

The Towers as a hospital was being wound up: as many as possible had gone home at Christmas. Gib was still in the Army, officially on convalescent leave. No mention yet of being demobbed. He himself never spoke of it. In fact, he hardly spoke at all.

Everyone was understanding about that too. Often, especially in the first week, he would go and spend all day with his father. At The Towers, he sat for hours on end up in their bedroom in a chair by the window. Once he asked for the key to the tower room where he and Alice had worked with their photography. She wondered if he worried about Alice, and dared one day to ask him. He looked at her with blank surprise.

So blank – it was almost dislike. She had to fight to keep back the tears. This was worse, much worse than the irritable, probably shell-shocked Gib of early 1917. The Gib who had shouted at poor Dougie . . .

The word that came into her mind most often was 'dead'. Once in bed at night she almost burst out: 'You might as well be –' Biting her lips, she caught the word in time . . .

Yet in truth there was nothing about him, or indeed the two of them as a couple, to remind her of life. They never made love. He had not touched her except formally since his return. (*How would they ever make a child?*) She could only believe, as others kept telling her, that in time he would be better.

One morning, shyly but with the same expressionless voice, the dull eyes, he handed her a small package:

'I want you to look after this, Teddy.'

'It's – what?'

He said flatly, 'A diary. Some thoughts, experiences – after they took me.'

She didn't know if she was meant to read it. Then decided that she could not, and put it away. That night, he made love to her. Anxious, awkward, mechanical almost. Silent and without tenderness. Cold arms about her in the cold December night – ghost of the gentle lover of summer 1917. Through all her months of desire, for all her longing for a child, she had never imagined this. This hurried, dry coupling.

'I slept with a dead man.' The words came into her mind next morning. '*I slept with a dead man . . .*'

The week after Christmas, Spanish 'flu appeared in Flaxthorpe. Erik and Lily and four of the servants were among the first victims. Then old Mr Nicolson and his household and lastly, Teddy herself.

She emerged weak, barely able to sit up, only to learn that Gib, who had been kept away from her, was now ill too. She insisted ('I'm immune now, surely . . .') on helping to nurse him. Wrapped in blankets she sat by his bedside. He was worse than she had ever been. His temperature rose steadily. A hundred and three. Four. Five . . . He didn't recognize her. Delirious, he called for Alice, and then for his mother. Over and over again for his mother . . .

Once he seemed to be laughing. Clutching perhaps at remembered happiness:

'Saint, there's a good chap, no, *my* turn . . . I give you Horace – *nam tua res agitur*, yes, *nam tua res agitur, paries cum proximus ardet* . . . cap *that*! . . . no, no, damn Horace and let's have tea . . . tell Vesey, don't be late . . . Only can't see Vesey . . .' His voice grew suddenly anxious, '*Can't see Vesey* . . .'

Eating nothing, he could of course only become thinner, more emaciated. With difficulty, a professional nurse was got in. The fever raged on – he was wrapped again and again in sheets wrung out in cold water. His furnace-like body dried them out.

Then, just when it seemed it could go on no longer, the fever died down. His first day without it, in the afternoon, he said to her weakly, as if recognizing her from a long way away: 'Thank you.' Then a little later, and as if surprised: 'Not chums, I think. It's Teddy isn't it? My head's quite clear now. A lot of love. Thank you . . .'

He fell almost at once into an exhausted sleep. Exhausted herself, she left him for a while. He slept through the afternoon and early evening. Next morning his face had become a dark bluish colour, almost purple. He was breathing with difficulty and did not appear to know her. The nurse and doctor took a very serious view of this new change. They used the word 'cyanosed'. She did not dare ask more, for she knew the answer.

He did not speak again. All that day there was his breathing – a harsh whistling sound. In the early evening, he died.

*

An astonishing number of people sent letters of sympathy. Even after four years of drawing on them, the wells had not run dry. The irony of his death – everyone remarked on that. To have survived so long . . . (But had he? *I slept with a dead man* . . .)

His few possessions he left to her. Small bequests and personal mementoes for George Sainthill and Arthur Vesey, from Cambridge days. Vesey of course was dead. But Saint, not yet discharged from the Navy, was in London working at the Admiralty.

He came to visit her. She did not know what to make of him. They talked self-consciously of Gib. Alice too. He was plainly surprised by what had been the turn of events, but she did not want to discuss it, was embarrassed by it (The letter, she thought . . .). Hastily telling him as much as she knew about Alice's present life, she changed the subject.

'What shall you do, when you leave the Service?'

'Something mad or bad,' he said drily. 'I might enter the lit world or Grub Street – or even go to Paris and try *la vie bohème*. Whatever's least like life on the ocean wave. And you?'

She murmured that she supposed she would pick up the pieces – much as other war widows.

He said, head on one side, looking at her quizzically, 'And you're truly only – eighteen, is it?'

She said, 'Gib was ruined by the spell in Pomerania. You'd scarcely have known him –'

'I fear so, I fear so.'

'He kept a diary there, which he gave me.' She hesitated. 'I haven't read it –'

'Do,' he said lightly, 'do. He'd want you to. Why else give it you?'

She had not thought of that. But still she left it in its wrappings. It was not till last year that she had read it.

She read it the morning after sleeping with Saint for the first time. Nearly three years after their first meeting. Then, casually, he had asked her to keep in touch. But in 1919, deep in her mourning, she could not imagine life beginning again . . .

Indeed it had seemed, the spring after Gib's death, that even nature had forgotten to renew itself. In the continuing wintry cold, leafbuds remained obstinately unfurled, hedges bare of anything but old leaves of brambles. Drystone walls glistened still with frost. From her window at The Towers, the view stretched grey and hopeless.

She lived through that year and the next somehow, as if waiting. Robert had become ill by then – she felt a detached concern; worried most for Sylvia. She went to Alice's convent to see her clothed, feeling that to allow Alice to forgive her, and to accept that forgiveness, was something she could do for both of them. For Gib too . . .

In the autumn of 1920, with her real father's death in Rumania, she became well off in her own right. When her mother began a complicated explanation of how the money came to be hers, she told her that she knew the truth . . . She did not betray Alice. Her explanation, garbled and emotional, suggested papers, a letter, accidentally glimpsed. Lily did not press her. On the contrary, she seemed glad Teddy knew. But neither of them, perhaps for their own reasons, had wanted to pursue it further. ('Of course, darling, anything you might want to know about him . . . any time. He was a War hero, you see . . . You – we – can be proud . . .')

In the summer of 1921, of age now, she decided to travel, to flee home and memories for a while. At Christmas, prompted by she didn't know what, she added on to her annual card to Saint: 'I'm thinking of a spell in Paris. Did you ever get there?' He wrote back from a Paris address to say he'd been there for the last eight months.

When she arrived, they drifted together. No other word for it. Irrationally, the first time she went to bed with him, she felt unfaithful, and then consoled herself with the idea that because it was Gib's friend, it was all right, better than it might have been, that he would not have minded.

The next day she read the diary.

Neat hand, schoolmaster's hand . . . shaking a little.

May 1918. All our talk is of food, and home – waiting to hear. Do they know yet, does *she* know? I have no feeling for time, it stretches out before me, beyond the barbed wire, the huts and rows of potatoes growing between . . . The sandy plains of Pomerania, which is at the end of the world . . .

We are about twelve British officers and some four thousand other ranks, of every possible nationality. Conditions are very bad. Starvation rations – No wonder all our talk . . . At first we spoke of meat, steaks – man's food. Now we long above all for sweets and more sweets. One of the officers, Marchant, recounted a dream today in which his uncle gave him for his coming of age a whole *shop* full of the damned things. He locked the door to the street and sat on the counter with them all piled round him – liquorice coils, Fry's chocolate cream, Farrah's toffee, Callard and Bowser, jelly babies, fondants, turkish delight . . . Our mouths watered to hear him. 'Aah, ah,' he said lugubriously, 'I was just about to feast, when I woke to *Heraus, heraus* . . .'

I talk of food too. As who should not? God knows our days are dark and hopeless enough . . . My weakened stomach, my teeth (sore bleeding gums), rebel at the coarse black bread, the foul stews, that curious tea, coloured pink and which Marchant says from studying the sediment at the bottom is canary-seed . . . Perhaps when, *if*, they hear about us, there will be food parcels.

June 1918. An account of how I came to be here . . . I was hit very early in the morning – we'd attacked just before dawn, my second day back in the line. The bullet, a rifle bullet, got me up by the neck. It seemed to lift my body, it was as if I flew upwards . . . I thought I was going to die, and was *almost happy*. The next thing I knew I was lying alone, in a shell hole in inches of water, blood, unspeakables. I tried to move but couldn't. I thought: Perhaps they have marked me and they'll send stretcher-bearers? Then I must have lost consciousness again, because next it was a dark sky overhead and stars. I felt intensely cold. The blood had soaked my front. I knew I would die. Just before dawn I heard the voices – skirt of a long grey coat . . . A torch flashed in my eyes. I saw a revolver and knew I was to be disposed of. Killed like a rat . . .

But there's kindness, humaneness. The wild movements I made to try and speak must have served . . . I remember little afterwards, until the terrible coming round at the Jerry clearing station. An RAMC doctor-prisoner, overworked and scared. Conditions terrible. No antiseptics, no anæsthetics. He feared not only gas gangrene, but typhus too. I was lying on a foul bunk thick with dried fæces. My first food, an evil-smelling bean porridge in a filthy encrusted iron vat . . . My time there is blurred in memory with the terrible days of the journey to Pomerania. Pain, thirst . . .

August 1918. Back in the present. The weather is suffocatingly hot. And, a lighter touch: fleabites. Marchant has a particularly spiky hairbrush which we all borrow to soothe our poor itching bodies . . .

September 8th. My dreams are growing worse – so that I dread the night now even more than the long days. I have decided that what I should do is collect together, like a treasure store to which I can keep returning, everything beautiful, everything happy that I have ever known . . . Any other way lies madness.

September 17th. Am tired of talking about food or the progress of my wound (Shall I be literally stiff-necked?). Our ill-health generally is surely the result just of being here . . .

September 22nd. I would have thought it easy, my treasure, store, but it isn't, *because of the dreams* . . . Marchant says its malnutrition and emotional starvation . . .

I want, dear God, to remember:

1. the countryside of my childhood.
2. being at Cambridge with Saint and Vesey.
3. last, but first, Teddy. *Everything* about her . . .

October 15th. They flee from me still, *those memories.* Every morning the same: last night's dreams crowding into my treasure store, grinning, setting up their abode . . .

I see myself: gaunt, unshaven, blood-encrusted figure, lying in the stinking shell hole . . . But when I look again (and in the dream I'm always compelled to), then *she's* there – my poor mother, my *little* mother . . . as she was at the end. Each day growing not just thinner but *smaller.* She shrank. She shrinks now every night. Wastes before my eyes . . .

It happened like that, of course. Only I don't want to remember, above all not now. *Then,* I was saved – by Alice. Perhaps that is why I don't care to remember . . . Without Alice, where or what would I have been? She was the rock in the stormy seas, the one sure . . . there when it mattered most. *Always* there. Sister, mother, lover, *everything.*

Why not wife? *What happened?* Nothing, of course – some bad part of human nature, something inherently evil. Original sin. The desire, need, to destroy good when we see it. *To take the wrong path* . . .

October 23rd. I can think only, over and over again, of the dreadful thing I did to Alice. In my dreams I don't know if it is her or Mother that I see – the horrible vision – it is *one and the same person now* . . . I only know that it is my fault, *my* doing . . . (Why did they bring me back, let me live? It would have been better if . . .)

November 4th. I have been thinking more and more of what I must do to gain forgiveness. To undo as much as I can the evil. I had thought to write to her, but my pen hovers over the paper, and the neck wound begins an unbearable throbbing . . .

November 7th. It would be easier if I didn't love Teddy (Theodora, gift of God) more than life itself – for *that is how it feels*. But each day that I realize my wickedness, each day I'm less and less worthy of her. It's all a pressing confusion. Head, neck – the pain runs from neck up into head so that my mind is clamped – giant pincers of punishment.

Why, *how*, can a gift of God be an instrument of wickedness? Who can I ask about this? I think of my dear gentle father . . . I wonder, did God allow the Devil to tempt me through Teddy? *No*. There the circle *begins again* – because *she is good*, but is tied to me – a monster of wickedness. *Wicked beyond forgiveness* . . .

November 20th. Nine days now since the Armistice . . . I can't really believe that in perhaps four weeks, if there are no hitches, I may be home . . . Last night I had the most terrible dream yet. I dreamed that all three of them, the women I loved – *I had killed all of them*. I woke up sobbing . . .

I thought this morning, does it matter, why should it matter if or when I go home? The best that could happen would be for me to die before – and be punished. For God will surely punish me in the next world. But those I love and loved will be free of me.

December 10th. I shall not speak very much in the future. Dead men have little to say. I dreamed last night that I was already dead and knew this morning that that is how it is to be. They will know I am dead. I shall say, 'Look, Teddy Bear, look . . .' The doctors, what can they do? They may insist as Marchant tries to now, that out of prison will cure everything. How little they know . . .

Some words from Revelations came to me this evening: '*And in those days shall men seek death, and shall not find it; and shall desire to die, and death shall flee from them* . . .'

How long, oh Lord, how long?

*

There seemed so many of them. American cousins. It was overwhelming at first. That, and the New World . . .

They all spoke at once:

'. . . My name's Jay. You're Cousin Teddy Bear . . .'

'Cousin Teddy, can you see whose sister *I* am?'

'Can you tell us, Teddy, why you've been so long coming to see us. David said –'

'Teddy, I sort of like *promised* Jay you'd sit with him . . .'

Even those who lived out of New York had come over to be there for her arrival. It was all part of that great lift of her heart she'd has as the liner came through the Narrows. Standing at the rail, seeing the Statue of Liberty. The New World (oh, how she *needed* a new world . . .).

Aunt Daisy. Her mother's sister. She hadn't expected her to be so like Lily. Photographs of the two as young girls – even later pictures – had not shown it. It was Mother's turn of the head, laugh, voice. Most of all – voice.

Nearly forty years now since she escaped to marry her Joszef. Teddy liked him at once. White-haired and frail, old for his age. Gentle. She wondered how, as her mother had said, two such gentle people had managed. Except Daisy had been strong with it. *Must* have been strong . . .

She talked freely to Teddy of the bad times. 'Some of it . . . your mother never knew. We wouldn't have wanted her to. And then in the end, she was *so good to us*. The money – I think it must have been the whole proceeds of her stage success . . .'

Teddy had wanted then, suddenly, to tell her about Rumania. This was, unlike her own mother, someone in whom she would find it easy to confide. Yet . . . (and I am able to tell casual acquaintances, shipboard friends like Daphne), she didn't feel it was her own secret to pass on. It was her mother's.

There had been money, but not so much of it until their eldest son, Joe, joined his father in 1905 at the age of eighteen. Within five years the business had taken off. Joszef's partner, approaching seventy, sold out. Joe, it seemed, had moneymaking talents inherited from who knows how many forebears. The Greenwood touch: he had that certainly.

He was thirty-six now, married, with three sons. The whole family came over for lunch the first weekend of Teddy's visit. Anna, the first daughter, came too, with her four children. David, the only member of the family Teddy had already met, had survived the War, but lived now in the West.

Ruth was the youngest. Her husband Lew had been killed in France in 1918. She and her four children lived now with Daisy and Joszef. Daisy said, 'We offered them a home at once – for selfish reasons. It's so lovely to have small children around all the time . . .'

For Teddy, passing several weeks with these grand-children, her cousins, was a happiness she tried not to grasp at too frantically. She thought sometimes they must sense her longing when she picked them up and hugged them, took them on excursions, sang to them at bedtime. It was worse even than the longing with the orphans in Paris . . .

Ruth's children. Jay and Harry were eight and five. The little girls, Esther and Lily, ten and seven, were dark-haired like their mother. Both were rivals over their dolls:

Esther: 'Cousin Teddy, my Gloria's cuter than her Laura, isn't Gloria *cute*, Cousin Teddy?' Lily: 'Estie's too *old* for dolls, Cousin Teddy . . .'

They liked stories from her at bedtime, especially stories of how it had been when she was a little girl. The boys liked songs:

'*I was born in Michigan and I wish and wish again*,' she sang:

'*Picking fruit seems silly, after Piccadilly . . . Oh how I wish again, I was in Michigan – Down on the farm . . .*'

Jay was the most talkative. He was learning the cornet and was very confident: 'Listen to me. I play a real mean cornet.' She had to sit while he tried over and over, *Black Sheep Blues*.

There were snowy days. Two red-cheeked little girls went to school by motor. Jay had a croup and had to stay home. He couldn't play cornet either. She sat with him and with Harry who was recovering from a fever.

'Say, can you play piano? When I'm not sick any more we could maybe play alongside each other . . .'

'I have to sing to Harry now,' she said. 'I promised.'

Harry climbed out of bed and sat on her knee.

'*I'm just wild about Harry*,' she sang, '*and he's just wild about, he's just wild about, he's just wild about me . . .*'

Jay asked, 'Cousin Teddy Bear, did you never have any children?'

'No.'
Puzzled, he said, 'Did you never want some?'
'Yes, Jay,' she said, 'Yes, I do.'

5

Her despair was terrible. The first week after Geoffrey's going, she wanted only to die. And, she thought afterwards, if she had known the best way, had had the courage, had not been given that puppy – what might not have happened?

Certainly the puppy needed her. The first night he cried piteously, so that she put the small basket up on the bed beside her, wrapping it round with an old blanket. When he cried, she cried. Outside the cold was intense and for a few days she had to stay in bed, still with the kidney complaint. She was treated by the new doctor with some nauseous alkaline mixture. She was told that she could expect to feel some sickness, and this she admitted to. Her real fears, she did not mention.

'What do you call him?' he asked of the puppy, which she had in the room with her now all the time, running to and fro squeaking, falling over his paws . . .

'Ludwig.'

'As in Ludwig van B, eh? Never thought to hear Jerry names chosen again. But time passes. Things not too good in Germany either . . .'

But it had been silly, absurd. She had named him after Beethoven only because of that first evening, the evening of the storm . . . How, why should she remind herself continually? And yet I do. Stupid. Unwise probably. Now she said only:

'He looks like a Ludwig. Don't you agree?'

She tried never to think at all of how far Geoffrey would be on his journey, of when he would arrive – of his new life, his *family's* new life. Tried but did not always succeed. On her second day up again, she went into Richmond and had her hair bobbed. When it was done, she would have liked not to have to look. But 'Yes,' she said politely to the hairdresser, 'yes, that's very nice.' She looked quite different: her face seemed surprised, fragile – her cheekbones accentuated. At home, her mother liked it. She herself knew the act to have been a punishment.

She had now passed the time for her second period. Panic seized her where before she'd been numb with despair. *I must do something*, tell someone. But who? Her mother – impossible. Teddy? I might. *If she were here* . . .

Three days later she received a Valentine from Reggie. She had no doubt it was from him. The handwriting, clumsily disguised, could have been no one else's. Postmarked in Argyll, it was a luridly coloured heart with attached arrow. Alongside he had written in capitals:

> Maid of Flaxthorpe, ere we part,
> Give, oh give me back my heart!
> Or, since that has left my breast,
> Keep it now, and take the rest!

Below he had added, 'How about marrying me?'

She smiled affectionately, for a second almost forgetting her despair. Then it swept over her again. I will wait one week, she thought, and then *speak to someone*.

Afterwards she was to reflect with surprise that it should have been *Reggie* to whom she spoke . . . It came about because he called at The Towers, driving a smart pony and trap, announcing that he was back in Flaxthorpe, and could he take her out?

She didn't suppose Mother would really approve. But she wasn't at home. Probably with Erik . . .

'To bob or not to bob?' Reggie said. 'Pity you couldn't have kept that hair . . .'

They took Ludwig with them on Sylvia's knee, wrapped in a rug. It was a mild sunny day, unbelievable for February.

'He's a wriggly little blighter. Terrier, good for rabbiting though. Shouldn't be surprised if he yaps . . .'

A little way out of Flaxthorpe on the Settstone road, he said, 'I didn't write that verse stuff – the Valentine, you know . . . Words by that bounder Byron. Maid of somewhere or other he said – so I put Flaxthorpe . . .' He paused a moment. 'How about it then? Any good a chap asking again, eh? Got quite a few prospects . . .'

'All right,' she said. 'Yes, I will, Reggie.'

He jerked suddenly on the reins, startling the pony.

Brought the trap to a smart halt. 'Phew! By George – that's the most extraordinary . . . Do you *mean* that?'

She was trembling, and put her gloved hands inside the rug where Ludwig lay sleeping, warm.

'It's not – I'm not –' she began, looking down all the time at the puppy. 'There's something dreadful I have to tell you . . .' And she burst into tears.

'Hold on, old thing. I mean to say –' Hooking up the reins, he turned so that he could put his arm about her. 'It can't be that bad – can it?'

But it was. Even in the version she gave him. The New Year party which she should never have attended, the man, visiting Yorkshire only, who'd paid her so much attention . . . the drink she wasn't accustomed to. Her *shame* when she realized . . . 'I'm not even sure of his name – only that he was married. I never thought . . . what happened to me, that it could . . .' She finished, 'So you see I have to be honest. I couldn't not be. But I can hardly expect –'

Soon it would be over: she would be despised, and the mistake she had just made wiped out. The terror would begin again.

'By Jove, that's a facer. Bloody good thing you haven't his name. His life wouldn't be worth much . . .' He pulled her closer, his mouth on her shoulder. 'You didn't think I'd take back my offer, did you, eh? That I'd be such a cad . . . I'm still there, if you want me.'

Ludwig had woken and was whimpering. 'Another kind of girl might have tried it on – deceit and all that. Getting *me* to, you know – well, *perform* . . .' He added: 'Wouldn't have minded a bit of that – except you're not the sort . . . That's why I *do* want you. If you'll have me –'

Yes, she would have him. There was no turning back now. For Geoffrey's child, a father. For her, Reggie . . . God's in his heaven, she thought suddenly, bitterly.

She picked up Ludwig and held him close but he wanted only to jump down and explore. He waddled and stumbled on the floor of the trap.

'. . . Luck,' Reggie was saying, 'don't usually get luck. Unless you count losing only one arm when it might have been both my – I'm sorry. Something I shouldn't say in front of a lady . . .'

She had to kiss him. It was not unpleasant although he tasted bitter (or was it her?). She felt a little faint as his empty sleeve pressed against her. He told her that he wanted a son. Very badly. 'Quite a thing with me, that is . . . Right through this last show I was thinking, *if* I come out – what I want is a son. A lovely little wife and a son . . . We'll sort out this little fellow first,' he told her. 'Then you'll have one for me, eh?'

Later, as they were driving back, he said, 'Look, old thing, if you're in this jam – the wedding, it'll have to be pretty soon, don't you think? Dashed soon by my reckoning . . .'

She did not have to decide not to think. She found quite simply that she could not. It was as if from the moment she had said 'Yes', and made her (false) confession, her mind had ceased to work. Practical matters such as telling her mother, those she could not escape. But *real* thoughts, she was spared. For the moment – she did not imagine it would last – she could not feel anything at all.

Her first concern now must be for the child. She would take care of herself, try to eat well, sleep more, walk in the fresh air. In the meantime she must tell her mother about the marriage. That, she dreaded. She would have to lie again.

She and Reggie had agreed that it would be better if she spoke, even though it was his place to do so. She told her mother in the evening of the next day, after dinner.

'Reggie Gilmartin – we want . . . what would you say – we thought, you see – of getting married . . .'

'*Darling* –' Her mother's face. Voice. Shocked. Displeased? Then, laughing almost, 'You're not serious?'

Oh, but she was. (*There must be no going back.*) She said over and over that really she meant it – that she and everyone else had misunderstood Reggie, that truly he was a much better person than he seemed. (And might not that indeed be true?)

'He's a fortune-hunter, *tout court* . . .'

But money had never been mentioned. He had not spoken of it, except to tell his ideas for making it . . .

'Daddy said something like that once, but not about Reggie. About men generally. Honestly, I don't think –'

'Darling, why not – wait a little? Postpone the whole notion and then see how you feel – say, after the Season? If it's real love –'

'But, Mummy –' (she could not bear, would not hear that word 'love'. What had this to do with love – except that it was *his* child?)

'Oh, do be civilized. I just make the suggestion –'

'But it *has* to be soon. The wedding, I mean. You see . . .'

Perhaps she had become better at telling lies, for this time it came out pat. 'I'm going to have a baby . . .' She phrased it so that she did not have to lie, did not actually say that it was Reggie's. Such foolish scruples amid such great deceit.

She was believed, of course. And her confession, as she had known it must, changed everything. Although Lily was at first inclined to blame Reggie:

'So much older. To have seduced you – it doesn't bear thinking . . .'

'But it was my fault, Mummy. And what a lovely old-fashioned expression, "seduced" . . . It was – we were just anticipating, you see, then there was Daddy's illness and – and . . .'

A lot of talking to be done. She did it all in the same airy, falsely happy tone. A dangerous excitement gripped her as if she played with death – or for very high stakes.

Her mother's voice broke. It sounded full of tears.

'I can't think – all my children . . . Teddy's marriage – such a rush, so little thought. But that had the excuse of wartime. I encouraged that marriage, which seemed so *right* . . . Just seventeen, younger even than you. Yet I who waited till twenty-seven –' she broke off. 'My plans, all my *hopes* for you, darling . . .'

She put her arms tight about Sylvia. She was weeping now. 'Forgive me. It's the shock. Perhaps we ought to . . . Please, *please* darling, think dreadfully carefully about this. That you are absolutely *certain* . . .'

But there was a baby. That altered everything. Her mother admitted that. And as for thinking . . . God, that I may never have to think again. Or feel again. May I be a good wife to Reggie. Above all, may I be a good mother to *his* child . . .

The rush to make arrangements started almost at once. Except for Angie and Mrs Fraser, his aunt, she knew nothing of Reggie's family. Both his parents were dead, but there was another sister, Bar, married to a doctor and living in Canada. Reggie spoke grandly of going out to visit her. There were some cousins in Argyll with whom he'd just been staying; others in Harrogate . . .

She wondered a little how Angie would react. She was staying with friends in Switzerland, but wrote immediately to Sylvia. It was a letter full of enthusiasm. '. . . All I could have wanted for the blighter – too marvellous for words – long to hear all details . . . perfectly sickening to see him so absolutely *pining* . . .'

The wedding date was fixed for April 6th, just after Easter, which that year fell on April Fools' Day. A coincidence she found sourly appropriate. The haste of course needed explaining, as would later the child's birth: even seven months could not be managed . . . But she had ceased to care about any of this and wanted only the ceremony and all the fuss that went with it over as quickly as possible. She knew there was some talk – gossip rather, not about the haste but because Reggie was (terrible phrase) 'not quite out of the top drawer'. Even her mother had said as much although she'd added, 'Since you love him, what's it matter? It's only if perhaps, later . . .' She left the rest unsaid. To Sylvia it all seemed much the same, since he was not Geoffrey.

Money too entered the picture. The family solicitor was sent for, and there was talk of settlements, a dowry, inheritance, jewellery, and of course, the Diamond Waterfall. Most of it was over her head, just as it had been when after her father's funeral they had read the Will. She knew only that at twenty-five she would be very rich. And that Reggie would not ever have to worry. Although he assured her, protested, that he could never live off her wealth. 'I've a sound business head, old thing, oodles of acumen – just need to find the best enterprise, get it off the ground. Bring Angie into it, perhaps . . .'

The arrangement was that as soon as she inherited The Towers, they would live there. Until then Reggie could find work if he liked. They would have her ample allowance meanwhile.

It was thought better if the birth did not take place in or near Flaxthorpe. In that way it would pass with less remark. The story was given out that Reggie had a post in the South of

France, in Mentone, deliberately vague but with diplomatic undertones. Because it must be taken up immediately, they would marry very quietly before he left.

They booked into the Carlton Palace for the first fortnight. Once out there, they would rent a house. Meanwhile she was measured for a wedding dress of cloth of silver. So far she had lost rather than gained weight. Only her breasts seemed to grow heavier by the day.

All her care now was for the child. She read somewhere that all one saw, heard, thought during the months of waiting could have its effect . . . Once a day in the last weeks before the wedding she went into the Norman church. Not to pray – she could not, just as she could not think – but to allow the prayers of others over the centuries to reach her and, through her, the child. Often during the day, she would say to her womb, 'I love you, Geoffrey's baby.' Sometimes, underneath her resignation and despair, she sensed something not unlike peace.

The night before the wedding she went very early to bed. But she could not sleep and about half past eleven saw a light still on in her mother's room. She went in, and for the next hour they talked. Or rather Lily talked, for Sylvia was careful to say little. One word, she thought, and I *shall say it all*. She longed that evening to tell the whole story. It would be so easy. Her secret would be kept. Geoffrey already gone away. Nothing truly could be altered now by her mother's knowing . . .

She said nothing. The moment passed. Her mother spoke of marriage with Erik at some future date. 'I'm sure you understand, darling, and can forgive . . .' She talked about her own family, the Greenwoods ('and you couldn't call *them* "top drawer" '), hinted at some of the difficulties in her own marriage. She asked too, as once before, if Sylvia was quite sure she wasn't confusing pity for Reggie's lost arm with real love:

'But then love itself, *that*'s not safe either, darling . . .'

Towards the end of their talk she said, 'The only really dreadful thing would have been to *do* anything about the child – That sort of thing can go horribly wrong. Can end – you'll probably know that one can *die* that way . . .'

But she spoke of something that had never been considered. In the worst of my terror, Sylvia told herself, I never thought of that. She clung though now to her mother as she kissed her goodnight. Was distressed to see that she was crying again.

When she had left her, instead of going back to bed she went downstairs. There was no one about. The servants in bed. She wandered into the kitchens and made herself a drink of hot milk. She thought it would be good for the baby.

As she came from the kitchens towards the hall, the telephone rang. She jumped with the sound, almost spilling the milk. It went again and again, shrilly, as she stood there. Death, disaster? Why a call at *this* hour?

She unhooked the receiver.

'Flaxthorpe two-seven –'

'Sylvia Firth, want to speak to *Sylvia* –' She could not mistake Reggie's voice. Even though drunk. Perhaps very drunk . . .

She said, 'This *is* Sylvia –'

'Get Miss Sylvia. Can't get any sense out of the servant class . . . You there, you –'

'Reggie, its *Sylvia speaking* –'

'You think I've been drinking, don't you? Don't you? I'll tell you something – no, don't hang up, you won't hang up on a chap, eh? I want to tell you, Sylvie. I'm a chap's never had a chance, that's why I'm rotten, you know. I *am* rotten blighter. Whole bottle tonight. Bottle and a half up the Line though, bloody needed it, had the wind up otherwise whole bloody time. Got to talk to you tonight, thought the bloody servants never going to answer . . . Listen, Sylvie, you're a good woman, white woman eh? Going to be a good mother. We'll have son, fine son – Listen there, Sylvia, not going to be like *my* mother . . . I'll tell you something, Mother didn't like all alone in bed, and Dad going away – can you hear, Sylvie? – She'd always ask someone in, you know. *In.* Right *in* . . . Then Reggie's back from school a day early and what's he see, eh? You guess . . . yes, they're bloody fucking . . . and *he* says, "What's that damned pipsqueak doing here?" and *she* says, wait for the laugh, you laughing, Sylvie? she says, "That pipsqueak's *my son.*" But Reggie's going to have fine son all his own – that right, darling? Don't go 'way, Sylvie, listen to me, I'll tell you something else – my little new wife's done a filthy thing but Reggie doesn't blame her – You'll see he doesn't, it was this filthy cad . . . got to protect her from cads, bloody bounders, prowling about after innocent girls. Sweet, sweet Sylvia . . . But you know you're filth, don't you? Are you there still, listening eh?'

'Reggie, why not go up to bed?' Her voice shook. 'It's *late* . . .' She couldn't believe what she'd heard. She held the receiver away from her now, unable to hook it up again. He is drunk, she told herself, it's better he gets it all said now, tonight.

'Bed, got to go to bed now – drank alone, didn't drink with friends. Always drink with chums, best friends chums fighting with, hear guns all together . . . Listen, Sylvie, tell you something else, though – you did a chap a good turn. Saved me a bit of juice eh? getting yourself filled up like that –'

'Reggie, that's *enough* –'

Before he could begin again, she hung up. She stood, trembling, for several minutes, afraid it would shrill again. Then picking up her cup, she crossed the hall. Her legs were unsteady. A thick cold skin lay over the top of the milk. Upstairs again, she was violently sick – hands on her belly, clutching the child.

She was not a bride upon whom the sun shone. It was a grey day, with an icy wind coming up as they left the church. Reggie, apart from a bad colour, showed no signs of his binge of the night before. And from the way he spoke, she felt certain he remembered nothing of it. *I must do the same* . . .

In Mentone the sun shone all day. About the fifth day there she felt the baby move for the first time, and was filled with sudden hope – almost as if it were her doing. She went that same evening into the church of St Michel in the old town, and sat quietly, saying, 'thank you'. Then she lit three candles: for the baby, for Geoffrey, and for Reggie.

Reggie. Here in the sun with money to spend, and on holiday, he seemed happy enough. He drank little, mainly wine, nor did he gamble except on one occasion at the end of the first week, when a visit to Monte proved expensive. He was very repentant.

Because she hadn't been able to think, she had not thought that she must sleep with him. She was surprised to find that by continuing not to think, it was possible for it not to matter at all. When he held her with his arm (the sight of the scarred stump that had been the other one aroused in her only pity), and muttered fierce words of love into her shoulder, it had nothing to do with anything that had gone before . . .

He was gentle. He said they must be careful with the child. He liked too to try and feel it move . . . That seemed to her odd – another man's seed. Sometimes he would say excitedly, 'We've just to get this little blighter landed safely, and all fit and OK – then we'll put in for a son of our own, eh?'

It was sometime in the first week in their rented apartment that she came across his revolver. Dark steel, lying in a drawer among his socks and suspenders, shirts . . . When she exclaimed in horror, he seemed taken aback. It was his Smith and Wesson, he said, his much loved trusty wartime 455. Double barrel.

'What would I do without it – always kept it, Sylvie. Makes a fellow feel safe . . .' He showed her his name engraved: PE Gilmartin . . . All that day she felt sick with apprehension. And anything but safe . . .

April turned into May, May into June. Perhaps most of all through the long days of sunshine she missed Ludwig, who would now be growing out of puppyhood without her. Reggie had suggested at first they bring him out with them. 'Easy enough to smuggle 'em back. Chaps in the trenches – we did it all the time.' But she told him 'No'. What she could not tell him was why Ludwig meant so much to her.

At the beginning of June Angie came out to stay with them. Sylvia, feeling much more pregnant now, found her hearty manner, her championing of Reggie which took the form usually of cheerful insults, and her extravagant praise of her, Sylvia, almost too much. As the days went by and Reggie talked more and more of this and that business venture which, having spoken with X yor Y, he *might* put capital into, she became unsettled and longed for home.

She had of course heard nothing from Geoffrey. But it was only when the weeks passed and she did not, that she realized how much she had hoped for some, any, sign of life. She could not help wondering if he had seen the notice of her wedding.

For he would by now be settled in, and surely all exiles in the colonies read avidly *The Times* foreign edition? (Oh, but then, what will he think when he learns? That I was soon consoled, that it did not take long for my heart to mend?)

The weather grew hotter: by the end of July, she was certain that she should come home. Reggie needed little persuading. Angie had managed to find work near Mentone as a paid companion and secretary, which would take her through the autumn and winter season. At least, Sylvia thought, she will not be living with us for a while . . .

They took a small house in the West Riding in a village outside Ilkley. As they had no transport they were thrown very much upon each other's company. Reggie began to look for work – he thought he might be a factor for a nearby estate. 'There is no need,' she told him, and then regretted her words. He often spent much of his disability pension now on gifts for her, sometimes even for the child.

She'd sent for Ludwig at once. She thought at first he had forgotten her, but within an hour he was curled against her skirt asleep. She was pleased to see Reggie was fond of him. 'Game little chap – He'll guard the babe. No bally cats getting in to smother.' She had not thought of anything so terrible . . .

She'd been told to expect the child about the third week of September. A monthly nurse had already been engaged. Her mother would come over to stay in the nearby hotel. Towards the end of August, Reggie's cousins in Harrogate invited them over for a few days' stay, to coincide with the unveiling of the War Memorial on the first of September.

She was reluctant to go at first, but then saw what it meant to Reggie. Two of his cousins were among those to be commemorated. A third, Malcolm, who'd been too young for the fighting, came to stay with them the weekend before. He would drive them to Harrogate.

She liked Malcolm and enjoyed his company, but about his car she was not so sure . . . The journey to Harrogate was exhausting, as it shook from side to side, and she with it. The baby too. The night of their arrival she could not sleep for the excited kicking and pummelling. Next morning found her with a low backache, and unbelievably weary.

It was a day of sheeting rain. The ceremony, to be attended

by Princess Mary and her husband, Viscount Lascelles, had drawn enormous crowds. Sylvia, standing beneath Reggie's umbrella, was hemmed in by a sea of other umbrellas. Reggie said, 'Trust the bally British climate . . .' He wondered if he should have brought her? But 'No, no, I'm all right,' she said.

She wondered if she was. Standing, the rain pattering down, beating on the umbrellas. Sodden Union Jack, stones of the square gleaming, wet lawn. A little bit away, near the dripping trees, people climbed on the tops of cars for a better view. The ranks of sailors opposite where she stood seemed to her to be swaying. She hoped only that, suddenly hot and cold as she'd become, she wouldn't faint. She fixed her gaze on the wall of The Prospect Hotel, with its sign, *Restaurant.* The writing sloped upwards.

Or did it?

From early evening when labour truly started, and then all through the night, she felt shock. Babies could come early or late: so why am I so surprised? Malcolm's family thought it was his car the culprit . . . As the hastily summoned doctor attempted reassurance, Reggie hovering anxiously (the very picture, she thought later, of the *real* father), she tried to rise above the waves of ever-increasing pain. '*I wasn't ready,*' she said over and over again.

And indeed she had nothing with her. None of the lovingly made layette. Her own belongings packed only for three days . . . But it wasn't that she meant. Simply she had expected more time, to be able to talk quietly in her mind to Geoffrey. To tell herself . . . *be brave.*

If Reggie was disappointed that the baby was a girl, he did not show it. Although he'd spoken often of 'the little blighter', she realized that naturally enough perhaps, it was only his own son he was interested in. Indeed the afternoon after the birth, he said as he peered into the (borrowed) cot, 'Feeling proud, old thing, Sylvie? Not long now . . . and we'll be having one of our own.'

He did not seem interested in a name for the child either. She was glad about this. Part of her not being 'ready' had been a reluctance to think about names. Now, looking at this brown-eyed, unusually long, fair-haired child, she kept saying to herself (and how afraid she'd been during labour that she might cry it out), '*Geoffrey's child.*' The second evening, falling asleep, she remembered suddenly his telling her once that his name, Selwood, meant 'willow wood'.

'What about Willow?' she asked Reggie.

'Willow Gilmartin – bit of a mouthful, old thing. But if you want it . . .'

It was decided she should stay on at the cousins' in Harrogate for at least ten days. Malcolm and his car were despatched with Reggie to fetch everything needed. The day they left, although summer, had a smell of autumn. It came through the open windows of the large guest-room where she had her lying-in. It had been just such a day when she and Geoffrey had met by chance in Richmond. Now as she lay back on the pillows, Willow asleep in her cot, milky-mouthed, fresh from the breast – she felt a strange autumnal happiness. *I have something of him* . . .

She didn't expect the feeling to last. That evening, back from his trip, Reggie leaned over the cot, poking a finger at the blanketed bundle:

'What about a little brother, eh? Eh?'

6

As soon as Teddy walked into the big whitewashed room which was the orphanage nursery, the children began to call out:

'*Tant' Teddie, c'est Tant' Teddie . . . Venez ici, Tant' Teddie . . .*' Several had soon gathered round her, the pleated panels of her blue woollen dress were tugged at, others had run off to fetch treasures to show her. The last to reach her was six-year-old Vincent, who had lost a leg two years ago. (The War will never be over, she thought, for he'd been the victim of one of the innumerable unexploded shells turned up each year by the plough on what had been the battlefields . . .) Now when he reached her, waited to be kissed, face alive with happiness, she thought: How easily they are made glad . . . Whereas she, she could only bring into this room, this October of 1924, her restlessness, her longing – *why could Gib not have left me a child?*

'*Tant' Teddie, Tant' Teddie – regardez ce que j'ai fait . . .*'

Vincent had drawn her a large smiling cat with a red bow. He explained that *le bon Dieu* had made him so excellent at drawing to make up for the leg. He asked her over and over, did she like his cat?

This most ordinary of cats – she loved it. She told him she would take it with her to England tomorrow.

'*Tant' Teddie, Tant' Teddie . . . Ne partez pas, Tant' Teddie . . .*'

She went from them to the Place Louvois to meet Saint who'd been working all afternoon in the Bibliothèque Nationale. They sat for a while in a café, both with a *fine à l'eau*. She smoked, lighting one up after the other because she hadn't done so at the orphanage – and because as always the visit had unsettled her. She thought idly, a little desperately: I might marry Saint. If he asked me. She pictured the children they might have . . .

'It's fairly discreet, I take it, your mother's wedding,' he said. 'I mean, the bells won't be pealing out across Yorkshire?'

'Very discreet, yes. Very quiet.'

She was happy for Lily that she married Erik at last. Her mother deserved this happiness. She looked forward also to the two months she was to spend at The Towers while Lily and Erik were away on a honeymoon cruise. Seeing something of Sylvia, perhaps, inviting Amy and her new husband, war veteran Gerald Vaughan, to spend time with her. Taking long peaceful walks in the autumn countryside.

'Your sister,' Saint was saying. 'The one who married Gilmartin – I thought *they* had The Towers –'

'No. When she's twenty-five. It's all rather complicated . . . But she'll get everything then. Diamond Waterfall. The lot. Reggie, I hope – I don't *think*'s a fortune-hunter . . .'

'Shall I marry *you* for your money? It might be an idea . . .'

'Why not?' She added lightly, 'Be good while I'm gone, and remember, I hate you . . .'

'And I hate you, darling . . .'

Sylvia at the wedding was pregnant. Reggie looked pleased with himself – and prosperous, although Teddy was unable to discovery anything he was actually doing. He had a number of ideas, Sylvia told her, but they would take time. And of course they were not actually short of money . . .

She thought Sylvia too pale. But said nothing to her. Nor did she want to worry Lily, who had seemed upset enough when the marriage took place. She asked herself yet again: Did Sylvia really have to marry him? I could have arranged something . . . France, Switzerland, a small village, 'widowhood', adoption . . . (I *must not think* how willingly, joyously, *I* would have adopted . . .) But she didn't confide in me.

I married for love. Sylvia . . . I wonder?

The first weeks after Lily and Erik had left passed pleasantly enough. She thought of inviting Saint to join her, but felt this might not be fair on her mother. Sylvia she had not managed to persuade. 'Come and stay in Paris later,' she said, 'after the babe.' She hoped Reggie would not come. He exhausted her.

Because she could do so little for Sylvia, she pressed gifts on her always. Luxuries. This time it had been a giant box of chocolates from Debauve et Gallais. I would much rather give her time, and love, she had thought. If I were allowed.

Colourful postcards came from Lily and Erik. From Saint, the occasional letter. She walked a lot, more than she had for several years. She took care to avoid paths and ways that she had been with Gib. Both outside and inside The Towers, in the church, near the Vicarage, she could never be certain a memory might not leap out at her. Here, we first kissed . . . In this bed . . . *Here* we believed we would be happy . . .

Days ran into each other. She knew that her restlessness only lay hidden . . . I could not be here *all* the time. When in early November a savage wind tore at the last of the leaves, howling round the house, she felt it mirrored something in herself. One night, not able to sleep, she foolishly read Gib's diary again, lying awake, thinking . . .

In the morning she felt sick and exhausted. Sitting at Lily's bureau in the drawing-room, she wrote to Saint. She was trying for a determinedly cheerful note, when one of the parlourmaids spoke:

'Mrs Nicolson, ma'am, two persons want to see the mistress – I said as how . . . It's a woman and a little boy, ma'am, but they're – They ought to . . . the *back* door, ma'am.'

When they were shown in, the woman was very red in the face. She appeared agitated. The boy, large, fair-haired, looked about five or six. She had hold of his hand. He gazed about him, staring at Teddy, who smiled at him. He smiled back slowly, revealing two missing front teeth.

The woman said:

'I'd best not beat about, Mrs Nicolson . . . It were Lady Firth I'd a mind to speak to. But – you'll do . . . I'm not one for writing, you see, so I thought it'd be best to come here, like, and – fetch the lad up too –'

The boy, interrupting, said to Teddy directly:

'I'm Michael – Michael –'

The woman slapped his hand sharply. He didn't seem to mind. She did it with a kind of hurried affection, going on talking then as if she hadn't been interrupted:

'It's Slader, they call me. Nellie Slader from Kingsbridge. Father – Mr Slader and I, we was married in 'ninety-nine. I'm North Riding, Pickering way. He's Devon. They're a strange lot down there, but they farm well enough.' She glanced over at Michael. 'Telling him off, made a confusion, it has. Where did I reach?'

Teddy thought: *What is all this about?* She couldn't take her eyes off the boy, who had left the woman's side and was sitting on a tall tapestry chair, swinging his legs . . .

'It's been a sad journey. But I wanted to fetch the lad up, to show, like –' she paused. 'To show Lady Firth her – grandson.'

'I'm sorry,' Teddy began, her voice puzzled. 'I don't think – I mean –' She felt the boy's eyes on her.

'Mrs Nicolson, I'd not have made this journey to tell fibs. This lad's a grandson right enough –'

Teddy was trembling. She lit a cigarette to calm herself, passing the cigarette box to Mrs Slader. She said, 'I shall ring for some coffee – or would you prefer tea? And perhaps some milk or lemonade for – Michael?'

Then in the silence that followed: 'If you could *please* explain?'

'My niece, that was his mam – she died it'll be three month, and the lad – I'd have bringed him up myself and I wanted to tell Lady Firth that. I'd have done the job only that my niece . . . She asked afore she went . . .'

She'd become flustered now in the telling of her tale. Teddy said gently, 'Can we go a bit further back? Perhaps to – the beginning?' She wondered too if the boy should be present? She said, 'Would Michael like perhaps to play with some toys?'

'There's nowt he can't hear, Mrs Nicolson. He's a good lad. There'll be nowt said, only what he's to be proud of . . .'

Teddy thought Michael looked as if he would like to cry . . . Her own mind raced.

'You're Lady Firth's daughter, that's right, Mrs Nicolson? Well, the lad – he's the son of your brother Henry. Hal, that was lost in the War. And his mam, you'll know her, she were Olive Ibbotson, from Lane Top Farm –'

Teddy said, interrupting her, 'But of course my mother would have wanted .. . at once. If she –' her voice faltered. 'She would only wonder, I know, that Olive wasn't in touch with us when – it first happened.'

She was still trying to take it in. That Hal . . . that all those years up at the farm had led to this – that he had got Olive into trouble. Had possibly never known . . .

'She were a stubborn lass, were Olive. Right from the start . . . I said to her then – for I'd the care of her – I said, "Olive, you've a duty to the lad. Tell them," I said. "Tell his folk . . ." But, "I'll not," she said, "I'll not. Hal knew that . . . I've never been beholden," she said, "and I'll not be it now . . ." I knew well, though, she worried on account of his schooling. There was times she'd be of two minds. We'd a happy house, though – I can promise you that, Mrs Nicolson. And Olive, she were a bonny girl. There's pictures here'll show you . . .'

Teddy, looking at the photographs (recognizably an Ibbotson sitting somewhere on a harbour wall, grimacing in the sun – in another, holding a baby in long robes and smiling), thought: How unreal all this is. Mrs Slader was putting them away – talking again:

'And then, when we'd all but lost Olive (it were consumption, like her mam afore her), she said then, those last days, "I've changed my mind, Auntie Nellie – I'll not burden you with him" – and I said to her, "It'll be no burden, we love him like as if he'd been ours" – She said then, "He's to go up to – *them*." She'd often call you "them" . . .'

While they spoke Michael had been sitting, head forward, his legs swinging from the high-seated chair. Now he began to swing them faster, faster, so they kicked continually against the wood. Mrs Slader stopped her talking, and slapped his legs.

Teddy almost cried, 'Don't!' but restrained herself. It was none of her business . . . Then realizing suddenly: But I'm more closely related than she is . . . *My nephew*, she thought.

Mrs Slader said, 'I've her lines here.'

Teddy, for a moment puzzled: 'Lines?'

Michael spoke up. He said in his Devon accent, 'Lines are for fishes . . .'

'Her *lines*,' Mrs Slader went on, as if he hadn't spoken, 'Her lines to show when she were wed. When she wed your brother, Mrs Nicolson.'

Teddy said, letting her breath out with a great sigh, '*What*?'

'Daft it were, all secret, like. I said to her, the times I said to her, "Wed in secret, all right," I said, "but not after, not after" . . .'

She brought out an envelope and removed a sheet of paper. 'The lines,' she said. 'Go on now. Take a look.'

Teddy, stubbing out her cigarette, unfolded the paper with care.

They were such happy days, those first ones with Michael. At first, thinking the break would be too sudden for him, she had wanted Mrs Slader to take him back to Devon for a week or two. She wasn't certain he realized he was actually coming to The Towers to *live*. But Mrs Slader assured her it had all been carefully explained.

'The sooner he's begun on his new life . . .'

At five, he was an unusually self-possessed boy. At the same time Teddy could see that often he was bewildered. Apart from the enormous difference between Nellie Slader's house and The Towers, there was the absence not only of his mother but of the person who'd taken her place these last months.

Once he suddenly stopped what he was doing, sat down, and cried heartbrokenly. The local girl who'd been engaged as a nurse for him, rushed to Teddy. But after saying half a dozen times, 'Think I'll go back to Mam, think I'll go back to Mam . . .' he got up just as suddenly, and ran off to play.

At night when she came to read to him, Teddy talked to him about Olive. Hal too. She brought down from one of the attics some of his books. *The Blue Fairy Book*.

'Soon your Grandma will be coming – she will love you *a lot* . . .'

Totally absorbed in settling in Michael, she could hardly bear to deal with all the implications of his arrival. She felt that until her mother and Erik came back she should do nothing. Tell no one. To the staff, she had half explained. And asked them to respect the confidence.

Sylvia she had told at once. That same afternoon, by telephone. Sylvia had wept with happiness. Had never for a moment doubted it was true. Had spoken of coming up to Yorkshire as soon as possible. But only a few days later Reggie had telephoned to say that she'd had a miscarriage.

Yes, yes, she was all right. His sister Angie was there to help . . .

Lily and Erik returned three weeks later. She travelled down to London to meet the boat train, wondering only if she should have left Michael even the day and night it took her to meet the honeymooners. Would he feel abandoned all over again?

That evening at their hotel, she told them. She saw that, just as she had been, her mother was completely overwhelmed. Shocked by happiness. But wary – more wary than Teddy had been. Erik too:

'The marriage certificate. The birth certificate. These are genuine?'

Her mother, calmer now: 'You're *quite* certain?'

'That he's Hal's child? Yes, absolutely. And you will be also.'

There had never been any doubt in her mind. Mrs Slader, odd, brusque, flustered woman, would never have lied . . .

'I talked to her, Mrs Slader, a long time before she left. Everything she said . . . it would be hard to see Olive as anything but a good person. A *proud* person . . .'

Her mother, hurt all over again. She remembered now Lily's pain, confusion, when after Hal's death, his clothes, his few personal effects had been forwarded to the 'Miss Ibbotson' listed as next of kin – back in the days when he had run away to be a soldier . . . They had spoken then of following it up. In their grief they had done nothing. Of what use to distress a much-loved girlfriend, also mourning?

She had been to see the family lawyer, she told them now. 'I felt he should be informed at once.' He had checked on all the documents. Robert's Will, made before Hal's death (and with only the codicil that cut her, Teddy, out after she received her Rumanian money), was quite clear. After the bequest to Hal, the straight inheritance, the words, '*or any legitimate issue*'. Sylvia, no longer the heiress, would have to be told. She would now have some capital of her own, the sum that would have been her dowry. But great wealth, the Waterfall . . . No.

Getting out of the motor at The Towers, Lily saw Michael. He was standing on the front step with the servants, his nurse beside him. Teddy thought: I need not have worried.

Michael stared at her a few seconds, then ran towards her. She gathered him up in her arms. Teddy, hiding tears, looked the other way.

Erik, standing beside her, said, 'We are having the best news since our marriage. And the best wedding present that is possible . . .'

'I think that too,' she said.

Back in Paris, she was greeted by Saint. He said, 'You behold me, fangs drawn, trussed for slaughter –'

'What's all this?'

'I'm to be married. Believe it or not.'

Her shock . . . And then, his explanation. The girl whose father was over on business for a year. A vague family connection. An invitation to dinner, months ago. Seeing more of her while Teddy was away. Being asked to paint her portrait and doing it very badly.

'I met her in the sort of dull circles you and I have always been so rude about. Just lately I've got to know her – fairly closely. It's come to marriage. Daddy wants it that way. So does she. And, we all come to it, don't we? I'm thirty-five, Teddy – forty's in sight . . .'

She asked dully, what sort of life was he going to lead? A semi-bohemian one still?

'I'm going into their family business. From today I shall cease to *épater les bourgeois* . . . Henceforward, I shall *be* bourgeois . . .'

7

'It can't go wrong,' Reggie was saying. 'A cert, absolute dead cert. Soundest scheme ever . . .' As he spoke he sipped a neat whisky. The two other men nodded in agreement. Claude Mulcaster, Sidney Johnson. New business acquaintances . . .

Sylvia looked at her own glass of weak orange squash with disgust. Perhaps she would have something stronger to be in this company – but she was two months pregnant, almost everything nauseous. More so than ever before. She had told herself that if this new one was not the longed-for son, she would have something fitted. Go to London and make some arrangement privately. Tell Reggie nothing. *I cannot go on forever.*

Willow, Lucy, Jessica, Margaret. Four little girls sleeping upstairs. Earlier, of course, the two miscarriages. And then the stillbirth – a boy . . . Reggie, saying it was not *her* fault and yet twice, after an evening spent with the whisky bottle, shaking her awake, hissing at her: 'You only carry sows – what about a *boar*, eh? How about a boar next time you're in pig . . . eh?'

The vulgar, the drunken side of Reggie – not seen so often but more often than once (never, never, please God, so alarming as that pre-wedding telephone call . . .) – who would believe in it now, looking about the pleasant drawing-room of their Surrey house, this autumn evening of 1932?

He turned towards her. (He's noticed me, she thought, that I am silent. But I am always silent at these gatherings . . .)

'What about a spot of music? I'll set the gram up. Jolly good gadget, this.' Moving about, skilful with one arm, 'Does six at once, you know. Drops 'em down.'

Perhaps the business discussion was over? She had not really been listening. Later tonight, if he hadn't drunk too much, he might elaborate it for her. Yet another doomed scheme . . .

'Don't be blue at all, it won't do at all . . .'

He liked a steady diet of dance music, although he never seemed able to recognize a tune. 'This a new one?' he'd ask of something he'd played daily three months earlier. Tonight the selection would be years out of date and never the numbers she heard from the wireless dance bands. Henry Hall, Carroll Gibbons, Jack Payne: when Reggie, and Angie if there, went out drinking, she would sit quietly, mending, and listening to them. She did not dance now. As for the piano – there wasn't one in the house. The person who had played at The Towers, who had offered refuge in the storm to Geoffrey, had been someone else.

Reggie, filling up glasses now:

'Feeling seedy, Sylvie? Angie be here soon . . . Help on Nanny's day off –'

Oh but, she thought, I don't want help from Angie. I don't want Angie here at all . . .

Angie, spending at least six months of every year with them since 1924 – and the first miscarriage. Coming to help then, sent for by a scared Reggie: 'to hold your hand, old thing, keep your calm –' So as not to lose *their* son . . .

But she never knew if it would have been a boy, for even lying quite still, not moving from the bed in the darkened room, she had lost it. Less than three months' old – indecent, messy, whisked away.

That 1924 miscarriage – *it was not necessary* . . . Because it had been his fault and his alone, Reggie had been scared, repentant . . .

She looked at him now, mellow with whisky, optimistic beyond reckoning over this wonderful new idea which was to make them all rich . . .

That had been the trouble, of course. There should not have been any need to worry. He'd thought, had he not, that he'd married money? At twenty-five she was to inherit. Everything held in trust for her – not least the Diamond Waterfall . . . (Limitless security through that alone.) A rich woman in her own right . . .

And then the happy (how could she ever see it as anything else?) arrival of Michael. Who could be unhappy that all of them, and especially Mother, had now something left of Hal?

People are the real riches, she thought. When an excited Teddy telephoned it had seemed to her good news from another world, beyond the grave. My big brother Hal *lives still* . . .

Perhaps that was it. Her great happiness, the expression on her face, tone of voice, rushing to tell Reggie that evening. (She had already told Willow. Willow, standing up in her cot, pulling at the strings of her jacket. 'Willow, Willow, Hal didn't die after all. You've a *surprise* cousin, my darling . . .')

To Reggie it had not been wonderful at all. She thought she would never forget: voice, face, *words* . . .

'What's all the smiling about, old thing?'

'I'm happy. I – Reggie, what –'

He'd turned away in exasperation. Then his so strong right arm shaking her – and again.

'You haven't *thought*? You really haven't – My God, good God, let me get a drink. A chap needs . . .'

Two double whiskies in quick succession. She had stood there trembling, feeling the happiness seeping from her, the nausea ignored all day rushing over her.

'*Money*, that's the matter. Ever thought about your father's Will? . . . Where's that damn bottle? Fill her up, steady now . . . Listen, Sylvie, little fool, in pig *and* a fool – *listen*. The money, all of it, the Diamond Waterfall, yes, the bloody *Waterfall*, they were all your brother's. *Or his legitimate issue*. Understand, eh? No hope the wretched little bastard *is* a bastard, I suppose? . . . The truth is you are not going to be bally rich – *we shall be bloody poor* . . .'

She could not believe her ears. She felt herself sway. 'I don't mind. I mean – it'll alter things, of course. But it's not –' (What was it not?). She reached for a chair . . .

'What rot's that you're saying? We're done for, you know. Every bloody hope and plan . . .' He paused: 'Are you *smiling*, Sylvie?'

She would not have dared. A frightened smirk only. But he'd been angry, she didn't want to remember now how angry – first with her, then with himself.

It was that evening he'd brought out the revolver. The one she had seen first in the South of France, in Mentone.

'Reggie – whatever? *Put that away* –'

He held it to his head, against the temple.

'*Reggie!*'

'Just fooling. Next time . . .' He tossed it on to the carpet.

Shaking and sobbing, 'How could you, how could you?' she had cried.

He only laughed. But when she couldn't stop crying he became angry again. He had been drinking before coming home. Now, four whiskies later, he was impossible.

Shaking her by the shoulder, jerking her neck. It wasn't that, she was sure it was not. Her body – a baby – could take more than that. Rather: the shock of happiness, followed so soon by a dreadful thought . . .

He didn't, couldn't have married me for my money. Alone in bed later – for he had stayed downstairs to drink – she had tried not to think that his kindness, the way he'd *rescued* her, had been only about that. It wasn't true . . .

But her body must have thought otherwise. Two days later she lost the child. Reggie, who seemed to have forgotten most of what he'd said, asked shamefacedly:

'I can't remember, old thing. In bed . . . Was I rough?'

She hadn't been able to bring herself to tell him anything. The evening was never referred to again.

'. . . *When fate designed my lucky star – there must have been a holiday* . . .'

Above the singer's voice, Reggie was talking about the new scheme. Telling Claude and Sidney: 'Sylvie's not listening . . . Listen, Sylvie, as I was saying – we've an accountant all but signed on the dotted line. *And* the director of another hotel – he ought to know what he's doing . . .

'. . . The old Smuggler's Inn on the London Road. We'll be developing a completely new hotel . . . Listen to this, Sylvie, our draft prospectus – listen: "A hotel enterprise represents without doubt a fruitful source of *secure* and *profitable* investment . . ." That's the sort of lingo, eh?

'. . . We'll be a public company with capital of over two hundred thousand . . . But raised through Belgium. That's the stroke of genius – a trust in London but the banking in Brussels. Stockbroker there – a financial wizard . . . gets advance commission, of course . . . We want to get contracts signed, plans approved, and get on with it. Mustn't miss the opportunity. *Really* hit it this time . . .'

'Why can't I be, like others are, whose life is like the month of May?'

My life, she asked herself, as the jaunty chorus went on, how would it have been if Geoffrey – But she must not . . . Some thoughts could not be allowed . . .

I have Willow, who must never know – just as Reggie must not. She marvelled still at his lack of curiosity. Once he'd spoken of 'bad blood'. 'Of course you can't tell, don't know . . . But first sign of any difficulties, anything odd – we must stamp on it quick.' He often spoke of being a firmer father, even a stern one – but when it came to it she did not think he cared. Or could truly play the part. He would indulge them suddenly – a cluster of celluloid windmills, a Mickey Mouse, Pluto in spongy rubber, a great box of sweets. 'Dolls' house, that's what the girls need, get them a dolls' house. Remind me, Sylvie.' It had been Lily who had in the end provided one.

'Shan't be putting much capital in myself,' he was saying. 'Don't need to. Haven't got it anyway – Not since your fiasco, old thing –'

How could he? (He was barely civil to Michael on family occasions . . .) Stung, 'What about Ireland?' she said. 'Your – our – hotel venture in Ireland?'

'Our mistake in Ireland, old thing, where we went wrong – not having people with us who knew the business. And living on the premises, trying to run it. All wrong . . . Now *this* . . .'

But Ireland – What had been the matter? It had been much more than a business venture gone wrong. She wondered if in the end the worst of it had not been Angie?

By that time, in the late 'twenties, her visits had been getting longer and longer, more and more frequent. She did not seem to have anything very definite to do. It was difficult to tell if she was interested in marriage, or had merely given up hope. She mentioned occasionally a man who had been killed in Italy, on the Asiago plateau, in 1918. 'Sort of an understanding,' she said once off-handedly. 'Don't know if it would have come to anything . . . I'm just one of the old maids washed up by the War . . . Then sickening beauties like you come along and take blighters like my bro . . .'

Reggie said she hadn't much capital, and an income so small she had to supplement it with *infra dig* jobs as companion to old hens with too much dibs . . . So of course it was better she could come to them. She was so much fun anyway. 'It's always fun when old Angie's around.'

Reggie had fewer fits of gloom when she was there. Angie did not allow gloom. Her relentless cheeriness, her predictable slang. Sylvia would wait with irritable dread . . .

'Look at what I've got for a bro – isn't he sickening, aren't you sickening, Reggie? Time to pip off now, *come* on, Reggie, Sylvie, let's *ooze* . . .'

The idea had been for Angie to help them in Ireland. The hotel was in Killarney. Distant Anglo-Irish cousins of Reggie's mother: their fine house mercifully spared from burning in the Troubles, to become a country house hotel. Reggie was to run it for them and to have a share in the proceeds, but without investing any capital. He was full of ideas . . .

It had seemed so safe. Good fishing, beautiful scenery. Irish-Americans would come in search of their roots . . .

Willow and the baby Lucy loved it. Ludwig who went with them seemed the happiest of all.

The first winter there she was pregnant. She was working very hard, determined to make the hotel a success. Reggie, always the genial host: willing, eager, to sit drinking of an evening with his guests. Sylvia, exhausted, would lie sleepless upstairs.

She carried the child to six months. A still birth, and the much wanted son. She felt certain that never again would she conceive a boy. That she had had her chance.

Guests came. But not enough. And sadly they never came twice. Sylvia wondered sometimes if it was Angie? Lying in bed after the stillbirth she could hear under her window Angie bossing, not just their staff but the guests too. Her tone ribbing, but also offensive . . .

'Why ever take a *child* up the Gap of Dunloe? They can't appreciate it.' . . . 'You didn't go in a jaunting car at *your* age?' . . .

Stronger, but not yet able to work, Sylvia would often sit with the guests. Delightedly finding things in common: someone whose sister was a nun in Alice's order, a couple who lived in Paris, even a love of the same book. And Ludwig, when he could be persuaded to come indoors, always won hearts.

Oliver Pulham, a bachelor, ex-Army (he did not care to reminisce with Reggie although they seemed to have been near each other in Flanders), was one of the guests the summer she was convalescing. A business man, he found that because of the war's effect on his nerves, he needed every now and then to escape somewhere peaceful. Over the weeks he was there, she had got into the habit of talking to him at morning coffee-time.

They had been drawn together by an instance of Angie's bossiness. When bustling through the morning-room where Sylvia sat reading, and Oliver, newly arrived, leafed through a magazine, she had cried:

'*Indoors*, Mr Pulham? This *sickening* rain we've had, and now when the clouds roll by, look at you, *frowsting* . . .'

'Crikey,' Oliver said, mopping his brow as Angie disappeared. Catching Sylvia's eye. 'Is she always?'

Sylvia had smiled, nodding conspiratorially. And then Willow, her main source of happiness in those days, had come running up, had sat herself on Oliver's knee . . .

She enjoyed their conversations, Willow often making a charming third. Oliver had a little niece of exactly the same age . . . Everything Willow said enchanted him.

And then – the dreadful evening . . . Sylvia, not able to sleep, going downstairs to make a hot drink. Seeing suddenly, in the hall alcove below the string staircase, avenging angel, Jaeger dressing-gowned figure of Angie:

'I know where you've been, Sylvie –'

Her whole manner, accusing.

'You've been in his room, haven't you?'

'What on earth –'

'That's where you've just come from, isn't it? That side of the hotel . . .'

Sylvia said patiently, 'Look, Angie – I came down for a warm drink. And now I'd like –'

But Angie blocked her way:

'Don't give me that sickening piffle. You can't keep your filthy eyes and hands off him, can you? I know *your* sort of girl, Sylvie. Major Pulham –'

'Angie, this is *nonsense*. And it's not the time –'

'It is. I have you *in flagrante delicto* – isn't that what they call it? I've a good mind to go and wake Reggie –'

'*Keep out of our room –*'

'Temper, temper! If Reggie *knew* . . . Only he shan't. He's been through enough. First to be *maimed* . . . And then deceived . . .'

'Angie – stop this nonsense. And let me pass by . . .'

'Accused of *lies*, am I? Any insult is good enough for an unmarried woman – the War's flotsam . . . You think because you snared a good man and now make a mockery of him you can throw your sickening insults about. My bro who deserved –' She suddenly lowered her voice as if ashamed. 'It's true, isn't it? That – Willow *isn't his* . . .'

Faint with shock, Sylvia thought: Of course Reggie told no one. (But a sister . . . perhaps he had thought a sister all right?)

'That child isn't Reggie's, it doesn't even look like him – Don't think Reggie blabbed, he was at a pretty low ebb when he told me, a bit tanked . . .'

'*For God's sake*, Angie –'

'Had enough, have you? It must be very uncomfortable hearing all these home truths. Who *is* the father anyway? I expect you lied about that too . . . Someone in Flaxthorpe?'

My God, help me. Two in the morning. I want only to faint away for love of Geoffrey. But I shall not weep, I shall not faint . . .

'I'm not surprised you don't answer. I'm too jolly well near the truth, aren't I? Want to know my guess? . . . I think it was Bertie F . . . That mother of his – it would have been terrible, wouldn't it? And you wouldn't want to marry *him* when you could have my bro, my lovely bro – So you didn't even tell Bertie . . . And Reggie, Reggie believes your cock and bull – sorry your cock and *cow* story –'

Sylvia pushed past her roughly. Surprised at her strength. She must be somewhere alone, to cry.

He did not marry me for my money, she repeated over and over as she wept alone in the linen room. (Where else could she feel safe?) *He did not marry me for my money*.

Next morning she was careful not to be in the coffee lounge at eleven. She stayed as much as possible in the living quarters with the children. When later she caught sight of Oliver, she walked hurriedly the other way. By taking care it was possible never again to have a direct conversation with him. She saw he was puzzled, and hurt. But she felt frozen. Fear made her cold. Distant.

Angie, the next day, was her old self. Friendly in an overwhelming, edgy way. It was as if the scene in the hall had never been. Perhaps I dreamed it? But she felt that it could happen again at any time. *I shall always be watched now* . . .

In the days following Reggie's announcement of the hotel scheme, it seemed to Sylvia that here at last was something that would work. Already it had progressed farther, faster than any previous one. Normally she might be cynical: all those evenings he'd come home the worse for scotch upon scotch, accompanied by a complete stranger, his future partner in some mad enterprise – selling this, that, setting up a golf club on ground which would only allow 8 holes . . .

No matter now in 1932 that there was world recession, economic crisis, massive depression and unemployment – it was explained to her that a hotel in a good situation could not fail since people had still to do business, and travelling, must stay somewhere. The very address 'London Road' showed the excellent siting . . .

As to his partners: Sidney Johnson, managing director of another hotel, brought with him expertise and, even more important, confidence. Individuals, banks and so on, Reggie explained, would invest if Sidney was involved. With his small tight body, toothbrush moustache and line in forced compliments, she was not sure she cared for him. But what matter? Enough if he was good for the scheme.

Claude Mulcaster, solicitor: clean cut, dark, slightly diffident, also exuded an air of trustworthiness. She didn't like being in his company either. He reminded her irrationally of the long-dead Uncle Lionel with whom she'd never felt at ease.

It was he too the cause of yet another of those distressing scenes . . . This time, a dinner out to discuss the enterprise. Angie invited along. Afterwards in the Ladies' cloakroom – probably she had drunk too much – she had hissed at Sylvia:

'I'm not going to say much now and certainly *not a word to Bro* – but it hasn't gone unnoticed, you know –'

Sylvia said tiredly, 'Not again . . . Who is it now?'

'Claude Mulcaster, you little fool – and *don't pretend.*

Something's going on between you two, *isn't it?*'

'You must be crazed –'

Angrily she had left the Ladies ahead of her. Then remembered her rings left by the washbasin. She had to hurry back, colliding with Angie in the corridor . . . When she'd returned to the table where they were drinking coffee, Angie had been laughing and friendly. 'Whatever kept you?'

Over the next few months plans for the hotel were drawn up and approved. 'Isn't it the tops,' Angie said. 'I think the blighter's really on to something . . .' Sylvia lent Reggie four hundred as his share of the advance commission to the financiers in Brussels. 'It'll be back soon, with interest of course. The three of us, we've borrowed up to the limit you see, to secure the hotel. Then there are the architect's fees and so on.'

The spring saw them showing signs of impatience. But it was *all right*, everything OK, Reggie told her, Sidney told her, Claude told her. Laughing at her expectant mother anxiety: 'Little Women – they're all the same. True, Reggie, old chap? Fuss, fuss, fuss . . .'

'Safe as houses,' Sidney told her, 'safe as *hotels* . . .'

'Like Killarney?'

'Sylvie –' Angie speaking – 'you're imposs . . . Killarney wasn't *Reggie's* fault . . .'

Work had begun on the conversion. Sylvia was driven with Willow to see the structure of the restaurant. She asked some questions. Where was the money coming from, since the trust had not received injections of capital from Belgium yet? Claude explained patiently that it had been borrowed from a London bank on a short bridging loan ('shows the confidence *they* have in the scheme'). It would be mad to miss the possibility of excellent trade in the summer months all through not being open . . .

Just after Easter she had her baby, two weeks early. Reggie, less put out than the monthly nurse who had had scarcely time to unpack her bag, seemed distracted – showing no disappointment that it was another girl. He remarked only, kissing her as she lay half propped with pillows:

'Looks all right to me, old thing. Quick enough, weren't you? Caught us all out . . .' He paused. 'Bound to be a bouncing boy next time. Better have a bit of rest, eh?' He seemed not to be concentrating. Spoke as if in caricature of himself. 'Have to go now, sorry can't be with you tonight of all nights but promised to dine with Claude – rather urgent talk. Hotel matters –'

'It's all right? Everything's all right?'

'Topping. Couldn't be better. Just some stupid hiccup . . .'

The baby was to be called Elizabeth after Reggie's grandmother. Willow's idea. Sylvia thought it a good one. But he scarcely listened when she told him.

Willow said: 'I'll call *my* first baby after *you*, Mummy. Sylvia's the bestest name.' She threw her arms about Sylvia, burrowing her head in her bedjacket.

Sylvia said, 'Babies *can* be boys, you know . . .'

Willow said nothing. She was bent over the cot: 'I expect we'll call her Beth. Isn't she dark? I'd like to be dark, my friend Janet that comes to tea sometimes, she has black eyes . . .'

Reggie, home unexpectedly early, shooed her out. 'I've business to talk to Mummy – There's a good girl.' Always affectionate, she stood on tiptoes and kissed his moustache.

At once Reggie sat on the easy chair beside the bed.

'Thing is, Sylvie, I'm in rather a rush . . . Need a yes or no quickly. Bit of a fix. Money's coming through any day from the Belgies – it's all in order, paperwork, all that – but we need to put up a bit extra just now. Before it comes through, you see –'

'How much?' she asked wearily. Suddenly overcome with tiredness.

'Rather a lot, old thing. Unfortunately. Not that it's a worry. It's just the inconvenience, and a chap hates asking.'

'Reggie dear, say, and be over with it. Nurse comes in soon – the five o'clock feed. I must stay calm.'

'How much is on deposit, old thing? You said once – I know with stocks and all that, one can hardly. Well, not in a hurry anyway –'

'Accessible? I suppose I could get – say a few thousand?'

'Make it ten, could you, old love? Ten would just about – in fact, *have* to have ten. To get us right. A week's loan. Two at the most –'

Knocking at the door. Nurse Matthews: 'I've had a lovely

walk, daffies out all over the park . . . Now we're going to have to ask Daddy to leave the room . . .'

Angie came to stay. But only for a long weekend. She had a post in Switzerland as companion-secretary until Christmas.

'The blighter's looking worried,' she remarked to Sylvia, 'Recognize the signs . . . When we were young, waiting for school report, knowing he'll get a pasting – Not that that sort of thing worried Mummy. She –' But she went no further.

Now she said, 'You're lucky Reggie's such a good boy. With you always in bed like that, having babies. But he never looks at anyone else. Piffle it may be, but I think men are much more faithful than women . . .'

She said it in an offhand, deceptively friendly tone. And, Sylvia thought, she can hardly accuse me, safe in childbed, of carrying on with Claude or Sidney.

Neither of them had been to the house for some time, although doubtless Reggie went out to meet them. Occasionally at night, between sessions with the whisky bottle, he became involved in long, long telephone calls. Sometimes after the ten o'clock feed, walking along the corridor, she would hear him.

She supposed that she should have seen it all coming . . .

He burst into her bedroom, white-faced, staggering almost.

She was in the armchair by the window, sewing. The baby in the organdie-trimmed cot by the bed was crying – she had been fretful all day. Sylvia thought it was worry affecting her milk. Nurse Matthews said it was soused herring. ('Really I should have some control over the kitchen and what Mummy eats . . .')

'Sylvie, there's been a bit of an upset. We've – Sidney and I . . . not Claude – *Claude's* all right, hasn't played the game. Fact is Claude's feathered his nest. Sylvie, old thing – take a deep breath. The hotel – whole thing, whole scheme. It's napoo.'

'Look, Reggie, just tell me quietly. *Are you in trouble with this?*'

His hand was shaking. 'No. No – it's all right, old thing. Just *shock* – put a lot into it, you know. Sidney too. We're both – bit shocked, you know. Claude – doing it on the quiet, you see . . .' He raised his voice suddenly, 'Stop that brat yelling, would you?'

'I'll ring for Nurse –'

'No, leave it . . . Can't think straight, old thing. All of a shake. Fact is there can't be a hotel enterprise – money, capital, all that, not enough's come through. We have to get out, sell up. You know the sort of thing. Belgies have made a proper mess of it – valued the place at something ridiculous – and say money can't be raised as a result. Meantime old Claude's done a deal behind our backs. Got some money off them in *his* name. Complicated thing – don't think there's a *chance* he'll be got for it. It's all through, over – napoo, old thing . . .'

'But *us*, Reggie, we're all right?'

'Of course all right, never been better. And look, can't stand that caterwauling – couldn't you feed it, or whatever it is you do?' He got up. She saw that his hand holding a cigarette trembled still.

She was not surprised when she couldn't sleep that night. She had anyway never been a good sleeper since the days of Geoffrey – and Willow. Perhaps it went back earlier, to her father's illness, when she would worry that he might die if she did not stay awake to *keep* him alive. Certainly she worried tonight for Reggie, who had gone out earlier leaving just a message with the maid that he wanted no dinner. She hadn't heard him come in. She looked now in his dressing-room, and in their bedroom. Then, seeing a light on in the hall, went downstairs.

He was in the small morning-room. The wireless, left on a wavelength without a programme, crackled and wheezed. He sat, head bowed. The usual empty glass and nearly empty bottle beside him.

'Reggie – don't you think –' She saw on his knees the Smith and Wesson.

'Whatever – Reggie, dear, *give it to me*.' When he didn't look up: 'You've been drinking – that's it, isn't it? A revolver, I've said before . . . too dangerous. Give it to me.'

He let her take it. Head still bowed, hand hanging by his side. 'Sorry, old thing. Sorry, Sylvie.' He began to weep. A noisy choking sound. 'Upset about everything . . . Children, haven't had a son. Nothing gone right. And for you – I though – best if I pipped out . . .'

'Oh Reggie, Reggie love.' She knelt down beside him, took his hand. '*Next time* a son. In the end . . . If you want it that much –'

'. . . At least Willow wasn't a boy – couldn't have stood that, you know. Another chap's. Cad. A *cad's* son. You'll have to watch her, watch *she* doesn't grow up . . . Blood will out. Women who can't keep away from men, bitches on heat – usually the best lookers, sort you can't say no to . . .' He was crying again.

Better he should go up to bed now. 'Reggie –'

'Chap who fucked you – pardon my French . . . Just tell me his name, old thing. Never pestered you before. But peace of mind. I stood by you – I'm the chap who –'

'Don't,' she began tiredly. He interrupted:

'Never *was* a chap at a party, was there? Guessed that. Told Reggie a fib, eh?'

'Yes,' she said. 'Yes, I lied.' She felt suddenly sick, shaky – and unbelievably sorry for him.

'The truth – a chap needs . . .' He shook his head, weeping still. 'Just give me the *truth*, Sylvie. Swear, I swear. Secret's safe with me, safe with Reggie. Wouldn't give a cad away –'

'Reggie, there's no question of a cad. He was a *good* man.'

She told him then. Hearing, unbelieving, the beloved's name out loud. (When had she last had occasion to say it?) 'He didn't know, never knew . . . He would never have left me to manage. It was my choice . . .'

She realized suddenly that he wasn't listening. Reaching now for more whisky, slopping it into the glass. Her confession, that she wished already unmade. Geoffrey's name, hanging there in the whisky-laden air. *I should never have done it.*

'Sylvie,' he said. 'It's a bit worse than I told you – Everything – *bit* worse. It's all gone. Finished. We're done for. Napoo . . .'

She couldn't speak: *Do I hear right*?

'That's why wanted to end it all. Everything lost –'

'The ten?' she said. 'Ah my God. *Ten thousand* . . .'

'No hope any of it. Shambles, nothing less. Sidney's got his hotel, of course – his job. Won't lose that.'

'We've got the house,' she said, slowly, trying to steady her voice. 'And ourselves. Our children. The bits, we can pick up the bits.' But she felt no confidence. Only shock. The ground opening up . . .

'You won't be prosecuted or anything? You're not in that sort of trouble?'

'Not done wrong, Sylvie. Just been a fool.' He stood up, turned away from her, hunched.

'About the house, old thing. Our house. Don't know what to say. That's . . . Collateral. Put it up, you know, before the ten thousand. Last ditch stand – that ten. Felt pretty confident or wouldn't have asked. No house now, though. Pretty serious, eh Sylvie?'

'Don't be blue at all, it won't do at all . . .'

Maddeningly the words of the song went round in her head. Jolly tune, jolly words:

'*Trouble and sin, how can you win? Don't hold everything, don't hold anything – just let everything go . . .*'

8

Winter of '33, through to winter of '34. The year of Ferdy.

So many men, Teddy thought, in and out of my bed, since Saint left me. Yet, once over the shock, did I really mind? What sort of a married couple would we have made? He chose well from all accounts, is happy. It was only my foolish longing to have a child which led me to think, ever, of settling with him.

Who is the better off, Sylvia with all that brood, a hearty but boring husband (I know, we know, he drinks), whose business dealings we can none of us fathom? Nowadays she tells us *nothing*. Her address, changed from Surrey to North London, and a part of it we don't know. She comes to us sometimes. We never go to her. Sylvia, who was so lovely . . . It breaks Mother's heart. (She says it smells of the Daisy story, but I think not. *That* was a love-match . . .)

What must it be like to bed with the same man for over ten years? Certainly not like anything *I've* known: Teddy Nicolson, married 1917, widowed January 1919. Mistress of Saint, 1922 to 1925 . . . And after? I wouldn't care to count the men.

She couldn't settle. Nor were her men often 'suitable' in the old-fashioned sense. (Once, yes. That General's son, who was quite desperate, proposing again and again – and much, much to young for me . . .) Some of course were married, and intended to remain so. It wasn't anything to do with the shortage of men, either. She seemed able to attract as many as she wanted. Often she did not want them for very long . . .

Ferdy was different. How? Not for a second did she contemplate marriage with him. It was from the start, light-hearted. 'You *are* fun, Ferdy!' It never sounded foolish to say that . . . It was all fun – as long as they kept off politics.

He was Belgian, from Liège. They spoke French together always (he remarked on her slight Belgian accent from Berthe, which she'd never lost) although he could speak English adequately. His business was cardboard containers, and he expected to spend a year between the firm's Paris and

London offices. To her English friends she said, 'Ferdy is in cardboard containers.' Because he didn't know the idiom, he was, the first time, genuinely puzzled by their laughter. Afterwards, he would pretend outrage.

They had such fun together. She had not been as silly since adolescent days with Amy (and we did not stay young or silly for long . . .). She remembered her mother telling her of happy years, just being 'foolish, giggling, childish', with a girlfriend, back in her early acting days. It was perhaps something like that.

They met in the late autumn of '33. She was just back from two months in Yorkshire. She would get sometimes this sudden longing, need almost, to be up there, and then would find herself soon restless. Although for the last nine years there had been the joy of being with Michael. She was as fond of him as she'd been that first memorable day. Michael, who had settled so well, who gave so much happiness to Mother. Already fourteen and just beginning his second year at Winchester. (The only pity that he and Willow did not get on, seemed to have loathed each other on sight . . .)

She and Ferdy met in the way she met so many of her men. Through friends of friends. At a party. He told her at once that she talked too much. 'However do you get a man?' Men didn't mind, she said. They gave as good as they got, or were happy to sit back and listen. Either way . . .

His first political remark then, and easily his most harmless. He distrusted the glib of tongue, he commented. 'Who was it said of Clemenceau, ' "*Si je pourrais pisser comme il parle . . .*" '

'I'd stop you midstream,' she said, in French.

That set the tone of their conversation. It seldom rose, often sank . . .

A week after that party meeting, he was her lover. Three weeks after that, she encountered his political views.

A late supper at Ledoyen's. The subject, Germany, who in the middle of that month had withdrawn from both the League of Nations and the Disarmament Conference. What were her intentions? The leopard doesn't change its spots, someone said. A journalist whom Teddy knew slightly, Didier, had a tale out of Germany:

'The other week Adolf Hitler was laying the foundation

stone of the German Art Gallery or some such – the idea being anyway to show Germany has no military ambitions, just cultural ones . . . The hammer should have tapped three times. It broke on the first, and the handle stayed in his hand. He was *furious*, evidently. Reporting forbidden, all photos destroyed. A few press boys who managed to circulate pics got threatened with a concentration camp . . . Personally, I saw it as I hope symbolic of the whole future of the insane Nazi movement.'

Ferdy said, 'God knows I've no affection for Germans – I was brought up on a Boche for breakfast – but it's *Communism* we should be worrying about. Here in France . . . You've got a Socialist ferment and a half. The Bolsheviks plan to rule the world, and I don't care to be there when it happens . . . If, to stop it . . . a little bit fascist . . . who cares?'

'I do,' Teddy said. Shocking him. She said afterwards, 'They're both bad. At the extreme. Why do you have to approve of *either*?'

'Dear Teddy . . . If both are bad we must find which is the least evil and encourage that to crush the other . . . Anyway, enemies change . . . We Belgians, not a century old, what are we to think? As for you English, it was only yesterday you said Bonaparte ate babies for breakfast. Now look at you . . .'

She took him up. He argued again. To his other views he added, perhaps not surprisingly, anti-semitism. She was reminded of Robert. They argued another half-hour and then it was over. They scarcely raised the matter again. After all, they weren't having an affair because of shared political views . . .

Quite a lot of her time was still spent at the orphanage. Ferdy affected to be amused. Occasionally he was impatient. 'Don't you take all this a bit too seriously? Orphanages manage to run without constant visits from well-meaning ladies. It's your money they want and need . . .'

He talked little of himself. She found she knew almost nothing, other than that he'd lost an older brother in the War. (We have that in common, she told him.) Once he was rude about marriage. 'Ah, marriage, pah . . . Spider's web, you shouldn't walk in.'

Most of the time was just – fun. He became part of her life. She went with him when he visited London for a week, prior to spending three or four months there in spring '34. She did not bother to go up to Yorkshire.

Their last night in London, Ferdy had a slight fever. She went alone to the Albert Hall for the Festival of Remembrance – and wished she had not. She had removed herself so much from her memories that to stir them was unbearable. And it was to begin all over again . . . From what she heard – sooner or later, probably sooner – war would come . . . The only possible excuse, justification for the sacrifice of Gib and Hal and the millions of others, had been that it would not happen again.

They sang, *There's a long long trail*, *Tipperary*, *Roses of Picardy* . . . She was back at The Towers Hospital – the twice weekly entertainments. Courage of the wounded and maimed, of the healed who went back . . . She thought: It is not the same for others who hear these songs. A million rose petals fell from the roof. The voice, boyish still, of the Prince of Wales recited: '*They shall not grow old, as we that are left* . . .'

They sang, '*Abide with Me, fast falls the eventide* . . .' She thought of Flaxthorpe church. And Gib, always of Gib. That night, sleepless in the small hours the idea took hold of her: If Gib came back, *what would he think of me*?

While Ferdy was based in Paris he went home to Belgium alternate weekends. She knew nothing at all about his life there. He spoke of his mother – the Boche-hater – and of how he had to drive her out on Sundays. He never suggested, which she was glad, that she should come with him. 'It's boring duty weekend again,' he would say. Grandpère was alive still, aged eighty-eight. He too liked a drive in the country . . .

Before Christmas he spent two weeks at his firm's Milan office. She could not resist joining him. The weather was atrocious. She hardly knew Italy and felt it a bad introduction. He had a few days free and they visited Verona, and then Venice. While they were there the weather worsened. The tide rose steadily, reaching several feet in St Mark's Square, which had to be nagivated by boat.

She and Ferdy found themselves talking about Gib one day. She mentioned him seldom, telling Ferdy as little as he told her about his past, or present. Sometimes just to speak Gib's name to someone like Ferdy, she felt was a betrayal.

Once he said, 'You're always so *solemn* when you speak of your husband – yet you laugh, talking about your brother. Could he have been, this Gib, just a very little bit *boring*?' In answer – the ultimate betrayal – she said, lightly enough, 'Might have been, Ferdy, might have been ... .' And felt his arm tighten about her as they danced . . .

How they danced. She thought afterwards: We danced across Europe . . .

London, February 1934. Henry Hall and his band playing a number called *Making conversation (when we ought to be making love)*. She and Ferdy slow foxtrotting. Occasionally his right hand, straying from her waist, would touch her elbow, lightly, beside the funny bone. Twisting it a little with his fingers. Secret signal of what would happen later . . . for him to touch her like that was as exciting sometimes as any direct advance. It said, later my fingers will do this, that . . .

Making conversation . . . making love . . . making *children*. Gib and I never made a child. She had heard of people who chose men, for eugenic reasons, to father their children. She could not imagine it: the calculating common sense of it all . . . She half smiled at the notion . . .

'*We walk about together, 'neath a magical moon above, Just making conversation . . . when we ought to be making love . . .*'

'What about a child, Ferdy? One of those little things I see at the orphanage – but made by us . . .'

He was never easily ruffled. He said smoothly enough, but she thought him a little embarrassed, 'Come along, Teddy – every little baby needs a father . . .'

'Precisely. And why not you?'

He must have taken her seriously, for he looked for a few seconds genuinely puzzled and uncertain. A little angry?

'Darling Ferdy – I'm only joking . . .'

'I must say, I thought for a moment – some accident perhaps . . .'

'Gawd, no . . . *Teasing* . . .'

'I should hope so.' He held her close, guiding her as they swung out on the floor. He sang with the vocalist, his head close to hers. She felt his breath on her as he crooned:

'. . . *We can't go on forever, counting stars in the sky above, Just making conversation, when we ought to be making love* . . .'

It became their song. He could always silence her with it.

The beginnings of an argument, perhaps, or when tired after some hectic social round. Before their arms went about each other: '*Just making conversation,*' one of them would say casually, barely singing the words, '*when we ought to be making love*–'

The last evening but one of their stay in London. The sitting-room of his suite was full of flowers. She'd arranged that. They were to eat upstairs before going out much later to dance. She was on the sofa, smoking and reading *Vogue*. She remembered afterwards that she wore a new dinner dress. Blackberry silk, with a high neck. Both the colour and cut flattered her.

Ferdy had just gone in the bath. Beforehand he had rung room service for champagne.

When there was a knock at the door, she thought: How speedy their service.

But it was a bell boy, with a telegram. She called through to Ferdy:

'A wire for you . . . Shall I bring it in?'

'God, no. Business . . . It can wait.'

He emerged a few minutes later, wrapped in a towel. 'Let's see,' he said. As he opened it, she saw him frown. For a moment, his face looked pinched, colourless.

'All right?'

'It's rubbish,' he said, shaking his head, 'the office really do pester me . . .' Crumpling it up, he threw it into the basket. 'Why are they taking so long with the champagne?' he said irritably. 'Ring again, darling. If it's not there by the time I'm dressed . . .'

She was ashamed, while he went through to dress, by her attack of vulgar curiosity. In the end she gave way to temptation. She so scrupulous of other's privacy, so jealous of her own, picked it out of the basket. She read it hurriedly. It was in French, oddly botched along the wires (scrambled deliberately?) but its meaning clear. An angry Solange told him she knew he was with another woman and that he was a *charogne* and a *crapule* and . . . ten indecipherable words . . . Ending: '*va te faire foutre . . .*'

She had already put it back in the basket as he came through. She said to him:

'I know I did wrong, but I read your wire.'

'Oh yes?' He looked uneasy.

'*Someone* feels strongly. By the sound of it she may even turn up here . . .'

'I don't think so,' he said. 'It wouldn't be her style.'

She said angrily, 'Why didn't you say? Some other woman – that you were in the middle of another affaire?'

'It's not an – affaire,' he said. 'She's my wife.'

'Oh Ferdy.' She could think of nothing better . . . Said it again angrily: 'Oh *Ferdy*. You could have told me –'

'Why?' He looked puzzled. 'We're not planning to marry. We haven't that intention. So what's it matter?'

'It's the deceit, the way I can't trust you. Why hide it all?'

'Why not? Who would it help if I told? To be honest, I didn't remember if I had or hadn't . . .'

'I don't believe that,' she said. 'If I'm to take someone's husband, I want to know that's what I'm doing. I've the right to know the wrong I'm doing –'

'I never heard such nonsense. *Casuiste*. I didn't tell you, and that's all . . . Anyway, she's been angry before. She's often angry –'

'Not without cause –'

'You didn't think, my darling, that you were the first?'

'No, nor the last.'

'Curiosity,' he said, 'it's the undoing of people, isn't it?' He added, 'What a charming way to begin our evening . . .'

At that moment the champagne arrived. The waiter offered to open it. Ferdy shooed him out.

'It's certainly put you in a bad mood,' she said.

They kept the argument up for another ten, fifteen minutes. Then ended it abruptly, by common consent. Teddy said, 'Whatever are we doing? Nothing but talking, talking, talking.'

His hand beneath her arm, other hand holding out a glass of champagne for her, he murmured in her ear:

'. . . *Just making conversation, when we ought to be making love . . .*'

9

'Cuckoo,' Reggie said in a loud voice. Then again, '*Cuckoo*, cuckoo . . .'

'Please,' Sylvia said, '*please*. Your voice. The little ones, their door's open –'

'Means nothing to them, Sylvie. Cuckoo, cuckoo in the nest –'

'Willow –'

'If Madam Titwillow hears something to her disadvantage – none too soon, is it, eh?'

'You promised. My God, you *promised*.'

'Can't learn too early what her bestest Mummy's like . . . Might have a bit more respect when she finds out what I've put up with . . . Eh?'

'She might have more respect if you weren't drunk five nights of the week –'

'Bloody rich, that – coming from you . . . Mote in my eye, beam in yours. Can't see it, can you, old thing? *Whoring* – that's what I have to put up with. Mess you've made of your hair, too . . . *permanent wave*, when we're on our uppers. It's to get men, isn't it? *Cave, cave* – mind we don't get another cuckoo's egg . . . Always room in the nest, eh? Titwillow. Cuckoo, cuckoo, cuckoo . . .'

The Lord is my Shepherd, I shall not want . . . I shall not want . . . I must believe this, Sylvia told herself, walking heavily round the small kitchen, flies buzzing in the summer heat, afternoon traffic rattling outside. I *do believe this*.

Homesickness made her long for the Norman church in Flaxthorpe. Sleepless at night, she would imagine herself going through the doorway, walking up to the family pew. Smell of beeswax, of roses, cool stone . . . She would people the church – old Mrs Matthews (was she still alive?), Mrs Fisher, Mother standing always so straight-backed, wearing the very latest in hats. Erik (yes, I knew he was her Lover), in his place on the left, four rows back. Let us sing. *Praise, my soul, the King of Heaven . . .*

The linoleum on the top landing. She saw as she came up the stairs, a big cut, the frayed edge showing. She hadn't noticed it before – yet it couldn't be new (oh God help us if we have to replace even the *cheapest* of floor coverings) since it was surely one of the younger children's work, and they'd been gone four days now: were Mother's worry for the next three weeks. An August holiday in a seaside hotel (and I hope, I *hope*, that Beth doesn't strip off the wallpaper beside her bed as she did last year at the Grand, Scarborough . . .).

Willow would look after them, of course – far better than the nanny engaged for the holiday. With her they were as naughty and difficult as a real mother. She did not seem to mind.

'Mummy, you look *worried* – don't worry. It's much better without a nanny, we see *lots* more of you. And the other girls at school, *they* don't have nannies . . .'

She leaned too much on Willow these days. She should not, really should not. Nor should one child be more precious than another – that had been the first wrong. So much love for Lucy and Jessica and Margaret and Beth – but for Willow just a little more, because she is Geoffrey's . . .

Cuckoo, cuckoo in the nest. It was that taunt drove her to burden Willow with the truth. (But I would have told her one day, surely?) The risk that she would learn from Reggie was too great. Drunk so often now (and that did not go unnoticed by Willow), he had twice already shouted out the truth . . .

So she told her. Willow, after staring at her, white-faced, burst suddenly into tears. Then flinging herself into Sylvia's arms:

'I'm so glad, so glad. I can't bear *he* should be my daddy – when he's so rude to you and doesn't care and –'

'But of course he cares, darling. It's because of the Great War – he got that habit of drinking too much. Lots of them did. And then he's had terrible business worries . . .'

'It's *you* I'm worried about, always tired . . . Oh Mummy, honestly, I *am* glad – I'm sure I knew somehow, even when he used to be nice, that he wasn't – that I'm not *his* . . .'

It was only afterwards she realized Willow had not asked a single detail. All she'd said at the end was:

'You looked so upset telling me, Mummy. I want you to sit on the sofa, with your feet up, and I'll put the rug over and make you some tea and then you've got to let *me* give Margaret and Beth their baths. Promise, darling Mummy?'

Perhaps she had wanted to ask, but could not. Meant to, and left it too late. Next evening they were fully occupied with a dying Ludwig. He was ill for two days only: losing the use of his back legs, then running a high fever. The third evening he died, Willow sitting one side of his basket, Sylvia the other. They both wept. Willow said she couldn't remember when there hadn't been a Ludwig. 'We're the same age, nearly, except he's *had* his thirteenth birthday.' Naughty Wig, who'd once stolen a whole leg of lamb, but who never snapped and was always, always obedient. Sylvia wept because she remembered Geoffrey, coming through the doorway, the puppy in his arms . . .

'One less mouth to feed, old thing,' Reggie had said, arriving home later. 'Don't go replacing him, will you?'

The younger children's grief didn't last long because of the excitement of going to the seaside with Lily. Up to the last moment Willow had tried to persuade Sylvia to come. Lily too. But she didn't want to. She was afraid to leave Reggie. What terrible thing might not he do, left on his own?

She wasn't sure which worried her the most: the heavy drinking – drink they could ill afford – or the suicidal rages and despairs it led to . . . When she'd spoken to the doctor, visiting the two youngest with measles, she'd either explained badly or been misunderstood.

'Is he ill with it? Hung over? How's his digestion?' But Reggie was able to tolerate vast quantities. That was not the problem . . . 'Of course I can't *make* him come and see me. So, better wait a little – shall we? And what about yourself? *You* don't look too good. Pop into the surgery sometime . . .'

She did not, could not, say that Reggie had struck her. Once on the breast, another time about the head. The first time but not the second he had remembered and been repentant. Too repentant. Abject: 'Got carried away, old thing. Went a bit too far. Was thinking, when we get our son, must never . . . Won't do to let a son see . . .'

'What about daughters?' she had asked. But he had not been listening. Of course they could not afford a son now.

Nor could she be for ever childbearing. It was that, and a painful miscarriage six months after they were ruined, that caused her to sell a few shares at a loss, and go to Wimpole Street to have a Grafenberg ring inserted. She did not tell him. What could he not do with the knowledge?

They had been hard days since the Crash . . . So much had had to be concealed from her family. She had forbidden the family lawyer to speak with her mother at all. She wondered sometimes how much they knew . . .

The terrace house in North London, its main advantage that it had no space for Angie, the grammar school where Willow was happy, the minor clerical job Reggie had found, and which she continually feared he would lose . . . The penny-pinching. Her own fierce pride. 'We're *all right* . . .'

Downstairs, she began the supper. The enervating August heat made food unattractive. She wasn't often hungry these days yet hadn't lost weight. Was puffy if anything . . .

She seldom felt well now. A dragging sensation, dizziness, sometimes blinding headaches. One was creeping up on her now. She tried to ignore it. She should have been at the seaside resting, but had fobbed Mother off with a story of going away later with Reggie. When he gets his holiday. Someone in to look after the children . . .

A salad: she carefully washed lettuce, peeled tomatoes, cut cucumber into patterns, the better to tempt Reggie. She had chopped up the last of Sunday's lamb and set it in aspic. Fetching it now from the larder, she heard the frantic buzzing of flies. She'd left the back door open to air the small kitchen – she saw outside the old wire mesh safe where Ludwig's meat was kept. The sound came from there and when she opened the safe, the smell too. Flies clustered thickly on his forgotten lumps of scrap meat. Even when she had dealt with it, throwing it away in several thicknesses of newspaper, the smell lingered. *How* could I have left it so long?

She found herself crying – for Ludwig again. He was only a dog, she told herself. Only a dog . . .

She went upstairs to have a cool bath, change her dress. The glass in the bathroom was clouded. Then as she stood there, it cleared, and her face stared back at her. Heavy black circles under her dull eyes, her skin rough, drawn . . . Stringy hair made worse by the perm which she had thought would simplify her life but which had succeeded only in enraging Reggie. Her hair was breaking – it had been perhaps too strong for it.

Even when some time ago her looks had begun to go, she'd thought: There is always my hair. Easy, gives no trouble. Hair that others had envied and she had scarcely appreciated. I was not vain, she thought. What I had was only wonderful, beautiful, because Geoffrey loved me . . .

1936. Fourteen years now since . . . Shutting her eyes, she opened them again quickly, head turned away from the glass. Thirty-two and she could have been fifty . . . *He would not know me now* . . .

She began to dress hurriedly, haunted by what she had seen. *Where did my beauty go*? It is not lying in wait for his return. *It is gone*. Destroyed. She felt a dull anger at the waste of years. Why not have trampled on everyone, fled after happiness? For we would have been happy. (If he had not felt guilt, if I had not felt guilt.) *We could have been happy* . . .

But what else could we have done, though? It was always doomed . . . I try now not to remember too much. To resist the recurrent temptation to trace him. Those letters (only a few over the years and always destroyed as soon as written):

'. . . You have a beautiful daughter, with fair hair and brown eyes. Willow, after the willow wood that is your name . . .'

But, of course, she thought now, *that's* where my beauty has gone. It lives safely in Willow. Together with his, because for me, *he* was beautiful too . . .

The front door slammed as she reached the top of the stairs. Reggie in the hall, called up to her:

'Sorry, late, old thing – sorry, Sylvie.'

She said, 'It's only cold supper. It doesn't matter.' She saw him sway a little.

'No hurry then, eh? Little drink. Some time together? Quiet without kiddies . . . Meant to give them something to spend – donkey rides, ice-creams, rock, that sort of thing. Always short these days, though – But your Mama – plenty. She'll give them a good time.'

He went into the sitting-room, which looked out on to the

small garden – the fence at the end backing on to another house. The French windows were shut. A bluebottle buzzed angrily.

'No hurry to eat, eh?' He opened the radiogram, picked up a stack of records and turned on the switch for the drop head. A Billy Cotton novelty number started up. He turned the sound louder. 'Let's have a little drink –'

'I don't feel like one really. I'd thought if we –'

'Always spoilsport, Sylvie. Not your fault. We need old Angie here to shake things up, cheer you . . . Life always better when Angie's around . . .'

He toyed with the food, breaking up the aspic jelly, grumbling about the lettuce: 'Lucy and Jessica's prize bunnies – give it them.' There was a boiled dressing. He poured it on lavishly, then pushed the plate aside. 'Get a drink . . .'

She had stewed some greengages. She said, 'What about pudding?'

'Drink – don't want any more till I've had a drink. You have one. Sylvie have a drink too.'

'Honestly, Reggie, no. Look, the meal –'

But he had gone through to the sitting-room. After a moment she followed him. The last of the records dropped down. Reggie, a full glass in his hand, drained it in two gulps.

'There you are. Now Sylvia have a drink too.'

'I said, no.'

'I'm feeling beastly. Reggie's down, pretty dumpy. Got dumps. Don't want to go on.' He turned. 'Come here and sit on a chap's knee.'

Yes, if it would give him pleasure. She felt sorry for him. How not?

He ran his hand over her hair. 'Hate those waves, curly stuff.' Hand over her breast, and on to her thigh. 'Wait a mo. A chap needs a drink. Got to drink if he's to make a son. Best thing we can do . . . what I need is *son* –'

Not now. Not that. She was safe . . . But Reggie maudlin was perhaps worse than Reggie rough, angry. And how quickly he could change from one to the other . . .

'Well, old thing, Sylvie – we've been long time now – no babe, eh? I don't pay attention I ought, have to try harder, make a son –' His voice changed. Suspicious. 'Not doing anything funny, are you?' He squeezed her breast, kneading it. 'Fellow I know, his wife had tubes tied, didn't tell him – poor chap found out too late . . . *Haven't had them tied, eh, Sylvie?*'

She shook her head.

'You wouldn't, old thing? Not the way to make a son, that. And those cap things, sponges, all those – Nothing like that, haven't been putting anything up, eh?' He pulled her dress up roughly, his hand parted her french knickers. Whisky-laden breath. She suddenly couldn't . . .

'Reggie – *enough* –'

He said angrily, 'Caught you out, eh? Haven't put it in – One of those dutch cap things – Marie Stopes nonsense. If I find one in, know what? I'll tear it out of you – yes, that's it, *tear* it out. Can't make our son that way.' He paused. 'You've been putting one in, eh?'

She said tiredly, 'No. No, I haven't . . . I'm going to make us some tea, Reggie –'

'Don't want tea,' he said sulkily. 'Don't want anything. Don't want to live. That's it – don't want to live.' He gave her a small push. 'Get me a drink.'

'Get yourself one.'

'I bloody well will. You have one. Come on –' his voice wheedling. 'Sylvie have a drink.'

'I don't want one. I said – a cup of tea. And you, certainly you've had enough.'

'. . . Telling me what I must and mustn't. So bloody good. *No* bloody good, that's what's wrong with you.' He reached for the whisky, drank some straight from the bottle, then pushed the rim against her mouth. 'Go on – I said, have a drink – *have a drink* . . .' He pushed her against the wall. She struggled – he forced a stream of whisky down her gullet. Rushing, burning, choking her. Her mouth open to cough, she felt more poured down. She gagged. As she tried to shut her mouth, the bottle rattled against her teeth. He tilted it and the whisky ran down her chin. Through the top of her linen dress. Trickling down her body . . .

She was whisky-sodden. Disgusting. She sobbed, 'How could you, how *could* you . . .' Running from the room. A bath, to wash it all away. Escape. Get out before Reggie turned angrier, rougher . . .

She had hardly reached the foot of the stairs when she

heard a bellow, as of pain. She rushed back in, her heart thumping.

Reggie had in his hand the Smith and Wesson. She said unsteadily:

'You fetched that quickly. I thought something had happened . . . That you were hurt –'

He waved the revolver in the air, then down again, brushing it against his empty sleeve. 'Can't go on, Sylvie. This time really going to pip out . . . Finish it all. Get us out of our misery . . .'

She was fighting nausea. Her head spun. She saw the brown patterned lozenges of the carpet grow dim, then clear again. *I will not be sick . . . O God our help in ages past, our hope in years to come . . .*

'Reggie, listen. Listen. Put that revolver away and listen to me. You only feel – it's the drink . . . Come up to bed, have a rest, Reggie –'

'Come to bed, that's it eh? *Come to bed.* What we want with any of that? Whore who goes to bed – have anyone in your bed . . . Wonder you haven't made money for us opening your legs, eh? Could have got us some of the ready, opening you –'

'Enough.' Her voice, meant to be sharp, came out wavering.

'Who are you, eh? Telling me enough . . . It's napoo, finee – just want to go, no money . . . We'd have been all right, listen to me now, Sylvie, all right if that bastard hadn't taken family money . . .' He paused. 'Know what?' He spoke as if a revelation had just come to him: 'Know what, Sylvie? You and that Doc you opened your legs for . . . I know what you did – *he* did it for you – Hurried off your father, hurried him off – that's what. Both of you to have money, Waterfall, all that. Be bloody rich. Only then *he went off you*, didn't he, after you'd been wicked? Knew you for a tart, eh? Sylvie, *queen of tarts*, didn't want Sylvie queen of tarts – So that's when old Reggie steps in, saves her . . . And what reward? Still a tart – But no dibs. Poor as a churchmouse. Poor churchmouse Reggie . . .'

She tried not to hear. Not to listen at all. To think only how to get the revolver from him. *How to stop all this.*

'*Why should I take Doc's leavings eh?*'

He waved the revolver again. Fear took hold of her. And anger.

She put her head down as dizziness washed over her. Then she came nearer to him. Slowly. 'Reggie, give it to me. There, there. Nothing meant. No upset.'

As she approached, he pointed it at her, directly.

Terror . . . A drumming in her ears. She said, trying to keep her voice calm:

'You don't mean it –'

'Never more sober.' He hiccuped. 'Never . . . It's napoo, finee. Both of us. Do you first, then Reggie goes. Clean like that. Want everything clean . . . Pity can't take – where's Cuckoo?'

'Reggie, darling – please, Reggie –'

'Where's cuckoo, eh? Cuckoo in the nest. Titwillow, *where's Titwillow*?'

'You know where. You know, Reggie – Quiet now.' She put out a terrified hand towards the revolver. Her hand was on his. Oh my God – he had only to press . . . If his hand would only relax, go limp. She fought dizziness – and again, dizziness, dizziness. Spinning world . . .

'No, *let* me. Got to . . . Going to . . . Sylvie say where Titwillow is . . . You hiding her? Got an idea you – she's getting a big girl now, soon be big tart, Titwillow give us a titshow, big tart learn from you –' His face so near hers was flushed, running with sweat. It shone dizzily. His saliva hit her face.

'Titwillow, little *tart* –'

Her hand was on the revolver. She forced the mouth of it away from her. Downwards. Felt his hand grasp and then grow limp. She had it safely. Safe. This spinning world of pain. And loss.

He reached out suddenly. Snatching it from her. She held on. Felt him try and bring it up to his head. He pushed his face against hers. 'Titwillow, *cuckoo* . . .'

She couldn't see properly. Blackness. Then haze. She swayed. Her hand over his still. Now he was turning the revolver. Towards her again. They struggled. Sweat ran down his face. Then again – he blurred. I can't see, I can't see.

As they struggled, she had hold of it again.

'Titwillow –'
Oh God our help in ages past, our hope in years to come . . .
Her fingers, round the trigger, pressed it.

10

In the boat train from the Gare du Nord, Teddy smoked incessantly. Hardly aware she was doing it. Amazed as they drew into Calais to see her cigarette case empty . . . On the crossing she sat with a brandy, eyes closed, trying to hurry the twenty miles to Dover.

I came as quickly as I could . . . It still did not seem quick enough. Returning to the apartment after a morning at the orphanage, finding the urgent message to ring Yorkshire. The distraught voice of her mother . . .

A Bad line, of course. Something to do with the storm the night before. Hearing the awful news in fragments (What, what, I can't hear, *I can't hear* . . .). But in the end she'd heard enough – enough to know she must leave *at once*.

Her maid Blanche gathering up clothes for her. Calling a cab, leaving a message for the man she was to have dined with this evening. Catching the train by minutes . . .

Reggie dead. Shot, by Sylvia. *By Sylvia* . . . Of course it was an accident. Her hand trembled, lighting up again. *How could it have happened?*

My little sister. Where was I when I should have been taking care? Always *next* year I was going to bother about Sylvia, to see she was all right . . .

She was not all right. When I last saw her – it must be already several months ago – she looked ill. Worn out I should think by childbearing and the worries about Reggie . . . That fierce loyalty to the hopeless Reggie. (But Sylvia was never a person to complain. Mother has been worried, often, but has always believed much too easily Sylvia's assurances. We were none of us confided in.) I scarcely knew Reggie. We could not manage five minutes conversation together. I cannot think of anything we had in common, except Sylvia. (I equally cannot think what she and he had in common, except the children.)

If I'd only been there all those years ago . . . instead of New York . . . Was it really necessary to *marry* him just because he got her with child? But my mores are not her mores . . . I would have kept the child and somehow, *somehow* . . .

Nothing seemed any better when, arriving at The Towers, she learned more. It made even less sense. Yes, it had been an accident. No, it had *not* . . .

It seemed Sylvia had rung the police yesterday evening, saying simply, 'I've shot my husband.' When immediately a constable came round, he could get no answer to his ringing. Getting in through the french windows, he found her slumped in a chair, and smelling strongly of whisky. She could barely be roused, and was apparently very drunk. It was only early in the morning they were able to get coherent talk from her, and the necessary information. Papers in the house gave them the addresses needed. Staff at The Towers had put them on to Filey and the seaside house Mother and Erik had taken for the children . . .

Mother seemed wonderfully composed. Only her lips with their slight tremble betrayed. The silver-haired Erik was as supporting and capable as ever, discussing with Teddy what they should do for the best. (As if there were any best, when something so terrible has happened . . .) They had brought back Willow with them from Filey, motoring over that morning. She had been told in an edited version what had happened. The little ones (the oldest, Lucy, was only nine) had stayed behind with the nurse.

Reggie's sister, Bar, in Canada, had to be cabled. They hoped later to speak to her. Angela, the other sister, telephoned *them*. Teddy took the call. She had been wildly hysterical, shrieking obscenities about Sylvia. When Teddy tried to calm her, to say, 'Look, I understand . . .' she had shrieked, 'You don't, oh no, you *don't*, I want to speak to a *man* . . .' Teddy had thankfully passed her to Erik.

Willow was unnaturally calm. Following Lily and Erik about, asking what could she do to help? Inquiring several times a day after her little sisters . . . With her long fair hair and troubled brown eyes, her composed little face wrung Teddy's heart.

Soon they would have to send for the other children. Someone would have to tell them what had happened. All of them for the time being would have to live at The Towers.

So many practical matters. Teddy found them curiously

soothing, numbing almost. Erik seemed to feel the same. Willow's school at Finsbury Park must be informed she would not be back for the new term due in a fortnight. The same for the younger children's school. There was the question of what to do about Michael, presently staying in Herefordshire with Stanley (Stingo) Hughes, a school friend who shared his motor-car madness. Should he be sent for, or left? Might he see something in the newspapers? Finally Erik spoke to the Hughes on the 'phone . . .

There was no bail for Sylvia. That sickened Teddy. What risk could there be in allowing her to be with her family, where she could be taken care of? Prisoner No. 793. It was Teddy who first visited her in Holloway. Taut with dread, she paid the taxi, stood before the formidable prison doors . . . She carried a profusion of late roses, a basket of fruit. She might have been visiting a hospital.

And that indeed was where she thought Sylvia should be. It was more than the drab prison dress, the strained eyes with their muddy whites, the bad colour. This was a sick woman. *I shall do something about it*, Teddy thought.

The visit was even more awkward, heart-rending, than she had feared. She told Sylvia the arrangements that were being made. 'You're not to worry about *anything*.' Erik was helping, she said. He and Mother would be down in a few days. They would find for her the best Defence Counsel money could buy.

It was impossible, though, to get from her a proper account of the shooting. 'It's difficult,' she told Teddy, 'when I can remember so little. You see . . .' But she went no further. Teddy could not have borne to press her.

A little before she was due to leave, Sylvia told her dully, 'Willow wasn't Reggie's child, you know . . .'

It is no use, Teddy thought, as gradually she learned the story, no use . . . Darling Sylvia, I would have *made* you let me take you to Switzerland, Italy . . . Rumania even. I would have adopted it for you. With a plausible tale. Everyone would have seen me not pregnant in the weeks before, there would have been no scandal, everything would have been all right. Her mind racing with these notions, she thought sadly: Of what use are they now?

Sylvia said, 'Willow knows. I had to say something – Reggie couldn't be trusted lately. I didn't say *who*. Don't tell her, Teddy. Unless she asks, until she asks you. Please. When she's ready . . .' Then just as Teddy was leaving:

'You'll be a mother to her, Teddy, if anything –'

'But it *won't*, darling. A good advocate, that's all we need. To explain to people, to get it across that it was all a horrible accident. You have told the solicitor – Kennedy, isn't it? – you have told him everything you remember?'

'What I remember, yes . . .'

In the taxi going back to her hotel, she thought: *Why drink?* How unlike Sylvia . . . And then to 'confess' like that immediately. Telling the police *she* had done it. 'There's been a terrible accident,' she should have said. 'And I shall say nothing until my lawyer comes . . .' *Why* couldn't she have kept calm and said he had committed suicide? Her fingerprints could easily be explained by her having picked up the revolver afterwards. And . . . and . . . Oh, I don't know. I am so ignorant of these matters . . . Maybe this, maybe that . . .

What horrors went on in her life that I knew nothing of?

11

To Stanley Hughes, Esq.,
Invalid,
From Michael Firth,
Scholar.

Winchester,
1st December, 1936

Dear Stingo,

Nice of you to send sympathy about my aunt. Everyone here's been pretty good. No ribbing, they'd certainly hear about it if there were. Might have been another story if I'd been in Junior Part. Little savages. But then so were we in our youth –

The trial opens at the Old Bailey on Monday. It's going to be a terrible ordeal for my grandmother – I worry for her a lot. The newspapers will have a field day – ('Edwardian beauty's daughter shoots husband'). With any luck though they'll be too busy with Mrs Simpson and our toppling throne. (New Christmas carol – 'Hark the Herald Angels sing, Mrs Simpson's pinched our King,' – heard it?)

Don't know why I'm trying to be funny – I don't feel it. Forget the facetious bits. The thing is I try not to think about my aunt's trial, but of course the thought won't go away. I think like I said that the wretched gun just went off and it was all a terrible accident and we've just got to hope the Judge is for her and her Defence is good. He's supposed to have a jolly fine reputation.

Awful thing to say – but all this has meant my eldest cousin Willow living up there (the other cousins may go to Canada to live, if things don't work out all right for Aunt Sylvia). She really gets under my skin. I get awfully fed up. Might be I'm jealous but don't think so. Girls *as a whole* just aren't very interesting. Not compared with cars!! Might make an exception of Lizbeth, not because she's your sister but because she's wonderfully unsilly. (You can tell her if you like!)

Am not expecting to have to see too much of Willow. My grandmother had laid on plans for me nearly right up till Cambridge next October (Down with Oxford, Stingo, what do you want to go to the *Other Place* for, you swine!) – I'm skiing at Semmering, then spending some time in Paris, gay Paree expect it will be, with my other aunt who lives there. Idea is to learn French!! I might go to Rumania after. Can use the French there! Some old family friends, Grandmother's arranging it. Hope they have some decent cars there.

The old 1914 Prince Henry Vauxhall I first learned to drive on (poop-pooping round the grounds age twelve – that beat even you!) has finally given up the ghost. Con rod went through the blocks – finis. Sad.

I still might get a motor for my birthday. I've rather set my sights on an Alvis Speed 25 – Charlesworth of course, I've seen just the one in a Salisbury garage, white, dark blue inside.

Really sporting of you to write to me from your sickbed. (Did you get them to put the appendix in a jar as a trophy?) You're not missing much here. I've a stack of chemistry notes to write up (physics is just possible, bit nearer to the inside of cars!) and feel a more than usually lazy cove so that's why I thought I'd drop you a line.

What about your Christmas? If you're really fit again, I could come and stay a few days – (tell Lizbeth!). It depends on the trial, though. Do you think your people will want me around if it all goes wrong?

Yours, Mike.

12

'Sylvia Maud Frances Gilmartin, you are charged with the murder of Reginald Peter Evatt Gilmartin on the twenty-first August last. Sylvia Maud Frances Gilmartin, how do you say, guilty or not guilty?'

'I plead not guilty . . .'

'May it please your Lordship and members of the Jury, the charge against the accused is that she murdered her husband, Captain Reginald Gilmartin, a business man, by shooting him . . .'

Teddy, reading the newspapers at the end of the first day, saw that the case merited only one column. Mrs Simpson was more interesting. The drama of the Throne took not only the front page but half of those inside. Thank God . . .

The second day, looking about the Court, her gaze ending up always on her sister, she thought: *They cannot convict her*.

All hope rested now with Counsel for the Defence. Ronald Spencer-Loring, KC, praised as 'invariably getting his man off . . .' Yet yesterday a hacking cough had interrupted everything he said. Today he blew his nose with a desperate trumpeting and was obviously running a temperature. Sweat poured down his face. His brilliance of eye was fever, not inspiration.

If *he* was a sick man, what of the prisoner in the dock? And yet remarks, inquiries Teddy had made to the authorities at Holloway had been greeted coldly. Yes, of course there had been a medical examination – if her sister was not well enough to stand trial, did Mrs Nicolson really think the Crown would . . .? Interference, they implied, usual behaviour of the rich and the privileged. No, a Harley Street consultant was *not* necessary . . . Yes, certainly the diet could be supplemented, if luxuries were felt appropriate.

Perhaps, Teddy thought, I was unlucky in those I spoke to . . . Sylvia's letters. Prisoner No. 793. They told me nothing. Lines written by a broken person and a sick one – I come back to that continually. *She never complains.* (Even as a child she never complained.) Sylvia, that gentlest of creatures . . .

Which is more than can be said of half the Jury. When I saw them sworn in, I was full of hope. Seven women and five men. A balance in her favour, I thought. The women will want her acquitted – at worst, a verdict of manslaughter. But three of them look righteous. Two others, timid – ready to be talked into anything . . . As for the men, they look as if their minds are already made up. Hard mouths, stiff necks, disapproving scowls. And then the Judge . . . To look at, not unlike Gib's gentle father. Oh, be like him, she prayed, be like him.

'I swear to tell the truth, the whole truth . . . so help me God . . .'

Angela Gilmartin, in a blue hip-length jacket, belted, with pleated skirt and a large fox fur. On her head a wide-brimmed felt hat.

Teddy thought: She has dressed to impress. (Just as I've dressed in a way I think suitable for Sister of the Accused. Mother, had she been here, in her elegant way would have done better still. Mercifully it has not been remarked on whose daughter Sylvia is – ageing Edwardian actresses not being particularly the thing just now.)

Angela Gilmartin. *I do not trust her.* I remember now she had that too gushing manner. All stupid emphasis. I can't believe she was a good influence on her dreadful brother . . .

'I am a spinster, presently living at . . .'

Red eyes. No, delicately pink-rimmed. The Court can see she has been crying recently. (Be fair – hasn't she lost a brother?) Already she has their sympathy.

She is being examined by Matthew Purchase, KC, for the Crown, a formidable man. Our man is looking worse by the minute.

'. . . You would agree then, Miss Gilmartin, that your brother was a man determined to make a success of his marriage, even if through circumstances beyond his control he was not to be successful in business? We could say that home life was to him of the utmost importance?'

'Oh yes. He – you see, our parents were not too happy together. Our mother . . . Shall I say?'

Mr Spencer-Loring rose suddenly. At first a sneeze impeded speech. 'Objection –'

'Yes, Mr Spencer-Loring?'

'The relevance of this excursion into family history of the deceased . . . What bearing can it have on the innocence or guilt of the accused?'

Objection not sustained . . .

'Now Miss Gilmartin, as you were telling the Court just now – your parents did not have a happy marriage?

'Indeed not. And unfortunately the unhappiness was made by our mother. She was –'

The Judge: 'Mr Purchase, where is this leading? It is not the deceased's *mother* on trial . . .'

'M'lud, if you will be patient with me – we are coming to the point . . . As you were telling the Court, Miss Gilmartin, your mother –'

'Our mother was – Forgive me, I don't care to speak of these matters. She – I think they call it a – nymphomaniac . . .'

The Judge interrupted: 'For the benefit of the Court, Mr Purchase, what is meant by this expression "nymphomaniac"?'

'I think, m'lud, it is best defined as an uncontrollable and morbid sex urge. In a woman, of course . . .'

'Thank you, Mr Purchase.'

'Miss Gilmartin, your brother was unhappy, was he not, even as a boy – about the home life of your parents?'

'I myself only knew what he told me. But, yes, he had seen, and heard – things which distressed him.'

'And as a result of this he had quite rightly a very high standard indeed of marital behaviour. By contrast . . . An idea that a wife should be above reproach –'

'Yes. He was looking . . . He thought he'd found in my sister-in-law a *good* woman . . .'

'But he discovered, did he not, that in fact history was repeating itself –'

Mr Spencer-Loring: 'I object most strongly.' (His voice came out most feebly.) 'Counsel is leading his witness in a quite blatant manner –'

'Objection sustained . . . Mr Purchase, you will kindly confine yourself to straight questions which the witness will then answer in her own words . . .'

But in seconds he was away again:

'Miss Gilmartin, what sort of marriage did your brother have?'

'Objection –'

'His marriage was a mockery –'

This, Teddy thought, is what they call Sensation in Court.

'In what way, a mockery? Please continue, Miss Gilmartin, even if it causes you distress. The Court must hear . . .'

'A mockery because – she was pregnant when they married –'

'And the father of that child?'

'Mr Purchase, you are leading your witness *again* –'

What is all this? What twist is this? Teddy thought. *Why, or why, does our man say nothing?*

'I apologize, m'lud . . . Miss Gilmartin, what effect did the accused's condition have on your brother?'

'He was greatly distressed. It was entirely for chivalrous reasons – he was always absurdly gallant – that he married her, knowing *it was someone else's child* . . .'

'How much did he tell you of this?'

'Only that it wasn't his. That it was the result of a casual encounter. Just as later –'

'Yes, yes, we shall come to that . . . Your brother was in the Great War, Miss Gilmartin?'

'He fought . . . he . . .' She sobbed.

The Judge said, 'The Court understands your distress, but I must ask you to try and answer clearly . . .'

'He fought at – he lost an arm, on the Meuse . . . the last month of the War.'

'Yes, yes. Tell me now – did his War service have any other adverse effects on him?'

'Yes, I'd say he had a great deal of nervous trouble. He was neurasthenic –'

'So that he suffered more than the normal person would when under strain?'

'Yes.'

'Would you tell the Court now what you know of your brother's marriage, after this – unfortunate beginning?'

'He suffered particularly. You see, he had business worries

which were made worse by his realization that my sister-in-law . . . that she consorted frequently with other men –'

'And you realized this first – when?'

'When we were trying to run an hotel in Ireland, and she took the opportunity . . . the run of men staying there . . . It was a paradise for her type. I had cause to speak to her. I said –'

Before there could be any objection, Mr Purchase:

'We do not need to deal just now with what you said. Rather, can I ask you what were your brother's reactions to this – behaviour?'

'After the first confidences, he didn't often discuss these – affaires with me. I know only that he was constantly distressed. Despairing –'

'There was never any question of his being that rather unattractive character, the *mari complaisant*?'

In the second's silence following: Dear God, thought Teddy. Are we to have *that* defined?

'Never. I know he spoke to her directly about these matters – angrily quite often. But of course without any results. On more than one occasion I was actually witness to – flagrant . . . to things I would rather not have seen . . . I was concerned too for the children –'

Teddy thought: Such a picture of our darling Sylvia. It is not possible people can tell such lies. Except that perhaps this woman *believes* her own lies . . .

'One last question, Miss Gilmartin. Did you not yourself intend to be married?'

'My – fiancé was killed. In nineteen-eighteen.'

'Thank you. That is all, Miss Gilmartin.'

Now, thought Teddy, she is made out to be almost a war widow . . . She had been watching two of the women jurors while Angela spoke last. One, in her early forties, whispered to another and shook her head sympathetically. No doubt that Angie had made a good impression . . .

The turn now of Sylvia's counsel to cross-examine. If only he did not look so ill. Where was that well-known thrust of the head, the sudden piercing unexpected question which would finish Angela Gilmartin? Puncturing the balloon of her self-righteousness . . .

'Miss Gilmartin, did you like your sister-in-law?'

'Of course I was fond of her. Why should you imagine I was not?'

'*I* am asking the questions, Miss Gilmartin . . . Now tell me, would you describe yourself as at all *jealous* of your sister-in-law?'

Objection by Matthew Purchase.

An apology. Then, sneezing and snorting, Mr Spencer-Loring resumed. Picking Angela up about this, about that. Getting nowhere. The fox fur trembled with outrage at the suggestion that any of her story might be biased, that Reggie's business failures were other than bad luck, that Sylvia could have been in any way provoked . . .

'Did you know that your brother was in the habit of drinking too much? Was dependent on drink to a great extent . . .'

'What is too much? My brother was used to it, from his days in the trenches. He was able to hold large amounts without apparent effect. It was quite different with *her* drinking. And of course if she was drunk at the time of –'

'Miss Gilmartin, you were not called into the box to make suppositions. That is the task of others. *You* are here to answer questions . . . Now tell me, did you actually see the accused, ever, the worse for drink?'

'Not actually *see* – I was not there so much of the time latterly. I was abroad, and . . .'

'Tell me, did your brother ever threaten suicide in your presence?'

'*Certainly* not!'

'Did you know that he had, lately, often threatened to take his life?'

'No – I . . . If he did – it would be to escape the hell *she* was making for him . . .'

'Miss Gilmartin, I must ask you again. These allegations of immorality . . . Now tell me, do you know whether he in fact spoke with the accused about . . . these alleged infidelities?'

'I don't – he did not say . . . Because he was unhappy and said it was to do with her, I naturally supposed . . .'

'We are not here to deal with supposition, as I think I told you before. I will rephrase the question. Did your brother *tell* you he had spoken to the accused of his suspicions? That it was an issue between them?'

'Not exactly. I . . . perhaps . . .'

'Thank you, Miss Gilmartin. No further questions.'

Teddy looked over at the dock. Sylvia in her little turquoise hat, worn on one side to the front of her head. A hat chosen by me, and sent in together with the suit, fur trimmed at lapels and cuffs. *My sister is a doomed woman*, she thought now. She hasn't even the wistful beauty which surely a few years ago would have won over the most hardened of jurors. All, all gone. I have been witness, slowly, inexorably to its departure. I did not notice enough when I should have done.

And now these terrible, false accusations . . . Sylvia the drunk, Sylvia the whore. (It is *I who am the whore* . . .)

The remainder of the trial passed for her in a haze. Words rolled over her head. She could not look at Sylvia, could not have borne to . . . There would be character witnesses – some one, someone surely would make it all right . . .

They came and went: the headmistress of Willow's school, the mother of one of her friends . . . Mr Purchase was rough with two of them. No one appeared to know Sylvia at all closely. She had not confided in her neighbours. Or in anyone.

'May it please your lordship, members of the Jury . . .'

Closing speech for the Crown:

'. . . we have heard all we need to show that the deceased was not only a man crippled in many senses, but a man provoked beyond imagining – ironically married to the very kind of woman who had made his youth such a shameful torment. A man who not surprisingly was driven to possess a revolver – knowing that there would be an honourable way out if all this should prove beyond his supporting. *Little knowing* it would be the very person driving him to this whose finger would be on the trigger . . .'

Listening, half listening to Matthew Purchase, Teddy could not understand his reasoning. She reminded herself that Ronald Spencer-Loring would have a chance after to refute everything, to turn it all upside down, *in Sylvia's favour* . . .

Mr Purchase still:

'. . . It is not important that no one comes forward other than her sister-in-law to state that she drank habitually. It is not necessary for the case that she should drink habitually. The question is, was she drunk enough *on this occasion* to cloud her judgment, so that she thought she was doing something other than killing her poor husband? You have heard the evidence of the deceased's sister: that the accused was in the habit of deceiving the deceased and that he was at the limits of his toleration. An evening was chosen when the children were absent . . .

'. . . it is not in dispute that the deceased was shot by the accused. We seek to prove that it was a deliberate, cold-blooded act. That she sought by this means to free herself of one who through no fault of his own had been unfortunate in business matters, and who now tried to curb and to interfere with her pleasures. That she took drink to give her courage – whether or no she habitually drank – and that her intention that night was . . .'

The closing speech now, on behalf of the prisoner Gilmartin . . .

What is our man making of the Defence?

He flounders, coughs, begs the pardon of the Court. As Teddy tried to concentrate, it seemed to her that his speech might as well be for the Prosecution. It rested as far as she could make out, on that struggle with the Smith and Wesson (Exhibit 24, horribly with them in Court). That in attempting to stop his suicide, in trying to wrest it from him, she accidentally pulled the trigger . . . (And indeed, in my own mind, I never for a moment thought anything else happened.) *But he does not sound as if he believes it.*

Now listen to his voice, tailing away to a murmur . . . This story that drink was forced down her. *I* believe it, but told by him it sounds the feeblest of defences. He seems too to be using as defence that, fuddled by alcohol, she did not know what she was doing . . . (This wretched business of drink. Sylvia never drank. No one will make me believe that she was a secret toper. And of course she had told me – us – nothing but: 'I shot him.' And words like, 'There can't be excuses for killing someone.' We are no further forward.

I can only hope, she thought, that the Judge (looking now more and more like Gib's father) will direct the Jury, those twelve good men and true, so that if she cannot be acquitted, if it cannot be called accidental death, at least it will be only manslaughter.

He has begun his summing up:

'. . . the fact that the accused is a person who has been guilty of immorality in circumstances which you may deplore has nothing to do with the case . . . You must judge the evidence from your knowledge of the world and experience – you are not supposed when you enter the jury-box to leave that knowledge and experience outside . . .

'. . . A man is presumed to intend the reasonable consequences of his act . . . if a man is so insane that he hits at somebody's head with an axe, believing that he is cutting down a tree, then he does not know what he is doing but thinks he is cutting down a tree. *That* is what is meant by not knowing the nature and quality of the act. He does not know what he is doing . . .

'We cannot have wives shooting inconvenient husbands who happen also to be drunk . . .

'. . . It is no answer and does not amount to insanity in law so as to make a man not responsible for his acts, that his resistance should be weakened or that his power of appreciation should be lessened. Therefore I have to tell you that, so far as that defence is concerned, you are bound to reject it upon my ruling . . .'

And now his last words:

'. . . I must also tell you what your duty will be if you come to the conclusion that although this lady fired the shot which killed her husband, she did so without intending to kill or do grievous bodily harm. I ought to say to you – it is material – that under those circumstances the accused would not be guiltless. She would be guilty of the crime of manslaughter, because manslaughter is killing a person unlawfully, without any intention of injuring him seriously, and of course without any intention of killing him . . .'

Too little, too late, Teddy thought, watching the jury file out. That may be the letter of the law but it is a different spirit he has conveyed. And he looked *so* like Gib's father . . .

Sylvia swayed, watching the world spin. Her swollen eyelids felt as though she had been crying. (If I were to weep, would I ever stop?) She thought: It's certain I am ill. It cannot be all nerves.

There had not been a time since that evening in September that she had been without headache. It was her familiar. Aspirin which they plied her with, only nauseated her, adding to the stomach pains, the burning throat. This *terrifying* headache. Blurred eyesight. Some days I cannot see properly at all . . .

She looked down at her fingers. Gloveless, they lay on her lap. She could feel the tingling starting up again. First a numbness, then pins and needles . . . The prison doctor says it is my kidneys, prescribes barley water and a bitter mixture in a bottle. Every other symptom is of nervous origin, it appears. The second doctor: 'You mustn't think, you know, you can get out of the trial through ill health . . .'

But I do not think at all. *Cannot* think. It is as if I listen to someone else's story. Mr Spencer-Loring's speech – I have seen no one impressed. Sympathy has been all with Angie. With her *lies* that she so firmly believes.

To think is to remember. *I thought I remembered nothing*. That policeman who has given evidence that he came in answer to my call. I telephoned, and cannot remember that. 'I have shot my husband,' I told him.

It was the nightmares brought it back first . . . They began the first evening in prison. The wardresses were, are, all kind. They *wanted* me to sleep well (sleeping draughts, phenobarbitone, but still I am half the night awake . . .), to feel better, to *be acquitted*. And yet how can I be? Since I did it. I pulled the trigger. *I wanted him dead*.

I can remember that – now. So long before it came back. Hazy memory. Of sudden flash, rogue thought, wild thought. Thought at the same time/in the same seconds that I held the revolver/gun. Such strength. How, weak as I am now, did I have such strength? That sudden . . . I would have liked to plead Guilty. If it weren't for the children.

Oh, my children. *My children* . . . Who will . . . what will . . . if the worst happens, who will help? Shall I be allowed to see Willow? *What shall I say to her*?

This is hell, nor am I out of it . . . my head, it will burst into a mass of – like Reggie . . .

Reggie is alive. So alive that in dreams he speaks to me, in *nightmares*. It's a dance at Dora Fisher's and I am young again. Captain Gilmartin, one-armed hero, wants to marry me. He asks me at the dance. My fingers touch a frock of pale orange georgette. The music goes on somewhere – always in another room – he asks me to marry him and when I begin to say no (there is some reason why I must not, *may not*), then his face changes . . . That is the nightmare, that terrible face – first drunk, angry, flushed – then changing, changing, dissolving, *bursting* into a mass of . . . *oh my God if only I could wake up then* . . . I've tried calling out, "I'm awake, I'm awake, it's not real,' just as I did as a child, as they told me to. I wake, and it is cold and half light, a grey half light from the first moment. I try and drag myself from it all – *And it is real* . . .

Once and once only – not a nightmare but a dream, of such happiness that I woke crying. Of course it was Geoffrey. It was our love again. Only why? When I haven't dared to think of him by day . . . In the dream we do not make love, we do not even talk. We only *are*.

'Members of the Jury, are you agreed upon your verdict? Do you find the prisoner, Sylvia Frances Gilmartin, guilty or not guilty of murder?'

'Guilty. But we should like to add a rider to that. We recommend her to mercy.'

'Sylvia Frances Gilmartin, you stand convicted of murder: have you anything to say why the Court should not give you judgment of death, according to law?

O thou who changest not, abide with me . . . The Lord is my shepherd, I shall not want, he maketh me . . .

'Sylvia Frances Gilmartin, the Jury have convicted you of murder with a recommendation to mercy. The recommendation will be forwarded by me to the proper quarter where it will doubtless receive consideration. My duty is to pass upon you the only sentence which the law knows for the crime of which you have been convicted . . .'

13

'Where is it?' Willow asked politely. 'Where is this convent?'

'East Anglica,' her grandmother said. 'It's the one where your aunt is a nun. Our Lady of Victory – or could it be of Sorrow? – I forget. But Erik and I, we were thinking . . .'

They were always thinking. That was part of the trouble, perhaps. Thinking always of her, and what would be best – when the best could only be to have Mummy back, and the terrible thing never to have happened. It wasn't mentioned in the house. No one mentioned it now. Because *Mummy is dead.* She had to go into the prison hospital the day after the trial. She was very, very ill. It was her kidneys, they said. Kidney failure. They don't have any cure when it's as bad as that. But oh, *I want her alive again.*

Aunt Teddy had invited her to come and live in Paris with her. But how could that do? She was frightened. Another strange place, she had thought. Another strange person. *I don't really know Aunt Teddy.*

She clung to Lily, as the time drew near for going. 'I want to stay with you. I'd much rather be here with you and Uncle Erik.' Grandma and Uncle Erik, with them she was safe. It was safe at The Towers.

Mummy told me about her childhood there. She was happy. And then the something terrible happened that made her marry the man I *used* to call Daddy. Who . . . Mummy told me about someone else being my feal father. Just a little about it. It frightened me. I don't know who I am. I don't want to find out. Something was said at the trial, I think. Aunt Angela. But she didn't say who *he* was. I think he has to have been wonderful for Mummy to have loved him. I know that she loved him – that is the one thing she said when she told me. I didn't ask her any more then. I didn't want to know. I don't want to know.

Everyone has been so kind to me, since she died. They try and say things to make it better, to show that it will be all right. *But it can't be* . . . There's this great yawning hole where there used to be my love for her. And hers for me . . .

She didn't need to die, why did she die? But if she hadn't, would they have – no, they would never have *hanged* her. But yes, women are . . . There was someone called Edith Thompson the year before I was born, and she hadn't even *done* the killing. There was to have been an appeal for Mummy, she would have been let off, everyone was absolutely certain. The Jury was never meant to say what they did. She would have had that other verdict – manslaying or something. She would have been a little in prison and then *come back to us*.

All five of us. Lucy, Jessica, Margaret, Beth. We were a family. The little ones cried because they didn't understand. I cried because I did . . . Little Beth clinging to me, not wanting to go to Auntie Bar. Canada is so far away . . . I've lost them. Although everyone says I may go and stay there. Not this summer – but perhaps the next, or the next.

It was raining as they turned into the convent drive. The motor drew up at the door. I shall be too proud to cry here, she thought.

Afterwards she could remember little of the first half-hour. They had been shown into the parlour and there had learned that they were a day too early. Term began tomorrow. Grandma had got it wrong. But it did not matter, they were told, Willow would be taken care of. The whole of her time there, she would be taken care of.

Reverend Mother smiled at Willow, taking her hand in a cold, dry one. 'Leave it to us, Mrs Ahlefeldt-Levetzau. We are quite used to – upsets. For such children the sooner there is a return to normal life, the better.'

She says it as if I were slightly deaf, or not quite present, Willow thought. I wish I *weren't*. All the time Reverend Mother spoke, she wore her proudest and 'cleverest' expression. It made her feel safer (and in the old happier days had made her friend Joyce laugh . . .)

But then, after tea in the convent parlour, when she'd kept back her tears, eating the last sandwich to make Grandma happy – in had come Aunt Alice.

Reverend Mother said, 'Mother Hilda has not been in the best of health. She is only able to do light work. Sacristy work . . .'

Aunt Alice was not at all what she'd imagined. She did not look particularly holy. Nor, except that they were both thin, could she see much family resemblance. But then Aunt Alice was only half Mummy's sister.

What to say to her? She didn't seem one for talking. She and Grandma discussed politely a few items of family news (the real news, the *bad things*, were not mentioned at all). They spoke of Michael going to Rumania. Aunt Alice said, 'Ah, Rumania . . .' as if she thought it the most boring country. Really, Aunt Alice wasn't very interested, or interesting. I can't imagine, Willow thought, what we shall talk about if we have to be together.

Then, suddenly, she was gone. Grandma had left. Sound of the motor turning out of the gates. Willow, alone in the parlour with Reverend Mother.

'I am ringing now for Mother Emmanuel, who will take you to your dormitory.'

'Oh, but just a sec. I forgot to give my aunt the present that –'

'Mother *Hilda*, I think you mean, Willow. Perhaps you would remember while you are here, for the sake of discipline, that Mother Hilda is a nun first, and your aunt second . . .'

'Whatever is that accent? Honestly, I never heard anyone talk like that unless they were being funny in a music hall or something. Is it Cockney? Are you Cockney?'

'I'm Willow Gilmartin.'

'And I'm Chrissie Leatherley. And no one I know talks like that. Where on earth did you pick it up?'

'What makes you think I got it on earth?'

'Just be careful how you speak to me, new girl. You may think you're the bee's knees and the camel's hips, Willow Gilmartin, but I can tell you *we* don't . . .'

There seemed so many of them. Although when she did a count it came to far less than at Finsbury Park. It was something to do with the way they'd formed cliques – had already made their friends last September, if not years before. She was the only new girl for the summer term. There were of course older girls, a head girl, three prefects, but they paid little attention to twelve- and thirteen-year-olds. People like Willow only got noticed if they made a scene or broke the rules in ways that couldn't be ignored.

None of the big girls seemed very interested in being at the convent. When they were overheard talking, it was always about the holidays. Joanna Mays was head girl but spent most of her time with a bay hunter she kept in the stables and which she rode to hounds in the winter and hacked in the summer. When Willow asked one of her own class if Joanna and her friends were taking School Certificate this summer, she'd met an incredulous face.

'Honestly! Whatever'd they want Matric for? They're not going into some stupid job. They do art and things. At Easter they went to Florence, with Mother Augustine's brother . . . Anyway you can't swot *and* hunt. There isn't time.'

She hadn't expected to be happy. But she hadn't expected to be quite so *un*happy. From the first miserable evening and night alone, on to the dreadful afternoon after, when in a seemingly unending stream the girls had returned from their holidays:

Pauline, Chrissie, Evelyn, Betty, Geraldine, Maureen, Priscilla . . . They didn't introduce themselves, or speak to her, but behaved for the first twenty-four hours as if she were not there at all. And she could almost have preferred that.

But of course it had not lasted. 'Are you the wallpaper, by any chance?' Maureen had asked. (Or the one she *thought* was Maureen.) Any answer to that would be wrong. So she kept silent, rather haughtily. That way there was no danger of crying. The worst imaginable would be to cry in front of *them*.

She shared a large room, almost a dormitory, with Evelyn, Betty, Pauline and Maureen. They were all Catholics except Priscilla. And even Priscilla knew when to genuflect, stand up, sit down, the words of the hymns, and what all sorts of things *meant*. Willow did not. She hadn't thought to discuss this with Grandma. And didn't dare say anything to Aunt Alice (sorry, Mother Hilda), whom she hadn't seen to speak to since that first day.

They wore summer dresses of blue striped material with navy blue sash belts and pale blue cardigans. All the uniform was blue. 'Our Lady's colour.' Except the brown shiny galoshes which in wet weather were worn over their blue punch-toed sandals. She was Form IVB and so her hair could not be worn loose. It had to be plaited: one or two plaits. Two was easier so she settled for that. The second morning she was struggling when Evelyn, who was nearly as tall as her, and very dark and silent, offered to help. She didn't speak at all while she was doing it. Then when the second plait was almost finished she tweaked Willow's head so roughly it brought tears to her eyes.

Maureen said, her smile like a pussycat's, 'Can't it do its own hair?'

'Just – it's, I've never had to do plaits on me. I used to plait my little sisters' hair, though . . .' Her voice faded away.

They were sitting on their beds staring at her.

'Did anyone speak?' Maureen asked. 'I thought I heard an odd sound –'

'Wallpaper can talk, you know,' said Willow.

Angrily Betty almost shouted, '*Chrissie* was meant to have that bed. Mother Augustine promised, absolutely *promised* that Chrissie could move in. It's a bit *much*. And she hasn't just broken her word, she's put a tree or a bush or something in with us instead. Willow will G.O. Agreed, girls?'

'Yes,' said Pauline. 'You go and ask to be moved, Willow. Then Chrissie can come in like she should.' Pauline had thick, short, tangled hair and a large nose. She poked her face now threateningly at Willow. But when Willow the next day did as they'd asked, she was reprimanded.

The days had a pattern. That was perhaps what saved her from despair. The pattern, and then the ticking off of the calendar: only so many more days to half-term. But first there was the Coronation. Several of the girls were taken out for tea by their parents. Grandma and Erik sent Willow a tin of toffees with Princesses Elizabeth and Margaret Rose on the lid. She wasn't sure about offering the toffees around. In the end she gave them all to the girls in Class III, two classes below her.

The lessons weren't too bad. She thought that probably she would have been able easily to do the work of Class IV A, and possibly Class V too, but because she had never done French or Latin and had studied the wrong period in history, she had been put with girls who were all younger. Most were only just thirteen. Not that any of the work was very difficult, but Mother Benedict had made the decision very quickly after asking a few questions. In fact it was this being in IV B instead of A which had caused her to be put in the room with Maureen and the others. She would otherwise have been on the floor below. Perhaps that would have been better? Impossible to tell really – since IV A and V didn't go out of their way to be friendly . . .

After the weekend outings for the Coronation she noticed something strange. It began with Betty, who said to her, in a casual voice, almost friendly:

'You never said your grandmother used to be a Lady –'

'Didn't I? Should I? I mean – what of it?'

'Oh, what of it –' said Chrissie who was standing nearby, 'what of it indeed? We know who she is, that's all –'

'She was very famous, on the stage,' Willow said. 'King Edward came to see her –'

'Stale buns for tea, it's something else we know, about *you* –'

'Go on then. Say it. Fire ahead.'

'Wouldn't you like to know, new girl?' said Chrissie. 'Wouldn't you like to know?'

I might have guessed, she thought. How could I have hoped, without a change of name, that no one would find out? Sooner or later. In spite of what Reverend Mother had said . . .

Two days later she was sent for during evening prep, and told to go to Aunt Alice in one of the parlours. They sat opposite each other awkwardly. Willow answered questions about her schoolwork, careful not even to hint she was unhappy at Our Lady of Victories . . .

Suddenly Aunt Alice remarked, her voice very precise: 'It was fortunate of course that the newspapers when gathering their information didn't know of my existence. And so did not embarrass the convent. There is something to be said for being buried alive . . .'

Willow, thinking her serious, bitter even, was surprised then to see a faint smile.

Someone came to fetch her. When she went back into the hall where they did their homework, lots of the girls turned to look. She blushed. It was like the way she'd been stared at when she visited the prison and later when she'd visited Mummy in the hospital there. She wanted to cry . . . could feel fifty, a hundred curious eyes on her . . .

At supper-time Maureen said, 'I hope you didn't go telling your aunt about us eating in the dorm. I bet you've been splitting on us . . .'

Pauline said she was surprised someone with a nun aunt wasn't a Catholic. 'You've never told us why you're not a Catholic –'

'Because my parents weren't –'

'Oh, your *parents*,' said Chrissie. 'Let's change the subject, shall we, girls?'

It was Willow's night for a bath. Mondays and Thursdays. There was a rota pinned up outside the washrooms. Just before running the water, she went into one of the lavatories by the communal washbasins. She was just about to pull the chain when she heard her name spoken.

'*You* know more about her. You sleep with her.'

'We wish we didn't –'

'Hey. Careful. Sure she's not –'

'Dead sure. She's gone for a bath.'

'Right. Honestly, though, wasn't it just the end, not telling us about a thing like a *murder*. I mean, if I'd known – Crikey. Gosh. When Mummy and Daddy find out . . . I bet that's why Reverend Mutt's kept quiet till now. I mean, if Pauline's mother hadn't happened to say . . .'

'Some of the big girls knew. I'm sure.'

'Honestly, I thought I'd die when Reverend Mutt put on that *awful* voice – the same one she used for telling us about that funny girl who wet her knickers . . .'

'Didn't she used to stink?'

'Like someone else I could mention . . .'

'But Reverend Mutt's voice. Honestly. "Girls, girls, what's this –" '

'You sound just like her, Maureen –'

' "*What's* this I've been hearing, girls? Ugly rumours about little Willow Gilmartin . . ." (Little, my foot, she's more like a beanpole.) "Yes, I'm afraid, girls, something nasty did indeed happen to Willow's parents . . . It is all very unsavoury and is on no account to be mentioned." *She's* got a hope! Honestly, we could have guessed a sneaky show-off like that would have something to hide –'

'But her mother's dead, that's awfully sad. And –'

'I think you're a bit soppy, Priscilla, if you want my opinion. How could she *love* her if she'd killed her father?'

'But it's still sad. I think –'

'Don't . . . I must say it's nice to know she got that showy-off expression because she's been in the newspapers. Or her family has. I mean that was one of the things Reverend Mutt said, that it might make her a bit proud.'

'I don't know . . . Have you read *Murder in a Nunnery?*'

'One of the big girls is going to lend it me. Don't spoil things by saying who did it, will you?'

Gradually the group broke up. She waited till there was no sound, then crept along to the bathrooms. The bottom of the bath was gritty with scouring powder. After, she cleaned it again, scrubbing with a kind of hopelessness. She said over and over, 'Mummy, Mummy . . .'

When she went back into the room, they were sitting on Evelyn and Maureen's beds, two on each. It was about fifteen minutes before lights out. Pauline was brushing her hair. No one spoke. Willow hung her towel up on the rail beside her bed.

'Fee fi fo fum, I catch the smell of an unwashed bum,' Maureen said.

'You were a long time in the bath,' Betty said. 'I hope you used some soap . . .'

Suddenly it was summer. They didn't need cardigans over the blue striped dresses. For a week or two the sun shone every day. The tennis tournament began, part grass, part asphalt – it was the luck of the draw which you played on. Willow was one of the oldest in the Junior section and although she had never really played before – only banged a ball about – she found she was quite good. When Miss Wedgwood, the games mistress, showed her the superiority of overhand serves, she developed quickly a deadly one with an unpredictable spin. 'Forty love, deuce, van in, van out . . .' For minutes at a time she forgot that she was profoundly, desperately, never to be cured unhappy.

That way the days passed somehow till half-term. (Half-term meant half over, half way to being back at The Towers for the long summer holidays.) But the few days' break was gone almost before she knew . . . She could not tell Grandma or Uncle Erik anything. Not even that the girls knew about her history . . . 'Yes, I'm very happy, honestly,' she said to their anxious inquiries, 'thank you.' How could she add to their unhappiness?

She was back again. With another six weeks to face. *I can't do it*, she thought . . .

They lay about on the grass in small groups. There was a Columbia gramophone, a portable which belonged to the convent. Some of the older girls had brought records, and these were played on Saturday afternoons, or weekday evenings while it was still light. When she was back from half-term, and quite despairing, she would hear the music coming over from the lawn. Their craze was Nelson Eddy, paired often with the steely voice of Jeannette Macdonald. *'Stout-hearted men'* and *'The Indian Love Call'* came from behind the rhododendron bushes. Joanna Mays, she of the roan hunter, perhaps she was sorry for Willow, because she invited her to come over and sit with them. Mary Woodruff, a prefect, and several others were there.

Joanna was lying on her stomach reading Agatha Christie.

'Have you guessed?' Mary Woodruff asked, 'I bet you haven't.'

'I think it's the Colonel, it *has* to be the Colonel . . .'

They were kind to her in a way she liked, by just talking among themselves, smiling at her now and then.

'. . . Are we bothering with an end of term play? Reverend Mutt hinted that the last offering . . . Let's do a *murder*, something juicy. What about *Night Must Fall*? That wonderful bit where Danny –'

There was sudden silence. Dorothy, the one who'd been speaking, went very red. Mary said hurriedly:

'D, you might wind the gramophone – a new needle . . .'

'I'll do it,' Willow said. 'Let me.' Hurrying, to show that although she had heard what they said, she had not taken offence, or been upset.

1937 was the Diamond Jubilee of Our Lady of Victories. The day fell by coincidence on the feast of Corpus Christi, so that as well as the usual procession, there were to be celebrations, a special meal, speeches. For two weeks before, one of the nuns read the history of the school aloud to them during meals. The silence they had to keep made them restless. There was face-pulling, note-passing, and kicks under the table. Willow often got kicked accidentally on purpose.

She rather liked the history part. Although the Order had three houses in Europe and one in Africa, it was an English one. The two women who began it all in 1877, Amelia Farringdon and Mabel Chesterton, had been childhood friends. One married very, very happily, but her husband was killed together with their only daughter, Laura, in a tragic accident in the Swiss Alps. The two friends both had a vision (or it might have been a dream – it wasn't quite clear) in which they were asked by Our Lady to found an order to teach girls the way they would have liked the dead Laura taught. But no one would listen to them: priests, bishops, nobody. What was wrong with existing convents such as Princethorpe, they were asked. Couldn't they become nuns in one of these? Sadly they had got nowhere when the unmarried friend died suddenly of a heart attack. Immediately after (and surely this was Mabel arranging things in heaven?) the Pope himself had decreed that Amelia might found an order and a school to go with it. And since she lived in East Anglia and possessed already a capacious family house . . .

'It really is *rot*,' Chrissie said. 'The only good thing is there's a rumour they're going to let us off next weekend. Friday till Monday. It'd better be true. Bags I come and stay with you, Maureen . . .'

They heard next supper-time after the reading that girls who lived nearby might go home, and girls who did not might go with friends. Telephone calls to parents would be booked immediately . . .

Maureen said, 'I suppose you'll spend the weekend with your *aunt*. With Mother Hilda. They can hardly expect you to go to Yorkshire for two days . . .'

Betty, who was tidying out her sponge-bag – slimy flannel, caked soap box, uncapped toothpaste – said casually:

'She could come back with me, I suppose.'

'Aren't you taking anybody?'

'No, Priscilla's got an aunt in Newmarket. She's going there . . .'

Willow wasn't sure whether she was meant to have heard.

'Well, do you want to come, yes or no?' Betty said.

The Friday morning they left there was a letter from Michael in Rumania. Betty was impatient to be off, 'Mumsy and Daddy are coming at nine. We've *got* to be ready.' But some of the others were impressed. Willow thought: He has a kind heart, after all. The letter was skimpy and didn't tell her too much, but it had some photographs with it. Mostly mountain scenes, and some peasants in national costume.

Betty's parents bustled the girls into the car straightaway and were off. Mr Lewin's driving was so swoopy it made Willow feel sick, stuck in the back as she was with Betty. A large red setter sat with them. His breath smelled terrible, and he licked Willow's face, hands, knees, more or less continuously. 'He likes you,' Betty said. 'Mumsy, Farmer likes Willow, isn't that good?'

Mrs Lewin said, 'You do ride, I hope? Betty didn't say.' She spoke briskly but kindly.

Willow was filled with dread, because when Betty had asked her about riding she'd said – curled up by the scorn on Chrissie's face: 'Bareback, I've only done bareback.' And Betty had said, 'Oh, that'll be all right . . .' Why ever had she made up such a whopper?

'Mumsy, I'm sure Willow will want to ride when she sees Clover.' Willow remembered the framed photograph beside Betty's bed. 'And she'll love Tootles . . .'

'Willow will, will she?' said Mr Lewin. 'Quite a name you've got there, haven't you, Willow?'

She kept wondering all the time if Betty's parents *knew*. They must, of course. Betty would have told them. But if they did, they made no reference to it . . .

The riding began almost immediately. Within half an hour of their arriving. A light drizzle had just started but Betty said it would take more than rain to stop her. 'When I'm older, the next pony – horse I have, I'll keep him at the convent. Like Joanna Mays.'

Tootles belonged to Betty's sister Audrey who was away at a different school. He was a fat pony, of uncertain temper according to Mrs Lewin. 'Perfectly safe, of course – just gets a bit pooky. *Lovely* soft mouth . . .' Willow was kitted out with jodhpurs too short in the leg and a hat belonging to Audrey. Also yellow string gloves because in the wet the reins would become slippery. On first seeing her, Tootles drew back his lips from yellow, very fierce-looking teeth.

'He likes you,' Betty said. 'Mumsy, I think Tootles likes her.'

Betty was much nicer to her than when they were at the convent. At the same time she seemed younger: the nine months between them longer.

'I think you're nearly too tall for Tootles –'

'I'll be nearer the ground and safer for falling,' Willow said.

'You aren't going to fall –'

But she thought she almost certainly would have done, if the drenching rain hadn't made them turn back after only ten minutes.

'After all, you've only got to *walk*,' Betty had said before, 'you haven't even to trot . . . And the place we're going to, you can just sit and watch me jump Clover . . .'

Luckily the rain didn't allow another attempt that day. The afternoon passed pleasantly enough with a drive into Bury St Edmunds for tea. By evening she was contentedly tired. Tucked up in bed in a room to herself – she'd thought she'd have to share with Betty – she tried not to think of the next day.

She hardly slept at all. There must have been some part of the plumbing system ran through her bedroom. Sounds of someone in distress: she tried to pretend it was a dragon in his death agonies but the fantasy didn't work very well. In the morning, the sun shone from a cloudless sky. There would be no escaping Tootles . . .

'Listen,' Betty said, 'stay in front of Clover all the time – away from her hind legs. She's a bit of a cow-kicker, Mumsy says it's the fault of her previous owner. Go on, Willow, up you get . . . No, you get on from the other side – can't you tell left from right? Left foot in stirrup, right hand on pommel – that bit there sticking up – Now lean a bit, right leg over . . .'

Somehow, giving Tootles little digs all the time as instructed ('I really ought to have lent you a crop for him. He's awfully dozy today, it's the grass – must be the grass'), she arrived safely to where Betty and her friends were to practise for summer gymkhanas.

The sun shone and it was a pleasant place. Betty and two other girls were going over jumps of increasing height. Betty had said, 'Back with you in a mo.' Now she seemed to have forgotten her.

Tootles pulled his head down. He seemed to want to graze. She let the reins go loose and he began to munch contentedly. She thought after a while, since he was so quiet she would dismount and tether him. Dismounting was easy. The ground was so near. While Tootles munched, she swung her leg back as she remembered from yesterday. Her left hand lay loosely on the pommel. She thought she had the reins. As her leg went over, she felt the pony move. 'Stop there,' she said. 'Whoa, Tootles.' But he was walking on. She hung for a moment. Oh gosh. Oh golly.

Then suddenly she was safe on the ground. Tootles, trotting, gathered speed.

It all seemed to happen in a moment. Betty saw at once, and she and her friend Monica rode over to rescue Tootles. 'Oh gosh, Willow – look what you've done . . .'

When they arrived back at the house:

'Mumsy, look, she's broken Tootles' reins! Tootles has put his foot through his *reins*, Mumsy . . .'

With that sort of beginning it amazed her that she agreed, even insisted on going out for a hack on the Sunday. It was a matter of pride. They set out straight after breakfast. She had been with them to early Mass. It was another hot still day. She was all right at first and managed quite well. A friend, Monica, went with them – she and Betty talked a lot. Willow was careful to keep away from Clover's hind legs. Tootles seemed in a good mood. I am quite getting the hang of this, she thought. She even opened a gate for them, getting her hands mixed up and ending up facing the wrong way – but managing.

'Jolly good,' Monica said. 'You've quite made up for yesterday.'

On the way back they were a few hundred yards from home, when without warning, Tootles broke into a canter. She remembered with horrow her own words – 'I've only done bareback – cantering about, galloping . . .'

She pulled hastily on the reins – I must not break this pair. Pulled harder. Nothing happened. She pressed angrily against him, her feet slipping farther into the stirrups. Betty shouted from behind, her voice sounding miles away: 'Turn him, try and *turn* him, you fool . . .'

She supposed this speed to be a gallop. She tried pulling to one side, to turn him. She slipped a little in the seat. Leaned forward – then backward to pull harder. She slipped further round in the saddle. And then she was down. But still attached to Tootles. Her head went bang, thump, bang. Her leg – shot through with pain . . .

'We've been told to be nice to you, that's why I'm here,' said Maureen, 'I've brought you some Kunzle cakes and the *Horse and Hound*. Betty says you were jolly lucky only to break a leg, she thinks you're the absolute end mucking up the weekend like that. People who can't manage ponies shouldn't get on them.'

When Willow didn't say much, she went on:

'Cheer up, do. When are they going to take the bandages off your head? We've all got to be in this ghastly outdoor tableau, it's a bit from St Lucy's life, her eyes were plucked out and she has to hold them on a plate – we're going to use peeled grapes or jelly sweets . . . Look, do open the cakes. I'm absolutely ravenous . . .'

Maureen was her third visitor in the convent infirmary. Betty and Josephine came first. Betty was warily polite – and brought well-wishes from her parents. Willow's left leg, in plaster of paris to above the knee, was stretched out in front of her. Her head would soon be out of its bandages, but the scabbed red healing on one side of her face made her not want to look in the glass. Luckily, although her visitors said some unkind things, they had not remarked on that.

At first after the accident she'd felt quite certain she would be allowed to go home. But after the first few days in hospital at Newmarket – where she was visited by a distraught

Grandma – she was told that ten days or so in the infirmary was all that would be needed. After that she would be able to get about and attend classes. It would be a pity to take her home, Reverend Mother told Grandma, when she'd settled in so well and made so many friends.

She had had three days now in the infirmary. She was the only person ill at that time and had a largish room with four beds all to herself. The meals were the same as in the convent dining hall. Mother Veronica who was in charge of her was a tiny bustling woman, permanently hurried. Willow hated to ask her anything.

There was medicine to take, of course. She didn't care for the one she was given for her head. It was cherry-coloured and sickly. It made her sleepy and after the sleepiness had worn off she always felt like crying.

Aunt Alice had been to see her each day so far. Willow was certain she had been sent. She sat at the foot of the bed and asked polite and, Willow thought, rather silly questions about her leg and head – although she reminded herself that her aunt had been a nurse in the Great War.

She and Mummy had the same father. Looking now, she tried to find some resemblance to her own mother but could see none.

'Do the girls come and see you? You're not too lonely? I'm sorry I could only bring some *Messengers of the Sacred Heart*, they're not very exciting –'

Willow burst out: 'You only come because you've been told to. You're as bad as all the rest. You've been *told* to be nice. I expect it was a penance in Confession or whatever –'

She had surprised herself. Her aunt looked not angry but amazed. Hurt.

'I didn't mean that, you know,' Willow said, 'my head aches and I get silly. It's very kind of you. Thank you very much for coming . . .' Then to her horror – it must be the medicine – she began to cry. She felt the tears fall before the sobbing began. Her cheeks were wet while her face was still composed. But then, once begun, she found she could not stop. Her head shook painfully. Her body heaved with sobs.

'Mummy,' she said, then over and over again, 'Mummy, Mummy . . .'

Without moving from the end of the bed, Aunt Alice said, 'You could tell me about it, if you wanted.'

'I expect you're going to say, "big girls, girls of nearly fourteen, don't cry –" '

'Indeed I shan't . . . You look as if you haven't cried enough.'

'What *is* enough?'

'I wish I knew. I cried for *my* mother for many years. Most of all when her place was taken. But then, I had my father, my home . . . I didn't have the – family tragedy you had. *Your* suffering . . .'

Willow had stopped crying now. She poured herself out a glass of lemon barley from the bedside table. 'Would you like some, are you allowed?'

'I saw your mother the day she was born, Willow. I was taken up to see her. She had hardly any hair, just a little pale fluff. Not like Teddy. But later – her curls –'

'Tell me, please, please tell me. Everything you can remember . . .'

She saw from the clock afterwards they had talked for over an hour. It seemed to her she had moved from the convent infirmary, with its white walls and cast iron beds, to some in-between land. She, who'd been too shy to ask Grandma the things she really wanted to know, even to talk about her mother very much at all (and oh, they meant well, how well they meant . . .), now could not stop:

'Did Mummy really, *really* – was she ever as naughty as that? When Margaret was very little she threw her sprouts on the floor once and Mummy said, "*I* never . . ." If we'd only known . . .'

She told Aunt Alice, 'I used to put the two smallest ones in the bath together. It was our happy time before Daddy – Reggie – came back from work. Sailing boats, blowing bubbles . . . The *very* first thing I remember in my *whole* life . . . the big bathroom we had in the Surrey house, I had this clay pipe and I was blowing bubbles, Mummy did it with me, hers were the best – we had Fairy soap and water . . .'

'. . . Floating soap, we had, Willow. Swan floating soap, it was called. And Nan-Nan used to allow me – my mother was never there at bedtime . . . Sylvia, your mother, I used to go in and give her her bath. She was so much younger – I felt more than a big sister. Almost a mother –'

'*I* was sort of mother too. To the little ones . . . Oh, I miss them so horribly. Canada's so far away. And if *they* cry for Mummy . . . I mean, Auntie Bar is sweet, but . . .'

Memories and more memories: 'The winter I was four, Aunt Alice, the snow began at Christmas time and just went on and on and on. Mummy made me a treat lots of nights – a twopenny carton of cream and she put it on my window-sill, then when I woke up it was *ice-cream* and so lovely . . .'

Oh, the luxury of talking to a *listener*, and someone who was Family. When Aunt Alice said that it was, alas, Benediction time, she made her promise to come back the next day, with lots of time.

As she got up to go, Willow said, 'Come here.' As her aunt approached, she threw her arms about her. 'That's for being wonderful and saving my life.' She covered her in kisses.

Her aunt looked pleased. 'I haven't done much, Willow. You know you can always talk to me. Any time.' She said as she turned away – she was very flushed: 'I wouldn't have kissed you unless you had first. I'm not a kissing person . . .'

14

'What a big boy!'

'*Isn't* he a big boy . . .'

'Michael, you're here exactly for *le five o'clock* . . . You tell us now everything of Paris – Mariana wants to know about *hats* . . .'

'Your aunt was telling us you are *little* – yes, I am certain she says *le petit Michel* . . .'

'Your French is very good. How was the jorurney? Say at once what you think of Bucharest –'

'Your grandmother knows my father who is coming in one minute – And she knew also his brother, my uncle Tino, who is dead, alas –'

Too many people, too much noise. They had come specially – all of them, to take afternoon tea in the town house of Ion and his wife Elena. (Ion, whom Grandma Lily had known, together with his brother Valentin, at the turn of the century.) Their married daughter, Mariana, was there with her husband Stefan and twin sons, Cristian and Corneliu, and little girl, Dina. Two more of Ion's daughters. Friends, relations . . .

The only one easy to distinguish was the redoubtable Sophie, whom Grandma had told him about. Eighty now, with features almost obscured by fat, she laid a plump hand gently on his.

'Your dear, dear grandmother, such friends we were. And my dear Teodor also . . . We spoke to her of course in English – her French was not like yours . . .'

They all congratulated him on his French, which in Paris had not been thought much of. Often Teddy couldn't wait till he found his words and wculd gabble for him.

There was a woman there, in her thirties he thought, whose name he didn't catch. Everyone, except for grey-haired Ion and Elena and white-haired Sophie, was dark. She was blonde. He wondered if it was natural? Taller than her, he took a peep at her roots later. Stingo said only barmaids had roots . . .

'We've so many plans for you – can you really stay until almost September? Yes, but we *love* visitors . . .'

'The Coronation, were you at the Coronation? The *affaire* before – this Mrs Simp*son*, it is impossible to understand. What a story . . .'

'Yours seems possibly worse,' he remarked, his first original venture since he had arrived. 'The King and –' He wondered if it was tactful to refer to the well-known liaison between their King Carol and the red-haired actress Magda Lupescu. For that, their throne had tottered . . .

'Soon it's very hot. Some of us go to the Black Sea, to Constanza where we have a villa . . . You like the sea?'

There was hardly time to eat. The food was richer than The Towers' afternoon tea. Only the *tarte aux pommes* reminded him of Teddy's in Paris. Everyone ate enormously. All sorts of little sandwiches, buns with thick sweetened cream, chocolate layer cake . . .

His head ached – the wheels of the Orient Express still revolving. Then the drive through Bucharest on his way here: being polite about their Arc de Triomphe – the first had fallen down, and this one didn't look much better – (and had he not just come from the real thing?) There'd been beggars – gypsies, he supposed. The women trailed long, brightly coloured skirts. When they had stopped the motor to buy a newspaper one of them thrust a hand in through the open window. There were cabs with weirdly dressed drivers. Peasants walking about, the women in embroidered blouses. He saw at least two very desirable cars – a Mercedes and an Alfa Romeo, both driven by young men who raced past, hooting . . .

'Young Michael – please call me Sophie – your grandmother writes you are passionate about motors . . . I think while you are here, my Ion has a small surprise for you. No, not so small . . . Something you will *like a lot* . . .'

Bucharest,
17th May, 1937

Dear Stingo,

Wish you were here! (So will you! See over the page!) Hope you've been getting my letters, and I wouldn't mind an answer some time – Haven't had a word since the card at Easter. I hope you're impressed with me getting out the old pen and paper. The only ink here is this frightful colour, but anyway here goes.

News from home is I *didn't* get that Alvis Speed for my birthday. They didn't say 18 was too young or anything but just to wait and see till I was back in England. Have changed my mind anyway and if the Trust will cough up I rather fancy a Lagonda LG45 – long stroke, four and a half litre. All right?!

They're a bit funny here but awfully kind really. I'm writing this in the garden by the fountain and may get interrupted any moment – lots of people about and they often get restless suddenly without warning. People are – Ion and his wife Elena (it's them I'm staying with), their daughters (there's a bachelor son too – I'm coming to that! who's on business in Brazil for three months). Then literally dozens of friends and relations. Sophie is the old aunt – her house is nearby but she treats this as a second home.

Now – this is the great news! I've got a motor, use of, and you'll be pea green when you hear, old Stingo. It's a Bugatti T57C!! She's a couple of years old but in magnificent tune, and she's MINE all the time I'm here. The bachelor son – remember what I hinted? it's his but I'm to be trusted with it. Though they did test my driving first. I didn't catch on of course what they were up to. Am I going to have a GOOD TIME with her?! Feel a bit mean telling you but – well, it beats anything, doesn't it?

There's an old lady here often, a family friend, but missing on a few cylinders, I'm afraid. Old age. Her name's Ana Xenescu and she lives with her daughter, Corina, who's a widow. The daughter's always round here, part of the great big family. She's actually just talking to Sophie now. She's a blonde (although it could come out of a bottle!) which is a bit unusual. I expect at any moment she'll come out here and say –'

'Let's all go to Cina's . . . Mikki, what do you write letters for, *you look terrible serious*. Isn't that a good bit of English? I like to show my bits of English . . . Now we speak French again . . .

Maman's been so trying today – she got some idea in her head that she'd been cheated by her milliner. I do all her accounts so it can't be, but she wouldn't be shaken . . . Then I realized she was thinking about a summer before the War, when I was still a child –'

'Oh Corina,' someone said, 'I am sure you were not even *born* before the War –'

'What lovely flattery,' she said. 'The truth is . . . It was nineteen hundred and two, my birth – and it was of great note because Maman was well over forty . . .'

Everything was different now he had the Bugatti. The first day that it came from the garage, where it had been lovingly cleaned and serviced, he went out in it with Ion. Once up the Chaussée and into the countryside, he took the wheel. I love her, he thought at once. He allowed his foot to press harder, harder on the accelerator – then out, full out, and off she roared.

'Good. Good,' Ion said.

He was at the wheel again today, going down to the Black Sea, across the wheat plains of the Dobrudja. A monotonous drive. He was taking Sophie and Ana Xenescu, and in the front beside him, Corina. This was because Nicu, the Bugatti owner, had he been there, would have taken them. Michael was not sure about Corina's company. Certainly the 'she' he preferred was the Bugatti.

'You drive well,' Corina said. Her hair, worn simply, was kept back with a jewelled clasp. Her lipsticked mouth was a vivid slash of red.

Ana, at the back, either chattered or, head lolling, snored. They stopped half way and drank champagne, iced, that they had brought with them. He was a little light-headed when they started off again, and surprised at how easily the Bugatti handled. I really know what I'm doing, he thought.

'You drive well,' Corina said again. She had been talking a lot on the journey. Her scent was heavy and obtruded. He thought that he preferred the smell of petrol.

On the whole, girls bored him . . . Although he was surprised sometimes to find himself suddenly for a whole ten minutes absolutely crazy about, for instance, Stingo's sister, Lizbeth. In Paris there hadn't been many girls, just women friends of Teddy's. They made a fuss of him which he didn't mind, except that they seemed to him rather old. As was Corina, really. She had even owned to it.

'We'll go swimming,' she said now. 'I'm sure you look magnificent in swimming costume. Such a big boy . . .'

He didn't like that at all. He said in a cross voice, the champagne wearing off, making his head ache: 'If you want to see someone really magnificent, look straight ahead . . .'

'What? What are you talking about?'

'The Bugatti of course. The most beautiful woman between here and Bucharest. Least, *I* think so . . .'

She was silent for a while after that. When she spoke again, she was like a small child who'd been scolded. She said in English:

'Don't you like that I am calling you "big boy"? Is that the matter?'

'Leave me alone, and don't tease –'

'Corina naughty, naughty!' called her mother in a sharp voice. A moment before he'd seen her in the mirror, asleep. 'Naughty girl, shan't have a cake!'

'Pay no attention,' Corina said to him. 'Ignore her. She forgets quickly, thank God.'

The sun didn't shine much for them during their stay at Constanza. Six of them were in a large villa outside the town in the direction of Mamaia. Nearby was a large hotel, the International, newly built. They went there to eat and to dance.

Corina needled him. 'You don't dance very well. You must let me give you lessons –'

He felt angry and said, 'It doesn't come easily to Englishmen. And anyway my aunt thinks I'm not bad – and a friend of mine, his sister, she tries all the time to get me as a partner.' He thought nostalgically of waltzing with Lizbeth. Uncomplicated, nothing expected of him. (What *was* expected of him here?)

Sophie asked him one day, 'You like all the family? Such nice girls, and these boys' (she called Ion a boy still), 'all so nice too. Corina . . . I ask you to be patient. She is sometimes nervous. Her husband – it wasn't a love-match, of course, but all the same . . .'

A gull perched on a rock. It was like any gull anywhere – it didn't know that it was a Rumanian gull. A sharp wind blew off the sea. Blue-black Black Sea, grey Black Sea. There was a monument to the poet Ovid who had died in exile there.

Sophie told him of how their 'old Queen', Carmen Sylva, had recited her terrible poetry through a speaking trumpet to the ships moored at Constanza. 'I think it was when the Russians planned perhaps to marry their sad imperial Olga or Tatiana Romanov to our Prince Carol. He didn't like how either of them were looking . . . But of course he would have made safe the life of one of them . . .'

On the drive back she sat in the front with him, taking a lot of space. Corina was behind, with her mother. 'He drives too fast,' Ana Xenescu called out suddenly. Then again, louder. He heard Corina soothing her. She was less impatient than he would have been. For that, he admired her.

The Bugatti. Oh, you beauty. Bugatti beauty. She was all he could think of. Her long body, with its great Scintilla head-lamps. Dark blue pigskin upholstery trimmed with softest glove leather. Beautiful wood of the steering-wheel, a stop-watch mounted in its centre: under the spokes near the rim, the four horn buttons . . . Strombos air horns . . .

The Sunday after their return from Constanza there was a luncheon-party at Corina's flat. Ion and Elena went, along with Michael, Mariana and her husband, Stefan, and their children. It was Michael's first visit there. They ate baby lamb roasted with wine and herbs which he found delicious. As a gathering, though, it wasn't entirely a success. The twins were over-excited on arrival. During the meal one then the other rushed out to be violently sick. Their sister Dina preened herself because she hadn't been, and got a telling-off which set her in a rage. Ana Xenescu, sensing a storm, joined in with querulous shouting: 'That's right, naughty boys and girls, that's right, we shall all be punished . . .'

By the time the meal was over and they sat drinking coffee, discussing whether to go for a drive, how to pass the rest of Sunday, the atmosphere was tense.

'Not long now,' Mariana remarked, 'until we go to the mountains. To Sinaia . . .'

All that week it had been hot, oppressive.

'Let's dance,' Corina said impulsively, jumping up, full of energy, eager to carry out the suggestion at once. 'Let's dance – it's almost *thé dansant* time . . .'

He knew she loved to dance. He didn't want to, remembering her taunts at the International. When she took his hand, leading him over to the gramophone, he said, 'I hope you're not going to give me a lesson . . .'

'Lessons are private,' she said. 'And very expensive.' She lifted a pile of six records above the turntable. 'Mikki, please don't be difficult.'

He said sulkily as the voice of Elyane Celis burst into *Piroulirouli*, 'It isn't for you to tell me off. I'm not one of Mariana and Stefan's offspring –'

'Oh absurd, you're absurd.' She put out her arms so that he was forced to clasp her to the music: 'That's better, much better. Arguing, it's so silly . . .'

He shrugged his shoulders in time to the music, smiled – and felt tired.

She said as they danced, 'Did Sophie ever ask you to be kind to me?'

'I don't remember – I don't know . . .'

'Well, if she does, pay no attention. I can look after myself.' Her voice had lost suddenly its flrtatious, bantering tone.

Soon after, Stefan came and took her away. 'We are old dancing partners,' he said. 'Watch us together.' Michael sat on the sofa at the side and talked to Sophie. The twins, recovered, ran in and out of the room playing Catch . . .

That night he dreamed he was in a large room with white walls, simply furnished. He sat drinking something sweet but tart also . . . He was at peace. There seemed nothing odd when Corina appeared suddenly, standing beside him dressed as if for a garden-party. Long white silk crêpe, a jacket trimmed with brown feathers, flowery picture hat worn on the side of her head . . . She sat on the arm of his chair. She didn't talk, or appear to want to. He noticed then that she had for a while been stroking the back of his neck. He didn't try to stop it. He felt her other hand stroke his leg beneath the trouser. 'Do go on,' he said. 'It's quite all right.' She was leaning forward, and he saw down the jacket that there was no real top to her dress. He asked her then if it was all right to touch her breasts. When she didn't answer, he knew that it was – for her hand now moved slowly, oh so wonderfully high, higher, from knee to thigh, inside thigh. Ah, but, he leaned over her breasts . . . I am going to cry, he thought in the dream. Sharp delight woke him. Sound of birds in the little walled garden . . .

'Nicu sends you best wishes from Rio where he is doing good business . . . and hopes you are a friend of his Bugatti, and that you are loving her a lot . . .'

Few letters seemed to come for Michael – he'd been waiting all that week for one. Nothing from Stingo, not even envious congratulations about the motor. From Grandma Lily only a short letter. Teddy, a scrawled card. He remembered he had promised to write to Willow, and resolved that tomorrow he would buy some postcards. He felt a great wave of homesickness.

The next morning they left to spend ten days among the painted churches of Moldavia. He met there friends of Ion and Elena's. Grandchildren for the twins and Dina to play with. Their nurse, a red-faced peasant girl with black button eyes, chased them good-humouredly. When she called them, they ran in the other direction.

His dream: it had stayed with him for two or three days, then grown fainter. It embarrassed him to remember it. Often as he drove the Bugatti he would find himself suddenly thinking of Corina. Wanting to tell her this or that. Wanting her approval – even, he wasn't sure why, her disapproval. He told himself: Really she's awfully nice and fun to be with, so *of course* I want to see her again.

And soon he would. For when he travelled to the Carpathians next week, they would all meet up. Sophie and Ana Xenescu – and Corina, who would stay in the villa which had belonged to her husband, Matei Draganesti.

'This very high Cross up on the mountain top,' Corina said, 'that's a memorial for the Great War. It's made from the remains of bridges destroyed in the fighting . . .'

He looked up at the high peaks, the remnants of snow, the dark patches of green forest. He had been longing for the heights. Mountain air, fresh in the June heat. Mariana had told him that in full summer, Bucharest could be as hot as India:

'The pavements boil and melt, it's unbearable . . . Then we don't eat in the evening until twelve o'clock – often we sit and watch the sun come up. We can sleep away our afternoons . . .'

Here he was now, in Sinaia, with his beloved Bugatti. He couldn't imagine sleeping away afternoons. He was full of energy and excitement. Also Corina was being very sweet and easy. She had not once teased him . . .

Today they were visiting the monastery on a hill outside Sinaia. Bearded monks wearing tall hats. Because she was a woman, Corina was not allowed into parts of the building. They found a memorial to one Take Ionescu, who in 1881 had married an Englishwoman, Bessie Richards, and later had been a hero of the Great War. Corina translated some words of his in 1917: 'I believe in our victory as I believe in the light of the sun . . .'

She said: 'The War was a terrible time . . .' Her scent with its exotic undertones became confused with the remnants of incense, there in the small golden chapel.

'Can you *remember* the War?'

'But of course. I was a young girl . . . You forget I've been here a long time . . .' She shrugged her shoulders: 'But it's all politics. I don't concern myself with that.'

On the hill coming down from the monastery, she stopped the Bugatti and said: 'My brother is buried here.'

They went in together. It was a small cemetery. Most of the graves were in good repair, with fresh flowers in small silver vases. He saw everywhere the word *Eroul*. Hero. She led him over to a grave where there was the photograph of a young man, moustachoied, with a centre parting and a high white collar. 'Lieutenant Xenescu, Mihail . . . 18.9.16.' And the place of death. '*In luptule de pe Vale Cerbului.*'

'I remember when we had the news he'd been killed. My mother . . . My husband, you know, was in the same regiment. He was a Major. He survived that battle, although I'm not sure it was good he did so. A man can have too many wounds.'

It was the most she had ever said about her husband. Coming out of the graveyard now, she shivered as if the air had grown cold. A cart was making its way up the hill. Two young children, feet dangling at the back, waved and called to Michael. She said, 'Your grandmother – she'll have known Mihail. They were all at Sinaia the summer she was there. They stayed at Teodor and Sophie's.'

'Yes,' he said, 'my grandmother told me about the house. Only now there aren't any borzois.'

'A lot of people coming and going,' she said. 'There was another Take, not the one there in the monastery. An anarchist. They used to drink at the Café Napoleon. My brother admired him a great deal. Too much. And Ion's brother, Valentin – Tino . . . oh, but he was *very* good-looking.' She laughed suddenly, lightly, 'Better-looking than you – yes, better even than you, Mikki.'

It was the first time since his arrival in Sinaia that she had needled him. It was over in a moment. As they got back into the Bugatti, she said:

'It's a nice thought in a way, where they've built the graveyard. There used to be dancing there. It was a special meeting place . . .'

He said, 'You don't talk much about your husband.'

'Why should I? He wasn't very interesting.'

From the monastery, a single bell. The sound carried in the high air.

'We go to the Casino this evening,' she said, in her more brittle voice, 'I hope you're going to be *daring*.'

The next day when he drove Sophie over to Corina's villa so that she might sit with Ana for the afternoon, he meant to go straight back.

He saw at once that Corina was in an odd mood. *I am really getting to know her*, he thought suddenly, and then was terrified. He remarked casually:

'You know, I'm really getting to know the Bugatti. She's more than a beautiful body. She's beautiful all through. And when I get inside her . . . the six bearing crankshaft, you see, it's turned from a solid billet . . .' He didn't know the words in French and had to paraphrase.

'Oh dear God,' she said, 'you really are boring.' The hall where they stood was for sitting also: there was a fireplace for damp or chilly days. In a low voice, she said:

'Sophie's going to read to Maman. Maman can follow a story if it's a book she knows. When they're settled, Mikki, stay for a while. Drink . . .

'I was going back –'

She said tartly, 'If you want to go – then go . . .'

As she spoke, the opened the door on his left. He had a glimpse of white walls, a carpet. White and gold furniture, not very much of it, a radiogram, bookshelves. *But this is my dream* . . . A white piano near the window. On it, a large photograph. He thought angrily: *That* wasn't there in the dream . . .

She said, 'You're looking at Matei. My husband. Didn't you see a picture of him in the apartment in Bucharest?'

'No.' This man looked about sixty or seventy – anyway at least *fifty*, and much much too old for her. He felt a wave of nausea. It's disgusting, he thought. Disgusting that someone like that should touch her . . .

'We'll have a drink now,' she said. 'We'll get it ourselves and not ring for anybody. After that, why don't we dance?'

She was hunting through records. 'I don't know,' she said, 'not much of a selection here. I mean every year to bring chic ones with me from Bucharest. Some of these are from Matei's time. Look, Viennese waltzes recorded only one side . . .'

Her scent came towards him. 'Put on something while I'm looking,' she said. Then as the music started, 'I don't like this. It's gypsy music, we can't dance to that.'

He liked the rhythm. He thought it might have belonged to the dancing that had gone on where now the soldiers slept neatly in rows – *Eroul* above them.

She gave a little scream of delight. 'Oh Mikki, look! Something in English –'

He went over. 'No,' she said, 'I can understand. *Little Boy Blue*.'

'No,' he said, '*Blues*.'

'Blue, blues, I shall play it at once. Who is this singing? June . . .'

'It comes from the 'twenties,' he said. 'I've heard of her. Grandma told me. June Tripp was her real name. She became Lady Inverclyde –'

'Your grandmother, she was also a *milady*, wasn't she?'

'Yes,' he said. He paused: 'My mother . . . She came from a farm.'

'Peasant blood, it's good. It's red and healthy. Why not?' she said, putting on the record. She put out her arms so that he would dance with her.

'. . . *Little Boy Blue is far too dreamy . . . He looks but he never sees . . .*'

'It's nice, it's rather chic,' she said. 'It must have been put there specially for us.'

They danced to it three times in all. She tried to pick up some of the words and sang in his ear.

'. . . I've got those little boy blues . . . I'd like to take him, make him open his eyes . . .'

They walked back to the gramophone and he thought she leaned forward to pick up her drink . . .

She was stroking his cheek, his hair, his forehead. 'I'm so lonely,' she said. 'So lonely.'

He said awkwardly, 'You've got lots of friends. In Bucharest anyway. And here too –'

'Oh, it's not that sort of lonely,' she said. 'Mikki, Mikki, look at me, Mikki.'

He didn't want to.

'You mustn't be shy,' she said. 'Are you frightened of me? Is that what it is now, you're frightened? Sit down. Let's sit down and finish our drinks.'

The chair she took him over to was like the chair in the dream. She sat on the arm of it. Her hand was stroking his neck and the back of his head. She ran her hands over his lips. He didn't protest. She buried her head in his neck. Then sitting up again, laughing:

'Which woman is it, Mikki, which *she* is the more beautiful – me or the Bugatti?'

'Comparisons are odious,' he said, 'that's what I was taught.'

She ran her hand suddenly along his thigh on the inside.

When it came to rest he knew it was the dream. Perhaps, he thought, I have brought it about. Willed it. But then it changed from the dream. Her hand didn't rest there. She put it about his arm, pulling him up. She said in a strange voice, lower than usual, urgent:

'Come with me, come, Mikki, please, please.' When he resisted a little, she said, 'You know you want to, you know you do.'

Then, 'Quietly,' she said, 'we must go up quietly.'

The rest, everything else, it was so different from the dream. All he could recognize was the sharp delight which in the dream had brought him from sleep to waking. Now it lasted longer. Happened later.

When she said, 'Let me teach you. I'll give you lessons,' he remembered suddenly about the dancing lessons and how he'd been angry. But these were lessons he could hope for again and again. They lay still, the sweat ran down his forehead. Then she sat up beside him in the bed. The sheet was silk. She pulled it round her. He said:

'What are you trying to hide?' He felt embarrassed to be speaking. She had turned away a little. He saw her bare shoulders above the silk slip. Her heavy-lidded eyes were closed. He said, 'Are you all right? You're sure you're all right?' All he could remember was a violence he had wanted and he thought she had wanted. He told himself: Of course I always knew it wasn't blonde hair . . .

Her hand lay on his belly. He could feel that he stirred again. I would, I would . . . he could think of nothing he wanted so much . . .

A small carriage clock chimed in the room. She gave a little cry. 'We must go, at once. If Sophie should want –'

At the dressing-table he watched as she put on more scent. It was a large flat-fronted bottle, Mitsouko of Guerlain. She said, 'I like this song, this record I found, it was clever of me. We must play it again, Mikki – shall we?'

He couldn't keep his eyes off Corina. His hands. That a few days ago had only thought lovingly of handling the Bugatti. Now I go every day on long journeys . . . learning . . .

'It's easy, Mikki,' she would say to him. 'Now I've shown you, isn't it easy?'

Yes, with her it was. He felt secretive about it. Could

not imagine ever mentioning it to Stingo. He remembered Ferguson Major at school, in his last term, boasting of three nights with a French actress. *But that is not the same thing* . . .

She loved the record. She spoke as if it were that that had brought them together. And she would sing with it, her husky voice beside the neat feminine one of Lady Inverclyde . . .

'. . . *I've got those little boy blues, my heart's right down in my shoes* . . .'

'*My* little boy blue,' she said to Michael.

'*Blues*,' he explained again. 'It's the blues, you know. Misery. Upset . . .'

'Oh *I know*,' she said offhandedly, a little impatiently. 'You're so sweet . . . And so *big* . . .

They lay in bed together, drinking wine. She was eating some small biscuits made of chocolate and walnuts. *Fursecuri*. Every now and then – often to stop him talking – she would pop one into his mouth.

'So *big*. It points up to the sky like a skyscraper. *Gratte ciel*. I never saw anything like it – and it is the first time, truly? I'm the first? That you should be so clever, all without any practice! I show you of course some little details . . . I teach you and then you will always be amazing. A Master. You will be able soon to make any woman happy –'

'But I only want to make *you* happy –'

'Oh you do, you do.' Her voice seemed to him suddenly so humble . . .

The days stretched out. Grandma wrote that Willow was in plaster, after a fall from a horse. Silly kid . . .

Sometimes he wondered if anybody here had noticed anything. Then he realized one day that everyone knew exactly what was happening – and thought nothing of it. One half of him was shocked, deeply. He even heard Stefan refer to him as Corina's *amant*. He wondered if Elena would like him to confide in her. She said once, 'You must always talk to me if something worries you.'

'No, no,' he said, 'there's nothing.'

'I see you're happy,' she said now. 'And that you make – friends.'

When he realized there were only three weeks left, it came

to him as a shock. He had been living in a world without minutes, hours, days . . . He thought: In three weeks *it will all be over*.

Corina said, 'What am I going to do when you've gone, Mikki? Shall I have Little Boy Blues?' She understood now what it meant . . .

'We'll write to each other –'

'Oh, I don't write letters,' she said. 'It's you I need – and *him*.' She looked down to where her hands encircled him lovingly. '*If I could shake him, wake him* . . .'

'Yes,' she said, 'I shall have those little boy blues . . .'

That was the day he told her about the Diamond Waterfall. He didn't mention his family often, and had told her only that his father had been killed and his mother was dead. Now he told her a lot about himself, and about others in the family . . .

She said, 'So this great house will be yours, one day. Do you become a *milord*?'

'The Sir's not hereditary. My grandfather got it for public services . . . Yes, I own The Towers at twenty-one. And of course, the Diamond Waterfall . . .'

She had been most interested in that. He had never given it much thought before. Now she made him describe it – gasping in amazement at *so many diamonds* . . .

'Ah,' she said, eyes open wide, 'what must a woman do to wear this wonderful *parure*?'

But that was easy. It came to him in a flash. The answer to everything. What could be more beautiful, he thought, than to be *always* with Corina? To see her naked – and then to cover her in diamonds. To see them trickle over her white skin . . . To take them off before . . . Best of all to have her beside him always. To be as happy as this for ever. That was what the fever in his blood *meant*: that he should make her happy and never, never lonely again . . .

That night he told himself that his father married before he was twenty. At University there'd been married undergraduates after the Great War. He could ask for his wealth in advance. There was plenty. When she saw The Towers, for all its vulgarity, she would – it would probably be the sort of place she liked . . . Grandma and Erik could continue to live there . . .

In the sun and the high mountain air, two, three days passed. He was at once nervous of asking her and impatient. He couldn't wait to make her happy. He thought he'd like to ask her, not in bed where it might seem obvious, but somehow in a celebration . . .

He told the others, 'I'm taking Corina out for a meal. Partly an early farewell, partly a celebration.' When they asked, 'What of?' he said, 'Does it have to be *of* anything?'

On the way there in the Bugatti, they met travelling gypsies. He saw it as some good omen. Their joint mood was one of absolute gaiety. He told himself: *She knows . . .*

The restaurant was open-air, vine-covered. She had taken a party of them there at the beginning of the holiday. He remembered it as a place where the tables were well separated. He wouldn't want to be overheard.

They ate pastrami and then crayfish with saffron. They drank a very dry Aligote. He was almost too nervous to eat. He felt instead a deep thirst. He said to her, 'You might look sad at my going.'

'I am,' she said, laughing. 'You remember where we were when I told you that. Yesterday. What we were doing . . .'

Then, 'Oh,' she said, 'what am I going to do?' Her face suddenly very solemn. She fingered her wine glass, looking out a little beyond him. 'Life isn't easy, Mikki.'

He started the wrong way, of course. He could have guessed he would do it wrong.

'Corina,' he began. 'You know I'm going to be very rich?'

She said, 'I'm very happy for you. Rich people – sometimes they're happy. I hope you will be . . .'

He said, 'That's not the sort of thing I meant.' He tried again. 'I've told you about the Waterfall. The Diamond Waterfall.'

'Oh yes,' she said, '*that*. So lovely.'

'You remember what you said?'

'What? When?'

'You said the other evening – *You remember where we were.* "What a lucky woman Mikki's wife will be. Diamonds trickling down her. *Lucky*," you said.'

'Certainly she'll be fortunate – and rich.'

'Corina, listen, please. Corina, Corina – now listen to me, *I want you to be that woman* –'

'What ever are you saying?'

'I want you to be . . . I want *you* to wear the Diamond Waterfall.'

She opened her mouth a little.

'Corina darling, I want you to be my wife . . .'

She put her head on one side. 'Oh Mikki – Mikki.' It was a funny little voice.

He said, 'You think I'm not serious?'

'Are you?'

'Corina, don't –' he trembled, felt the sweat grow cold on his forehead – 'don't I look serious? Look, darling, I've thought it all out –' He could hardly look at her as he explained everything. All that he had pictured. Planned.

'You'll like England – and there'll be money enough to travel, to shop in Paris – and Rome and . . . You see, my father married very young, and . . . two of my aunts . . . It's meeting the right person, it's *knowing* . . .' His head was turned away.

An unexpected sound distracted him . . . Yes. No. Yes, she was *laughing* . . . She put out a hand: 'Mikki, you are a funny little boy –'

'What's funny? What do you mean, *funny*?'

'All right, funny *big* boy . . . It's just so –' and she started to laugh again. 'It's just the idea. You, me –'

'Well, what's wrong with *us*?'

'Oh Mikki, it's – absurd, Mikki. Mad. Crazy. You're a dear boy, and of course you make me happy, and we have fun – and we're perhaps a little in love, but – to be *married* . . .'

Cold with anger, he said, 'It is *not* funny –'

'But it is,' she insisted, 'it can't be that you haven't seen . . . we've been having *fun*, that's all, Mikki.'

'Funny,' he said, '*fun*. What about love?'

'Well, what about love?'

'It's what I feel for you. God, it's what I feel for you. And I think, I thought it's what you felt for me. You said –'

'Mikki, darling Mikki, please – your voice down . . . Look, Mikki, of course when people are in bed, and they say it, they mean . . . And I do, I *do* love you – when we are having fun . . .'

He couldn't speak. Couldn't answer her.

'Mikki,' she said, 'it's been a holiday and soon it'll be over. You go back to England, to your university. You forget me. I – forget you. That's all. And our memories are happy.'

'I don't want memories,' he said. 'I want *you.*'

'Oh well,' she said, her voice had an edge of impatience now. 'You can't have me then, can you?'

'But why?' He said it again, like some lesson he couldn't understand, 'Why? I thought you loved me. That all this was *serious*. You said –'

'Mikki, please. We have had a good meal, we are going to have a drive. We go back to the villa, maybe have a little sleep –'

'No,' he said, 'No. Corina, please, please be serious. I love you. I want to *marry* you –'

She stood up from the table. Refastened her hair clasp. Picked up her handbag.

'Where are you going?'

'Look,' she said, 'I go to the Ladies' Room – it's allowed, yes?'

She was gone five or ten minutes. Perhaps she meant him to calm down. He poured more of the wine. Tapped on his glass for the waiter, called out, '*Domnule*!' twice. He ordered a ţuică, then one for her, and more coffee.

She came back. 'What's this? Do we start again?'

'Yes,' he said, 'I want to talk to you. Please, can we talk about it?'

Her voice snappy: 'No, we can't. I thought while I was out there, I thought – Mikki is being a nuisance, Mikki is spoiling it all . . .'

'How can loving you be spoiling it?'

'Listen,' she said, 'listen. How can I say this? Now you know how to do it, what we do together, then really one cunt is as good as another . . . Maybe even, one cock . . .'

He didn't or couldn't answer. She accused him then of sulking.

He paid the bill. He felt strange, his head which had been clouded was now clear. Anger, that he couldn't distinguish from pain . . .

They went out to the Bugatti. There she stood in all her beauty. He thought then: *Something is going to happen* . . .

She got in beside him. He hadn't showed her in. She didn't speak. He started up the Bugatti almost before she had shut the door. She was still arranging some things in her handbag. The car shot forward and everything fell from her lap.

'Mikki,' she said. 'Look, Mikki –'

Oh beautiful Bugatti. Nought to thirty in seconds. They drove towards the afternoon sun.

'Look, Mikki, what's that – you're crazy, that's – you're on the *left* of the road . . .'

Anger growing, he swerved back to the right. They were near a corner. He took it at great speed. The car swooped. She called out, '*Don't drive like that* –'

I want the world to end. The world must end soon. *Soon.* And her with it . . . He drove faster still as the road sloped downwards. The speedometer – seventy-five, eighty . . . On either side were the pine woods.

'*Stop that*! It's much too fast. You're *crazy* . . .'

Her scent. Mitsouko, Mitsouko, came over in waves. She must have put more on when she left him in the restaurant. She was desirable, disgusting, beautiful, she could not mean to be so wicked. *She never said all that, she could not have meant it.*

I shall drive faster and faster. We shall . . . where shall we go? *Something is going to happen.* I shall make it happen. His rage and sorrow terrified him . . . Faster, faster.

Something will happen to her. But it must not. She must be saved. At once. He pulled the car across the road, brakes on suddenly. The tyres screamed. She fell forward – putting out a hand to guard her face.

'My God,' she said, 'You're mad. Save me, God –'

'Get out,' he said, 'you whore. Get out. Out. Whore.'

She was already opening the door. He gave her a push. She stumbled a bit, then, righting herself, stood on the grass edge by the roadside. Her red slashed mouth was open in fear. He banged the door shut.

And away . . . Bottom gear, second, third . . . she can do seventy uphill in third . . . Top gear . . . Foot down. Speedometer rising . . . Eighty, ninety, ninety-five . . . Of course I should be driving on the left. *You drive on the left* . . .

The engine roared in his ears. A hundred, hundred and five, hundred and ten . . .

The sun made a pattern through the trees. A way through the pines. The sun fragmented, like stars.

Oh my God – oh my God, my God . . . *Something is going to happen . . .*

15

Send for Teddy, Teddy to the rescue. It was Sophie who telegraphed Paris: MICHAEL IN MOTOR ACCIDENT STOP NO DANGER STOP PLEASE COME . . . Later, Mother had called from Yorkshire.

She was glad she'd postponed the trip she was planning to the States – she had been about to sail on the *Mauretania* the first of September. Now instead, here she was on the Orient Express . . .

Michael was in hospital in Brasov when she arrived, but the next day came back to Sinaia. A broken arm, cracked ribs, neck injuries, multiple cuts and abrasions . . . It should have been much, much worse. Everyone thought it a miracle he had survived. He had been protected of course by the long bonnet of the Bugatti.

The Bugatti – or what had once been a Bugatti . . . What business had they, she thought angrily, allowing him the freedom of such a powerful animal? The sheer folly of it . . . (Although of course I knew. He enthused enough, in the few letters he wrote . . .)

And then, there was something else. When she spoke to Ion and Elena they were guarded, even enigmatic, looking at each other before speaking. Punctuating remarks: '. . . perhaps he was over-excited. And this motor . . . so easy to go too fast . . . We ask ourselves whether . . .'

'Well, at least he was alone,' she said. 'A passenger would have been killed . . .' The right-hand side of the car, she had seen it. Nothing but buckled twisted metal.

'Oh yes,' Mariana told her, 'it was such a good thing that this friend he was with – you will hear that he was with a family friend – that she wanted to take a little walk, and so got out first . . .'

This was not the way she had wanted to come to Rumania (*if* she had wanted to come to Rumania . . .) There seemed little time for the luxury of emotion about being at last in her father's country. She thought: I learned what I learned too late. When I already had Gib. And now, I no longer want a father.

She met Sophie and liked her very much. It was only when talking to her, giving her loving messages from her mother, that any references were made to the past . . .

'You are my dear Lily's child, I am so *so* happy to meet you . . . Your mother was happy here. I think she took some of Rumania back with her in her heart . . .'

Not only in her *heart*, Teddy thought. She could almost have smiled.

Sophie said: 'She has known such *fine* people here. Men, one man perhaps who was very good –'

Now is my chance, she thought. I can say that I know everything, can ask about this Valentin who loved my mother, *who was my father*. Photographs, memories – Sophie would give me all those if I asked. But somehow, for some reason, it is all too late. I do not even *feel* very Rumanian. And if not here, in what is partly my native country, then where?

I am not even sure that I like Rumanians very much. Individually, yes, although they seem sometimes almost childishly irresponsible. And charming with it. But charm is not enough. Altogether, *en masse*, they will not do . . .

Echoes of what was already happening over too much of Europe. Germany, Italy, Spain. What she learned through conversation (as a family they did not seem interested) of the political situation here, did not reassure her. A king who had abdicated twelve years ago over his affair with the red-haired Magda Lupescu. Divorced by his wife in 1928, then back on the throne in 1930. 'I like being King . . .' he was reported as saying. The same man who as a young prince at the Front in the Great War had been dubbed Carol Bolshevicul and accused of stirring up Socialist agitation, now reigned surrounded by his green-shirted Iron Guard – Fascists all. And everywhere a distinct smell of anti-semitism, boding ill.

She had to speak to Michael after a day or two. Had to voice her suspicions that the accident was not quite what it seemed. But she was all the same surprised when he confided in her, very briefly, head averted as he spoke. I can't bear it, she thought, when he had finished. I can't bear the weight of it all, others' sins added to my own, others' failures, wounds . . . Then she thought cynically: He's young, he'll get over it . . .

She betrayed neither shock nor surprise. Comforting him as best as she could. 'We need never speak of it again,' she said. 'Unless *you wish to* . . .'

She thought perhaps she should meet this Corina. But from the day of her arrival, Corina had been indisposed. A migraine which apparently would not yield to any drugs.

The day before she was to take Michael back, Teddy called on her. She came downstairs wearing a swandsdown wrap. She was utterly charming. Her nephew was a dear boy, she told Teddy.

'Dear Mikki,' she said, 'I think perhaps your family has sent him out too young. This experience he had. It was too much. Such a *big* motor . . . A Bugatti is a very –'

'Ah yes, the Bugatti,' Teddy said. 'Of course . . .'

The next day they left for Bucharest.

16

Michael lay on the swing seat, near the lily garden at The Towers, and thought about his father. Through half-shut eyes he saw the September sun dapple the leaves of an oak. The moors in the distance, a hazy purple.

By the time he'd arrived back from Rumania, Willow, fit again, had been just about to leave for two weeks on the Yorkshire coast. They were taking her to Runswick Bay.

'No, thank you, I don't want to come . . .' What would he do all day in the company of an (almost) fourteen-year-old who might herself be bored? How would he manage, trying to hide his shame, his secret knowledge, his shattered world? And, yes, yes, they had agreed, he probably wasn't well enough yet . . . Left arm still in plaster. Cracked ribs still giving pain. The neck brace uncomfortable. And those ugly facial bruises . . .

He and Willow. Her mishap had been honourable. A fall from a pony, *an accident*. While his . . . He thought: *I meant something to happen* to Corina. The first words he'd said in hospital (he had heard his own voice as if another person spoke), 'Is Corina – Corina's not hurt?' And that, he thought, must have meant that really deep down I didn't want her harmed. It was only my anger – *then*.

She had been loyal, with her story of 'getting out for a walk'. But I didn't want to see her . . .

Lying in hospital in Brasov he'd felt, still stirring amid the shock, the memory of his anger. He did not want to look too close. *What I said to Corina, what she said to me*. And – afterwards. The Bugatti, unleashed . . . I can see the speedometer . . . I pushed her beyond. *Something happened*. She spun and spun . . . Once? A thousand times?

And afterwards, all those *ifs*. If I had been on the right side of the road as I went into the trees . . . If, driving on the left as I did, *she* had been in the passenger seat . . .

Telling Teddy. He didn't want to relive such shame . . . Guilt festered in him all that September. Cambridge, and

Clare College, would not begin till October. He could not imagine his new life. *How shall I manage?* A student, an undergraduate . . .

His father was meant to have gone to Cambridge . . . Perhaps because he himself had been so near to death, he kept thinking of his father and death – and *war* . . .

That word spelled for him his father's lonely death (he had always known it was lonely). His mother – that was different. She had been so strong. Even when he had spoken to her for the last time, and not *known* it to be the last time, she had been strong. She is all right, she is in Heaven, he had always said to himself. And others had told him. Never raging against the waste. Auntie Nellie particularly (dear Auntie Nellie, he thought now – Christmas cards, little notes, and never back to see her), *she* should have raged that both of them had gone, leaving her with the problem that was me . . .

What sort of a person was she, my mother? Who could so easily have laid claim after the War to comfort and care and money – and recognition. She called herself Ibbotson. I thought Ibbotson was my name. 'Michael Isbitton,' I used to say . . . 'Ibbotson', Auntie Nellie would say patiently, correcting me for the *n*th time. Then suddenly I had to become Firth. I was proud of it. That explosive *F*irth . . .

I must have been sturdy, emotionally. Except for sudden bouts of homesickness, I managed the changeover quite easily. Forgot, too soon perhaps, my early life in Devon. Aunt Teddy, immediately mother to me – I could *see* she was family. Showing me photographs of my father, my father at *my age*. A whole new world opened . . . Bewildering. A child in wonderland, I couldn't believe it when they said to me, 'Here is your pocket money,' and there was a whole sixpence to spend . . . Soon after came all those other delights: the giant pedal car, the tricycle, the car that had a sort of engine . . . All the way up to driving the Prince Henry Vauxhall.

Prep school three years later might have been difficult. But it was easy, I liked it, I made friends, I was popular except when I lost my temper suddenly, ferociously. Even then I had people on my side. And how little curiosity, when there's nothing to arouse it, boys of nine show . . . By Winchester I *was* Michael Firth, might never have been Michael Ibbotson. I could hardly remember him myself. And the family, intentionally or not, never bothered to keep fresh the memories I did have . . .

All through those weeks of lying up, he tried to make sense of everything. I love my family, he thought, of course I love them. But it was as if they had chopped off a limb to make him grow stronger, and he had later become used to its absence. *I need to know*, he thought suddenly.

'Tell me,' he said to his grandmother. Question after question, about his father, his mother . . . About his mother's home. The farm . . .

It wasn't that her answers were evasive, just that she did not seem to know very much. She had never been to the Ibbotsons'. Had spoken only a few times to Stephen (my *Uncle* Stephen). Barely knew Olive . . .

Teddy had been the most willing to talk. She told him all she could remember. 'It isn't much. As children, Hal and I fought. And then as soon as possible went our own ways. Sadly, I think now . . . He was often with Stephen – your uncle. And then, there was Jack . . .'

Ah yes, Jack. But that was another story . . . And now there was Christopher Hawksworth. A nice enough chap. But we've never been friends, he thought. Too big an age difference. Straight into the Army from school, and now posted to India. We shan't see him for a while . . . He's anyway too handsome. Surprising he's so nice with it . . .

Willow went back to her convent. He asked questions again. And again. His manner must have been irritating, since it caused Erik to say:

'Be a good chap now and don't keep worrying your grandmother. She's had a big concern already that you have this accident. You mustn't be pressing her more . . .'

Why didn't I ask years ago? he thought. *Why didn't I bother, why didn't I care?*

For a while as a small boy, he had let them read to him from the Andrew Lang Fairy Books – Blue, Yellow, Red, Violet . . . They had all belonged to his father, to Hal Firth. Together with *John Bargreaves Gold* and *The Red Cockade*, they stood on the shelves in his bedroom. They had never really been to his taste. Now, in his present questing mood he took another look. It was no better. These kings, queens, princesses in distress, princes who were tested and won the hand of fair lady, wicked uncles turned into frogs . . . *So what*? A world, his father's, that he could not enter.

And then the Diamond Waterfall (I don't want to think about what I said. What I *did. All that madness* . . .), the priceless Diamond Waterfall lived now in a vault in a bank in York. Grandma did not want to wear it. It waited for him now. But the precious gems in the Stones Room – the very ones that Fräulein had helped herself to and his uncle had been falsely accused of stealing – he had looked at them only a few times in his life. Now he asked suddenly to see them.

Emeralds, rubies, black opals, fire opals, coral, pearl, amber, lapis lazuli, topaz, peridots, citrines, moonstones, sapphires . . . Such beauty . . . It left him cold. Reminded him only of scented bejewelled courtesans (I know where I get *that* idea . . .) Yet one more of his father's worlds he could not enter.

The Ibbotson farm had been called Lane Top. It was on the map, of course. And it would be easy also to ask locally. Perhaps in the Fox and Grapes . . . The Ibbotsons had left it some time during the Great War, he knew. His mother had been already living in Devon when she married his father. He remembered a few times when she'd spoken of her childhood:

'We had this dog Tess. Your Uncle Stephen – he'd take her rabbiting along the walls. How vexed our dad was . . .'

He saw on the map that he could reach it by road the longer way, or from the thicket behind the orchard at The Towers, going uphill and then down again into another valley. He had to decide. A bicycle. The motor. Or on foot – the way his father had usually gone. ('Hal, always wandering off . . .' They had at least told him that.) He decided he was fit enough to do the walk. It was the pain in his ribs he feared most, when he tired. His arm was in a sling now but his neck had still to be in a brace. He felt that it made him literally stiff-necked.

And indeed when he'd been walking nearly an hour, following the stone wall up the hillside, wanting to look back, he had to move the whole of the upper part of his body . . . From where he had reached he could see (*just as my father must have done*) the river winding below, the square church tower, the bridge, the drystone walls criss-crossing the hill . . .

It was a fine day. Just breeze enough to send the small clouds racing. He was going along by the stone wall that separated the grazing land from the moor. Up and up. For a while he followed a small beck. Pebbles gleamed in its clear water. Up on the high moor – blobs of grey-white – sheep were being rounded up . . .

And into the next valley. Down a grassy lane. Up again. A cow house in a walled field – the upland meadow where hay was gathered. A mile, half a mile away?

Smoke came from the farmhouse chimney. A dog barked and barked. Just outside the cobbled yard a rowan tree, heavy with red berries. The dog, a collie, could be seen now – angrily barking still.

His feet seemed to ring on the cobbles. He wondered about stroking the dog, or trying to calm it, when a voice called,

'Down – hush . . . give over, Glen . . . Hush!'

In the doorway: a bald, middle-aged man with a friendly face. He said to Michael, 'Don't mind t'dog. He's a soft bugger.' Then:

'Who'll you be, eh?'

'I'm Olive Isbitton – I mean *Ibbotson*'s son.' He felt confused, unhappy . . .

'And I'm Thwaites, Tom Thwaites. If you'd not told me, I'd have said you were the Firth grandson. From The Towers, aren't you?' And when Michael hesitated:

'You'll come in, then? We're all at our tea . . . The wife, she's over Richmond way . . . There's our lads here, though. And him, by the fire – the wife's father . . .'

The two sons had brown hair – much more of it than their father. They sat in shirtsleeves, putting away large doorsteps of bread, smiling, acknowledging Michael with their mouths full. The old man by the fire had one tooth only, which he bared at Michael in a pleased grin.

Tom said, 'Been in t' wars, have you?'

'A car accident – abroad.'

'Well, that should larn you to stay home. Them as went off to fight in Spain, they'll agree. When I seen you, knocked about like that – I thought: Maybe he's one of them . . .'

He said to his sons then, 'This likely lad – his mam used to live here. Twenty year since.' Sitting at the table, sleeves rolled up, he told Michael:

'I'd not have minded wedding her missen – your mother. She were the best cook . . .'

They had just finished their tea. (No, he didn't want any, thank you. Although it looked good, so good . . .) Earlier in the afternoon Tom and his sons had been on the moor gathering up the wethers to take to Settstone market tomorrow.

He was shown around the farmhouse. The dairies, whitewashed, smelling of fresh milk. A bedroom: 'When I were first here,' Tom said, 'this were mine. Afore, it were your Uncle James's, that he'd to share with Stephen and Will, I think they called him . . .' The bigger room upstairs had been Michael's grandparents'. There was also a little cupboard bed Tom showed him.

'Your man were there when she were a small un. Arthur that was with us in wartime, he slept there a while. Went to New Zealand, did Arthur. 'Twenty, 'twenty-one . . .'

He liked to think of his mother – Olive – running from room to room. Carrying great jugs from the dairy, baking in the kitchen, cooking for all those menfolk . . . Yes, they told him, much of the furniture was the same. The dresser, some of the china, the fire tools. The flagstones . . .

He was thinking he should leave, when Tom said:

'I've a few things put away I'd not the heart to throw out. Your man's. You'd best have them . . .'

He wasn't sure what he'd expected . . . Something secret, hidden in this cardboard box, which would alter his whole life?

They were school books. Little problems about yards of lace and pounds of sugar. Handwriting exercises (*Monday's child is fair of face, Tuesday's child is full of grace* . . .) A composition: *A Summer's Day.*

. . . *Tim and Pat O Rork come from Kery in Irland to help our dad with the hay, they like a feest and to drink a lot of beir when it is al over* . . . Olive Ibbotson, aged ten years and 4 months, 15th September 1907 . . .

Thirty years. The space of thirty years. And it's not just the world that has changed . . .

'You'll tak a sup with us? There's ale at the back –' But he didn't want to stay . . . He thanked them. Excused himself . . .

He made his way home, almost at peace. Twice he found himself smiling, in spite of his extreme fatigue.

'I'm very tired,' he said when he got back. He went to bed without any supper.

'That's not like you,' Erik said.

'I'll be fine in the morning . . .'

He was. No sooner upstairs, no sooner between the sheets, than deep, deep sleep. Dreamless too. The best sleep he'd had since the accident.

I know, he thought in the morning, I know who Michael Ibbotson Firth is . . . It might even be possible to live with him . . .

17

Any umbrellas, any umbrellas, to mend today . . .

That song follows me, Willow thought, hearing it come from the open door of a small house near Flaxthorpe church. The wireless turned up loud. A man in his shirtsleeves playing with a kitten.

He'll mend your umbrellas and go on his way, singing toodle looma looma, toodle ay . . . A sunny September day. A war that might break out any moment. There was a Crisis: Mr Chamberlain had been twice already to Germany to meet Herr Hitler.

Tomorrow, she went back to Our Lady of Victories. It could not be escaped. It would be her fifth term there. And she had to admit that in fact her first year had ended better than it began. For after the days in the infirmary, there'd been the friendship with Aunt Alice. (Never, never would I have thought, looking at that face, that here was someone who would understand so *exactly*.) Then at long last, end of July 1937, the summer holidays . . .

Flaxthorpe, Grandma, Erik. And no Michael . . . When he did arrive back after his terrible accident and brush with death, he was nothing like as awful. Quite nice, in fact. A bit quiet, going off for solitary walks. He wasn't even motor-car mad any more . . .

The convent, though, had had to be faced again that September. She had wanted to curl up in a little ball and hibernate. In the end she'd managed it by stages. (I've lived through a day, a week, a *month* . . .) The class work was easy: she'd caught up with everything. And the girls were just possible. By being around she'd grown acceptable. She couldn't say she was popular but at least the heat was off.

Christmas 1937 she'd been lucky. She became ill. Too ill to go back to the convent. Only a septic throat to begin with – but then, oh joy, the throat no sooner healed and her temperature down, than she had stomach pains. They turned out to be sub-acute appendicitis, which one night became suddenly acute. By the time she'd been operated on and convalesced there wasn't enough term left to make a return worthwhile.

She caught up again with the work in the summer. She was able to keep going because of the treat that awaited her: a visit to Canada to see the little ones and dear Aunt Bar.

Then just three days before she sailed, she lost any good will she might have had from the nuns by her performance in the school play, *Murder in a Nunnery*. (The subject-matter hadn't worried her – it had none of it anything to do with real life.) Joanna Mays and her friends had held auditions. All Willow's class wanted to be in it. The play's heroine, Verity, a convent pupil who got in the way of all the investigations, was the big speaking part. Willow wanted it, but it went to Chrissie. They told her she was to play one of the nuns instead. Joanna said Deirdre had seen her doing a *scrumptious* imitation of Mother Ursula, and would she please do it for the play? She did. And frightened herself in the process. She was so exactly Mother Ursula . . .

Afterwards she had asked Aunt Alice, 'Did I – was I a bit *too* much?' And Aunt Alice had answered tactfully, 'You should have met your uncle – he could take off *anyone* . . .'

They had known. The Reverend Mutt in her speech afterwards: little digs, allusions. I should have left out Mother Ursula's sniff, she thought, and the way she scratches the dandruff under her veil with a fingernail. And the spit, lots of it, that gathers when she has a sentence of more than about twelve words . . . In rehearsals she'd moderated herself. On the night there had been no stopping her. A few girls thought she'd gone too far. 'Just because your grandma was an actress . . .'

Her report was terrible. A potential bad influence, must be more serious and responsible in her attitudes; Willow's head is easily turned – in the wrong direction. Mother Ursula had contented herself with, 'A disappointing performance.' Others might think the reference was to Geography, but Willow knew . . .

Canada was wonderful. Just to be with the little ones again . . . But she had had to remember to take care – for after all Aunt Bar, dear as she was, was Reggie's sister. Certain things could not be said. When the talk skated near *the terrible thing*,

Aunt Bar would cleverly, and with a laugh usually (she was a happy person, and easy, and she made the little ones so happy), move on to something else.

But underneath all the time was the sadness. It wasn't possible, ever, to forget. It was there. And she never knew when it would surface to blacken a day, a night. The best, this year was that she had been able, once or twice, to talk about it with Aunt Alice. 'I'd like to know something, anything about my father. I'd like –' but she was never sure what it was she would like. For him to walk through the door? And be seen to be horrible? And wicked, because he had left Mummy with all the worry . . . Some people thought that was a smear, made up by awful Aunt Angie at the trial. I know otherwise. I *don't look like Reggie.*

She had heard while she was in Canada that Aunt Alice was ill. A cough she'd had during the summer had worsened and they were afraid for her lungs. 'My mother was consumptive,' she wrote, 'but since she was no blood relative of yours, *you* mustn't fear . . .'

Willow's birthday had been while she was in Canada. Yesterday she had had another celebration at The Towers. The dread of returning hung over the tea-party like a thick fog. Her throat felt choked. Upstairs sat the big green trunk, its trays already full of regulation blue blouses, gym tunic, hockey boots, shin pads, navy blue knickers, white knicker linings . . .

'Here come the bee's knees *and* the camel's hips – Willow Gilmartin you've grown disgustingly taller – Look, everyone, Willow's got *freckles* – Didn't you bring us back a Mountie? *Have* you seen the air raid shelter? The Reverend Mutt had it all organized before . . . Chrissie's brother's in the Air Force . . .'

She'd been right to feel doom. When she asked for Mother Hilda ('My aunt' brought only the response, 'I think you mean Mother Hilda, Willow . . .), there seemed a conspiracy of silence. Then Mother John told her that her aunt was in Switzerland, in their house in Sion. East Anglia was too damp, too chill. The doctor had said . . .

Why no letter, though? She wrote one herself immediately and gave it to a girl going out to tea with her parents the first weekend of term. She wrote to Grandma too, asking did *she* know if there was anything to worry about?

The first week or two the days were sunny, it could still have been summer. She thought she might manage somehow. One way of making things bearable at night-time was to read down the bed with a torch after lights out. Geraldine, who had the end bed and was very moody, had smuggled in a lot of detective novels. When she was felling sweetptempered she would lend Willow one. Like *Murder in a Nunnery*, they weren't *real*, had nothing to do with what happened to *people*, to Mummy, to Reggie . . . Agatha Christie, Dorothy Sayers, Nicholas Blake, Margery Allingham . . . Snuggled down, half afraid of the shadows in the silent dormitory, she read herself into sleepiness.

Lessons. She waited always for them to become interesting. The monsoon countries, the tundra, the Repeal of the Corn Laws, causes of the French Revolution, past definite and pluperfect of *dire*, *recevoir*, *pleuvoir* . . . She would find herself half way through a class not realizing which subject she was studying. All were covered in a uniform greyness. The coming of winter, scurrying of leaves in sudden autumn gusts . . .

'Willow – Willow Gilmartin – step out here, please. No, up to the dais. Willow, perhaps you would like to tell us what you find so amusing about the Seven Sacraments? The rest of the class, who with the exception of Priscilla are Catholics, want to know what you find so mirth-provoking. Your own church is sadly lacking in sacraments by comparison, could it be that you are jealous?'

'Yes – I mean *no*, Reverend Mother.'

'Take that smirk off your face, please – at once, Willow. And come and see me after prep this evening . . .'

'Willow Gilmartin, what is your explanation for not wearing a veil at Benediction? An uncovered head, even of a non-Catholic, is an insult to the Blessed Sacrament . . .'

'My veil blew out of my hand when I was opening the dormitory window, Mother.'

'. . . Reverend Mother, I have had to give Willow Gilmartin five bad conduct marks. The most any girl has had this term . . . Willow is not to sit in the library with the juniors, Mother John considers her a bad influence. . . . Willow answered Sister back in the laundry . . . went for a walk outside the school grounds . . . had three trashy novels hidden under her mattress . . . hasn't handed in her ordnance survey map to Mother Ursula . . .'

It was difficult, almost impossible to be alone unless you were ill. She walked out of the gates one afternoon, and half a mile to the next village – where she sat in the Protestant church. It had medieval wall paintings of devils with forks and gleeful expressions.

She'd brought with her, her favourite photograph. In it Mummy was about seventeen and very, very beautiful: her hair shining and thick, and the expression on her face so sweet that anyone – anyone – who saw her would want to love her. *My father* must have known her then, she told herself. Sometimes she imagined Mummy saying, 'I love you, I love you,' to this shadowy person. Laying her head on his shoulder. Mummy would have inherited the Diamond Waterfall if it hadn't been for Michael. (How beautiful she would have looked . . . But she had told Willow she never wanted it.) She shut her ears now to the memory of Reggie drunk. That ugly, angry voice coming up the stairs . . .

She sat there a long time just feeling peaceful. Around her, Harvest Festival fruits, grains, flowers . . . She put two sixpenny pieces in a box for the upkeep of the paintings and bought a booklet about them. When she got back to the convent they were going in to tea after hockey. She was in trouble, and got another bad conduct mark.

No letter came from Aunt Alice. But she heard from Michael which surprised her – and gave her a nice warm feeling. That he should have bothered . . .

> I really like it here, even better than before. Second year has everything. Cambridge looking very fine just now. I'll have to arrange for you to visit – maybe in the summer? Have been wondering about trying to do some acting, ADC or Mummers (Grandma coming out?) Trouble is it can easily take up all your time if you're not careful. I expect I shan't bother – I'm a lazy so-and-so . . . Guess what? One of our American cousins is here! Ex Harvard and doing I think international law at Peterhouse. Any-

way there was a note for me at the porter's lodge. I expect to meet him some time . . . And now a quick line to Stingo – I might go over to the Other Place (Oxford!) for a visit, if I can't persuade him here . . .

She became ill again. This time it was miserable. Her bladder. It began with a terrible burning pain and then there was blood as well so that she had to go and speak to Mother Vincent in the infirmary. The doctor was sent for. He said it was cystitis. Her grandmother was telephoned, and as a result she heard she was to stay in the infirmary for at least a week. They were afraid for her kidneys. It had been something to do with kidneys that had killed Mummy.

Betty and Maureen came up to see her. They said that Mother Ursula was very cross because Willow still hadn't handed in her ordnance survey map. 'Honestly, *do* get it done. She's being really frightful on account of you. I'll lend you my mapping pen if you like. And here's some Turkish Delight . . . Hard luck you're going to miss half-term.'

Homesickness hit her suddenly. It was just as she'd felt that first term, only worse. It came in great waves – it was truly named sickness. And now she would *miss half-term as well*. Grandma sent a parcel of tuck, but she had no appetite. The chocolate cake smelled of home and The Towers and was too precious to eat. The pain in her bladder was almost gone, the bitter medicine which burned her mouth dry almost finished . . . In two days the week would be up.

Mother Ursula came to see her. Willow had the map ready. It lay on the wide bedside table, together with the framed photo of the little ones, taken with Ludwig on Jessica's knee.

She was looking at the photograph of her mother when the nun came in. By staring hard she could imagine Sylvia Firth, young girl, at The Towers. See her lips move, hear her voice – younger, brighter . . . It was like travelling in time . . .

She put her hand over it when she heard Mother Ursula. *Don't let her see*. She turned back the sheet to cover it.

'I did the map, Mother. I'm sorry it's late. I've been in here –'

'The delay was long before that, Willow. You can hardly use illness, if it *is* illness, as an excuse . . .'

'It's not worth a visit to the infirmary just to tell me that –'

'Willow, I have already put up with an unprecedented amount of impudence from you . . . Nor is malingering attractive. It seems that whenever you wish to escape class work, you take to your bed. Is that not the truth?'

I shan't answer her, Willow thought. No answer is the best answer of all . . .

The spit had gathered at the corners of Mother Ursula's mouth:

'Did you hear me? You are perfectly fit, and should be back in class.' She stooped and peered at Ludwig and the little ones. 'Those are your sisters, Willow?'

Willow turned her head away. Please God make her go . . .

'I see we are not even civil enough to reply to a question. If you cannot take a reprimand . . . I notice also there is no photograph of your mother. I have never seen one in the dormitory . . . The other girls . . .'

'I don't want a photograph of her there. That's why.'

'Why ever not? Your own mother . . . Willow, my child –'

'I said I *don't want a photograph of her there.*'

'It's usual to add "Mother" when addressing me. I've had to speak of this before . . . Willow, I read the trial, your mother's trial. I know everything. I know it in all its sordid details –' Spit landed on the sheet. 'You should be praying for her, Willow. Even as a non-Catholic, you have learned surely to pray? Why not put out a photograph and show the world that you are not ashamed of her? For you are, are you not? Is that not the reason why we never see her? You too could be a sinner of that sort. Anyone, anyone can fall in that way.' She grew more and more impassioned. Carried away by her rhetoric. 'You *are* ashamed of her, aren't you? You should be ashamed of that shame, Willow –'

The words were like sharp pointed stones. Pain stretched tight across Willow's throat.

'*Ashamed*, Willow!'

She is sick, Willow thought. It is she who should be in the infirmary . . .

Mondays, Wednesdays and Fridays were hockey days. Sometimes Mother Benedict took them, wearing leather boots and with the skirt of her habit tied up. The weather had turned colder. Willow's hands were stiff and sore as she tightened the laces of her hockey boots. Chilblains already on three of her fingers . . . She felt tired all the time. And sad.

They had made her play wing first, then centre forward because with her long legs she could run so fast. Dribbling the ball, faster, faster, pass to Maureen who passes to Geraldine who passes to Chrissie who trips and falls headlong . . . Oh gosh, what miserable bad luck, oh *bad luck*, Chrissie . . .

The afternoon was raw and she caught her breath painfully as she ran. When the whistle sounded across the pitch, she was reminded suddenly of prison. Her mother had been in prison. The last time they took me to see her, she was in the prison hospital. *She died in prison* . . .

Armistice Day came and went. In the two minutes' silence in the big classroom, she thought of Uncle Hal whom she had never known, of Uncle Gib who had survived prisoner of war camp only to die of Spanish 'flu, of Teddy who had never married again . . . She thought of all the sadness in her family and in herself and could not bear it . . .

She was in trouble with the nuns almost every day now. Her sadness taken for sulks, her pent-up misery for impudence. She found she could not remember, even if she'd wished, the lists of this and that – Corn Laws, Polonius' advice to Laertes, the principal exports of Malaya. Mother Ursula watched her all the time.

I cannot go on. She remembered often Michael and his kind letter. Dear, dear Michael, who was *family* . . .

It was Betty's birthday next Saturday and her parents were taking her out to lunch. 'Mumsy says I can bring someone. We're going to the Angel at Bury St Edmunds and then on home. Who's coming? Eeeny meeny miney moe catch a nigger by his toe . . . Willow, it's you . . .'

Geraldine lived at Bury St Edmunds and often went home on Saturdays. She'd invited Willow twice. Willow told Betty: 'I won't stay for the weekend. I'll go on to Geraldine's for tea. Her parents can bring me back.'

She hadn't seen Mr and Mrs Lewin since the opisode of Tootles in her first term. Mr Lewin teased her about it now. The smelly setter Farmer was still there in the car. She wore her school mac over her navy blue Sunday dress and had been allowed to wash her hair because of the outing. Also, she could have it loose. The plaits made it very wavy. She had ten shillings pocket money with her, the remainder of the pound she had for the term. Betty had said they might shop afterwards.

At the Angel at Bury St Edmunds when she had just been served with some mushroom soup, she stood up: 'Excuse me, I need to go to the Ladies' –'

'But you went when we arrived,' Betty cried indignantly. 'Mumsy, she's just *been* –'

Her mother murmured something and her father said, 'Manners, Miss Elizabeth.'

She went straight to Reception, then changed her mind. They would remember her, later. She walked a few yards down the street, trying not to shiver in her serge dress. In a newsagent's, she asked, 'Can you tell me anything about trains to Cambridge?'

They had taken her soup away to keep it warm. 'I'm awfully sorry,' she said, sitting down again. 'I haven't been very well.'

'Willow's always in the infirmary, Mumsy,' Betty said. 'Because she's *infirm*, you see.'

'Ha, ha,' said Willow with a sudden burst of spirit. She felt an enormous sense of excitement. And yet was so tense . . . she could scarcely eat the large vanilla and strawberry ice she felt forced to order.

When they had drunk coffee in the lounge and talked for a while, Willow said she would go on to Geraldine's.

'Are you sure you're fit enough?' Mrs Lewin asked.

'Yes, yes,' she said hastily. 'And I know which house it is, thank you.'

Betty said, 'Table tennis. I bet my big present's a ping-pong table. *Is* it a pingpong table, Mumsy?'

As soon as she left them, Willow went to the post office. She sent a telegram to the convent: WILLOW GILMARTIN REMAINS WEEKEND WITH US NO REPLY NECESSARY GOOD WISHES LEWIN.

At Geraldine's home she told them, 'I just came in to say thank you very much, I've decided after all to spend the weekend at Betty's. I expect they'll lend me a sponge-bag . . .'

A few yards from the house she broke into a run. When she

reached the station she was breathing heavily and there was a pain near her appendix scar.

She'd pushed her horrid distinguishing school scarf down into the top of her mac. It gave her an odd-looking bust.

'The Cambridge train?' A porter pushed her through. There wasn't time to buy a ticket. A fat woman puffing even more heavily, hurried through with her. They looked as if they were together.

Once sat down, she shook. To still herself, and to feel safer, she shut her eyes and feigned sleep.

Long, long station platform. Long, long straight road leading from it. No sign of a university . . . 'Excuse me, could you tell me which bus goes nearest to Clare College, please?'

Even when she got off the bus, she had to ask twice. It was dark now which made it more difficult. I must not appear remarkable, she thought, as she came to the porter's lodge.

The porter had his back to her. 'Where do I find Mr Michael Firth, please? I should know – I forgot . . .' She clutched the brown leather purse in her pocket, playing with the fastening.

He turned his head: 'C staircase, miss. Left. He came in just ten minutes ago –'

How could she have been so stupid? If he had been *out* . . . Could she have said he expected her and asked to wait? It'll be all right, she told herself. Once I'm with Michael, it'll be all right . . .

She crept up the wooden staircase. And knocked.

When he came to the door it was his feet she saw first. He was wearing the dark green house slippers she remembered from home.

'Christ Almighty. *Willow* . . .'

'I'm a surprise, Mike, I –'

'Anyone else from Our Lady of V? Is it some poisonous school excursion?'

She had meant to throw her arms round him. *Dear* Mike. But it wasn't working out like that . . .

'You'd better come in. And explain –'

'Have you had any tea?' he asked as he closed the door behind them. 'I was just going to make a pot. Though it'll be Hall in less than an hour. I've some crumpets somewhere . . .'

'I had a big lunch, thank you.'

The room had a plump chesterfield, brown leather, buttoned. She sat down stiffly on it.

'I'll put the kettle on all the same.' She glimpsed a small room. Sink, gas-ring. 'And now – as you were explaining?'

'I haven't. It's rather difficult . . . I want to stay with you. Here, in your college. Till –'

'You must be crazy.'

'Only for a few days, Mike. Just till – I need to be away, I need –'

'Too bad, Cousin Willow. Too bad. Whatever you need . . . I mean, come up to tea, OK, but you can't . . . Christ. You can't *sleep* here.'

'Just hide me a couple of days, Mike. *Please.* I –'

'But it's a *ghastly* risk for me . . . Can't you go to a hotel or something or get a train up home? Why run away from the wretched place in the first instance?'

'I just . . . I couldn't be there another *moment* –'

'It came on rather suddenly, didn't it?'

'They . . . Listen, Michael, this is the sort of thing they do, I can't bear –'

'Hang on. The kettle –'

When he came back she tried to tell him something of what she'd been feeling. But despair, she thought, can't be talked about. Only felt. And worse, she began to cry.

'Not content with turning up like a bad penny, you're going to drown me as well . . . Look here, Willow –'

But he must have had a kind heart because he toasted her some crumpets as well as giving her tea.

'I don't know what else you'll get to eat. You can hardly come down to Hall . . .'

'I can stay, then? You mean I'm staying?'

'If you won't go I haven't any choice . . . But, God, you'd better keep your head low . . .'

His black gown lay the other end of the chesterfield. He dragged it on, then went through to the bedroom and changed the house shoes. In the gown, he looked a different person.

'And for God's sake, stay put. Don't answer any knocks. I'll shut the outer door, sport my oak so no one will . . . If you want the lavatory or anything –'

The doors banged behind him. A minute later, he rushed in again. 'Look, if you get peckish . . . I mean, lunch must have worn off and you're going to need *something*.'

'I'm all right, Michael. Honest.'

'There's some fruit cake Grandma sent in a tin somewhere, and some savoury things from GP Jones . . .'

'I'm OK,' she insisted. When he'd left again, his gown flying behind him, she sat a few moments, eyes shut. Waves of fear, of *might have been* swept over her.

Of what might yet be . . . Even now they could be distrusting the telegram, checking it. The *search may be on.* She felt a mixture of light-headed fatigue and restlessness, and after a little she got up and began to pace the room. The rug on the stained oak floor, she recognized from home. In the bookshelf were some of the books from his untidy, warm, confused room at The Towers. She went through into the bedroom. Everything quite neat, for Michael. A huge wardrobe, a washstand by the window.

Coming back, she put some more coal on the fire, got coaldust on her fingers and wiped them vigorously on her school dress. At least she wasn't wearing her horrid gym tunic . . . As it was, the dress had this wretched Our Lady of Victories badge sewn right over her heart. In the bedroom she'd seen a Fair Isle pullover. She slipped it on. Although much too big across the chest, it wasn't bad for length.

In the bedroom she thought she heard a knock at the door. Don't answer, Michael had said . . . But a man already had his head round the sitting-room door. He saw her.

'Hi – I was looking for Mike . . .' He wasn't quite as tall as her. He had a lively, bony face and moved quickly. He spoke with an American accent. He too wore a gown.

'He's in Hall? Right, can you give him a message? I feel bad *barging* in, but well, I guess the outer door was open so . . . Can you tell him, please, his cousin Jay came by and that the girl I was bringing tomorrow, she's had to go away for the weekend. I figured he'd need to know for the numbers . . .'

As he spoke she thought he looked oddly at her face. She tried to change her expression to a more grown-up one.

Curling her lip. Her hands with their bitten nails lay in her lap.

As soon as he left, her quaking began again. She wanted too to go to the lavatory. When Michael came back she would have to ask about that. Then the terrifying thought came to her: Perhaps he had not really gone down to eat in Hall? Perhaps he had gone to book a telephone call to Crandma, or the convent? She could not bear it.

They have telephoned, she thought. The convent has telephoned Betty's home to say it isn't all right and they are a little surprised, Geraldine's father has told Reverend Mother he thought it odd nothing was said to *him*, *he* would have given the message, Geraldine's parents have telephoned Betty's . . . Oh please, dear God . . .

She ate some of the fruit cake, using the lid of the tin as a plate and throwing the crumbs in the fireplace.

When Michael came back, she said:

'Your cousin dropped in. He –'

'Look, what did I *say*? I must have left it not shut . . . Christ, you didn't *tell* him anything, did you? Didn't turn on the waterworks –'

She was hurt, but dignified. 'I just took a message for you, that's all. He obviously thought I'm your girlfriend –'

'Girlfriend, my foot . . . As if anyone would – in that get-up. Smuts too or something, all over your face.'

'It must be coal,' she said. Embarrassed. 'And I'm sorry, I borrowed your pullover.'

'That's all right. Mustn't let you catch cold.' He made the fire up again. 'Well, what *was* the message?'

When she'd told him: 'Dimwit,' he said, 'I suppose you didn't realize he's *your* cousin too . . .'

Emotion, upset, fatigue, must have thickened her brain. She felt stupid.

'I'm sorry, really –'

'Forget it. Jay's all right as they go, but a bit electric. Live and all that. Quite keen, though, to be friends.'

'I thought he looked nice.'

'Great-aunt Daisy. One of her daughters' sons. Don't ask me which . . .'

'What's the party tomorrow?'

'I'm giving it with another chap in his rooms. They're

larger. I expect it to be quite a good thrash. One girl the less isn't serious . . .

'Have you got a girlfriend?'

'Wouldn't you like to know?' he said, but not unkindly. 'No, thank you. As it happens . . .'

They sat a few moments. He leafed through a magazine. She asked for the lavatory: it was quite a way away and oddly enough was called Lady Clare.

'If they do look for you,' he said, 'I bet they'll think of here first. I mean, they're not going to think it's an abduction, when you laid the false trail yourself.'

'Someone else could have done that,' she said. 'My kidnapper.'

'Oh, who'd want to ransom you?' he said irritably. Then immediately repentant: 'Are you sure – about eating? We could slip out to a café . . . Or I could have something sent up . . .'

'I'm not hungry, *honestly*.'

'I've told someone,' he said. 'The friend who's giving the thrash with me. Chas. He'll be up later and we'll have coffee.'

Chas had flashing eyes and teeth which showed a lot of pink gum. He seemed amazed at the whole business. 'It's very Naughtiest Girl in the Fifth, Madcap Maisie and all that. Poor Michael's scared out of his wits. I've told him not to worry. We'll look after you . . .'

While Michael was filling the percolator, he said:

'She's coming to our thrash, I take it?'

'God, no. Sunday. It's just when they'll be starting their search . . .'

'Best thing. Hide her in a crowd . . .'

Michael said reluctantly, 'I suppose we could dress her as a man. Boy anyway. I don't know. It's all *mad*.'

Willow burst into tears.

'Whoops,' he said, 'there she goes again . . .'

She woke almost every half-hour in the night. A clock struck outside with a high-pitched tone. Footsteps up and down the staircase. Footsteps beneath her window. Voices. Once a burst of singing . . .

She lay in her liberty bodice, vest, and blue knickers and linings. She kept her woollen stockings on too though the suspenders poked a bit. She had Michael's bed. He'd insisted, saying he would sleep on the chesterfield. 'I'm OK. Just *you* don't go wandering out of the room . . . *For anything*.'

After a while she heard him snoring. He coughed at intervals too. She wished she hadn't drunk the coffee which she thought was keeping her awake. And filling her bladder. If she were to catch again that awful complaint which had kept her in the infirmary . . .

In the morning she was looking out, her hand on the curtain, when Michael rushed in. Pulling her by the arm, he opened the wardrobe and pushed her inside.

'Ssh,' he went, '*Ssh*,' his face looking agonized.

She crouched in the wardrobe which smelled tweedy and a little sweaty. She daren't move in case she fell against the door and pushed it open. She heard a woman's voice:

'All right if I come in, Mr Firth, sir? Had your breakfast, have you?' Her voice was louder than Michael's. Willow thought she would never go. She sighed and puffed as she went about the room. 'Bed'll be done in a jiffy, Mr Firth . . .' Then Michael saying: 'I hadn't wanted you to bother this morning . . .'

When he opened the wardrobe door suddenly, she almost fell out.

'Phew!' he said. 'That was my bedder. I'd meant to get you out somehow or hide you – but I overslept. In spite of the discomfort. And you?'

'Oh, I slept *very* well.'

She was raw with fatigue, sick, empty and more frightened today than yesterday. Very soon she was going to have to think, be calm, make a decision. Chas came down to see about the party. He and Michael wanted simply to put her on a train for York. Telephoning home first. Obstinate with panic, she refused. She felt even less able to leave Michael's room.

During the day they were busy with their party. They brought her food which she tried to eat. Every now and then one of them would put a hand to his head and say,

'We'd better do something about all this. It's . . . she's a real problem. Tomorrow she's positively absolutely *got* to go.'

She felt weakly obstinate. 'They can come and get me.'

'It's putting my whole Cambridge career in jeopardy, your cussedness,' Michael said.

Chas (the very one who'd said last night, 'We'll take care of you,') said now, 'I suppose we could turn her in?' He no longer seemed to find it a joke. To Michael it had *never* been one . . .

The party began about eight. They'd never meant seriously that she should come to it. She thought of going to bed and burying her head under the sheets and *forgetting*. But when she'd been alone in the sitting-room for about half an hour she grew uneasy. Betty would be back at the convent by now. Perhaps the search had already begun?

Her school dress looked even more awful today. She saw there were food stains on the skirt. She sponged them off in the gyp room. In Michael's chest of drawers she found a penknife and cut away the convent badge. The dress looked worse without it so she took another of his pullovers, a smaller one this time. Then she washed her face. Her hair was still wavy from the plaits. She brushed it with one of his brushes. Then she felt light-headed and thought perhaps she should eat: she took some of Grandma's fruit cake and a glass of water.

Then she set out up the staircase, following the sounds of voices, laughter, music . . .

'Hullo, hullo, hullo, and who is *this*?' She was taken firmly by the arm and whirled into the room by a man with glasses and hair like a dishmop. She thought he might be a little tiddly.

Clinking of glasses, babble of voices. Faces blurred and merged . . .

'Blooming Naiad,' the man with the dishmop head told her, 'that's what you are.'

Chas had seen her. Michael too. In a minute he was by her side. He whispered in her ear:

'For heaven's *sake*! What are you doing? And my yellow pullover –'

'It looks nice,' she said cheekily.

'Kid sister, you look a real kid sister.' But once again he didn't go on being angry for long. He found her a glass of lemonade, then introduced her to a group of people over in a corner, whispering first, 'You're on your own now and serve you right . . .'

'My Cousin Willow,' he told them, 'she's staying with friends nearby to do some riding.' (*How could he*?) 'Hence the absence of party togs . . .'

They were very nice to her. She steered the talk away swiftly from horses. Remembering that Tootles had been a cow-kicker, she said, 'It's been a sickening weekend, too dreary for words . . . My mount was a cow-kicker. I just can't *bear* to talk about it.'

She hoped they wouldn't guess she was only just fifteen. One of the men kept calling her 'fair coz,' leaning towards her: 'How like you this, fair coz? What think you of that, fair coz?' She found it very trying. Mostly she let the conversation flow round her. In another corner a radiogram played. She recognized Stephane Grappelli. *When day is done. Solitude.*

Fragments of conversation floated over:

'. . . All Quiet on the Red Front . . . the gospel according to St Marx . . .'

'Rugger yesterday – that pitch – wind blew straight from Siberia . . .'

'. . . was caught doping champagne cocktails . . . I mean, he'd been gated already . . .

'Colour? a sort of Beverly Nichols green, I suppose . . .'

'. . . was a chucker-out at the Dot Ball . . .'

'Say Hullo to God, don't wait for God to say Hullo first . . .'

'. . . All mains, HMV, five valve. Second-hand of course.'

'The whole beano got out of control . . . rugger songs . . . then a whole set of crockery in smithereens – Andy giving one of his CUSC speeches . . .'

'ARP Evacuation practice . . . really brings it home . . .'

She hadn't noticed that someone stood behind her.

'Hi, there. We met last evening . . .'

She turned, the lemonade sploshing in her glass. When she saw who it was, she said:

'You didn't realize – I'm your cousin –'

'Fair coz, but whom else?' interrupted the annoying man.

'Is that true?'

Willow said, 'Well, if you're our American cousin, yes. I'm Michael's cousin, you see –'

'Let me guess. Are you the one with the fancy name? *Lovely* name. Willow?'

She nodded. Spilling some of the lemonade.

'Well, I'm Jay. Like I said . . . Willow, let's go over there, not too near the radio – and you tell me *everything*.'

She thought at first he knew something. And Michael *promised* . . . She looked round to see where he or Chas had got to. Both were opening bottles near the door.

But it was about family he wanted to talk.

'I remember your aunt. Teddy, Cousin Teddy. She visited once when we lived with our grandmother . . .'

'She told me. Your sisters. A brother. Years ago –'

'Nineteen-twenty-three. I must have been seven, eight. She sang *I'm just wild about Harry* to my kid brother – imagine that. He's just started in medical school . . .'

'I never know who's who –'

'My mother's Ruth. The youngest of Daisy's children. She'd be first cousin to *your* mother . . . Dad was killed in the War, before I was even born. Mom married again in 'twenty-six. He's a banker, and a fine person.'

She asked what he was doing here, and for how long?

'International law. How long's up to Adolf Hitler . . . As it was, I almost didn't . . .' He took her empty glass: 'Our side of the family, yours too, we're really bad about keeping in touch. Our grandmothers exchange news, but us . . . apart from I've seen something of Michael, I've done *nothing* . . .'

While he spoke, she'd been feeling safer than at any time since she'd run away. Then suddenly, glancing at her watch – half past nine – panic. Surely by now?

'Hey there – something not right?'

'The nuns,' she said. 'They'll be coming after me any moment . . .' Her mouth felt weak, but stiff at the same time.

'Willow, this is *some* story . . .' Then, as if he really meant it: 'Why don't I help you? I can run faster than any nun.' He added, 'Serious, though. If there's anything I can do?'

'I can't tell you here – it's too difficult . . .'

'Let's go down to Michael's rooms – if it's OK by him.'

She didn't bother to ask Michael: telling Jay that of course it was OK. Michael didn't see her go, nor Charles.

They sat on opposite sides of the banked-up fire. It was easy, because she'd been wanting to tell someone. It meant going right back to the murder and the trial – he knew something of that, of course. He listened very carefully, to everything. When she'd finished he asked a few questions. Then he sat very still – although he didn't *seem* still. (Electric, Michael had said . . .)

He told her then what she must do. 'But only if you want to . . . You see, I reckon you just don't need to stay there at all. Only you have to tell the right people so they can do something about it. And that means your Grandma . . .'

'What you do first, is write the nuns. Very politely, courteously, but saying where they get off. Your grievances. And how really sorry you are they don't have a better school. They won't answer – but *you*'ll feel better.'

But she must do it soon, he said. Tomorrow's post. No later . . .

Then, 'Stay right here,' he said. She sat not daring to move. He was back in what seemed seconds.

'I spoke with Mike – he says everything's fine by him, and goodbye and good luck . . .'

It all seemed to be happening suddenly very fast . . .

'You didn't have any luggage?'

'Just my school coat and scarf . . .'

'OK. Then you come with me. We'll write that letter together first thing tomorrow. Right now I'm going to check you into the University Arms. After that we'll call your Grandma. The hue and cry – it'll have just about started up . . .'

'Yes,' she said. 'Yes, please.' She felt weak with relief.

'We'll tell the hotel you missed your train, that's why you've no luggage . . . No, better, we'll get a cab to my rooms and you can borrow a bag. Maybe some pyjamas. I reckon you're a half inch taller, but what the hell . . .'

Yes, Jay. No, Jay. Whatever you say, Jay . . . Bed and sleep, she thought, and safety. And then home . . .

18

'If you wish to smoke, Mrs Nicolson, please feel at liberty. I shouldn't like you to think you must behave as a *pupil* of this convent –'

'None of the girls smoke, Reverend Mother? How times have changed. I thought all schoolchildren surreptitiously puffed . . .'

The nun smiled icily. 'Perhaps, Mrs Nicolson, it is precisely this frivolous attitude to wrongdoing which has led your niece so astray?'

Teddy, folding her legs, stared across the room at the Infant Jesus of Prague, crowned and cloaked above the fireplace. 'I'd be happy to think I'd had any influence on her at all. I admire her a great deal.'

'It would seem we are speaking about a different person. The girl to whom I refer has, among other outrages, sent us *this* –' As if they were unclean, she held up two sheets of paper covered in Willow's large unformed hand: 'Mrs Nicolson, perhaps you would like to read what your niece has written?'

Oh my God, what am I doing here, Teddy thought. It's always me to the rescue. This time it was only luck she'd been available. She'd decided soon after the Munich crisis to go to the States for a month, returned a week ago on the *Normandie*, and then suddenly wanted to be in Flaxthorpe . . .

She had been there when Jay telephoned . . . His call had come ten minutes before Reverend Mother's:

'There is as yet no call for panic, Mrs Ahlefeldt-Levetzau, but we are a trifle concerned that little Willow hasn't returned yet from a visit we *thought* to be sanctioned . . .' It had been some time before she realized she was talking to Teddy. She behaved then as if she'd been fobbed off with brass instead of gold:

'That is not Mrs Ahlefeldt-Levetzau? In whom have I been confiding, then? Her *daughter*? I am speaking to an adult, I trust –'

Silly woman, Teddy had thought. She thought it again

now, as she skimmed through Willow's manifesto. Spelling mistakes apart, it was quite impressive. Jay had mentioned to her that Willow would be 'telling them where they get off . . .'

'I hope you are shocked, Mrs Nicolson . . . Naturally I have not allowed any other member of the Community to see it. There is enough suffering in the world without inflicting unnecessary wounds on innocent persons –'

Teddy thought, I shall not comment on what Willow has written. I shall not play into her hands at all. I need not even have come. It was at Mother's request, and indirectly for Alice's sake . . .

'Which brings me, Reverend Mother, to the matter of my stepsister. Of Mother Hilda. A subject mentioned here –' She held up Willow's letter.

'An unjustified and embarrassing grievance. Mother Hilda has in fact written to your niece – I speak to you now in the strictest confidence. Three letters have arrived. Since I did not permit the first I naturally cannot pass on subsequent ones. The tone of that letter – I feel pained to tell you this – I can only call it subversive. Highly critical not only of the Order but of the school, and our treatment of Willow. I could *not* allow it – I do not like to think what worse excesses Miss Willow might have committed as a result. Mother Hilda – must be excused, of course. Her illness, there can be effects on the mind, the balance . . . And then, her time of life . . . She *cannot* be held responsible. I have written to her Superior in our Sion house –'

Teddy said tiredly, 'Perhaps you would care to make your own arrangements about this matter, Reverend Mother, and we will make ours. As a family.' Her anger was such that it had turned to exhaustion. 'It was a mistake to come here. We do not see eye to eye. *I* see a child who has been thoroughly wronged, and who has felt a need to state her case . . .'

Reverend Mother leaned forward. 'May I say just one thing, Mrs Nicolson? This child, who was not a Catholic – and remember, convents are primarily for Catholics, for those *inside* salvation – this child was taken as an act of pure charity because of the terrible case of the mother. You are a woman of the world, Mrs Nicolson. You must see that I risked soiling the school. Risked, too, losing pupils. God does not ask that we abandon all common sense when we are charitable. Prudence –' she smiled – 'in our excess of charity, I had almost forgotten that most important of virtues. Prudence surely would dictate that we had had enough. That even without this –' she picked up the letter – 'your niece would have had to go . . . This convent does not *need* Miss Willow Gilmartin.'

She said it triumphantly. There seemed little point in continuing, Teddy thought. She itched to smoke but was too proud . . .

She decided suddenly to go. Getting up, saying, 'No, no, thank you, Reverend Mother, I can see myself out.'

Reverend Mother in acknowledgment gave a gracious half-smile. She will be glad to be rid of me, Teddy thought. Going out, she stopped and turned, her hand on the door-knob. 'By the way, Reverend Mother –' She spoke slowly, drawling almost.

'Yes, Mrs Nicolson?'

'My sister Sylvia had more charity in her little finger than you have in the whole of your body . . .'

She did not bother to say 'Good day' or 'Goodbye'. Also, she left the door very slightly ajar. That always irritated them . . .

19

Have a good time while you may . . . May, May Week. That fortnight in June of unwinding after exams. Of celebration. College Balls. Last year he had taken a blind date, a second cousin of Chas's. It had not gone well. The conversation had never got off the ground – like his dancing. He seemed to have grown clumsy, even the Palais Glide too much for him. This June, he thought, I shan't bother. Then he thought: The whole world may be about to end soon. Bang or whimper, perhaps he should go . . .

'You might find your own popsy this year,' Chas said. 'What about a local bloom? Save you the trouble of having one shipped in.'

He had heard through a friend that Jay was very tied up with a girl from the town. 'Jack and Jill, *Jay* and Jill,' the friend said. A town girl. For some reason he imagined the traditional tobacconist's daughter, barmaid . . .

He'd hardly seen Jay since Willow's escape last winter. A couple of arranged meetings, both of which had fallen through. A chance encounter in the KP café. He felt mildly irritated when he thought of him: Jay had managed the Willow business well. Handled by him, it had seemed so simple (take hold of her, tell her what to do, and make sure she does it *at once*). He wondered now why *he* couldn't have frogmarched her to a hotel that first evening, put her on a train to Yorkshire next morning, rung the convent or Grandma – let someone else take over . . . His absurd feeling that he mustn't do anything sneaky, that he was in some way being tested . . . Then when he'd had all the discomfort, along comes Mr Cleversides who'd only met her for two minutes before, and off she goes like a lamb . . .

Of course Teddy had taken over afterwards. Just as, two years ago, she had rushed to Sinaia. *The time of Corina*. He didn't often think of Corina now, or of Rumania at all. There was too much guilt.

And the happiness, fulfilment, he had known with her,

what was he to do with that? Sometimes he felt it had happened to someone else. He could give, had given, very great pleasure to a woman. It seemed here and now useless knowledge . . . From their talk he knew that his friends would be incredulous, doubting, or plain surprised . . . He had changed, too. Dirty jokes, the hearty, nervous laughter that went with them, he couldn't . . . Sometimes when they'd all been drinking, someone would turn on him accusingly: 'Mike's po-faced . . . You've shocked him . . . Make sure it's all good clean fun when Mike's around.'

All the time, too, this feeling of uncertainty. The air heavy with it, making him question the point of being here at all. Why bother with exams? Is it worth going on? From there, a short step to the whole misery. 'You can't sport your oak against Herr Hitler,' someone had said. Did anything matter, if war was coming?

He drank with others at the Mill. Some people had their own tankards there. The water rushed through the millrace. He stood and watched. Smelling the river smell . . . It didn't matter whether he sat his exams, passed or failed. War would come . . . He felt it in his bones. Old bones. *My father's bones.* Rotting, manuring the earth somewhere in France, in Belgium, where soon there would be a battlefield again . . .

Memories from the cinema: men living like troglodytes, waiting their turn, rushing out now over the top, falling like ninepins. Lying across the wire. Lying in no man's-land.

Since January he had been having flying lessons with the University Aero Club. Flying a Gypsy Moth. When it all happens, I shall go up in the sky, he thought. I shall rise above it. Then came that familiar sinking of the heart, sudden wave of terror, never really lost since the accident – *something is going to happen* . . .

He had a dream about Corina. She was on a train waiting in the station, where he also waited. For what? She leaned out, elbows on the sash window. When she saw him she laughed and chatted as if nothing had happened . . . 'It's Mikki, isn't it?' He asked her was she all right? So much unrest in Europe . . . In Rumania . . . 'But of *course*, Mikki.' She was smoking, talking to a man in uniform – someone he'd never seen before. Thirtyish, very good-looking. 'Mikki promised me *diamonds*,' she told him, 'a whole waterfall of them – Mikki, you won't forget, will you? *Where are they*, Mikki?' It was all light-hearted, though – he had only to explain that they weren't for her after all. She said, 'I make a joke only, Mikki –' And then they were all laughing. She leaned out farther as the train began to move. He could see it for a long time – almost as if he moved with it. Running effortlessly. Floating . . . He was so happy . . .

'. . . You fly from Croydon. Dutch airlines. Berlin by lunch-time, Budapest by tea . . .'

The man talking leaned back on his heels, swayed pompously. Adjusted his collar and tie – caused Michael to fiddle with his. It was infectious.

He had only been ten minutes at the party and already he was bored. He wasn't sure what he was drinking: it had floating fruit and a lot of greenery, and an indefinite taste. Like this party, he thought . . .

'What about Bucharest?' someone asked, 'isn't that vaguely in that direction?'

Awed by his own wit, the man said, 'Yes, well, Bucharest for *cocktails* . . .'

'And Ruritanian nights, I suppose,' said someone else.

Ruritania. *Rumania*. He thought Chas was about to say something:

'This chap –' Chas began (oh dear God, *no*!) – '*this* chap here, Firth, knows something about flying. Up in all weathers. He's really keen . . .'

The party was being given by some friends of Chas's family. Chas went there occasionally to Sunday lunch. The house was at the Barton end of Grange Road. In the long downstairs room the French windows were open: the garden was lawn, fruit trees, a gazebo. It was still light. Amid the clinking glass and the chatter, he could hear birdsong.

'Exams,' the pompous man said. 'Half the young chaps here this evening are Gown, not Town – aren't you meant to be living on black coffee with wet towels round the head?'

Chas said, 'I've made quite enough sacrifices. No flicks, a moratorium on boozing at the Mill . . . It's Roll on May Week, maidens, madrigals. I shall really hit the burg –'

'Now if you were a *rowing* man –'

'Which-thank-the-Lord-I'm-not-sir . . . Dancing's more my line. I'm on the Committee for our College Ball . . .'

Michael said, 'Chas's feel really flash . . .'

'The Big Apple, the Dance you Dare not Do, that's old hat. I'm learning something called the Camel Stomp. I –'

Michael turned, looked about him. He seemed to have been here years. And there was supper to come yet . . .

In another group, two girls were talking to a man with glasses and a bald head. One of them, dressed in coffee-coloured silk, had her back to Michael. Blonde hair, caught with a slide. Line of neck. Tilt of head. He caught his breath. For a single absurd second: *Corina is here* . . .

'You weren't listening,' Chas said. 'Our friend here . . . He can get one at cost. We ought really to tell the Ball Committee.'

'Excuse me a moment,' he said, 'I saw someone arrive . . .'

He felt sick with fear, anticipation, disgust. He moved purposefully to where she stood. Perhaps sensing his gaze, she turned. Caught his eye. Smiled.

How could he have ever? Such an ordinary *quiet* face. Not even very pretty. Gentle lips tinged with pink where the slash of red had been. Her smile, slow and friendly.

The balding man put out a hand. 'Look, can you settle an argument? The seven dwarfs, Snow White . . . We've got stuck. The seventh one –'

'Which do you have already?'

'DopeySleepyDocBashfulHappyGrumpy . . .'

'Sneezy?'

'Well done . . . it's unbelievable how irritating . . . on the tip of the tongue . . .' He turned to the girl. 'Now, Jilly, Someday Your Prince Will Come . . .'

'I'm Wishing . . .' she said, smiling again. The talk moved via Donald Duck and Goofy to Hollywood. A tall bustling man joined the group. After a few moments the other two moved away with him. Michael was left with this girl who wasn't Corina.

He said straightaway, 'Some people are out in the garden – would you like to go there?' He saw an iron seat empty near some rose-bushes. The light was going now.

'I'm Michael Firth, and you're –?'

'Jilly Russell.'

'Are you sure you're warm enough?' he asked.

'A moment later she said, 'Have you a cousin, an American, at Peterhouse?' When he said yes, she said, 'I thought I recognized the name. I was meant to come to a party of yours in the winter . . .'

'You're Jill, then, of *Jay* and Jill?'

'Yes. He'd have been here tonight – but his ears are glued to the wireless. Transatlantic broadcast, improvised swing from New York. Lionel Hampton and other gods of his . . .'

She came from London, she told him, but was living in Cambridge working as secretary to a professor at Emmanuel. 'He's a friend of Daddy's, and promised to employ me even before I could do twenty words a minute . . . Actually a lot of the work's not shorthand at all. Some of it's terribly interesting . . .'

Jay, she had met in Miller's shop, buying records on her afternoon off. They'd both wanted the same one. The last in stock.

'Who got it?'

'Oh, Jay of course. His arguments for keeping it were so impressive. I couldn't . . . So I agreed to come back to his rooms and listen to it . . .'

She smiled and he thought: How easily we could have met before, if . . .

'He's a good chap, my cousin,' he said bravely.

'Yes, he is. Tell me something about *you*, though.'

The wonderful thing was that she really wanted to hear. Sitting there, in the fading light, he talked easily. His only worry, that someone would come over and take her away . . .

They went in together for supper. He fetched her chicken and chocolate mousse. A plate piled high.

'I can't eat all that.'

He thought if he gave her enough, she would have to stay with him until it was finished.

Some couples had begun to dance. 'Shall we?' The tune was a quickstep: he managed well enough. He would have preferred to glide languorously to a slow waltz. There was a vocal: . . . *the future's looking bright . . . and now she's in love with me, the girl in the upstairs flat . . .*

He wanted to say: You reminded me of somebody. Otherwise I might never have seen you, I might have passed you by, or talked to someone else. *Wasted my evening* . . . How important was chance. With a dry outsider's eye he saw how many better-looking girls were there.

'Jay's taking you to a May Ball?'

She shook her head. 'He's tied up playing the cornet – Quinq Stompers or something . . . So I expect not . . .'

Then just when he felt the evening was really beginning, right in the middle of a deep conversation, Jay came to collect her.

'Jilly, your carriage is at the door,' someone said.

He couldn't bear it. Seeing Jay standing there, looking in his sports jacket momentarily quite English. He remembered how he'd once described him as 'electric'. Now when he went out with Jilly into the hall, he thought it again. Electric.

'Look what the wind's blown in,' he said, half joking. He thought afterwards: I meant to be rude . . .

Jay only said, 'Mike, I haven't seen you in ages. Of all the . . . have you two just met this evening?'

Michael nodded. Feeling suddenly flat, drained. Seeing her go a few moments later, he thought: I can't bear the empty night . . .

Chas said, '*You* did well. Who's that you got off with? Not that I did badly myself, of course . . .'

He thought at first he had a fever. Over the next few days he could not eat, could not work. From desk to gyp room and back to the sitting-room, where he would stare out of the window, and find half an hour gone . . .

Earlier, he'd questioned the value of going on with the exams at all. But now that he was actually interfering with his chances, he panicked. Once when the mood to work came on him, unheralded and almost too late, he began straight after Hall in the evening and continued all night. Strangely enough, the following day he felt better than at any time since he'd met Jilly. Eleven days ago now. His first exam was tomorrow. He went to a kiosk and rang Emmanuel College. But when she came to the phone, he couldn't think what to say.

'I just wondered how you were?'

Her voice, gentle, easy, unsurprised.

'*Very* well . . . How nice to hear you. And you?'

'I've got my first exam tomorrow morning . . .'

She wished him good luck, and he said, 'I remembered you have an afternoon off tomorrow. Would you like to come up to tea? And records, of course. I've quite a few . . .'

'I'll bring some,' she said. 'Jay just gave me a lot . . .'

His preparations were elaborate. He put flowers in three places. Early roses, yellow and pink-tinged, on the desk near the window. The afternoon sun would come through . . .

Anyone would think . . . I'm mad, I know. I must tell myself I'm asking Jay's girl (Jay's popsy, that's how I must think of her) to have tea with me. *And that is all.* Yet he couldn't rid himself . . . an image of some great whirlpool, of which she was the still centre. In her is my peace.

It went well from the start. All that agonizing about what he would say to her, and there it was: easy.

He had bought two sorts of cake from Fitzbillie's Café, and a big selection of biscuits, as well as Chelsea buns. 'What are you trying to do?' she asked, laughing. 'That great plate at the party and now all this. Do I *look* so greedy?'

She wore a navy blue spotted dress with Peter Pan collar and short puff sleeves. It didn't look fussy on her. He could see that she might easily become plump. But that would be lovely, it would suit her . . .

The records she'd brought, about half a dozen, were mostly Ella Fitzgerald, some Benny Goodman, and several Al Bowlly, including the tune they'd danced to at the party. She had quite a collection of Al Bowlly. 'Jay says he's Bing Crosby with sex . . .'

But he didn't want to hear what Jay said.

They sat together on the window-seat. Outside, it looked as if it might come on to rain. He told her about Willow hiding out up here. She'd heard something of it from Jay. That was the only thing wrong – Jay in the room too . . .

'Jay says . . .'

'Are you going to marry him?' He was horrified when he'd said it. The words coming out abruptly. Intrusive, personal . . .

'What a question . . . He hasn't asked me, Michael.'

'*Would you* if he did?'

She hesitated. 'I'm not in love with him. But he knows

that. I'm *very*, very fond. No one could not like Jay.'

'I could,' he said. 'Easily.'

She shrugged her shoulders. 'Relations,' she said, smiling. 'Family. It's not a fair comparison . . .'

He thought of some answer to that. Then was distracted, seeing her look at her watch:

'Don't go till we've played through all the records. Please.'

He wondered how soon and when and where he could kiss her (the same man who had lain long afternoons in Corina's bed . . . how *could* it be so different?) The best now would be if they could sit for ever on that window-seat, looking through the small-paned window, out on to the gateway to the Backs, and the grey summer sky.

'How much time do you get at lunch? I'm often at the Mill . . . In the evening what time do you finish? Do you like the river? We could take a punt up to Grantchester . . .'

And that was how it was. For about ten days. Hurrying after his morning exam, waiting leaning over the bridge at the Mill, watching the water rush and then looking up and seeing her. Evenings, tap-tap of her heeled sandals, hurrying to meet him. 'Jay says . . . Jay says . . .' But he never listened now.

A punt moored in the willows, upstream. Early evening, smell of summer grass.

'Jay says he's so pushed this week he's had to renounce all sorts of things – including taking me out.'

He'd asked her once, did Jay know she was seeing *him* as well? 'Oh yes,' she had said, 'I've mentioned it often. He says we should all three get together one evening . . .'

He did not like that at all. Also, he had become very determined. When a little later, he held her in his arms, sitting there on the river bank, he wanted to say, almost said, 'I love you, Jilly.'

The days were passing. It was almost May Week. 'About that Ball,' he said. 'Are you going to one or not?'

She laughed. 'Not that I know of . . .'

'You know of now . . .' he said. 'You're coming to Clare Ball with me.'

As simple as that. Too simple perhaps. For two days afterwards he walked about in a happy dream. (I do not have to think about France and the trenches and gas masks and aeroplanes shrieking over Guernica . . .)

So he was all the more surprised when it happened.

Jilly was away for the weekend, at home. He was restless so Chas took him to a party in Pembroke. He left early and came back to his rooms, sleepy with beer. It wasn't much after ten. He lay back on the chesterfield for a few moments and was almost asleep when a knock came on the outer door.

Jay stood there. 'You didn't get my note?'

'I've had nothing from you. Haven't seen you since –'

'Since you stole Jilly from me . . . I don't know where the note went – I wrote the damned thing . . .' Then: 'Can I come in? I'm *going* to come in.'

He sounded as if he had been drinking too. Lively still, but a very slight slur to his speech:

'You might have kept your hands off her –'

'Why?'

'Because she's mine.'

'That's not what she thinks . . .'

'Look, all I know is – I get tickets for a Ball, I ask her – she says no, sorry, I'm already going with your cousin . . .'

'She doesn't *have* to come. She's coming because she likes to be with me –'

'She's liked to be with me, since the fall. Since we met.'

'Perhaps she needed a change?'

'Jilly's *not like that*.'

'You say so. You're just angry because you didn't think to ask her yourself. Too busy with your jazz. And now you're singing *Somebody Stole my Gal* . . .'

'I don't think in song titles, thanks –'

'You're not engaged or anything. I know because I asked.'

'We were a couple, for Chrissake . . .'

'Yes, Jay and Jill . . .'

He kept expecting to be angry, kept waiting for it to happen. He felt only calm, sleepiness all gone – almost superior. Jay, *who always does it right, who sorts everybody out, tells everyone what to do . . .*

He said mockingly, 'Jack and Jill . . . You know what

happened, Jay? *Jack fell down and broke his crown* . . .'

And Jill came tumbling after . . . He remembered the next line as soon as he'd spoken . . .

Jay said, 'There's no law to stop you poaching on another guy's territory. I can't stop you. You're free, white, and twenty-one –'

'Twenty.'

'OK, twenty . . . I'm just hurt, you see. And I holler when I'm hurt –'

'Doesn't say much for the way you were brought up. Barging in here, raising Cain when you can't get what you want –'

'I'll take remarks from you, OK, but don't you say anything about the way I was raised – *you leave my family right out of this* . . .'

It was about then it turned ugly. He wasn't sure who started it, who was abusive first. The insults bounced from one to the other.

'. . . when I've finished with you, you won't know if your arsehole's bored or punched.'

'Poopstick –'

'Runt, you little *runt* –'

'Get wise to yourself, would you, and *grow up*!'

'You just made me a year older, remember?'

'I don't give a bitch's curse – and play *that* on your piano . . .'

'There's no need to blast me to high heaven –'

'Right then – swords or pistols? Do we go up Gog Magog?'

'*That* Cambridge apology for a hill? Look, for heaven's sake, Jay, just calm down . . .'

'. . . if I want to raise *Hail, Columbia*, I'll raise it – and I don't need your leave . . .'

It ended lamely. 'Look, you'd better go,' Michael said. 'Get out, would you. Whose rooms are they?'

'OK, OK, I will –'

'Clear out – and look where you're going down the steps. Just keep on singing *Somebody stole my gal*.. . .'

'Don't worry, I will . . .'

'And pull all the stops out . . .'

He could only think, in his shaken state afterwards, how it would upset Jilly. She must never know . . .

An apology, written, came from Jay. He thought perhaps he should send one back (. . . we both behaved badly . . .) In the end he did nothing. He thought: I never liked him very much anyway.

Jilly knew about it, of course. He supposed she had been given an edited version because she said only, 'Jay says you've had words over me . . . How could you? Two little boys squabbling. Really, Michael. Jay has a quick temper, of course – How about you?'

Anger. Corina. *Something happening*. He changed the subject.

He was dressing for the Ball. White shirt, starched front. Starched single cuffs. Square-cut gold cufflinks. Tie with narrow knot, wide ends.

They were quite a large party, eight or ten. Sitting out would be in Chas's rooms, since they were the largest. Jack Harris's Band was to be the main attraction.

They all had dinner first at the University Arms. He could not take his eyes off Jilly. She wore a mid-blue taffeta dress which rustled and billowed. It had the same embroidery at waist and neckline . . . He saw that the sun of the last weeks had faintly dusted her face with freckles.

After all his talk, Chas had imported his sister's best friend. She was very smart and wore a dress with padded shoulders, and her hair up with an Edwardian look. She told Chas, 'I had Jack Harris for my coming out dance. He's all right. You should have got Jack Payne. He's far more robust.' She said to Jilly, 'Don't you smoke? I'm just *lost* without my filigree holder . . .'

When they were sitting upstairs between dancing, he had to ask her how it had been with Jay. He had meant not to.

'Well, yes, he *does* dance better . . . But then . . .'

Another guest was saying, 'In life, you see, the girl with the least principles draws the most interest . . .'

Someone else said, 'You know this one? He: May I have the pleasure of this dance? She: What do I have to lose? He: *You* ought to know . . .'

Chas said, 'She had to go and lose it at the Astor, I suppose . . .'

Groans. Oh well done, Chas. Stick to dancing and leave the cabaret to others . . .

Chas said suddenly that he, and two others who should be nameless, had a book on the first of their crowd to be married. He looked meaningly at Michael . . . 'Want to know *your* odds, Firth?'

Jack Harris played Gershwin's *Bei mir bist du schön*. Jilly said, 'Jay says . . . we should have tried to get George Lewis for cabaret. He seems besotted with his clarinet playing. Runs up to London after him. In fact, Jay says –'

I don't mind, he told himself. She is mine now.

They went outside together along the Backs. There was little or no moonlight. They leaned over the bridge to where the river ran below. A bat swooped, just missing her bent head. Bats were gothic, part of the river smell, the willows, the scent of summer evenings.

'Watch out . . .'

'I'm rather fond of them,' she said. 'The babies specially. Mice with wings. Flying mice. That makes them sound quite ordinary – not at all sinister.'

Sound of a cornet, a saxophone, carrying across the water. Coming from the Ball. I shall not think of Jay . . . He will go back to the States. Will have to, if the war . . .

'Is it all right,' he asked, 'about Jay?'

'Of course it isn't.' She said it gently. 'How can it be all right when he loves me and I don't love him back? I don't come out of it at all well. I would have come out of it even worse if I'd pretended . . .'

They went back to dance. He held her very close now. Whatever happens, I shall, *we* shall, have had this night. A ball on the eve of Waterloo. Because of the accident, perhaps, and what he had glimpsed, because of his father even, he would freeze suddenly in the middle of a dance, thinking: *Who of us will be the first go to?*

They walked out again just when dawn was coming up. The sky lilac. They held hands. He could feel tiredness and exhilaration run together . . .

'The idea is to go up to Grantchester for breakfast. The whole party . . .'

'Yes.' He wanted already to be back with her in his arms

on the dance floor. Feel her breath on his cheek when she spoke . . . Close, closer, closest . . .

'Could I meet your people?' he asked. 'I'd like to do that. If you don't mind.'

'Of course. It's only London . . . I –'

'Time seems so short somehow. I'm not twenty-one yet – not till next year. But with the balloon about to go up . . .'

Their hands tightened. His mouth then, in her hair. Kissing her.

'I love you so terribly,' he said.

They were silent a few moments. She said, with a sigh:

'We ought to turn back, I think – if we're all to get into punts . . .'

'I suppose,' he said, 'it's much too soon to ask you to marry me . . .'

'I suppose it is. Honestly.' She turned to him, smiling. 'But I wish you would . . .'

20

Once she had used to be excited by dinner-parties. Somewhere in that decade between life with Saint and the year of Ferdy, the very invitation would excite her, with its wonderful Perhaps. Always the possibility that here, invited quite by chance, would be *the* person: the beloved, the husband, father of my children . . . Unreasonable to hope – and yet . . .

Then I gave up. Each invitation means less and less. Until tonight *I can hardly be bothered* . . .

She looked down the dinner table. I should have had babies. If I hadn't the orphanage . . . When I follow their progress now it's as if they were my own. One-legged Vincent, who has been able to study law, who will be all right if– when – the war comes . . .

'Pierre was ill today, Pierre at Desfosse. He *always* does my hair.' Denise de Lanessan, sitting opposite, had a hard face which closed up as soon as she finished speaking. In her hair, some sort of bird on the wing, jewelled. It reminded Teddy of the extravagances of guests dining at The Towers. Glimpsed as a child . . .

It seemed to her this July of 1939 that social life had become like the set for a costume movie. Paris slipped back into the eighteenth century. Last season peasant kerchiefs had abounded, encrusted with jewels at night-time. This year they were worn by tandem riders in culottes, hooted at in the Rue Royale. To be smart now was to wear a velvet hood and cloak with a picture frock. And why not? It made a change, to appear a little romantic. Or was it just Marie Antoinette again, playing at shepherds and shepherdesses?

Easy enough to understand how it had come about. The near miss last autumn, Daladier back from Munich, the invasion of Czechoslovakia . . . Events since then had only made the final outcome more likely. Here in Paris, they did not talk about it much . . .

The guest on her right turned. 'Everyone here tonight has

spoken a little of themselves – but you, nothing . . .' His voice raised, a question-mark.

'Probably because there's nothing to say.' Her tone was almost rude. She did not feel flirtatious tonight . . .

'That I find very difficult to believe,' he said, smiling. She liked him even less when he smiled. She had been displeased at being sat next to him. Earlier when they had drunk champagne upstairs, balcony window open on to the Paris evening, she had wished she had known a few more of the guests. Her hosts were not close friends.

And he, this man (M. Seydoux – or was it Feydeau, Peydeau, who cared?) seemed known to no one. A man guest had cried off this morning and other guests, a Colonel Martin-Galliflet and his wife whom she didn't know either, had brought a business acquaintance, in Paris for a few days. He was about her height with dark thinning hair and glasses. His face was keen, his look could even be described as piercing. She noticed the fourth finger missing from his right hand. She felt that he was critical of her. Let him have something to be critical about, she thought . . .

'That I find very difficult to believe,' he repeated. He was still smiling.

'Hardly. Since I lead a completely idle life.'

'These days? It's impossible? Yes, of *course* it is . . . If a person wishes –'

'I do wish,' she said. 'I wish to be completely aimless and trivial and all the other adjectives which are waiting to balloon from your mouth, like those cartoons . . .'

'I do assure you –'

'Please,' she said, 'you're boring me . . .' She lifted her glass. The giant ruby and diamond ring (Firth inheritance, reset in platinum for last decade's fashion) caught the light, matched the colour of the wine.

No one heard, or commented. Everyone else from the party of twelve seemed otherwise occupied. Perhaps Aimée Ribourel, her hostess, noticed something, for as Teddy turned, she leaned forward, asking M. Seydoux whether he knew Paris well?

'Alas, I only visit her for business, and even then it's so short always – I sail for Canada next week . . . Our office in Montreal. For about three months.'

A little further down the table, brightly, the voice of Michèle Rochard, telling a story a little too loudly:

'. . . on the corner . . . Raspail, Montparnasse, they have this flower wagon on the pavement and it's too priceless. They stop for lunch but *completely*. Table, chairs, four courses. A sideshow in itself. Mouth-watering dishes simmering all morning among the blooms. I tell you, some people know how to live . . .'

Now it was Denise de Lanessan again, on one of her two topics: clothes and her appearance, usually combined.

'. . . the house of Patou . . . No, it is *not* the same . . . Since his death . . . Barbas is not Patou, and that is all . . .'

Someone said, 'What is this *absurd* nickname the President suddenly has? Pouh-Pouh indeed! Our youngest son used to be called that – as a baby . . .'

'Precisely,' said Colonel Martin-Galliflet. 'He was being filmed for the newsreels, one of his grandchildren cried, he took it on his knee, didn't realize the sound track was on and sang "Pouh-pouh . . ." The nation apparently was enchanted . . .'

'Who would be President today? Who could *wish* to?' M. Seydoux to his other neighbour. Conversation settled into gossip. Teddy, who knew hardly anyone discussed, glanced at him to see if he betrayed boredom. Unfortunately she caught his eye.

'No contributions? Don't your idle moments give you anything juicy to add?'

She made a small angry noise. He said:

'I think really you are perhaps not so idle, and spend your days – say, rescuing – fallen women? Am I right?'

'What is *your* business, which by the way you seem unable to mind, that it makes such a contribution to society?'

'A business of no importance whatsoever,' he said, 'which wouldn't be missed if it went tomorrow. It's a living. A life. I am not particularly convinced of the value of it.'

She thought absurdly: If I didn't dislike him so I would probably rather like him. She feared that later in the evening there might be cards, which she detested, and that she might be partnered with him. But it was not like that. After Denise de Lanessan's husband, with a little persuasion, had given a very bad imitation of Fernandel, their host said, 'This can't be the only talent present. Do startle us, someone . . .' Teddy was surprised when without any shyness, M. Seydoux said:

'. . . Only what I can remember. Do keep on talking . . .' Accompanying himself, he sang in a light assured voice. Different styles: a gravelly Jean Gabin, changing his face so that he almost *was* Albert Préjean, Georges Milton for comic effect. Fréhel. Then: 'One of Mireille's best,' he said. *'Depuis que je suis à Paris.'* His voice had the caressing intimate notes of Jean Sablon.

'What a talent,' someone said.

'A touch of the boulevardier. I had a father who was the life and soul . . . it was expected of us all.'

Aimée said, 'And that was – where?'

'The Haute Savoie. My real home. I'd go back there tomorrow if business permitted . . .'

It had grown late. The party broke up soon after. A flurry of chauffeured cars collecting. Teddy would go as she had come, in a cab. Mme Martin-Galliflet said, 'Oh, but our friend's hotel . . . he would have to pass in your direction . . .'

So, what she had not wanted, she found herself in a taxi with him. She said, 'Do you mind if I smoke?' adding, 'You're favoured. I should ask, but don't always.'

As she tried in the rocking taxi, turning a corner, to light her cigarette:

'One moment, I have my lighter.' She was disturbed by the hand so close to her face. Flash of white cuff, of expensive cufflinks. A successful man who does not need me, whom I do not need . . .

'There's something with this lighter. Wait –'

She saw again, the missing finger. She said in a careless voice, 'Forgive my asking. I'm not only idle but idly curious – your hand, that finger . . . were you born –'

'No, not congenital. The War.' He said it half-angrily: 'I was fortunate, don't you think, that I lost only that?'

She didn't answer. He went on:

'Four brothers. I'm the fifth son and the only survivor. A story you could hear any day, anywhere in France.' He paused, adding more gently, 'Or England for that matter . . . I forgot for a moment. You speak so well, one doesn't immediately think, English . . .'

She said, 'It *was* worse here. The figures show it. It just feels the same, if you –'

'I really am sorry. Brothers? Father?'

'One brother . . . And – my husband.'

'Forgive me. I hadn't thought. You seemed too young –'

'I married at seventeen.' She thought: Why should I tell him Gib wasn't killed? She felt again – sudden chill: *I slept with a dead man* . . .

The taxi had stopped. She said in a forced, bright voice, 'We're in the middle of a conversation. Won't you come in – a cognac, a whisky?'

Leaning to open the cab door, 'Yes, yes. Delighted. Why not?'

Why not indeed? Here I am again, she thought, about to allow – no, invite – a comparative stranger into my bed. It will be all right. Probably it will be quite enjoyable. In the morning I shall be disgusted, and glad he has left early to creep back to his hotel . . .

'Who are these?' He was looking at the photographs, a collage of them on the wall above her bureau. 'Not all nephews and nieces, surely? You must be very blessed . . .'

She told him then a little, not too much, about the orphanage. In spite of herself she heard her voice soften. She could not keep hidden her enthusiasm, her love for these children. The one *certain* thing in my life. I shan't let him mock it . . .

He said: 'You didn't tell me whose work this is?' A drawing, violently coloured, of a fat woman and even fatter man sitting side by side, smiling. Benoît, whose parents while they were alive had beaten and starved him, had done it for her last week. He couldn't or wouldn't remember the bad times . . .

'A little boy,' she said. 'He has drawn his parents.'

While they were speaking, they stood close together. She was terrified by the violent attraction. Perhaps that's what has been wrong all evening? Involuntarily she shivered. (Soon he will take me in his arms and it wiil be all right. For the next few hours, it will be all right . . .)

'Now I must leave,' he said, 'and surprise the night porter. I've so enjoyed the cognac, and the talk –'

She leaned forward very slightly. Hardly knew that she

was doing it. He put his arms round her quickly, trapping her. Their heads bent, lips met. She shut her eyes. Already, her legs . . . it was as if they had begun the walk to the bedroom . . .

But he was standing back, smiling. 'I do have to go –'

It seemed to her he almost hurried. Thinking about it later, she realized he had left calmly, politely.

And for ever.

She lay awake, unable to still her racing heart. Why is this thirty-nine-year-old woman lying sleepless, sixteen again and kissed by Gib in the library? I'm no older and wiser, merely more cynical – would it have been any better *if*–?

She opened a barely begun copy of *La Passante de Sans Souci*. Slit a few pages. Her attention wandered. It is a love-story, she thought, I do not need to read about love . . .

Waking from a short sleep, drugged almost, she saw it was ten o'clock. She was glad she hadn't arranged to go to the orphanage . . . Blanche the maid, who had been here two hours already, brought her coffee.

At half past ten the telephone rang.

'Good morning, Henri Seydoux here. We met last night . . .' She held the receiver in one hand, the cup of black coffee in the other. '. . . I unfortunately have only a little time free in the day. At lunch-time. I hope you have too . . . Prunier's, downstairs . . . Yes?'

Yes. She had two hours. It wouldn't be enough. I am absurd. Half an hour wasted while I try on three different outfits. A bath run, then left to grow cold. Scent – too much, too little? More jewellery, less? And the hat. Too far forward, the wrong tilt?

She settled for a suit, simple and well cut, and with it a white brocade waistcoat. I am an empty-headed social butterfly flitting from man to man. But looking at herself in the glass, she saw she was not dressed for the part.

As she came into Prunier's, seeing first the little pots of caviar on ice, lobsters, crayfish, langoustes, on her right the caisse, she did not dare to look at the tables . . .

He said, 'You are not late – I was very early. And now, please –'

She ate prawns, and then goujons of sole. The minutes ticked away, faster than she would have thought possible.

'I chose here because it's good fast service – and delicious. It's unfortunate I have these three appointments this afternoon . . .'

Because she was afraid (what if he should *see* that I care?) and through nerves, she was at her most brittle:

'You were lucky to find me at home. My engagement book –'

'Last night, in your home,' he said, 'you weren't like this. Would you stop it, please?'

Her voice came out small and humble: 'I'm sorry. I –'

'At some risk,' he said, 'allow me to tell you you're very much attracted to me. Although not as much as I to you. But you're wary, and that's the form it takes. Am I right?'

'Perhaps –'

'No *perhaps*. Certainly I'm right. But by itself – all that – it's not enough. You invited me to your home and then you were angry, I think, or disappointed, when I left you almost exactly as I found you. But why not? Why shouldn't I respect you?'

'Oh, respect,' she said. 'Respect. Whatever next? You sound like an Englishman proposing marriage –'

'Instead of a Frenchman proposing – I think you know – what.'

'By all means – if you can spare the time . . .'

He held up his right hand. She was mesmerized by the missing finger. 'Enough, please. I'll order coffee. You shall pretend we're back in the taxi again. You were rather charming then, and natural –'

She felt her mouth work. I certainly don't need to cry here. Among the lobsters and langoustes.

'Are you free tonight?' He spoke hurriedly now. Suddenly the worried one. 'I have nothing, but –'

'Quite free.'

'You see, I have only three more days. Then the weekend out of Paris. Monday, here from midday. On the Tuesday, Le Havre, and Montreal.'

'Oh,' she said in a small voice. 'Oh well –'

'Yes – oh well. You're thinking already that I wasted last night? Perhaps I did . . .'

The bill had come. He was busy with that. Then suddenly, both hands cupped over hers, holding them down:

'Tonight I shall come straight to your apartment. About seven. We'll see then where we go . . . There's a great hurry, you know. You'll see . . .' He lifted his hands slowly.

'Where do you want to go now? I'll call you a cab . . .'

It was beyond excitement. She was beyond excitement. There were four hours to live through. She went to her favourite lingerie shop in the Rue de Rivoli, and came out with a nightdress that was almost a dinner gown – halter-necked with a fitted bodice, burgundy chiffon and georgette. I am extravagant, and ridiculous . . .

Evening. *La Route Enchantée* was showing not far away. Charles Trenet sang exuberantly of the country of love: come with us and you'll see . . . love, love . . . It seemed to her at first wasteful they should sit in the cinema when they might be alone – but the quiet couple of hours, holding hands as if young again, were somehow calming . . .

When they came out: 'You could add Trenet to your repertoire,' she said.

'I was listening carefully, Teddee . . .' She liked very much how he pronounced her name. It made her seem in a way a different person . . .

They ate at a small restaurant, a café really, a few corners down from her apartment. During the soup, she asked him, 'Do you have a wife? I want to – must know, if you're married.' It suddenly mattered terribly . . .

'I was – until about six years ago. The marriage wasn't good and I'd become attached elsewhere and wanted to regularize that. She, Christine, had been my mistress for over eight years. I got an annulment – very difficult, causing great distress – so that we might marry. I think she became frightened. Or met someone better – who knows? But within a week of my freedom it was all off. Since then, I've been very careful . . .'

'I'm always careful,' Teddy said. 'Children?'

'One daughter, already married. She lives near Cahors.' He said: 'You haven't married again. Did you wish to?'

'Yes, in principle . . . Though *maybe* . . . In case you hadn't noticed, there's a shortage of worthwhile men. My sister found a rotter, married him, and shot him dead.'

His eyebrows went up. 'That is a story.'

'It was.'

'Later you can tell me about her, perhaps? Now, it's *your* story I want to hear, Teddee . . . You do have one, I think?'

That first night he shouted in his sleep. She woke in a fright, thinking: Some disaster. A burglar. A heart attack . . .

'Are you all right, what is it, darling? Henri, *what is it?*' She woke him up. She could not bear it. He said only:

'My God, one of my nightmares. I could have done without . . . Forgive me . . .'

She wanted to comfort him . . . But it was nothing, he said (nothing, she thought afterwards, when he had told her, *nothing* . . .) Only a shell that had exploded in '16, burying him. Hardly an uncommon experience, he said – and at least he had survived. Since then, occasionally, if he became nervously excited it could happen: this reliving through a nightmare. Clutching, clawing, desperate to reach air . . .

He said, 'I don't expect to have it again while we're together.'

While we're together . . . That was the giveaway, that the time they would be together was so short. Only two more days and then he must leave for the weekend. After that, one more day, and he would be gone completely.

Over the next two days, except when they went to a restaurant or he had to meet business contacts, he was seldom out of her apartment. Much of the time was spent talking, when they were not making love (and all of that so perfect that superstitiously she did not dare to tell him. Accept, give, but do not appear vulnerable . . .) A lot of the talking was done by her. It was not that he was secretive – he answered questions frankly, but he seemed to have taken it on himself not only to listen to the story of her life, but to shape and alter her memories . . .

She noticed it first when, as they lay together on the double bed, she told him more about Gib than she had ever told anyone (Ferdy – how to imagine telling him those secrets of the heart? Saint, who had been his friend? Even less . . .)

She ended her tale with the diary. The diary that had been not only comfortless but a death knell too. *I slept with a dead man.*

'Afterwards, when he came back –'

'You should remember only the Gilbert you loved . . . The man of the diaries – wasn't Gilbert. I know, because for years after – the reason in the end why I had no marriage, was that I was no longer Henri, nineteen-fifteen. I *understand* this dead man you speak of. I was buried alive, you see. I too came back from the dead . . .'

She got his name wrong, when she chanced to use it one time: "Feydeau."

'I'm not a farceur,' he said, laughing. He didn't correct her, though. 'Call me what you like – though Henri would be better.'

'You don't have a pet name?'

'Give me one –'

'Later,' she said, 'later. When we have more time together . . .' She was certain now that they would. But whether they did nor not would depend on her. He had said so. Suddenly very serious, he had explained that he did not see it just as an affaire, although she might. On the other hand, she must not rush into anything. Above all, she must give herself a breathing space. The dreaded weekend that he was to spend in the Loire: 'I can't avoid it, since it's business . . . But while I'm gone, you must think, *very seriously*.'

'Couldn't I come too, as your secretary?'

'No. You're meant to be thinking, Teddee. Neither of us, you see, can afford a mistake . . . So, Monday we shall meet for lunch, and you can tell me. We can tell each other. If you are frightened, have changed your mind, then it's enough not to keep our appointment. That way it is very simple. I shall know – but you will have been spared telling me . . .'

He went on, 'But if all is well, Tuesday we can go to St Lazare together. Hoping that Danielle Darrieux isn't travelling the same day – that happened to me once, not a porter left to pay attention . . . We can plan then what we'll do, when I'm back from Canada. Or if you would wish to come out too . . .'

She wanted to say: But I've thought already. I think I'll come now. Try even to get a passage for Tuesday . . . But to show so much certainty . . . It would not do.

On their last evening, the Friday, they ate outside Paris on the edge of the Bois de Verrières. She wore a black moiré suit with tight-fitting jacket, and vest and jabot in pale pink organdie. They were at a group of restaurants with tables up in the trees. Everyone wanted to be up a tree – the waiters naturally encouraged them to take tables on the ground.

He told her, 'During the weekend I shall want to telephone you. But I won't . . . It wouldn't be right or fair.'

They arranged that when – *if* she came on Monday, it would be to the little café two corners from her apartment, where they had eaten the first night, and sat drinking twice since. It was usually so crowded as to give a sort of privacy.

'I *promise* that if you are not there I shall do nothing. I shan't run round to your apartment saying, "But I thought you love me . . ." '

'It's wait and see then, isn't it?' she said in her cooler, teasing voice.

'I woke up this morning,' he said, 'when you were still asleep, and thought: I shall go to the Avenue Matignon to Max and buy her a wild mink – full length. I didn't, of course. But that is the sort of mad impulse I've been having . . .'

'If you *do* get one, I shall want only the best . . .'

'Naturally . . . Teddee . . .'

She didn't expect to sleep on the Saturday night, so was surprised when drowsiness overcame her about two in the morning. *Sunday* now. Already she'd managed one whole day. When she woke she would go straight to the orphans, spend the day with them, then early to bed. In the morning it would be Monday. And then at lunch-time . . . '*Yes, yes,*' she would say, 'I want to be with you always, *forever* . . .'

Then after the happy-sad-happy night they would wake and dress, and take a cab to the Gare St Lazare. She would go with him to Le Havre. See the boat off. Then decide about following him and how soon it would be . . . Meanwhile, about the war . . . We have the Maginot Line, she repeated to herself like a charm, we have the Maginot Line. France will be safe.

And anyway, it would be all right once they were together. I feel so sure, she thought. The whole of today I was absolutely certain (as only someone who's made hundreds of mistakes could be). Ever since Gib I have been looking . . .

The telephone woke her with shocking suddenness. Groping for the light, knocking the receiver off . . . She could not at first make out the voice: faint, then more clear. Repeating patiently:

'Erik, this is *Erik*. Teddy . . .'

Oh dear God, she could not hear properly. Mother- . . . No, not *dead*. But the doctors . . . she had been ill about a week, now they were of a sudden worried last night – had arranged to operate early Monday. 'They want to see what's happening with her . . . the liver, we don't know what we must think . . .' The normally unruffled Erik, agitated. She remembered his telling her his father had died under the knife – a pioneer operation for appendicitis . . .

'Erik, I'll come *immediately* – the first boat . . .'

Yet another time of rushing. For Sylvia . . . To Rumania for Michael. She should be used by now . . .

The time was half past three. She had already pulled on her wrap, reached for a cigarette and lit it before she realized. Sunday now. The orphans, that would be all right. But *Monday*?

I shall tell him what's happened. She threw clothes into a suitcase, mentally composed notes, instructions for Blanche . . . I'll send a letter to his hotel which will make it absolutely clear. A telegram to Le Havre. A telephone call from Yorkshire . . .

She would leave these practicalities till the last moment. If she did everything quickly she could get a cab in about an hour. The first train out of Paris, an early boat, England by the afternoon, Yorkshire late this evening . . . She thought about 'planes. A Sunday. By the time I've found out the details I could be half across the Channel . . . (That man, lover, years ago, who said: 'If ever you want flying anywhere in an emergency, just call me.' *At four in the morning*?)

She'd begin by ringing the night porter at Henri's hotel, to leave a message. But – oh dear God . . . *Which hotel*? She had never asked or known. Try ringing some likely ones – so popular at this hour – asking whether they have staying there a M. Henri . . . a M. Henri . . . M. Henri *who*?

Oh, but it's not possible . . . I'm mad. Dearest darling Henri, *of course* I know your name. We were introduced at that dinner party . . . Since then she *must* have heard him use it . . . He had perhaps left a card? She began a frantic search. He had not.

Feydeau, *Feydeau* ran round in her head. The playwright. That wasn't it, but it was somewhere near. Daudet, Feldeau, Feydoux . . . No . . . Aimée Ribourel, she gave that party, he was brought as an extra guest – *by whom*? She would know. But one couldn't ring her house now. And . . . of course, they have left for the country. Somewhere in the Romanche, I think. I never bothered to find out.

I could wait till Yorkshire. I must. It is Mother who is important. I could leave a note for Blanche that she try to do something . . .

The *café where they were to meet* . . . She ran downstairs and along the deserted street. Perhaps there are late drinkers still, someone will remember us, give a message?

The shutters were up. Refuse piled outside. A grey alley cat scavenged. Mewing, it came over, rubbing its face against her leg. What message could she leave? 'If a dark monsieur with glasses seems to be waiting for a guest, tell him that Teddee . . .'

Impossible. She felt paralysed with sadness, worry, panic. Where was that so sophisticated, so unflappable Teddy? Haunted by images of death, disease, she began already to reject the happiness she had known. *It was not meant to be.*

All the way home, cab to train to boat to train and train again, she was sick with worry. If Mother should die before I arrive. And if, ungrateful, always absent, always wayward daughter, I should miss her because of my love-life – my unsatisfactory, desperate love-life . . . A mess yet again. I didn't get it right. *It was not meant to be* . . .

21

'. . . I have to tell you now that no such undertaking has been received, and that consequently this country is at war with Germany . . .'

So that's it, Teddy thought. Seeing Willow's strained face on the sofa opposite (her birthday yesterday scarcely noticed; it had not been a time to celebrate . . .) We have come to this – the war to end all wars, in vain.

The Towers: suddenly full of memories. I walk the corridors, flapper, little help, reading to the officers, singing for them, dancing, *falling in love with Gib* . . . Thank you, God, for nothing . . .

Sunday today. By Tuesday evening The Towers would be more or less a children's home. It would have been sooner had she not insisted they have the chance first to bury Lily quietly, and with dignity . . .

About forty children would descend on them, to be housed in dormitories of ten. Children of whom the eldest would be only five or six. I shall have my work cut out, but I want that. For the next few months every minute of every day will be occupied. There will not be enough moments . . . I shall have to borrow time.

No question now of going back to Paris. She had been in touch with Blanche's father to try and arrange some caretaking. Her friends would so what they could. All that life, an Englishwoman in Paris, must be forgotten for the moment.

As must Henri . . . When she thought of that episode now, it no longer seemed real. She was surprised not to have suffered more. After those first terrible few days, it had been bearable, because numb . . . I got what I deserved, she thought. The way I've been behaving all these years . . . But had I been *truly* ruthless I would have found a way. He too . . . Except he was proud, and had promised he would not question my decision . . .

The pattern of my life . . . Now it's to be good works, and casual loves again. That should suit wartime. But children,

I'm to be allowed to love *them* as much as I want . . . And that is not nothing . . .

There had never been any hope for Lily. The exploratory operation had told them only that her liver was beyond healing. No time was given. It had not occurred to Teddy then to return to Paris. (I could not bear another rush back across the Channel, heart thumping, wondering if I will be in time?)

Willow, and Erik to some extent, hoped. Willow because she hadn't been told enough, Erik because it was in his nature. Besides Teddy, the only person close to Lily to be realistic about her chances, had been Sadie Hawksworth. And she had worries of her own: for several months Charlie had been showing symptoms of an undiagnosed illness.

Michael had had compassionate leave for his grandmother. He was in the RAF – not having waited to see if war would be averted . . . He was engaged to a girl from London, unexpectedly suitable. It wouldn't be long before they married.

Willow was waiting for the results of her Matric exam. She had been a weekly boarder at a York school since January, and planned to stay on for at least another year.

Two Austrians, mother and daughter, were living at the Vicarage. In those difficult days of nursing Lily, bolstering Erik, taking care of Willow, Teddy went there twice a week for German lessons. She didn't imagine there was a great demand for these just now, nor that the Austrians would knowingly accept charity. She paid as highly as she dared. Surprisingly, she found the lessons restful, and easy. She remembered more than she realized from the days of moon-faced Fräulein.

Meanwhile Willow must not be left to languish. Teddy tried with small tennis parties, teas . . . Sadie was as kind as ever. Her soldier son was home on leave from India – the handsome Christopher, who as a baby had been so ugly . . .

To look at, he was nothing like Jack as Teddy remembered him. Nor Sadie or Charlie particularly. Undoubtedly a Hawksworth, though. The nearest resemblance, a portrait at the Hall of the grandfather who'd fought at Sebastopol.

It became obvious those early days of August that Willow

had quite a crush on him . . . Strange, Teddy thought, considering I was in love with Gib at sixteen, I never think of Willow, and boys, and love.

But . . . that furious blushing when we met him in the village shop. That watching him under her lashes in church – to see without being seen. Then when I arrange a tennis afternoon, she is struck dumb. She plays with him in mixed doubles and every time he speaks to her she turns bright pink, unable to say a word . . . It's unlikely she will tell me anything about it . . . He seems scarcely to notice her, being as he is the centre of attraction. I would have expected him to be spoilt. He is not.

It had seemed an obscenity, this hive of activity, as August wore on – warm, dry, reminding her of the dry hot July of 1914. As one event succeeded another, it became apparent the time had passed for going back to Paris. Military reservists were called up. There were mass evacuation plans, including the children they were to take in here. A scurry of preparations. People's cancelled or curtailed holidays.

Christopher had rejoined his regiment, to be ready to go to France. Lily had not died. Her pain and discomfort, her terrible colour . . . Erik's distress. Teddy told him: 'If, when, something happens to Mother, you'll go to Denmark? It's what she would expect . . .'

And indeed the next day Lily said: 'You'll make sure Erik goes home? He's been a long time away. And on my account too . . .'

Some days she was lucid, some not. It was when her mind wandered, she said the most. She spoke of Val (*my father*, thought Teddy), and once or twice imagined it the turn of the century, that she was in Rumania again. One very hot day, she told Teddy, 'It will be cooler of course as soon as we get up into the mountains. Sophie's villa in Sinaia, we shall be comfortable . . . And Val, although he may go shooting, will come back to us . . . He was always faithful, you know, *in his heart* . . .'

Lucid, she gave all her love to Erik. Telling him again and again, in Teddy's presence, in Willow's, that he had saved her life. 'You don't know, never will know though I've tried to tell you . . . How you came and saved me when it was impossible. When it was *all impossible* . . .'

Listening to her, Teddy thought: If I could have hoped for something like that . . . But Mother was older than I am now. I *should* hope. Only where are these people? Erik, Henri (but *I must not think of him* . . .) Where are they to be found?

She had been uncertain whether or not to do something about Henri. In a moment of sudden hope she had thought: I could try and get Aimée Ribourel's address in the Romanche – she will know who were the guests who brought him . . . An advertisement in the principal Montreal newspaper? Saying that if Henri will contact Teddee, he will hear something to his advantage . . . There was something pathetic, distasteful even, about that notion . . .

War grew nearer by the day. So did Lily's death. When on the first of September, Hitler invaded Poland, she was comatose and semi-delirious. That evening, in a voice tired and pain-filled but clear as that of a young girl, she told Teddy, 'I have been so happy, I was so lucky. Try to be happy, Teddy darling . . .' Willow, who had sat by the bed all day, was holding her hand. 'And Willow too . . . Willow . . .'

She was unconscious most of Saturday the second. Then late in the evening:

'Strange,' she said, 'we've been having a little tea-party under the trees. Sadie in the hammock. She expects her baby any moment . . . No . . . The War . . . Christopher was born the week . . . July nineteen-fourteen . . . Now another war starts. And I'm dying. Strange . . .' Then she added matter-of-factly: 'I think I shall have to go, soon.' Three hours before Chamberlain's broadcast, she died.

Teddy wrote to the American relations. Daisy wrote back, sad about Lily's death. She included some family news. One of her grand-daughters, Jay's sister Esther, had just married. Jay was home again in New York but she wasn't certain of his plans. There had been girl trouble. She didn't say in which country. Teddy wondered . . . Hadn't Michael's fiancée been his girl? He will recover, she thought. She'd met him only once since 1923 but had thought: I recognize in him (mixed with whatever other heritage) that fall-on-your-feet, survivor's streak that darling Sylvia lacked, and Mother did not. Which old Grandad Greenwood had almost too much of . . .

Alice, still in Switzerland, wrote that she would be staying on there. She promised Mass offerings for Mother. She was well and happy, she said. Her tuberculosis, it seemed was either quiescent or cured, and her spirits good. Whatever the crisis had been . . . She enclosed a letter for Willow. Willow did not show it to Teddy, but told her: 'I shan't worry about Aunt Alice now . . .'

Underneath the spreading chestnut tree, Neville Chamberlain said to me, 'If you want to get your gas masks free, join the blinking ARP . . .'

But they were free anyway, Teddy thought. To everyone. The little children at The Towers had Mickey Mouse ones. Some panicked, some found them fun. Dear God, may it never be for real . . .

They slept on little canvas camp beds, with donated patchwork quilts . . . By six-thirty every morning they would be running around. They were dressed, given breakfast, and potted – she had not done much potting at the orphanage . . . Then except for the really tiny ones, they sat in a ring, Teddy in the middle, while she read to them. They all had to blow their noses before she began.

"*. . . and Bay Bear said, WHO'S been sleeping in MY bed?*"

At lunch they sang grace: *Thank you for the world so sweet, thank you for the food we eat . . .* The older ones waiting on the younger. In the afternoons they ran about, then after a bath at six were read to again. By seven they were tucked up. They cried for their mothers regularly.

The arrangement was only temporary. Other plans were being made for them. A convent on the Yorkshire coast might be evacuated here instead. But meanwhile, she loved the children . . .

Sadie, typically, had turned the Hall into the permanent wartime home for a hospital of crippled children. Rows of small white cots, little ones hopping on crutches (reminding Teddy of Vincent all those years ago). Charlie stayed quietly in the rooms set aside for the family. His disease, diagnosed now as Parkinson's, had become since the beginning of the War rather worse. Sadie was in her element with these children: Teddy imagined it kept her mind off the worry of Christopher, already over in France.

Although nothing much was happening there . . . From the copies of French *Vogue* she continued to receive, and from letters, it seemed light-hearted still in Paris . . . While here, Christmas in sight already, and not a sign of a bomb. The Bore War, the Funny War, they called it . . .

As expected, Erik had gone to Denmark to join his daughter and her family. 'After all, Erik dear,' Teddy told him, 'it's your own country. Here in Yorkshire you only have memories. However happy . . .'

The blackout was bad, but must be much worse in the big towns. Here it was simpler not to venture out after nightfall. Rationing had not yet begun. It would start in the New Year, they were told. They would get four ounces of bacon and four ounces of butter a week.

Finland, oppressed by the Russians, suffered. There was an appeal for furs. Teddy sent Lily's Persian lamb, and her own white lamb. Then wondered if she should have sold them and donated the money.

Henri offering to buy me a wild mink . . . What world, what life was that in?

22

Willow is in love. His name is Gerry and he's dark and a little taller than her, provided she wears flat shoes. He is not the first: she's spent the time between her sixteenth birthday on the eve of the War and now, March 1941, falling in love. One time it lasted three months, another – three weeks. Once it was all of three days.

She told Teddy: 'It's funny. Each time I'm quite absolutely certain. I mean, it *feels* right – and then . . . All these princes that turn into frogs . . . When it's finished, I can't think how I ever.' It was all tremendously exciting . . .

She did wonder sometimes: thinking how Teddy had married so young, and had lots and lots of men friends. 'Teddy's boyfriends,' someone had remarked once. 'They'd make a rugger fifteen, *and* the opposing side.' Perhaps she had inherited a tendency like that herself? But seventeen, she thought, was a bit young to hang a label on oneself. And much too young to be serious about anyone . . .

Or so she'd thought, before she met Gerry.

She was living with Teddy now, and had been since the New Year. There had been a difficult patch last year when The Towers was turned over to a girls' convent, evacuated from the East Coast. She found some irony in this transformation of her home into a *convent*. (Whenever she thought now of Our Lady of V, she shuddered . . .)

Teddy was driving ambulances. She worked very hard on alternating day and night shifts. After leaving the north a year ago, she'd rented a mews flat in central London. Willow had pleaded to join her. But although before Dunkirk it had looked possible, after it had not. When the raids had begun in earnest it seemed foolhardy for her to be there rather than somewhere safe. 'It's quite different for me,' Teddy had explained. 'Someone has to work her. Anyway I've *had* my life. Yours is yet to come . . .'

Then the raids had eased off. Living with them had in any case become a way of life – although sometimes when she saw

Teddy looking worried, she would think that perhaps she shouldn't have persuaded her . . . But she hated the idea of being sent up to Flaxthorpe . . . A couple of weeks ago they'd had the worst snowstorm there since 1888. Snow falling for over fifty hours and the troops in to clear the roads. She had liked imagining The Towers Convent (they called it St Anne's) under siege . . .

Since January she'd been doing a secretarial course at the Triangle in South Molton Street, and enjoying it a lot. Shorthand was a wonderful blend of secret code, pictorial art, drawing puzzles, and a foreign language – she found each new series of squiggles more exciting. The other girls thought her mad, although they said so very nicely. She liked typing too. Playing the piano in the dark was how she thought of it, those early days with the keyboard covered up . . .

As well as attending the college, she helped at the Feathers club, doing lunches or breakfasts. It was there she'd met Gerry, or rather Gerry's mother and later, Gerry. He was in the Navy, at present working at the Admiralty, though he expected, and Willow feared, that soon he would be back at sea.

She liked living with Teddy. They seemed to get on well and be friends – perhaps because they did not have to spend too much time together. Mostly too they kept off any very deep subjects. Once, though, almost by chance, they had begun talking and then gone on far into the night.

That was the time Teddy told her *who* her father was. The man that Mummy had Loved . . . It wasn't she who asked. She could see too that Teddy was surprised she hadn't done so before . . . It gave her a curious feeling, *knowing*. It meant nothing. He wasn't a *person*. Just a father . . .

She didn't even ask what he was like . . . It was Teddy who said:

'I expect you'll want to know something about him . . . Of course Mother, your grandmother, would have known more. I only met him once, when I came over for Robert's funeral. He was tall. Thin. Your build – lanky. Gentle. He had an invalid wife. Three children . . .' (My half-brothers and sisters, Willow thought.) 'He was in Flaxthorpe less than a year. Went abroad. The Colonies – Kenya, Rhodesia, somewhere like that . . .'

The information sank like a stone. That was just how it felt. A stone in her heart.

Teddy wasn't at all strict. In the four weeks she'd known Gerry, Willow had been allowed a lot of freedom. They went out usually in the early evening, not staying late. It was light till well after six now that the clocks had been kept forward. Once they went to the Savoy with Gerry's parents and danced to Carroll Gibbons's Orpheans, playing underground. Sometimes they ate at the Causerie in Claridge's. She got on very well with his parents. There was another brother, John, in the army, who had been captured at Dunkirk.

Teddy had a protégée, Isabelle, the daughter of French friends. She'd got out of Paris last year before the invasion and now worked at the Free French club. She and Teddy sat and gossiped sometimes. Occasionally there would be a night out when Isabelle and a partner would join Teddy and Willow and *their* men.

And that means Gerry, Willow thought. She had a photograph beside her bed of him in his Lieutenant's uniform. His hair grew very thick and he had beautifully chiselled lips and very blue eyes. He was in love as well. With Willow.

Isabelle would be twenty-one on March 9th, a Sunday. Teddy wanted to make up a party for her. 'It will have to be the Saturday,' she said. 'A nightclub. Four or six of us. I'm on an early shift that day . . .'

Willow told Gerry. 'You'll come, won't you? In fact you're officially invited . . .'

He 'phoned her:

'Mama says why not the Cafe de P? Douglas Byng's in cabaret there, I *think* we like him . . . It was a favourite pre-war haunt of John's. Little brother never got asked along . . .'

Teddy agreed. 'A better idea than Quag's or the Four Hundred – or that one that used to be the Stratton before a bomb took it. The Suivi, is it?'

Willow bought a new evening dress, without asking Teddy's advice. It was pale blue organza with a tiered skirt and wide straps above a square neckline, and with artificial flowers at the waist and one shoulder. She liked it when she'd bought it, although she thought it made her look a little frail.

The party was for Saturday the eighth. On the Thursday evening, she had a gritty throat. I'll ignore it, she thought. Every day in every way I am getting better and better . . . But when she woke it was swollen and sore. Teddy said, 'It doesn't look suitable for taking out dancing . . .'

'I'll be all right,' she said. (I shall be too.)

But Teddy wanted to cancel the party: 'Postpone it, rather. Isabelle won't mind . . .'

'Go without me,' Willow said. 'It's just that . . . Gerry and I – we were *terribly* looking forward . . .' She sneezed.

Although very snuffly, she was a little better on the Saturday. 'You've had your way,' Teddy said, 'you can give everyone your cold . . . We're going, definitely.'

Teddy had invited a Major Beazley. One of her Men, Willow supposed. Although a bit old. Fiftyish. But perhaps Teddy needed them older and older. She was *forty*, after all.

On the evening Teddy wore a lovely midnight blue velvet dress. Isabelle, her hair a mass of dark curls, wearing a very bright lipstick and a dark red dress, arrived in a taxi with a Capitaine Raoul Lemercier of the Free French. She was bubbling with excitement. She told Willow, who was dabbing at her sore nose: 'I never forgive you if you shouldn't have come to my *anniversaire*.'

Willow had two pairs of silk stockings for her, but refused to tell anyone where she'd got them. She felt hot and cold, a little feverish: very much wanting Gerry to arrive. Now that she had seen Isabelle's dress with its tight-fitting bodice and simple cut, she wasn't quite so sure about her new one. She longed for Gerry to tell her she was beautiful.

And suddenly, here he was. The beloved, looking so wonderful in his uniform. Better even than in white tie and tails . . .

They sat for a while drinking sherry. The Major seemed boring. He stared at Teddy a lot. The best, Willow thought, was knowing Gerry watched *her* all the time as she talked and laughed – and sneezed.

'Bless you,' the Major said predictably.

Gerry said, 'You know what I heard, blast it? No Douglas Byng after all. He's been pinched for a Charity do.'

'Oh,' Willow said, looking at him. 'Oh well. Worse things happen at sea.'

It was a moonlit night. They got into two taxis. The Café de Paris was underground, in Coventry Street, off Piccadilly. A cinema above it. As they went down the long flight of stairs to the foyer, Gerry said, 'Know what this place used to be, darling?'

'No.'

'A bearpit. Honestly. That's why it's below ground, sunken like this . . .'

'All to the good these days,' the Major said. 'We shan't hear a damn thing . . .'

Willow came out of the cloakroom, and stepped on to the balcony encircling the restaurant. Gerry stood beside her. He said, 'I'm the captain, this is the bridge of my ship. I'm looking down on the quarterdeck . . .'

'You are silly,' she said. Then: 'I'm so happy, and excited . . .'

The double curved stairway led down to the dance floor and tables. The bandstand was between the stairs. Teddy and her Major went down first. Willow wondered if he perhaps bored her? He seemed, even as a companion for someone of forty, rather heavy going. When they were home again, she and Teddy might have a laugh about him . . .

The mirrors round the walls gave a sparkling effect. Most of the men dining and dancing were in uniform. There were even a few kilts. It was very crowded – and exciting. Willow thought: I like it that way. Squeezing Gerry's hand as they sat down at their table.

He said, looking around, 'That's another thing. This whole decor and everything, when they first turned it into a ballroom – nineteen-ten or eleven – it got modelled on the dining and ballroom of the *Titanic* – first class, of course . . . which was just being built. That's what I meant by being Captain on the bridge . . .'

'You do know a lot,' she said.

'Brother John told me. He's a mine of information on all such matters. *And* on the best dancing places . . .'

Teddy was ordering cocktails. Willow said, 'I want to try a Between the Sheets –'

Raoul asked what that was. Teddy didn't know. The Major said he thought Willow would be better to have a Maiden's Blush. Isabelle frowned as if not quite understanding, and then laughed. She had a frank, infectious laugh. Gerry said, laughing too, 'Willow's only ordering that sort of thing because she thinks it's smart.'

Teddy said, 'Cocktails were meant to be so wildly decadent when I was young, but Mother always said the fast set among the Edwardians – she may have included herself – had been drinking them for *years* . . .'

The music was Ken Johnson and his Caribbean Band. Snakehips Johnson, he was known as. 'Isn't he wonderful?' Gerry said. 'His *Snakehips Swing*. One of us should tell him it's your birthday, Isabelle. He might play a request.'

Teddy said, 'I've got this mad urge to sing to him *Tell me, are you from Georgetown*? which he is, to the tune of *Tell me, are you from Georgia*? She paused. 'I used to have that sort of cheek . . .'

Gerry asked, 'Did you never want to sing and dance, Mrs Nicolson, like your mother?'

'We're not concentrating on *food*,' Teddy said. 'If we don't give our order soon . . .'

The Major said, 'Drink's easy. We're sticking to champagne. Beats me, though, why you spoil a fine taste with cocktails –'

When they'd finally made up their minds, Raoul asked very politely if the lamb would be pink: 'If it will be brown I don't choose . . .' Isabelle told him off. 'You've escaped from the Germans – and you worry about pink lamb . . .'

'But that's what it's being – to be free,' he protested. Isabelle held a cigarette out for him to light, shrugging her shoulders, laughing. Seeing Teddy take one out too, the Major fumbled for his lighter.

'While we're waiting,' Teddy said, 'I'll just go and have a quick word with Harry –'

'Harry?'

'McElhone. Harry's New York Bar. The Rue Daunou. He got out when the Germans came. Raoul, you're Parisian, you'll know? He's barman here now . . .'

Willow didn't enjoy her Between the Sheets. She made Gerry drink most of it. The Major said, 'I told you you should have a Maiden's Blush.' But by this time the first of the champagne had arrived. Seeing it beaded, bubbling in her glass, she felt a sudden surge of happiness, excitement . . .

'Willow,' cried Teddy, coming back now to the table, 'you'll never guess who's here –'

'Reverend Mutt from Our Lady of V.'

'Darling . . . No, *Jay*. With a glamourous blonde. They're at the bar, just arrived. *And* he's in uniform. Ours . . . He's a horse gunner. He came back last May. Wicked, I said to him, not telling us a *thing* . . . In a little when they've ordered, he's coming over to talk . . .'

She explained Jay to the others. How they were always losing touch. 'I sang lullabies to him and his brother Harry, once upon a time . . . More recently, he was dreadfully kind to Willow when she was in a fix, just after Munich . . .'

Willow thought: I want to see him, I want to show him Gerry. She thought too that she'd like to be seen by Jay in *her* glamour. Grown up.

As their first course was served, Teddy said, 'By the way there's an alert outside, Jay says. The banshees are wailing . . .'

'Couldn't be in a better place,' the Major said. 'Good as a shelter.' The waiter brought another bottle. Rattle of the ice-bucket. 'Champers, that's the stuff . . .'

Raoul had lit up after finishing his soup. He seemed a heavy smoker, like Teddy. Willow thought of becoming one too. So far she'd never managed to keep a cigarette alight.

Her champagne glass was full. Gerry looked across at her and then, as the music started: 'I'm going to ask the birthday girl for a dance, darling,' he said. He turned: 'Isabelle?'

She felt a sickening wave of jealousy. Isabelle, in her red dancing frock, so poised, so vivacious, her hair just right. Her hands, small, neat, the nails well shaped, a vivid scarlet. *Why do I bite mine*? Gerry had remarked on it. From tomorrow, I shall stop . . .

Before the evening began, I was so certain . . . As the band struck up *Oh, Johnny, Oh*: I can't bear it, she thought. Gerry and I love this tune. Gerry has the Orrin Tucker record at home. We've played it together. He could have, should have, asked me . . .

As Gerry swept Isabelle on to the floor, away out of sight. '*Oh Johnny, oh Johnny, how you can love* . . .' Raoul smiled at Willow. She thought: *He's* going to ask me. She was trying to decide if she should say yes (he was after all shorter than her –

they might look odd) when, stubbing out his cigarette, he turned to Teddy . . . As they moved off, Willow thought: He just wants to chatter in French . . .

She was left with the Major.

'*You're not handsome it's true, but when I look at you, I just* . . .'

'Old tune, this,' he said, wiping his moustache. 'Fourteen-eighteen – goes back to the last show . . .'

'. . . *And when you're near I just can't sit still a minute,* . . .'

The rhythm was bouncy. She wanted to bounce. She imagined herself out on the floor there. Why can't . . .

When she said nothing, the Major went on, 'Not too keen on this sort of dancing. But – been to worse spots. Dreadful, some of them. Shuffling around, floor the size of a dumb waiter . . .'

'*You make my sad heart jump with joy* . . .'

The Major drummed his fingers on the table. '*The Times* goes up to threepence next month. Bad, that. The whole world's going to pot . . .'

Second chorus now. '. . . *Oh Johnny, oh Johnny, please tell me, dear, what makes me love you so* . . .'

Willow, feet tap-tapping, craned to try and see Isabelle and Gerry. They must be over by the band. Gerry might be trying to get a request. Stemming her irritation, she said, 'Can't you read it in your Mess or Club or whatever? Save money that way?' What an old fogey he was . . .

'My dear girl –' he began.

She lifted her glass. And then it happened.

Something . . . her head . . . as if she'd been kicked by a giant. Then suddenly – darkness.

Where am I? She was sitting on the ground. In the silence. Half-light. Eerie *silence.* At the table she could see the Major . . . He stared at her. He was staring and staring. Covered in dust. She was covered in dust. Everything . . . She opened her mouth to call out – but no sound came. It's the silence of death, we are all dead. She saw the Major's mouth move. She couldn't turn her head. His mouth opened and shut.

How long was it? Minutes, seconds . . . Her head felt loose suddenly – trembled, jerked from side to side, uncontrollably.

Then screams, groans, wave upon wave of *sound* – as if suddenly a door had opened somewhere. More, more. She could turn her head properly now. She saw that *something terrible had happened.*

Just near her, a figure lay twisted. Bleeding. Blood everywhere. Someone screaming, louder than the others, above the whimpers. Still the Major didn't move.

Her mouth was full of dust. Dust coated everything. She said thickly, 'Teddy, *where's Teddy*?' Reaching out, wanting to shake the Major. She was afraid to move from where she was. Something worse might happen. A voice behind said, 'Bombs, they were *bombs* . . .'

But *where was Teddy*? And Gerry, oh where was Gerry? She called out, 'Gerry – where are you?' Her legs buckled under her as she stood up. She went a few yards on her hands and knees. She saw her hand was covered with blood. Not my own, not my own. Just as it's not *me* screaming . . .

She stood up again. The waist of her dress was ripped. Her foot caught in it, so that she stumbled. A man in a kilt helped her up. 'Where's my aunt Teddy?' she sobbed, 'my aunt, my aunt . . .' 'Don't fret,' he said, 'We'll find her . . .' Before she could speak again he was gone.

She could see light now up on the balcony. But oh, the balcony – it was about to fall . . . Bodies. People everywhere. Somewhere was Teddy. And Gerry and . . .

A woman's voice, whimpering, 'Help, help *here*. Someone *help* –'

She saw the woman was holding the bloody head of a man.

'I can't, I don't – I'll try and do something.' She saw then a large man in khaki was helping. Lifting the man.

'Oh, *where's Teddy*?' she sobbed, 'please, where's –'

From behind a squeaky-voiced young man cried, 'They're dead, all dead, this table. Look, all dead.' Excited, almost hysterical. She looked quickly. But *they're alive* . . . she thought. She did not want to look again.

A hand came round her shoulder.

'Hey there, Willow . . . Willow, are you OK?'

She turned. And then clung to him. 'Oh *Jay*.' Her voice was someone else's. 'Jay, oh Jay. *Teddy* –'

'OK. OK, Willow – Laura and I, we'll help you find her.' A blonde girl came up beside him.

'We're fine,' she said. 'God, if we weren't lucky . . . We're trying to give a hand now, Jay's doing what he can –'

Willow held on to Jay still. 'The far end, by the band, I haven't been . . . Gerry was dancing –'

They made their way nearer to the double staircases. She made out one side, blocked with dust and debris.

The flare of a cigarette lighter. A man, sitting on the floor near them.

'Put that out. At once.' Jay's voice, peremptory, sharp. Voice of authority. 'For Chrissake, we'll *all* go up. Gas. Gas . . .'

Then suddenly: Teddy. Black hair white with dust. Clasping Willow to her *like a mother*. 'Darling, darling . . .'

She had Raoul with her. Jay said, 'Thank God –'

Willow sobbed, 'Your Major's all right, I saw he was all right.'

Teddy said, 'I've been there – to the table, looking for you. But he couldn't talk. He's . . .' She held Willow close. 'Darling – Gerry and Isabelle –'

'Where's Gerry? I was just going. I –'

'Don't go. Not that way. Isabelle –' Her voice raggedy. 'Gerry too . . . Both of them.'

'I want to see. Where's Gerry, *where is he*?'

'Hush,' Teddy was saying. 'Hush. You don't want . . .'

'They're not dead, they can't be dead . . .'

She was never sure how she got through the next hour or so.

Teddy kept saying angrily, 'The ambulances – why aren't they here?' She couldn't understand, she said. Her own section was just nearby . . .

Teddy, Jay, and Laura too were the efficient ones. Raoul and Willow just did as they were told. Raoul seemed stunned, bewildered. Someone had rigged up a light with flex from a point out in the passage. They congregated there. Dinner napkins, torn-up tablecloths – they used them as rough bandages, or to staunch blood. Champagne poured over a wound, cleansing it. 'Alcohol, any you can find,' Teddy said. 'That'll do.' Stretchers were made from screens . . .

Jay was directing things. Teddy too. Willow found that because of them, she too could help, be calm, *seem all right* . . .

She had a cut on her neck – it must have come from a piece of glass. She couldn't feel anything but she saw now that there was blood on her dress as well as the blood from the people she was helping . . . It didn't hurt at all. There was a lot of glass about, broken. Great jagged pieces, slivers like stilettos.

And over all – a horrible bitter, pungent smell which stung her nostrils . . .

The Major was given more brandy. He continued to sit in absolute silence. Willow wanted to ask: Can he talk? She thought with horror – he might be dumb for the remainder of his life . . .

She said, 'Fancy Isabelle escaping from France – and then this . . .' As she spoke her mouth kept drying up. She was shaking. She said twice, 'Say he's not dead, they're not dead.' She thought then: They never let me see Mummy. I saw her in the prison hospital while she was ill. But afterwards, when she died, I *never saw her* . . .

They left the Café de Paris. Staggering up from that same entrance that only a few hours earlier . . .

A girl who had followed them up said to her partner: 'I don't give a damn. You have to *show* them . . . I'm going on to the Suivi, I'm going to keep on dancing . . . Grab a taxi, would you, darling?'

People had congregated, of course. It was only natural. And disgusting. Jay had his arm round Willow. Laura and Raoul, and Teddy and her Major came up behind. Perhaps there weren't as many people as she thought – there only *seemed* a lot. But it was as if they pressed on her and Jay – on all of them, as they came out. Her eyes met those of a fat man in a blue muffler, his mouth half open in curiosity . . .

The six of them went into a hotel just near. A number of survivors of the raid were already there. She walked dizzily, supported still by Jay. Once she turned her head: a looking-glass on her left. She said, 'Oh, who's that?' in a foolish trembling voice. Scarecrow almost, blue organza in stained tatters, white dust over all, blonde hair gone a greyish yellow, an ageing face. Blood ran down her neck.

Teddy was in a fury still. 'Jay, I have to tell Isabelle's parents –'

Gerry's family. Willow said, 'Who's telling Gerry's family, parents? I can't – you won't expect . . .'

She sat in a chair. Brandy, she had to sip brandy. They

looked at her neck more closely. She had said over and over it was nothing, that it was other people's blood. But Jay said now that it almost certainly needed stitching. Charing Cross Hospital was dealing with casualties. He said he'd take her. Laura, who seemed easy and friendly and eager to help, said she would come too. Teddy was taking care of the Major, and Raoul, who still seemed very shocked.

At the hospital they asked her if she wanted to stay in for the night. They said that she too was shocked.

She told the nurse who was attending to her, 'Last time I was stitched up was when Tootles bolted with me.' (Oh easy nuisance . . . no matter of life and death . . .)

'Well, what about staying in, Willow? Resting . . .'

But she wanted to go back home to Teddy.

'Tell me Gerry's not dead,' she said flatly.

'If I did, it wouldn't help,' Jay said. 'Look, little cousin –'

She felt numb still. Not just where they had stitched her neck, but all over.

She knew she didn't believe about Gerry and Isabelle. It isn't true, she said to herself, how can it be true? *I can't bear it to be true . . .*

23

'*And when you turned and looked at me, a nightingale sang in Berkeley Square . . .*'

Teddy's dress was crêpe, in a vivid orange. The bodice ruched, the shoulders wide and padded. Large bishop sleeves billowed as she danced.

Dancing . . . She had thought once: I shall never dance again. I never expected to want to, ever.

She told her escort:

'Nearly two years ago now, to the day. The Café de Paris. Thirty dead – sixty or so wounded. Two killed out of our party of six. And I'm angry still. It produced in me such a rage against the enemy, like nothing in the last War, nothing I saw in the Blitz. It's irrational . . . but I have this hatred now. All things German. Nazi – no, *German.* If I could actually *do* something . . .

'You seem to me to be doing a lot . . . Working all hours . . .'

He was a colonel, in his mid-forties. She'd met him a few times before, refused two dates, and now given in. He was pleasant, even if he didn't dance well.

'. . . *there were angels dining at the Ritz, and a nightingale sang* . . .' She said, 'Dreadfully sentimental, but can you imagine an evening without their playing it?'

His grip tightened slightly. 'Who started it all?'

'That revue, *New Faces.* Dunkirk time, about. Someone called Judy Campbell sang it . . . And then all that blitzing of Berkeley Square . . .'

The tune had changed: '. . . *I haven't said thanks for that lovely weekend* . . .' Vera Lynn had sung it. She said something . . .

'Oh yes, well, Vera Lynn,' he said. 'What must it be like to be Forces' Sweetheart?'

'Rather nice, I should think. We all want to be loved.'

'Agreed. Only some of us go about it in an odd way.'

He spoke light-heartedly enough but with a bitter undertone. She thought probably he was referring to his wife. The marriage she had heard was not good. She wondered idly: Am I beginning another affaire? On balance probably not . . .

'The song's been banned in the States –'

'Why's that?' he asked.

'Because it doesn't actually *say* the couple are married . . .'

'Ah. Yes, a dirty weekend . . .'

They were back at their table, and drinking Algerian wine. Dining and dancing in 1943 – it was what one must expect. And the food . . . Ubiquitous rabbit. Fricasseed or, as tonight, curried. (Is it cat sometimes? she wondered.)

They danced again. *The last time I saw Paris.*

'This is better – quickstepping's more my mark . . . *The last time I saw Paris* . . . Nineteen-thirty-seven. A two-hour wait for the Dijon express, and just the Gare de Lyon restaurant for sustenance. Could have been worse.' He twirled her round . . . 'And when did *you* last see Paris?'

'Oh, 'thirty-nine. July . . .'

'Last fling, was it? Know her well?'

'I lived there.'

Voice, face, alert . . .

'Really? That's interesting –'

'Why?'

'Oh . . . Other people – what they do, why they do it . . . Did you live there long?'

'Since nineteen-twenty-two.'

'So if it hadn't been for Jerry . . . Nearly twenty years. French good?'

'Possibly somewhat Belgian . . . Yes, very . . . I learned it well in the last war – a family from Bruges. The daughter was my age . . .'

'Which is? A gentleman never asks, but I'm interested – you look too young. A small child then, in the last war?'

'I age with the century. It's convenient, and I don't have to think . . .'

'Fit? Are you fit?' He asked it idly enough, but she sensed interest. My God, she thought, he can't be planning Free French basket-ball . . .

'I don't play games –'

'I didn't suggest . . . Health, stamina, resilience?'

'You're quizzing me. I can run for a bus without noticing

and I'm never ill. Good enough?' Her tone was sharp.

'Sorry. I'm being boring . . .'

At the table he picked up the empty bottle. 'Another Algy? I'll summon the waiter –'

'It can give one a frightful head, and I have to be up early. I'm on a seven a.m. . . . And these cold mornings . . . One thinks sometimes it will *always* be wartime.'

'Please sit down, Mrs Nicolson. I'm sorry, this room does have a somewhat depressing appearance . . . Wartime and all that. A hotel bedroom of the smaller variety . . . I wrote to you, invited you here, Mrs Nicolson, because I think you could possibly be of help to us. I know your present war work is essential –'

'Driving ambulances? Yes. Though with the bombing a little quieter –'

'Let's hope it stays that way . . . I'm told your French is excellent and that you know France well. Paris in particular . . .'

'I lived there, yes.'

'And you hope one day to go back?'

'Not *hope* . . . *Shall* –'

'I see. Good. And the day now perhaps not so far away as it was once . . . A lot nearer than when your French friend was killed in March of 'forty-one.'

'You seem to know a great deal about me. Who's been talking to you?'

'Yes, I think so. But favourably. A suggestion that you are perhaps the sort of person . . . Intelligent, fit. The Stage in the family – so acting ability, perhaps? French-speaking, habituée of Paris. Not young but with mature outlook, experience of life . . . There might be something for you . . . Work –'

'Work where I could use the language? I –'

'Work where you'll be able to use no other . . . In the country itself. In France.'

'That's ridiculous . . . And hardly likely –'

'Mrs Nicolson, what does the word *agent* mean to you?'

'Spy . . . Anarchist . . . Joseph Conrad.'

'I see. Yes. Well. Let me put it this way, then . . . We are an organization. We train men and women to work in France alongside the Resistance movement there . . . Our agents are dropped into the country – where they act as wireless operators, saboteurs, couriers . . . Sabotage is a very important part of our work . . . Messages have to be taken – often long distances – people accompanied . . . A great deal of the work is boring, monotonous. Quite unlike any possible fantasies you may have of the spy world . . . But however humdrum – it is *never* without danger . . .'

'Scarcely surprising . . .'

'For an agent, the penalties of being discovered are very serious. There's always the possibility he or she will fail to return The Geneva Convention . . . You would count as a spy . . .'

'How many have *failed to return*? In ordinary language – how many have you lost?'

'That's not the sort of information –'

'Two can play at question and answer . . . And by the way, aren't you, and this place, something to do with the War Office? Perhaps you could tell me the truth, then, about the Dieppe raid last summer? I wasn't happy with the official line . . .'

'Not our department. Mrs Nicolson, I think perhaps . . . to change the subject . . . Can we go back a little? I'd like to ask you something more about yourself – if I may? What have you, who have you, in the way of dependants? Close relatives?'

'A nephew, married, in the RAF. A niece – she's nineteen, working for the Ministry of Aircraft Production.'

'Yes . . . I want to ask you also . . . Could you *live a lie*, Mrs Nicolson?'

'It depends on the lie . . . Yes, I could.'

'Are you courageous?'

'Possibly not . . .'

'Or possibly – yes? Mrs Nicolson, what I've told you, all I have spoken of today, is of course confidential. I would expect you to respect this confidence . . . I should like you to think about it all very carefully. In fact, it is very important that you give it considered thought . . . Remember, there is *no shame* in refusing. Better to refuse than find later you should never have accepted . . .'

Her mouth was dry. She looked for water but could see

none. A handbasin in the corner. What must have been a simple hotel bedroom . . .

‘Go home quietly. As you drive your ambulance around in the next week or two, think about what I’ve said .’.’. When you’re ready, then let me know . . . Yea or nay.’

‘If it’s yea,’ she said, ‘how soon could I start?’

24

'Well then,' Mrs Parr told Willow, 'there's been a big victory in Africa. They've got that General von something and I don't know how many took prisoner. They said it on the news, you'd have heard if you'd not been snoring . . . And what about your breakfast? It's all dried up now is your scrambled egg.'

Willow stifled a yawn. Waiting to hear from her landlady that if only she didn't stay out so late nights, she'd be bright in the morning. That was as may be. The other piece of good news, which Mrs Parr had told her before the news of victory in the North African campaign (which *must* mean Jay would be safer. *Please*, God . . .) was that another girl would be coming to share her billet. Three weeks alone with Mrs Parr had been much too much.

She looked at her plate, and felt nausea. Its origins as dried egg powder were very obvious. Bright orange undissolved lumps . . .

'I have to queue, you know,' Mrs Parr said. 'You girls don't have the worries I have. Sitting on your backsides all day, coming home to a nice hot meal . . .'

'I meant to say I'm not in for tea tonight. Some of us are going to a dance in Knaresborough.'

It was her second billet since coming up to Harrogate. The first had been a really lovely house in York Place, also run by a widow. They were four girls there – then the landlady had become too ill to have billetees.

Altogether Willow had been nearly three months in Yorkshire. She did clerical work for the Ministry of Aircraft Production, using some of the typing skills she'd learned from the Triangle. She had never finished there, because she'd left London almost immediately after the Café de Paris incident.

Mrs Parr had three overalls in flowery patterns: a red, a blue and a yellow, all with a brown background. She wore curlers in the morning, and if she planned to go out in the evening would be wearing them still when Willow came back at six. With them out, her hair looked like two rows of greasy sausages, and reminded Willow horribly of their owner's cooking . . .

Till now Willow had been the only billetee, succeeding a Miss Mason who had gone back south. She'd realized from the first day that it wasn't going to be easy . . .

The piano, for instance. The piano took pride of place in the small front room:

'You'll not touch that?' Mrs Parr had said, the day she arrived.

'I can't actually play the piano,' Willow had explained.

'I just want it clear between us at the start . . . If folk *play* it, there's anything might happen to a piano. It does it no good, having its keys struck . . .'

May 1943. Two years and two months since the Café de Paris. She thought she must be over it by now, but was not sure. It didn't seem like it when the dreams came. The nightmares. It was as if the two terrible times in her life had joined together and made one. She was back in the eerie half-light, in the Café de P. Her legs buckled under her. She was rooted then. *She could not move.* She was looking for her mother. If she could *move*, then she'd be able to rescue her. Only she could save her. 'I'm coming,' she would try to call out. 'Don't worry, *I'll save you.*' But just as she couldn't walk, neither could she talk . . .

Once the dream was almost happy, because she found her. It wasn't the mother she remembered, but *Sylvia*, from the photograph. She was so beautiful. The air raid, everything had been a mistake. They even laughed about it. They were all dancing together. *Sylvia* was dressed in white and at her neck and throat and almost down to her waist she sparkled with diamonds. They were reflected in the glass at the sides of the dance floor. She was waltzing with a tall man, and looked wonderfully, wonderfully happy. She shone even more than the diamonds. Willow could see only the man's back as he danced by. But she knew, in the dream, that he was her father.

Sometimes now she would think: Mummy, Gerry . . . *to lose people, I only have to love them.*

She'd thought for so many months afterwards about Gerry. She felt certain it had truly been love. It would have lasted – even though separated they would have grown closer to each other. She imagined herself writing to him every day, watching anxiously for the post. Getting to know him better and better through *his* letters. They had already so much in common . . .

Now over two years had passed, and the terrible thing was *she couldn't remember what he looked like*. Isabelle's face, yes. The Major's . . . as if it were yesterday. But Gerry was just a face among dozens of others. A sort of amalgam of all the good-looking young men who'd chatted her up, escorted her since 1939.

Here in Yorkshire, in Harrogate, she was busy building up a *new* life. She had made friends at work (even if one of them was a mischief-making hard-faced girl called Olga, who wore a turban and slacks and too much lipstick, and smoked all the Lucky Strike she could get from the Americans at the camp). She went out dancing with the RAF, the Free French, the Poles, the Czechs. The days, the evenings, weren't long enough . . .

Her day went something like this. Two very loud alarm clocks ten minutes apart, then Mrs Parr banging on the door . . . A quick wash in the chill bathroom – as many as four days a week the bath would be full of Mrs Parr's washing, cold soaking. Requests for a bath were greeted by: 'What's wrong with a good *stand up* wash? At least you know you're clean . . .' She couldn't trust Willow either, she said, not to go over the line, painted in bold red paint, showing the limit for patriotic bath water. 'My last billetee, I could see by the ring she left. Never bothered scouring, didn't Miss Mason.' Miss Mason had been so terrible that Willow thought she must be better just by comparison . . .

The Ministry had taken over a hotel, the Harrogate Hydro. After breakfast there was the walk – no, the *run* up there, to sign on by nine. At ten past, a red line went in the book and latecomers had their pay docked. She couldn't afford that. She had to live on her pay and a very small allowance. Even if she'd had the coupons to spare, she couldn't have bought half the clothes she wanted . . . Teddy who'd arranged all her finance, kept her on a strict rein. The money Grandma had left her was all tied up.

She hadn't seen anything of Teddy for a long time. Teddy, once a second mother to her, who'd become a *friend.* She wrote to her every fortnight. Teddy's letters, not too frequent, were mostly concern about Willow, that she was coping all right.

A few months ago she had joined FANY. First Aid Nursing Yeomanry. The uniform was smart and suited her. They wore silk stockings. Willow supposed she was still driving, but officers now, not ambulances. It seemed somehow less useful work . . .

In a way, if anyone could be said to have taken especial care of her, it had been Jay. At least until he'd gone to fight in North Africa. For a while after they'd met in the raid, she had been so upset that only he had really been able to help. Teddy had been too close, too much part of it all.

The day after the raid he had telephoned the flat on his way back south again, to see if both of them, she and Teddy, were all right. She wrote him quite a long letter of thanks the next day. She remembered she'd never thanked him properly for all he had done when she'd run away to Cambridge. (Yet it was *his* fault, wasn't it, that they'd lost touch?)

Now it was twice he'd saved her . . . She had told him in the letter that she felt worse now than the night of the bombing. Much, much worse. 'But I don't want to worry Teddy with it . . .'

He telephoned her when he was passing through London about ten days later. He'd already answered her letter.

'How is it?' he asked. 'Did it get better at all?'

'It comes and goes,' she said.

'And right now?'

'Bad,' she said, beginning to cry. She was so *weak* . . .

'I can't get to see you, not this week . . . But listen, Willow . . . Write me. Whenever it comes on bad, write me. Exactly how you feel, right that moment. It'll be safe with me.'

'You'll destroy – them?' she'd asked anxiously. For some reason she imagined them left lying around carelessly – as she had seen letters from Stingo strewn about in Michael's room . . .

'Sure I will. Sure.' She had begun the habit then of writing to him. Sometimes he wrote back a quick scrawl, sometimes long pages of advice. He seemed rather to like it when she told him she hadn't taken the advice. 'That's right, I've made you *think* . . .' She took to putting near the end, when she'd said what was worrying her, large or small, 'What does Jay say?' She liked the sound of it. She signed herself 'Willow the Wisp', because of a teasing remark he'd made. Often he would mention girls' names. For a while it was Laura, the one she'd met in the raid. But usually a name would appear in two or three letters, then disappear.

Now she was more than thrilled by the news. Relieved. A victory in North Africa . . . She had only gradually realized how much she'd counted on his coming through safely. Family . . . She had not so much of it that she could afford to lose any more. Aunt Alice – she had not of course lost Aunt Alice, nor did she worry about her since she was safe in Switzerland, but there was no chance of being with her until the War was over, and won . . . How I would have loved it, she thought now, if she could have been there after the Café de Paris: we would have talked about it, woman to woman, in a way that I cannot even with Jay. Aunt Alice knows all about War . . .

There was other family. The little ones (she still thought of them as that, absurdly. Lucy must be nearly sixteen by now . . .) sent letters and photos. One day she would go and see them again, they would come and see *her* . . .

Her fellow billetee arrived two days later. Diana Howe. She was much smaller than Willow and had naturally curly black hair which she wore very short. She told Willow, 'I'm frightfully easy to get on with. Except I giggle a lot.'

They discovered there were only two weeks between their birthdays. Diana had two older sisters, both in the WRNS, and a brother in the Navy. Her family lived near Ilkley so she hoped to see them quite often. 'They're wonderful,' she told Willow, 'I've been so lucky. I've *always* been happy. When I see what families some people have . . .'

About the second week, when they were eating chips sitting on the end of Diana's bed (she'd been given the larger, better room), Willow told her about her mother, and the trial and the whole terrible time. 'He wasn't my real father, of course,' she said. 'But my little sisters – he was their father . . .'

As she talked, she felt stirring an unease, a disease almost: the sudden need to know something more about her own father. Then it was gone again . . .

Diana listened wide-eyed. She was quiet for several minutes afterwards. Then: 'How absolutely *terrible*,' she said. 'I don't know how you managed. I never thought of things like that happening to anyone I *know* . . .' Her chips grew cold and greasy in their newspaper.

Willow said, 'We'd better wrap those up in something – I'll open the window and get the smell out. She's sure to notice . . .'

It was good to have an ally against Mrs Parr. Not that Diana was worried by her. Altogether she was much bolder than Willow. Very bold, really. One evening when Mrs Parr had gone out for a church meeting, Diana said she wanted to play the piano.

'I expect it's got the moth *and* mouses' nests,' she said. Willow had never bothered, or dared, to open it.

'It's ghastly,' she told Willow later, 'half the keys don't work, and the pedals . . . one's gummed up and the other gone loose. There *might* be mouse dirt . . .'

Not long after her arrival, there was trouble over food. Mrs Parr decided that if a meal wasn't eaten and properly appreciated, they would have to do without most of the next. Two mornings later they didn't eat the spam provided for breakfast, and that evening found only bread and beetroot and lettuce, with vinegar. 'I'd polony planned to have alongside, but as you don't like meat, I've not bothered. I know when something's not wanted.'

'I suppose we could complain to somebody,' Willow said. 'I'm sure we're meant to be properly fed. She's got our ration books. She *gets* all the stuff . . .'

'Honestly,' Diana said, 'People like that, doesn't it make you want to spit?'

Michael was flying Liberators, protecting Atlantic convoys from U-boats. Jilly was expecting a baby, and he wrote to Willow that he was sending her to Harrogate for a rest, and for Willow to look after . . . She had always liked Jilly and the ten days they spent together that May was for her a great happiness. More *family* . . . Jilly stayed at a small hotel in Harlow Moor Road and Willow walked over to see her each day after work. The baby was due at the beginning of September. She let Willow feel it kick.

Olga told Willow, 'That smashing Flight Lu who has his eye on you – someone else will get him. You're never around . . .'

Willow didn't worry – there were plenty more where he came from . . . (and Poles and Czechs and Americans – though Mrs Parr was very down on Americans. 'I don't want to see any of your *gum chums*,' she said. 'None of that going down Pennypot Lane after those Yankees. Gum chums indeed . . .')

Michael came to fetch Jilly. He had a week's leave and they were to spend it in Ryedale.

When he and Jilly came together to the billet in Valley Mount, Diana said he was so big and fair and strong-looking he made her feel quite *faint*. 'Isn't it just my luck he's already married?' she said. She listened goggle-eyed while Mike, sitting on the sofa with the knobbly springs, told them both about an adventure from last week which *could* have ended badly . . .

'Oh thank God,' Jilly said, 'when he told me last night, I thought: Thank God . . .'

It had been his thirteenth mission, and he'd *felt* superstitious:

'. . . A really bad show. The ship had a full bomb load. We were heading out over Scotland, and had begun climbing at about fifteen hundred a minute – but got engine trouble almost at once. Visibility was pretty bad, less than two thousand, so we couldn't crash land . . . I didn't dare jettison bombs, because of the towns below. So after we'd both wrestled with the controls, I gave the order to bale out – then headed her out to sea before going over the side myself . . . that sort of kite's a real death trap if ditched. I was just floating into the overcast when I saw her wheel into a gentle bank. Christ, I thought, Christ . . . But the Observer Corps heard her – and some Spitfires were sent up . . . Ack-Ack were alerted . . . And to cut a long story short, they shot her down with *some difficulty*. She ended in the drink . . . Her wings chewed off. Christ, when I think what could have been . . .'

Willow, watching Jilly, saw her quiet pride in Michael as she listened, hands clasped over the bump beneath her smock. Her face was at once grave and tender. Oh, I *do* like her, she thought.

In early June there was a spell of really fine weather. One Monday evening both girls said they wouldn't be in for a meal. Diana had a date with a Pole, Jan, whom she was crazy about: 'I thought Free Frenchmen were really exciting, even though their English isn't special, but now I've met some *Poles* . . . Jan just oozes charm – and I don't trust him one inch.'

Willow, who'd decided she didn't after all like Andrew, the Flight Lieutenant she'd been going out with on and off since the beginning of May, thought she'd just go for a walk after work. She would think quietly. Then perhaps get herself something to eat.

It was sunny, with very little wind, even on the corner of James Street. She sat by herself on a bench near the Cenotaph. Because of the good weather there were lots of servicemen and civilians about. She remembered her mother telling her about the day it was unveiled. And how while she was standing there Willow had begun to be born. She'd been to see the house in Hereford Road where the birth had actually taken place – Reggie's cousins no longer lived there.

Pangs of hunger. There was a café in Cambridge Crescent that would do . . . She stopped outside the Regal which was showing Hayworth and Astaire, *You Were Never Lovelier*, and looked at some of the stills. Rita Hayworth lay back in Fred Astaire's arms, in the middle of a dance. Breasts high, hair thick, glossy. A man in army uniform on the opposite side was looking at stills of the supporting film. Something about the shape of the head was vaguely familiar.

He turned, and saw her:

'It is, isn't it?'

'Yes. It is,' she said. 'And it's Christopher –'

'Indeed it is. Look, this is wonderful. Really. I thought just now: That must be Willow . . . But since your grandmother died, and since the convent came to The Towers, I'm all behind with the news. Mother can't have known or she would have mentioned it – my being stationed here . . .

She had forgotten how good-looking he was. And how, summer of 1939 while he was home on leave, she had used to watch for when he would walk up the village. How, one afternoon, she had *played tennis with him.*

He was saying again, 'This is really good, our meeting, I'm so glad. We could so easily have missed each other . . .'

He asked her then: 'Were you going in to the film? I can't believe anyone so lovely would be going in alone. Two splendid Czechs have been watching you ever since we spoke . . .'

She explained about the spam and Mrs Parr. 'I just couldn't face it . . .' She thought it might be bad form to add that she'd turned down her date.

'Let *me* take you for a meal, will you? Then we can talk. Catch up with everything . . .' He suggested a little restaurant about ten minutes' walk away. 'If you don't know it – it's Italian and really jolly good. Even if you're not sure these days what's in some of the sauces . . .'

They sat at a table near the door. Almost at once the owner, a small woman in black, grey hair in a knot, came over to speak to them. Christopher told her Willow came from the same village as he did. Afterwards he said:

'A friend, Tim, and I came in a couple of times, then one day got talking to her. Her husband was one of the aliens interned in the Great Scare in 1940. Then a casualty on the *Andorra Star* when it was torpedoed. Bad enough losing him for the duration – but to lose him altogether like that . . .'

He said suddenly, '*You* had a tough time, Willow. Some years ago. I wasn't around at the time – but I thought you were frightfully brave. The business of your mother, I mean. And then of course, the Café de P.'

'Yes,' she said. 'I did, really.' She didn't want him to say any more about it. Turning spaghetti round her fork, she said, 'I was born here in Harrogate, by the way. But quite by accident.' When he said, 'Tell,' it was a relief to talk . . .

He filled her in with Flaxthorpe news. He said that two of the convent girls had walked into the Fox and Grapes last month – a bet or something – and ordered six *crème de menthe.*

The landlord had got quite fussed and rang the Reverend Mother, who seemed remarkably *un*fussed by it all. 'What was said to them in private, I don't know . . .'

'It doesn't sound like *our* convent. At Our Lady of V –' She stopped. Another subject she didn't care to talk about.

Twice he mentioned a girl's name – the same one – saying, '*We* did this, *we* did that . . .' She wasn't surprised. What else could she expect?

When she'd asked him about his work and whether he expected a posting overseas soon, they discussed the fact that they both had American cousins. They seemed to have plenty to talk about.

She said to him then, 'I used to think you were super.'

'Oh dear – don't you any more?'

'The time we played tennis together, when you were just back from India, I really muffed it by being absolutely tongue-tied and blushing horribly.'

'You *were* rather red in the face, now I remember . . .'

He poured out the last of the wine, and said, 'Have you seen that film, the Astaire one?' She shook her head. 'Because I've a confession to make. I was just about to go in to it this evening . . . So I wondered, why don't we see it on Thursday, if you're free? It's on all week and I can come over that night. Please.'

She thought: What wonderful thing is happening? I'm sitting opposite the handsomest man I've ever known, and he's *asking me out again*. Part of her wanted to be home, curled up on the end of Diana's bed, telling her all about it.

When she did, Diana was amazed. 'How *wizard*. Some people get all the luck . . . My evening was *ghastly* . . .'

She'd been given some bars of Cadbury's Orange chocolate and Willow managed one in spite of the meal. Diana said, 'He sounds really keen. I've got a romance going for you already.'

'I rather think he's got somebody . . .'

They came out of the Regal. Her head was full of rhythms. Fred Astaire singing *I'm Old-Fashioned* to Rita Hayworth. All that swinging hair and voluptuous figure. To dance like that, to *look* like that, must be marvellous. As they walked down James Street, she hummed '*You were never lovelier . . .*'

'*You* were never lovelier,' Christopher said. 'No, I'm not just shooting a line. You are very lovely – and I expect you've heard *that* lots of times before.'

She had, now she came to think of it. She said, 'It depends, of course, who says it . . .'

He took her hand. She'd been surprised he hadn't done so in the cinema. 'I've another confession to make . . .'

'Again?'

'Well, no, not a confession – something I ought to tell you. On Monday when we met I'd just finished a – love-affair. At least, I'd just posted the letter. It was when we were stationed in Edinburgh, after Dunkirk. I thought I was serious at the time. Just lately I realized it – wouldn't work. So I wrote to her . . . I was feeling a perfect heel when I ran into you . . .' He paused. 'So the truth is that I'm quite free. Nature abhors a vacuum.'

When he walked her home it was a lovely velvety evening, the light because of the clocks doubly forward, only just going . . . She felt certain he would kiss her on the step. But as they reached the portico, Mrs Parr was just letting the cat out. She had on her dressing-gown but her curlers weren't in yet. Willow had to introduce Christopher.

'He looks a nice lad, your latest,' she said next morning. She glared at Diana. Her Pole had called to her outside the window on Tuesday night. Mrs Parr claimed to have had no sleep at all. 'I'll send for the law next time.'

'A nice class of boy. Nice manners. And a *Captain* too. If he ever visits at the house, I'd not object – he could have a little go on the pianoforty . . .'

Willow and Diana got the giggles on the way to work. 'I don't even know if he can *play*,' Willow said. And, 'The very idea,' Diana said . . .

The few days left of May, and on into June, July, she spent more and more time with Christopher. Since that first outing to the cinema, the tone had changed irrevocably. Once he'd said, 'You're very lovely,' they had stopped being two Flaxthorpe people meeting, enjoying a ready-made acquaintance. 'Nature abhors . . .' he'd said.

'I told Mother we were seeing lots of each other. She's

thrilled about it. She still misses your grandmother enormously, you know . . . She said to especially give you her love.' Of the Parkinson's which was making life so difficult for all the family, he said only 'My father's illness. It's pretty grim . . .'

Whenever he could get into Harrogate and she was free, they were together. Olga at work complained there were an awful lot of long faces now Willow was never available. 'That smashing Flight Lu you cast off . . .'

She found she was thinking about nothing else but the next meeting. The kisses under the portico were long and lovely. They always had lots to talk about too. She refused weekend invitations to Diana's home to be with him – even missing the chance to meet Diana's beloved brother, Peter, on short leave from his ship.

They borrowed bicycles and cycled to Fountains Abbey. Another time he got hold of some petrol and drove her out to Malham Cove. They took the footpath to Gordale Scar. Waterfalls rushing down a steep gorge . . . made her think of the tale of his brother Jack. Perhaps he had not thought when planning the outing? But when they had walked a while, and were away from the waterfalls, he said:

'I was thinking . . . You and I, we're closer than we realize. Your Uncle Hal and my brother jack – inseparable, evidently. Hal was there when it happened. And so of course was the boy who was Michael's uncle. Stephen – the one who took them fishing that day. The whole thing,' he said, 'a shadow over my life. Mother in some ways has never got over it. It wasn't that she was over-anxious when I was small – in fact she went out of her way *not* to be. But I could feel it like an atmosphere. My father's never wanted to talk about it. Always changes the subject . . .'

Another day he was able to take her out to the moors near Linton. It was a fine day, and they lay out in the sun and talked and kissed and talked.

'You know what's happening, don't you?' he said. 'I'm twenty-nine and *very* serious – about you. How is it with you, darling? Darling Willow. Do you like it when I hold your breasts?'

She said, 'I wish they stuck up like Rita Hayworth's.'

'Oh, that's all done with mirrors,' he said. 'And anyway it's the girl that goes with the bust matters to a chap. Honestly. You're just so . . . Brown eyes, fair hair. To me you're just gorgeous. And if that's corny, I'm unrepentant. Now, let me show you I appreciate you . . .'

She felt safe with him. 'I'm only asking for this, lots more of this. I'd never ask . . . I'm old-fashioned, just like the song in *our* film. Not that it isn't what I want more than anything, here with you now . . . but I do feel enormously protective. You mustn't worry, because I won't – you won't be taken advantage of . . .'

'What if I'd like to be?' she asked. Sick with sudden excitement.

'In that case –' He broke off suddenly. 'Look, we ought to be going. One more kiss before you do your blouse up . . . I think there's something very serious I'm going to have to say to you . . .'

'Is it a telling off? I'm pretty used. After the convent and Mrs Parr . . .'

'It's not. And if you go on looking so lovely and not buttoning up your blouse – no, you won't get kissed again. Only surprised by those Home Guard just coming over the bridge . . .'

Christopher's friend, Tim, joined him a couple of times and they went out in a foursome with Diana. Diana was very aggravated with her Pole. He'd been seen at the Roxy cinema in Knaresborough with a friend of Olga's. Or so Olga said. Tim was almost as good-looking as Christopher but in a swarthy way. His moustache was an RAF handlebar. The second time Christopher and Tim came to collect the girls, Mrs Parr made them promise to cme back for a cup of tea.

She came and sat with them. She had her curlers out and wore a blue dress with yellow marguerites which looked not unlike the overalls. She brought up the subject of the piano again. Christopher, warned by Willow, explained that he couldn't play a note.

It appeared Tim could. Before Mrs Parr could say anything, he had crossed to the piano stool.

'I'm sure that'll be all right,' she said feebly. Willow felt almost sorry for her.

'Bit dicky, your ivories, Mrs Parr,' he said. He picked out with one finger, *I've got sixpence*, then began to vamp with his left hand. A few agonizing chords . . . The sounds were terrible. He moved a vase off the top of the piano: 'Excuse me.' Then, looking inside: 'You've got moth in your dampers, Mrs Parr. I should get that seen to . . .'

Sitting down again, he went straight into *You are my sunshine*. 'And now one our hostess is sure to know . . . *Kiss me good night, Sergeant Major . . .*'

'. . . *Sergeant Major, be a mother to me . . .*' All four sang, and enjoyed it. Willow was amazed to see Mrs Parr, sausage curls nodding, as Tim thumped, trying to coax out notes. She seemed to have forgotten that pianos weren't meant to have their keys struck.

Afterwards: 'This moth now, Captain Jennings,' she said. 'What's best to do about it?'

Willow *had* to ask Christopher. She felt it was foolish not to find out if he knew something. At the same time she couldn't *tell* him anything . . .

So one day when they were talking casually about his spinster sister Edie, now doing very well in the ATS, about his sister Amy, her grown-up children all in the Services, she said to him:

'When you were small do you remember a Dr Selwood?'

'Selwood? The faintest of bells . . . Dr Ash, I remember Dr Ash. So will you. Dr Sowerby when I was very small . . . But Selwood –'

'He wasn't there long,' she said, 'I think less than a year. Anyway – you don't remember anything?' She didn't want to press him. Blurred memories of a child . . . what would she gain?

'Sorry, no. Why?'

'I just wondered. Something I'd heard about him.'

Something I'd heard about him. I heard that he was my father. How's that for a laugh?

Her excitement . . . In the daytime, bent over her typewriter, she often pinched herself. It wasn't real. As if part of her life were a fairy tale. Diana said, 'It's all so – it's *absolutely* . . . If you're not in love with him, you jolly well ought to be . . .'

She supposed she was. In love. Since it was all much more intense than with anyone before – even Gerry, and she'd certainly been in love *then* . . .

But sometimes, suddenly, she would feel that she was standing a long way away, watching both of them. Walking in the Valley Gardens, kissing . . . They were two other people. Willow and Christopher. But Willow is *me* . . . Then she would shiver, icy. Once he said, 'Shivering on a hot day. Did someone walk over your grave?'

'Yes.'

But it was another Yes that worried her. Only a matter of time now . . . Even then it took her by surprise.

'I know you're not quite twenty . . . I hope you don't think, just another wartime romance. I hope you realize I really am terribly, terribly serious. We've had two whole months to get to know each other. What I'd love best . . .'

'Marrying,' she said, 'I hadn't thought.' (What a lie . . .) 'It's a big question. I wouldn't want to say yes unless I was absolutely sure. I know you love me. I *do* love you. I just want time to think . . .'

At the same time she was excited, wildly so. Christopher Hawksworth *wants to marry me*. It was suddenly so very serious and grown-up. If she said yes, when would they be married? She knew he could not be for ever stationed in England. If and when he went overseas, would they be married first?

When he left her on the step, very late, she hurried upstairs to Diana's room . . . Hoping she was in, wanting to sit on the end of the bed and talk about *getting married* . . .

Yes or no? To be or not to be?

But Diana was sitting, fully dressed, on her bed. Her face puffy with weeping.

'Diana, love –'

'Peter – his ship . . . He's dead. Mummy and Daddy heard this afternoon, they rang, it was terrible, they rang and Mummy was crying – I'm going home first thing tomorrow, we want to be together, I'm the only one who can get home . . .' The tears started again.

Willow had her arms round her. It was a long while before

she could be calmed. In bed at last, she sobbed desperately, 'I can't cope . . . Willow, help me, and make it morning soon. Willow, I can't bear . . . You see, I *only know about being happy . . .'*

25

The German officer was reading the menu when Teddy first noticed him. Her drink was almost finished. She was about to pay – and get out. She glanced at her watch. Her Resistance contact whom she'd arranged to meet here plainly wasn't going to turn up. And that meant worry . . . Although he could simply have been delayed, he could have been arrested. Or rounded up in a street *rafle*, to be sent to Germany for forced labour. The train bringing him to Paris, bombed by the Allies . . . All those possibilities. And useless to tell oneself not to worry. I shall go back to the apartment and telephone. Try to keep the fear out of my voice. *He wasn't there . . .*

Half past midday. In half an hour drinking time would be over until six this evening. Less drink available was said to have lowered the figures for death from alcohol. That was as maybe . . . But the Germans had taken the wine, four million litres by one reckoning. It did not endear occupiers to occupied.

She was sitting inside the glass verandah. Outside a pale December sun. The German officer was examining something on his cuff. He looked up. And for a second, jolt of her heart, she thought – *Gib*. The smooth freckled face, something about the cheekbones . . . Their eyes met. She veiled hers with boredom. But it was too late.

'Allow me,' he said. He stood beside her. He had brought his high-peaked cap and his *Pariser Zeitung* over with him. 'This chair isn't taken?'

'I was just leaving. I called the waiter –'

'Please don't,' he said in excellent French. 'You see, I noticed you earlier. I think you were expecting someone?'

'Perhaps . . . Men are all the same. Not to be relied on . . .' She reached for her bag. The waiter was hovering. 'I must go. I'll pay and –'

'No, no. Please take a drink with me. What was it you had? Cinzano?'

A guitarist in the café began to play, singing along with his instrument in a high melancholy voice.

'You have to be somewhere? If *he* had come, you would be with him now . . . So you have the time, I think?'

It was not Gib. Just an uncanny look of him. And that was the end of the matter. It was something I shouldn't have so much as noticed. I am not meant to have a heart now. I am not really meant to have feelings at all. Safer not. Unless they are feelings of hate, the better to spur my loyalty . . .

I am an SOE agent. Specials Operations Executive. F for French section. Code name: Lucienne. My cover name is Monique Liebert and I am the Belgian widow of a French businessman from Peronne (where all records were destroyed). To supplement my small income I sell cosmetics made from ersatz ingredients, and travel about France with my samples . . . This is the cover for my work as a courier. I have a second identity, if needed, as a supply schoolteacher. Nothing and nobody can shake my story.

She said, 'Why shouldn't it be a work colleague I'm meeting?'

'Oh, by the way you looked at your watch. Then over at the clock. A little tremor of anxiety.'

I'm not meant to be glamorous, she thought. I'm not meant to look like someone who meets lovers in cafés. These sensible dark-rimmed spectacles I wear. The grey I've allowed to grow at my temples . . . My straight hair permed, so that my looks are quite altered. I do not attract, nor am I attracted . . .

To change the topic from this mythical lover, she said, 'You speak French very well. It's a pleasure . . .'

'My grandmother was French – although I must admit I scarcely knew her . . . But my mother spoke the language perfectly. We often holidayed in France. I am Austrian. I expect you recognized the accent . . .'

Their vermouths arrived. She wondered how quickly she could drink hers, and leave. If her contact were to arrive *now* . . .

'I'm very fortunate, to be sitting here in Paris. Paris is so beautiful. Before my wife – before she left me, I was able to send her so many gifts from Paris . . .'

'I'm sorry,' she said.

'Sorry? That I buy such lovely things?'

'That your wife left you.' She regretted at once saying it.

He remarked: 'You said just now, Men – they are not to be relied on . . . Well, I had wanted to say, women . . . Yes, she left me. She – met someone while I was at the Russian Front. We have a little daughter of eight. Lore.'

The guitarist played and sang now one of the medieval airs from the film *Les Visiteurs du Soir*. Occasionally she cast an eye to the door.

'. . . I haven't wanted to be in the army, really. In the War at all. I would like to be a singer. It's – my life. I –'

'What do you sing?' She felt now on safe ground.

'Lieder. Schubert, Schumann, Loewe. Some oratorio. But lieder is where I'm happiest.'

She thought he might be. Sudden image of him, in plain clothes. Singing. No doubt beautifully. An ordinary man. We shouldn't be at war with such persons. She clasped her glass tightly. Let it go, afraid it would snap. She saw his eyes on her hand, on her wedding-ring.

'You're married, you'll –'

'A widow.'

With gentle pressing she told him a little about herself. Her so well rehearsed cover story . . . Yes, grown-up children. Two daughters. One in French Canada, one in Provence. She worked, yes. She dealt in cosmetics.

'So you see, it's a simple life.' Her drink was almost finished.

'You'll take another?'

'No, I do have to go . . . But it's been interesting. And I wish you well with the singing.'

He hesitated. 'I know I'm very hopeful. But I'd like you to hear. I sing . . . This is not a common pick-up. I'd like to *talk* to you. It . . .'

'I have to go out of Paris. My work.'

'When? Immediately?'

'Soon . . .'

'Your address, madame? Perhaps – we . . . what I should like is to take you to a meal. The Claridge perhaps? Or the Fête Foraine. We can . . . Something that would be a treat . . .'

'I can't,' she said. 'No, truly, thank you. The . . . man who didn't turn up. That one, he gets insane with jealousy. I kept worrying just now that he was going to come in and make a scene . . .'

When she left, she saw that he was hurt. Puzzled. She wondered: Will he come after me? But to the last his manners were courteous.

He made no move to follow her. She knew he would not. That would be the end of that. Such people are not meant to be charming, courteous, kind. Sympathetic. For those few minutes she had been with someone who in any other circumstances she would have liked.

And now, she must find out what had happened to her contact . . . Although it did not show, by the time she reached her apartment she was shaking with fright. Damp with fear. As always.

When had it begun, this fear? Certainly it had been with her all her time in France. It was a familiar. She slept with it (cat mewing, a shout in the darkness, feet on the stairs, a gunshot . . .), woke with it. It followed her round Paris, and further . . . At railway stations, as she got on, got off trains. She could not remember how it had been without.

But it had been another emotion that had brought her here in the first place. Anger. Simple anger. After the Café de Paris, all through that spring and summer of 1941, it had burned in her. So that she would realize suddenly: *I hate.* I hate them for what they have done . . . for what they may be doing somewhere that we don't yet know of . . . In the evenings, after a day of unremitting hard work, she would find herself alone in the flat, precious brandy and water beside her, tiredness draining out of her and, in its place – rage. Rage with no shape. Formless. But directed towards the enemy . . .

Then eighteen months later, she had dined and danced with that colonel. From there . . .

To the outside world: Ensign Theodora Nicolson, First Aid Nursing Yeomanry. A lady, in well-cut uniform and *silk* stockings (no making do with cotton lisle, rayon . . .)

In those days, training to be an agent, she had not been frightened. Anger still, but no fear. Not yet. It wasn't there through all the unexpectedly tough physical training, or the tests of enterprise. Wasn't there when she learned to shoot. The shooting was good for the anger. Nor when she learned tricks (oh, may I never have to use it) of silent killing.

Perhaps it was the company she kept. She had found it easy to be friends – she had been the oldest of the women, on her mettle to see how well she could do. She had been confidante, 'aunt', mentor. Shared sense of purpose. The dangers to come were for all of them. Loneliness came later.

Perhaps the fear began, yes, certainly it had – with that first mock-Gestapo interrogation – in the middle of the night. Such a necessary part of the training. Such an important test. Little point if it had not been thorough, and convincing, and tough . . . But for a few terrible moments she had found herself *believing*. These people whom she already knew, play-acting to such effect . . . She had felt she was fighting for her life, rather than for the right to come over here, and possibly lose it . . . She had not done well in that test. Her cover story which for days she had soaked herself in, had been exposed in three weak areas. But it appeared she had done well enough. If the real thing should happen – perhaps she would be all right.

But from then on, fear had stalked her. Growing rapidly worse after the landing from the Lysander plane, and the first days of living a lie in an occupied country. Her fear, after all, was not unfounded. One slip was enough, and God knew, easily enough made even by the experienced. She herself, her fourth week, tired after an endless railway journey, checking in at a hotel in Nantes, what did she do but write on the reception slip, T. E. Nicolson . . . The pen hardly put down before, sick with fear, the realization, she had said hurriedly, easily, 'Oh, give me that back . . . I promised my children I wouldn't spell it that way . . .' Scratching out the offending word, writing boldly: 'Monique Liebert . . .'

Oh, the strangeness of living in Paris – where everything was at once familiar and yet not. Occasionally perhaps, sitting in a café at a pavement table, looking out on to perhaps the Champs-Elysées, it was possible in the autumn sunshine to think oneself back again. But then . . . The swastika flags, the signposts in German directing the Wehrmacht north, south, east, west. And, biggest change of all, everywhere, grey-green blot on the landscape, the Germans themselves.

Bicycles . . . The streets were full of them. Gone with the petrol famine, the hooting taxis: the only cabs now, apart from horse-drawn ones, were *vélo taxis*, rickshaws almost, except it was not a coolie but a cyclist providing the power. Official German motors aside, there were only the odd-looking *voitures à gazogène*, fuelled by a natural gas cylinder at the rear and needing to stop frequently for refills. Buses, which ran only when the Métro didn't, were cumbersome with this device. She didn't bicycle herself here, but used her feet or the Métro. But when her courier work took her into the countryside she would ride one.

It was a Paris of queues – for clothes, films, making a claim, petitioning . . . but above all, for food.

Soon after their arrival in 1940 the Germans had quietly removed all the good things of France – the butter, the pastry, the steaks, the wine . . . '*Ils nous prennent tous*,' the cry had gone up. Now, at the end of 1943, they were still taking everything. But more of it . . . When she had seen part of the Tuileries dug up, with carrots and beans growing, she wasn't surprised (visiting Willow, had she not seen the beautiful grass of Harrogate Stray turned to potatoes?) It was the hungry, the undernourished, look of so many that appalled her. Thin children – that she could not bear.

To think in England I ever bothered about curried rabbit, fussed over our shortages. *We* were never truly in want. But here it would seem that everything was made of, or had in it, *swedes*. (Cattle food to them. At least *we* are used to eat swedes with haggis . . .)

Food, food, food. The obsession. The first page, often the only page to be read of the Vichy-controlled newspapers ('Any copies left of *The Liar*?' she had heard in her newsagent's) would be the one listing the latest allowances – what each food ticket was worth . . .

The black market flourished. How not? And who was not of it? Certainly everyone knew someone, who knew . . . And the only good meals she herself had eaten had been either in those restaurants which didn't take tickets, charged a lot of money and fed one very well indeed, or in the homes of Resistance colleagues who knew where and how . . . It was all as it was, and that was that. She was reminded often of the saying 'A standing prick has no conscience.' Nor, she thought now, has an empty belly . . .

She felt part of this Paris. It had been her home. Now, she was more French even than when she'd lived here. Before leaving England every possible trace of her own country had had to be removed. French trivia to replace the English trivia in her handbag. An array of beautifully forged papers and permits. A full set of food tickets, clothing tickets (a death pill too – but she would not think of that). Clothes with French labels sewn in, shoes carefully without that tell-tale 5 for size . . .

Although she wasn't living now anywhere near her previous home, she must not, dare not, go near it. It might be that her old concierge was sympathetic and a *gaulliste* – and it might not. And Blanche, her maid? Who knew? It was not safe to find out. But how tempting once when she was only two blocks away just to look in . . . And then the orphanage – greatest temptation of all. But, no risks. Training, hadn't they been told again and again that no one, however well known, however intimately known (those I have been to bed with?), *no one* is to be trusted. And that, she thought sadly, would have to mean Henri – if ever by some wonderful, wonderful chance he were to be seen walking about Paris . . .

Indeed, one of her frights in the last month had been a possible sighting of Ferdy in the *Colisée* – all among the *zazous* and the black marketeers. The more she thought of it afterwards, the more she was certain it *had* been Ferdy. And why not? Agreed, he had *used* to live in Liège, yet wasn't he often in Paris? But she had been walking past, he had been reading a newspaper. She had not lingered to find out . . .

People she knew in Paris – there was always this fear of seeing them. The fright on Monday of last week when she had seen a rather odd, gossipy woman, Céline Gauchet, a friend of Aimée's, whom she'd met a few times in 1939. 'Greetings! Surely it's . . .' Cutting her, 'refrigerating' her, as Saint had used to say in the 'twenties . . . 'You have made a mistake, madame.' The puzzled but genuine apology . . .

Back in her apartment again, she picked up the 'phone. 'Lucienne here. The person I should have met. He didn't . . . I thought of coming over?'

The voice answered, 'Don't come this evening. It's not convenient. No one will be in.'

She hung up, satisfied. She hadn't heard the dreaded formula, telling her that the Gestapo had been, or were there. 'Yes, *do* come, we've visitors here, you're expected . . .' A child's form of code, playing contrary. But it made for safety. So far it had worked.

As well as a second cover story she had another address in Neuilly which she had told to *no one*, and to which she could escape if in danger. Her present apartment she had been in for about six weeks. It was in a street not far from the Gare de L'Est. Her balcony was patched up, the wrought-iron broken. The family on the floor below, with a much larger balcony, had until recently been keeping hens on theirs. Anything to help with food . . .

It was already a home of sorts to her. The stairs, with their inescapable smell of stale alcohol, old polish, bleach, herbal tobacco . . . Two other apartments, also small, were on the same floor as hers and had in them a commercial traveller and an engineer, both of whom were either bachelors or living singly. She saw them very little, hadn't exchanged more than a dozen words with either. The Chevillons, the henkeepers of the floor below, were a different matter. Although she had naturally to be careful whom she got to know, it would have been difficult to ignore this family.

The husband, an industrial chemist, was a prisoner of war in Germany. His wife Jeanne looked after the three children as well as her mother-in-law . . . Old Granny Chevillon, with her pebble glasses, her down-at-heel shoes and her heavy body, seemed to clump up and down stairs most of the day – either sitting with the concierge, or going out to queue for Jeanne. Or visiting Teddy. She loved to talk.

Xavier, the eldest boy, was a *zazou*. This statement made by more or less rebellious adolescents was illustrated by outrageous clothes (wide shoulders on huge jackets, greased hair worn long, dark glasses, exaggeratedly tight trousers and a general air of being out to shock). Teddy could understand it so well. It could not be easy being seventeen in these times . . . All around, the inevitable compromises made by many of their elders, compromises which often slipped over into collaboration. Sometimes she would think with dread of how it would be after the War. Those who had nothing to be proud of, or worse, something of which to be truly ashamed, would have to pay for it. And *all* would have to live together . . .

Xavier was on bad terms with Gabrielle, his sixteen-year-old sister: a tall, round-cheeked, striking brunette who looked already completely grown up. The youngest, Daniel, was the one Teddy saw the most of. He was nine, an afterthought perhaps – the baby of the family. He played ball near the concierge's room and in the doorway and generally made a nuisance of himself. Mme Dastien, the concierge, whose husband had died just before Teddy came, suffered from nervous headaches and would shout at him. Another time he might be found teasing the German soldiers, the *frises*, bursting paper bags behind them. No wonder Jeanne Chevillon looked careworn . . .

Once, on the stairs, Teddy was introduced to Jeanne's sister, Pauline. She was a small wiry woman, very busy and efficient, who worked for the Red Cross. Her husband had been killed flying reconnaissance in early 1940, in the *dròle de guerre*. Jeanne had explained that Teddy travelled in cosmetics and had difficulty in getting ingredients. Pauline was just saying she thought she knew someone . . . when Xavier had come out of the apartment – the complete *zazou* – on his way to a café. Jeanne had let loose a torrent of criticism and exasperation . . . His aunt had been more tolerant. She said, 'His energies have to go somewhere. It's harmless enough, if he isn't too cheeky with it . . .' But Teddy knew that they worried he might be picked up in a street *rafle*. There was no peace of mind.

Pauline had been there earlier this week when Teddy had visited the Chevillon apartment, by invitation. Jeanne had returned home in the evening the same time as Teddy. They had met in the hallway:

'Come in for a *tisane*,' she said. Then, once inside: 'I know you don't have a radio down there – Do you want to listen to . . . you know – the *BBC*? Everyone does it. They know we do it . . .'

But they weren't lucky. The reception was very fogged, impossible to decipher. Then some anxious knob twiddling brought, loud and clear: '*Sie hören die Deutsche Rundfunk* . . .'

'*Merde*,' Jeanne said. Pauline also. She struggled with the set but with no success. Daniel changed '*Rundfunk, rundfunk*,' and roared with laughter. Jeanne cuffed him. '*T'es dingue . . .*'

The circuit to which she was attached for her work met in different places. Cafés, as well as each other's homes. Her apartment was seldom or never used – particularly as there was no exit other than the front door. They were a small group. Jean Luc, their organizer, had strong views on this. Paris had had enough trouble. A chain, he said, precious cigarette dangling from his lips, was only as strong as its weakest link . . . Painfully obvious, and yet . . .

Jean Luc was a railway inspector for the SNCF and so, helpfully, was able to travel about easily. In the 'fourteen-'eighteen war he had rescued a German from a burning house near Amiens, and had been awarded an Iron Cross. He wore it now in his lapel. 'What could possibly make me safer?' he would say. 'They daren't insult *that* . . .'

Teddy had said the first time she met him, 'Perhaps they'll think you bought it?' He'd shrugged his shoulders and laughed.

'And what about other Frenchmen? Mightn't they misunderstand?'

'I'll worry about that when it happens . . .'

Then, she hadn't yet realized what a subtle art blending in was. How to *seem* to be *collabo*, the better to take advantage . . .

Another agent, code name Olivier, was a librarian. He was one of those who had a *laissez-passer* to travel after curfew, that much sought-after permit with its Gestapo stamp of love-birds. (When Teddy had first heard it described, memory had played a trick. Sending her from one war to another: She and Gib in Brighton, 1917. Watching the love-birds at the Metropole. '*That's us*,' he had said . . .)

Olivier and his Breton wife, Annick, lived on the Ile de St Louis. Annick cooked wonderfully and one of Teddy's real pleasures since coming back to Paris had been eating with them, Annick managing always to get hold of something both substantial and mouth-watering . . .

There was also Claude, a radio technician, and Marc, a postal worker . . . Besides Teddy, the only other British person was their Wireless Operator, seconded from the RAF. Code name Vincent, he had been trained before her so that she had not met him at any of the schools. He had a French mother and had grown up bilingual. Shortish, with already receding hair and a dry sense of humour, he was very quiet. Everyone liked him.

Then there were the sub agents scattered about the countryside. Every one a possible weak link. Or a great strength. Some Teddy marvelled at, such as the bee farmer in Normandy who moved his bees about, ammunition hidden in the hives. What official would be brave enough to examine a hive of bees?

Tonight they were arguing as so often, now that the Allied invasion, the Second Front, could not be far away, about the best way of doing everything. To go in for large-scale sabotage before, or after, the landings? Already they'd been successful with small efforts, stage-managed by Jean Luc. Sometimes nothing more dramatic than altering a lading bill so that goods went to a wrong destination. At other times a line put right out of action. Jean Luc didn't approve of the RAF bombing, and would try to needle Vincent. He argued, rightly Teddy thought, that a small bomb in the right place, planted by the Resistance, could do more damage than fifty hit or miss . . .

But mostly they saw eye to eye. All were in equal danger from the Gestapo – the dreaded *Geste*. She and Vincent faced possible torture, deportation, death. So, if discovered, did the rest – but *they* involved their families. The punishments for sabotage were fierce. All male relatives over eighteen, sons-in-law included: shot. Women, sent to forced labour in Germany. Children taken away – God knew where . . .

How to live, she thought, *as we all must live*, with this ever-present threat. And if caught – to give nothing away. Or at the least to hold out forty-eight hours so that everyone concerned could go to ground. To fear for yourself, that you might be the one to break down and 'finger' a colleague . . . Tales of the dreaded water torture alone had given her nightmare upon nightmare, of drowning, of suffocation . . .

Four days later the weather turned cold, sharp. In two weeks it would be Christmas. If anyone had told me last year that I should be in *Paris* . . .

Tomorrow she had a long train journey. Limoges. She would be alone both going and returning. How tired she had grown of station officials, French gendarmes who weren't too bad, milice who were despicable, Germans – including sometimes the *Geste* – all looking inside her samples case, that pathetic collection of ersatz cosmetics. The coarse rachel powder, the hard lipstick. Crudely scented creams . . . 'Yes, I make some of them myself . . .'

It was just after midday. She put some bean soup on to heat. She thought she felt hungry but wasn't sure. Perhaps what I really need is a *good* cigarette . . . She heard clumping on the stairs. A snatch of song, '*Où es tu, mon Espagne*', in a nasal voice. Then a knock at her door.

Three guesses . . .

'Come in, Mme Chevillon. No, of *course* you don't disturb me.'

There was a faded torn leather armchair which Teddy never sat in, finding it uncomfortable. Mme Chevillon settled into it at once. She asked Teddy, 'Did you see Xavier just now? Rushing out just when his mother told him to be in – and going without his lunch. You'd think, a growing boy . . . Jeanne had some *escalope de poisson*, I queued for it – she won't keep his for him if he's not back.'

Better, Teddy thought, not to offer her an *apéro*, even some non-alcoholic *grenache*, or her tongue would become even more loosened. 'Excuse me,' she said now, 'something on the stove –'

'The trouble my daughter-in-law has with that boy, you don't know. But it's how they have to be when they're growing up . . . My son after 'fourteen-'eighteen – the wild ideas . . . Now it's *his* son. Oh, he says, Grandmère, I'm *terriblement swing* . . . He thinks it's smart to talk like that. They all do. They get together in these places. I passed and saw him once, in the Select Bar, with all the pansies. I don't know where they get the clothes, they oughtn't to be allowed . . .'

Teddy, from the kitchen, made the right noises.

'I'll tell you a secret (Jeanne, she'd be so angry if she knew

I was up here gossiping – You've got to stop talking all over the place, she told me . . .), little Gabrielle – she goes out with *German officers*. And her with an angel's name too . . . My daughter-in-law, naturally she doesn't approve, but with a girl like that, and so tall she looks twenty-two, what can you do?'

As old Mme Chevillon tut-tutted behind her pebble glasses, Teddy remembered she had been frightened just to see the uniform. The girl and the German, there in the hallway, out of sight of the concierge, embracing. Breaking off hurriedly as Teddy came in sight . . .

'Perhaps she has other friends who do it, and she doesn't want to be left out?'

'Oh, you young mothers – you're too easy-going . . . I'll tell you something, *I* know how it's going to end. A girl like that and a handsome Siegfried . . . one and one can make three all too easily, and *then* where shall we be? It's the same whenever there's a war. A young aunt of mine in 'seventy when the Prussians came . . . If anything happens, *I told you so*, I shall say to Jeanne . . . Over *eighty thousand* babies so far, they say . . .'

She eased her feet deeper into the slippers: 'To tell the truth I'm more afraid for Xavier, thinking how they might pick him up just for being *odd*. He's a saucy one, he'll give some answer he shouldn't and find himself behind bars, and *then who knows*?'

It was only necessary to listen . . .

'. . . I wanted to try and borrow a little pink cotton thread from you, just to mend this old camisole, but the truth is I like a little talk – hearing your news. I've always had this interest in other people's lives, stuck as I am in that apartment all day –'

Jeanne rushed in, agitated, full of apologies. 'Really, Belle Mère,' she could be heard saying down the stairs, 'you *must not* make a nuisance of yourself . . .'

26

41 Valley Mount,
Harrogate.

Saturday, 18 December 1943

Dearest Jay,

This will have to be my happy Christmas letter to you. I wish we could find a way to spend some time at Xmas together. I've got lots to talk to you about. And things to ask you. You're a wonderful listener – although when *you* do the talking, you're awfully bossy, so there – that's to stop you getting a swollen head!

Well, 1943 is nearly over and the best thing that's happened in it (apart from me being an *aunt*!) has been you coming back from North Africa, *safe and sound*. Why do you have to be up in wild, wild Wales where I can't see you, why can't you get yourself station *in Yorkshire*? (Don't get sent abroad again just yet, PLEASE!)

The latest is that I'm going to spend Christmas with Diana and her family. It's the first since her brother's death, so it's really a sad occasion. She has been quite a lot better just recently, but this will open up all the wounds.

She has a different Pole now. This one is really super and I think it *may* be serious . . . Her parents have met him and they like him a lot. He was almost a lawyer before the War.

She sends you her love. She thought you enormous fun when you were here, but says we'd look better together if you were a bit taller. (Moral: I shouldn't have worn my smart new Joyce wedges!)

Isn't it lovely – I've had a letter from *Aunt Alice*! It was brought over by a Major who escaped through Switzerland and who'd been staying with some people who have a daughter in my aunt's convent – work that one out! He visited there and offered to bring it. Of course it isn't the same as seeing her and talking to her (we used once upon a time to have such lovely *family* talks), but after the long silence it feels awfully nice and warm. And she sounds well and really very contented. She's taken up photography again!

There's been one letter from Teddy since I saw you. But it didn't *say* anything and it didn't answer any of my questions or say anything about my news. It's a bit fishy, à mon avis . . . I wish I had an exact address in Scotland. I wonder if it's remotely near Michael? My geography was always terrible, and anyway I don't believe the postmark is where she actually *is*. If it didn't worry me so horribly it would make a nice bit of detective work. Makes me a bit orphan Annie, if I didn't have Michael and Jilly and you (and my nephew! by the way, Jilly says he's beginning a tooth *already*! *Is this a record*?!)

Life here goes on much as usual. Diana and I were in trouble yesterday because our supervisor suddenly asked to see our gas masks. It was just as we were leaving. And – yes, you've guessed, our masks weren't inside our cases. Honestly it's such a *frightful* nuisance carrying them everywhere, we might as well make use of the cases. We both had make-up in them and lots of bars of Fry's Sandwich and Aero chocolate – Diana knows this Free Frenchman who runs canteen supplies. We said we'd bought other people's sweet rations for them, Girl Guides' honour (have you got that, Girl Guides' honour I mean, in the States? It goes down really well with supervisors). We got a WARNING for this time!

I nearly forgot. Weren't Diana and I lucky!! Glenn Miller came to play at the US Camp in Pennypot Lane. *And we were there*! We had a really wizard time.

There've been two letters so far this month from Christopher – I get that sinking feeling every time the newsreader says *Sicily*. Worrying, it's a habit, isn't it? And how could I not? I think of darling Mrs Hawksworth and her other son going all those years ago. Oh Jay . . . Now do tell me I'm just silly when I wonder if they brought you back from Sidi Rezegh so you could go to France for the Second Front (which *must* come next year, mustn't it?) Try and stay a *long time* in Welsh Wales.

You don't mention any girls at all – are you losing your touch or won't they go out with you any more? Please give me a proper account of how many Welsh beauties you've charmed. After all, *I* tell *you* everything!

I got involved in a chain letter, a really stupid one, called Luck of London. It's been *they say* three times round the world. You have to send four copies on and then see what happens in six days. Bad luck comes if you don't. That sort of thing really frightens me – I can hear you laughing – so I expect I'll do it! Diana was all for tearing it up but I pointed out that it's *me* who'll get the bad luck. (I might send one of them to you – so there!)

I keep putting off writing the serious bits. I'm still worried about not having said Yes (or No) to Christopher before he went. If I said Yes, and then had to write that I'd changed my mind, that would be a terrible thing to do to someone under fire. I suppose I *sort of* said No. I mean, he knows he's quite free. It's just he so very much wants to marry me when and if he gets out of all this. And the trouble is, Jay, some days I really think it would be all right. I know they say if you have to ask if you're in love then you're *not* (If I didn't have you, Jay, I'd *seriously* think of writing to a magazine – Evelyn Home or something . . . because Diana's no help. She just thinks I'm mad not to say Yes. Stark staring!) But sometimes it feels like love, and sometimes it doesn't. I feel *all of a muddle*. I hope being 21 in the summer will help. The awful thing is I wouldn't die of misery if he married someone else, I think I'd just feel hurt. So *that* doesn't sound like love . . . And – off we go again! *What does Jay say*? Tell me what you think. Honestly . . .

Now, dearest Jay, thank you very much again for all the shoulder to weep on you've given me for five years now if you count it starting in 1938. I don't know how you managed to cope with my ravings when you were fighting a War in Africa.

If I've left it to the end to say anything about you looking for my father, it's *not* because I'm not grateful. I am, Jay, I wouldn't have known where to start. Now, if you say the Medical Directory is a dead duck and the Medical Register only gives qualifying dates and all that, where do you go next? The 1935 Cox and King's address you wrote to, I awfully hoped for something from that. Did it really just come back Gone Away, are you sure it didn't say Deceased? I know I'm always expecting people to die and I'm silly. Sorry. I feel altogether I'm asking you something *really difficult*.

Except *you* suggested it, you said, 'I could maybe find out something for you or I could maybe help – if you wanted it.' And when I asked *how*, you said, 'Where there's a Jay there's a way.' (You do make the most *awful* puns, Diana remarked on it!)

I'm just off to the flicks now, we're going to a matinee. Someone famous is at the organ all this week, Reginald Foort I think. The film is Deanna Dustbin – *Hers to Hold*.

Lucky you getting that parcel from your parents. Gosh, it'll be wizard if they really mean to send Diana and me one too. Thanks for arranging!

Lots of love, and a big kiss,

Willow the Wisp . . .

27

Teddy sat in the crowded railway carriage. She decided that while they talked round her she would sleep. She'd long ago lost fears she might sleep-talk in English.

She had been reading before. Nose buried in Vialar's *La Grande Meute*, hoping not to be spoken to. Now she shut her eyes. Her spectacles lay on her lap. (Would they ever seem anything but a nuisance? That time they had needed to be mended and the optician had said, 'But, madame, they are hardly worth the wearing . . . such a weak prescription – it would be better for your eyes if . . .')

She dozed almost. The train swayed. Opposite her was a thin dark man in a beret, who had in the rack above him, from the smell, some cheeses, as well as meat and wine. A visit to the country.

The talk washed over her. It was almost predictable, now that she travelled so often.

'Everyone will be a *gaulliste* soon . . .'

'Nothing's going to make me, I can tell you. What is he? He's just an *arriviste* . . .'

'. . . the Maréchal's done his best. He's an old man. If *you'd* been there in 'fourteen-'eighteen –'

'. . . running late again. These trains. All we need now is for the Allies to bomb us . . .'

'All we need . . .'

'. . . it says here, the GA ticket, it's worth 25 grams of oil . . .'

'What are we meant to do with *that*?'

'My little grandson – he's hardly grown a centimetre this last two years. And we're a big family. Big bones . . .'

'. . . and with the cold we've been having.'

'. . . they were pruning these trees near the Chaussée and René got a lot of firewood. Everyone was after it . . .'

'. . . people ought to pray more. He says it's because France has turned away from the Sacred Heart . . .'

'No – from the Blessed Virgin. It's the Blessed Virgin we should be praying to . . .'

The fat woman beside her shifted her weight, pushing against Teddy. Eyes half opened, she glanced away from the window and towards the corridor. A man walking down it carefully as the train swayed. His head turned, idly looking in the compartments. Ferdy . . .

Ferdy saw me . . .

She closed her eyes again quickly. Feigning sleep. The door slid open. She tried not to hear it. I shan't open my eyes. By not a flicker shall I show fear . . .

His voice. 'Teddy, what a surprise! Wake up, didn't you see me?'

The fat woman's voice. 'Someone's speaking to you, madame.'

He persisted. 'Didn't you see me? Teddy, it's *me*, *Ferdy*.'

She opened her eyes. Look at him coldly.

'I think you have made a mistake. My name is Liebert. Madame Monique Liebert.'

'Teddy, surely –'

'That's enough. You've made a simple mistake – and now, if you would kindly –'

The thin dark man in the beret said, 'You're upsetting the lady . . .'

She saw the once well known face, puzzled now, indignant, closing the sliding door. Off down the corridor. Gone.

'A complete stranger,' she said, shrugging her shoulders.

'Anyone can make a mistake,' said the man with the beret but the fat woman said, 'He went on too long. It was a pick-up. Men . . . They're all the same.'

They were all silent for a while. Then slowly they started again. She tried to sleep. Then read for a bit. They came round to check papers, and although she had nothing to fear, *I am Monique Liebert, a traveller in cosmetics*, the restlessness was still there. It affected her bladder. She would have to go to the lavatory. She dreaded that Ferdy would be in a compartment close by, where she must pass. She tried to think: Had he gone away to the left or the right?

When she hurried down, it seemed safe. But then when she had come out and was half way to her seat, she felt a hand on her shoulder.

'Teddy, look, *what is this?*'

She went on. Shaking him off, saying angrily, 'I don't know who you are, monsieur, but if this is an attempt to introduce yourself, *you have not succeeded . . .*'

'We don't need introducing, we know each other . . . very well. *You* know how well, Teddy . . .'

She had reached the compartment door. 'There are police on this train. If you don't remove your unwelcome attentions . . .'

His hand touched her elbow. Touched her, in that particular way. He said, in English, '*Making conversation, when we ought to be making love . . . You know me*, Teddy . . .'

'I don't know what language that is, but I don't understand it. And take your hands off . . .'

She slid open the door, was safely inside. He stood outside. But didn't attempt to open it . . .

'Oh dear,' she said, sitting down again. Her knees trembled, ached.

'He's not still at it?' said the fat woman. Her shoulders shook. 'Men will try anything . . . That's how I met my husband. *Certain* he was, he knew me from somewhere or other. I didn't believe a word. But of course he got round me . . . He still does . . .'

Only half an hour till Paris, unless the train was delayed again further. She didn't try to sleep any more, but kept her spectacles on, burying herself again in *La Grande Meute.*

The train drew into the Gare St Lazare. The great thing, the essential now, was not to hurry. How many times had she been taught, how well she knew, *don't hurry* . . . To hurry is to draw attention. And as well, flurry doesn't make for a cool mind . . .

She didn't hurry. But walked patiently, purposefully, calmly. She saw, as she had dreaded, that it was a day when the Geste were looking at papers. She flooded her mind with details of her cover story. All the little frills that went to make it *real* . . . Cousin Mathilde has terrible asthma and often when she can't manage I go to help her . . . I'm worried about Uncle Benoît because his lungs have been troubling him, you always worry about consumption in the family . . .

Ferdy may be behind, he may be watching for me, may be very near now. I shall not look round.

She went into the lavatories. She was surprised how she was shaking. As if I didn't have enough anxieties without Ferdy too . . . Someone had written on the cubicle wall, misspelt, 'Money has no smell, a Jew has.' She felt sick.

Back on the platform again, she looked around casually. There was no sign of him. She wondered if she should do a detour on the Métro, just in case . . . But why, when she was so exhausted.

Daniel waylaid her as she came into the vestibule. He was jumping from one stone stair to the other, two at a time. He looked a candidate for a sprained ankle.

'Ssh,' he said, looking behind him and then over at Mme Dastien's room. 'Are we alone?' He came up close to her, 'Madame Liebert, do you know what a Boche is?'

She had been caught out once – saying solemnly, 'It's a slang, rude name for Germans . . .'

'No,' she said, 'what is a Boche?'

'He's a lean German pig, fattened in France, salted in the Channel and tinned in England? *Voilà*!'

She was so tired that she went to sleep almost at once. She had thought she was hungry, but there was nothing in the apartment and she could not bear to go out. The restaurant nearest had been closed for the last two days because of insufficient stocks. She was invited tomorrow to Oliver and Annick's. She would eat well there.

She dreamed one of her anxious dreams. A face that was, almost, Gib's grew larger, smaller, approached, receded. A voice called from somewhere, echoing down a corridor, calling in French, 'Save me, save me . . .' The person who wasn't Gib said, 'If you could hand over the Diamond Waterfall, you could save yourself and all of us. They'll do anything for money. They're only human, they're only German. Where is it?' She said, 'It doesn't belong to *me* and it's in England. I can't . . .' He said quietly, 'You must, if you want us to be saved . . .'

'Help me,' she cried. She woke suddenly, thinking she heard a banging on the door. But it was only a loose shutter blowing in the March breeze.

She was busy the next morning. In the afternoon she went to the hairdresser. It took nearly three hours, another permanent. How she disliked her new looks . . . On the way back she was caught up in an air raid. What an irony, she thought, if I were in the end to be killed by the RAF.

Passing a piano shop on her way back she had heard someone picking out '*Le Premier Rendezvous*'. This song of Danielle Darrieux, from the film which she had seen twice already, oddly and cruelly reminded her of Henri, with whom it could have nothing to do. A song heard everywhere. Violin, accordion, guitar, as haunting air, jogging foxtrot, whistled, from doorways, through open windows . . . The first meeting, the heart tired of beating alone . . . That is me, that was us . . . She thought: If I survive, if I live to tell the tale, *this* will be the song which will reawaken it all. She would remember that they had never danced together. Silly, *why didn't we*?

Loss of Henri: over the years it had settled to a dull ache, occasionally, like a wound in damp weather, flaring up into acute pain. She thought yet again, sadly: It could have been something. For four days we were lovers, and friends. She had still to tell herself, *it was not meant to be* . . .

She would dress now to go to Olivier's. To be certain to be there early so that, leaving, there would be no problem about the last Métro.

It was still light. She looked out from the balcony. A cart drawn by oxen rumbled by, laden with parcels, going towards the Gare de l'Est. She imagined it to be yet more of France's good things, on their way to Germany . . .

She finished her make-up. Cleaned her glasses – hateful things. At least she would not need to wear them at Olivier's. As she sorted her handbag by the door, she thought she heard steps on the stairs. Ah no – unmistakably old Mme Chevillon.

'Mme Liebert, Monique dear,' her voice came through the door, before she knocked.

Teddy opened it. 'I was just going out . . .'

Then she saw. Behind the old lady, bounding up the stairs, Ferdy.

'Oh no,' she said, 'oh no.' She would have shut the door but Mme Chevillon stood inside it.

'Here's a friend of yours, dear, he was looking for you, there I was, taking care of things for Mme Dastien, she's had to go to the doctor again for her head, and I saw him come in. When he asked for you, I'll take you up I said, the exercise is good for me . . .'

The voice went on. Ferdy had stepped from behind and past her. He was there, inside.

'. . . so I'll leave you now, dear, old friends have a lot to talk about . . .'

'What's this?' she said angrily. 'How did you get here?'

'I simply watched you – yesterday. You looked around, but not quite enough. Hiding in the lavatory indeed –'

'Just get out,' she said.

'Aren't you going to offer me an *apéro*?'

'No.'

'Teddy, you might tell me what this is about? What's all this monique Liebert nonsense?'

She took a deep breath. 'I'll tell you . . . I didn't get out in time. In 1940. And I reckoned to be British might be difficult. After all, the French aren't at war with the Nazis – we are. I didn't want to be interned at Porte St Denis . . . So, I'm a Frenchwoman. It's as simple as that. You must know people can get papers if they need them. Obviously I'm at risk, but . . .'

'Anyway our enemies aren't Germans. They're Jews and Bolsheviks and Freemasons . . .'

'I see your politics haven't changed.'

'Your story, as a story,' he said, 'it stinks.'

'It's the only one I've got.'

'Look, Teddy. You know me well. We . . . used . . . You asked me once to father a baby for you –'

'I must have been mad.'

'What about for old times' sake – we could just . . .' He pointed to the bedroom. 'There – it's a good double bed.'

She tried a line of attack. 'What are *you* doing here?'

'I come to Paris on and off. I came to be here when our Belgian Fascist, Léon Degrelle, speaks. The Place Chaillot on Sunday.'

'Léon Degrelle. Jean Hérold-Paquis. Two of a kind.'

'It doesn't follow I *agree* with him. I'm not a *collabo*.'

'I dare say not. Just an honest *attentiste*, waiting to see how it goes. Well, it's not going too well, is it . . .'

'I'll take a risk and ask this. Are you a *résistante*?'

'What if I were – as if I'd tell you . . . But no, I never did have anything to do with politics. You should know that. I'm just here – and when it's all over I'll be Teddy again.'

'We're back again,' he said, '*making conversation, when we ought to be making love.*' He put out a hand. 'For old times . . . Come down to a café and drink with me –'

'No. And I was going out. I shall be late.'

'You smell different,' he said suddenly, lunging forward.

'It's different scent. I used to use Lanvin. Now I can't afford it if I could get it –'

'No, your skin. You . . . I could want you more than ever. Teddy, *remember* . . .'

'I do – remember. And it's over. *Over*. Finished. That was nineteen-thirty-four. Now it's 'forty-four. I'm not the same person.'

He said, 'You don't smell the same. You smell of deceit. Something's going on . . . If you're on some secret mission, if you're helping your country . . . Supposing *I* wanted to help? As long as you're not working for the Bolshies, I'd like to help. I travel to and fro. I could do a lot . . . Can you put me in touch with anyone?'

'I couldn't. And now – I want to go out.'

He had tight hold of her. Pinning her arms to her body. He tried to reach her lips, as she shook her head.

'No, Ferdy, *no*.' She struggled. Undignified. Mussed hair. His heavy breathing.

'Get out,' she said, breaking free. 'Go on, *get out*.' She itched, with her high-heeled wooden shoes, to *kick* him.

She said at dinner, 'I was late because of this man . . . I don't trust him. I shall move apartments tomorrow. Vincent can radio London . . .'

She returned unbelievably tired again. She wondered almost if the meal out had been worth it. Walking from the Métro, she thought: If London suggest I go home for a spell, I'll take the offer. It's spring fever, or end of winter tiredness. I would never *ask* – but I'd accept . . .

For a while, overtired, she lay awake. She thought of getting up and packing her few belongings for the move. The flit. She would miss the Chevillons . . .

The banging on the door that woke her at four in the

morning – she could not have mistaken it for a shutter in the wind . . .

The man had a clever face, with deep-set eyes and a firm, not unsympathetic mouth. His voice was gentle.

'I'd much rather talk in English, Mrs Nicolson. My English is much better. It's nonsense we should conduct all this in *French*. You are not French –'

'For the fifth, sixth time – I'm Belgian. Walloon. French is my tongue.'

'Belgian. Like this man you said . . .'

'I wouldn't know where he comes from. Possibly he's Belgian. I told you, I never saw him before yesterday.'

'You expect me to believe that?'

'He picked me up. We . . . It was not a success. He was impotent. And disgusting with it. I told him so. I'm used to something better. Just because I'm a widow in my forties –'

'An *intelligent* widow, I suspect. You really think we don't know this is all a nonsense, Mrs Nicolson?'

'I'm used to something better, as I said. The goods were not delivered. I expressed myself insultingly. You're a man – would you take that? I imagine this person – he even gave me a false name – I imagine he had a motive for vengeance. Hence this tawdry slander, attempt to get me into hot water, give me a fright. Now, please can I go home? I had a promise of some calico if I reached the shop before two –'

'You talk a lot, Mrs Nicolson. You have a lot to say.'

'Mme Liebert, *please*. Of course I talk. You must be able to see I'm outraged by this. I thought you Germans were to protect us here in Paris – all these fine words nearly four years ago. Now innocent women are –'

'Our soldiers have behaved impeccably. Often under considerable provocation. But you are not a French citizen talking to a German officer. You are a British citizen – and I wonder, perhaps more than that? Refusing to answer reasonable questions from a member of the Gestapo.'

The best thing to do is to think about Henri. Imagine he is here with me. He stands behind me and encourages me. Try to think of the words of a French song. Henri at the piano, try and remember the words . . . It was so light a voice for a person of such wiry strength . . .

'Now please be sensible, Mrs Nicolson. You have known this man for at least ten years. You and he even spent time together in your own country, England. In nineteen-thirty-four.'

'The Stavisky affair. January nineteen-thirty-four. I was *here* for that. I can tell you all about the Stavisky –'

'Please do not try to evade the issue with digressions about French politics. A sordid scandal, it was in all the newspapers . . . I should like you to talk *quite soon*, Mrs Nicolson. We are not making very good progress. My patience isn't unlimited.'

'You just accused me of talking too much. I can't do right.'

'On the contrary, it is quite easy for you to do right. You have merely to tell me about your real self. And about your *friends*. We know what we know. But we need to know more. And you can tell us.'

'I have nothing to say.'

'Is that the new line? I thought you were Mme Liebert who needed to get to the draper's . . .'

'I *am* Monique Liebert, and I shall go to the draper's. When you've stopped this nonsense –'

'These cosmetics you peddle, Mrs Nicolson . . . No, on second thoughts I shall not bother breaking that thin disguise.' Picking up the cheap suitcase, he upset the contents. He seemed to be doing it as displacement for his anger with her. She could not see any other point. Then, but too late, she said:

'My samples – how dare you! It's enough bringing me in here unlawfully without prejudicing my livelihood. The scent might have broken . . .'

'You were very slow to react for one whose livelihood they are meant to be. Now you overdo it . . .'

'It's just as I said. One can't do right. Minding my manners, trying not to be too angry –'

'Pick them up. Now,' he said suddenly, his voice edgy, ugly. 'You are a tiresome woman.'

She was surprised, but somehow not displeased. Kneeling down, not far from his feet, she felt she was given time to recover, time to think. She was blushing furiously. As she sat down:

'You have a very good colour.'

'I should think so. Bending down. And it's – my time of life. I blush because of that. It's unexpected. The doctor says –'

Leaning across the desk, he struck her. His hand with its heavy wedding-ring catching her cheek. She drew her breath in quickly. Wincing. Her heart began to drum.

'That is just to show I am serious. That I am angry with your . . . that you should think us so *stupid*. You are a good actress. The *real* person is more sophisticated. A lot more obstinate. And that I shall break. Now – the truth about yourself. And – your associates.'

'I have nothing –'

He struck her again. She could see that his irritation had now gone beyond his control. That he was angry with himself.

He said, his voice calmer suddenly, almost coaxing, 'Would it surprise you, if I told you that *not* talking is useless? Your *SOE*, we have penetrated it. Our agents are everywhere. They are there. And so – we know all about you.'

She said in a cold voice, her fear calmed suddenly by an icy anger. 'If you know so much, why bother asking me?'

She thought he would strike her again. He moved some papers with an abrupt gesture. 'We are neither of us any longer in the mood. I shall go for my lunch. Then I shall order a good meal for you. Better than you have been eating. After you have enjoyed it – and please tell the Hauptmann whether you like cognac with your coffee – we shall have a civilized talk this afternoon . . .'

It was a mistake she was surprised he should have made, allowing her time to think. She decided to make the most of the meal. To give herself strength. She was weak from lack of food, dizzy. She had not eaten properly since Olivier's two days ago. Beware the alcohol. She drank the coffee, poured some more, drank half and then poured the cognac into the cup. She left it.

'I see you have made a good meal. And the cognac – it was good? We have been appreciating the good things that come out of France. And your steak? It was done the way you like?'

'I have nothing to say . . .'

Half an hour later, he struck her again. It seemed he could

not stop. Left right, left right. His face was barely flushed. It was pressed close to hers.

'What stupidity. We shall get everyone, everyone. If not at once. Soon. *Soon*. There are always others more sensible. The rewards are great. You don't seem interested even in considering them. I am out of patience.' He struck her again. 'You don't want rewards. Then it will be punishments.'

He rang the bell again. As the uniformed man came to take her away, he said in a brisk, businesslike voice without looking up, as if he were an employer to his secretary:

'We shall see what a holiday in prison – with some amusements of course (at least, *we* shall find them amusing), we shall see what that will do for you. And for *us* . . .'

28

'This is the BBC Home Service. Here is a special bulletin, read by John Snagge. D-Day has come. Early this morning, the Allies began the assault on the North-Western Face of Hitler's European fortress . . .'

At last, at last. Wanting it so much, the Second Front. Except that it couldn't happen without people being killed – and that could mean *Jay* . . .

1944 had been black enough, grim enough already – because of what had happened in January . . .

Jilly and the baby had gone to spend the New Year with Jilly's parents in Battersea. Why, why, *why*? Sudden violence of renewed raids, after a lull. The Little Blitz, it had been christened since. Big or little, it killed. Among the victims in a street where six houses were razed: Jilly, her parents, the baby . . . Willow, no Teddy to weep with, wired frantically to Jay. White-faced, she sat with Diana and wondered what they could do for Michael.

When she spoke to him on the 'phone, she wanted him to cry like she was crying. But he talked in an odd sort of voice so that she knew he *ought* to be crying. 'It's a really bad show,' he kept saying, 'a knock like that. A bad show . . .' She thought how he didn't have anyone now because of Jilly's parents. She had had a brother a prisoner in the Far East, that was all. Probably there were aunts, uncles, and so on. But . . .

Both Michael and Willow had leave around Easter and she tried to arrange for him to come with her to Wales. Friends of Diana's had a cottage near Colwyn Bay. But she couldn't persuade him. All he said was, 'I want to keep on flying, I'm all right flying . . . I'll pay them back. I'll *get* them . . .'

It started the dreams off again, of course. The mixed-up dreams. They always went back to the Café de Paris, as if somehow that violence had set a pattern. (Except the violence went back, didn't it, to Reggie, and the *terrible thing* . . .)

When she had tried to picture, after seeing newsreels, the fighting in Italy, and how it must have been for Christopher, her mind had filled with images of Isabelle and Gerry. Gerry she couldn't see properly, but Isabelle in her red frock and her black curls covered in dust (*I never saw her dead*) lay like a broken doll. Perhaps the other dead looked like that too. Jilly, the baby . . .

And, oh please, God, what is happening to Teddy, *what is she doing*? I'm under no illusions now. When I was informed it was secret work somewhere in Europe . . . I should like to be told more so that I would at least know *what* to worry about . . .

The absurdity of the messages. The latest one told her only that Teddy was 'well when we last heard . . .' (and when might that have been?) In her dreams too, men, women, children wandered over Europe, *without homes*, lost. She hated now so terribly that word Lost. I lost my mother, Michael lost his wife and son, Teddy lost . . . Losing, LOSS, LOST . . . She remembered something Teddy had said about *her* war, in 1914. The sound of weeping. So now, everywhere, millions must be *weeping*. Such tears, why doesn't the world drown? Why are we not drowned?

The first excitement of the landing armada – four thousand ships. Willow and Diana sat huddled over the wireless in the evening. At tea-breaks, devouring newsprint. Fingering the names of Norman villages in the atlas, tracing the steps forward – and too, the steps back.

In the meantime Germany had a secret weapon. The flying bombs. They called them doodle-bugs, and they were perhaps the most frightening of all. Some mothers and children, evacuated, arrived in Harrogate and the district. She tried not to be reminded of Jilly.

And then Jay – there *must* be ways of keeping him safe. She woke in the mornings dry mouthed, fearing that something had happened to him and *she didn't know yet*. Each day, all day, she hedged him round with love, what else? We must all love each other – what is left of our family.

Christopher, who had gone into the bag in Italy. She thought: I have to believe he is safe. Is isn't like what we've heard about prisoners of the Japanese . . . He *should* be all right. But she had not been able yet to tell him yet that he and she were all right. That they would marry as soon as Victory came . . .

She thought sometimes these days of the Diamond Waterfall, lying in its bank vault in York. Once to have been worn by Jilly. She could not remember what it looked like, if she had ever really seen it, what it looked like . . . She imagined it sometimes, its brilliance hidden, resting on its velvet bed, in a case within a case within a metal container box, underground. If they had found anything of Jilly and the baby, were they in a box underground?

It was very hot, very dry weather. The grass looked parched. Diana said one morning:

'This evening we'll sit with our parachute silk . . . I've got a cami-knicker patter off Olga . . . If Dame Parr has a church meeting we could have the wireless to ourselves . . .'

Straight after work, she went to the library in Victoria Avenue, and Willow sat in the Valley Gardens, reading the new *Picture Post* with photographs of the landings. Looking at them, like looking at the Pathé newsreels in the cinema only made her more worried for Jay. She tried to imagine a life *without Jay*. Her stomach knotted. She felt cold and shaky.

She walked up Harlow Moor Drive, turning off for Valley Mount. When she came into the billet, Diana wasn't back yet from the library. At once she heard Mrs Parr, loud with indignation:

'. . . at the fishmonger's, I'd to queue *one hour* all on account they said there was cod come in and then what do I get? "Oh Mrs Parr, I'm sorry there's only its head left . . ." Well, you girls will just have to make do . . .' Her voice rose and fell.

'There's post for you . . .'

A letter waited on the tray in the hall, near the umbrella stand. Addressed to her with a box number. She didn't recognize the writing – the sender's name on the back was G. M. D. Selwood.

'Dear Willow,' it began . . . She couldn't concentrate on any of it . . . She looked again at the envelope. *G. M. D. Selwood.* The name swam, suddenly in blacker ink . . .

'Don't just stand there,' Mrs Parr said, 'it's not bad news, is it? That comes in telegraphs. And where's Miss Rowe? She never said about not having her tea. Half an hour and it'll be

on the table, all washed up before *Monday Night at Eight* . . .'
The handwriting was impossible . . .

. . . such a difficult letter to write there isn't a way it can be done right . . . Now perhaps, Willow, you won't be so very much surprised to receive this, I've just learned that you've been looking for me . . . If I'd known about you, *I* would have looked for *you* . . .

It's very important that I *do write* this, however much I despair of expressing myself . . . Willow, I knew nothing. Not even the *sad, terrible* story of your Mother. I know now that it was made much of in the English newspapers, but that year, 1937, I was working where we didn't have time or inclination to keep up with news, unless it was of wars and alarums. And even then –

I know if I *had* read of it – I would have broken my self-imposed silence and written to your mother, and to others in your family. Would have tried desperately if it had not been too late to do *something*. But *I knew nothing*. And above all *I knew nothing of you*. If I had even seen all those years ago the announcement of your birth – I should have known. I would never have mistaken you for premature . . . I would have understood everything.

Your mother was so brave, and beautiful. It is more than twenty years now since we met – I won't say anything now about the whole sad story, for which I take *the whole blame*. You, I think, must be the most lovely, most happy thing to have come out of so much sadness.

For myself, my wife died in 1929. And that was the only time I made any attempt to find out how things had gone with your mother. Before, we thought it wrong – for either of us. Even then I didn't write directly to her. I wrote to the Vicar at Flaxthorpe, asking for general news of the Firths. His words, which I remember so well, he said '. . . Sylvia married several years ago and lives in Ireland where they run a hotel. There are at least three children of the marriage . . .' I felt then that I knew enough, that she was all right. And better off without me.

After my wife's death I stayed in the same sort of work because of the children, but by 1935 the youngest was able to cope and I fulfilled an ambition, a calling I suppose that

I had had for years to work among the really poor here in Africa. I've been at this Medical Mission since 1940, and was in another in the north, even more hidden away, from '35 to '40.

Now, if you are wondering *how* it is you have heard from me – it was my stupidity and carelessness making me so difficult to trace . . .

The newspaper advertisement. Did you place it? It was sent to me by a Reverend Muncey in Nairobi. He knew me some years ago in my first mission. In fact the cutting was sent to me by several people. But with Muncey, something in the name rang a bell with him – he followed his hunch, looked up everything – and told me what *I wish need never have happened*. Dearest Willow, what you too must have suffered . . .

I should tell you I have a married daughter in New York State, and a son in the Navy, in South Africa. Another daughter is a nurse in Rhodesia . . . It would be nice if the post allows an exchange of photographs. I shall send you mine in a few days' time and I shall expect one from you.

I would have come to England on some sort of leave in about 1940 if it had not been for the War. Now, Willow, I shall *certainly* come when all this is over. And I can't believe now that it can be so very long . . . I shall visit the States . . .

Mrs Parr was almost shouting. 'I don't think you've heard a *word* I've been saying . . .'

Oh, but she was overwhelmed. Thank you, thank you, Jay, thank you . . .

She thought it was the worst about Jay when, three days later, she heard the news of Michael. First from the family lawyer, then later that day, with more details, from one of his RAF friends. Michael's Liberator had gone after a Focke-Wulf Condor which was stalking and attacking a convoy in the Atlantic. He had damaged its port engines so badly that it had crashed. In the meantime he too had been hit . . . And he too had crashed.

The tears, deep down as in a well – they just waited . . .

This time it was she who sobbed in Diana's arms. She said,

'I know, I know . . . why should his luck be better than anyone else's? But he's lasted so long . . . I don't think, Di, he really wanted to go on after Jilly and the baby. In a way, they took away what he was fighting *for* . . .'

She thought: To find a father and lose a dear cousin, all in three days . . . Dearest Michael, that I ever thought I didn't like you . . . Remembering the time at Clare, hiding in his wardrobe.

Laughing, crying, she said to Diana, 'I gave him a terrible time . . . his friends . . . then going to his party and spoiling it for him . . . I was a bit of a brat. And oh, I did love him . . .'

29

She knew they were being deported. Even if the prison guard had not told her, she would have guessed from the route the coach was taking. The Boulevard de Strasbourg, the statues of two women above the clock at the entrance to the station. The Gare de l'Est for travellers to Germany . . .

There were about eighty of them in two ordinary coaches with unblacked windows. They had been warned not to knock, wave, or cry for help. Not to draw attention to themselves.

On the way they had been held up by a convoy of troops. Bound she supposed for Normandy. She had learned of the landings a few weeks back, on the prison grapevine. Although it had raised morale, it had done nothing for prison conditions. Panic reigned, the anger of those cornered. But they were not yet so desperate they would ingratiate. A rumour had started almost immediately that many prisoners were to be moved. No chance of her being here to be liberated . . .

It was a warm summer's day yet, tired, undernourished, unkept, dirty, verminous, she felt a cold in her bones as if she brought prison damp with her. The dank smell of defeat. The nightly screams. The sobbing (her own). Although the pain had only been in the first days, when they still thought she had information. They must in the end have become suddenly bored. Have come to believe she knew nothing, was just silly Monique Liebert. But of course she must stay here, even though half forgotten, mixed up now with political prisoners, people apprehended for any number of different offences.

Loneliness. Who knows, she thought, what will become of me now? I don't regret what I did, it is not as strong as that, but where has the anger gone, the *pride*? Only the fear remains . . .

I know of course that it was Ferdy. Shopped by Ferdy. For what? Money? What was I worth? What he knew about me was able to tell them, was very little. And nothing at all about my *real work*. Yet he, they, were not stupid. As they said, an Englishwoman, a former resident, living under a false name, pursuing a career quite out of character – what else were they to suppose but clandestine activity?

She felt a great wave of anger, and helpless fear. How odd, she thought with desperation – nearly sixty years ago my mother was imprisoned by her own father. Locked in her own room – and escaped. Helped by the Uncle Harry I never met, who died on the eve of my birth.

What will become of me? She was haunted by some lines of poetry. *La vie est brève, un peu d'espoir, un peu de rêve, et puis – bonsoir* . . . The shortness of life. Death which in 1914 had been all round her, which since last year had threatened her daily, had become now a near certainty. Germany. A camp. Starvation, disease. Death might seem the least of the horrors.

They were not handcuffed, for that she was thankful. Together with their guards they formed a milling crowd in the courtyard of the Gare de l'Est. Their train was at six-thirty. It was only six-ten as they arrived. She spoke to a woman who had sat beside her on the coach, staring straight ahead, rigid. The woman continued to stare, not answering. It is that, Teddy thought, to be quite hopeless.

A Red Cross van was drawing up in the courtyard. There was hope, perhaps, that they would receive a hand-out. Something to tide them over a journey bound to be long and slow. Already it was seven or eight hours since the thin gruel she had eaten, or rather drunk, this morning.

The van circled, and stopped not far from her. On the far side a woman got out, and walked round to the rear, which she opened. The driver, also a woman, had her head turned towards the passenger seat, writing something. As Teddy moved nearer, she looked up. Turned her head. Caught Teddy's eye.

She was Pauline. For a second they stared at each other. Then, '*Put on your white coat* . . .' Pauline said. '*It's in the rear of the van* . . .'

Teddy looked about her – at the guards, at the other prisoners – then, shufflling past the van, head bent, she side-stepped. Rolling her right shoulder a little, moving sharply towards the open van rear. And up into it. She saw the coat at once, hanging on the left.

'Who, *whatever*?' said the woman in the van. She was small with a pug's nose.

'Mme Perronault' – thank God that she knew the name – 'she sent me . . .' And in a moment there *was* Pauline.

The pug-faced woman said, 'You should tell me, Mme Perronault, if there's extra help coming. Three just clutters the van, do we have to fit her in the front seat? And she's taken your coat . . .'

Bread. Barley coffee. It crossed her mind fleetingly that she was weak, hungry. Steam from the urn. Rattle of cups. She worked with frantic, feverish strength, wearing the white coat as if it were hers. Oh, life-saving uniform . . .

She couldn't have said afterwards if it was an hour, two hours, three – or a mere ten minutes. She didn't look at the other prisoners, if they had been shepherded away. When would they be counted? Would there be a list as they boarded the train?

Steam, rising from the urns, pricked her face. Opening up now, to see how much was left. Tap on, off, on – fill cup after cup. 'No, one bread only, *please*.' And Pauline saying 'If only it were Christ and the five thousand.'

How could a white coat cover that distinctive smell, her grubbiness, that she could smell herself? Working close to the pug-faced woman, she tried to forget she smelled. Plainly the woman could not. I smell, therefore I live. *I live*.

On the drive back, although the woman, not understanding, had protested (I never meant to complain . . .'), she was in the closed-up rear, for safety. Safety for how long? She could not be being delivered to her old apartment. She could not go there. She saw herself suddenly, dumped on the pavement, no papers, no belongings or signs of stability. What if we are stopped for papers now? If they open up the van? The Red Cross, they do not have immunity from rules . . .

The van stopped once. Since nothing happened, she supposed it was pug-face getting out. After what seemed an age it stopped again. She thought she heard army tanks. Then another fifteen minutes perhaps, and they stopped a third time. Pauline opened up the back. 'Quickly,' she said. 'And keep on the coat.' Then she said, 'We were held up. All those tanks in the Boulevard Suchet. Off to Normandy . . .'

They entered an apartment block. She didn't know the street. Pauline said casually, 'The Geste came back, to search your apartment. My sister . . . The children are barely over it. Xavier got a real fright, thinking the Geste were after *him*.'

She said only the briefest of words as they went up the stone staircase – the concierge watching.

'I'm leaving you with friends. You'll be safe here. I'll be back tomorrow morning, or evening.'

The door opened. An elderly maid stood there. Pauline said, 'Tell your mistress, there's a lady here wants sewing work . . .'

A pleasant-faced woman came in, 'So you want sewing work? I place a lot of people. It depends where you would like to be . . .' Then as the maid left the room. 'I will show you where to go. Please don't move until one of us comes for you. We will feed you as best we can.' She locked the door – spoke urgently.

'You are among friends, you can speak freely . . . We're more used to men, you see – airmen especially – but we have a password for women too . . . Hence the "sewing work" . . .'

Teddy told her only the bare essentials, giving away nothing that could connect her to code name Lucienne. 'I need to get out,' she said simply.

'We'll do what we can. You'll have to lie low until we've got something arranged. Some papers together . . . I think you will go down the line to Switzerland.'

She knew she must have nothing to do with Jean Luc or Vincent, or any of her group. She could not risk even trying to contact them – however much she might wish to radio London. What 'safe house' might not have become a death trap in the months of her absence? That she should not harm them was her prayer . . . thought . . .

Over the next few weeks she was moved slowly, uncomfortably, across France. She who had once been a courier was now escorted herself. She had lost her nerve. Armed with the password, she could have gone from one 'cut-out' to another. But she could no longer give a cover story . . . She shook at the thought of answering simple questions. She travelled usually as someone's middle-aged aunt – hard of hearing, and rather slow. 'She's *stupid*,' her escort would say, 'come on, Auntie, pull your hat over your face and go to sleep . . .'

Switzerland drew nearer. Although she trembled still, had not yet recovered her nerve, physically she was much better. She had lost the look, feel, and smell of prison. She even *believed* that she would arrive safely over the frontier.

But there was still, over and over, the *mauvais quart d'heure*, as it was known – when, left by one contact, she must wait for another. The cut-out. Each unknown to the one before. And she must hold in her head the password. The code. A simple question, a simple answer. The password.

The sun shone in the park. She had been left on a bench to wait. To appear natural, normal, and to pass the time, she read: a well-thumbed copy of Guilloux's *Le Pain de Rêves*. She could not take in one word of it . . .

I am to hear: '*Do you know somewhere near I can get my shoes heeled*?' I shall answer: '*M. Andre is the only person still offering this service*.'

Today when her contact came, she would be driven to the village of Bossey, near Annemasse. From there, if all went well, she would be able later this evening to cross the frontier into Switzerland.

Un mauvais quart d'heure. Yet another long, worrying quarter of an hour . . . And how slowly . . . A small black terrier came running past, tripping up, rolling over . . . She went back to her book.

A voice said, 'Excuse me, madame – do you know somewhere near I can get my shoes heeled?'

It was the hand she saw first. There was a finger, the fourth, missing on the right hand.

'*M. Andre is the only person still offering this service*.'

She looked up. He was looking down at her. Afterwards she was never sure who had been the more surprised.

'Our appointment,' he said, eyebrows raised. Amused. 'I rather thought we had an *appointment* . . . You are almost five years late, Teddee.'

30

The Diamond Waterfall lay on its bed of ivory velvet. Willow stared. In the subdued setting of the bank vault, its beauty seemed unreal. Out of time.

Two bank officials stood by. Jay said, 'You were going to try it on . . .'

She put out a fearful finger to touch it. He lifted it out for her, placed it around her neck – over her Aertex shirt and slacks and zipper top. How incongruous . . . She turned her head. Looked round at him. She felt that as she moved it moved with her – and it was heavy, so heavy. There was no looking-glass. She was glad of that.

Because she felt that she ought, she kept it on a few moments. But would rather have not. Its place was – back in its box.

'Like it, Willow?'

'Jay, it's not a liking or not liking sort of thing. You just . . . It's beautiful.'

'It's yours.'

'Yes,' she said sadly, 'it's mine – now.'

They walked out of the bank and into the streets of York. The sun shone. For April, it was unusually warm. Near the station, above the Roman Wall, daffodils moved in a slight breeze.

'They say nineteen-forty-five's going to be a wonderful summer. The old style weather prophets that is . . . After a winter like last one, we need it.'

The War news was very good now. Troops had crossed the Rhine. They were advancing daily. Victory Day, in Europe at least, couldn't be far away.

Jay, who had been wounded quite severely last September at Epinal, was convalescent now, although still not at all strong. He was allowed to go out and about a little and Willow who had a week's leave due to her, had arranged for them both to board at a farmhouse in Wensleydale. Before setting out for there, they had arranged this visit to York – for Willow to see the Diamond Waterfall.

She had not wanted to see it. But she had a nagging sense of compulsion that she could not explain. She told herself that she *ought* . . . And with Jay there, it would be all right.

With Jay, everything was all right, always. Except – lately she was not so sure . . . There was this new awkwardness with him. Her awkwardness.

He said now, 'Wisp, I'm going to take you out. How about a cup of British tea?'

'At the *station*?'

'Goof . . . No, I'll take you to Terry's. Hot margarined toast. Wartime afternoon tea – but one of the best . . .'

'Your ankle, your side – they're not bothering you? You can walk that far?'

'Fine, fine. I'm just fine, Willow.'

Their conversation, once so easy, seemed to her suddenly stiff, considered. I'm upset by the Waterfall, she thought.

The teashop wasn't full. It was still quite early. Sitting at a table against the wall, he asked her:

'OK?'

It was her turn. 'Fine,' she said, 'I'm fine . . .'

They were both silent. Then: 'Well,' he said, 'you've worn it at last. The famous Waterfall. You'd truly never seen it?'

'*Might* have done. But not to remember . . . I – tried not to think about it. You see, I heard Reggie say once . . . It was always "If we'd had the Waterfall, *you* lost the Waterfall . . ." I don't want to remember. He was drunk. And he's dead . . . Mike never spoke of it. I can only recall him mentioning it once. Talking about Jilly. And then of course the War came. Diamond necklaces and war don't go together somehow. Although my grandfather nearly gave it to the War Effort in nineteen-seventeen. The great gesture that was to elevate him – I don't know – hereditary peerage? Bought from Lloyd George RIP . . .'

'You're not about to do the same? Give it away, I mean?'

'Jay, I might, I just might. I must do *something* with it . . .'

Tears filled her eyes suddenly. 'What had to happen for me to own it. Mike, Jilly, their baby. I don't want it. All those refugee children. Flotsam of war. Imagine what one could do with the money . . .'

When they'd given their order for tea, she said, 'I couldn't ever ever ever want to wear it. I don't think that after the War it's going to be that sort of world . . .'

'You show a touching faith, Willow. It'll be much the same old world, I guess, just rearranged a little. Reshuffled . . .'

'Problem is, in that reshuffled world, who'd wear such a thing? It doesn't seem to belong, Jay . . . If I sell it . . .'

'If you sell it . . . Maybe an eastern potentate'll buy it for his queen, or a movie star for his paramour of the moment. I agree it's not for afternoon tea . . .'

'My great-grandmother wore it then. Or so they say . . . I suppose really it's very Empress Eugénie. She was a great one for diamonds. Teddy told me this story once . . .'

'I want to hear it OK, but *are* you going to pour the tea?'

'. . . What happened was that Eugénie saw some actress on stage wearing this magnificent diamond parure from her waist to her ankles. Paste, naturally. But you know how theatrical stuff glitters . . . Apparently nothing would satisfy Eugénie but she must have one just the same. So she commissioned it, using diamonds left over from her Imperial Crown – She was in a great hurry about it, wanting to wear it for some particular function. She badgered the poor workers who had to stay up all night. Finally, it was ready five minutes before the ball . . .'

'Don't tell me. It all fell apart . . .'

'Worse. When it was put on her, because the diamonds weren't paste, their weight raised the back of her crinoline so high she showed several inches of *leg*.'

'And we weren't amused?'

'We weren't. And she never wore it, ever . . .'

She realized she was still holding the teapot over the strainer. Half of Jay's cup poured. None of her own.

'I'm a pretty patient guy,' he said.

'Jay, I'm sorry . . . Teddy told it jolly well. She heard it from her Henri . . .'

'Sure. Henri. And how are they?'

'Married . . . I feel goofy again, I'd meant to say . . . I heard just last week. Although one's hardly *surprised* . . . But it's been good the authorities letting her go back to Paris, though it's the least she deserves. Now It Can Be Told, and all that . . . A secret agent. She had a dreadful time –'

'And a wonderful escape –'

'Oh, so wonderful. When she was over here at Christmas and told me, I couldn't believe . . . I mean, and knowing Henri before the War and everything. Though he wasn't anyone she'd ever *mentioned* . . .' She stirred her tea thoughtfully. 'I've always wanted Teddy to be happy. Now she is . . .'

'Will they live in Paris?'

'For the moment, yes. But they want to work with refugee children. He's very rich, evidently. Anyway that's what they plan. He'll stop his business – and then they'll devote themselves to that. She always did love children . . .'

'Right. That's Teddy settled and happy. What about *you*? That's the one set of plans doesn't get mentioned in letters. What Willow Gilmartin's going to do when the Ministry of Aircraft Production's finished with her . . .'

She picked up a finger of toast. 'Oh, me. Oh well . . .' She got margarine on her thumb and rubbed it off vigorously. She said, 'We haven't decided. The Waterfall. What I'm to do with it . . .'

'You don't think if you sell it, your children might ask after it? Why you didn't keep it for them?'

'Could be . . .'

'I had a thought,' he said.

'That's not very remarkable, they're not rationed, you know . . .'

'You're very acid suddenly . . . OK, second try. I've been thinking – we've got this week together. Maybe we should do some talking . . .'

'What about?' Her voice was sharp again. Feeling herself suddenly threatened. Edgy. The sun gone in. *Don't go away and leave me, Jay.*

'About Christopher. The Eighth Army's liberated a lot of camps already. He'll be appearing before long. By the summer surely . . .'

'I'm going to – I'll tell him . . . No. Even if he's been hoping. It'd be only fair. I feel *terrible*. But that's not important, how I feel. For him, it's awful. After being a POW. But it's been really difficult to decide . . .'

'You know *why* it's been so difficult?'

'Yes . . . No . . .'

'Because you love me.'

'You've got a nerve –'

'If it's not true – why do you look like that?'

'What?'

'Open your bag and get out your mirror. Like *that* . . . See? Say it's true. It's true, isn't it? I used to think maybe how you are with me it's because you're grateful . . . Like – I found your father. All that. But it isn't, is it? I watched you all today. I thought . . . For Chrissake, I thought, I'll say something over the teacakes . . .'

'Look, I didn't mean –'

'I've just loved you – rather a long while I reckon . . . I'm not sure it didn't start back when I saw you in Mike's sweater with coal dust on your face . . .'

'Jay, it couldn't –'

'It could.'

'Anyway I'd have to think. I don't know if . . . You might *organize* me. You know – "You do what you want, Willow, so long as it's what I want . . ." '

'You could say No if you don't like something. You always did before . . .'

She saw his teacup was empty. She leaned over and tossed the dregs into the slop basin, then refilled the cup without asking.

'Willow, just tell me . . . What were you going to do when peace breaks out – if not marry me?'

She didn't answer, feeling suddenly panicky amid the teacups. Panicky with happiness. (Of course I shall say Yes, of course it's what I wanted and hadn't even dared to think of . . .)

She said obstinately, 'If I did – marry you, would everything happen here, or the States? I know you'll want to get back. You propped up Britain in her Darkest Hour. But now –'

'I guess I will want to get back. For a while at least.'

'Well, I'm not so sure, not just like that, that I want to live over there.'

'You never tried –'

'I mean I just don't want it *assumed* we go where you want to go.'

'OK. So maybe I haven't decided yet. Look, it's only a problem if we make it one. We've got a week to talk it all through – and other things. Like how much I want to kiss you. And more . . . And more . . .'

'I love you a lot, Jay. And the Diamond Waterfall *not at all* . . .'

Probably it was all right to be happy. Probably . . .

'Oh, but what shall I *do* with it?' she cried suddenly. 'What does Jay say?'

'I say the hell with it . . . It can't be that difficult. Where there's a Willow there's a way . . .'

'You do make the most terrible puns,' she said happily.

She had this sudden picture – it was so lovely – of Aunt Alice's face when she heard the news. Aunt Alice would understand best of all. Aunt Alice who had not wanted to be an alone child. Who too had loved and lost her mother. Who had hated the Waterfall (what must it have cost her to tell me of those photographs?) She said:

'I know it's a bit soon and there's no hurry, darling, but you weren't planning . . . we won't have an alone child?'

'There you go again. Problems.' He smiled. 'That one . . . Well, I guess that one won't be very difficult . . .'